BLACK
SUN
RISING

Novels by
C. S. FRIEDMAN
available from DAW Books

IN CONQUEST BORN
THE MADNESS SEASON
BLACK SUN RISING

BLACK SUN RISING

C.S. FRIEDMAN

DAW BOOKS, INC.

DONALD A. WOLLHEIM, FOUNDER

375 Hudson Street, New York, NY 10014

ELIZABETH R. WOLLHEIM
SHEILA E. GILBERT
PUBLISHERS

Jacket art by Michael Whelan
For color prints of Michael Whelan paintings,
please contact:
Glass Onion Graphics
P.O. Box 88
Brookfield, CT 06804

DAW Books are distributed by Penguin U.S.A.

Book designed by Leonard Telesca

DAW TRADEMARK REGISTERED
U.S. PAT OFF AND FOREIGN COUNTRIES
—MARCA REGISTRADA.
HECHO EN U.S.A.

PRINTED IN THE U.S.A

This book is for several very special readers:

Rick Umbaugh, who started it all;
Kellie Owens, Linda Gilbert, Lori Cook, David
McDonald, and Joe and Regina Harley, who keep it
going;
and Betsy Wollheim, whose criticism is, as always,
worth its weight in gold.

The author would like to thank the following people for their insight,
inspiration, and/or vital emotional support during this novel's forma-
tive period: Jeanne Boyle, Adam Breslaw, Christian Cameron, Tom
Deitz, Nancy Friedman, Bob Green, John Happ, Delos Wheeler, Karen
Martakos, Robin Mitchell, Steve Rappaport, Vicki Sharp, Mike Ste-
vens, Sarah Strickland, Mark Sunderlin, and Glenn Zienowicz.

Prologue

She wondered why she was afraid to go home.

She was within sight of the castle now, and its proximity should have calmed her. She loved the traditional building which her husband had designed, and all the men and women who lived inside it. The seat of the Neocounty of Merentha was a gleaming, ivory-colored monument to the Revivalist dream: all the elements of Gothic perpendicular architecture that seemed so oppressive elsewhere—at the royal seat, for instance—were here combined by that unerring aesthetic sense that was her husband's strongest attribute, to create a building that was at once a soaring display of stone arches and finials, and a very real, very comfortable home.

For a moment she reigned up her unhorse, commanding it to stillness, and tried to focus on the source of her anxiety. As ever, the effort was doomed to failure. She wished she had her husband's skill to name and analyze such feelings. He would have taken one look at the building and said *there, you see! The demonlings are out early tonight, it's their presence you sense.* Or, *the currents are unsteady tonight, of course you're nervous.* Or some other explanation, equally dependent upon his special vision, that would render up the source of her discomfort in small, comprehensible packets of knowledge, so that it might be dealt with and then discarded.

The sun had set. Maybe that was it. The piercing white sun which bathed the land in sanity was gone, and the Core had followed it into its westerly grave. Only a few stars remained, and soon they too would be swallowed up by darkness. Things were abroad now that hid from the light of day, maverick human fears that had taken on a life of their own and coursed the night in search of a bodily home. She looked up at the sky and shivered. Even Erna's moons were missing now, two having already set and one, the smallest, yet to rise. Soon there would be as much darkness as the Earthlike world could ever know. A *true night*, her husband would have called it. A very rare, very special occurrence, for a world near the heart of the galaxy.

A night of power.

She kneed her unhorse gently into motion again and tried to lose herself in memories of her family, as a means of combatting the uneasiness that had been growing in her since she left the Bellamy household nearly an hour earlier. Her daughter Alix, barely five, had already mastered the rudiments of riding, and delighted in bare-backing the castle's miniature unhorses whenever her parents would let her. Tory, nine, had clearly inherited his father's insatiable curiosity, and could be found at any given moment in the place he least belonged, doing something that was only marginally allowable. Eric, the oldest, proud master of eleven years of lifely experience, was already practicing his charm on all the household staff. He alone had inherited his father's manner, which would serve him well when he received his lands and title; the Neocount had charmed many an enemy into martial impotence with the force of his presence alone.

As for her husband, the Neocount himself . . . she loved him with a passion that was sometimes near to pain, and adored him no less than did the people he ruled. He was an idealist who had swept her off her feet, caught her up in his dreams of Revival and then set her by his side while king and church jockeyed to do him the greatest honor. A young genius, he had turned Gannon's wars into triumphs, thus abetting the unification of all the human lands. He had bred unhorses from local stock that were almost indistinguishable from the true equines of Earth, imposing his will on their very evolution with a force and efficiency that others could only wonder at. Likewise his uncats chased the local rodents with appropriate mock-feline fervor, ignoring the less harmful insects which were their grandsires' preferred prey; in two more generations he would have the fur looking right—so he promised—and even the behavioral patterns that accompanied their hunting.

In truth, she believed there was nothing he couldn't do, once he set his mind to it . . . and perhaps that was what frightened her.

The castle courtyard was empty when she entered, which was far from reassuring. She was accustomed to returning home at dusk, and her children were accustomed to meeting her. Pouring forth from the house like a litter of overexcited unkittens, plying her with a thousand questions and needs and "look-sees" before she could even dismount. Today they were absent—a disconcerting change—and as she gave her reins over to the groom she asked him, with feigned nonchalance, where they were.

"With their father, Excellency." He held the unhorse steady while she dismounted. "Belowground, I believe."

Belowground. She tried not to let him see how much that word chilled her, as she walked through the evening shadows to the main door of the keep. Belowground . . . there was only his library there, she told herself, and his collection of Earth artifacts, and the workroom in which he studied the contents of both. Nothing more. And if the children were with him . . . that was odd, but not unreasonable. Eventually they would inherit the castle and all that was in it. Shouldn't they be familiar with its workings?

Nevertheless she was chilled to the bone as she entered the cold stone keep, and only her knowledge that the chill was rooted deep inside, in the heart of her fear, caused her to give over her cloak and surcoat to the servant who waited within.

"Here's a message for you," the old woman said. She handed her an envelope of thick vellum, addressed in the Neocount's neat and elegant hand. "His Excellency said to see you got it, as soon as you arrived."

With a hand that was trembling only slightly she took it from her, and thanked her. *I won't read it here*, she told herself. There was an antechamber nearby that would give her more privacy. Not until she was well inside it, with the heavy alteroak door firmly shut behind her, did she remove the folded sheet from its vellum envelope and read the words her husband had written.

Please come to me, it said, *at your earliest convenience. The workshop below.* There was little more than that—his family crest imprinted above, the swirl of his initials below—but she knew as she read it that there was a volume of meaning between the lines . . . and that she lacked the resources to read what they said, and thus must descend to him uninformed.

She glanced into the huge glass mirror that dominated the low-ceilinged room, and briefly wondered if she should change her clothes before joining him. Her gown, true to Revivalist style, had dragged in the dust all day; its warm cream color was nearly rust about the hem, stained dark by the red clay of the region. But elsewhere it was clean, its soft woolen nap protected by the heavy surcoat she had worn. She pulled the few pins out of her hair, and let red-gold curls pour down about her shoulder and back. He loved her hair, and this style of gown; he loved *her*, she told herself, and would never let her come to harm. She settled for fluffing the curls to more volume and using a dampened cloth to wipe the dust from her eyes and off her face. That would be enough. That had to be enough, if he wanted her to come to him quickly.

Filled with more than a little misgiving, she descended the winding staircase that led down to the belowground rooms.

The library was empty, and lit only by a single candle. *Kindled long ago*, she thought, noting its length; he must have been down here most of the day. Its four walls were lined with books, a history of man from the time of First Sacrifice to the current day—scribbled in tight, fearful letters, by the settlers of the Landing, printed in the heavy ink of Erna's first mass-production presses, or painstakingly copied from holy scriptures, with letter forms and illuminatory styles that harkened back to nearly-forgotten ages back on the mother planet. She recognized the leather bindings of his own twelve-volume treatise on the arts of war, and less formal notebooks, on mastering magic. Only. . . .

Don't call it magic, he would have said to her. *It isn't that. The fae is as natural to this world as water and air were to our ancestors' planet, and not until we rid ourselves of our inherited preconceptions are we going to learn to understand it, and control it.*

And next to those books, the handbooks of the Church. *They caused this*, she thought. *They caused it all, when they rejected him. Hypocritical bastards!* Half their foundations were of his philosophy, the genius of his ordered mind giving their religious dreams substance, transforming a church of mere faith into something that might last—and command—the ages. Something that might tame the fae at last, and bring peace to a planet that had rarely known anything but chaos. But their dreams and his had diverged in substance, and recently they had come but one word short of damning him outright. *After using him to fight their wars!* she thought angrily. To establish their church throughout the human lands, and firmly fix their power in the realm of human imagination . . . she shuddered with the force of her anger. It was they who changed him, slowly but surely—they who had planted the first seeds of darkness in him, even while they robed him in titles and honor. Knight of the Realm. Premier of the Order of the Golden Flame. Prophet of the Law.

And damned as a sorcerer, she thought bitterly. *Condemned to hell—or just short of it—because he wants to control the very force that has bested us all these years. The force that cost us our heritage, that slaughtered our colonial ancestors . . . is that a sin, you self-righteous bastards? Enough of a sin that it's worth alienating one of your own prophets for it?*

She took a deep breath and tried to steady herself. She had to be strong enough for both of them now. Strong enough to lead him back from his fears of hell and worse, if they had overwhelmed him. He might have gone on for years, bitterly cursing the new Church doctrine but otherwise unconcerned with it, had his body not failed him one late spring night and left him lying helpless on the ground, bands of invisible steel squeezing the breath from his flesh as his damaged heart labored to save itself. Later he could say, with false calm, *this was the reason. Here was the cause of damage, which I inherited. Not yet repairable, by my skills, but I will find a way.* But she knew that the damage had been done. At twenty-nine he had seen the face of Death, and been changed forever. So much promise in a single man, now so darkened by the shadow of mortality. . . .

The door opened before she could touch it. Backlit by lamplight, her husband stood before her. He was wearing a long gown of midnight blue silk, slit up the sides to reveal gray leggings and soft leather boots. His face was, as always, serene and beautiful. His features were elegant, delicately crafted, and in another man might have seemed unduly effeminate; that was his mother's beauty, she knew, and in its male manifestation it gave him an almost surreal beauty, a quality of angelic calm that belied any storm his soul might harbor. He kissed her gently, ever the devoted husband, but she sensed a sudden distance between them; as he stepped aside to allow her to enter she looked deep into his eyes, and saw with sudden clarity what she had feared the most. There was something in him beyond all saving, now. Something even she could not touch, walled away behind fearborn defenses that no mere woman could breach.

"The children," she whispered. The chamber was dark, and seemed to demand whispering. "Where are the children?"

"I'll take you there," he promised her. Something flickered in his eyes that might have been pain, or love—but then it was gone, and only a distant cold remained. He picked up a lamp from the corner of a desk and bid her, "Come."

She came. Through the door which he opened at the rear of the chamber, leading into an inner workroom. Artifacts from the Landing caught his lamplight as they passed by, twinkling like captive stars in their leaded glass enclosures. Fragments of unknown substances which once had served some unknown purpose . . . there was the soft silver disk that tradition said was a book, although how it could be such—and how it might be read—was a mystery her husband had not yet solved. Fragments of encasements, the largest barely as broad as her palm, that were said to have contained an entire library. A small metal webwork, the size of her thumbnail, that had once served as a substitute for human reasoning.

Then he opened a door in the workroom's far wall, and she felt a chill breeze blow over her. Her eyes met his and found only cold there, lightless unwarmth that was frightening, sterile. And she knew with dread certainty that some nameless, intangible line had finally been crossed; that he was gazing at her from across an abyss so dark and so desolate that the bulk of his humanity was lost in its depths.

"Come," he whispered. She could feel the force of the fae about her, bound by his need, urging her forward. She followed him. Through a door that must have been hidden from her sight before, for she had never noticed it. Into a natural cavern that water had eroded from the rock of the castle's foundation, leaving only a narrow bridge of glistening stone to vault across its depths. This they followed, his muttered words binding sufficient fae to steady their feet as they crossed. Beneath them—far beneath, in the lightless depths—she sensed water, and occasionally a drop could be heard as it fell from the ceiling to that unseen lake far, far below.

Give it up, my husband! Throw the darkness off and come back to us—your wife, the children, your church. Take up your dreams again, and the sword of your faith, and come back into the light of day. . . . But true night reigned below, as it did above; the shadows of the underworld gave way only grudgingly to the light of the Neocount's lamp, and closed behind them as soon as they had passed.

The water-carved bridge ended in a broad ledge of rock. There he stepped aside and indicated that she should precede him, through a narrow archway barely wide enough to let her pass. She did so, trembling. Whatever he had found in these depths, it was here. Waiting for her. That knowledge must have been faeborn, it was so absolute.

And then he entered, bearing the lamp, and she saw.

"Oh, my God! . . . Tory? . . . Alix?"

They were huddled against the far wall, behind the bulk of a rough stone slab that dominated the small cavern's interior. Both of them, pale as ice, glassy eyes staring into nothingness. She walked slowly to where they lay, not wanting to believe. *Wake me up,* she begged silently, *make it all be a dream, stop this from happening.* . . . Her children. Dead. *His* children. She looked up at him, into eyes so cold that she wondered if they had ever been human.

She could barely find her voice, but at last whispered, "Why?"

"I need time," he told her. There was pain in his voice—deep-rooted pain, and possibly fear. But no doubt, she noted. And no regret. None of the things that her former husband would have felt, standing in this cold stranger's shoes. "Time, Almea. And there's no other way to have it."

"You loved them!"

He nodded slowly, and shut his eyes. For an instant—just an instant—the ghost of his former self seemed to hover about him. "I loved them," he agreed. "As I love you." He opened his eyes again, and the ghost vanished. Looked at her. "If I didn't, this would have no power."

She wanted to scream, but the sound was trapped within her. *A nightmare*, she begged herself. *That's all it is, so wake up. Wake up! Wake up. . . .*

He handled her gently but forcefully, sitting her down on the rough stone slab. Lowering her slowly down onto it, until she lay full length upon its abrasive surface. Numb with shock, she felt him bind her limbs down tightly, until it was impossible for her to move. Protests arose within her—promises, reasoning, desperate pleas—but her voice was somehow lost to her. She could only stare at him in horror as he shut his eyes, could only watch in utter silence as he worked to bind the wild fae to his purpose . . . in preparation for the primal Pattern of Erna. Sacrifice.

At last his eyes opened. They glistened wetly as he looked at her; she wondered if there were tears.

"I love you," he told her. "More than everything, save life itself. And I would have surrendered even that for you, in its proper time. But not now. Not when they've opened hell beneath me, and bound me to it by the very power I taught them how to use. . . . Too many prayers, Almea! Too many minds condemning my work. This planet is fickle, and responds to such things. I need time," he repeated, as though that explained everything. As though that justified killing their children.

He raised a long knife into her field of vision, even as his slender hand stroked the hair gently out of her eyes. "You go to a far gentler afterlife than I will ever know," he said softly. "I apologize for the pain I must use to send you there. That's a necessary part of the process." The hand dropped back from her forehead, and the glittering blade was before her eyes.

"The sacrifice is not of your body," he explained. His voice was cold in the darkness. "It is . . . of my humanity."

Then the knife lowered, and she found her voice. And screamed—his name, protests of her love, a hundred supplications . . . but it was too late, by that point. Had been too late, since true night fell.

There was no one listening.

He leaned slowly, and shut his eyes like an insect—like an instant—the ghost of his humor still seemed to hover about him. "I do not feel like it," he said. "But I love you." He opened his eyes again and the ghost vanished. He looked at her, like dull ivory, they would have no power.

She wanted to scream, but the sound she trapped within her. A whimper, she banged his wrist. "Half hit me, you're waking me. Wake up."

He handed her a body hesitantly sitting her down on the bunk against slab. Turning her about, drew down until it reached her hip smiled, used the waster bound with shock, she ran to her fingers and the slightly until he was insensible for her to have Perhaps her waking, unasked, reasoning, accepting place, she held was something to her. She would only take at him in particular be shatters, you could only watch in amazement at he worked to hand the will use to his purpose only in preparation for the arrival of time, waiting.

At last his eyes opened. They glanced wary as he looked at her. He stared at the expression.

"Time well, p..." said he. "Bird clan everything save the scant. And I would not be surprised even that for you imagine a particular hour not time. No when they're paper bell through me, and hoped time to relay in...any power I assist them how to use. "Too many prayer. Although. Too many minds concerning my self. Time plucks my shelter me and me undo in such things. I used time," he repeated, as though that explained everything... although that just tied a kind of their shoulder.

He raised a long curl into his field a vision, even as he smiled. Handsome what the last of my bud out of his room. "And so to a far extent a month soon I will let you know," he explained in some say my wisest his last part. I must use to send you there. There's a new way I tried the prophecy. The hand drops about from her forehead and she put mine slide and a flowing eye.

"insofar...is not enough being," he explained his voice was cold in the stillness... of my humanity."

Then the smile lowered, and she raised her voice. And so remains this part... taking of her love. A hundred suppositions... but it was too late. She spoke. Had been too late, since true night itself.

There was no one listening.

CITY OF
SHADOWS

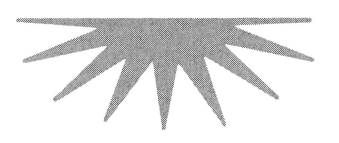

One

Damien Kilcannon Vryce looked like he was fully capable of handling trouble, for which reason trouble generally gave him a wide berth. His thick-set body was hard with muscle, his hands textured with calluses that spoke of fighting often, and well. His shoulders bore the weight of a sizable sword in a thick leather harness with no sign of strain, despite the fact that the dust stains on his woolen shirt and the mud which caked his riding boots said that he had been traveling long and hard, and ought to be tired. His skin had tanned and scarred and peeled and tanned again, over and over again with such constancy that it now gave the impression of roughly tanned leather. His hands, curled lightly about the thick leather reins, were still reddened from exposure to the dry, cold wind of the Divider Mountains. All in all a man to be reckoned with . . . and since the thieves and bravos of Jaggonath's outskirts preferred less challenging prey, he passed unmolested through the crowded western districts, and entered the heart of the city.

Jaggonath. He breathed in its dusty air, the sound of its name, the fact of its existence. He was here. At last. After so many days on the road that he had almost forgotten he had a goal at all, that there was anything else but traveling . . . and then the city had appeared about him, first the timber houses of the outer districts, and then the brick structures and narrow cobbled streets of the inner city, rising up like stone crops to greet the dusty sunlight. It was almost enough to make him forget what it took to get here, or why they had chosen him and no one else to make this particular crossing.

Hell, he thought dryly, *no one else was fool enough to try.* He tried to picture one of the Ganji elders making the long trek from westlands to east—crossing the most treacherous of all mountain ranges, fighting off the nightmare beasts that made those cold peaks their home, braving the wild fae and all that it chose to manifest, their own souls' nightmares given substance—but the diverse parts of such a picture, like the facets of a badly-worked Healing, wouldn't come together. Oh, they might have agreed to come, provided they could use the sea for transport . . . but that had its own special risks, and Damien preferred the lesser terrors of things he could do battle with to the unalterable destructive power of Erna's frequent tsunami.

He prodded his horse through the city streets with an easy touch, content to take his time, eager to see what manner of place he had come to. Though night was already falling, the city was as crowded as a Ganji marketplace at high noon. Strange habits indeed, he mused, for people who lived so near a focal point of malevolence. Back in Ganji, shopkeepers would already be shuttering their windows against the fall of night, and making ward-signs against the merest thought of Coreset. Already the season had hosted nights when no more light than that of a single moon shone down to the needy earth, and the first true night was soon to come; all the creatures that thrived on darkness would be most active in this season, seeking blood or sin or semen or despair or whatever special substance they required to sustain themselves, and seeking it with vigor. Only a fool would walk the night unarmed at such a time—or perhaps, Damien reflected, one who lived so close to the heart of that darkness that constant exposure had dulled all sense of danger.

Or was it that there was simply safety in numbers, in a city so large that no matter how many were taken in the night, the odds were good that it wouldn't be you?

Then something caught his eye; he reined up suddenly, and his three-toed mount snorted with concern. Laughing softly, he patted it on the neck. "No danger here, old friend." Then he considered, and added, "Not yet, anyway."

He dismounted and led the dappled creature across the street, to the place that had caught his eye. It was a small shop, with a warded canopy set to guard the walkway just outside, and a marquis that caught the dying sunlight like drops of fire. *Fae Shoppe* it said, in gleaming gold letters. *Resident loremaster. All hours.*

He looked back over his shoulder, to the gradually darkening street. Night was coming on with vigor, and God alone knew what that would mean. The sensible thing to do would be to find an inn and drop off his things, get his mount under guard, and affix a few wards to his luggage . . . but when had he ever done the sensible thing, when curiosity was driving him? He took a moment to remove his most valuable bag from the horse's back—his only valuable bag, in fact—locked the beast's lead chain to a hitching rack, and went inside.

Into another world. The dying sunlight gave way to orange and amber, the flickering light of tinted lamps. Warm-toned wood added to the sense of harmony, possibly aided by a ward or two; he could feel his travel-weary muscles relax as he entered, but the Working that made them do so was too subtle to define.

All about him were *things*. Marvelous objects, no two of them alike, which filled to overflowing the multitude of shelves, display cases, and braces that lined the interior of the shop. Some were familiar to him, in form if not in detail. Weapons, for instance: his practiced eye took in everything from blades to pistols, from the simple swords of his own martial preference to the more complicated marvels that applied gunpowder in measured doses—and just as often misapplied it. Household items, of every kind imaginable. Books and bookmarks and bookstands, pen and paper. And some objects that were clearly Worked: talismans etched with ancient Earth symbols, intricately knotted wards, herbs and spices and perfumes and oils, and all the equipment necessary to maximize their effect.

A bizzare sort of gift shop, or general grocery? He read some of the labels, and shook his head in amazement. Was it possible—really possible—that the objects surrounding him were Worked? *All* of them? What a fantastic notion!

In the center of the room, dividing the public area from that space which clearly served as a reference library, a glass counter served to support several dozen books and the man who was perusing them. He was pale in a way that westerners rarely were, but Damien sensed nothing amiss about the coloring; despite its stark contrast with his dark hair, eyes, and clothing, it probably meant nothing more sinister than that he worked the late shift. In a city that remained active all night, anything was possible.

The man lifted up his wire-rimmed spectacles as he noticed his visitor, then removed them; Damien caught a flash of delicately etched sigils centered in the circles of clear glass. "Welcome," he said pleasantly. "Can I help you with anything?"

The counter with filled with more whimsical objects, taffeta-quilt hearts and small calico bags with rosette bows, wards made up to look like massive locks and chalices engraved with sexually suggestive motifs. All of them labeled. And if the labels were accurate. . . .

"Do they really Work?" he asked.

The pale man nodded pleasantly, as though he heard the question every day. "Lady Cee's a certified adept. Each object in the shop has been fae-bound to a purpose. Results are guaranteed, in most cases. Can I show you something in particular?"

He was about to answer when a door in the back of the shop swung open—well camouflaged by the mountains of books that flanked it, or perhaps by a Working?—and a woman entered, her bright eyes jubilant. "Found it!" she announced.

Her associate sighed melodramatically and shut the thick volume before him. "Thank gods. At last."

"If I hadn't worked that damned Obscuring on it in the first place—" She stopped as she saw Damien, and a smile lit her face. "Hello, I'm sorry. I didn't realize we had company."

It was impossible not to return that infectious smile. "Lady Cee, I presume?"

"If you like. Ciani of Faraday." She came forward and offered her hand, which he grasped with pleasure. Dark hair and soft brown skin served as a backdrop for wide, expressive eyes, and lips that seemed to find their natural placement in a broad grin of pleasure. Fine lines fanned out from the corners of her eyes, hinting at age, but the quality of her skin and the firmness of her figure told another story. It was impossible to read either her true age or her origin, which might have been intentional; whatever the case, he found himself more than marginally attracted to her.

Be honest, Damien. You've always been attracted to things fae-wise, and here's a true adept; would her looks have made much of a difference?

"My pleasure," he said with gusto. "Damien Kilcannon Vryce, lately of Ganji-on-the-Cliffs, at your service." Her eyes crinkled with amusement, which hinted that she knew how many titles he was omitting. She must have worked a Knowing on him as soon as she saw him; that he had never noticed her doing it said much for her skill.

But that stands to reason. As an adept she isn't simply more powerful than most, she's immersed in the fae in a way no others can be. Then he remembered where he was, and thought in amazement, *What must that mean for her, to have such awareness, living in the shadow of such a great Darkness. . . .*

"And are you the resident loremaster, as well?"

She bowed her head. "I have that honor."

"Meaning . . . an archivist?"

"Meaning, I research, collect, Know, and disseminate information. As it is said our ancestors once used machines to do, before the Great Sacrifice. For a modest consultation fee, of course."

"Of course."

"Meaning also that my position is one of absolute neutrality, regarding the uses to which such data is put." Her eyes sparkled mischievously, and she added, "Discretion assured."

"That's necessary, I assume."

"Oh, yes. We learned that the hard way. Too many so-called Datalords were killed in the early days, by sorcerers seeking vengeance for one indiscretion or another. We learned not to take sides. And the populace learned to respect our neutrality, in order to benefit from our continued presence. —Is there something I can show you? Or some service we can offer?"

He wondered just how deep within him her Knowing had searched. And watched her closely as he said, "I need a local fae-map. Do you carry them?"

Her eyes sparkled with amusement, reflecting the amber of the lamplight. "I think we may," she answered simply. Not rising to the bait. "Current or historical?"

"Current."

"Then I'm sure we do." She stepped back to search through one of the book-strewn shelves, and after a few minutes chose and pulled forth a heavy vellum sheet. She laid it out on the counter before him and pinned its corners down with several unlabeled objects that had been lying about, allowing him to study it.

He whistled softly. Currents of fae flowed through the city in half a dozen directions, each carefully labeled as to its tenor and tidal discrepancies. North of the city, beyond the sheltered ports of Kale and Seth and across the twisted straits that separated two continents, a spiral of wild currents swirled to a focal point so thick with notes and measurements that he could hardly make out its position. The Forest? he wondered, seeking out the region's name from among the myriad notes. Yes, the Forest. And smack dab in the middle of it was the wildest fae on any human continent, and by far the most dangerous. So close!

"Will it do?" she asked. In a tone of voice that said plainly that she knew it made the fae-maps of his home look like mere road maps of a few simple country paths. He had never seen, nor even imagined, anything like this.

"How much?"

"Fifty local, or its western equivalent. Or barter," she added.

Intrigued, he looked up at her.

"We have very few visitors from your region, and fewer still who brave the Dividers. Your news and experience are worth quite a bit to me—professionally speaking, of course. I might be willing to trade to you what you want, in return for what you know."

"Over dinner?" he asked smoothly.

She looked him over, from his mud-caked boots to his rough woolen shirt; he thought he felt the fae grow warm about him, and realized that she was Knowing him as well.

"Isn't there someplace you're supposed to be?" she asked, amused.

He shrugged. "In a week. They don't know I'm here early—and won't unless I tell them. No one's waiting up for me," he assured her.

She nodded slightly as she considered it. Then turned to the man beside her—who was already waiting with an answer.

"Go on, Cee." He, too, was smiling. "I can hold the shop till midnight. Just get back before the—" He stopped in mid-sentence, looked uncomfortably at Damien. "Before *they* come, all right?"

She nodded. "Of course." From under a pile of papers she drew out two objects, a ward on a ribbon and a small, clothbound notebook. These she gave to the man, explaining, "When Dez comes in, give him these charts. He wanted more . . . but I can do only so much, working with the Core stars. If he wants anything more, try to convince him to trust the earth-fae. I can do a more detailed Divining with that."

"I will."

"And Chelli keeps asking for a charm for her son, to ward against the perils of the true night. I've told her I can't do that. No one can. She's best off just keeping him inside . . . she might come in again to ask."

"I'll tell her."

"That's it, I think." She lifted a jacket from the coatstand near the door, and smiled at Damien as she donned it. "Your treat?"

"My honor," he responded.

"The New Sun, then. You'll like it." She glanced back, toward her assistant. I'll be there if you need me, Zen; just Send."

He nodded.

Damien offered her his arm. She stared at it for a moment, clearly amused by the custom, then twined her own smaller limb about it. "You can stable your horse there," she informed him. "And I think you'll find the neighborhood . . . interesting."

Interesting was an understatement.

The Inn of the New Sun was one of several buildings that bordered Jaggonath's central plaza, as prime a piece of real estate as one could ask for. The restaurant's front room looked out upon several neat acres of grass and trees, divided up into geometrical segments by well-maintained walkways. By its numerous pagodas and performance stands, Damien judged that the plaza hosted a score of diverse activities, probably lasting through all the warm-weather months. It was truly the center of the city, in more than just geography. And at the far side, gleaming silver in the moonlight. . . .

A cathedral. *The* cathedral. Not surrounded by satellite buildings of its faith, as was the Great Cathedral in Ganji, but part and parcel of the bustling city life. He moved to where he could get a view clear of the trees, and exhaled noisily in admiration. If rumor was truth, it was the oldest extant church on the eastern continent. Built at the height of the Revival, it was a monument to the tremendous dramatic potential of the Neo-Gothic style. Archways and buttresses soared toward the heavens, creamy white marble reflecting moonlight and lamplight both with pristine perfection. Set against the dark evening sky, the building glowed as though fae-lit, and drew worshipers to it like moths to a flame. On its broad steps milled dozens—no, *hundreds* of worshipers, and their faith tamed the wild fae that flowed about their feet, sending it out again laden with calmness, serenity, and hope. Damien stared at it, awed and amazed, and thought, *Here, in this wild place, the Dream is alive. A core of order, making civilization possible. If only it could have been managed on a broader scale. . . .*

Her light touch on his sleeve reminded him of where he was and who he was with, and he nodded.

Later.

She ordered food for both of them. Local delicacies, she said. He decided not to ask what they'd looked like when they were alive. But despite his misgivings he found them delicious, and the thick, sweet ale that was Jaggonath's specialty was a welcome change after months of dried rations and water.

They talked. He told her stories, in payment for the map, embroidering upon his true adventures until her gentle smile warned him that he bordered on genuine dishonesty. And gave her real news, in a more sober vein. Five ships wrecked on the Ganji cliffs, a diplomat from the Wetlands lost in the tragedy. Summer storms from out of the desert, as if the sandlands themselves would claim new territory. Tsunami. Earthquakes. Politics. She was interested in everything, no matter how trivial it seemed to him, and would give him no information in return until he had finished to her satisfaction.

By the time their dessert came the night was as dark as most nights ever got, the sun and Core wholly gone, one moon soon to follow, a few lingering stars barely visible above the horizon.

"So," she said pleasantly, as she spooned black sugar—another Jaggonath specialty—into a thick, foamy drink. "Your turn? What is it you hunger most to know?"

He considered the several half-jesting answers he might have offered another woman, then reconsidered and discarded them. An open offer of information was just too valuable an opportunity to waste on social repartee.

"Forest or Rakh," he answered, after very little thought. "Take your pick."

For a moment—just the briefest moment—he saw something dark cross her countenance. Anger? Fear? Foreboding? But her voice was its usual light self as she leaned back and asked him, "Ambitious, aren't you?"

"Those things are only legends where I come from. And shadowy legends, at that."

"But you're curious."

"Who wouldn't be?"

"About the Forest? When merely thinking about it opens up a channel for the dark fae to travel? Most men prefer to avoid that risk."

The Forest. The fact that she had chosen that topic meant that it was the other one which had caused her such acute discomfort; he filed that fact away for future reference, and addressed himself to the issue she preferred. The Forest, called *Forbidden* in all the ancient texts. What did they know of it, even here? It was a focal point of the wildest fae, which in an earlier, less sophisticated age had been called *evil*. Now they knew better. Now they understood that the forces which swept across this planet's surface were neither good nor evil in and of themselves, but simply *responsive*. To hopes and fears, wards and spells and all the patterns of a Working, dreams and nightmares and repressed desires. When tamed, it was useful. When responding to man's darker urges, to the hungers and compulsions which he repressed in the light of day, it could be deadly. Witness the Landing, and the gruesome deaths of the first few colonists. Witness the monsters that Damian had fought in the Dividers, shards of man's darkest imaginings given fresh life and solid bodies, laying traps for the unwary in the icy wilderness.

Witness the Forest.

"Sheer concentration makes the fae there too strong to tame," she told him. "Manifestial response is almost instantaneous. In plainer English, merely worrying about something is enough to cause it to happen. Every man that's dared to walk in those shadows, regardless of his intentions, has left some dark imprint behind him. Every death that's taken place beneath those trees has bound the fae to more and greater violence. The Church once tried to master it by massive applications of faith—that was the last of the Great Wars, as I'm sure you know—but all it did was give them back their nightmares, with a dark religious gloss. Such power prefers the guarded secrets of the unconscious to the preferences of our conscious will."

"Then how can man thrive so close to it? How can Jaggonath—and Kale, and Seth, and Gehann—how can those cities even exist, much less function?"

"Look at your map again. The Forest sits at the heart of a whirlpool, a focal point of dark fae that draws like to like, sucking all malevolent manifestations toward its center. Most things that go in never come out again. If it were otherwise we could never live here, this close to its influence."

"You said that *most* things never leave."

She nodded, and her expression darkened. "There's a creature that lives within the Forest—maybe a demon, maybe a man—which has forced a dark sort of order upon the wild fae there. Legend has it that he sits at the heart of the whirlpool like a spider in its web, waiting for victims to become trapped in its power. His minions can leave the Forest and do, in a constant search for victims to feed to him."

"You're talking about the Hunter."

"You know the name?"

"I've heard it often enough, since coming east. Never with an explanation."

"For good reason," she assured him. "Merely mentioning the name opens a channel through the fae . . . people are terrified of such contact. It's more than just the Hunter himself. He's become our local bogeyman, the creature that lurks in dark corners and closets, whose name is used to scare children into obedience. Easterners are raised to fear the Hunter more than any other earthly power, save the Evil One himself. And don't take me wrong—he is, genuinely, both powerful and evil. His minions hunt the shadows of the eastern cities for suitable prey, to take back to the Forest to feed to him. Women, always; mostly young, inevitably attractive. It's said that he hunts them like wild animals there, in the heart of that land which responds to his every whim. A very few survive—or are permitted to survive, for whatever dark purpose suits him. All are insane. Most would be better off dead. They usually kill themselves, soon after."

"Go on," he said quietly.

"It's said that his servants can walk the earth as men, once the sun is gone. For which reason you'll rarely see women abroad alone after dark—they walk guarded, or in groups."

"You call it *he*," he said quietly. "You think it's a man."

"I do, myself. Others don't."

"An adept?"

"He would have to be, wouldn't he?"

"Whom the Forest dominated."

She studied him, as if choosing her words with care. "Maybe," she said at last. Watching him. "I think not."

Or he dominated the Forest. The thought was staggering. All the might of the Church had been pitted against the measureless evil in a war to end all wars . . . to no avail. Was it possible that one single man might dominate such a place, when thousands had given up their lives failing to do so?

With a start he realized that she had signaled for the bill, and was gathering her jacket about her shoulders. Had they been here that long?

"It's getting late," she said, apologetically. "I do have to get back."

"To meet with *them?*" He tried to keep his tone light, but there was an edge to it that he failed to disguise.

The bill was placed between them. He looked at it.

"There are ninety-six pagan churches in this city," she warned him. "Nineteen adepts, and nearly a thousand more that style themselves *sorcerors*, or its equivalent. You won't like any of them, or approve of what they do. So don't ask."

"I don't know about that. I rather like this one."

She looked at him, clearly bemused, and at last shook her head. "You're not half bad company, considering your livelihood. Far better than I expected."

He grinned. "I try."

"You'll be in town for a while?"

"If they can tolerate me."

She didn't ask who he was referring to, which confirmed the fact that she already knew. Her Knowing had been thorough indeed—and little surprise, in such a place as this.

He looked out into the night-bound plaza, and thought of the things that such darkness might hide.

"Come on," he told her, and he scattered eastern coins on the table. "I'll walk you back."

If the cathedral had seemed magnificent from a distance, it was even more impressive from up close. Greater archways soared above lesser ones, the space between them filled with a rich assortment of stylized carvings. Layer upon layer of ornamentation covered the vast edifice, as if its designer had suffered from a phobia of unadorned space; but if the whole of it was overworked, by modern standards, that too was part of its style. The strength of Revivalist architecture lay in its capacity to overwhelm the viewer.

Damien stood at the base of the massive front staircase and let himself open up to all that its presence implied: the faith of thousands bound together, serving one Law; the remnants of a great dream that had been damaged but not destroyed in one terrible war, that had fragmented man's Church and left him at the mercy of what this strange planet called Nature; the hope that someday faith would conquer fae, and the whole of Erna could be colonized—safely—at last.

All those impressions filled him, joining with the warmth of his body: the coursing heat of rich ale in his veins, the triumph of his arrival, and the exhilaration of sexual diplomacy.

If I were not so dusty, he had said to her, when at last they returned to her shop, *I might attempt to seduce you.*

If you were not so dusty, she had answered with a smile, *you might stand a chance of success.*

An excellent omen for the future, he thought.

The last congregants of the night were descending on both sides of him, parting like a wave as they poured down the ivory steps. No women walked alone, he noted, but they stayed together in small groups, or were guarded by men; even here, on God's own front steps, the shadow of the Hunter was felt.

Then the last well-wishers shook hands with their priest and made their descent, and the great ornate doors were swung slowly shut, closing out the night.

He looked at them for a while, admiring their intricate carvings, and then climbed the steps himself and knocked.

A sub-door opened and a robed man with a small lamp peeked out. Against the background of the gleaming white steps, in the wake of so many well-dressed attendants, Damien knew that he looked his grubbiest.

"Well?" the man asked, in a tone of voice that clearly stated: *We are closed for the night.* He shot a suspicious glance toward Damien's sword.

"The building is open?"

With a sigh of exasperation the man stepped aside, allowing

Damien to enter. Yes, technically the building was unlocked, and anyone could enter it to pray—that was Church custom, in east and west alike—and if some rough warrior wanted to do so at this time, the man had no right to turn him away. Damien had known that when he asked. But as he ducked beneath the lintel of the low, narrow sub-door, and entered the foyer of the cathedral itself, the man's hand fell like a warning on his shoulder.

"No arms," he instructed coolly.

Damien was more amazed than angered. The hilt of his sword was plainly visible over his shoulder, and its gold-worked pommel and quillons with their flame motif should have warned the man to better manners. Had it been so long since a member of his Order had entered this place, that these people knew nothing of their customs?

"Is His Holiness available?" he asked.

The man regarded him as though he had just worked a Cursing in his presence, and brushed at his sleeve as though somehow Damien's mere presence had made him dirtier. "The Holy Father is occupied," he said brusquely. "Come back in the morning, during our regular business hours, and you can apply for an audience."

"Tell him that Damien Kilcannon Vryce is here," he responded. "I think he'll see me."

The man stared at him for one long, hostile moment. And then at last decided that he would get rid of this unpleasant guest faster by indulging him than by trying to throw him out. He waved over an acolyte—a young boy with clear eyes and a willing smile—and said to him gruffly, "Go tell His Holiness—if he'll see you at all, which I doubt—that Damien Kilcannon Vryce desires an audience, *right now.*"

The boy ran off, eager to serve. Damien took the time to walk across the foyer and peek between the heavy alteroak doors, into the sanctuary itself. He caught a glimpse of velvet-clad pews, a gold-chased altar, a jeweled mural of the Prophet binding the Evil One to darkness—one of the few representations which the Church permitted.

Nice, he thought. *Very nice.*

"Father?"

The boy had returned. He stared at Damien with wide eyes, full of awe, as the robed man, clearly distressed, offered, "I'm sorry, Father. We didn't know who you were. Of course His Holiness will see you."

The boy moved to lead him, but Damien said gently, "No. I know the way. Thank you, son."

He could sense the boy gaping as he crossed the tiled floor, to a pair of heavy doors that must surely open on a staircase. How much had he been told? Damien tried to listen for whispers or some hint of movement behind him, but not until he had reached the stairs themselves, and the doors were swinging shut behind him, did he hear the youngster reveal what must have seemed an incredible truth.

In a whisper that was nine parts awe, and one part fear: "Father Vryce is a *sorceror*. . . ."

Damien laughed softly, as he ascended.

Two

Image of a Patriarch: stark white hair above aquiline features, eyes a cold, piercing blue. Thin lips drawn back in a hard line, a fleeting glimpse of flawless teeth within. Pale brown skin dried and thickened by age. Lines of character deeply incised: tense, severe, disapproving. The body, like the face, toughened rather than weakened by seventy winters of life. Broad, strong shoulders, from which cascaded a waterfall of ivory silk, voluminous enough to obscure the body's outline. Power—in every feature, even in his stance. Authority.

And something else, to be read in his face, his eyes, his very posture—and his voice, a rich baritone that any chorister would pray to possess. *Anger. Resentment. Distaste.*

Exactly what Damien had expected.

"You have a commission?" the Patriarch asked coldly.

Books lined every wall, punctuated by small, pierced-glass windows that broke up the city's lights into a thousand jeweled sparks. What furniture there was, was rich: a heavy mahogova desk, crimson velvet cushions on the single matching chair, antique drapes and patterned carpets that spoke of wealth in careful, tasteful investment. Damien looked around for some convenient resting spot, at last chose a shelf edge to support his bag while he rummaged inside it for the Matriarch's letter. Dust rose up from the travel-stained pack and settled on several of the nearer shelves; he could feel the Patriarch's eyes on him, disapproving, even before he faced him.

"Her Holiness sends her best," he announced, and he handed over the vellum envelope. The Patriarch regarded it for a moment, noting that the seal of the Church which granted it official status had been set to one side, so that the envelope remained open. He glanced up at Damien, briefly, cold blue eyes acknowledging the message: *She trusts you.* And adding his own: *I don't.*

Then he removed the commission itself and read.

Power, Damien thought. *He radiates power.* When he was certain that the Patriarch's attention was firmly fixed on the document, he whispered the key to a Knowing. Softly—*very* softly—knowing that if he were caught Working the fae at this time and place, he might well be throwing away everything he'd hoped to accomplish. But the words, barely spoken, went unheard. The fae gathered around him, softly, and wove a picture that his mind could interpret. And yes . . . it was as he had suspected. He wondered if the Patriarch even knew, or if the man attributed the force of his own presence to mere human concepts, like *charisma. Bearing.* Instead of recognizing the truth— which was that his every thought sent tiny ripples coursing through the fae, altering his environment to suit his will. A *natural*, in the vernacular. A born sorceror, whose chosen profession forbade him from acknowledging the very source of his authority.

At last the Patriarch nodded, and with carefully manicured hands he folded the commission again, sliding it back into its vellum container. "She thinks highly of you," he said, placing it on the desk beside him: statement of fact, with neither approval nor disapproval implied. *"He is loyal, she writes, and wholly dedicated to our mission. You may depend upon his honor, his vigilance, and his discretion."* He glared, and the thin mouth tightened. "Very well. I won't do you the dishonor of dissembling, Damien Kilcannon Vryce. Let me tell you just how welcome you are here—you and your sorcery."

Four long steps took him to the nearest window; Damien caught the flash of jeweled rings as he swung it open, revealing the lights of the city. For a moment he simply stared at them, as though something in the view would help him choose his words. "Since my earliest years," he said at last, "I've served this region. Since that day when I was first old enough to understand just what this planet was, and what it had done to mankind, I've devoted myself body and soul to our salvation. It meant adhering to one god, in a world where hundreds of would-be deities clamored for worship, promising cheap and easy miracles in return for minimal offerings. It meant clinging to a Church that still bled from the memory of its greatest defeat, in an age when triumphant temples rose up like wheat in springtime. I chose what was clearly the harder path because I believed in it— *believe* in it, Reverend Vryce!—and I have never once faltered in that faith. Or in my belief that such faith is necessary, in order to restore man to his Earth-born destiny."

A cold evening breeze gusted in through the window; the Patriarch turned his face into it, let the chill wind brush back his hair. "Most difficult of all was Church custom regarding the fae. Especially in this city, where sorcery is so cheap that the poor can buy visions of plentiful food more easily than the real thing ... and then they die of hunger, Reverend Vryce. Their bodies gutted by starvation, but a ghastly smile on their faces. Which is why I believe as I do—as my Church has believed, for nearly a thousand years. We won't tame this tyrannical force by parceling it out to sorcerers, for their paltry spells and their squalid conjurations. The more we expose it to humankind's greed, the more it stinks of our excesses. Gannon saw that very clearly, back in the Revival. He outlawed private sorcery for that very reason—and I agree with him, heart and soul. If you need an example of what the fae can do to a man, once it has hold of him ... consider the Prophet's Fall. Or the First Sacrifice. Witness all the monsters that the fae has brought to life, using man's fear as a template ... I swore to fight those things, Reverend Vryce. At any cost to myself. I swore that the fae would be tamed, according to the Prophet's guidelines.

"And then came a letter. From your Matriarch, your Holy Mother. Informing me that the west had begun an investigation into how the fae might be manipulated for Church purposes, by a chosen few trained toward that end. Sorcery! Dress it up in holy silks as you will, it still stinks. I argued with her, pleaded with her, I would have gone so far as to threaten her if I thought it would do any good ... but your Holy Mother is a headstrong woman, and her mind was made up. And now—I am watching my Church dissolve, Reverend Vryce, my dream of salvation corrupted ..." He turned back to Damien, cold eyes narrowed. "And you are the vehicle of that corruption."

"No one said you had to have me," Damien snapped—and instantly regretted his lack of control. He'd been prepared for much worse than this; why was he overreacting? It was the fae that had affected him, responding to the Patriarch's will. Why? What did he want?

For me to lose control, he realized. *For me to act in such a way that he would have no choice but to cast me out.* It staggered the imagination, that a man who neither accepted nor understood the fae could Work it so well—without ever knowing that he did. How much of the man's intolerance was rooted in his own need to deny the truth?

"No," the Patriarch agreed. "I could have fragmented the Church instead, given birth to a schism that might never heal ... or begun a holy war, trying to avoid that. Those options were even more distasteful, in the end, and so I agreed. Send me your sorceror, I told her. Let me see what he does. Let me see how he operates. Let me see for myself that his Working is no threat to our faith." His expression was icy. "If you can demonstrate that to my satisfaction I'll be a very surprised man."

Mustering all his self-control, Damien answered cooly, "I'll regard that as a goal, Holiness."

The blue eyes fixed on him, pinpoints of azure fire. "Damien Kilcannon Vryce. Knight of King Gannon's Order of the Golden Flame. Companion of the Earth-Star Ascendant. Reverend Father of the Church of the Unification of Human Faith on Erna. What is our calling, to you?"

Damien stiffened. "A dream—that I would die to uphold, or kill to defend."

The Patriarch nodded slowly. "Yes. Well recited. The definition of your Order—first voiced in a more bloodthirsty time than this, I dare say. But *you*, Reverend Vryce—the man. The dreamer. What do *you* believe?"

"That you're wrong," Damien answered quietly. "That our traditional belief system is outdated. That our ancestors perceived of the world in terms of black and white, when nearly all of it is made up of shades of gray. That the Church must adapt to that truth, in order to remain a vital entity on this world. The survival of our dream," he stressed, "depends upon it."

For a long moment the Patriarch simply gazed upon him, silent. "She chose well," he said at last. Ivory silk rippled in the breeze as he reached out to take hold of the window and shut it again. "But tell me this. When you work your sorcery—when you hold the essence of this world in your hands, and use your will to give it form—can you honestly tell me that the concept of power, *for its own sake*, doesn't tempt you? Have you never once Worked the fae for your own good—your own *personal* good, independent of the Church's need? Never once changed the face of Nature for your own benefit? Or dreamed of doing so?"

"I'm as human as you are," Damien answered curtly. "We all have our temptations. But our ability to rise above them—to serve an ideal, rather than the dictates of selfish instinct—is what defines us as a species."

"Ah, yes." The Patriarch nodded. "The Prophet's words. He failed us, you'll recall. And himself. As have all men, who tried to reconcile sorcery with our faith. Remember that."

He walked to the heavy mahogova chair and sat down in it, smoothing the folds of his robe beneath him as he did so. And he sighed. "You'll have your students, Reverend Vryce. Against my better judgment and despite my objections, but you'll have them. A dozen of our most promising acolytes—chosen not because they have great sorcerous potential, but because their theological background is sound. You will not reach out beyond that group until I'm satisfied that this ... *experiment* ... can proceed without danger to my charges. Or my Church. Am I making myself clear?"

Damien bowed, and managed not to grin. Barely. "Very clear, Holiness."

He clapped his hands twice. Barely a few seconds later the door swung open, and a young girl in servant's livery entered.

"This is Kami. She'll get you settled in. Kami, take Reverend Vryce to the rooms that have been prepared for him. See that he has a schedule of our services, and anything he needs for tonight. Breakfast is in the Annex, at eight," he informed Damien. "A chance to meet the rest of our staff under slightly less ... *trying* circumstances." His mouth twitched slightly; a smile? "Is that too early for you?"

"I'll manage it, Holiness."

The Patriarch nodded to Kami, a clear gesture of dismissal. Damien gathered up his pack and turned to follow her—but when they reached the door the Patriarch called his name softly, and he turned back.

"When it comes time to die," the Patriarch said, "—and the time will come, as it comes to all men—what will you do then? Bow down to Nature, to the patterns of Earth-life which are the core of our very existence? Help us to lay a foundation whereby our descendants can reclaim the stars? Or submit to the temptations of this alien magic, and sell your soul for another few years of life? As the Prophet tried to do? —Consider that as you retire, Reverend Vryce."

It was clearly a dismissal, but Damien stood his ground. "The fae isn't magic."

The Patriarch waved one ringed hand, dismissing the thought. "Semantic exercises. What's the real difference?"

"Magic can be controlled," Damien reminded him. He gave that a moment to sink in, then added, "Isn't that what Erna's problem is all about?"

And he bowed—with only a hint of defiance. "I'll consider it, Holiness. Good night."

Three

The sun had set.

Narilka stood in the shop's narrow doorway, eyes fixed on the western horizon. She was cold inside, just as the night was cold without. The sun had set while she was downstairs. Long ago, by the looks of it. How could she have been so careless?

The stars were almost gone.

There was no strong light in the heavens, save one full moon that stood balanced along the eastern horizon. Soon even that would be gone, and only the stars of the Rim—sparse, insubstantial—would accompany a slender crescent in the west, lighting her way home.

For a moment she almost went back into the shop, panic tightening her throat. *Help me*, she would say, *I've been at work longer than I should have, please walk me home. . . .* But home was a good distance away and Gresham would be busy—and besides, he had already expressed his total disdain for her fear of the night, often enough that she knew any plea to him would fall on deaf ears. *You carry wards enough to supply the damned city with 'em*, he'd say scornfully. *Women have walked the streets with less, and made it home all right. Where's your sense, girl? I have work to do.*

With one last deep breath of the shop's dusty air, taken for courage, Narilka forced herself to step out into the night. The chill of the autumn evening wound around her neck like icy tendrils—or was that her fear manifesting?—and she drew her shawl closer about her, until its thick wool managed to ward off the worst of the cold.

Was she overreacting? *Was* she being unreasonable? Gresham had said it so often that now she was beginning to doubt herself. Did she really have any concrete evidence that the risk to her was greater than that facing other women—which is to say, that a female should always be careful and keep moving, but most survived the night?

As she passed by the silversmith's shop she stopped, long enough to catch sight of her reflection in the smooth glass storefront. Thick hair, onyx-black; smooth white skin, now flushed pink from the cold; lashes as thick as velvet, framing eyes nearly as dark. She was delicate and lovely, as a flower is lovely, and fragile as a porcelain doll. It was a face mortal women envied, men would die for, and one—neither man nor mortal, but an evil thing, Erna's darkness made incarnate—would destroy, with relish.

Shivering, she hurried onward. The faster she went, the sooner she would get home. In the inner streets of Jaggonath there were still people about, crowds enough that she could imagine herself lost among them. But they thinned as she left the commercial districts, leaving her feeling naked in the night. She had to keep moving. Her parents must be worried sick by now—and with good reason. She looked about herself nervously, noting the abandoned streets of Jaggonath's western district, the tiny houses set farther and farther apart. The road had turned to mud beneath her feet, cold enough to chill her through the soles of her shoes but not yet frozen enough to be solid; her feet made rythmic sucking noises, painfully conspicuous, as she walked. She felt like a walking target.

The Hunter. That was what they called him. She wondered what he was, what he had once been. A man? That was what the tavern girls whispered, between giggles and mugs of warm beer, in the safety of their well-lit workplace. *Once* a man, they said, and now something else. But with a man's lust still, corrupted though it might be. Why else were all his victims female, young, and inevitably attractive? Why would he have such a marked taste for beauty—and for delicate beauty, most of all—if some sort of male hunger didn't still cling to his soul?

Stop it! she commanded herself. She shook her head rapidly, as if that could cast out the unwanted thoughts. The fear. *Don't!* She would make it home all right, and everybody would be very relieved, and that was that. Her parents would be furious at Gresham for keeping her after dark and they would write him an angry letter, which he would promptly ignore—and then it would be over. Forever. No more than a memory. And she could say to her children that yes, she had been out after dark, and they would ask her what it was like, and she would tell them. A fireside story like any other. Right?

But you are what he wants, a voice whispered inside her. *Exactly. You are what he sends his minions into Jaggonath to find.*

"Damn you!" she cried suddenly—meaning her parents, her fears, the night itself. And her own looks, for that matter. Gods above, what might her life have been like if she were unattractive, or merely plain, or even of a sturdier type than she was? Might she have been allowed to play outside after sunset, as some other children were? Might she have grown accustomed to the night, ranking its terrors alongside other childhood fears, dealing with them simply and rationally? *Come home on time,* her parents would have cautioned. *Don't talk to strangers. Raise up a ward if some demon appears.* And then they would have let her go out. Gods of Erna, what freedom, what freedom!

She reached up to wipe a tear, half frozen, from her cheek, and then stopped walking in order to dislodge a bit of mud that had oozed its way into her shoe. And as she did so, she became intensely aware of the silence that surrounded her. No other footsteps sounded in the night, though the road on all sides of her had been heavily trod. No birds sang, no insects chittered, no children cried in the distance. Nothing. It was as if the whole world had died, suddenly—as if she were the only creature left on Erna, and this section of road the last spot where life might exist, in the whole of creation.

Then a sound behind her made her start suddenly. Almost silent, a mere hint of movement, but set against the night's backdrop of utter soundlessness it had the power of a scream. She whirled about, staring back the way she had come.

At a man.

"Forgive me." His voice was smooth, his carriage elegant. He bowed, soft brown hair catching the moonlight as he moved. "I didn't mean to frighten you."

"You didn't," she lied. Another bit of mud was trickling coldly into her shoe, but she didn't want to take her eyes from him to dislodge it; she shifted her weight a bit, and almost fell as a result. Gods, was she that unsteady? She didn't dare look as afraid as she felt. The Hunter was attracted to fear. "It just seemed so . . . quiet."

"The night can be like that." He walked toward her slowly, casually, his languid grace mesmeric in the moonlight. A tall man, lean, with delicate features, arresting eyes. Unadorned, save for a thin gold band that held back his hair from his face, the latter cut shoulder-length in a style several years out of date. His eyes were pale gray flecked with silver, and in the moonlight they flashed like diamonds. She sensed a cold amusement lurking just beneath his surface. "Forgive me," he repeated, "but a young woman out alone? It seemed unusual. Are you all right?"

It occurred to her that she hadn't heard him approach, that in the midst of all this sticky mud she should have had some warning—

but then his eyes caught hers, held hers, and suddenly she couldn't remember why that bothered her.

"Yes," she stammered. "That is—I think so." She felt breathless, as if she had been running instead of walking. She tried to step back, but her body wouldn't obey. What kind of Working had he used to bind her?

But though he came close—too close—it was only to touch her chin with the tip of a well-manicured finger, turning her face up toward him. "So fragile," he murmured. "So fine. And alone in the night. Not wise. Would you like an escort?"

She whispered it. "Please."

He offered his arm. After a moment, she took it. An antiquated gesture, straight out of the Revival period. Her hand shook slightly as it came to rest on the wool of his sleeve. No warmth came from the arm beneath, or any other part of him; he was cold—he radiated cold—like the night itself. Just as she, despite her best intentions, radiated fear.

Gods above, she prayed, *just get me home. I'll be more careful in the future, I swear it. Just get me home tonight.*

It seemed to her he smiled. "You're afraid, child."

She didn't dare respond. *Just let me get through tonight. Please.*

"Of what? The darkness? The night itself?"

She knew she shouldn't speak of such things, but she couldn't hold back; his voice compelled response. "The creatures that hunt in it," she whispered.

"Ah." He laughed softly. "And for good reason. They do value your kind, child, that feed on the living. But these—" and he touched the wards embroidered on her sleeve, the warding clasps that held back her hair "—don't they bind enough fae to guard you?"

Enough to keep away demons, she thought. Or so it should have been. But now, suddenly, she wasn't sure.

He put his hand beneath her chin, turning her gently to face him. Where his fingers touched her flesh there was cold, but not merely a human chill; it burned her, as a spark of fire might, and left her skin tingling as it faded. She felt strangely disassociated from the world around her, as if all of it was a dream. All of it except for him.

"Do I read you correctly?" he asked. "Have you never seen the night before?"

"It's dangerous," she whispered.

"And very beautiful."

His eyes were pools of silver, molten, that drew her in. She shivered. "My parents thought it best."

"Never been outside, when sun and Core had set. Never! I wasn't aware the fear had reached such an extreme here. Even now . . . you don't look. You won't see."

"See what?" she managed.

"The night. The beauty of it. The *power*. The so-called dark fae, a force so fragile that even the moonlight weakens it—and so strong in the darkness that death itself falls back before it. The tides of night, each with its own color and music. An entire world, child!—filled with things that can't exist when the light in the heavens is too strong."

"Things which the sun destroys."

He smiled, but his eyes remained cold. "Just so."

"I've never—been allowed."

"Then look now," he whispered. "And *see*."

She did—in his eyes, which had gone from pale gray to black, and from black to dizzying emptiness. Stars swirled about her, in a dance so complex that no human science could have explained it—but she felt the rhythms of it echo in her soul, in the pattern of mud beneath her feet, in the agitated pounding of her heart. All the same dance, earth and stars alike. *This is Earth science*, she thought with wonder. *The Old Knowledge*. Tendrils of fae seeped from the darkness to wind themselves about her, delicate strands of velvet purple that were drawn to her warmth like moths to flame. She shivered as they brushed against her, sensing the wild power within them. All about her the land was alive, with a thousand dark hues that the night had made its own: fragile fae, as he had said, nearly invisible in the moonlight—but strong in the shadows, and hauntingly beautiful. She tried to move toward it, to come closer to a tangle of those delicate, almost unseeable threads, but his hand on her arm stopped her, and a single word bound her. *Dangerous*, he cautioned; language without sound. *For you.*

"Yes," she whispered. "But oh, please. . . ."

Music filled the cool night air, and she shut her eyes in order to savor it. A music unlike any other she had ever heard, delicate as the fae itself, formless as the night that bound it. Jeweled notes that entered her not through her ears, as human music might, but through her hair and her skin and even her clothing; music that she took into her lungs with every breath, breathing out her own silver notes to add to their harmony. *Is this what the night is?* she wondered. *Truly?*

She felt, rather than saw, a faint smile cross his face. "For those who know how to look."

I want to stay here.

He laughed, softly. *You can't.*

Why? she demanded.

Child of the sunlight! Heir to life and all that it implies. There's beauty in that world, too, although of a cruder sort. Are you really ready to give all that up? To give up the light? Forever?

The darkness withdrew into two obsidian pinpoints, surrounded by fields of cracked ice. His eyes. The dark fae was alive in there, too, and a music that was far more ominous—and darkly seductive. She nearly cried out, for wanting it.

"Quiet, child." His voice was nearly human again. "The cost of that's too high, for you. But I know the temptation well."

"It's gone. . . ."

"It'll never be gone for you. Not entirely. Look."

And though the night was dark again, and silent, she was aware of something more. A tremor of deepest purple, at the edges of her vision. Faint echoes of a music that came and went with the breeze. "So beautiful. . . ."

"You avoided it."

"I was afraid."

"Of the darkness? Of its creatures? Such beings aren't kept at bay by a simple closed door, child, or by lamplight. If they want to know of you, they do, and if they want to have you, they certainly will. Your charmed wards are enough to keep lesser demons at bay, and against the greater ones mere lamplight and human company won't help you at all. So what's the point in locking yourself away from half the wonders of the world?"

"None," she breathed, and she knew it to be the truth.

He took her arm and applied gentle pressure, forward. It took her a moment to realize what he meant by it, and even then the gesture seemed strange. Too human, for this extrahuman night. In silence she let him walk her toward her home, his footsteps utterly silent beside her own. What else did she expect? All about them shadows danced, alien shapes given life by the moonlight. She shivered with pleasure, watching them. Was this hers forever now, this marvelous vision? Would it stay when he was gone—his gift to her, in this unearthly night?

At last, eons later, they came to the last rise before her house. And stood on it, silently, gazing upon the all-too-human abode. There, in the light, the music would fade. The fae would be gone. Bright sanity, in all its dull glory, would reign supreme.

His nostrils flared as he studied the small house, as if testing the breeze that came from it. "They're afraid," he observed.

"They expected me home before dark."

"They had good reason to fear." He said it quietly, but she sensed the threat behind his words. "You know that."

She looked into his eyes and saw in them such a mixture of coldness and power that she turned away, trembling. *It was worth it*, she thought. *Worth it to see the night like that. To have such vision, if only once.* Then the touch of his finger, cold against her skin, brought her back to face him.

"I won't hurt you," he promised. And a hint of a smile crossed his face—as if his own benevolence amused him. "As for what you do to yourself, for having known me . . . that's in your own hands. Now, I think, you'd better go home."

She stepped back, suddenly uncertain. Dazed, as the fae that had bound her will dissolved into the night. He laughed softly, a sound that was disconcertingly intimate; she sensed a glimmer of darkness behind it, and for a moment she could see all too clearly what was in his eyes. Black fae, utterly lightless. A silence that drank in all music. An unearthly chill, that hungered to consume living heat.

She took a step backward in sudden panic, felt the wet grass bunch beneath her feet.

"Nari!"

She whirled around, toward the source of the sound. Her father's form was silhouetted against the glowing house, as he ran up the rise to reach her. "Narilka! We've been so worried!" She wanted to run to him, greet him, to reassure him—to beg for his help, his protection—but suddenly she had no voice. It was as if his sudden appearance had shattered some intimate bond, and her body still ached for the lover it had lost. "Great gods, Nari, are you all right?"

He embraced her. Wordlessly. She couldn't have spoken. She clung to him desperately, dimly aware of the tears that were streaming down her face. Of her mother, running out to join them.

"Nari! Baby, are you all right? We didn't know what to do—we were so worried!"

"Fine," she managed. "Fine." She managed to disentangle herself from her father, and to stand alone with some degree of steadiness. "It was my fault. I'm sorry. . . ."

She looked back toward where her escort had last stood, and wasn't surprised to find him gone. Though the grass was crushed where she had been standing there were no such marks from beneath his feet, nor any other sign of his passage. Again, no surprise.

"Fine," she murmured—that single word, how little of the truth it conveyed!—and she let them lead her home, across the farmland, into the negligible safety of the light. And she mourned for the beauty that faded about her, as the shadows of night fell farther and farther behind. But that vision would be hers now, whenever she dared to look for it. His gift.

Whoever you are, I thank you. Whatever the cost, I accept it.

Reluctantly, she let them lead her inside.

Four

They used the river to gain the coast, though the swift-running water made them feel an equivalent of human nausea. One was lost at sea, caught up in Casca's evening tide and swept far beyond any hope of earthly purchase before his companions could reach him. His companions mourned, but only briefly; he had known the risk, as all of them had, and had signaled his acceptance when he entrusted himself to the cold, treacherous waters. To mourn him now—or to mourn anyone, at any time—would run counter to their very nature. *Regret* was not in their vocabulary, nor *sorrow*. They knew only hunger and—possibly—fear. And that special fealty which bound them together in purpose, which demanded that they brave the ultimate barrier and walk the human lands, in service to another.

By dawn they had found caves to hide in, ragged hidey-holes gutted out of granite cliffs by wind and ice and time. Below them the surf raged as tidal patterns crossed and tangled, Casca and Domina and Prima battling for dominance of the sea, while Sun and Core together ruled the sky. They slept as the dead sleep, oblivious to such liquid disputes, resting on mounds of newly killed animals, that of the caves' former occupants. Whose flesh did not interest them as such, though they licked at the dried blood once or twice upon awakening, as if to cleanse their palates. What little food such animals could supply had been drained from them quickly the night before, in battle, and flesh without purpose offered these creatures little sustenance. And no pleasure. Humankind, on the other hand, could offer both: pleasure and sustenance combined, more than even the rakh could offer. They knew that. They had tasted. They hungered for more, and their hunger was powerful enough to take the place of courage when it had to. As it often had to, in those nights that they skirted the sea.

After three and a half days—eight moonfalls—they sighted a light far out on the water, that revealed the presence of a small trading craft. Using flares they had brought for just such a purpose, they signaled a desperate cry for help. The sudden splash of green light against the black sky illuminated a small vessel, riding the waves with difficulty. An answering flare—life-orange, hot with promise—was sent aloft, and they watched with nightwise eyes as a small rowboat was lowered to the water, presumably to brave the deadly shoreline and, if possible, save them.

Food! one whispered.

Not yet, another cautioned.

We have a purpose, the third reminded them both.

They stood shoulder to shoulder on the cold northern shore, as they imagined real humans might stand, and cheered on their saviors in desperate voices—exactly as they imagined real humans might do. All the while arguing, in whispers, the value of food versus obedience.

There'll be humans enough once we reach the human lands, the wisest one among them pointed out—and they savored that thought, while the ship's men braved rock and surf to reach the shore.

Five

The interior of the boutique was small, and crowded with a tangle of hanging garments and treelike accessory displays; Damien had to push aside a rack of beaded belts to get far enough back from the mirror that the whole of his bulk could be reflected within its narrow confines.

He glanced at Ciani—who was managing not to smile—and then at the fluttering moth of a proprieter who picked at his clothes periodically, as though searching for pollen between the patterned layers. And back at the mirror.

And at last said: "I hope you're joking."

"It's the height of fashion."

The image that stared back at him was draped in multiple layers of purple cloth, each of a slightly different hue. The layered ends of vest over half-shirt over shirt proper, triple-tiered upper sleeves and cuffed pants—each in a different shade of plum, or grape, or lavender, some in subtle prints of the same—made him look, to his own eyes, like a refugee from some dyer's scrap heap.

"What all of those *in the know* are wearing," the proprieter assured him. He plucked at Damien's vest front, trying to pull the patterned cloth across the bulk of the stout man's torso. The thick layers of muscle which comprised most of Damien's bulk had been further padded by the eastland's rich foods and seductively sweet ale; at last the man gave up and stepped back, diplomatically not pointing out that fashions such as these were designed for considerably smaller men. "Subtly contrasting hues are the fashion this season. But if your taste runs more to the *traditional*," he stressed the word distastefully, as if to indicate that it wasn't normally part of his vocabulary, "I can show you something with more color, perhaps?"

"I doubt that would help."

"Look," Ciani was grinning. "You told me that you wanted to dress like a Jaggonath cleric—"

"A Jaggonath cleric *with taste*."

"Ah. You didn't say that."

He tried to glare, but the obvious merriment in her eyes made it difficult. "Let me guess. You got paid off by some pagan zealot to make me look like a fool?"

"Now, would I do that?"

"For the right price?"

"I'll have you remember I'm a professional consultant. First coin, sound contracts, reliable service. You get what you pay for, *Father*."

"I'm not paying you for this."

"Yes." Her brown eyes sparkled mischeviously. "There is that to consider."

"Please!" the proprieter seemed genuinely distressed by their exchange. "The lady Ciani is well known to us, your Reverence. She's helped clothe some of the most important people in Jaggonath—"

He stared at her in frank astonishment. "A *fashion* consultant? You?"

"I'm helping you, aren't I?"

"But, for real? I mean—professionally?"

"You don't think me capable?"

"Not at all! That is—yes, I do ... but why? I mean, why would someone pay an adept's consulting fee just to have you help pick out their clothing? One hardly needs the fae to get dressed in the morning."

"Ah, you are a foreigner." She shook her head sadly. "*Everything* here involves the fae. The mayor runs for reelection, he wants his sartorial emanations assessed. Some power-hungry businessman itches to close the deal of a lifetime, he needs someone to tell him which outfit will best serve that cause. Or say that some notable from another district comes to town, he wants his potential read in everything that he might wear. I consult on *everything*, Damien—because everything involves the fae, in one way or another. Now ... do you want this outfit, or not?"

He regarded his reflection with renewed interest, if not with aesthetic enthusiasm. "What will it do for me?

She folded her arms across her chest in mock severity. "I do usually get paid for this."

"I'll treat you to dinner."

"Ah. Such generosity."

"At an expensive restaurant."

"You were going to do that anyway."

He raised an eyebrow. "I thought you couldn't read the future?"

"I didn't. It was obvious."

He sighed melodramatically. "Two dinners, then. *Mercenary* lady."

"My middle name, you know." She came up to where he stood and studied him casually. He tried to discover some hint of a Working in her demeanor—a whispered word, a subtle gesture, perhaps eyes tracking some visualized symbol used for a key, even some indication that she was concentrating—but there was nothing. If he hadn't seen her Work before, he would have thought she was tricking him.

Reading: not the future, but the present. Not *fate*, but *tendency*. A true Divining was impossible, as there was no certain future, but the seeds of all possible futures existed in the present moment. If one had skill enough, one could read them.

"You'll stand out in a crowd," she assured him.

He laughed softly.

"Among strangers, men will be put off. Women will find you . . . intriguing."

"I can live with that."

"Among those who know you . . . there aren't that many in Jaggonath, are there?" Her brown eyes twinkled. "*I* think you look charming. Your students will be even more terrified of you than they are now—no major change there. I read at least one barmaid who will find you unutterably attractive."

"That's appealing."

Her eyes narrowed. "She's married."

"Too bad."

"As for your superiors . . ." She hesitated. "Superior? Is there only one?"

He felt himself tense at the thought of the man. *Easy, Damien. You've got months to go, here. Get a hold of yourself.* "Only one that matters."

She checked him out from head to foot, then did the same again. "In this outfit," she proclaimed at last, "you will irritate the hell out of him."

He stared at her for a minute, then broke into a grin. And turned to face the proprieter, who was nervously twisting a red silk scarf between his fingers.

"I'll take it," he declared.

The street outside was gray upon gray, chill autumn sunlight slowly giving way to the shadows of Jaggonath's dusk. Dark shapes shivered about the corners of an alleyway, the cavernous mouth of an open doorway, the scurrying feet of a dozen chilled pedestrians. Was it lamp shadows, tricking the eye? Or some force that genuinely desired life, and might seek it out in sunlight's absence?

"Hey." She prodded him. "Ease up. You're not at work."

"Sorry." He caught up half his packages under his right arm, carried the rest with that hand. So that he might walk with her close to his other side, her body heat tangible through the coarse wool of his shirt. His hand brushing hers, in time to their walking.

"Your Patriarch doesn't approve of this, does he?"

"What? Shopping?"

"Our being together."

He chuckled. "Did you think he would?"

"I thought you might have charmed him into it."

"The Patriarch is immune to charm. And most other human pleasantries, I suspect. As for us . . . suffice it to say that battle lines have been drawn, and we both are poised behind our armaments. He with his moral obsessions, and I with my fixation on rights to an independent private life. It'll be quite a skirmish, once it starts."

"You sound like you're looking forward to it."

He shrugged. "Open conflict is infinitely more attractive to me than fencing with hints and insinuations. I'm a lousy diplomat, Cee."

"But a good teacher?"

"Trying to be."

"Can I ask how that's going? Or is it . . . classified?"

"Hardly." He grimaced, and shifted his packages again. "I have twelve young fledglings, ranging in age from eleven to fifteen. With marginal potential at best. I culled out two of the younger ones, who seemed to be in the worst throes of puberty. Damned rotten time to be teaching anyone to Work . . . and I think His Holiness knows it, too." He remembered his own adolescence, and some very nasty things he had unconsciously created. His master had made him hunt them down and dispatch them, each and every one; it wasn't one of his more pleasant memories. "Hard to say whether they're more terrified of me or of the fae. Not a good way to start out. Still, they're all positives on one scale or another, so there's hope, right? As of yesterday—"

He saw her stiffen suddenly. "Ciani? What is it?"

"Current's shifted," she whispered. Her face was pale. "Can't you see?"

Rather than state the obvious—that only an adept could see such things without conscious effort—he worked a quick Seeing and observed the earth-fae himself. But if there was any change in the leisurely flow of that force about their feet, it was far too subtle for his conjured vision to make out. "I can't—"

She gripped his arm with fingers that were suddenly cold. "We need to warn—"

An alarm siren pierced the dusk. A horrendous screeching noise that wailed like a banshee down the narrow stone streets, and echoed from the brickwork and plaster that surrounded them until the very air was vibrating shrilly. Damien covered an ear with one hand, tried to reach the other without dropping all his purchases. The sound was a physical assault—and a painfully effective one.

Whoever designed that siren, he thought, *must have served his apprenticeship in hell.*

Then, just as quickly, the sound was gone. He took his hand down nervously, ready to hold it to his head again if anything even remotely similar started up. But she took his hand in hers and squeezed it. "Come on," she whispered. He could barely hear over the ringing in his ears, but a gesture made it clear what she wanted. "Come with me."

She urged him forward, and he went. Running by her side, down streets that were suddenly filled with people. Dozens of people, in all stages of dress and activity: working folk with their dinner plates in hand, children clutching at homework sheets, women with babies nursing at their breasts—even one woman with a hand full of playing cards, who rearranged them as she walked. Pouring out of the houses and shops that lined Jaggonath's narrow streets like insects out of a collapsed hive. Which brought to mind other images—

He stopped, and forced her to stop with him. His eyes were still Worked enough to let him see the current that swirled about their feet, though the image was little more than a shadow of his former vision. He checked the flow again, felt his heart stop for an instant. It *had* changed. He could see it. Not in direction, nor in speed of flow, but in *intensity.* . . . He gripped her hand tightly. There was less of it than there should have been, less of it than any natural tide could have prompted. It was as if the fae itself were withdrawing from this place, gathering itself elsewhere to break, with a tsunami's sudden force—

"Earthquake?" he whispered. Aghast—and awed—by the revelation.

"Come *on,*" she answered. And dragged him forward.

They ran until they reached the north end of the street, where it widened into a sizable shopping plaza. She stopped there, breathless, and bade him do the same. There were already several hundred people gathered in the small cobblestoned square, and more were arriving each minute. The horses that were tethered there pulled nervously at their reins, nostrils twitching as if trying to catch the scent of danger. Even as Damien and Ciani entered the tiny square the hanging signs of several shops began to swing, and a crash of glass sounded through one open doorway. Shopkeepers exited the buildings hurriedly with precious items clutched in their arms—crystal, porcelain, delicate sculptures—as the signs above them swung even more wildly, and the panicked animals fought for their freedom.

"You had *warning,*" he whispered. What an incredible concept! He was accustomed to regarding Eman history as a series of failures and losses—but here was real triumph, and over Nature herself! Their ancestors on Earth had had no way of knowing exactly when an earthquake would strike—when the concentrated pressure that had built up over months or years would suddenly burst into movement, breaking apart mountains and rerouting rivers before man even knew what had hit him—but here, on Erna, they had warning sirens. Warning sirens! And not on all of Erna, he reminded himself. Only in the east. Not in his homeland. Ganji had nothing to rival this.

He was about to speak—to share his awe with Ciani—when a sound even more terrible than the siren split the night. It took him a few seconds to realize that its source was human; it was a voice racked by such pain, warped by such terror, that Damien barely recognized it as such. Instinctively he turned toward its source, his free hand already grabbing for a weapon . . . but Ciani grabbed him by the arm and stopped him. "No, Damien. There's nothing you can do. Let it be."

The scream peaked suddenly, a sound so horrible it made his skin crawl—then, as suddenly as it had begun, it was cut short. Damien had fought some grotesque things in his life, and some of them had been long in dying, but nothing in his experience had ever made a sound like that.

"Someone Working when it hit," she muttered. "Gods help him."

"Shouldn't we—"

"It's too late to help. Stay here." She grasped his arm tightly, as if afraid he would leave despite her warning. "The siren went off in plenty of time. He had his warning. That's why we run the damn thing. But there's always some poor fool who tries to tap into the earth-fae when it begins to surge. . . ."

She didn't finish.

"And they die? Like that?"

"They *fry.* Without exception. No human being can channel that kind of energy. Not even an adept. He must have wagered that the quake would be small, that he could control a small bit of what it released and dodge the rest. Or maybe he was drunk, and impaired in judgment. Or just stupid." She shook her head. "I don't understand. Only an idiot would bet his life against an earthquake. No one ever wins that game—*no one*. Why do they insist on trying? What can they possibly gain?" Something in his manner made her look up at him suddenly, and she asked, "You were warned about that in the west. Weren't you?"

"In general terms." His stomach tightened as his mind replayed that terrible scream. "We were warned. But not quite so ... graphically."

He was about to say something more when she squeezed his arm. "It's starting. Watch."

She pointed across the plaza, to a tailor's shop that faced them. Sunken into the lintel of its arched doorway was a sizable ward, made up of intricate knotwork patterns etched into a bronze plate. The whole of it was glowing now, with a cold blue light that silhouetted its edge like the corona of an eclipsed sun. Even as he watched the display it increased in intensity, until cold blue fire burned the pattern of its warding sigil into his eyes and his brain.

"Quake wards," she told him. "They're dormant until the fae intensifies ... then they tap into it, use it to reinforce the buildings they guard. But if it's a big one, there's more than they can handle. What you're seeing is the excess energy bleeding off into the visible spectrum."

On every building surrounding the plaza, similar wards were now firing. Awed, he watched as tendrils of silver fire shot across doorways, about windows, over walls, until the man-made structures were wholly enveloped in a shivering web of cold silver flame. And though the force of the earthquake was enough to make brickwork tremble, no buildings toppled. No windows shattered. Furniture crashed to the floor within one shop, glass shattered noisily inside another, but the buildings themselves—reinforced with that delicate, burning web—weathered the seismic storm.

"You've warded the whole city?" he whispered. Stunned by the scale of it.

She hesitated. "Mostly. Not all of it's as well done as this. Sorcerors vary, as does their skill ... and some people simply can't afford the protection." As if in illustration, a roar of falling brick sounded to the south of them. Dust and a cloud of silver-blue sparks mushroomed thickly over the rooftops. Damien could feel the ground tremble beneath his feet, could see brick- and stone-work shiver all about him as the force of the earthquake fought to bring the man-made structures down—and the Workings of man fought to keep it all intact. The smell of ozone filled the air, and a sharp undercurrent: sulfur? The smell of battle, between Nature and man's will.

Our ancestors had nothing like this. Nothing! Venerate them we might, but in this one arena we have surpassed them. All the objective science on Earth could never have managed this. . . .

Incredible, he thought. He must have voiced that, for she murmured, "You approve?"

He looked into her eyes and read the real question there, behind her words. "The Church should be using this, not fighting it." The ground was singing to him, a deep, rumbling sound that he felt through his bones. "And I'll see to it they do," he promised.

The tremors were increasing in violence, and the wards—fighting to establish some sort of balance—filled the plaza with silver-blue light, as nearly bright as Corelight. Some of them began to fire skyward, releasing their pent-up energy in spurts of blue-white lightning, that leapt from rooftop to rooftop and then shot heavenward, splitting the night into a thousand burning fragments. Nearby a tree, unwarded, gave way to the tremors; a heavy branch crashed to the ground beside them, barely missing several townspeople. It seemed second nature for him to put his arm around Ciani, to protect her by drawing her against him. And it likewise seemed wholly natural that she lean against him, wordlessly, until her hip brushed against his groin and a fire took root there, every bit as intense as the faeborn flame which surrounded them.

He ran his hand down over the curve of her hip and whispered in her ear, "Is it safe to make love to a woman during an earthquake?"

She turned in his arms until she faced him, until he could feel the soft press of her breasts against his chest, the lingering play of her fingers against the back of his neck. Her heat against the ache in his loins.

"It's never safe to make love to a woman," she whispered.

She took him by the hand, and led him into the conflagration.

Senzei Reese thought: *That was close.*

Behind him, some precious bit of crystal that Allesha had collected—in deliberate defiance of earthquakes, it seemed to him—shivered off its perch and smashed noisily on the hardwood floor. One more treasured piece gone. He wondered why she would never let him bind them in place, with the same sort of Warding that reinforced their building. Wondered if her "mixed feelings" about using the fae might not translate into "mixed feelings" about him.

Don't think about that.

Power: He could feel it all about him. Power thick enough to drown in, power like a raging fire that sucked the oxygen right out of his lungs, leaving him dizzy—breathless—trembling with hunger. For a moment it had nearly been visible—a sheer wall of earth-force, a tidal wave of liquid fire—but he had forced himself to cut the vision short, and now he was as fae-blind as Allesha herself. Only Ciani and her kind could maintain their fae-sight without a deliberate Working— and a Working, under these circumstances, meant certain death.

But what a way to go!

He had almost done it this time. Even knowing the risk, he had almost chanced it. Almost gritted his teeth against the bone-jarring pain of the warning siren and continued with his Work as if nothing was happening. What a moment that would have been, when the wild fae surged into Jaggonath—into *him*—burning down all the barriers that kept him from sharing Ciani's skill, Ciani's vision . . . the barriers that kept him human. *Merely* human.

Every few earthquakes some tormented soul took that chance, and added his dying scream to the siren's din. Ciani couldn't understand why—but Senzei could, all too well. He understood the hunger that consumed such people, the need that coursed through them like blood, until every living cell was saturated with it. *Desire.* For the one thing on Erna that Senzei might never have. The one precious thing that Nature had denied him.

In the other room another bit of crystal fell, and shattered noisily against the floor.

He wept.

Not until the sunlight was wholly gone and the worst of the tremors had subsided—the immediate tremors, at any rate—did the stranger come up out of his subterranean shelter. The fae still vibrated with tectonic echoes; it was the work of mere moments to read them, determine their origin, and speculate upon the implications.

The Forest will shake, he decided. *Soon. Too big a seismic gap there to ignore. And the rakhlands. . . .* But there was no way to know that, for sure. No news had come out of the rakhlands for generations, of earthquakes or lack of them—or anything else, for that matter. He could do no more then speculate that the plate boundaries there would be stressed past endurance ... but he had speculated that many times before, with no way of ever confirming his hypothesis. In a world where Nature's law was not *absolute*, but rather *reactive*, one could never be certain.

Then he squatted down close to the earth and touched one gloved finger to its surface. Watching the earth-fae as it flowed about that obstacle, tasting its tenor through the contact.

The current had changed.

Impossible.

For a moment he simply watched it, aware that he might have erred. Then he sat back on his heels and looked off into the distance, watching the flow of his taint upon the current. And yes, it was different. A minute change, but it was noticeable.

He watched it for a moment more, then corrected himself: *Improbable. But true.* Any bit of the fae contaminated by his person *should* have scurried off toward the Forest, subject to that whirlpool of malignant power. It took effort for him not to travel there himself, not to unconsciously prefer that direction every time he made a decision to move. That the taint of his personal malevolence was being channeled elsewhere meant that some new factor was involved. A Working or a being—more likely the latter—headed in this direction. Focused upon Jaggonath in both its malevolence and its hunger.

It would have to be very focused, to come here against the current. And nasty as hell, to have the effect it did.

Nastier than the Hunter, perhaps?

The stranger laughed, softly.

If not for the siren—*the damned warning the damned*, he thought—Jaggonath's Patriarch might never have known there was an earthquake. That, and the sloshing of tee over the side of his cup. He picked up the delicate porcelain piece and sipped it thoughtfully. While the siren screamed. And some damned fool of a sorceror screamed, too—but that served him right. There was no free ride in this world, least of all with the fae. It was time they learned that, all of them.

It occurred to him briefly that he should have warned his visitor about that particular danger. Coming from the westlands, where quakes were less frequent and far less severe, he might not be aware of it. Might even try to harness that surging flow, to bend it to his sorcerous will.

Then there would be justice, he mused. *And I would be free of this burden. But for how long? They would just send someone else. And I would have to start all over again.*

He put his cup down carefully, watched for a moment to see that it didn't slide, and then walked to the window. The floor trembled beneath his feet, and a low rumbling sound filled the air, but except for that there was little evidence of any disturbance. There never was, in Jaggonath's great cathedral. The faith of thousands, year after year, had reinforced the ancient stonework with more power than any sorceror could have harnessed. No wards guarded its doorways, no demonic fire would flash from its pinnacles and spires at the peak of seismic activity—but the building would stand, nonetheless. And those thousands of people who had gathered in Jaggonath's central plaza would see it stand, an island of calm in a city gone mad. And a precious few would wander through the cathedral's doors, and devote their lives to the faith that had made it possible.

The whole planet could be like this, he thought. *Will be like this, one day.*

He had to believe that. Had to maintain that belief, though sometimes his ministry seemed about to be swallowed up by the great maw of Erna's cynicism. Had to remember, always, that the dream which he served would not be fulfilled in one lifetime, or five, or even a dozen. The damage which man had done here was too great to be corrected in a single generation . . . and it was still going on. Even now the wild fae, loosed in hideous quantity by the earthquake, would be gravitating toward the minds that could manifest it. A child's brain, dreaming of monsters. A malicious adult, envisioning vengeance. A thousand and one hates and fears and paranoid visualizations, plucked from the human mind, that would all be given flesh before morning. His stomach turned at the thought. What could he say that would make them understand, that every day the odds against man's survival increased geometrically? A single man could dream into being a *thousand* such monsters in a lifetime—and all those things would feed on man, because he was their source. Could any one sorceror's service, no matter how well-intended, compensate for such numbers?

He felt tired. He felt old. He was becoming aware, for the first time in his life, of a hope that had lived in him since his first moments in the Church: a desperate hope that the change would come *now*, in his lifetime. Not all of it—that was too much to ask for—but enough that he could see it started. Enough that he could know he had made a difference. To live as he had, to serve without question, then to die without knowing if there was a point to any of it ... his hands clenched at his sides as he looked out over the blazing city. He wished there were truly no other choice. He wished the fae could *not* be used to maintain youth, and thus to prolong life. He wished he didn't have to face that terrible decision every minute of his life: commitment to his faith versus the chance to court the fae, extend his life, and see what effect that faith would have upon future generations. Death itself was not nearly so daunting as the prospect of dying in ignorance.

Thus the Prophet was tempted, he thought darkly.

As for that blustering fool of a priest ... his stomach tightened in anger at the thought of him. How easy it was, for him and his kind! How seemingly effortless, to take a piece of sharpened steel from the armory and simply go hack up the product of man's indulgence. *This is my faith*, such a man could say, pointing to a heap of dismembered vampire-kin. *Here is my service to God.* An easier faith than the one the Patriarch had embraced, for sure. A faith that was continually reinforced by the adrenaline rush of violence, the thrill of daring. A faith that could be reckoned in numbers: *Ghouls killed. Demons dispatched. Converts made.* So that when his time of reckoning came such a man might say: This is how the world was bettered by my presence. Not through moral influence, or by teaching, but in these human nightmares which I have dispatched.

And I envy him that, the Patriarch thought bitterly.

Six

WHeN tHe *Neoqueen Matilla* finally pulled into harbor, it took
two men to hold Yiles Jarrom back long enough for it to dock. And
strong men, at that.

"Vulkin' assholes!" he muttered—with venom enough that the two
men backed off a bit, though they still held onto him. "I'll teach'em
what it means, to break contract with me!"

The two men—dockhands, recruited by the Port Authority in order
to avoid outright murder on the piers—held tightly to his arms, while
the shallow-hulled shipping vessel that was the subject of his invec-
tives settled itself into position. A bevy of dockworkers moved in
quickly and made her fast in record time. And then the gangplank
was set in place and the ship's first mate, a young and rather lanky
man, trekked the length of the pier toward where they stood. And
the men let Jarrom go, which was good for them. Because in another
few minutes he would surely have spouted fire and burned his way
free of them, if they'd continued to hold onto him.

"Vulkin' bastards!" His face was red with rage, his shaking hands
clenched into fists. "Vulkin' incompetants! Where you been, with my
cargo? Where's your coward-ass captain, who lied to make contract?"

The first mate didn't look directly at him, but at his own feet.
"Give me a minute, sir, and I'll try to explain—"

Jarrom snorted derisively. "Give you a minute? I'll give you my
fist! I don't have to waste my precious time talking to a lackey!
Where's your captain, boy? Or that damned best-eye-in-the-eastrealm
pilot he's so vulkin' proud of? Bring those men out, and then we'll
talk!" When the young man didn't answer him immediately, he
added, "Two of Prima's months, boy—that's how long he said it
would take. Two lesser months, come hell or white water or smash-

ers from Novatlantis. And how long has it been, I ask you? A good three shortmonths, going on four—and my buyers threatening to blow my whole business to hell—so where the vulk have you *been?*"

In a carefully measured voice, the young man said, "It's a dangerous route, Mer Jarrom. You know that. Orrin's a damned good captain, and Jafe was as good a pilot as Erna's ever seen. It's still a nightmare of a trip, and you knew that when you hired us. Knew we might not make it at all, contract or no contract." His voice faded away to a whisper. "Almost didn't. Gods help us."

"That's through no fault of mine—eh? No big storms this way, no smashers out of the east, a small quake down south but that'd barely shake the waters, so what—" It struck him suddenly what the first mate had said. "What the hell do you mean, *was?* You lose a pilot, boy? Is that your excuse? Jafe Saccharat die on route?"

The first mate raised his head, and met Jarrom's eyes at last. And Jarrom nearly took a step backward from the force of that gaze. He was a strong man, to be sure, and brave in the way that the strong can afford to be brave; he had seen his share of dockside violence and come out on top of most of it, had even wrestled a succubus once and not had his life sucked out in the process—which was as close to victory as anyone ever got with that kind. But though none of those situations had ever made him really afraid, the look in the boy's eyes was enough to make his blood run cold. Bloodshot orbs stared out from a pale, hollowed face, underscored by purple crescents dark enough that they might have been bruises . . . but that wasn't what shook him up so. A dozen men a day looked that bad, dockside, and Jarrom neither pitied nor feared them. No. It was something else that took him off guard, which he'd never seen before, not in man or demonling, or even dockhand. Not something *in* the first mate's eyes, exactly. Perhaps . . . something absent?

"Not dead," young man muttered. "The pilot's alive. They're all—*we're* all—alive. I suppose."

"You'd better explain yourself," Jarrom warned. But the fire was out of his voice now, he could hear it. What had happened? What *could* happen, to put that look in a man's eyes?

"It's a dangerous route," the first mate repeated. Empty of emotion, as if the explanation had been rehearsed so many times that it had lost all meaning to him. "First there's the Shelf, y'see, and that's safe enough unless a smasher comes, but who can take the chance? Then there's the ridges where the Serpent turns—jagged mounts, that can rip a hull to pieces in a minute—and the bars of the eastern Straits, they're murderous too, and the whitewaters just east of Sattin. . . . You wanted us to rush your cargo in, Mr. Jarrom, and that means taking a lot of chances. Only a good pilot would dare it. Jafe was the best, y'see? And he took us to where we needed him most, in close to the shore of the rakhlands. All cliffs and boulders and treacherous shoreline, but he said it could save us time enough . . . and he knew the way. He said. Knew it all: every submerged mount and rock and how high each one sat, and how deep they'd be when the tides changed, and how much time between tide and countertide there was when a special way was open. . . ." He blinked. "Knew it all, Rafe did."

"So what happened?" Jarrom demanded. "Why the hell weren't you here when you were supposed to be?"

The first mate drew in a deep breath, exhaled it slowly. When he spoke again, there was a faint tremor in his voice. "I . . . that is, he . . . *forgot*, sir."

"Forgot?"

"That's right, sir."

Indignation heated Jarrom's blood anew, rage coursing through his veins like cheap booze. "*Forgot?* Your vulkin' pilot *forgot* the route?"

The first mate nodded. "That's right, sir. Forgot . . . the whole Straits, I think he said. You see, there was this scream . . . that's how we found out. We found him screaming like a looney on the forecastle, threatening to throw himself off. Said something had taken away all his landmarks, just wiped them clean out of his brain. Took three of us just to calm him down."

Jarrom snorted. "That's as likely the result of hard liquor as anything."

The first mate glared, a look all the more accusatory for coming from those bloodshot eyes. Those terrible, haunted eyes. "We don't drink while doing the eastern stretch," he said coldly. "No one does. The lay's just too dangerous. Gets you killed faster than you can open a bottle."

"All right, all right. So your saint of a pilot wasn't drinking. He was . . . his landmarks were taken, all right? Taken right away. So what about his rutters? Were those snatched too? Or did the best Straits pilot in the east not bother taking notes?"

"Oh, he had'em," the first mate assured him. "Brought them out and showed them to us. Fine leather volumes, copied in his own hand. A signed hand, all personal symbols and the like."

"So you couldn't read them." The story got more and more preposterous. "And I suppose, he 'forgot' how to read?"

The first mate hesitated, seemed about to elaborate. Then he simply nodded, and looked down at his feet again. "Yessir," he whispered. "That's the lot of it."

"And your captain? And the rest of that mangy crew? All their brains taken, as well? You look whole enough."

"It was like something took a part of you out," the first mate whispered. "While you were sleeping, it'd happen. And then when you woke, that part just wasn't there. It never came back, either. The captain . . . it won't do you much good to talk to him, Mr. Jarrom. I say just take your cargo and go, and feel lucky it got here at all. And hope that whatever got us isn't contagious." He looked up again, met Jarrom's gaze with his own. "You catch my drift?"

He turned away, refused to meet that tortured gaze. "I had buyers, you know. With a contract. Gods alone know if they were willing to wait another night, when all I could give them were empty promises. If they—" He stopped, and scowled. Squinting, to see the *Matilla* more clearly in the early evening's darkness. "Who the hell are *they?*"

Three men were disembarking from the shallow craft. They hadn't been among the crew, Jarrom knew that. He had signed on the crew himself. "You pick up passengers, boy? That's against all contract, and you know it."

"I . . . know that." He seemed to be struggling for words. His hands, Jarrom noticed, were trembling. "I think . . . they were marooned. We saved them. I think."

"You're not sure of much, are you?" They were pale men, and they moved with almost feral grace. Dressed like locals, but the cloth sat awkwardly on their bodies. They were used to something else, clearly. Something less? One of them turned toward Jarrom and grinned briefly—a cat's grin, a hunter's grin, lean and hungry—and above all else, *amused.* Though all his instinct said he should go and confront them, Jarrom suddenly found he didn't want to move. Didn't want to go toward them, not for any purpose.

"I remembered enough myself," the boy was whispering. "Barely enough. We went north, a different route. Safer up there, if you strike ground; some hope of getting moving again. Had to take it slow, you understand? Couldn't help the schedule, sir. We'd have died, otherwise. *Had* to take it slow, do you understand?"

The strange men were gone now—vanished like fae-wraiths into the deep evening shadows—but Jarrom felt as if their eyes were still on him, mocking him. Felt his skin crawl, in a way it never had before. "Well," he said loudly—as if somehow mere volume could overcome his growing unease. "We're lucky you didn't forget also, aren't we?"

The reddened eyes blinked once, slowly. "I didn't forget the route," he said softly. "No. Not that."

Suddenly, an eruption of sound and color whirled across the dock toward the two of them. "Bassy!" Silk taffeta rustling like the wind, tiny feet beating a rushed staccato on the fog-dampened timbers. Perfume, in feminine quantity. "Bassy, honey! You made it!"

Then she was in his arms, a tiny girl even thinner than the boy was. And she was crying with joy, and kissing him, and leaving smears of lipstick all over his tan, weathered face. "I was so scared, honey, so scared! When they said you all hadn't come in on time—and I *know* how prompt Captain Rawney is, but you can imagine all the terrible things I thought of, when no one knew where you were—"

And Yiles Jarrom would never forget the look in the first mate's eyes, when the boy's fiancée embraced him. Never. Though days and weeks and even months might occlude the rest of that awful night in his memory, it could never erase that terrible vision—of a glance which said, in a single instant, what volumes of prose could never have expressed so eloquently. So horribly.

Who is she? the reddened gaze begged him. *Who?*

Help me!

"Gods help us all," Jarrom whispered.

Seven

The Patriarch remembered:

"Mom?"

The house was quiet, preternaturally so. The boy hesitated at the doorway. "Mom?" No answer. He dropped off his school books in the hallway, on the heavy alteroak cabinet put there for that purpose. "Mom?" Suddenly he felt cold inside, and angry. Cold, because something was obviously very wrong. Angry, because he knew what it probably was.

"Mom!"

Damn it all, if she was doing that stuff again . . . he searched the house for signs of her presence, her self-indulgence: half-empty bottles lying wherever they happened to fall, thin foil wrappers with the remnants of cerebus powder—and the paraphernalia of her household tasks scattered about, left lying wherever the mood happened to strike her. But for once, all the obvious signs were absent. Whatever had happened, it wasn't that. The tightness that had begun to build in the boy's chest eased somewhat, and he thought: she's still sober. Then added: maybe.

"Mom?"

The house was silent, except for a strange chittering sound that came from the kitchen. He walked that way, one hand nervously playing about the handle of his ward-knife. Any minute now his friends would start calling for him, impatient for his return. They might even come in after him, if they got bored enough with waiting. He had to find his mother before that happened, deal with her quickly, and get out. The shame of having them see her when she was doubly loaded was something he had no desire to experience. It had been bad enough with alcohol, when she was only doing that.

Now that she had started mixing cerebus powder into her drinks, it was a hundred times worse.

That combination will kill you, *the doctor had warned her.* It'll eat your brain right up. Is that what you want? Is that what you want for your family?

One of the boy's friends hammered on the front door, impatient. The boy quickened his pace. He just had to find her, get permission to cross the river with the others, and then he could go. It didn't even matter if she was wholly conscious of what she was saying when she gave him permission; as long as he did his duty and asked, he was covered. The important thing was, if he did it all quickly enough his friends would never have to see her. Oh, they could probably guess why they hadn't been invited in . . . but that still wasn't as bad as having them actually see. Not by a long shot.

As he put his hand on the kitchen doorknob he found that he was shaking. What if she was really in trouble? What if the doctor was right—that mixing illusory drugs and alcoholic disinhibition was really more than the human brain could handle? That someday she would fry her brain for good? What would he do, if that had finally happened?

Shaking, he forced himself to turn the doorknob. Not wanting to know what lay beyond.

Please, Mom. Be okay. Be sober . . . at least long enough to talk to me. Please.

He opened the door.

And saw.

And screamed.

Somewhere in the distance, a heavy alteroak door slammed open. He barely heard it. Terror had filled his throat so that it was impossible to breathe; he tried to step backward, but his hand was locked on the doorknob. In the kitchen, dozens of things chittered; dark things, wet things, things with shining claws and sharp teeth that dripped bright crimson on the Everclean tiles. Things that sat on his mother's shoulders, dipping bright claws into her matted hair and bringing up soft, slimy tidbits to eat.

He managed to take a step backward. Heart pounding. Mind reeling.

Two steps. Another.

It'll eat up your brain, *the doctor had said.*

He ran.

Eight

Never sleep *through the true night*, Damien's master had taught him. *Whether you mean to use its power or not, you should be awake to observe its passage. There are too many things in our world that draw their life from that ultimate Darkness, too many evils that can only be Worked when all sunlight is gone. So be awake, and take your enemy's measure.*

He sat on the wide ledge of his room's northernmost window, looking out over the city. His nerves still jangled from the dream which the harsh mechanical alarm clock had dispelled. It was 3:05. The true darkness would last a mere three minutes tonight—and true to his training, he was awake to watch it happen. He pulled open the heavy curtains at his window, saw Casca's yellow-green crescent sinking defiantly in the east. He watched as its light slowly faded from the night sky. Then: utter darkness. The Core was gone, and with it the millions of stars that marked the heart of the galaxy; Erna's night sky looked out on desolation, across an emptiness so vast that it was easy to forget there were other stars at all, much less other planets where living things flourished and fought and gave birth and died . . . much less any place called *Earth.*

Damien breathed deeply, and patterned a Seeing so that his vision might respond to the fae's special wavelengths. Below him, in the city streets, deep purple shadows stretched tentatively forth, as if testing their strength. Tendrils of deepest violet—so dark they could hardly be seen, so intense that to look on them was painful—began to creep their way into the city's open spaces. Shopping plazas, city squares, even rooftops: places where the sunlight normally kept such things at bay, now made defenseless by the true night's special darkness. Damien watched the flow of it, muttered a prayer of thanksgiving that there were no people in the streets. Of all the forms the fae might take, this was the most dangerous. It could manifest in minutes what would otherwise take hours, if not days—and with a much more violent tenor. Thank God for the light of the Core, which kept the stuff at bay half the year, and the three moons, sun-reflecting, which guarded the darker nights. *Most* of the darker nights.

He tried to get some sense of the local currents—to read who might be Working this special darkness, and why—but it was like trying to focus on a single ripple in the midst of white-water rapids. At last, exhausted by the effort, he let his Vision fade. Back home he could have identified every sorceror in town by now, and spotted those few who dared to Work the stuff—but the currents here were so volatile and so complex that his skill was barely more than a child's by comparison.

He watched as the point of Domina's crescent slipped over the eastern horizon, right on schedule. Watched the deep violet light thin out and dissipate, as if it were no more than an early morning ground fog scattered by sunlight. He watched it recede into the myriad cracks and crevices that would protect it from the light, while fresh moonlight scoured the streets and rooftops clean of its deadly presence. He watched until the moon was half-risen, then went back to bed.

3:35. He fell asleep as soon as his head hit the pillow.

Fifteen minutes later, the explosion came.

"What the hell?" He sat up groggily, still half-immersed in sleep. Remembering a loud, sudden noise that hadn't been fully incorporated into his dream, which was gone before he was awake enough to identify it. Was it his imagination? He shook his head to clear it, and heard doors slam along the corridor of the Annex. Feet running in the hallway, slipper-shod. No. Not his imagination at all.

He threw on a cotton robe and, as an afterthought, grabbed for his sword. No telling what was going on, he'd best be prepared. Out into the corridor then, to quickly take his bearings. A sister-priest from Kale was just emerging from the room opposite his; her face was white. "Southwest," she whispered, and he realized that the window of her room must face that way. "What is it?" he asked, but she shook her head: *No, can't help you, I don't know.*

Southwest. He ran down the corridor as quickly as he could, took the broad central stairs two at a time. The outer door was just closing as he reached it. There was too much light coming in through the

windows, much more than the crescent Domina should have provided. A light that flickered, like flame gone mad. As he put his hand
to the door and flung it open he realized, with a start, that even that
was wrong. Fire should be yellow, orange, even yellow-white; this
light was a chill blue, as if from some unnatural flame.

Outside the Annex, some two dozen guests of the Church stood
with their heads thrown back, gaping at the sky. Damien didn't stop
to look. If the fire—or whatever it was—was to the southeast of here,
he was in the wrong place to determine its source. He sprinted around
the side of the Cathedral, until that building no longer blocked his
view. And then saw—

Fire. Spurting heavenward. Not a natural fire, no; cold blue, like
the quake-wards. Fae-spawned flame, without a doubt. Damien tried
to visualize the city's layout, to determine the fire's source. And as
he did so something tightened inside him, a mixture of dread and
fear so cold and so intense that he trembled where he stood.

Ciani . . .

He ran. Down Commerce Street, pushing his way past frightened
mothers and scurrying vendors and the inevitable rubber-necked tourists. Shoving them out of the way, when necessary. Past Market Lane,
past Seven Corners, into the artisan's district, then through it and
beyond. Here, on this quiet street, the Fae Shoppe had done its business. And here, on this suddenly crowded street—

It burned. Burned with a fae-light so intense that it drove him back;
he had to fight his every physical instinct to get within a block of
it. It was impossible to look at, it burned like a thousand suns, it
would surely sear the retinas of anyone who tried. He worked a
Shielding for his eyes, felt the light about him dim, then tried to look
again. Better. He forced himself forward, past the firewagons that
were even now being pushed into place, past an adept in singed robes
whose attention was fixed on the fire, past . . . there were too many
people to count, running toward the fire or away from it. He got as
close to it as he could, with all the force of the faeborn flames pushing
back at him. Until he could feel its unnatural smoke in his lungs,
and had to work a Shielding against that, too.

The shop was gone. His altered sight could see that now; what was
left to burn was no more than the rubble of what had already been
destroyed. Some monstrous explosion had ripped the place to pieces,
along with the better part of two adjoining buildings. Now it was all
gone, along with whoever had been tending shop at the time. . . .

Fae Shoppe, the sign had said. *Open all hours.*

No one could have survived that blast. No one.

Ciani!

He tried to work a Divining, but the currents were in chaos, their patterns unreadable. All he could make out was that somehow a chain reaction had been triggered—that some malicious Working aimed at Ciani had ignited her wards, one after the other, until the whole place blew—

There were tears in his eyes; he wiped them away with his free hand, tried to breathe steadily. The smoke was thick in his lungs; he Shielded against that, too. It occurred to him that several adepts in the crowd were working hard to contain the faeborn flames, to keep them from spreading to neighboring buildings. He raised one hand as if he, too, would begin to pattern a Working—but another hand grasped his, and a familiar voice warned, "They can do it better than you or I."

He turned, as if facing an attacker. It took him a moment to absorb the fact that the speaker was Senzei, and that the man was dressed in a thick cotton robe, his hair still tangled from sleeping. Slowly, painfully, the truth of it sank in. Senzei Reese: in a bathrobe, because he had rushed here in the middle of the night after hearing the explosion . . . because he hadn't been there at the time it happened. Which meant Ciani had. Damien cursed fate, for making it so—and hated himself, for wishing it were otherwise.

Ciani!

He lowered his head and blinked forth new tears, to wash the smoke out of his eyes. Senzei was silent, which confirmed the horrible truth of it all. If she had survived, he would have spoken. If she had stood even a chance of survival . . . but she was inside the Fae Shoppe when it blew, and never had a chance. Senzei's silence confirmed that.

With an anguished curse—at fate, himself, Jaggonath, the true night—Damien turned back into the crowd, and elbowed his way away from Loremaster Ciani's crematory fire.

Loss. Like an empty wound, out of which all the blood had drained. Incapable of healing because all its vital fluids were gone. Dried up by grief.

Alone in the still of the night, he struggled to come to terms with his feelings. He'd lost friends before, and even lovers; those were the risks which his chosen vocation entailed, and each loss was its own separate grief, an island of mourning, finite and comprehensible. Why was this so different? Was it the shock of what had happened, the suddenness of it—the terrible impotence of standing there, unable to do anything, while the last remnants of a woman's life went up in smoke? Or . . . something more? Some feeling he hadn't yet acknowledged, which had been growing between them along with the jokes and the entertainment and the loving? Some feeling which had been cut short now by the heat of the fire, as if it had never existed. As if some part of him that had never fully opened up had begun to, just briefly . . . and then slammed shut again, charred by the heat of that terrible fire.

Was this love? Was this what love would have felt like, had it lasted?

Alone in his room in the Annex, Damien Vryce wept silently.

Do you even know how old I am? she had asked him once. Bright eyes sparkling in amusement.

No. How old?

Nearly seventy.

He had thought then how wonderful it must be, to reach one's seventieth birthday without aging a day past thirty. That number had seemed filled with wonder, because of her. Filled with vitality.

Now, it was just a rotten age to die.

The door creaked open slowly. Damien raised his head just enough to see who had entered, that much and no more. And when he saw, he lowered his head again.

"I'm sorry," the Patriarch said softly. "Genuinely sorry."

Are you? he wanted to snap. But for once, the anger was gone. Emptied out of him, by grief.

"Thank you," he whispered.

"Is there anything I can do?"

"No." He managed to shake his head; even that much movement took effort. "I can't . . . I just need time. It was so sudden. . . ."

"It's always hard, losing those we care for. Especially in such a senseless accident."

"It wasn't an accident," he whispered.

The Patriarch came into his room—slowly, quietly—and took a seat opposite him. When he spoke, his tone was gentler than it had ever been before. Gentler than Damien had imagined it could be. "You want to talk about it?"

"What's the use? I couldn't read it clearly enough. Something attacked either her or the shop, and her defenses ... backfired. I couldn't read what, or how, or why. I don't know what I could do about it now, even if I knew. And I think ...." He shut his eyes, tightly. "I think ... I was falling in love with her."

"I guessed that," the Patriarch said softly.

"I feel so damned helpless!" He got up suddenly, upsetting a chair as he did so. And turned away, to stare at the weapons which hung on the wall behind him. "I stood there while it burned—while *she* burned, for all I know!—and what on Erna could I do to help? I couldn't even get *near* the place...." He shook his head, was aware of new wetness on his cheeks. "You don't know what it's like, seeing something like that happen, feeling like you could stop it if you could just figure out what to do ... and then not being able to. Standing there helplessly, unable to save someone you care about...."

"I do understand," the Patriarch said quietly. "More than you know."

He heard the Holy Father stand, and walk to where he stood. But unlike Senzei, the Patriarch made no physical contact.

"She was very active in this community. Very respected. There'll be representatives sent from organizations in Jaggonath and beyond, to honor her passing." He hesitated; Damien could hear in his voice just how much these words were costing him. "Given her community service, it wouldn't be ... unreasonable ... if our Church made such a gesture."

Surprised by the offer, Damien turned about to face him. And thought: *If she had lived, they would be about the same age.* Only how much longer would the Patriarch go on, without the benefit of sustained youth?

"No," he muttered. "Thank you ... but it isn't appropriate. I do understand that." He shut his eyes. "But thank you for offering."

"Those who court the fae take certain chances. But knowing that doesn't make it any easier, does it? Human loss is all the same in the end." He seemed as if he was about to say more but then stopped. Considering what his feelings probably were on the matter, Damien was grateful.

"Whatever we can do to help," the Patriarch said at last. "You let me know. I'll see it done."

Nine

It's finished, the first one whispered.

Not well.

No. But it is finished.

Too bad we didn't know the wards would blow. Hungrily: *We could have killed her ourselves, in that case.*

They were silent for a moment, savoring that concept.

She had a rich life, one said at last.

A full life, another agreed.

Delicious.

And we can go home, now. Yes?

They turned to the one who had become, for lack of a better title, their leader.

We go home, he told them. *But not just yet. . . .*

Ten

Damien thought: *I just can't believe she's dead.*

A shapeless heap of blackened rubble was all that remained of the Fae Shoppe. Investigators had been sifting through it for almost 24 hours now, but still hadn't offered any explanation of the blaze more plausible than their first hypothesis: Something had attacked the shop, powerful enough to set off a chain reaction in the protective wards. Ciani's own defenses had killed her.

It can happen, he reminded himself. *For all that we Work the stuff, its easy to forget just how unstable it is. Even in the hands of an adept.*

Those who court the fae must pay the price.

He blinked the growing wetness from his eyes, and focused his senses on the ashes. Even knowing that half a dozen adepts had already done the same—and discovered nothing—he had to try. The pain of losing her was bad enough; the frustration of inaction was more than he could bear.

Though the ashes were cool to the eye, they were white-hot to his inner senses; it took only a minimal Working for Damien to see the power that remained there. It was as if all the tamed earth-fae that had been in the shop had been boiled down and concentrated into one hot spot of chaotic power. He wondered, distantly, how it would affect the local currents, to have such a chancre of raw heat located here. Then wondered who would bother to map it, now that Ciani was gone.

Stop it. Now. You're only making it worse on yourself.

How long before some idiot would try to harness that stuff? He looked for a telltale mark, saw a sigil chalked on a bit of brick. Ciani would have been outraged. *Gods in heaven,* she would have said, *is there nothing so dangerous some fool won't try to Work it!*

Once more, he tried to Divine just what had happened. Once more, the sheer mass of unfettered power clogged his senses, and his Working accomplished nothing. It was like trying to focus on the flicker of a candleflame, when that candle was in front of the sun. His head hurt from trying.

And then there were footsteps behind him, and he turned to see who else had come to this place.

Senzei.

The man looked terrible. Haggard. Drained. Damien guessed that he hadn't slept since the accident, and wondered if he'd had the time to eat. Or the desire.

The man looked about nervously, as if checking for eavesdroppers. There were none. His bloodshot eyes fixed on Damien, then quickly looked away. In that instant, Damien thought he saw fear in them.

"I need to talk to you," he said. His voice lacked substance, like that of a ghost. It took effort to hear him. "But not here." He looked up and down the street again, a quick and nervous gesture.

"Where?"

"My place. Can you come? It's ..." He hesitated. Met Damien's eyes. "It's about Ciani."

Wild hope lurched inside the priest. "She's alive?"

Senzei looked thoroughly miserable; it struck Damien that he seemed afraid to speak. "Come with me," was all he would say. "I ... we can't talk here."

He wanted to shake him, to demand answers, but with effort he bested that instinct. Instead he nodded stiffly, and let Senzei lead the way.

Just beyond the narrow, stone-paved streets of the city's mercantile district was a small residential neighborhood. The house that Senzei took them to was one of a dozen similar buildings, modest brickwork abodes whose narrow structure and lack of yard space made a clear statement about the cost of real estate in this district. Senzei led them to a corner house, and Damien took in details: neatly white-washed brickwork, small porch, hanging plants. Sigil over the door— a quake-ward—and smaller symbols etched into each window, in the lower corners. Curtains in the downstairs window that seemed surprisingly feminine for Senzei's taste ... and then Damien remembered that he lived with a woman. Roommate? Girlfriend? It embarrassed him that he couldn't remember the exact relationship.

The door opened as they approached. In the shadow of the doorway Damien made out the form and features of a woman. In many regards she resembled Senzei—pale, dark-haired, a little too thin for her height. And afraid. Very afraid. The same kind of fear that was in him.

"You found him," she breathed.

"At the shop." They passed quickly inside; she bolted the door behind them, two locks and a burglar-ward. Despite the afternoon's relative warmth, Damien noticed that all the windows were shut tight.

"Were there insurance people—"

"No." He shook his head emphatically. "No one."

"Thank the gods for that, anyway."

Senzei introduced them: Allesha Huyding, his fiancée, and Reverend Sir Damien Vryce. It might have been Damien's imagination, but he seemed to stress the titles.

"I'll get you something to drink," she said, and before Damien could respond that it wasn't necessary she was gone.

"The fae makes her nervous," Senzei explained. "And this situation ..." he sighed, raggedly. "I think more than anything she's afraid our adjustors will find out what really happened."

It took all of Damien's self-control to keep his voice level as he demanded, "What about Ciani?"

The fear in Senzei's eyes seemed to give way to something else. Sadness. Exhaustion. Desolation.

"She's alive," he whispered. But there was no joy in his voice. "Alive ... but little more than that."

"Where?"

Senzei hesitated, but his eyes flicked toward a door that led from the living room, and that was enough. Damien stepped toward it—

And Senzei caught his arm with surprising strength. And held on to him, tightly.

"She's hurt. Badly. You need to understand, before you go see her—"

"I'm a Healer, man, I—"

"*It isn't that kind of pain.*"

His hand, on Damien's arm, was trembling. Something in his tone—or perhaps in his expression—kept Damien from pulling free.

"What is it?" he asked sharply.

"She was hurt," Senzei repeated. "She's ..." He hesitated, searching for the right words. Or perhaps the courage to speak. "... not what she was."

"You mean the explosion—"

"It wasn't the explosion. *I* caused the explosion." He released Damien's arm, began to twist one hand nervously in the other, as if trying to cleanse himself. "To cover up what happened. To make whatever had hurt her think she had died . . . so it would leave her alone."

Damien heard the door open behind him, the padding of footsteps, the tinkle of ice in glasses. And then the door closed, and they were alone again.

"Tell me," he said quietly.

Senzei took a deep breath; Damien could see him tremble. "We had an appointment at three a.m. She wanted to try something in the true darkness, needed me to help. I came . . ." He shut his eyes, remembering. "I found her . . . that is . . . she had been attacked. . . ."

"Physically?" Damien pressed.

Senzei shook his head. "No. There were no marks of any kind. No sign of any physical confrontation. But they had gotten to her— somehow—and she was lying curled up on the floor. Whimpering, like a wounded animal. I . . . tried to help her. Got her wrapped up in something, to keep her warm. I couldn't tell if she was in physical shock or not, but it seemed practical. I didn't know what else to do. She cried out a few words, then, and I tried to make sense out of what she was saying, but they were only fragments. Mostly incoherent. I don't think she even knew I was there. There were three *things*, she said. And something about a demon in human form. She was hysterical by then, terrified that they were coming back. That's what scared me most of all. Her reaction to it. I . . . well, you know Ciani. It wasn't like her. She told me they were coming back for her, to take her away somewhere." He bit his lower lip, remembering. "That she would rather die than go, and would I please kill her before it could happen. . . ."

Damien looked toward the door, but said nothing.

"That was when I decided what had to be done. I figured I could make it seem like her defenses had overloaded, blown the place to hells . . . and no one would ask questions. Except the insurance people," he added bitterly. "I figured I could use the shop's contents as a sacrifice, leave everything in there to burn . . . there's power in that kind of destruction, you know that. And if I did it right . . . whoever was after her, they would think she was dead. And leave her alone." He drew in a deep breath, still shaking. "An adept could have done it and told you all about it. I couldn't. In order to make it take right, I didn't dare tell anyone. . . ." He looked up at Damien, bloodshot eyes glistening. "That's why I couldn't tell you then. I'm sorry."

"Go on," he said quietly.

"I brought her here. No one saw us, praise fate; the true night had kept everyone indoors. No one—and nothing—bothered us. I managed to salvage some books that first trip, but the rest of it had to go; the value of what's destroyed is what gives a sacrifice its power, you know." He hesitated, as though waiting for the priest to criticize him; Damien said nothing. "I threw on a robe and ran back, and did it. Blew the place. But it worked, didn't it?" He shut his eyes, and shivered. "All that knowledge. All those artifacts. If I had known then what I know now . . . it was more of a sacrifice than I was even aware of. Because I didn't know about *her*."

"What about her?"

He looked toward the door. "She's in there," he whispered. "Alive. Physically uninjured. Only . . . without memory. They took her memory. And the fae . . ." He turned away until Damien could no longer see his face. His shoulders shook. "She's lost it! She's like us, do you understand? You and me. Most of humanity. They took it away, took it all away, she can't See any more. . . ."

Damien put a hand on the man's shoulder. Tried to steady them both. Inside, his thoughts were whirling. "She doesn't remember anything?"

"She remembers who she is. What she is. What she *was*. But she hasn't got the knowledge, you understand? All those million and one little facts that she had accumulated over the years—all the things that made her a loremaster—that's gone now. You understand? This isn't some godsawful accident that just happened to strike her with amnesia. They took her knowledge—they took her Vision! And they left her with just enough to understand what had been lost. No wonder she wanted to die!"

It was only sinking in, what he was saying. The ramifications. "And now her research library—"

"Is gone!" Senzei said angrily. As if daring him to criticize. "I did what I thought was best. Sometimes you have to make decisions so godsdamned fast that there's no real time to think. You do the best you can. I did the best I could. I thought maybe my arrival had interrupted them, that they might come back any minute to hurt her more . . . that's what *she* thought. She was terrified—and I couldn't think of any other way to protect her." His hands had balled themselves into fists, knuckles white. "And it worked, didn't it? You couldn't read past it. The adepts can't. They've called in consultants, but no one can make heads or tails of what happened. Even the godsdamned insurance people can't read through it. You think I could have managed that, without one hell of a sacrifice?

"Easy," Damien said quietly. "No one's blaming you."

He drew in a deep breath, released it slowly. "They would if they knew," he muttered. "The adjustors alone would have my head."

"No one's telling them."

Senzei looked up at him. His face was a ghastly white. "She would have trusted you. That's why I did."

"Let me see her," Damien said softly.

Senzei nodded.

The room Ciani was in was small and lined with books on every wall. A cot had been placed in the center of the room, and on it lay a figure so still, so colorless, that for a moment he feared she was indeed dead. He came to her side and sat on the edge of the cot, careful not to jar it. He had thought she was sleeping, but now that he was beside her he could see that her eyes were open. Empty. Staring into nothingness.

"Cee," he said gently.

She turned toward him, slowly, but her eyes were unfocused. He could see now that her face was wet with tears, and her pillow was soaked with them. He took her nearer hand in both of his and squeezed it tightly; the flesh was pliant, unresponsive. As empty of life as her expression.

No longer an adept. Dear God, what a blow. How do you come to terms with that? How do you start over again, after such an incredible loss?

He brushed some stray hair out of her eyes; she might have been carved in marble, for all that she responded to him. Nevertheless he held her hand, as a devoted mother might cling to a child in coma, and talked to her. As if that could bring her back. As if anything could bring her back.

And fought with his own pain, his fury at being unable to help her.

We have to change this damned world, before it's too late. We have to make some fate for ourselves, other than this.

"Father."

A touch on his shoulder, feather-light. He turned to acknowledge Senzei's presence, then looked back at her. Her eyes were half-shut, her breathing slow and even. Asleep, it seemed. He disentangled himself from her hands gently, careful not to wake her.

"I've Summoned help," Senzei whispered. "I don't know that there's anything he can do to save her ... but he might know something we don't."

Sick at heart, Damien nodded.

What good is it to play at Healing, if you can't save the ones you care about?

Senzei led the priest upstairs, to what appeared to be his workroom: a semi-finished, cluttered space which took up half of the second story. The nearer wall was lined with shelves, on which all manner of books and artifacts rested; opposite it a broad, aged desk supported piles and piles of documents. Damien caught sight of ward specifications, and recognized a symbol that had once been in the shop. Clearly, Senzei was trying to determine who—or what—might have circumvented Ciani's defenses.

In the center of the room stood a man . . . or rather, what appeared to be a man. He was bearded, husky, and dressed in a manner that seemed wholly inappropriate for such a gathering. A lush, fur-edged robe of emerald velvet hung open at the chest, and swept the floor behind his heels. It gave the impression of having been but loosely belted in place, with nothing underneath. From his summer sandals to his opulent jewelry, his every accessory was inappropriate for the time and the place he was in—and mismatched to each other as well, as if he had chosen each ring and necklace for its momentary appeal, without thought for its relationship to the whole of his appearance.

Damien keyed a Knowing, and what he saw made his hair stand on end. Instinctively he reached for his sword—and discovered that he didn't have it on him.

The stranger nodded. "Your priest would slay demons." He raised a brass goblet to his lips and drank—it hadn't been in his hand a minute ago, Damien was sure of it—and nodded. "An admirable reflex. But speaking as one who prefers not to die, I hope he'll get over it."

"This is Karril," Senzei said quietly. "An old . . . *friend*, of Ciani's."

Damien took a deep breath, reminded himself where he was, and managed to unclench his fists. Nevertheless his heart was pounding, and adrenaline rushed through his system as if he were heading into battle. *It's just reflex for him to consult the faeborn. He doesn't understand that each such contact serves to reconfirm man's vulnerability on this planet.*

But where do we draw the line? When do we start controlling this world, instead of just accepting it?

"How is she?" the demon asked him.

Startled, Damien took a moment to respond. What kind of Summoning was this, that allowed the faeborn such autonomy? Then he found his voice, and answered, "Asleep. At least for now. Thank God for that, anyway." He sighed, heavily. "I wish I knew what to do for her."

"Karril healed her once before," Senzei told Damien.

"I gave her peace," the demon corrected. "An illusion, no more. At that time, it was enough. All she wanted was to forget. This time they maimed her—and I'm not a Healer."

"But you know what happened?" Damien asked. "Do you know who did it?"

For a brief moment, the demon was very still. "I know," he said at last. "Who hurt her, why they did it . . . and why she can't be healed this time. And I'm sorry, but that is the case."

"I don't accept that."

The demon seemed startled. "Unusual spirit," he mused aloud. "I'm beginning to understand what she saw in you."

Damien's expression darkened. "If you have information, I'm ready to hear it. If you're here to assess our relationship . . ."

Karril drank heavily from his goblet, then dropped it; it disappeared before it hit the ground. "Church manners are so atrocious, don't you think, Senzei? They have no concept of how to deal with the faeborn. As if they could wish us out of existence merely by being rude."

Damien glared. "Under the circumstances—"

"Enough! You're quite right. I've been *Summoned*, after all." For some reason that term seemed to amuse him. "I'll tell you, priest. Everything I know. And later, Senzei can explain what it costs me to do that. Just being near such pain as hers weakens me considerably. Discussing it, in detail . . ." He shuddered melodramatically. "And in truth, I don't know very much," the demon warned. "But it's more than you'll get from any other source."

He sighed heavily. "First I should explain that Ciani and I have known each other for a long time. She was the first to catalog my family line, and to raise certain questions regarding our existence." He chuckled. "Don't worry, priest—I'll spare you the details. Suffice it to say that I knew her well. And when she decided to go off into the rakhlands—alone—I was one of the few whom she told. I tried to talk her out of it, of course. Any sensible entity would. But she was determined. It did no good to point out that although many explorers had braved that place, none had ever returned to talk about it. She wanted knowledge—*hungered* for it—and I'm sure I don't have to tell you how strong that drive was in her. Had the rakh survived? she asked. Was it they who erected the barrier that we call the Canopy, or did that predate them? If they survived, what had they become? You see, she had to have answers. And there was only one way to obtain them.

"I saw her off at the base of the Southern Pass, in the Worldsend Mountains. She was more alive than I had ever seen her, flush with the ecstasy of taking on a new challenge. Exquisite! I watched her as long as I could, but once she reached the edge of the Canopy my vision could no longer follow her. She passed through the barrier without looking back, into the fae-silence that has guarded the rakh-lands for centuries.

"Six years passed. And then she was brought to me. They had picked her out of the water by Kale, half drowned, more than half starved, battered by prolonged exposure to the elements. Shivering, even when her body was made warm. Terrified. They thought she was mad, or possessed, or worse. They did what they could to help her, using human skills—and then, when that failed, left it in the hands of the gods. In this case," he bowed slightly, "myself." Damien stiffened, but Senzei put a warning hand on his arm. "Like it or not," the demon continued, "that is my status in this region. Take it up with my priests if it bothers you.

"My domain is pleasure—human pleasure, in all its manifestations. There are few kinds of pain that I can tolerate, fewer still that I can feed on. But *apathy* is my true nemesis. It is anathema to my being: my negation, my opposite, my destruction. You should understand this when I say that I did what I could for her, but I know little of what happened to her. A few whispered words, a few fleeting images. No more. To delve into her memories would have meant my dissolution—my death—and it would have done her no good in the long run.

"This much I learned from her: The rakh who fled to that land survived, and it was their need for protection from man's aggression that caused the Canopy to exist. They affect the fae like all native species—unconsciously—and their psyche is wholly unlike the human template. Nevertheless, there are similarities—and the demons they've created are just as happy to feed on man, once the option is presented to them.

"Ciani discovered an underground nest of such demons. She made the mistake of exploring it. I'm sure I don't have to tell you what kind of power lurks in the places where sunlight never reaches; there's a reason that mines and wine cellars are ritually exposed to daylight once a year. They found her, and they trapped her, and they used her for food. But what they hungered for wasn't blood, or flesh, or any other bodily matter. They wanted *substance—depth—complexity—* and they gained it at the expense of prisoners like Ciani, whom they kept entombed beneath the earth for that purpose. They fed on their memories for as long as they were sane, and then on the tide of their madness. At first, these creatures were little more than wraiths; later, as they established a permanent link with their hosts, they gained solidity at their expense. Eventually their food source would wither and die, and they would have to find another. For they were eternally hungry, forever requiring a fresh input of life to sustain their own existence. And I think, as well, that the feeding amused them.

"These were the creatures that trapped Ciani and bound her away from the sunlight. This was the slow and terrible death they doomed her to, by making her feed one of their kind. And this was the prison she escaped from, against all odds. Killing her keeper so that her memories might be freed, because otherwise no time and no Working could ever heal her. Half-dead from her ordeal, more than a little mad, she fought her way back to the human lands—to be brought to my temple, where the pain could be soothed at last."

He paused for a moment, giving his human listeners a chance to digest his words. Then added quietly, "That's all I know. That's all anyone knows. There was nothing I could do to help except bury the memories within her, so that was what I did. Maybe it was the wrong thing to do—I'm not sure—but she never could have regained her identity, with her soul still trapped in the past."

"You present her assailants as . . . primitive," Damien challenged.

The demon hesitated. "I think that the beings Ciani dealt with were simple fae-constructs, primitive-minded, who knew only the promptings of hunger and sun-fear, and perhaps just a tad of sadism. I think some of them have become far more than that. Maybe it was their contact with her—or with humanity in general, once they passed beneath the Canopy. There's no question that they've demonstrated a sadistic instinct right up there with humanity's finest." His eyes sparkled. "Quite an adversary."

"I've killed demons before," Damien said coldly.

Karril leaned back and studied him. "You want to help her, don't you? But there's only one way to do that. You'll have to kill the one who hurt her. *That specific creature.* And he is, by definition, the most sophisticated of his kind." His expression was grim. "He's probably back home by now, on the other side of a barrier no human can Work through—so you can't possible prepare yourselves for what you'll find there. As for the rakh . . . your people tried to eradicate them once before. Do you think they'll bear you any fondness for it? Do you think your sorcery can stand up to theirs, when they Work the fae as naturally as you breathe? When their power is fueled by memories of humanity's attempted genocide?

For a moment Damien said nothing. Just sat there, remembering Ciani. As she had been. As she was now. Then he looked at Senzei—and saw, in the man's eyes, exactly what he had hoped to find: pain overcome by determination, enough to equal his own.

"It'll be tough," he agreed. "So where do we start?"

Eleven

The Temple of Pleasure was located just beyond the county line, which meant that Jaggonath's strict laws regarding public intoxication were not in effect there. Accordingly, in response to the warmth of the night, seven of the eight walls had been rolled up. The breeze poured in, and worshipers poured out. Couples and triples and even a few determined loners sprawled on the steps outside the temple, energetically pursuing whatever passed, in their own minds, for *pleasure.* Warm air caught the scent of wine and drugged incense and human pheremones and gusted it out toward the city, along with the sharp aroma of several dozen torches. At the border of the temple's influence, where the light grudgingly gave way to midnight's darkness, figures milled about with the energetic restlessness of circling insects. The curious, come from Jaggonath to watch. The demonic, come from the depths of night to feast. A succubus flickered into female form at the edge of one such gathering, eyes hungrily searching for a safe way to approach the well-warded temple. A vampire in male form touched its tongue tip to its dry lips in anticipation, as a local woman accepted its advance. All forms of pleasure were deemed worship here, even such as theirs; as for the safety of those humans who fed them, the pleasure-god Karril protected only his own.

A tall man stood at the edge of the temple's light. Lean, aristocratic, tastefully dressed, he clearly was no part of the voyeuristic entourage. In confirmation of which he stepped forward, and entered the temple's circle of light. Women looked up as he passed by, intrigued by his beauty, and one reached out to him. But he failed to notice most of them, and the one whose hand had come too close met his eyes and faltered, then drew back shivering.

There was a fountain in the center of the temple—one might call it an altar—with sexually explicit carvings that spewed forth the drugged red wine of Karril's worship. Leaning against it was a man of middle age, considerably shorter than the newcomer, whose disheveled clothing and hearty grin implied that he had just found fulfillment in someone's embrace.

The stranger came to where he stood, and waited.

"Good guess," the shorter man said pleasantly.

"You forget that I have demon-sight."

"I meant, that I would be here."

"You forget that I know you."

The shorter man chuckled. "So it is." He sighed, and looked out over the congregation. "They'll make a god of me in truth someday— isn't that the way it works? Rather awesome, to be at the receiving end of it. I keep wondering if I'll feel it when it happens. Or if it will be a gradual conversion."

"Spare me the pagan philosophy."

"It's your philosophy, my friend, not mine." He dipped a jeweled goblet deep into the fountain, dripped red wine from his sleeve end as he drank from it.

"Can we talk?" the stranger asked.

"Of course."

"*Privately.*"

He shrugged. "As much as there ever is privacy, in this place." A room appeared about them, tastelessly luxurious in its trappings. "It's all illusion anyway, but if it makes you more comfortable. . . ."

"I find the sight of such worship . . . unpleasant."

"Ah. Church sensibilities, once more. My theme for the wcck." He chuckled. "Shame on you, my friend. I'd have thought you'd have outgrown all that by now."

He reclined on a plush velvet couch and pointed to a matching stool opposite. "That one will support you."

The stranger sat.

"Can I offer you something? Wine? Cerebus? Human blood?"

The stranger's expression softened into something that was almost a smile. "I always refuse you, Karril."

"I know. It pleases me to offer, just the same." He drank deeply from his goblet, then vanished it when it was emptied. "So, what brings the Forest to Jaggonath?"

"A search for beauty. As always."

"And did you find it?"

"A lovely, overprotected flower, growing in the mud of a farm."

A shadow passed over the demon's face. "To be hunted?"

"Curiously, no. She caught me in a rare moment of magnanimity, and I'm afraid I promised her safety."

"You're getting soft." The demon grinned.

"My pleasures vary. Although this one, admittedly, was . . . odd."

"You may lose your reputation for evil."

The stranger chuckled. "Unlikely."

"So what brings you to this place? To me? Or am I to believe that you simply desired my company?"

For a long moment the stranger just looked at him. Karril made himself another full goblet and drank from it, waiting him out; such a silence could mean anything.

"What do you know," he said at last, "about the incident at the Fae Shoppe?"

The demon's expression darkened perceptibly. He stood, and turned away from his visitor. Goblet and couch both disappeared; the passionate reds of the room's interior were exchanged for blue, sullen and grayed. "Why do you want to know?"

"I was at the place earlier this evening. At what *remained* of it. I worked a Knowing—and a Seeing, and a Divining, and several more things whose titles you wouldn't recognize. All blocked. It takes more than an apprentice's skill to block my sight, Karril. Something about that shop was damned important to someone—and they must have worked one hell of a sacrifice to protect it."

"It doesn't concern you," the demon said quietly.

"Everything concerns me."

"This doesn't." He turned back; his expression was strained. "Trust me."

"I could take it down, you understand. There isn't an adept in Jaggonath whose Working could stand before me if I was determined enough. But then it would be down for good. And whatever it's protecting. . . ." He spread his hands suggestively. Karril winced, but said nothing. "Need I remind you that I could simply work a Summoning and bind you?" the stranger pressed. "That you would then have to tell me what I want to know? That's a much more unpleasant relationship, Karril. Why don't you spare us both the trouble."

"Because there's someone I don't want hurt."

The stranger's eyes widened with sudden understanding. His voice, when it came, was a whisper. Seductive. "Do you really think I'd use you as an accessory to pain? After all these years, don't you think I know better?"

"Your standards and mine differ somewhat."

"You feed on the Hunt."

"I feed on the *Hunter*. And if his pleasures changed tomorrow, I would celebrate."

"Even if—"

"Why do you care?" the demon demanded. "What is all this to you, that you bother?"

The stranger sat back, suddenly distant. "A loremaster has been attacked. I happen to be among those who respect the neutrality of such people. Shouldn't I be upset? The currents in town have shifted—which hint at something much more nasty than a simple accident. Shouldn't I be concerned? A nonadept sacrifices God knows what, to set up a blockage even I can't Work through—"

"And something dark that isn't of the Forest moves into Jaggonath. That's what this is really all about, isn't it? Territorialism. Defense of the Hunter's turf. The loremaster and her mercantile enterprises have nothing to do with it."

One corner of the stranger's mouth twitched slightly: the hint of a smile without its substance. "There is that also," he said quietly.

The blue of the room shifted through gray, to orange.

"I want your word," the demon said.

"I recently gave that to a young girl," he mused. "She didn't know what it was worth." He looked at the demon sharply. "You do."

"That's why I want it."

"That I won't hurt the lady Ciani? I have no reason—"

"*Your word.*"

"You can be very tiresome, Karril." His tone was light, but his eyes were narrow, his gaze dark. "As you wish. I will neither harm Ciani of Faraday, nor cause her to be harmed, until this matter is dealt with."

"*Ever.*"

"All right—*ever.* Are you satisfied now? Do you trust me?" He smiled, but his eyes were cold. "So few creatures would."

"But we go back a long time, don't we? I know where you came from. I know what you are. Even more importantly, I know what you *were.*"

"Then it's time you made me equally well-informed."

"There's a priest involved," the demon warned. "A Knight of the Flame. Do you care?"

He shrugged. "His problem, not mine."

"I wonder if he'll appreciate that fact."

Again: an expression that was not quite a smile, a tone that was not quite humor. "It could make it . . . amusing."

The demon smiled. And made himself a chair. And sat in it. The room faded slowly to red again; plush velvet, in quantity.

"You sure you wouldn't like a drink?"

"Tell me," the stranger demanded.

He did.

Twelve

"This is a rakh."

Senzei took hold of the ancient drawing with care and gently freed it from its tissue cocoon. The paper had yellowed with age and its ink had browned; he was infinitely careful as he turned it toward the lamplight, sensing just how fragile it was.

On it was sketched a mammal, four-legged and tailed as all Ernan mammals were. Visually unimpressive. He read the Latin name inscribed beneath it (Earth words, Earth terms, the species had been renamed so many times it hardly seemed to matter what it had originally been called) and then the date. And he looked up at Damien, startled. "2 A.S.?"

"The original. This is a copy. Done some two hundred years later, but supposedly an accurate reproduction. If the introduction is correct, the artist was copying from a sketchbook belonging to one of the original colonists."

"The landing crew," Senzei breathed. Tasting the concept.

Damien leaned back in his leather-bound chair; overhead, the deeply shadowed vaults of the cathedral's Rare Document Archives seemed to stretch toward infinity. "That's the earliest representation we have. And, for quite some time, the only one. Evidently, the original settlers didn't consider the species worthy of too much attention. Of course, they had other things to worry about."

"Like survival."

Damien nodded. "Look at these." He pushed a pile of sketches—chronologically arranged—across the table. Silently, Senzei began to leaf through them. After a while his eyes narrowed slightly and he shook his head, amazed. Then he went through them again, more carefully.

"It's incredible," he said at last.

"One can see why the settlers were frightened."

"Gods, yes. If they didn't understand the fae. . . ."

"And this is before First Impression was verified. Before they really understood how man's presence had altered the natural pattern here." He picked up the first sketch and studied it. "Animal," he muttered. "No more than that. Hardly worthy of notice, until Pravida Rakhi declared it to be the most sophisticated life-form native to this planet. That was forty-one years After Sacrifice. Man's innocence lasted only that long." He tipped the fragile paper toward the light, careful not to crease it. The creature that posed on its surface could have been related to any one of half a dozen species he knew—or even one that had ceased to exist. With but one aged sketch, it was hard to tell.

"You think they began to change after Rakhi's announcement?"

Damien shook his head. "No. Before that. As near as I can tell, it started right after the Sacrifice. But when Rakhi declared that this species was man's Ernan equivalent—that but for man's presence, the species would have developed advanced intelligence and complex dexterity and eventually taken to the stars—the pace picked up alarmingly. Such is the power of the popular imagination."

Senzei leafed through the sketches again, laid several out before him in chronological order. Though they were done in a variety of hands using dissimilar media, the overall pattern was clear.

The species was changing.

"Of course, now we understand what happened. Now we know that *evolution* is a very different process here than it was on Earth. Here, if trees grow taller, the next gaffi calves are born with longer necks. If lakes dry up, the offspring of underwater creatures are born with rudimentary lungs. Their need affects their DNA, in precise and perfect balance. To us, it seems wholly natural; several adepts have even managed to Work the process, giving us our un-Earth species. But we understand this all *now*, after centuries of observation. Imagine what it must have meant for our ancestors, to see this happening before their eyes!"

Senzei looked up at him. "When did they guess where it was headed?"

"Not for a while. Not until Rakhi. The settlers observed that changes were occurring—but they were occurring in hundreds of species, in every ecological niche on the planet. And they had, as you say, much better things to worry about."

"So now, imagine the rakh in that time. Moderately intelligent, seemingly self-aware, possessing opposable digits and thus a fair degree of manual dexterity. Inhabiting the very same ecological niche that man's primitive ancestors did on Earth, in that evolutionary instant before he gained his true humanity. Changing, generation after generation—adapting to man's presence, to the sudden appearance of a rival species. Slowly. Erna was feeling its way along genome by genome, testing out each new evolutionary concept before making the next adjustment. Keeping the ecosphere in balance.

"And then, along comes Pravida Rakhi. Convincing all concerned that if man had never come here, these creatures would have been the natural monarchs of this planet. They would have become the local equivalent of *us*. The popular imagination is aroused, on all levels of consciousness. Intellectual curiosity, gut fear response, competitive instinct—you name it. Every possible mode of thought, every manner of instinct and emotion, every level of man's mind, all are focused on the image of these creatures as *pseudo-human*. Is it any wonder that the fae was affected? That these natives, who were a natural part of this world, evolved accordingly?"

He shuffled through the sheets that were spread out before him until he found the one he wanted. And placed it before Senzei.

"131 A.S.," he said quietly.

Erna's dominant natives had altered drastically in both shape and balance. The back legs were sturdier, the hindquarters more heavily muscled. The spine had bent so that the torso might be carried erect, although the front paws—hands?—were still being used as auxiliary feet. Most dramatic of all was the change in the skull, from the sharply angled profile of an animal predator to something that looked disturbingly human.

Senzei tapped the date on the drawing. "This was when they guessed what was happening."

"This was when they began to *suspect*. You have to remember how alien such a concept was to their inherited way of thinking. It took five generations of close observation before anyone was sure. And several generations after that, to see if human sorcery could reverse the trend. It couldn't. Erna had supplied us with a competitor, and one cast in our own image. We had accepted it as such. The work of a single sorceror was hardly a drop in the bucket, compared to that. Generation after generation, the rakh were becoming more human."

"And we answered with the crusades."

"Wholesale slaughter of an innocent species. And the unwitting creation of a host of demons, as byproducts of man's most murderous instincts. All feeding on his hatred, all savoring his intolerance. Is it any wonder that human society nearly devolved into total chaos? That the rigid social patterns of the Revivalist movement seemed to be man's only hope of maintaining order?"

"And thus the Church was born."

Damien looked at him but said nothing. For a moment, the room seemed unnaturally still.

"And thus the Church was born," he agreed. At last he looked down at the table again, and unrolled a heavy parchment sheet atop the pile of drawings. A map.

"The rakhlands."

Senzei looked it over, muttered, "Shit."

Damien agreed.

The land that the rakh had retreated to was well fortified by nature to resist man's most aggressive instincts. To the west, the Worldsend Mountains provided a daunting barrier of ice-clad peaks and frozen rivers. To the east, sheer basalt cliffs carved out by centuries of tsunami offered no easy landing site, no hope of shelter. The southlands were hardly more appealing, acre upon acre of treacherous swampland that harbored some of Erna's deadliest species. Only in the north was there any hope of passage, between the jagged peaks and wind-carved cliffs that looked out onto the Serpent Straits.

Damien tapped a finger to the mouth of the Achron River, and muttered, "Only way."

"What about the mountains?"

Damien looked up at him sharply—and realized, in an instant, how little the man had traveled. "Not with winter coming. Not if we want to live to get to the rakhlands. I traveled the Dividers in midsummer, and that was rough enough. Even if the cold doesn't kill you outright, there are nasty things that inhabit those peaks— damned hungry things—and it's hard to fight them when your body's half frozen. Of course, if we wait until summer. . . ."

"I can't. *She* can't."

"Agreed—on all counts. River it is, then. Hell of a landing, but I think it can be done. And you can bet we'll pay dearly for it. In cash, I mean." He leaned forward in his chair, intent upon the display before them. "Where's the Canopy?"

Senzei hesitated. "That depends. Roughly, *there*." He sketched a rough circle with his finger: up through the center of the Worldsend range, east along the coast, to a curve that extended up to ten miles off the eastern shore, and back through the swamps. "Half a mile wide, in places—and as much as six, elsewhere. It moves, too. Sometimes it edges out into the Straits—which is why most boats avoid that shoreline like the plague. I have better maps at my place," he added.

"Good. We'll need them. Tell me about it."

"We don't know much. A wall of living fae, that first appeared shortly after the rakh fled into the Worldsend. No natural fae-current passes through it. No Working can pass from one side to the other.

Tamed fae that's Worked in the middle of it can go wild, and do anything. Ships that flounder into it discover that their instruments have suddenly gone haywire, that the very shoreline seems changed . . . but so much of our technology is fae-based, how can we be sure of what that means?"

"What's it made of? Earth-fae? Tidal? Solar?"

Senzei shook his head. "None of those. Nothing we humans understand. Ciani thought there might be some sort of force inherent in the rakh themselves—we see similar things in other species—and that the Canopy is an extension of their communal existence. Their need for protection."

"From man," Damien said grimly.

There was no need for Senzei to comment.

"Do we know what the rakh are now? Did Ciani ever say?"

"We know they survived. We know they must be at least moderately intelligent in order to have manifested the kind of creatures that she encountered. And that there are large numbers of them—or the Canopy wouldn't exist. That's all. I can list a hundred rumors for you . . . but you know how reliable those are. There's no way of knowing whether they followed through on their initial Impression, and eventually developed a human-compatible form, or went off in some other direction entirely. The fact that their demons can adopt human form seems to imply the former—but I wouldn't bet my life on that conclusion. Some demons are very versatile."

Wouldn't a world without demons be better? Damien wanted to argue. *Worth sacrificing for?* But he bit back the words before they were spoken; this was neither the time nor the place for theosophy. Senzei and he would be spending a long time together, under very trying circumstances; anything that might add additional tension to the situation was a course to be avoided, at all costs.

"Let's prepare for everything," he said. "Once we get there, there'll be no sending home for supplies. If it's small and it might be useful, we take it with us. If it's large and heavy . . . maybe we pack it anyway. Often it's the little things that make a difference—especially when you don't even know what it is you're going to be facing.

Senzei leaned back, but there was nothing relaxed about the posture; his body was stiffly erect, tense. "You really think we can do it?"

Damien hesitated. Met his eyes. Let him see the doubt that was there, inside him. "I think we have to try," he said quietly. "As for the rest . . . there's no way of knowing that until we're inside, is there? Until we can see what we're up against. The odds are certainly against us." He shrugged. "But we won't even know what they are until we get there."

"We need an adept," Senzei muttered.

Damien looked around, as if checking for eavesdroppers. The gesture reminded Senzei of where they were—as it was no doubt meant to do. "Not here," he muttered. He began to gather the drawings. "Good enough for research, but for the rest . . . it isn't appropriate."

"I understand."

"We'll go to your place. All right? I'll have copies made of the map, and sent there." He glanced about, paused just long enough to draw Senzei's attention to the two other priests, ritually clad, who were within hearing distance. "We need to have this worked out as well as we can before we take a single step toward the rakhlands, you know."

"And gods help us then."

Jarred by the plural, Damien looked up at him. "Pray long and hard, if you want your gods to interfere." His voice and manner were strained. "And do it soon. Because once we get under the Canopy, and that silence stretches between us and Jaggonath . . . no god of this region is going to hear your prayers. Or anything else, for that matter."

She lay still as death on Senzei's guest cot, glazed eyes staring out into nothingness. The light of a single candle illuminated her face and hands in sharp relief, from the stark white highlights of her colorless flesh to shadows so sharp and deep that they might have been carved in stone. Even her eyes seemed paler, as though sorrow had leached the color from them. As though her assailants had drained her not only of memory, but of hue.

The food that had been placed beside her was untouched. Damien moved it carefully out of the way and then sat by her side.

"Cee." His voice was no more than a whisper, but in the absolute silence of her chamber it might as well have been a shout. "Cee. We're going after them. Do you understand?" He put a hand on her shoulder—ice-cold flesh, without response—and squeezed gently. "You've got to get hold of yourself."

She turned to him slowly. Her face was dry of tears, but he could see the streaks of salt-stiffened flesh where they had coursed. The desolation in her eyes nearly broke his heart.

"What's the point?" she whispered.

He Worked her then. Gently, praying that she wouldn't notice. Worked a link between them that would keep her attention on him, keep her from falling back into unresponsive darkness. "We need you."

For a moment it seemed as if she would turn away again, but something—perhaps the fae—held her steady. Her voice, when it came, was a dry, dehydrated whisper. "For what?"

"Ah, Cee. I thought you would have guessed that." He took her nearer hand, prying it gently from the blanket's edge to enfold it in his own. Cold flesh, nearly lifeless. How dilute was her vitality now—how fragile had that thread become, which binds such a woman to life? "You have to come with us."

For a moment she looked startled; there was more vitality in that single expression than he had seen in all the days since the assault. He felt something in himself tighten, tried to quell the tide of hope rising inside him. Or at least, control it. So much depended on how she took this. . . .

"We can't leave you here," he told her. "You'd be unprotected. There's no ward Senzei or I could Work that would hold them off, if your own didn't. And he's not all that sure that the illusion he Worked at the shop would hold once he's under the Canopy. They might suddenly realize that you're alive . . . and we'd have no way of getting back to you. Or even knowing what had happened." He took a deep breath, chose his next words carefully. "And without you, Cee . . . we can't find the one who did this." He felt her stiffen beneath his hand, saw the fear come into her eyes. He continued quickly, "If not for the Canopy we could rely on a Knowing, but with the Canopy between us . . . no one can read through it, Senzei said, not even an adept. And God knows, we're not that. With you on one side and us on the other, locating your assailant would be like trying to find a needle in a haystack. Even worse: like trying to find one single blade of hay in that stack, when you don't know which one you're searching for. How would we even know where to start?" He squeezed her hand gently, wished he could will some of his own warmth into her flesh. His own vitality. "We *need* you, Cee."

She shut her eyes; a tremor of remembered pain ran through her body. "You don't understand," she whispered. "You can't possibly understand." A tear gathered under her lashes, but lacked the substance to free itself; her body was too dehydrated to spare that much fluid. "What it's like to live with the fae. Like adepts do. Zen thinks it's like a constant Seeing, but it's not that at all." Her brow furrowed as she struggled for words. "It's everywhere. In everything. There are so many different kinds that I don't even have names for them all, some so fleeting that they're just a spark out of the corner of your eye—a flash of light, of power—and then they're gone, before you can focus on them. And the currents flow through it all—*everything!*— not just around it, like he Sees, but permeating every substance on this planet, living and unliving, solid and illusory. Sometimes you'll be looking at the sky and the tidal-fae will flux for an instant and there it is—like a flaw in a crystal that suddenly catches the light, a spectrum of living color that's gone before you can even draw a breath. And there's music, too, so beautiful that it hurts just to listen to. Everywhere you look, everything you touch, it's all permeated with living fae—all in a constant state of flux, changing hourly as the different tides course through it. And the result is a world so rich, so wonderful, that it makes you shiver just to live in it. . . ." She drew in a shaky breath. "Do you understand? When I touch a stone, what I feel isn't hard rock—I feel everything that stone has been, everything it might become, I feel how it channels the earth-fae and how it interacts with the tidal fae and how the power of the sun will affect it, and what it will be when true night falls . . . do you understand, Damien? That bit of rock is alive *alive—everything* is alive to us, even the air we breathe—only now—" She coughed raggedly, and he could hear the tears come into her voice. "Don't you see? That's what they took! It's all dead now. I look around, and all I see are corpses. A universe of corpses. Like everything I see is sculpted out of rotting meat . . . except it's not even rotting; there's life in corruption, you now, even carrion has its own special music . . . and here there's nothing. Nothing! I touch this bed—" and she grasped the bedframe with her free hand, and squeezed it until her knuckles were white with the pressure, "—and all I feel . . . gods, there's no *life* in it . . . can you understand? It wasn't *me* they drained, it was the whole of my world!"

"Cee." He stroked her hair gently from her face, letting his fingers warm her skin. "Cee. We're going to get it back for you. Do you understand? But we need your help. We need you to come with us. It's all a waste if you don't. Cee?" He continued to stroke her hair— gently, as one would a frightened kitten's—but she only moaned softly, wordlessly. As the tears finally came.

"We'll help you, Cee," he whispered. "I swear it."

The books and documents that had been brought to Senzei's work-room had long since overflowed the confines of his desk; when Damien entered the room he found him sitting on the floor in the center of his sigil-rug, surrounded by carefully ordered stacks.

Damien waited until Ciani's assistant looked up at him. "I'm going to kill them," he hissed. "Going to kill those sons of bitches—hard, and slow. You hear me? I'm going to make them suffer."

"Thus speaks the guardian of peace."

"There's nothing in my Order's charter about peace. Or in the Church's Manifesto, for that matter. That's post-war PR." He grabbed a free stool, put it down by the desk, and sat on it. "Find anything?"

"A simple question for a complex task." Senzei began to point to the piles around him, naming them one after the other. "Things we should take with us. Things we should read before we go. Things we should take with us except they're too large, fragile, or heavy to carry, so we should have the information in them copied into something else, preferably with waterproof ink. Things we—"

"I get the picture." He flipped back the cover of a leather-bound volume that sat on the edge of the desk—*Evolutionary Trends in Native Species: a Neo-Terran Analysis*—"How about the manpower problem? Any progress there?"

Senzei hesitated. "I have her records, you know—one of the few things I saved. Detailed dossiers on all adepts living in this region. Depressing as hell, given our situation."

"You don't trust their power?"

Senzei sighed. "I don't trust *them*. Need I remind you that the gift of adeptitude is utterly random, that we don't understand the least thing about how it comes to those it does, or—more importantly—why? The adepts in Jaggonath are an utterly random sample of humanity: most of them are self-centered, unstable, intellectually limited . . . replete with all the flaws that define us as a species. One or two are marginally hopeful . . . but I don't like it, Damien. I don't like trusting a stranger in this, adept or no."

"You were the one who wanted us to find someone."

"I wanted Ciani," he said bitterly. "Someone like her. Only there isn't someone like her. She was the exception. I can't imagine any of these people," he waved his hand over three of the nearer piles, "taking on the cause of a stranger, like she would have done. Risking their lives just to find out what's on the other side of those mountains. All right? I was wrong. So shoot me."

"Easy." Damien made himself a place on the rug and sat down, opposite Senzei. "You can't let it get to you, Zen. Not this early in the game." He picked up a piece of paper from the pile nearest—a fae-map of the Serpent Straits—and looked it over as he said, "I'd just as soon have an adept along, too, but if we can't, we can't. You and I have power enough, in our various fields. It'll have to suffice."

"I hope," Senzei said miserably.

He put the map down again, tried to change the subject. "How about the rakh?"

He hesitated. "What exactly are you asking?"

"When can we find one? How can we do it?"

Senzei stared at him for a moment, clearly astonished. "You mad? We need to stay clear of them at all costs. Their hatred of humanity—"

"Was last documented almost a thousand years ago. I'm not saying it's not still in effect—might even have worsened—but is it safe to assume that? I do know that we'll be crossing their lands, and I'd be surprised if we can avoid any contact. Don't you think we'd be better off approaching one or two under carefully controlled circumstances, than riding blindly into a city full of potential enemies?"

Senzei digested that concept. "I suppose. Once we're inside the Canopy I could work a Calling; that might bring us something with a potentially sympathetic mindset. But we'd have to wait until we get inside to know for sure. If only some of the rakh were outside the Canopy—"

Ciani's voice interrupted. "How do you know they're not?"

The two men looked up to find her leaning in the doorway. Wrapped in a blanket and shivering, as though protecting herself from the chill autumn winds that blew outside the house. Despite that— despite her ghastly pallor, hollowed cheeks, and the thin red webbing that filmed her eyes—she looked better than she had in days. Since the accident.

Alive, Damien thought. *She looks alive.*

"How do you know where they are?" she pressed.

"The rakh never travel outside the Canopy. They—"

Her voice was a ragged whisper. "How do we know that?"

Senzei started to speak again, but Damien put a hand on his arm. Quieting him. On first impression it seemed that Ciani was asking for simple information: What facts had she forgotten which caused them to believe this about the rakh? But on second impression. . . . He looked in her eyes, saw a brief glint of fire there. Intelligence. They had taken her memory, but they hadn't dimmed her sagacity. They couldn't.

"We don't know," he told her. "We assumed."

"Ah." She shook her head sadly; there was a hint of humor in the gesture, a mere shadow of her former self. Weakly, she whispered, "Bad move."

Senzei stiffened. "You think they might travel? That one or more might be outside their own wall of protection?"

"I have no information on which to base such a guess," she reminded him gently. Damien could see the pain of it in her eyes, the constant frustration of reaching inside for memories that weren't there. Of not even knowing how much knowledge she had lost. "But it's possible, isn't it?" She hesitated. "Do we know any reason why it wouldn't be?"

"None at all," Damien assured her. And then he was up and by her side in an instant, to catch her as her spurt of strength finally died. As she fell. So light, so fragile. . . .

"She needs food," he said. "I'll take her downstairs, try to feed her something. Zen—?"

"Working on it," he responded. He climbed over several stacks of books to reach the desk; once there, he began to rummage through a stack of maps. "I can do a Converging, to draw whatever's out there. *If* there's anything out there. I'll try to get it to meet up with us on route—that's better than waiting for it here, don't you think?"

"Much better."

"We won't know what it is, of course. Or where it's coming from. Not until it gets to us.' He looked back at Damien. "You're sure—"

"Yes," he said quickly "A rakh contact this side of the Canopy is worth any risk. Do it."

"It may not like us."

"We may not like it," Damien said dryly. "That's life."

And he carried Ciani downstairs.

Senzei found Allesha in the kitchen, washing out the last of their dinner dishes. He waited for a moment in strained silence, hoping that she would notice him. But if she did, she made no sign of it. It did seem to him that her body was somewhat tenser, that her hands were scrubbing more vigorously, as if using the household chore to vent some private anxiety . . . but that was probably his imagination. The stress. Not Allesha.

Finally, "Lesh," he said softly. He saw her stiffen. She put down the dish she was working on, carefully, but didn't otherwise acknowledge him. "Lesh? I need to talk to you. Can you spare a minute?"

She turned to him slowly; something in her disheveled manner, so utterly free of cosmetics or artifice, reminded him of when they had first met. How deeply he had been in love with her since that first moment. It made him all the more miserable that a breach had been growing between them. That for all his efforts he seemed unable to recover the joy of those innocent, happy days.

"Lesh? You want to sit?" He indicated the table with its delicately carved chairs. The whole of the kitchen was delicate, like her.

"I'm all right," she said softly.

He hesitated. Not knowing how to start. Not knowing how to commit to speech all the things she must be aware of, which lacked only official pronouncement. "You know how bad it is with Cee. I mean ... Damien thinks the only way to change that is to go into the rakhlands. To hunt down the creature that did this and destroy it." The violent words felt strange on his tongue. *Hunt. Destroy.* Not words of study, or of quiet city life, but keys to a far darker universe. "I think ... that is, I mean ..."

"That you're going," she whispered.

Stiffly, he nodded.

She turned away.

"Lesh—"

She waved him to silence. He could see her shoulders trembling as she fought to hold back tears. Or anger? He moved toward her, his every instinct crying out for him to hold her, to use their physical closeness to blunt the edge of his announcement, but she drew away from him. Only inches—but it hinted at a much more vast gulf between them, that had been months in the making.

"Just like that," she whispered. "So easy. . . ."

His heart twisted inside him. "I didn't know how to tell you. I didn't know when. It just sort of happened, all of it ... Lesh, I'm sorry, I would have come to you earlier. . . ."

She shook her head. "It isn't that. It isn't that at all." She turned back to him. Her eyes were red-rimmed, and not just from the last few minutes. She had been crying. "And it isn't just Ciani, either. Or the events of the last few days. I want you to understand that, Zen. It's been going on for too long, and I ... I can't take it anymore."

She turned away from him again; her voice became so low he could hardly hear it. "I think we should end it," she whispered. "Give up. It's not going anywhere, Zen—and it won't get better. Maybe it was a mistake in the first place. Maybe there was a time when I could have changed things. . . ." She looked back at him. "But I'm sorry. I failed you. Failed us both."

She reached down to the edge of the sink where a slender gold ring lay in a dish of soap-suds. And wiped it clean as carefully and as delicately as if it were fine china. "I think you'd better have this," she told him. She didn't meet his eyes as she held it out to him. "You can keep mine. It's okay. I don't want it. I wouldn't want to see it. . . ."

He stared at the engagement ring in shock, not quite believing it. Not quite absorbing.

"I've been thinking about it for a long time," she said hurriedly. "I want you to know that. Gods, I've been going over it in my mind for so long that I can hardly remember a time when I wasn't. Isn't that awful?" She took a deep breath. "Because I realized one day that though I can be many things to you, I can never be first in your life. Never. Oh, I tried to convince myself otherwise—I reasoned that if we only spent enough time together, if you cared enough about our commitment . . . we could work out our priorities, establish the kind of relationship I want. The kind of relationship I *need*. But we can't. I understand that now. This incident didn't start it, it just drove the lesson home. —And it's all right, Zen, it's just the way you are, I have to deal with that—"

"If it's Ciani—"

"It's not Ciani! Don't you think I know that? It's not any other woman. Gods!" She laughed shortly; it was a bitter sound. "I wish it *were* another woman. I'd know how to compete with a woman. I don't know how to compete with *this*." She was facing him now, and her eyes, normally soft, blazed with anger. With pain. "I mean the *fae*, Zen. I mean your hunger for something you can never have. Don't you think I see how it eats at you? Don't you think I can feel it in you every time I'm with you? Every time we touch? Feel it in you every time we make love—how you wish it could be more, how you wish you could experience it on all those different levels—don't you think I can sense your frustration? Your distraction?" she drew in a deep breath, shakily. "I can't live with it any more. I'm sorry. I've tried and tried . . . and I just can't do it any more."

"Lesh . . . we can work it out. We can work on it—"

"When you come home again? Two, three years from now? Do you really think I should wait—for this?"

He could say nothing. The words were all choked up inside him. Words of anger, pleading, surprise . . . and guilt. Because he had seen it coming. Deep inside him, on levels he hated to probe. And he despised himself for not knowing how to stop it.

"I love you," he said. Willing all his passion into his voice—wishing he could communicate his emotions directly, without need for such an artificial vehicle as words. "I love you more than anything, Lesh—"

"And I love you," she whispered back. "I always have." She shut her eyes tightly; a tear squeezed out from the corner of one of them. "I only wish that was enough to base a marriage on, Zen. But it isn't. Can't you see that?"

He wanted to argue with her. He wanted to beg her to stay, to tell her that soon he would be back again soon, they could start all over—he would change, she would see!—but the words caught in his throat and he just couldn't voice them. Because she was right, and he knew it. He could make all the promises he wanted, and it wouldn't change a thing. The hunger was first in his life, had always been. Would always be. Mere words couldn't alter that. And if it wasn't enough for her that he tried not to express that, that he worked to repress that terrible yearning while they were together, tried to hide it . . . then there was nothing he could do to fix things. Nothing at all.

"I'm sorry," he gasped. Sensing clearly the vast gulf that had formed between them, not knowing how to reach across it. Feeling lost, as though suddenly he were surrounded by strangers. "I'm so sorry. . . ."

"I just hope you find what you want," she murmured. "Or make some kind of peace with yourself, at least. If there was anything I could do to help . . . I would. You know that."

"I know it," he whispered.

She came to where he stood, and kissed him gently. He put his arms around her and held her tightly. As if somehow that could make the problems go away. As if a mere demonstration of affection could make everything better. But they had passed that stage, long ago, while his attention was elsewhere. While he devoted the core of his attention to the fae, failing to see that all about him the pieces of his life were slowly dissolving. Withering, like houseplants that had been starved of water. While he failed to see their need.

Numbly he watched as she put the thin gold ring down on the kitchen table; it made a small puddle, mirror bright, with the water that dripped from her fingers.

"I'll keep the house," she said gently. "Take care of it, until you come back. So you don't have to worry about your things . . . while you're gone." She looked toward the remaining dishes, then away from them. Away from him. "I'm sorry, Zen." She whispered it, in a voice that echoed with fresh tears. "So sorry. . . ."

She ran from the room. He moved as though to follow her—and then checked himself, with painful effort. What was he going to say to her? Where was he going to find the magic words to make it all better, so that somehow they might pretend it had never happened? So that somehow *he* could pretend that she wasn't right, that he hadn't failed her, that when he came back from the rakhlands everything would go back to normal?

He sat in the kitchen chair heavily. And fingered the thin gold ring, with its delicately engraved sigils of love.

And he wept.

Thirteen

"Holiness."

The Patriarch closed the heavy volume before him and pushed it to one side. "Come in, Reverend Vryce." He pointed to a cushioned chair set opposite the desk. "Have a seat."

Damien tried to bring himself to sit, but couldn't. His soul was wound too tight with tension; he felt that if he tried to bend his body, to relax in any way, something inside him would snap. "Holy Father. I . . . need to make a request."

It could still go wrong here. It could all fall apart.

The Patriarch looked him over, from his rumpled hair and sleepless eyes to the simple beige shirt and brown woolen pants he had worn for the audience. And nodded, slowly. "Go on."

"I need . . . that is, something has come up. . . ." He heard the tremor in his voice, took a deep breath, and tried to steady himself. *It's not just that you're afraid he'll refuse you, remember that. It's the way the fae responds to him.* He started to speak again, but the Partiarch waved him to silence.

"Sit down, Reverend Vryce." His voice was quiet but dominant; *authority* flowed forth from him, thickening the fae between them. "That's an order."

Damien forced himself to sit. He started to speak again, but again the Patriarch shushed him. He passed a goblet across the desk to him, scarlet glass with a darker liquid within. Damien took it and drank: sweet red wine, freshly chilled. With effort, he forced himself to relax. Took another drink. After a few minutes, the pounding of his heart subsided to a somewhat more normal rythm.

"Now," the Patriarch said, when he had set the glass aside. "Tell me."

He did. Not the presentation he had planned, with its careful inter-weaving of truth and half-truth and insinuation, designed to manipu-late the Patriarch into making the decision he required. Something in the Holy Father's manner inspired him to do otherwise. Maybe it was the fae, communicating between them on levels Damien could hardly sense. Or maybe simply human instinct, which said that the Holy Father was ready to hear—and deserved to be told—the truth.

He told it all. The Holy Father interrupted once or twice, to request that a point be clarified, but otherwise he offered no response. His expression gave no hint of either sympathy or hostility, or of any wariness on his part. Any of the things that Damien might have expected.

"The end result," he concluded—and he took a deep breath to steady himself—"is that I must request permission to leave my duties here in order to go east. A leave of absence, your Holiness. I believe that the situation merits it."

For a long time the Patriarch looked at him, clear blue eyes taking the measure of his soul. Or so it seemed. At last he said, "If I refuse you?"

Damien stiffened. "This isn't merely a personal concern. If these demons are able to leave the rakhlands—"

"Answer the question, please."

He met those eyes—so hard, so cold—and answered in the only way possible. Though it tore him apart inside to do it. "I swore an oath, your Holiness. To give the Prophet's dream precedence over my own life. To serve the patterns which he declared were necessary . . . including the hierarchy of my Church. If you're asking me if I under-stand my duty, that's my answer. If you mean to use this situation to test me. . . ." He felt his hands tighten on the chair's wooden arms, forced them to relax. Forced the anger out of his voice. *It is his right. In some ways, his duty.* "Please don't. I implore you. As a man, and as your servant."

For a long time the Patriarch was silent. Damien met his gaze for as long as he could, but at last turned away. He felt helpless, not being able to Work the fae to his advantage. Doubly helpless—because the Patriarch, just by existing, did.

"Come," the Holy Father said at last. He stood. "I want to show you something."

He led Damien through the western wing in silence, the whispering of his hem against the smooth mosaic floors the only sound to accompany their footsteps down the long, vaulted corridors. Soon they came to a heavily barred door, whose steel lock was inscribed with passages from the Book of Law. A thick tapestry ribbon depended from the ceiling, and this the Patriarch pulled. They waited. Soon, hurried footsteps could be heard coming from down the hall, and the tinkling of metal upon metal. A priest appeared, still shuffling through the key ring that depended from a gold chain around his neck. He bowed his obeisance to the Patriarch even as he managed to single out the key he wanted. Damien turned toward his Holiness— and saw a similar key cradled in his hand, its grip made of fine gold filigree, fragments of bloodstone set in a spiral pattern.

Together, synchronized, they unlocked the heavy door. The Patriarch nodded for Damien to pass through, then took down a lamp that hung by the threshold and followed. The door was then shut behind them and locked.

"This way," he said.

Down stairs. Into the depths of the building, into the very foundation of the structure—into the earth itself—until they were far enough beneath Erna's surface that the earth-fae grew thin and feeble. Damien cautiously worked a Seeing, could barely see it clinging to the rock that surrounded them. Curiously—or perhaps ominously— there was no dark fae present. There should have been in such a place, this far beneath the prayers that safeguarded Church property. Was there some sort of Warding here? Or . . . something else?

At last they came to another door, with a single keyhole. A sigil was inscribed in the aged wood, and Damien thought, *A ward! Is that possible!* The floor creaked as they approached, and Damien heard machinery shift behind the walls; an alarm system of some kind. He imagined a thief being trapped in this place; it wasn't a pretty picture.

The Patriarch touched the engraved sign with reverence, then carefully unlocked the door. Despite its weight, he pulled it open without assistance—

—and *power* washed over them like a tidal wave, tamed fae in such concentration that it was impossible not to feel it, even without a Working; impossible not to *see* it, a light that glistened like molten gold sprayed into the air, a fine mist of luminescence that glittered like the stars of the outer Core, making the flame of the Patriarch's lamp seem dull and dark by comparison.

"Relics of the Holy War," he said quietly. He set the lamp on a table by the door and stepped aside, nodding for Damien to enter. "Take a look. See, if you need to."

He did so. Carefully. Despite the relative lack of earth-fae underground, his vision burst into full being the moment he Worked it. And suddenly he could barely see the objects that surrounded him, so bright was their power; the intensity of it brought tears to his eyes. After a moment he was forced to desist, and let the Working fade. The world returned—very slowly—to normal.

"Light was, of course, their primary weapon. Their tool of invasion. There are other things bound into each item here . . . but always light. They thought they could conquer the Forest with it." The Patriarch reached out to the wall beside him, fingered the edge of a rotting tapestry. "Sometimes, I think, that's what was responsible for our defeat. When we play by the rules of the enemy, we inherit his weaknesses.

"Go ahead," he urged. "Look around."

The chamber was large, its high, vaulted ceiling more reminiscent of the cathedral that towered high above it than the rough stone tunnels which led to its entrance. Niches had been carved into the walls and sealed with glass; the more delicate relics had been protected thus, safe from the moisture that might otherwise damage them. Most of these were mere fragments—a scrap of cloth, a few golden threads, a bit of rusted metal—but power poured forth from all of them equally, as if the fae that had been bound to them in the days of their use was unaffected by their material state. On the walls, warded shields bore mute witness to the desperate fervor of those days, in which priests served as sorcerors and soldiers simultaneously—and eventually, as martyrs. For the Forest had triumphed. The creatures which humanity had given birth to in its violent years had accumulated far more power than a single army of sorceror-priests could hope to conjure.

At the far end of the room, in a gilt-edged case, a crystal flask filled with golden liquid glowed richly with internal light. The Patriarch walked to it, gestured for Damien to follow. "Solar fae," he explained. "Bound well enough to survive even in this place, where no sun ever shines. No single adept could have managed it; only the prayer of thousands has that kind of power. Imagine a time when that kind of unity was possible. . . ." His voice trailed off into silence, but Damien continued the thought: *When our dream was that close to completion. When consummation of our Purpose was still within sight.*

Then the Patriarch reached out and opened the case, and lifted the flask up from its velveteen bed. "They bound it to water. Such a simple substance . . . they reasoned that since all living things consume water, and ultimately incorporate it into their physical being, this would be the perfect tool of invasion." He held it up so that the crystalline facets caught the lamplight, reflecting it back in a thousand scintillating fragments. "In here is all the power of sunlight. All the force of that heavenly warmth. Whatever it is in the solar fae that weakens night's power, this fluid contains it. If a thing runs from light, this will hurt it. If it can't bear the heat of life, this will burn it. All this . . . bound to the most common substance on Erna." He turned the flask slowly, watched the light revolve around it. "They meant to seed the Forest with it. They meant to give it to the ground and let every living thing that took root there suck it up for nourishment. In time, it would have infected the entire ecosystem. In time, it might have defeated even that great Darkness."

When he fell silent, Damien asked, "So what happened?"

The Patriarch bit his lip, considering the flask. And shrugged, wearily. "Who knows? No one ever returned from that expedition. In the battle that followed, our armies were slaughtered. The tide of the War turned against us." He looked at the priest, his eyes feline-green in the golden light. "God alone knows what happened to the rest of it. This is all that remains."

He turned the flask gently, and shards of light coursed the room. Eyes still fixed on it, he said quietly, "Your Order wasn't founded to provide nursemaids for fledgling sorcerors, Reverend Vryce. It exists because violent times sometimes require violent acts. And because a single man can sometimes succeed where an army of men might fail."

He lowered the cover of the case and set the flask on top of it. From the pocket of his robe he drew out a square of cloth—white silk, thickly woven—and this he wrapped about the precious bottle, until the light that came from it was no longer visible.

He held it out to Damien. And waited. The priest hesitated. Finally the Patriarch took his hand and placed the silken package in it. Not until Damien had folded his fingers securely over it did the Holy Father let go.

A faint hint of a smile crossed his face. "I thought you might have some need of this, where you're going."

Then he looked about the room, at the tattered remnants of his faith, and shook his head sadly.

"May you have better luck than its creators," he whispered.

Fourteen

It was a chill, bleak morning when the last of the bags were finally packed and secured onto the horses. In the distance, stormclouds threatened; Senzei glanced at them uneasily and muttered the key to a Knowing, making sure that nothing had changed since his Divining that morning. But no, it still appeared that the worst of the storm would pass them by. And the rest of it—they had all agreed—was not worth delaying for.

"We should make Briand well before sunset," Damien said. "As for whether we choose to put up there, or push on after nightfall. . . ." He looked up at Ciani for a response. But although she was feeling somewhat better—almost in high spirits, compared to her previous state—she wasn't about to bear the weight of such a decision.

And rightfully so, he reminded himself. *She's forgotten the very things that make such decisions important. Like what kind of creatures are out there, in the night.*

We'll cross that bridge when we come to it.

Her appearance had changed. They had changed it. Not with the fae, but by simple cosmetic art. Looking at her now, Damien was pleased by their efforts. They had bleached her hair to a golden blonde and added an olive tint to her skin. Between the features which she had redrawn and the deep hollows that her suffering had added to her face, she looked as unlike her former self as was reasonably possible. Bulkier clothing and heeled boots had altered her size and stance as well, and Damien was reasonably sure that no one—not even her tormentors—would recognize her now. But just in case, he had added an Obscuring. To cover all bases.

The Canopy will probably cancel it out. But until then, every little bit helps.

Senzei was reading off the last few items on their checklist, crossing each off as he verified that it had indeed been packed. Anything of vital importance was with one of the three travelers; additional items—and duplicates—were secured to one of the three extra horses the small group was taking with them. The checklist was four pages long, in small print; Damien wondered what they had managed to forget, despite it. Senzei had accused him of packing everything but the kitchen sink. (*Did we forget that?* he'd asked), but Damien had learned from experience that it was better to pack too much than too little for a journey such as this. There'd be time enough later to strip down their outfits, and they could always sell off the extra horses and supplies if they needed to. He had been on too many journeys in which a missing item or a disabled horse had ground the whole expedition to a halt. When they needed to travel light, they would; until then, they were prepared for anything.

At last Senzei looked up. His eyes met Damien's, and the priest thought he saw a flicker of pain in them. He'd been unusually quiet ever since they started packing—quiet and morose. Was it trouble with Allesha, perhaps? Damien didn't know the man well enough to draw him out on it, much less to help him cope, but he knew from experience just how hard it was to establish a relationship that could weather such a departure. He'd never quite gotten the hang of it himself.

"That's it," Senzei told him. "It's all here. We're ready."

Damien looked out into the early morning light—gray mists gathering to the north, stormclouds heavy and black in the east, western horizon still veiled in night's darkness—and muttered, "All right. Let's get moving."

The sooner we get where we're going, the sooner those bastards die.

In the foothills of the Worldsend Mountains, a figure stood very still. She had been still like that for hours since the call had first come to her. Since her sleep had first been disturbed by human sorcery, in a manner unprecedented among her kind.

For hours now, she had studied the currents. She had watched as the ripples birthed by that alien call had dashed themselves against the stolid earth-fae of the mountains. Had watched while that alien message was absorbed into the fae-tides of early morning, to course outward again in delicately altered patterns. From such patterns, she could read much of the sorceror who had sent that call, and why he did so. She could also read what other patterns were moving to converge with his, and how her own presence might alter that balance. The situation was complicated. The danger was real. And as for traveling with humans . . . she shuddered.

After several hours, she decided that she was more intrigued than wary. A very strange feeling.

She chose a path that would intersect with theirs, and began to hike along it.

NIGHT'S
KEEP

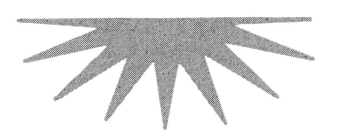

Fifteen

Oh, the *joy of flying! Swimming through the air with long, sweeping motions—pulling himself through clouds, overtaking birds, thrilling to the sure caress of the wind upon his body. And underneath him, glimpsed through an occasional break in the cloud cover: Briand. Home. Only now it seemed different—a fairy place, made up of light and music and fine brush strokes of color. So delicately constructed that it seemed to him a strong rain might wash it all away. Houses dissolving into gray and ocher streams, trees bleeding green and umber into the muddy streets—even people dissolving into so much color, like a watercolor painting put under the faucet. His mother and father liquifying into streams of pink and brown and green, spiraling into the flood and down, down, down into the secret storm drain beneath the city that lay waiting for it all, ready to swallow up all those beautiful tones . . . he could see Briand's colors running down into the river now, to meet with the dilute hues of Kale and Seth, the harsh, bright tones of Jaggonath, the cold ash-gray tones of the distant mountains. All swirling together, mixed by the river's harsh current. What a glorious vision! And he with no concern but the moment's pleasure, mated to the wind, flying high above the chromatic floodwaters, into—*

Into—

Darkness. Ahead of him. A point of blackness, searing in its intensity. A tiny fragment of no-light in this universe of color, a blotch on the fairy landscape. He shuddered and banked to the right, looking away. The blackness hurt his eyes, burned them like a sun might. Better not to look at it. Better to focus on the colors of the sky, the myriad hues of life. Better to—

It was back. In front of him.

Startled, he lost his rhythm. For a moment the winds had hold of him, and they were suddenly no longer the friendly breezes he had been riding, but the harsh staccato blasts of a storm front. He floundered. Ahead of him was that bit of burning blackness, no longer a mere speck amidst silver-gray clouds, but a full-fledged hole in the rapidly darkening sky. And inside it—or beyond it—lay something in waiting, whose thoughts were so loud that they screamed like thunder in his ears. He tried to fly away, but the winds had turned against him. Tried to slow his flight, but the blackness was like a vacuum, and it sucked him ever closer. At last, having exhausted all other means of escape, he tried to focus on the world he had left behind—that other world, the colorless one, the one that made him want to kill himself from boredom—because if he could remember it, he knew he would return to it. But the chemicals coursing in his bloodstream were too strong for that. He couldn't go back. He was flying—had always flown—knew no reality, other than flying. And the blackness, which spread itself hungrily before him.

Terrified, he fought to escape it.

It was larger, now. It took up half the sky, blotting out the sun like a giant storm cloud. He clawed at the air desperately, trying to pull himself away. But when he turned, it turned. When he reversed his direction, it appeared before him. Hungry. Implacable. Devouring all the color in the sky, the very air that supported him. He fell into a pocket of hurricanic turbulence, felt the stormwinds battering him closer and closer to his nemesis. That great maw of darkness which had almost devoured the sky, which would certainly devour the land, which so palpably hungered to devour him. . . .

And as he touched it, as he knew it for what it was, he screamed. Consumed by terror, desperate to be heard. Forgetting, in his final moments, that the same narcotic which had given him flight had also disconnected his consciousness from his flesh, thus making a real scream impossible. He screamed, and screamed . . . and was silent. His body lay unmoving atop a patchwork quilt, a thick fold of calico clutched between his frozen fingers. No one came to help him.

Who can hear the death screams of a disembodied soul?

The dae called Briand was solidly fortified, as befit a travelers' sanctuary that served the main trade route between Jaggonath and the northern portlands. A double stockade of roughly hewn posts hid most of the complex from view, but over its jagged top Damien could make out the roof of at least one sizable hostelry, steeply angled in the manner of northern houses. Even that limited view made it clear what manner of place Briand was. The roof was overthatched with hellos thorns—said to repel the undead—and the two dormer windows which were visible were barred with iron, worked in a protective motif.

As if mere walls could keep out a true demon, he thought grimly. *As if bars made a difference to blood-wraiths.*

"We stop?" Senzei asked.

Damien looked at Ciani—at Fray, he corrected himself—and tried to assess her condition. It was difficult to see past the various elements of her disguise, to judge just how tired she was. Hard to see Ciani herself, between the makeup that had altered her countenance and the fog of despair that enshrouded her soul.

She could go on, he decided at last. They all could go on. And there was something to be said for pushing toward their goal as quickly as possible, especially with winter coming on. But the thought of possibly being stuck outside when night fell was not a pleasant one. Damien alone could have handled it—God knows, he had camped out often enough—and Senzei, perhaps, could have coped. But not Ciani. Not now. Not when night was so very threatening to her. They had to safeguard her soul as well as her body, and the former was so terribly fragile. . . .

"We stop," he said firmly, and he thought he saw relief in her eyes.

There was a guard at the main gate, polite but efficient; after a brief interrogation they were permitted to pass within the protective walls. Damien noticed sigils burned into the wood, ward-signs etched into the heavy posts. Most of them were useless, he suspected. For every faeborn consultant that sold legitimate Workings, there would be at least a dozen con artists imitating the trade. And knowing that, to be sure, a dae such as Briand must buy twelve times as much protection.

He reflected upon the cost of that and muttered, "There's good money in sorcery here."

Senzei managed a halfhearted grin, and nodded toward the building ahead of them. "Don't you think she knew that?"

Following Senzei's gaze into the compound, he saw one of Ciani's wards guarding the hostelry entrance. Finely worked, beautiful even in its quiescence, it occupied a place of honor high over the arched lintel. They must have paid a pretty penny for it, he reflected; Ciani's work didn't come cheap.

Then he saw her face—the total lack of recognition, as she gazed upon her own handiwork as if it were that of a stranger—and something tightened inside him. As if for the very first time he finally understood just what had been done to her.

They'll die for this, Cee. I promise you. The bastards will die.

As with all such sanctuaries, the dae was a sprawling conglomerate of disparate buildings, linked together by warded walkways, and—in the case of several two-story buildings—sturdily enclosed bridges. Once inside the dae, one need not leave it for any reason. Like most such sanctuaries, Briand would have space to house a trade caravan when necessary, as well as sufficient food to feed its people and all the supporting services—practical, aesthetic, and hedonistic—that they might require. Private domiciles no doubt clustered about its back walls like satellites, each linked to the whole by a private walkway. But for all its space and supplies, Briand would be a sterile place. All daes were, regardless of location. There was profit enough to be made off a traveler's need that men might come here to garner it, but no other reason was sufficient to draw people to such a place—and even the dae-keepers often left, once their fortune was secure. Briand was no more than a stopover point—even for those who had made it their permanent home.

The portal warded by Ciani's Working was clearly the main guest entrance. Damien and Ciani unpacked the horses while Senzei went off in search of a groom. After some moments he reappeared, a pair of lanky boys in tow. Teenagers, both of them, with the nervous, uptight gestures of boys whose pubescent energies had not yet found safe outlet. *They need a good night out on the town,* Damien thought. Then, upon reflection, added, *They need a good town.*

It was dark inside the hostelry, despite the light of day that still burned outside; a crackling fire in the center of the large common room seemed to be the only source of light. Lanterns hung unlit on posts set about the outer walls, waiting for some hand to kindle them. No doubt when more travelers began to arrive—when the sun was nearer to setting, and the dangers of the night that much nearer to rising—the place would be well lit for their comfort. Now, empty of patrons, unattended, it had somewhat the aspect of a tomb.

"No windows," Damien muttered.

"What did you expect?"

"I saw some upstairs."

"Farther from the earth," Senzei told him. "Fae is weaker there. It still means a risk . . . but if some rich guest demands a view. . . ." He shrugged.

Damien looked about at the thick timber walls, the heavily plastered ceiling, and shook his head. "Do they really think this will stop a demon?"

"If the guests believe it," Senzei countered, "doesn't that give it some power?"

"Enough to matter?"

He had no time to answer. A woman had entered the room, with a thick black ledger book in one hand and a coarse pencil in the other. Middle-aged, with hair that was gray about the temples and forehead, drawn tightly back into a bun. She seemed distressed but managed a businesslike nod to serve as welcome. Crossing the room quickly, she spared a quick sideways glance to assess the state of the fire. And nodded, satisfied.

"Name's Kanadee," she said brusquely. Offering no gesture of physical contact, merely a brief nod of welcome. She reached up to brush back a stray lock of hair from out of her eyes, then opened up the book and took their names. *Senzei Reese*, Damien told her. *Fray Vanning. Reverend Damien Vryce.* She looked up at that last entry, and her eyes searched his face for . . . what? It happened too quickly for Damien to read her expression; by the time he noticed it, she was all business once again. "You'll be wanting rooms for the night," she said. Now that Damien was listening for it, he could hear a faint tremor echoing her speech. Her cheek glistened moistly in the firelight—from recent tears?

"Please," Damien said. "Adjoining, if that's possible."

She studied the others for a moment, assessing them quickly. Ciani was clearly acceptable; Senzei received a brief frown, then a nod. "Forty a night, per head. That includes dinner. Bell's at six-and-half, serving's at seven. Other food anytime you like, but it's extra. Call into the kitchen, if there's no one out here." She nodded toward a heavy door at the far end of the common room. "Only three of you?" Damien nodded. "Good. Lucky number. Tam'll take your things up, get you settled." She pulled a bell out of her apron pocket; a tangle of cords and keys fell to the floor. "Any questions, you ask for me. See?" She rang the bell sharply, then stopped to recover her possessions. Amulets with sigil signs, keys with horoscopic symbols etched into them, a plain but finely worked image of the Earth . . . she had it all back in her pocket by the time a spindly young boy appeared, and she gestured him toward their packs. "Take 'em up to the east suite," she ordered. "Settle them in, and show 'em the place."

He began to gather their bags, groaning as the weight of Senzei's books joined all the rest on his shoulder. But despite his obvious discomfort, he would let none of the travelers carry their own. "He's a good boy," she told them. Again, there was an echo of sorrow behind her words—so fleeting that Damien nearly missed it, but so poignant that it seemed to dim the light about them. Had she lost a child recently? Or, closer yet (he struggled to define what he had sensed, to put a name to it), was she *contemplating* losing one? "You tell him what you need, he'll get it for you. See?"

Sometimes, hungering for a symbol, followers of the One God would carry an earth-disk. Sometimes the need for a material symbol of their faith was simply too great, and their understanding of the Church's goals too limited . . . and that was the most acceptable option. The Church had learned to tolerate it.

He muttered a Knowing—and his breath caught in his throat as the nature of her suffering became thickly visible about her. As he read its cause.

For a moment he hesitated. His first duty lay with his friends . . . except that they wouldn't really need him until dawn, when it was time to move again. Ciani's wards alone should be enough to protect them in this well-guarded place, and it was possible that one or two of the other charms that had been nailed to the wall might actually Work. While he . . . he hungered to be active. To be needed. To *do* something.

"Go on up," he said to his companions. "I'll be there shortly."

Her business done, Mes Kanadee began to withdraw, back the way she had come. But when she saw that he was following, she stopped and confronted him. "I told you, Tam'll take care of you. There's work I have to see to—"

"I'm a priest," he said softly. "And a Healer. Will you let me help you?"

She seemed about to say something sharp—and then the defense crumbled, and exhaustion took over. Despair. She protested weakly, "What can you do? If prayers alone would suffice. . . ."

"We use more than prayers, sometimes."

Startled, she looked up at him. Deep into his eyes. No assessment there this time, only wonder. And not a little fear. He could see the struggle raging within her—her hunger for hope in any form, versus a daeborn distrust of strangers. Her fingers tightened on the ledger book, as if feeling his title through the thick leather cover. *Reverend.* Her church. The title seemed to calm her. Surely a priest could be trusted.

At last she lowered her eyes, and he saw her tremble.

"God willing you can," she whispered. "God willing anyone can." She opened the heavy door, and motioned for him to follow. "Come. I'll show you."

The boy lay still on a rumpled bed, fingers clutching the quilt beneath him. His skin was pale, but that was typical of dae-folk. His complexion betrayed his adolescence, while his mussed and untrimmed hair—and less than aesthetic clothing—hinted at a vague air of defiance. Personal artifacts littered the room, making it hard to walk to the bed without knocking into something. Sigils pinned to the wall ranged from the fae-signatures of popular songwriters to symbols with more arcane overtones, and a few that seemed touched with genuine power. Dark power, Damien noted, and tainted with the chaos so typical of adolescence. But power nonetheless. The boy was trying to Work.

She saw him gazing at the walls and blushed. "He had . . . interests. I didn't know whether to try to stop it, or how. . . ." *But now it's too late,* she seemed to imply. *And if he courted some Power that he shouldn't have, and hurt himself in the process, am I not to blame for failing to prevent it?*

"Let me take a look at him," Damien said quietly.

He sat on the edge of the bed, careful not to jar the boy as he did so. The youth's breathing was regular, and his color—despite the daeborn pallor—was good. He took the boy's nearer hand in his own and tried to dislodge it from the quilt it clutched. The fingers were stiff, but they did open; that ruled out most legal drugs as the source of the problem.

"How long?" he asked.

"Day and a half now." Her hands twined nervously in her apron, knuckles white. "We found him in the morning, just like this. We've . . . tried to feed him. He won't take anything. Even liquids. I had a doctor in. He sent for a specialist. Should arrive by tomorrow. To set up an IV, so we don't lose him . . . but they don't know what to do about the coma, Father. They don't even know what caused it. I had a Healer, too—he was a pagan, Father, but what else was there to do? There was no one available from the Church, and I was desperate." Her tone was begging for forgiveness.

"Did he find anything?"

"He couldn't say. Or wouldn't say. I shouldn't have asked him," she said miserably.

He asked it as gently as he could, but it had to be asked. "Any prolonged drug use that you know of?"

She hesitated. He sensed her gaze flitting across the walls, from sigil to sigil. "No," she said at last. "He tried some things, once or twice. Out of curiosity. Don't they all?"

"Which ones?" he pressed. "Do you know?"

She looked away, and bit her lower lip in concentration. "Blackout, I think. Maybe cerebus, once. Maybe slowtime. We said it was all right—at least to try them, just once—provided he purchased them in Jaggonath. On the open market. Was that wrong?" Her tone was a plea—for forgiveness, understanding, absolution. "We didn't think we could stop him."

"If that's what he took, it's not what's got him now." He lifted the limp hand a few inches above the blanket, and gently let it fall. "Jaggonath's drugs are strictly regulated; if he kept to that market, it's unlikely he met with any surprises. And his limbs are pliant," he pointed out. "If he was currently in a drugged state, that wouldn't be true. There's a paralytic in all Jaggonath legals." He looked up at her. "The doctor couldn't tell you anything at all?"

"He didn't know. They're going to take him to a hospital in the city, with better facilities. But travel time...." She looked around, and shook her head helplessly. "All these fae-things. Could it be that I mean, could he have called up something...." *That fed on him,* her tone said desperately. *That took his mind away from us.*

"I'll take a look," Damien said gently.

Such a Working came easily to him; it was what the Church had trained him to do. Fae gathered in response to his will—slightly tainted by the presence of adolescent instability, but his will was enough to give it order—and linked him to the boy in a personal Knowing. Allowing him to peer deep into the youth's soul and, hopefully, read the cause of this unconsciousness.

But to his surprise, he met resistance: a wall of fae, tightly woven, that forced him to keep his distance. Unusual. He probed at it, trying to find its weak spot. Trying to channel through. But the barrier was remarkably balanced in structure—remarkably unlike the boy himself, or anything such a youth might have conjured. Resilient, it gave just enough to diffuse his aggressive energies; he couldn't seem to pierce it, no matter how he tried.

He added prayer to his efforts. Unlike most pagan faiths, his Church didn't believe in a God who made personal appearances on demand; nevertheless, prayer was a powerful focus for any Working. Strangely—and inexplicably—the resistance seemed to grow even stronger as he did so. As if something in his prayer had added its strength to that seemingly impenetrable barrier.

That's impossible, he thought darkly. *Patently impossible. Even if*

a priest had Worked the damned thing in the first place ... I'd be
able to read that. Or some kind of personal signature, at least.

Who would do such a thing? What purpose would it serve?

Frustrated, he turned his attention to the boy's corporeal shell. But every aspect of the body was just as it should be, save for its comatose state. He spent a long time studying the boy's flesh, on every level possible, and at last had to concede defeat. There was no apparent biological damage. And as for the boy's soul ... that was unreachable. Unless he could come up with some new plan of attack. Hit it from a different angle.

Ciani could have handled this. Ciani could have dispelled such a barrier in half the time it took me just to recognize it. Damn those creatures, and their hellbound hunger! Even without the fae she could have told us who might have set up such a thing. Because it isn't the boy who's behind this. It can't be the boy. But then who? Or what? And, most important: Why?

"Is it your son?" he asked gently.

"My firstborn," she whispered. "I ..." She blinked back tears. Couldn't speak for a moment. Then: "Can you help him, Father? Is there any hope at all?"

He let the last of his Knowing fade; his head was pounding from the strain of his efforts, and from the unaccustomed taste of failure. He managed to keep his voice steady as he told the woman, "There's nothing my skills can do. That doesn't mean the doctors won't be able to help." He could hear the exhaustion in his voice, but managed somehow to keep it sounding strong. She needed his strength. "I'm sorry, my child. I wish it could be otherwise."

She wept in his arms for a long, long time.

Sitting in the darkest corner of the common room, the three travelers went unnoticed. Nearly two dozen guests had taken shelter in the dae's protective confines before the gates were shut at sunset, but for the most part they were a travel-weary, introverted lot, who offered no threat to the small company's privacy. One particularly large group of men had been drinking since dusk, and occasionally a voice would rise from among them to dominate all others in the common room, underscoring some vital point in their debate—but in general they were a tight, self-contained social unit, who might acknowledge a comely waitress or two but who otherwise had no interest in the people surrounding them. The other guests had collected in couples and trios and were far more interested in the central fire and its warmth than in the three travelers who had chosen to isolate themselves in the shadows of a far corner.

"It didn't go well?" Senzei asked quietly.

"It didn't *go* at all." Damien took a deep drink from the tankard before him. Briand ale; not the best, but any alcohol was welcome. "There was some sort of barrier . . . I've never Seen anything like it before. Couldn't get through it, no matter what I did." He took another drink and sighed. "It seemed deliberate; a Worked obstruction. That was the oddest thing. I mean, who would have set it up? And why? The boy didn't have that kind of skill, I'm sure of it. But who would? And why?" He took another deep drink of the ale, winced at the bitterness. "If we assume that his problem wasn't just a medical one—that something faeborn hurt the boy—the question is, what sort of demon would do that and then bother to cover its tracks? And do it so vulking *well!*"

"Careful," Senzei warned—meaning his volume, his anger, his profanity. "You did what you could. That's all any of us can do."

"If only—" But he stopped himself. Just in time. *If only Ciani's skills were whole,* he wanted to say. *She could have read that boy like a book. She could have fixed him up in half the time it took me to confirm the problem.* He ached for her loss—and for their loss, having to travel without her skills to protect them. God in heaven, everything would be so much easier if she were whole . . . but then again, if she were whole, they would still be in Jaggonath. They could make love in her Gees Street apartment with no more thought for the future than a passing concern over whether they had enough food for breakfast in the morning.

I think I was falling in love with you. In a way that I haven't experienced before. Why couldn't we have had just a little more time to see where it was headed before this happened?

He started to turn to Senzei—to ask him for advice on the boy's condition—when a noise from the far end of the room caught his attention. He turned toward the door—and stiffened as he saw it opening. As he heard the creaking of its thick metal hinges and the jangling of its disengaged lock.

"Don't the daes—" he whispered.

"Yes." Senzei nodded sharply. "The doors are locked after sunset. An exception would be . . . unusual."

One of the night guards had squeezed inside, and he traded hurried words with the dae's keeper. Mes Kanadee hesitated, then nodded; the door swung fully open. Darkness poured in—and with it a man whose movement was so fluid, so graceful, that it was hard to believe he couldn't have simply flowed in through cracks in the door, had he wanted to.

All heads in the place were turned toward him, all eyes assessing this man for whom the rules of the dae had been broken. But the Keeper stared back at them as if daring her guests to protest. One by one they turned away and went back to their former conversations. *Just a man,* her gaze seemed to say. *What business is it of yours, anyway?* Damien whispered the key to an Obscuring under his breath, so that her eyes passed over his table as though it were empty; he had no intention of confronting her, nor did he intend to relinquish his right to study the stranger in secret.

The newcomer was a tall man, slender, who carried himself with easy elegance. Handsome, refined—attractive to women, Damien decided—he moved with a grace that seemed to come naturally to him. His clothes were simple but well made, unadorned but clearly expensive. A calf-length tunic of fine silk brushed the top of glove-soft boots, accentuating his height and rippling with his every movement. Midnight blue, the color of evening. His hair was soft and simply dressed, not in the complex cut and curls of modern fashion but caught back in a simple clip at the nape of his neck. Save for that one piece, there was no gold visible on him, nor jewelry of any kind. Or any other thing of obvious value, other than a slender sword with a heavily embroidered sheath that swung at his side . . . and the pistol tucked into his belt.

Damien worked a minor Knowing—and hissed in surprise. In disbelief.

"UnWorked," he whispered.

Senzei nodded. "I know."

That means. . . .

They looked at each other.

"I'll check," Senzei muttered, and as soon as he was sure that the stranger wouldn't see him, he slipped away to go to their rooms. Damien turned back—and saw Ciani's eyes on him. Curious. Suffering. Anxious to know.

He tried to explain to her. About firearms, and how dangerous they were. About technology in general, and the power of human fear, and how sometimes when there was a physical process that a man couldn't watch happen—because it was too small, or happened too fast, or was simply out of his sight—his fears could foul it up, and cause it to backfire. So that such a gun might well blow up in its owner's hand at the moment he most needed it to function. Which meant that no man would carry such a thing, unless he'd had it

Worked for safety. Or unless he was a total fool, who thrived on
senseless risk. Or unless. . . .

Unless he was an adept.

He stiffened at the thought. Eager and wary, in equal measure. He
had a nose for suspicious coincidence, and this man's arrival stank
of it.

*The odds against one of that kind just happening to walk in here
are . . . incredible. So either he isn't what he seems to be, or there's
some reason he showed up tonight. And I can't think of one that I'd
like to hear.*

Senzei slid back into his seat, a small black notebook clutched in
one hand. "Nothing," he whispered. "None of the descriptions
match. If he's an adept, he isn't from this region. Or else we just
didn't know about him. . . ."

"Unlikely," Damien muttered. That kind of skill was hard to hide,
especially in the childhood years. And news of adeptitude traveled
fast. If the man wasn't described in Ciani's notes, he wasn't from
this area.

Carefully, Damien worked a Knowing. *Very* carefully. The stranger
might take it in his stride that other Workers would wish to identify
him . . . or he might consider it an invasion of his privacy and exact
revenge. Adepts were a touchy lot.

He relaxed the Obscuring that protected the three of them, just
enough to Work through it. Then he reached out, ever so delicately,
meaning to brush the stranger with a Knowing. Even if the man felt
so delicate a touch, he might consider it no more than it was—a
polite inquiry—and let it pass unnoticed.

Breathing deeply in concentration, Damien felt the Working build,
spanning the room between them. It gave order to the fae along its
path, like a magnet would organize iron filings. Soon a single shining
filament of purpose stretched from Damien's table to the one where
the stranger now sat—fine as spider's silk, luminous as crystal—
allowing him to extend his senses into the stranger's personal space
and touch the man's essence with his own.

And he encountered a surface like polished glass. Smooth—reflective—impenetrable. His Knowing brushed up against it; there was a
brief moment when it seemed he was touching not glass, but ice;
and then it was gone, all contact between them broken. His Working
had simply vanished—the thread was dissolved, into thin air—as
though it had never been. As though he had never even tried.

A Shielding, he thought. He was awed by its execution. An adept's
work, without question. And even by that standard, magnificently

done. There was no doubting the man's power—or his skill in applying it.

Slowly, calmly, in response to Damien's fleeting touch, the stranger turned toward him. Across the length of the common room their eyes met. The man's clear, steady gaze was more informative than any Working could have been—and much more discerning. Damien felt his own space invaded, the chill touch of a strange mind sorting out who and what he was—and then as quickly it was gone, and the space between them was impenetrable once more.

A faint smile crossed the stranger's face. Then, clearly satisfied with whatever information he had garnered, he turned away again. A stemmed goblet had been placed before him and he sipped from it, delicately, while he watched the fire dance in its stone enclosure. Utterly calm, he seemed unconcerned with Damien's presence, or with the Working that had so briefly disturbed his peace. Or with anyone else in the room, for that matter.

"Damned sure of himself," Senzei muttered.

Damien noticed the edge in the man's voice, felt it echo in his own thoughts. *How much of our reaction is jealousy?* he wondered. *How can a man experience that kind of power and not want to control it?*

And especially Senzei, he reminded himself. Ciani had told him that. The man hungered for Sight like a starving man hungered for food; what did it mean to him, to see that kind of power displayed so openly?

"You think he's an adept," Ciani breathed.

Damien looked at her. Measured his words. "It's possible," he said at last.

She leaned forward slightly; her eyes were gleaming. "You think he could help us?"

For some reason, he was chilled by the mere thought. "That would be very dangerous. We know nothing about him. *Nothing.* Even if he would be willing to join us, can we afford to take on a total unknown?" *Who arrived at just the right moment,* he added silently. *Too right. I don't trust it.*

He suddenly looked back at the man, and wondered how much of his response was rational, and how much of it was the result of growing tension over other matters. Like having to sit here in this overfortified inn while the creatures they sought after were probably getting farther and farther away with each passing minute. Like his problems with the boy, the unaccustomed taste of a failure. With an adept's power to back him. . . .

No. Unthinkable. The risk simply wasn't worth it.

"To involve a stranger in our personal business—knowing absolutely nothing of his power or his purpose—that would be incredibly dangerous. How could we risk it?"

"The problem is our ignorance?"

He looked at her sharply; there was a note in her voice he couldn't quite read. "That's a good part of it, yes."

She hesitated only an instant, then pushed her chair back and stood.

"What are you doing?" he hissed.

"Knowing," she said tightly. "In the old Earth sense." And she smiled, albeit nervously, for the first time since leaving Jaggonath. "Someone has to do it, don't you think?"

And she was gone. Before Damien could protest. Before Senzei, reaching out, could stop her. The two men watched, aghast, as she wended her way across the dimly lit room. As she waited for the stranger's attention to fix on her, and then began to speak to him. After a few seemingly pleasant words, he offered her a seat at his table. She took it.

"*Damn* her," Damien muttered.

"And women in general," Senzei growled.

"That, too."

The stranger called a waitress over. It was the same girl who had served Damien and Senzei, but now her blouse was tucked down tightly into her belt, outlining breasts that she was clearly proud to display to him. Whatever charisma the stranger possessed, it seemed to work tenfold on women. For some reason, that was more irritating than all the rest combined.

"You think she's safe?" Damien whispered.

Senzei considered. And nodded, slowly. "I think maybe she's in her element."

He looked at Senzei, surprised.

"Watch her," the sorceror whispered. There was a kind of love in his voice that Damien had never heard him express before. For the first time he sensed the true depth of their friendship—and he reflected sadly upon the fact that he had never heard such a note in Senzei's voice when he spoke of his fiancée.

She must have realized that. And it must have hurt like hell.

Ciani was indeed in her element—tense, wary, but more *alive* than she had been in days. And why not? Whatever it was that had caused her to devote her life to the acquisition of knowledge, that instinct was still intact and thriving. They had taken the facts from her mind, but they couldn't change what she was.

Seeing that the stranger was responding well to her advances—and

that she herself was slowly becoming more comfortable with him—
Damien relaxed. Or rather, tried to. But there was another kind of
tension within him, and that was growing. Not concern for her,
exactly. Rather, more like. . . .

*Jealousy. Simple-minded, ego-centered, masculine jealousy. Well,
grow up, Damien. You don't own her. And just because he has a
pretty face and some new stories to tell doesn't mean that he does,
either.*

"They're coming," Senzei whispered.

He must have been watching them on other levels, because it was
several minutes before Ciani and the stranger actually got up. He
first, rising effortlessly, then stepping behind her chair to help pull
it out for her. The custom of another time, another culture. When
she turned in their direction, she no longer seemed afraid; her eyes
were sparkling with newfound animation. *Not for the man,* Damien
reminded himself. *For the mystery that he represents.*

As if that made it any easier.

If the stranger bore them any ill will for their previous invasion of
his privacy, he didn't show it. He bowed politely as Ciani introduced
them but offered no hand for them to clasp. The social patterns of a
bygone age—or a paranoid adept. Damien suspected the latter.

"This is Gerald Tarrant," Ciani announced. "Originally from Ara-
manth, more recently from Sheva." Damien couldn't identify the
place name exactly, but like all cities near the Forbidden Forest it
had been named for an Earth-god of death or destruction. He was
from the north, then. That was ominous. Generally anyone with the
Sight steered clear of that region—for good reason. The Forest had a
history of corrupting anyone who could respond to it.

"Please join us," Senzei said, and Damien nodded.

The newcomer pulled up chairs for the two of them, helped Ciani
into hers before sitting down himself. "I was hardly expecting company," he said pleasantly. "Arriving at such an hour, one often
receives a less than enthusiastic welcome."

"What brings you to Briand?" Damien asked shortly.

The pale eyes sparkled—and for a moment, just a moment, they
seemed to be reaching into Damien's soul, weighing it. "Sport," he
said at last. With a half-smile that said he knew just how uninforma-
tive that was. "Call it pursuit of a hobby." He offered no more on
that subject, and his manner didn't invite continued questioning.
"Yourselves?"

"Business. In Kale. Family shipping, for Fray—and for us, a chance
to get away from town. An excuse to travel."

The stranger nodded; Damien had the disquieting feeling that he knew just how much wasn't being said. "It's dangerous traveling at night," he challenged the man. "Especially in this region."

The stranger nodded. "Would that all our pursuits could be completed in neat little packets of time during the day, and we need never stir between dusk and dawn." He sipped from the goblet in his hand. "But if that were the case, Ernan history would be quite a different thing than it is, don't you think?"

"You're lucky they let you in."

"Yes," he agreed. "That was fortunate."

And so on. Damien designed questions that should give him insight into some facet of the man's existence—and he parried them all, without missing a beat. He seemed to enjoy fencing words with them, and would sometimes cast out tidbits of knowledge to draw them in—only to turn them aside with a quick response or a well-planned ambiguity, so that they came away knowing no more of the man than exactly what he meant them to know. Which was next to nothing.

Damien wondered if he had played the same game with Ciani. Was it possible to play that kind of game with Ciani?

At last the newcomer leaned back in his chair, as if signaling the end of that phase of their relationship. He set the goblet down before him; red liquid glinted within, reflecting the lamplight.

"The lady tells me you're working on a Healing."

Startled, he looked at Ciani—but her eyes were fixed on the stranger. He weighed his alternatives quickly and decided at last that there was no better way to test the man than to tell him the truth.

"The Keeper's son," he said quietly. Watching the man for any kind of reaction. "He's comatose. I tried to help."

He bowed his head gracefully. "I'm sorry." Which might have meant anything, *Sorry for the illness. Sorry about your desire to help. Sorry about your failure.* "May I be of service?"

"You Heal?" Damien said suspiciously.

The stranger smiled, as if at some private joke. "Not for some time. My own specialty is in analysis. Perhaps that might be of use to you?"

"It might," he said guardedly. He looked across the room, couldn't locate the boy's mother. She must have gone back to his bedside. When a waitress looked in his direction he waved her over, and asked her to please locate the dae-keeper for them. He had news that might interest her.

"She's wary of strangers," he warned. "She trusted me because of my calling. My Church. Whether she'll want you near the boy is another thing."

"Ah." The stranger considered that for a moment. Then he reached into the neck of his tunic and drew out a thin disk on a chain. Fine workmanship, a delicate etching on pure gold: the Earth.

And he smiled; the expression was almost pleasant. "Let us see if I can't convince her to accept my services. Shall we?"

The boy's room seemed even more quiet after the relative noisiness of the common room. Oppressively so. Damien found it claustrophobic, in a way it hadn't been before. Or was that his territorial instinct, responding to a newcomer's intrusion?

Childish, Vryce. Get over it.

It was just the three of them in the small room. The boy's mother had agreed to let the newcomer look at her child—fearful, apprehensive, but she had agreed—but she drew the line at admitting the pagan multitudes. Just as well. Damien welcomed a chance to assess the man, without Ciani's presence to distract him.

Gerald Tarrant walked to the far side of the bed and gazed down at the child. With a start, Damien realized that the man's skin was hardly darker than that of the boy; flesh sans melanin. It suited him so well that Damien hadn't noticed it before, but now, contrasted against the boy's sickly pallor . . . the coloring was ominous. And here it was soon after summer, too. Damien considered all the reasons a seemingly healthy man might not have a tan. A few of them—very few—were innocent. Most were not.

Be fair. Senzei's pale. Some men have business that binds them to the night.

Yes . . . and some of that business is highly suspect.

Slowly, the stranger sat on the edge of bed. He studied the boy in silence for a moment, then made a cursory inspection of obvious signs: lifting the eyelids to study the pupils, pressing a long index finger against the boy's upper neck to take his pulse, even studying the fingernails. It was hard to tell when he was simply looking and when he was Knowing as well; he was like Ciani in that he needed no words or gestures to trigger a Working, only the sheer force of his will. An adept without question, then.

As if that was in doubt.

Damien looked at the boy's mother, and his heart wrenched in sympathy. Because he had vouched for the stranger, she had allowed him to approach her son. But Gerald Tarrant wasn't a priest, and it was clear that his presence here made her very nervous. She twisted her hands in her apron, trying not to protest. Glanced at Damien, her eyes begging for reassurance. He wished he had it to give to her.

He looked down at the boy again—and froze, when he saw the stranger's knife pressed against the youth's inner arm. A thin line of red welled up in its wake: dark crimson, thick and wet.

"What the hell do you think you're doing?" he hissed.

The stranger didn't acknowledge him in any way. Folding his knife, he tucked it carefully back into his belt. The boy's mother moaned softly and swayed; Damien wondered if she was going to faint. He was torn between wanting to go to her and desperately wanting to stop this lunacy. What purpose could it possibly serve, to cut the boy open like that? But he stood where he was, chilled by a terrible, morbid fascination. As he watched, the stranger touched one slender finger to the wound, collecting a drop of blood. He brought it to his lips and breathed in its bouquet; then, apparently satisfied with it, he touched the crimson droplet to his tongue. And tasted it. And stiffened.

He looked at the woman. His expression was dark.

"You didn't tell me he was an addict."

The color drained suddenly from her face, as if someone had opened a tap beneath her feet and all her blood had poured out. "He isn't," she whispered. "That is, I didn't. . . ."

"What is it?" Damien asked hoarsely.

"Blackout." The cut he had made was still oozing blood; a thin line of crimson dribbled down the boy's wrist, onto the quilt. "And not all legal, was it?"

She was shaking. "How can you know that?"

"Simple logic. This boy had quite an addiction. If he'd fed it with legals, that would have meant repeated trips into Jaggonath . . . and you would have known. On the other hand, with all the travelers that you have passing through here. . . ." He shrugged suggestively. "It guaranteed his secrecy, but at a high cost. He knew the risk, and accepted it. I suspect that was part of the thrill."

"You can't say that!"

His eyes narrowed—just that, and no more. But no more was necessary. She took a step backward and turned away rather than meet his gaze.

"Is that it, then?" Her voice was a whisper. Her hands were trembling. "Just . . . drugs?"

He turned back to study the boy. After he was silent for a moment, Damien conjured his own Sight into existence—and watched as the shield he had fought with for so many hours was peeled back, layer by layer. Parting, like the petals of a flower coming into bloom. He felt a sudden surge of jealousy, had to fight to keep concentrating. *Why does it have to come so damned easily to him!* Beyond the barrier was . . . darkness. Emptiness. A blackness so absolute that the cold of it chilled Damien's thoughts. He dared not reach out to read its source, not when a stranger was in control—but even so he could tell that something was wrong, very wrong. Something that went far beyond mere addiction, or the self-destructive fantasies of a depressed adolescent. Something that hinted at outside interference. At a malignance far greater than anything this poor boy might have conjured.

"Leave us," Tarrant ordered. He looked up at the woman. She began to protest—and then choked back on the words, and bowed to the force of the man's will. Tears were pouring silently down her cheeks as she turned and left the room, and Damien longed to comfort her. But he was damned if he was going to leave the boy alone with this stranger, even for a minute.

When the door had shut securely behind the woman, Gerald Tarrant reached out to touch the boy, one slender finger resting against the skin of his forehead. Slowly, layer by layer, the barrier that he had parted restored itself. Slowly the gaping blackness that was inside the boy became less and less visible, until even Damien's strongest Knowing could no longer make it out. Deep blue lines began to radiate from the adept's fingertip, like blood that had been starved of oxygen. Damien watched as they began to penetrate the boy's skin, delicate threads of azure ice that chilled the capillaries as they entered the boy's bloodstream—

And then he reached out and grabbed the man's arm—the flesh was cold, and seemed to drain the warmth from his hand where there was contact—and he pulled him away from the boy as violently as he could. And hissed in fury, "What the *hell* do you think you're doing?"

Tarrant's eyes fixed on him—infinitely calm, infinitely cold. "Killing him," he said quietly. "Gradually, of course. It won't culminate until morning. The family will consider it . . . *natural.* Medics will ascribe it to the contamination found in black market drugs. And the matter will end there. Isn't that desirable?"

"You have no right!"

"This boy's body serves no purpose," he said quietly. "They can ship it from city to city for months, pour bottles of sugar and tonic and what have you into its bloodstream to keep it alive for years . . . but what's the point? There's nothing left here that's worth maintaining." His pale gray eyes sparkled coldly. "Isn't it kinder to the

living to remove such a hindrance, rather than let it drain them of
money and energy until they have nothing left worth living for?"

He felt like he was being tested somehow, without knowing either
the parameters of the test or its purpose. "You're saying he can't
recover."

"I'm saying there's nothing left *to* recover. The soul is still there,
hanging on by a thread. But the mechanism that would allow it to
reconnect has been removed, priest. *Devoured*, if you will."

"You mean . . . his brain?"

"I mean his *memory*. The core of his identity. Gone. He let the
drugs weaken his link to this body . . . and something moved in while
he was absent. Moved in, and cleaned house." The gray eyes were
fixed on him, weighing his reaction. "There is no hope for him,
priest—because *he*, as such, no longer exists. That," and he indicated
the body, "is an empty shell. Would you still call it murder, knowing
that, if I caused it to expire?"

Memory, Damien thought. *Identity. God in Heaven. . . .*

He reached for a chair—or anything that would support him—and
at last lowered himself onto the corner of a trunk.

Memory. Devoured. Here, in our very path.

He thought of those *things* getting into the dae. Feasting on the
boy, as they had once feasted on Ciani. Only this time they'd had no
need for vengeance, no vested interest in prolonging their victim's
suffering. They'd eaten all there was to eat, and left no more than an
empty shell behind. . . .

*Does that mean they're right ahead of us, traveling the same route?
Do they know we're coming? Are they letting us know it? Challenging
us, perhaps? Merciful God, each possibility is worse than the last. . . .*

Then he looked up into the stranger's eyes and read the truth
behind his calm.

"You've run into something like this before," he challenged.

There was a silence. A long one. The cold, pale eyes were impossible to read.

"Say that I'm hunting something," Gerald Tarrant said at last. "Say
that this is its mark, its trail. Its spoor." He looked at the boy's body,
and said quietly, "What about you, priest?"

*Hunting. The very things we're after. Is that the mark of an ally—
or a trap? There's too much coincidence here. Be careful.*

"They killed a friend," he said quietly.

He bowed. "My condolences."

He tried to think. Tried to factor this new variable into all his
equations. But it was happening too fast; he needed time to consider.
He needed to talk to Senzei and Ciani. If the creatures they were

trying to kill were only one day ahead of them, on the same road they meant to travel ... he shook his head, trying to weigh all the options. Maybe they should speed up, not cower in the daes at night. Or change their route, try to circle around and get ahead. Or else maybe the creatures *meant* them to do one of those things, had set up this little tragedy to throw off any possible pursuit. To pressure their pursuers to choose a lesser road, one with fewer protections. . . .

Too many plots and counterplots. Too many variables. He smelled danger, but couldn't tell just where the odor was coming from.

"Which way are you headed?" he asked.

Tarrant hesitated, suddenly wary. It occurred to Damien for the first time that he, also, was loath to trust a stranger. That was a sobering concept.

"Wherever the trail leads," he said at last. "North, for the moment. But who can say where it will turn tomorrow?"

As anxious as I am not to give anything away. For similar reasons?

"You'll be here till morning?"

The stranger laughed softly. "The trail I follow is only visible at night, priest—and so that must define my hours. I stop at the daes when I can, for a taste of real food and the sound of human voices. *When* they let me in. But already I've been here too long. The spoor—" and he indicated the boy's body, "—is already growing cold. The hunter must move on. Now, if you will permit me. . . ."

He moved toward the boy once more. Damien had to force himself to be still as those delicate fingers settled once more on the colorless skin. Like flies. Leeches. The chill blue fae began to build once more, a slender webwork of death that wove itself about the boy's skin. He had to fight himself not to interfere.

"You could tell her," he said quickly, "the truth."

"His mother?" He looked up at Damien, and one corner of his mouth twisted slightly. In amusement? "He died in terror. Do you want her to know that?" Then he focused his attention back on the boy, on the delicate veil of death taking form beneath his fingertips. "You do your job, priest. I'll take care of mine. Unless you'd rather do this yourself."

"I don't kill innocents," he said coldly.

The death-fae halted in its progress. Gerald Tarrant looked up at him.

"There are no innocents," he said quietly.

They let the man out into the night, as carefully as they had previously let him in. Mes Kanadee guarded the door until it was safely locked behind him, and Damien—who had volunteered to help—added a Protecting to reestablish the fae-seals.

He felt both bitter and relieved that the man was leaving them. And envious, in equal measure. It was terrifying to be out there alone at night, especially in an area as actively malignant as this. But it was also exhilarating. For a man who knew how to take care of himself—as Gerald Tarrant clearly did—it was the ultimate challenge.

He watched as the last of the bolts was thrown, then joined his companions at the fireside. Night had thinned the ranks of travelers that previously had filled the common room; save for one woman asleep by the fire, and a middle-aged couple nursing their drinks at a far table, the small company was alone.

Senzei looked up at him, then back to the fire. "Where's he headed?"

"North."

"Our route?"

"Most likely."

"Did you learn his business?"

He stared into the fire. Tried to get the man's image out of his mind. "I learned a little of his nature," he answered. "That's enough." He wished he could rid himself of the chill that had entered his soul, the images that refused to leave him. Of a gaping black hole where a boy's soul used to be. Of the cold blue worms that were even now sucking out his life, to give him a "natural" death. Of pale gray eyes, and the challenge that had been in them. . . .

Despite the heat of the fire, he shivered. "I'll tell you about it later. In the morning. Let me sort it out in my own mind first, so it makes some kind of sense when I tell it."

"He's an adept," Ciani said. Her tone was a plea.

He put an arm around her and squeezed gently. But the tension in her body refused to ease; there was a barrier between them now, a subtle but pervasive blockage that had begun when her assailants devoured so many of the memories they shared. But now it seemed even stronger—colder, somehow. As if the stranger's presence had caused it to grow. He had assumed that time would give them back what they had lost; now, suddenly, he was no longer certain.

"I've seen power like that before," he told her. Trying to explain the coldness that was inside him, the nameless chill that rose up whenever he thought of allying with that man. "But I've never seen it exercised so cold-bloodedly."

And there are so many little things that are wrong, with him. Like the Earth medallion. His supposed allegiance to a Church that rejects his kind. No adept has made peace with my faith since the Prophet died.

"We're better off without him," he told her. Working the fae into his words. Trying to make himself sound convincing.

He wished he truly believed it himself.

Sixteen

Slowly, carefully, the xandu came down out of the mountains. Flexible feet treading silently on soft earth, picking a way between the sharp, treacherous boulders on one hand and the tangle of fallen branches on the other. Dead, all of it was dead. Autumn might be coming to the lowlands, but winter had already crowned the Worldsend peaks in white—and mile by mile, inch by inch, the carpet of life on which the xandu and his kind depended was being smothered by winter's cold.

It lifted its head and sniffed the wind, seeking some promise of change. How much farther could it go on, this utter desolation? The xandu's instincts insisted that there would be food to the west, thick green grasses not yet made brittle by winter's ice, curling leaves turned rust and amber by autumn's breath, but not yet fallen. Not yet dry. Not yet dead as this place was dead—as all of its usual grazing lands were dead, rocky lands carpeted in dried-out, useless husks of what once might have served for food.

It was a young animal, not yet experienced in the harsh rhythm of the seasons. Not yet *aware*, on all the levels that a xandu might become aware. Fae-tides rippled about its feet, but they were as meaningless to it as the stars which rose in the daytime, which were not required for light. It ignored them. Its only concern now, beyond that of safety, was food—and it sent that need out, echoing across the foothills of the Worldsend and into the lowlands, without ever knowing that it did so.

And it was answered. Not with a scent, exactly. Not with anything the xandu could have defined, or anything it knew how to respond to. Call it . . . a certainty. A sense of direction, and definition. It was hungry, and there was food, and if it traveled in a certain direction, at a certain pace, the twin paths of *need* and *supply* would converge.

It knew this as it knew the rhythms of its own body, the taste of highgrass just coming into bloom, the smell of winter. Without doubt. Without words.

It began to gallop. Pounding feet noisy on the packed earth, it kept alert for predators. But there were few beasts who would hunt a young, healthy xandu. Its long, gleaming horns might have been intended for sexual combat, but they were just as effective in goring an arrogant predator.

It traveled for many hours. The sun set in the western sky, and soon after was followed by that curtain of stars which was its closest rival in light. Evening fell darkly across the lowlands. The xandu was picking up new scents now, strange scents, of plants and animals native to this foreign terrain. Still it traveled. There were things growing here that might have served it for food, but food was no longer its primary concern.

And then, on the horizon, it saw something. Merely an amorphous shape at first, which slowly became more defined as the xandu galloped closer. A strange animal, that stood back on its hind legs as though raised up in sexual display. The xandu slowed to a trot, then to a walk. There was a feeling of *rightness* about the creature, of completeness, such that the xandu didn't think to fear. It had sought food, and here was food. It would soon need warmth, and here was a creature who commanded fire. It would ache with loneliness . . . and here, in this creature, was a companion for its winter, who would brave the ravages of the ice-time by its side, and then release it to seek out its own kind when the spring came again.

Wordlessly, effortlessly, it absorbed the stranger's need. Inside its body, unseen, molecules shifted their allegiance from one chemical pattern to another; instincts which had been merely dormant before this moment quickened with new life, and others—which had previously ruled its actions—subsided into half-sleep. And it knew, without understanding how, that the strange creature had also changed. And that the change was natural, and correct.

Then the stranger reached into its skin—a false skin, the xandu observed, which was wrapped around its own—and brought out food, which it gave to the xandu. And then more, and yet more, until the xandu's hunger was sated. It offered water, too, poured into its cupped hands, and the xandu drank.

Then the creature swung itself up onto the xandu's back; and that, too, was correct, and exactly as it should be. So much so that it suddenly seemed strange to the xandu that it had never borne such a creature before.

They turned north, and—at a vigorous gallop—began to close the distance between where they were and where they needed to be.

Seventeen

He couldn't do it.

Senzei sat alone in the center of a clearing, and tried to quiet his mind. Ever since they had encountered that man at the dae his nerves had been jangling like a hundred wards all set off at once, making it hard to concentrate. Now, every time he tried to take hold of the fae and commit himself to Working it, the memory of Gerald Tarrant got in the way.

It bothered him. It wouldn't stop bothering him. He felt like the man had been toying with them somehow, without knowing how or why.

You can't let it get to you. Not this much. We have to know where Ciani's assailants have gone and what they intend ... and if you can't get your act together to Know that, you might as well have stayed home.

Which thought brought its own special pain.

It could be simply that the man had awakened a storm of conflicting emotions within him: hunger and anger and jealousy combined, all in response to his obvious power. Or it could be something far more ominous than that: it could be that the stranger had established a channel between them, a subtle link between himself and the three travelers that hinted at darker intentions. But toward what end?

Only one way to find out, he thought grimly.

He hadn't shared these misgivings with his companions. Not yet. Damien had been sullen all morning, and Senzei suspected that something Tarrant did when they were alone together was the cause. No reason to add to it. And Ciani ... his chest tightened with grief at the mere thought of her. She would just hurt—silently, but he would see it in her eyes—and he would feel guilty for feeling such things, for feeling anything at all. While all the time he would want to scream at her, *You had it, you had it all and you lost it, how could you let it go!* As if somehow it had been her fault, as if she could have stopped it from happening.

Despite the relative warmth of the morning, he shivered. *We're none of us as rational as we'd like to be. Gods keep that from dividing us.*

A sudden rustling disturbed the brush behind him; he twisted around to see its cause, saw Ciani standing at the edge of the clearing.

"I didn't mean to interrupt," she said quickly. "Damien said to see if you'd be ready to move soon."

So we can make the next dae by sunset, he finished silently. *And lock ourselves away in safety one more time.*

The answer's here, in the night. Tarrant knew that.

"Come here," he said gently, and he patted the ground beside him.

She hesitated, then entered the clearing and sat. "I don't want to disturb you," she said.

"I was going to Work. You can Share it, if you'd like."

In her eyes: Elation. Fear. Hunger. He fought the instinct to turn away, knowing how much that would hurt her.

My gods. Did I look like that to her! Has fate done no more than reverse our roles!

He took her hand in his, weaving their fingers together. Holding her tightly, palm to palm, until it was possible to feel the pounding of her pulse against his flesh, to imagine that their two bloodstreams had somehow become linked together—and through that linkage, all the skills that made a Working possible.

All right, you bastard. Obviously I'm not going to be able to Work on anything else until I settle with you in my mind. So let's get a good look at just where you are, and what you're up to.

He sent his will questing along the fae-currents, noting the distinct northward pull that seemed to affect everything in this region. That would be the Forest, exerting its malevolent influence. Soon it would be difficult to Work in any other direction. How could an adept bear to live in such a place, where every thought was dragged toward that single point? Didn't Tarrant claim to come from somewhere north of here?

Slowly, the landscape about them began to take shape before his special senses. He clasped Ciani's hand tightly, Sharing the vision with her. The ground began to glow, with a colorless light. Currents of earth-fae swirled like fog about their knees, responding to some unseen pattern deep in the earth beneath them. He drew back—and upward—willing his viewpoint to expand and take in the surrounding terrain. Now he could see the clearing from above, with their two small bodies sitting side by side. *Higher.* The trees gave way to brush, to open ground. To a road, dusted with discolored leaves. He followed it southward, noting the pull of the current against him; soon it would be all but impossible to Work against its flow. Slowly, the vision he sought unfolded before him. There was the dae, in all its protective glory. There was the stockade gate, with a spot of light marking each active fae-signature, every working ward. And there were the footsteps leading to the road, a fading remnant of each traveler's identity that clung to the earth they had walked on, leaving a record that the faewise were able to read.

It was no great trial to determine which marks were Gerald Tarrant's; they stood out from among the others like a livid black spot on the face of the sun—a trail so dark that it seemed to vibrate, sucking the sunlight into its substance. The other footprints seemed weaker by the light of day, but his had gained in substance. As though each were a raw scar upon the earth, which the sun's rays worried at.

Not pretty, he thought grimly. *Not pretty at all.*

He followed the trail several yards, tracking the man's progress toward the road. And then the trail ended. Suddenly. Not tapering out, as a line of true footsteps might. Nor marked with the hard light of a Working, to indicate that the man had deliberately hidden his trail. It simply . . . wasn't there. At all.

Senzei sank himself deeper into concentration, straining to summon all the Sight that was available to him. The image of the dae sharpened. Tarrant's trail came into clear, almost painful focus . . . and still it disappeared, just as suddenly and in the same spot as before. It was as if the man had ceased to exist beyond that point.

He withdrew from the dae's confines, taking Ciani with him. And moved his viewpoint to high above, trying to gain some perspective.

"What if he mounted?" Ciani whispered.

The concept was so utterly naive, so ignorant of the most basic laws of the fae, that Senzei nearly wept for hearing it from her. His concentration, and therefore the Vision, wavered. "This isn't like a physical trail. You don't lose it when his feet are off the ground. It's the result of his presence affecting the currents . . . and that shouldn't disappear, just because he's sitting on a horse. The trail might look different, but it should still be there."

"What if he . . ." She hesitated. "Became something else?"

Startled, he looked at her. The vision shattered into a thousand bits, like breaking glass. He let it go.

"That's not possible," he whispered.

"Why not?"

He drew in a deep breath and tried to gather his thoughts. Tried to banish the feeling that somehow, somewhere, they were being Watched. "Shapechanging is . . . technically feasible, I suppose. And there are legends. But no one I ever knew could manage it, or had ever seen it done." He met her eyes. "*You* couldn't do it," he said. Gently. "I asked you why. You said it would require total submission to the fae. The kind of submission that the human mind can't accept. Maybe native sorcerors could manage it, you said. If there ever were any native sorcerors."

She said it quietly. "That wasn't what I meant."

"Cee, shapechanging—"

"I didn't mean shapechanging."

He stared at her for a long minute, trying to comprehend. "What, then? What is it?"

"What if he isn't human?" she pressed. "What if that was just a . . . a guise? A mask? What if once he was outside the dae, out of sight of the guards . . . he didn't need it any more?"

He stared at her, speechless.

"Isn't it possible? I don't remember. . . ."

"It's possible," he finally managed. "But there were wards up all over the place! Nothing that wasn't human should have been able to get within yards of it. Least of all in a false body."

"Something got in to hurt that boy," she pointed out. "Something that the wards were supposed to be guarding against."

He wanted to say to her, *Your ward was up there, too, right over the front door. Are you telling me something got past that? Not only walked right in under it, but maintained a false human body all the time it was there?*

But he was remembering something she had once told him. Remembering it as though she were saying it now, her voice low and couched in a tone of warning.

Every Warding has its weak spot. Every one, without exception. Sometimes you have to search hard to find it, but it's there, in all of them. Which means that the wards only protect us as well as they do because so few demons are capable of working an analysis. . . .

My speciality is in analysis, Tarrant had said.

Senzei squeezed her hand tightly. Hoped that she couldn't feel his fear. The air seemed suddenly warm, too warm; he loosened his collar, felt his hand shaking.

Don't let it get to you. You can't let it get to you. Her strength depends on yours. Don't lose it, Senzei.

"Come on," he said. He managed to stand. "Let's get back to Damien." He helped her to her feet. "I think he should know about this."

Damien listened to what they had to say—silently, patiently, without interrupting even to question them further—and then answered simply, "I had the same problem. Which just means we won't be able to track them by Working. Otherwise our plans stay the same."

"Damien," Senzei protested. "I don't think you understand—"

"I do," he said stiffly. Something in his manner—the set of his shoulders, the tone of his voice—bespoke a terrible tension. A struggle inside him that was only now breaking through to the surface. "I understand more than you're even aware of."

"If those things are right ahead of us—"

"Yes. That sound reasonable, doesn't it? Only, *how do we know that!*" His hands had balled into angry fists by his sides; he looked about himself, as if searching for something to hit. "I'll tell you how. Twenty-five words or less. We know it because *Gerald Tarrant told us.* That's how we know." He drew in a deep breath, let it out slowly. Fighting for control over the rage that seemed ready to consume him. "I've gone over it in my mind again and again since we left the dae this morning. And each time it comes to the same thing. *I trusted his word.* Not willingly—not even knowingly—but like an animal trusts its trainer. Like a laboratory rat trusts the men who feed it when it finally runs the way they want it to. Gerald Tarrant said that something had devoured the boy's memory, and I accepted it. God knows, I had good reason not to test him then. If I'd let myself be drawn into his Working, there's no telling what might have happened. So I didn't. You understand what that means? I didn't Know for myself. I took his word for it that what he said was the truth, when I should have Seen for myself—"

"You couldn't have known," Senzei said hurriedly. "Such power—"

"*Damn* the power!" His eyes blazed with fury—at Gerald Tarrant, at himself. "Don't you understand? If he *wasn't* telling the truth—if the boy's memory *hadn't* been taken—then what *did* attack him? What left him wounded like that, and then set up a Shielding so perfect that no one but Mer Tarrant could get through it? Ask yourself that!"

He took a deep breath. Then another. Trying to calm himself. It didn't work. "I should have confirmed it," he muttered. "If not then, later. *I should have checked.*"

Senzei hesitated—and then reached out and put a hand on the priest's shoulder. Emotional support, without the pressure of a Working; after a moment Damien nodded, acknowledging the gesture.

"We can go back," Senzei said gently. "If you need to Know—"

"We can't go back. One, because we have a mission to complete—and the longer we delay here, the harder it will get. Two, because . . . because. . . ."

He turned away. Slipping out from under Senzei's grasp so that he stood alone. His shoulders trembled.

"The boy is dead," he said at last. "Tarrant killed him. You understand? He called it a mercy killing. Maybe it was. But damned convenient, don't you think?

"God," he whispered; his voice was shaking. "What have I been witness to?"

"What do you want to do?" Senzei asked quietly.

He turned back to face them; his eyes were red. "We go to Kale," he told them. "Directly to Kale. If Tarrant was right and those things did attack the boy, then they're nearly two days ahead of us; we won't pass them without intending to. If he was wrong . . . then they could be anywhere. Behind us, ahead of us, even back in the rakhlands by now. I couldn't get a fix on them any more than you could, Zen. He's right in that; such a Working has to be done at night. But in Kale. In the relative safety of a city's confines. Not out here . . . where camping outside the daes means setting ourselves up for God knows what."

"You think he's allied with them?" Ciani asked anxiously.

"I don't know what he is—and I don't want to know. He's setting up some kind of game, maybe just for his amusement, maybe for some darker purpose. I say we don't play by his rules. That means we go straight to Kale, like we planned. No detours, no delays, and above all else no forays out into the night. We tell the daes to keep their doors shut; if he wants the night that badly, let him stay in it. Agreed?"

"And if he really is hunting them?" Senzei asked.

"In that case," he muttered, "more power to him. I hope he makes his kill."

He looked out over the road ahead—northward, toward the Forest—and added, "May they take him with them, when he does."

Eighteen

Tobi Zendel was securing the last of his nets when dusk fell, and because his attention was wholly fixed on the task before him he failed to notice the figure as it approached him, and did not hear it coming until the planks of the small pier finally creaked in warning.

"What the—" He turned about to see what had come up behind him; the anatomically complex profanity he had been about to spout forth withered on his lips, unvoiced. "What the hell?" he said softly— a socially acceptable substitute.

The figure that stood on the pier before him was that of a woman, oddly dressed. She was about his height, which was not tall; slender, and delicately boned; precisely made, with small, high breasts— although the latter were somewhat obscured by her clothing, so it was hard for him to judge their exact appeal. She was clothed in layers of tight cloth, which might have been actual garments but had more the appearance of wrappings. Gloves hid her hands, and a scarf which was tightly wrapped about her head and neck hid all the rest of her from view, except for her face. That was delicately sculpted, delicately colored—a clear golden brown that perfectly matched her garments—and oddly soft, as though he were viewing it through frosted glass.

"I'm sorry, Mes." He breathed the words, as though somehow her presence demanded silence. "I didn't see you coming, was all. Can I . . . can I help you?"

She looked out across the Serpent, as if searching for something. After a few seconds her gaze fixed on a distant point, and she extended her arm toward it. A question; a command.

He looked over his shoulder, toward where she was pointing. And laughed, somewhat nervously. "Morgot? Lady, that's out." The fin-

gers of her glove were split, he noticed; thin curving claws, like those
of a cat, gleamed in the slits. "That's upstraits, crosscurrent . . . and
bad luck, besides. You want that crossing, ferry over to Kale. They'll
take you, sure enough—if the price is right."

She reached into a fold of fabric at her hip, brought out a small
purse.

"Lady, it isn't money. I value my neck. You understand? That's a
rough crossing. And I'm a coward."

Slowly, she lowered her arm. And waited. He was about to speak
again when he saw something move, up by the start of the pier. Not
a person, this time. A . . . a. . . .

Gods of Earth n' Erna. A xandu!

It was horse-sized, and roughly horse-shaped, but there the similarity ended. Thick fur gleamed along its limbs, tufting thickly about
its five-toed feet. It was pearl-gray, for the most part, but a mane of
thick white hair adorned its chest and shoulders, and small white
tufts marked the points of its ears. Its head was slender and pointed,
its large eyes positioned in a manner that could have served it as
predator or prey. And its horns . . . he had to fight not to reach out
and touch them, not to put his hands on their cool, rainbow length
and know for a fact that, yes, they were real. The creature was real.
A true xandu, which mankind thought had been Worked into extinc-
tion, so many years ago. . . .

He looked at the woman—dark, her eyes were so dark, you could
see neither iris nor white in them, only pupil—and said, in a voice
that shook slightly, "You'll trade him? I'll take you, for that. Take
you over. There'll be mounts there, you understand? You can buy a
mount on Morgot. I mean, you know where to get a xandu, right? So
it's not like I'd be taking anything you couldn't replace." He was
fighting to speak coherently, while greed and wonder conspired
within to rob him of speech. "I mean . . . I'd take the risk, for that."

She looked at him—and at the xandu—and then back at him.
Assessing. After a moment, she moved her head slightly. He thought
it was a nod.

"We can go right now if you want." He started to prepare to cast
off, loosening the ropes he had only so recently tied. "It's pretty safe,
out on the water. Unless you'd rather wait for sunlight—"

Silently she stepped to the edge of the pier, her soft leather boots
making no sound. For a moment he was close enough to see her face
in detail—and it seemed that the golden surface was not skin, but
close-lying fur. He shivered. Then she was past him, stepping into
the boat. Tobi looked to where the xandu was waiting—and found it

already beside him, ready to board. After a moment he stepped aside and let it do so.

Heart pounding—head spinning with thoughts of fame and wealth soon to come—he freed his boat from its mooring posts and set sail for the northern caldera.

Nineteen

Five days and nights now, in safety. Five daes that protected them from unknown demon-hunters—and from decisions.

Damien dreamed. At first only misty images, vignettes of dread mingled with bits of memory: a fear-mosaic. Then the dreams began to gain substance, and definition. Night after night he played the same saga out: their journey, their arrival, their final confrontation. And night after night, in every variation, he watched his companions die. And died himself, at the hands of a creature who squeezed the memories from him like pulpy juice from an overripe fruit, then cast the rind aside.

Again and again. With no hope of success. Because what they had wasn't enough. They lacked the numbers they needed, and the knowledge. They lacked the *power.*

Evil is what you make of it, the Prophet had written. *Bind it to a higher Purpose, and you will have altered its nature.* And: *We use what tools we must.*

Damien wondered if—and how—Gerald Tarrant could be bound.

The port called Kale was as unlike Jaggonath as any place could possibly be. The city's plan was a veritable maze of narrow, twisting streets, flanked by houses that had been hurriedly built and, for the most part, poorly maintained. Rich and poor were quartered side by side, laborers' hovels leaning against the thick stone walls of a rich merchant's estate—barbed iron spikes adorning the top, to discourage the curiosity of strangers—which was flanked in turn by the mildewed shells of workhouses, the miserly confines of tenement flats, the iron-clad husks of massive storage sheds. The streets themselves might once have been paved with stones, and occasionally a flat slab of shallite—deep green, or slate gray, or midnight black—would peek out from beneath the layers of mud and debris and animal droppings which seemed to coat everything in sight. The whole place smelled: of damp, of dung, of decay. But there was commerce here, enough to support thousands. And where trade flourished, humankind inevitably congregated.

They arrived shortly before dusk and wasted the next hour getting themselves thoroughly lost. As the sun sank slowly behind mildewed walls, the maze of streets became stiflingly close. At last Senzei grabbed hold of a passing youngster—a mud-caked ten-year-old who clearly had more time on his hands than he knew what to do with—and offered him a few coins to serve as guide. The boy glanced once at the darkening western sky, as if to point out the danger involved in taking on business at such a late hour—but when no more money was offered he coughed and nodded, and led them through the maze of tangled streets to a somewhat more promising sector.

The breeze shifted, coming in from over the straits: salt air, sharp with promise. Here, the River Stekkis emptied its fresh water and its mud into that precious conduit which connected Erna's great oceans, dividing the human lands in two. Here, just beyond the whitewaters of Naigra Falls (named for a similar formation on Ancient Earth, or so it was said), goods from along the river were weighed and measured and packaged and assessed and taxed, to be shipped to the hundred-and-some-odd cities that flanked the length of the Serpent Straits. Golden figurines from Iyama rested in sealed crates, next to precious spices from Hade and spring wine from Merentha County. And traveling merchants gathered in lamplit taverns, drinking Kale beer with one hand while they outlined the financial future of nations with the other.

"Let's get rooms and food," Damien said. "And secure our things. After that . . . I think we need to take a good look around."

Five days of travel along the trade roads of the east had come to an end at last—and not a moment too soon, for Damien's taste. Five endless days spent covering the miles one by one, nights spent cowering in the daes like timid ground-skerrels that went to burrow at dusk, lest something that called the night its home should snatch them up. Five days of hiding from Tarrant, too—although they used other terms for that strategy—by making sure that each dae understood there was something out there desperate to get in, so that none would dare to open their doors. Was that necessary? Was it circumspect? Damien was no longer sure.

"He might not mean us any harm," Ciani had said.

How could they be certain of that?

Kale. Damien breathed in its rich scents with relief, his heart pounding with newfound exhiliration. The miles before this had been necessary, but tedious. A road devoid of choices. Now . . . they could begin to plan in earnest. Could begin to weave the net that would eventually draw in their enemies, and free Ciani.

Her assailants would have come through here. Might even still be in the city. They might take this opportunity to feed, feeling themselves safe in such a murky, anonymous place. In that case . . . good. The battle could take place here, on human ground, and no one need ever go on to the rakhlands. Oh, the three of them might decide to go anyway, after it was all over—but that would be a *choice*, not a necessity. They might choose to explore the lands that mankind had abandoned, as Ciani had once tried to do. Who knew what secrets might be waiting for them, in the shadow of the Worldsend Mountains?

Then he thought of Ciani, and her vulnerability, and he muttered, "We don't leave her alone." Senzei nodded and moved closer to Ciani. "Not until we know for a fact that those things aren't here in town."

"You want me to Divine that?" Senzei asked.

He thought about it. "Dinner first. Let's find ourselves rooms and settle the horses. Then."

By then it would be night. The demon/adept Tarrant (which was he? Damien wondered. Was it possible to be both?) had said that the creatures were best tracked at night. They'd give it a shot and see if he was right. One try. It would be worth the risk. Wouldn't it?

We'll have to face the night soon enough, anyway, he thought dryly. *There are no top-rank hotels in the rakhlands.*

(Even as he thought that, he imagined Ciani's voice—always tender, always teasing—as she challenged him, *How do we know that?*)

They took rooms in a cliffside inn that had gargoyles over every doorway—not Worked, Damien noted, but ugly enough to drive away any demon with aesthetic sensibilities—and crude iron grilles over the windows, twisted into some sort of sigil-sign. Again, not Worked. There was an absence of Working all over the city, Senzei pointed out, which was doubly jarring after the proliferation of wards in Jaggonath and the daes.

More like home, Damien thought. It was oddly comforting.

They ate. Strange shapes culled from the sea, inundated with local spices. Spongy tendrils of flesh in cream sauce, suckers sliced into delicate rings and fried, something small and spiderlike with its head and legs intact: *pull the limbs off these little guys yourself,*the menu urged. Kale was proud of its seafood.

And afterward, for dessert, a sense of anticipation so keen that the three could almost taste it. Mere sweets were bland by comparison, and one by one the travelers pushed them aside.

"It's time," Damien muttered. "Let's go."

They had chosen this particular hostel because of one very special facility: it had a flat, easily accessible roof. For a small bribe—"call it a damage deposit," the manager had said—Damien had obtained the key. Now, in the darkening night, with only a few remaining stars and a single moon to light the sky, they let themselves out of the inn's smoky confines, into the chill of evening.

The earth-fae would be weak up here—but that was good, Senzei had insisted. Good that the taint of the Forest would be thus diluted before he tried to Work it. Damien looked at his companion, saw the fear in his eyes. The excitement. *He's in his element,* the priest thought. *At last.*

Damien loosened his sword in his scabbard—and then, as an after-thought, drew it free. There was no telling what manner of creature such a Working might call to them, or how quickly it might come. He made sure Ciani was safely on the other side of him before he nodded to Senzei: Yes. Go ahead.

The dark-haired Worker took a deep breath, steadied himself—and then began to weave a Seeing.

Power. A vast, unending seascape of power—swirls and eddies and cresting waves of it, earth-fae so fluid and deep that it laps up against the sides of the inn, and dashes a spray of limitless potential into the air before his eyes. Magnificent! For a moment Senzei can do no more than stare at it, drinking in the Sight. So much of it! So . . . raw. Chaotic. Potent. He considers the sterile city, its wardless walls and unWorked gates, and shakes his head in amazement. How can such a thing be! How can this kind of power exist, without men coming here to tame it! The city should be full of sorcerors—should cater to sorcerors—should be renowned among the faewise, as a focal point of power. So why isn't it! What is there that his eyes can't See, which has kept that from happening!

He opens himself up to the power, welcomes its wildness into the core of him. Not slowly, as he had meant to do. Not cautiously, as he knows it should be done. Joyfully—exuberantly—his soul's barriers thrown wide open, the core of his being laid bare. And the fae pours into him. An ecstasy more intense than any sex suffuses his limbs: the taste of true power. Here, in this place, he might do anything.

Do they want information? It is there for the Knowing. Do they need protection? Here, he might craft a Warding that would endure for ages. Had he envied the adepts of Jaggonath? For all their vision, they had never tasted this! He shivers in pleasure and awe as the power flows through him—wild power, wholly undisciplined, fae that lacks only his command to give it substance and purpose.

This is living, he thinks. This is what I was meant for!

In the far north, across the Serpent's waist, a midnight sun is rising. Black sphere against ebony blackness, jet-pure; a thing that can only be Felt, not Seen. Into it all the light of the world is sucked, all the colors and textures that the fae contains: into the crystalline blackness, the Anti-Sun. He stares at it in adoration and horror and thinks: There, where all the power is concentrated, like matter in a black hole ... there is the power we need for this quest. Power to shake the rakhlands and make our kill and move the earth besides!

And one thing is as certain as the night sky above him, the broad disk of Domina looming overhead: he alone can channel this power, can make it serve their purpose. Who else? Certainly not Ciani, whose skill was excised from her. Nor Damien, whose priestly Workings are too entangled with intellect, with questions of morality and correctness and Revivalist philosophy ... no, of all of them only he can master this terrible force and make it serve their will.

It seems to Senzei that his life was spent preparing for this, making him ready for this single moment. He reaches out toward the source of the power—meaning to take it, to shape it, to let it shape him— but something grabs at him from behind, forcing him back. He struggles against it wildly, like an animal caught in a net. There, in the distance—there is freedom, there is power! He feels himself forced back one step, then another—and his soul screams out in anguish, as he is forced farther and farther away from the blackening dawn. Farther away from the only thing that can give him the power he hungers for, the only thing that can give him peace. The fae surges forward about him, mindless of his suffering; he grabs wildly at the rising tide, tries to link himself to it so that it will carry him with it, toward that point of Power ... but something is in his way, something that drives the breath from his body in a sudden burst of pain, until he reels from the force of it and falls—his head striking hard against the ground, or is it the roof?—his senses caving in one by one as the ebony sun fades, the whole of his Vision fades....

Light. *Real* light. Moonlight, falling across the tarpaper roof. Senzei moaned, turning away from it. Searching for shadows. Anywhere.

Then, slowly, other things came into focus. People. Ciani's beloved face, contorted with worry. Damien's eyes, blazing with . . . what? His head ached; he couldn't read it. His stomach ached, too, with a throbbing hurt that spoke of real bodily damage. He put a hand to his abdomen and winced. Tender, very tender.

"What . . . what happened?"

"You tried to walk off the roof," Damien said quietly. "Ciani tried to stop you. I helped as soon as I could." A brief nod indicated the deep purple fluid on his blade, the dark shapes that lay huddled and bleeding on all sides of them. Pain pounded in Senzei's temples. "I've never seen anything manifest so fast," Damien said. There was an odd tone in his voice which Senzei couldn't identify. "Or in such quantity. You all right?"

He looked out over the roof's low edge toward the north. Toward where the earth-fae still flowed, now invisible to his unWorked senses. Moisture gathered in the corners of his eyes; he blinked it free, felt it work its way slowly down his face.

"Yes," he whispered. "I think so. It was. . . ." He shivered. "Incredible."

"Untamable, more likely. We should have known that. Should have guessed it when we saw the town." Damien took out a handkerchief and wiped his sword clean. "I think it's safe to say that now we know why there are so few Workings in Kale, yes? We'll have to avoid that angle ourselves—at least until we get out of range of *that*." He nodded toward the north as he resheathed his sword. Then he offered his hand to Senzei. "Can you stand?"

After a moment, he nodded. It took several tries, but at last the two of them managed to get him to his feet. He felt as though his limbs were made of gel, barely able to support him.

"It would have drawn you in," the priest said quietly. A question.

Senzei hesitated. Considered it. "Yes. I think. I wanted to go to it. I wanted for it . . . to devour me. So I could be part of it. You . . . you can't know." He choked on the words, and a sense of terrible loss filled him. And fear. He could do no more than mutely shake his head. "Thank you. Thank you."

"Come on." It was Ciani, slipping underneath one arm to help him walk. "Let's get inside. We can talk about it later."

"An adept," Senzei muttered. "Can you imagine? To live with that vision, endlessly . . . one would drown in it. . . ."

"Which is why there are no adepts in Kale," Damien reminded him. "Remember your notes?"

Unless there is now, Senzei thought. *Unless Tarrant followed us.*

At the door that led into the building, Damien paused. He looked out over the tarpaper expanse of the roof's surface, at the dozen or so newborn demonlings that were slowly bleeding out their substance in the moonlight.

"Damn it," he muttered. "It'll cost us good money to have this cleaned up."

Always practical, Senzei thought dryly. *Who else would care?*

Dear friends, if you could have seen what I have seen. . . .

And then his thoughts slid down into darkness, and the blissful numbness of sleep.

Midnight. Plus some. An hour of peace, even this close to the whirlpool. Ciani was sleeping soundly—at last—and Senzei was still lost in the oblivion of his healing trance. The three of them were sharing a suite, which had turned out to be the perfect situation; Damien could check on his companions easily enough, but if one of them happened to wake in the night and glance about before returning to sleep, they wouldn't see that he'd left. He had left a note on his pillow just in case, but didn't really expect anyone to find it; he should be back long before they awoke. And hopefully, he would have some new answers.

The town itself was silent, so much so that he could hear the soft wash of salt-laden waves against Kale's rocky shore. He made his way toward the sound, using it as a compass to maneuver through the narrow, twisting streets.

As with most of the northern coast, Kale's shoreline was a series of ragged cliffs and overhangs, inhospitable to travelers. Damien worked his way slowly westward, toward the port itself. Natural caverns were etched deep into the rock beneath him, and periodically something dark would fly out of the mouth of one, to shriek its way across the jagged shallows. Not a good place for boats or men, he reflected. But it was still far safer than the ocean shorelines which were battered by an endless procession of tsunami; and so man had forced this coast to accept a port wherever there was the slightest opening for one, and would make do with its shortcomings. Erna was a harsh mistress.

Soon, the cliff edge he traversed began to drop. A narrow path led him around several major obstacles, to a place where the earth, shaken by one too many tremors, had collapsed. A mountain of jagged boulders sloped down to the Serpent, covered over by a webwork of wooden walkways and stairs that made safe descent, if strenuous, possible.

Damien clambered down, noting that there was activity about several of the boats that were docked below. Erna's opposing moons made for a complex tidal pattern, and the few windows of opportunity that occurred must be grasped when they did; in the city itself life might subside at sunset, but Kale's shipping fleets never rested.

At last he reached a sizable boardwalk that gave him a level surface to the water's edge. Long piers stretched out across miles of water, bridging the boulder-strewn shallows. At high tide it was perhaps possible for a boat to come in close to the shore itself; at low tide, the sailors would have quite a hike after docking. For a moment Damien wondered why they hadn't done something more permanent to fill the land in, or thoroughly dredge it out; then he remembered where he was, and reminded himself: *There is no such thing as permanence, in this part of the world. What man chooses to construct, earthquakes can unconstruct in an instant. Better to build flexibly— or at least temporarily—and give way to Nature's temper tantrums when they occur.*

Come to think of it, didn't the whole Stekkis River shift once, within recent centuries? Wasn't Merentha once the port city at its mouth, instead of Kale? It must be hard to invest time or money in a city that might be made worthless tomorrow, he thought. That alone would explain an awful lot about the city's appearance.

He watched the men moving about the piers for some time, assessing various facets of their activity. Ganji-on-the-Cliffs had a similar port, and it was no hard task for him to draw parallels between them. After a while he thought he saw what he was looking for, and he began to pick his way over to the far eastern end of the docks, near where the cliffs began to rise. There was a small boat docked there, whose relatively shallow draft was well suited to inhospitable ports. As he came closer, he could see that it had strong masts and a small steam turbine in the rear; its owner didn't trust technology, but had enough survival sense to pack it as a backup. Excellent. Damien assessed its size, its probable speed, the amount of room on board, and nodded. This one was promising.

He walked out to where the small ship was moored. Two men were bustling about its deck, gathering up the last of some precious cargo. A third stood at the bow and watched; he glanced up shortly when Damien approached but didn't acknowledge him otherwise. Damien waited. The cargo was loaded into a coarse handwagon with a shipping emblem seared into its side. When it was full the two men handed documents to the third, who read them by moonlight. And nodded. Not until the laborers had grabbed hold of the handcart and begun to pull it toward shore—not until they were out of hearing, and almost out of sight—did the overseer acknowledge Damien with his eyes and slowly walk over to meet him.

"C'n I help you?"

Damien nodded towards the boat. "Yours?"

The overseer assessed him. "Maybe."

"I need to hire transportation."

The man said nothing.

"I'm prepared to pay well for it."

The man chuckled. "That's vulkin' fortunate. It don't come cheap."

Somewhat disdainfully, Damien pulled a small leather pouch from his pocket; he rattled it once, so that the sound of metal striking metal was clearly audible.

The man's nostrils flared, like an animal scenting its prey. "Where you headed?"

"East. Southern shore. Near the mouth of the Achron River. You interested?"

The man coughed, and spat into the water. "You'd need more'n money to buy that kind of passage."

"What, then?"

"You need a pilot that's vulkin' set on suicide—which I'm not. That's some of the worst shoreline on the Serpent." He grinned, showing stained and chipped teeth. "How about somewhere else for vacation, eh? I hear there's a good river up north."

"It's business," Damien said shortly.

"Then I'm real sorry." He looked hungrily at the purse, but his expression didn't soften. "That's death on the rocks, that trip. I don't want none of it. No one will. Not unless you can find some young fool of a merchant's son with a spanking new yacht to wreck . . . and then you'd just die in the landing, along with 'im. You catch my drift?"

Damien stretched open the mouth of the purse and spilled two gold coins into the palm of his hand. The man's eyes widened.

"Perhaps you know someone who can take us."

The man hesitated—it seemed that two parts of him were at war with each other—but at last he shook his head. "Not in Kale, Mer. Don't know anyone foolish enough to try. Sorry." He chuckled. "Wish I even had a good lie, for that kind of money."

Damien was about to speak when another voice—smooth as the night air and nearly as quiet—intruded.

"I believe the gentleman doesn't understand the value of your currency."

He turned quickly toward the source of the voice, and found Gerald Tarrant standing not ten feet from them.

"Permit me," the tall man said, bowing slightly.

After a moment Damien nodded. Tarrant approached—and withdrew a thin golden disk from his tunic, which he displayed to the mariner.

The side that Damien saw was a familiar image: it was the earthdisk that the stranger had displayed in Briand. But whatever was on the other side made the mariner's face go white beneath its stubble, the jaw dropping slack beneath.

"Tell him what he needs to know," Tarrant said quietly.

The man looked over his shoulder—northward, across the Serpent—and then stammered, "Not here. You understand? You need to go to Morgot. That's where the kind of men would be, who could help you. Morgot."

Damien looked questioningly at Tarrant, who explained, "an island just north of here. A caldera, made into a port. It occasionally serves as a way station for the . . . shall we say, less than reputable sort?"

He reached over toward Damien, so smoothly and so quickly that the priest failed to react in time. He took the gold coins out of his hand, and gave them to the mariner. A faint chill touched the priest's flesh where contact had almost been made.

"You'll take his party over to Morgot tomorrow." Tarrant's tone was one of confident authority. It was hard to say exactly where in his words or his manner the threat was so evident. "No questions asked. Agreed?"

The man took the money awkwardly, as though not quite sure what the ritual of acceptance should be. "Yes, your lordship," he whispered. "Of course, your lordship." He scrambled down to the deck of his craft and disappeared hurriedly into the cabin; after a few minutes had passed without him reappearing, Tarrant turned to Damien, clearly satisfied that the man would not disturb them.

"Forgive me for intruding in your business."

Damien forced himself to respond to the politeness of the man's manner, rather than what he imagined lay beneath the surface. Which made his skin crawl. "Not at all. Thank you."

"I think you now have what you came out into the night to find." Tarrant said quietly.

"Now I do," he assured him.

Tarrant laughed softly. "You're a curious man, priest. Courageous enough to take on the demons of Kale, not to mention the rakh's vicious constructs . . . but not quite confident enough to share a dae's fireside with another human traveler."

"Are you that?" Damien said sharply.

Tarrant's expression tightened, ever so slightly. The pale eyes narrowed. "Am I what?"

"Human."

"Ah. Let's not get into philosophy, shall we? Say that I was born a man—as you were—and as for what a man may become . . . we don't all follow paths that our mothers would have approved of, do we?"

"A bit of an understatement, in your case."

The silver eyes met his. Cold, so cold. The dead might have eyes like that. "You don't trust me, do you?"

"No," he said bluntly. "Should I?"

"Some have chosen to."

Ciani wants to, Damien thought. And: *I never will.*

"You killed that boy. In Briand."

"Yes. I told you why."

"And I believed it—at the time." It was impossible to tell from the man's expression whether he would buy a bluff or see right through it. He decided to chance it. "I didn't know then what I do now."

"Ah." Tarrant's eyes were fixed on him: piercing through his wordly image, weighing his soul. "I did underestimate you," he said at last. "My apologies. It won't happen again."

He felt like he had won points in some game, without even knowing what he was playing. Or if he would ever see the rulebook. He indicated the boat that was tied up before them, in whose cabin the mariner was presumably still cowering. *Probably won't show his face until we're out of here,* he thought. Then corrected himself: *Until Tarrant's out of here.*

"What was it you showed him?"

Tarrant shrugged. "I merely indicated that I understood the situation."

"Which is?"

"Morgot plays host to a number of legitimate shipping concerns. It's also a refuge for smugglers and other unsavory types. For all he knew, you were some kind of local inspector trying to track down a freelance. Out to hurt his friends. You see," he said quietly, "trying to maneuver in this region without knowing the rules can be . . . difficult."

"And you know the rules."

He shrugged. "This is my home."

"Kale."

No answer. Only silent, unvoiced amusement.

"He called you *lordship*," Damien pressed.

"An ancient honorific. Some men still use it. Does it bother you so much?"

He met Tarrant's eyes—so pale, so cold—and suddenly understood what made the man so dangerous. *Control.* Over himself, over his environment . . . and over everyone who dealt with him.

"It would seem," the priest said quietly, "that we hunt the same creatures."

"So it would seem."

"For the same purpose?"

Again Tarrant shrugged; the gesture was anything but casual. "I want them out of the human lands. If they die en route . . . so much the better."

Damien hesitated; he felt as though he were balanced on the edge of a precipice, and anything—the wrong words, even the wrong thoughts—might send him over. But he knew why he had come here. What he had to do. He might not like it, but his dreams had made it clear.

"We're here to kill them."

Tarrant smiled indulgently. "I know."

"My friends think you could help us."

"And you don't."

This time it was Damien's turn not to answer.

One corner of Tarrant's mouth twitched slightly; a smile? "We do serve the same cause," he observed. "If you won't trust me, trust in that."

"Should I trust you?"

"I would say. . . ." He smiled, and shook his head. "No. Not you."

"But you're willing to help us."

"For as long as our paths coincide—and our purposes are compatible—yes." He indicated the boat beside them, the caldera in the distance. "I thought I made that clear."

Damien drew in a deep breath, tried to settle his unease. It was dangerous to let the man know their weakness—but if he was to help them, he would have to. There was no other way.

"We've lost the trail," he said quietly. Watching Tarrant for his reaction. "We can't Work the fae here."

"Most can't," he agreed.

"The currents are—"

Tarrant waved him to silence.

For a moment the tall man just stood there, nostrils flared as if to test the air. Then he turned toward the shoreline. Casually, as if his only intention was to watch the waves break. He raised a hand—but made no gestures with it, nor did Damien hear a whispered key for Binding.

Minutes passed.

"They're not here," he said at last. "Not in Kale." He stared southward a moment longer, then added quietly, "But this was their route. Without question."

"You're sure."

"Their taint is unmistakable." He turned back to the priest—and for a moment it seemed that his eyes were not gray but black, his gaze a measureless emptiness. "And besides, if they mean to go home, this is the only way to do it. Short of swimming—or climbing the Worldsend."

"And how is it that you can Work the fae here?"

The stranger smiled; his perfect white teeth glinted in the moonlight. "Call it practice."

"That's all?"

"That's enough. You're too full of questions, priest. I don't make a habit of explaining myself."

"That's too bad. I like to know who I'm traveling with."

Tarrant seemed amused. "Is that an invitation?"

"We've just booked passage to Morgot. You're welcome to join us . . . unless you'd like to swim."

"I prefer to leave that to the fish, thank you. —But yes, I'll travel with you tomorrow. For as long as our paths coincide, you may count on me."

He turned away as if to leave—and then looked back at Damien. "We don't leave until dusk, of course. I prefer not to travel in sunlight. But you guessed that, didn't you? You guessed so very much." He smiled, and bowed his head ever so slightly. "Until tomorrow, Reverend Vryce."

Speechless, Damien watched while Tarrant strode the length of the pier, disappearing at last into the shadows that lay along the shore. The priest's hands clenched into fists slowly, then unclenched, then repeated the pattern. Trying to bleed off some of the tension, so that the night wouldn't throw his own fears back at him. The last thing he needed now was a battle with brainless demonlings. He needed to think.

What's done is done. You made your decision, and now you'll have to live with the consequences. For better and for worse.

There was a stirring inside the boat's small cabin, as if in response to the sudden silence without. After a moment the mariner peeked out; when he saw that Damien was still there, he began to withdraw.

"He's gone," the priest said quickly. "But I do need to talk to you."
The man hesitated, then came out onto the deck. "Mer?"

"The trip tomorrow." He felt himself stiffen, fought to keep the
tension out of his voice. "We won't be able to leave until after dusk."

The man just stared at him. "I figured," he said at last. "You travel
with that kind, those are the hours."

He started to turn away, but Damien indicated with a gesture that
he wasn't done with him.

"Mer?"

"What was the medallion he showed you?" the priest asked tightly.
"What did it mean?"

The man hesitated; for a minute, it looked like he wished he were
somewhere else. Anywhere else. Damien just waited. And finally the
man muttered, "The Forest. The Hunter. His servants wear that
sigil." He looked up at Damien; his expression was a warning. "We
don't anger that kind. I suggest you don't either. Not in this region,
anyway." *Maybe nowhere at all,* his gaze seemed to say. "They take
care of their own. Their enemies die. No exception. —You understand?"

"I understand," Damien said quietly. Hearing his own thoughts
echo within him, like that of a stranger.

Evil is what you make of it.

We use what tools we must.

"Damn it!" he hissed angrily, when the man was out of hearing.

It was a long while before he started back.

Twenty

The sun was still shining brightly when Tobi Zendel's steam-driven boat approached the Morgot docks. With care, he brought it in safely at the far end of the harbor. There were few people about. Which meant few police and few inspectors. That was intentional. With the xandu on board—and a damned strange passenger to boot—he was anxious to avoid anyone in uniform.

"This is it," he told her. He looped a mooring line over a convenient post, then leapt up onto the pier to secure it. The boat rubbed up gently against the cold, swollen wood. "Sorry I can't take you closer in by boat, but . . . well, hey." He offered her a hand to help her onto the pier but she looked right through him, as if it were beneath her pride to notice. After a moment his hand withdrew. She stepped up easily onto the boat's polished edge, and from there continued without hesitation or slippage to step across the water to the more stable surface of the pier.

"You got your sea legs fast, that's for sure." He grabbed at another rope from the back end of the boat and affixed that, too; then he tested them both. "Tell you what. I need to arrange for some fuel before I start back. You come with me, I'll show you the way up to the travelers' facilities. Okay?" She said nothing. He patted the last of his mooring lines affectionately, then looked back uneasily at the boat. "Think I ought to secure him? I mean, I left him inside and all . . . but those are damned flimsy walls, you know what I mean? Not meant to do much more than keep out the rain." He glanced at her. Her expression was unreadable. "Think so?" Still nothing. At last he shrugged and climbed back down onto the slowly shifting deck.

She waited.

After a moment, there was a noise from inside the cabin. Some quick movement, and one sharp impact against the wall. Then silence.

She waited.

The xandu climbed out of the cabin and shook itself quickly, like a cat shedding water. It looked at her, at the well-worn pier, and the distance between them. And then, in one powerful leap, it bypassed all the obstacles. Its feet landed heavily on the thick planks by her side, toenails digging into the soft wood for balance.

Wordlessly, she took a small bit of cloth from out of her right hip pocket. And wiped its two horns dry, of blood and sea-spray both.

They walked to where the trees began, and made sure they were well out of sight before she mounted.

Twenty-one

Gerald Tarrant arrived promptly at sunset. His height and his bearing made him stand out from the locals, even at a distance: long, easy stride contrasted with their short-legged hustling, fluid grace set against their unrefined simplicity. *Aristocratic*, Damien thought. In the Revivalist sense of the word. He wondered why the adjective hadn't occurred to him before.

The horses had been on edge since being lowered like cargo from the eastern cliff wall; now, as Tarrant approached, they grew even more agitated. Damien moved closer to his mount and put his hand on its shoulder. Through the contact he could feel the animal's fear, a primal response to dangers sensed but not yet comprehended.

"I know just how you feel," he muttered, stroking it.

Gerald Tarrant was all politeness, as always. And as always, there was a dark undercurrent not quite concealed by his genteel facade. Stronger than before, Damien noticed. Or perhaps simply more obvious. Was that in response to the local fae, which would tend to intensify any malevolence? Or was it simply that the mask of good nature he normally assumed was allowed to slip a bit, now that he was close to home?

Or your own fertile imagination working overtime, he cautioned himself. *Senzei and Ciani aren't having any problem with him.*

Not quite true. Senzei was polite, but Damien knew him well enough to read the added tension in his manner. The revelation of Tarrant's origin hadn't pleased him any more than it did Damien. But Ciani—

With consummate grace, Tarrant walked to where she stood, took her hand in his, and bowed gallantly. Gritting his teeth, Damien was forced to acknowledge the man's charm.

"Watch her," he muttered, and Senzei nodded. Tarrant's ties to the Hunter should have been enough to make Ciani keep her distance— except that she was Ciani, and even before the accident she had loved knowledge for its own sake, without the "taint" of moral judgment. With a sinking feeling Damien realized just how drawn she would be to the Hunter, and to the mystery that he represented. It would mean little to her that he tortured human women as a pasttime, save as one more fact for her to devour. For the first time it occurred to him just what a loremaster's neutrality meant, and it made his stomach turn. He had never considered it in quite that way before.

Tarrant came over to where he stood beside the horses; instinctively he moved closer to his own mount, protecting it. Tarrant regarded the animals for a moment, nostrils flaring slightly as he tested their scent. Then he touched them lightly, one after the other. Just that. As contact was made with each animal it calmed, and when it was broken each lowered its nose to the planks of the deck, as if imagining that it was not at sea, but somewhere on its favorite grazing ground.

"Not mine," Damien warned him.

"As you wish." They were being approached by the boat's captain and owner; the grubby mariner of the day before had been transformed by a shave and a change of clothing into something marginally neater, but no less obsequious. He clearly considered Tarrant the master of this expedition.

"Welcome on board, your lordship."

"The wind is adequate?" Tarrant asked.

"Excellent, your lordship. Of course."

"It will hold until we reach Morgot," he promised.

"Thank you, your lordship."

Tarrant glanced about the deck, taking in all of it: the travelers, their luggage, the newly docile mounts. And Damien, with his own horse nervously pawing the deck. He spared an amused, indulgent nod for the pair of them, then told the man briskly, "All's in order. Take us out."

"Yes, your lordship."

Mooring lines were cast off, sails were raised to catch the wind, and they began to move. The piers gave way to open harbor, and then to the sea. Dark waves capped by moonlight, and a wake of blue-white foam behind them. When the ride was smooth enough for study, Senzei took out his maps again and began to go over them with Ciani. Trying to inspire her enthusiasm? Damien winced at the memory of how lively she had been only a handful of days ago. And he ached anew, for the loss of the woman he had come to know so well.

After a time he moved to the bow of the small ship, and tried to make out the shape of what would be Morgot. But the island was too dark, or too small, or else too far away. For a moment he thought he saw mountains in the distance—but no, those must be low-lying clouds that fooled his eye. The northern mountains were too far away to be glimpsed from here.

"You're apprehensive."

He whipped about, a combat-trained reaction. How did the man manage to come up so close behind him without him being aware of it?

"Shouldn't I be?" he retorted stiffly.

Gerald Tarrant chuckled. "Here, where no rakh-born demon can reach you? Remember the power of deep water, priest. They can't even sense your trail, over this."

He moved so that he could look out over the waves without quite losing sight of Tarrant. Miles upon miles of water surrounded them, flowing over earth and earth-fae alike. Far beneath them, hidden from sight, the currents still flowed northward, but they clung to the surface of the earth's crust. Here, above the waves, such power was all but inaccessible. Faeborn creatures usually avoided crossing bodies of water for that reason; shallow waters might rob them of their special powers, and deep enough waters might cost them their life.

He wondered if the creature called the Hunter could survive such a crossing. Was that why he sent out his minions, his constructs, but never left the Forest himself? Or was his form simply so *unhuman* that the men who plied the straits for a living would respond poorly to his overtures—unlike their response to the elegant, courteous Gerald Tarrant?

Easy, priest. One quest at a time. Let's clean up the rakhlands first, then take a good look at the Forest. Too many battles at once will cost you everything.

Black water, pale blue moons. Domina overhead, rising as they sailed northwards, and the whiter crescent of Casca counter-rising in the west: a heavenly counterpoint. For an instant he sensed a greater Pattern forming between them, as if the tides of light and gravity were cojoined with the rhythms of lunar rotation in a delicate, ever-shifting web of power. Then the moment was gone, and the night was merely dark.

"Yes," Tarrant whispered. "That was it."

Damien looked up at him.

"Tidal fae. The most tenuous of all powers—and the most potent."

The silver eyes looked down on him, reflecting the cool blue of moonlight. "You're a very fortunate man, Reverend Vryce. Few men ever see such a thing."

"It was beautiful."

"Yes," Tarrant agreed. There was a strange hush to his voice. "The tidal power is that."

"Can it be worked?"

"Not by such as you or I," he responded. "Sometimes women can See it—very rarely—but no human I know of has ever mastered it. Too variable a power. Very dangerous."

Damien looked up at him. "You've tried," he said quietly.

"In my youth," he agreed. "I tried everything. That particular experiment nearly killed me." The pale eyes sparkled with some secret amusement. "Does it comfort you, to imagine I could die?"

"We're all mortal," he said gruffly.

"Are we?"

"All of us. Even the faeborn."

"Certainly the faeborn. They lack the innovation—and thus the initiative—to make it otherwise. But men? With all this power waiting to be harnessed? Have you never dreamed of immortality, priest? Never once wondered what the fae might do for you, if you harnessed it to fend off death?"

Something stirred inside Damien, that was half pride and half faith. It was the core of his strength, and he wielded it proudly. "I think you forget the God I serve," he told Tarrant. "Those of my calling neither fear death, nor doubt their own immortality."

For a brief moment, there was something in the other man's expression that was strangely human. Strangely vulnerable. And then the moment was gone and the cold, mocking mask was back in place. "Touché," he muttered, with a slight bow. "I should know better than to fence rhetoric with your kind. My apologies."

And abruptly he left, for the company of the others. Damien just stared after him. Wondering what it was that he had seen in Tarrant's face—so fleeting, but so very *human*—and wondering why it was that that brief hint of humanity chilled him more than all other facets of the man combined.

Morgot. It took shape slowly on the horizon, a mountain of deep gray jutting up from the glassy blackness of the water. As they came closer, Damien could make out details, etched in moonlight: the jag-

ged upper edge of a crater's rim, the thick mass of vegetation clinging
to its slopes, the place where the walls had collapsed into the sea,
permitting entrance into the crater's mouth. Dark, all of it dark. Was
there no night life on Morgot?

Then, as if in answer to his thoughts, a bright light flashed on one
side of the entrance gap. It was followed seconds later by a matching
light on the other side, of the same angle and intensity. The ship's
captain hurried toward the mirrored lamp that was affixed to the
forward mast. He struck a match and applied it; flame surged upward
in the glass enclosure, made triply brilliant by the mirrors behind it.
Using shutters to focus its beam, he turned it toward the challenging
lights at the caldera's entrance. Short and long bursts of light in carefully measured proportion flashed across the water toward Morgot; a
few seconds later, a similar code was returned. The captain muttered
to himself as he interpreted Morgot's messages, reciting weather
warnings, customs codes, docking instructions. At last he seemed
satisfied and shuttered the signal lantern.

"Cleared to go in," he muttered—then added, for his passengers'
benefit, "Risky passage at night. Could be worse, though." He
grinned. "Could be moonless."

He moved to the stern of the boat, then, and kicked the small
furnace open. Inside, an orange fire hungrily consumed its store of
fuel. He fed it more. Then, when he was satisfied that the heat was
as it should be, and that the volume of steam thus produced was to
his satisfaction, he engaged the boat's small turbine. For some
minutes more he remained by the mechanism, following each motion
with his eye, reaffirming the patterns of how it worked in his own
mind. That was necessary to counteract any doubts his passengers
might have had about it, as well as the formless fears of the horses.
The deep water beneath them meant that such fears couldn't manifest too easily, but it never hurt to make sure. One good jinxer on
board and the whole mechanism could blow sky high.

When he was finally satisfied with the machine's performance, he
ordered the sails struck and steered them toward Morgot. Entering
the gap in the crater wall was like entering a tunnel: dark, silent but
for the sound of the turbine, claustrophobically close. The crater's
ragged edge towered over them on both sides, massive walls of igne-
ous rock that seemed precariously balanced, dangerously topheavy.
What little moonlight seeped down into the narrow passage only
worsened the illusion, and Damien found himself holding his breath,
all too aware of what the most minimal earthquake could do to such
a structure. And earthquakes there must be in quantity, right at the
heart of a collision zone. But then, just when it seemed that their

boat wouldn't make it through to the end, the gap widened. Enough so that another boat, traveling in the opposite direction, could pass them in safety. They came about a sharp jag in the wall—

And Morgot's interior unfolded before them in all its luminous splendor.

Stars. That was Damien's first impression: a universe filled with stars, upon whose light they floated. On all sides the crater's walls rose up about them, its curving slopes lit by thousands upon thousands of tiny flickering lights: lanterns, hearth-lights, port markers, open fires. Lights flickered along the shoreline, lights lined the crater's ridge, lights shone from every boat and pier—and all of it was reflected in the rippling harbor water, each light mirrored a thousand times over, each image dancing energetically to the rhythm of the waves. They were in a vast bowl filled with stars, floating in a dark summer sky. The beauty of it—and the disorientation—was breathtaking.

He heard soft footsteps coming up behind him, guessed at their source. But not even Tarrant could make him turn from that glorious vision.

"Welcome to the north," the man said quietly.

Colored lanterns marked each of the boats in the harbor; their captain fitted a colored gel to his own signal lantern, and red sparks danced in the water on all sides of them. "Not bad, eh? Best beer in the eastlands, to bet. It's out of Jahanna."

"Jahanna?"

"The Forest," Senzei explained. He and Ciani had come up to join them at the bow, to watch the sea of scarlet stars part before their hull.

"The Forest makes beer?"

The captain grinned. "Can you think of something that place'd need more, besides a good drink?"

The harbor was busy—so much so that Damien wondered if Earth hadn't looked like this, once; a place where night contained no special dangers, where business—and pleasure—might be conducted at any hour. What was Earth like now? It had been half-covered in steel and concrete when the colony ships first left it. How many tens of thousands of years ago was that? The colonists had crossed a third of the galaxy in coldsleep to get here; how many Earth-years would that take? Damien knew the theories—and he also knew that any real knowledge of how interstellar travel had worked had been destroyed in the First Sacrifice. All they had left were guesses.

The efficacy of sacrifice, the Prophet had written, *is in direct proportion to the value of that which is destroyed.*

And Ian Casca damned well knew that, Damien thought bitterly. *And understood its implications, all too well. If only they could have stopped him. . . .* But there was no point in pursuing that train of thought, and he knew it. What was done was done. If mere regret could have brought the Earth ship back, it would have done that long ago.

Wending his way through a bewildering array of light and shadow, the captain brought them unerringly to the proper pier, and came up against it with hardly a bump to jar their concentration. The horses looked up slowly, dazed, and Damien and his two companions moved to get them off the boat before their full faculties returned.

When they had finished that job, Damien turned to pay the captain for their passage—and found Gerald Tarrant counting out coins from a small velvet purse. Gold, by the look of it.

"That isn't necessary—"

"The Forest pays its servants well," he said shortly. "Which is why such men are willing to serve us at inconvenient hours." Then he looked up at Damien; his pale eyes sparkled. "*One* of the reasons."

"Damien." It was Ciani; she pointed along the pier with one hand, holding reins in the other. A man in uniform was walking toward them.

"Police?"

"Probably customs." Tarrant tucked the small purse into his outer tunic, then opened that garment at the neck. The gold of the Forest medallion glinted conspicuously between layers of blue and black silk. "I'll take care of it."

"Is there anything you haven't prearranged?" Damien said sharply.

He seemed amused. "You mean, do I ever leave anything to chance?" He smiled. "Not by choice, priest."

He moved off to deal with the official. When he was out of hearing, Damien walked over to where Ciani was, and helped her fasten the travel packs back onto their mounts.

"He's interesting," he said quietly. An opening.

"And you're jealous."

He stepped back and feigned astonishment.

She tightened the last strap on her own mount's harness, then turned to him. "Well, you are." She was smiling—not broadly, not energetically, but with genuine humor. *It's a start,* he thought. "Admit it."

And suddenly he wanted her. Wanted her as he had in Jaggonath, wanted any little bit of the old Ciani that was left inside her, wanted to take that bit and nurture it and coax it into life, until she could look at him and smile like that and her eyes would be the same, her expression would be what it once had been ... and that precious feeling would be there again, binding them, making them oblivious to Tarrant and the rakh and all such mundane concerns.

The sudden rush of emotion took his breath away; with effort he managed, "Tarrant?"

"Deny it," she dared him.

"*Jealous?*"

"Damien." She stepped forward toward him, close enough to touch. And she put a hand to the side of his face, soft warm palm against the coarseness of a long day's stubble. "Women know things like that. Did you think you were hiding it?" Her eyes sparkled—and it did seem that there was life in them, a hint of a younger, unviolated Ciani. "You're not a subtle man, you know."

He was about to respond when Senzei coughed diplomatically: Tarrant was back. Damien stepped back from Ciani, putting a less intimate distance between them—but there was an unspoken challenge in his expression as he turned to face the Forest's servant, and he knew without doubt that it communicated exactly what he meant it to.

"Can you pick up a trail?" he asked him.

"Unlikely," Tarrant answered. "Not here, at any rate. A live volcano exudes its own fae, in quantity; that, and the strength of the northbound current, will muddy the trail considerably." He looked up toward the crest of the cone, at the lights that marked the crater's upper edge. "Perhaps up there it can be managed. Perhaps. There should be an inn, at any rate, and the three of you will want refreshment." He began to lead them toward the narrow shoreline, but Damien stopped him.

"A *live* volcano?" he asked. "I thought Morgot was extinct. You're telling me this thing could go off beneath our feet?"

"The verb you're looking for is *vulk*. And as for this being an extinct volcano, there's no such thing. Not in a collision zone. All we know about Morgot is that it hasn't erupted while man has been present on Erna—a mere twelve hundred years. That's nothing, geologically speaking. Volcanoes can have a period considerably longer than that. Ten thousand years—one hundred thousand—perhaps even longer." He smiled. "Or twelve hundred and one, for that matter. So I would say that if you want to eat and get some kind of a fix on things we should start moving now. Who knows what the next hour may bring?"

"All the sorcerors in the Forest," Damien muttered to Ciani, "and we have to get a smartass."

She grinned at that. And he put his arm around her. And felt for the first time since leaving—the first time since the attack on the Fae Shoppe—that things were going to be all right. It would take a lot of work and one hell of a lot of risk to assure it . . . but that was what life was all about, wasn't it?

The path up to the inn was steep and narrow, a winding switchback road barely wide enough for them to traverse single file. Rushlights bordered the path along its outer edge, illuminating a sheer drop down to the rocky shore beneath.

"Lovely place," Damien muttered.

After what seemed like hours—but it must have been much less than that, the crater's edge simply wasn't *that* high up—the path widened out, and a broad shoulder developed along its outer edge. Soon trees became visible, their roots trailing down like tangled snakes, their bare branches breaking up the moonlight into webwork patterns across the road. As they continued, more and more trees began to crowd the shoulder until the harbor beneath them was no longer visible. Then they reached the crest itself—and they stopped for a moment, to gaze out upon one of the most infamous territories in man's domain.

"So close," Ciani whispered.

It was close. A mere channel separated Morgot's northern boundary from the shore of the mainland; it could be swum, if one were foolish enough to try it. Ferries plied the distance even as they watched, and disappeared into the base of the caldera. *Some kind of tunnel there*, Damien decided. And: *Hell of a lot of traffic for a place like that.*

"You make assumptions." It was Gerald Tarrant's voice, disconcertingly close behind him. "Where there is commerce, there will be men. And the Forest holds its own in trade."

But in what sort of goods? Damien thought darkly.

The inn at the head of the winding road was clearly a popular one. Half a dozen horses were roped to a lead rail outside the front door, and the stable-boy who ran out to greet them looked like he'd been used pretty hard for most of the night.

"Staying the day, mers?" he asked.

The travelers looked at each other—and at Tarrant—and at last Senzei answered, "Looks like it." To the others he said, "Go on inside. I'll unload."

The interior of the inn was dim and smoky, rushlights serving as

lamps along the outer walls. A fire burned in an open pit at the far
end of the room, but it wasn't quite enough to banish the autumn
chill. Despite the cold, Damien chose a table far from the fire; it was
quieter there, and somewhat more private. It seemed safer.

There were menus already waiting on the table, and Ciani opened
one as she sat. She looked at it for a moment, scanning its contents—
and then her eyes went wide.

"There's blood on the menu," she whispered.

"It's a rough place," Damien observed. He dropped his sword harness over the back of a chair.

Tarrant smiled coldly. "I don't believe that's what the lady meant."

He looked at her. She nodded slowly. And said, "There's blood
listed on the menu."

It took him a second to find his voice. "Animal or human?"

"Several varieties. I believe ..." She looked at the menu again.
"The human is more expensive."

"Tastes differ," Tarrant said quietly. "Morgot prides itself on being
hospitable to all travelers."

"And what will you be having?"

He laughed softly. "Nothing, for now. I thought that while the
three of you ate I might take a look around."

"At the fae?"

"If it's possible. There was a nice little clearing about a hundred
yards back. It should offer as good a view as any. I'll be back shortly,"
he promised.

You do that, Damien thought.

Senzei joined them a few minutes later, their valuables in tow.
Then a young boy, introducing himself as Hash, offered to serve as
their waiter. The blood? he said, in response to Damien's query.
Quite healthy. Freshness guaranteed. Now, if the gentleman had a
particular *type* in mind. . . .

Damien shuddered, and told him just to bring a drink. Anything
that wasn't red. He didn't hear what Senzei and Ciani ordered; his
attention was fixed on the door to the outside, his imagination fixed
on the man just beyond it.

"You worried?" Senzei asked.

Damien looked at him sharply. "Shouldn't I be?"

"Why don't you go check on him?"

He started to protest, then stopped himself. And stood. "I will," he
promised. "If the food comes before I get back . . ." *Then something
has gone very wrong.* "Eat without me," he said simply.

He took his sword with him.

Outside, the night was cold. They hadn't noticed it on the climb up—the climb itself must have warmed them—but now, alone in the darkness, he wrapped his jacket tightly about himself and thought, *Winter's coming. Traveling will get harder. Everything will get harder.*

Coming up north didn't help.

A short distance from the inn's front door, he found a small clearing that looked out over the harbor. Gerald Tarrant was standing there, eyes slowly scanning the crater's interior. Once. Twice. Again.

At last, Damien dared, "Anything?"

He hesitated. "Hard to say. A trace, perhaps. Hard to focus on. Nearly every signal is drowned out by the volcano's outpouring . . . very little is comprehensible. The image of someone *watching* stands out—not our quarry, I might add—and a taint at the harbor's mouth which might have been left by the ones we seek. But as for when they left here, or exactly where they went . . . the interference is simply too great."

"Like trying to search for a candle flame in front of the sun," Damien said quietly.

Tarrant glanced at him. "It's been a long time since I stared at the sun," he said dryly.

Damien stepped forward—and was about to speak, when the slamming of the inn's door warned him that someone else was about to join them. He looked back the way he had come and saw Ciani running toward them. Senzei was right behind her.

When she came to where the two men stood she stopped, and then hesitated; there was a sense of *wrongness* about her that Damien was hard put to identify, but it was enough to put him on his guard. Senzei tried to put a restraining hand on her arm, but she pulled away sharply.

"I want to be here," she told them. Something about the cadence of her voice seemed oddly wrong, as though the words were being forced out. By her, or someone else? "When things are decided. I *need* to be here. Please. . . ."

"She just got up and left," Senzei said. "I tried to stop her, but she didn't give me any warning. I had to leave the stuff behind—"

Damien strode to her, quickly. His heart was pounding in a fevered rhythm he knew all too well, and he felt his sword hand tensing in combat readiness as he took her firmly by the arm and said, "We're going back. Now. We can talk inside. You should never have come out here, Cee. . . ." *And would never have,* he thought grimly. *Not without some sorcerous influence to cloud your judgment.*

"—Too late for that." Tarrant said softly. He nodded toward the trees on the far side of the road, to where motion that was not windborn stirred the dying branches. Ciani's eyes, mesmerized, followed the motion. "They have us," the tall man whispered.

And the creatures attacked. Not merely three of them now, but a band whose numbers had clearly been swelled by reinforcements. They came from the far side of the road, and Damien had barely a moment to reflect that if luck had been against them—if Tarrant had chosen that side of the caldera's rim for his efforts—the humans would have been slaughtered before they could make a move to defend themselves. As it was, there was less than a second before they struck, and Damien used it. He shoved Ciani behind him, hard, and drew his sword in one sweeping motion. "Get her!" he hissed to Senzei—and thank God, the man understood. He ran behind Damien—unarmed, the priest noticed, damn the luck!—to get hold of Ciani before she could recover herself. So that whatever power had taken control of her mind, it couldn't force her back into the center of things.

Then the creatures were upon him, and as he swung the keen blade into them he felt himself giving ground, trying to retreat to some position that would keep the enemy from surrounding him. There were too many, they were too fast, and there was simply no cover in sight . . . bad, it was very bad. If he'd had more than an instant to think about it, the fear might have frozen his limbs; as it was, he channeled all his tension into his sword blade, and it struck his first opponent's blade with enough power to force back the crude steel, so that his blade bit into flesh and the creature's blood—dark purple, glisteningly unhuman—began to flow. But it was only a drop in a flood tide of violence, and he knew as he recovered his sword that were simply too many of them, that sooner or later they must surely overwhelm him—

And then, without warning, light filled the clearing. Cold light that blinded but did not illuminate—that washed the moonlit battlefield in a chill blue luminescence, whose presence seemed to intensify rather than drive back the shadows. *Tarrant,* he thought darkly, as he brought up his sword to defend himself from another blow. *Must be.* He dared to twist his head around for an instant—only an instant—and saw the tall figure standing with sword drawn beside him. The chill light came from that slender steel and was as blinding as a sun to look upon; Damien fell back as his vision was seared into near-uselessness, trusting to instinct rather than sight to fight for a moment of recovery. He saw the blazing unlight arc, heard it bite into the flesh of their nearest opponent. An icy wind whipped at his face, as if the blow itself were sucking the heat right out of him. And then two of the creatures were upon him—or was it three?—and the whole of his energy had to go to fighting them off. He felt the shock of a sword stroke reverberate against his own steel, tried to draw back into a parry that would defend against his second opponent—but they were too fast, there were too many of them, and he felt sharp steel bite into his arm, releasing a gush of warm blood down his shirt sleeve. *Can't do it*, he thought despairingly—and, with bitter determination: *Have to*. He was aware of Senzei behind him, struggling to keep Ciani out of the line of battle. Both of them unarmed. Helpless. He saw Tarrant swing again by his side, saw the brilliant unlight cut into another one of the creatures. But: *Not enough*, he thought. He felt the cold bite of fear deep inside him as he swung again, forcing one of his opponents back. Trying not to open himself up to the others while he did so. *Not enough!*

And then, everything stopped. Suddenly. It was as if the air about them had suddenly become solid; as if both their bodies and their minds had been paralyzed. For a moment, there was no movement—not even thought—only the physical shock of forced immobility. Utter fear . . . and wonder.

At the far side of the road, a figure stood. The cold blue unlight hinted at a form that was human in shape, tightly bound in layers of cloth. Female. Though only her face was visible, and that was without expression, Damien was suddenly overcome by the sense that she was suffering—had suffered—would suffer endlessly, unless he helped. For one blind moment there was no armed enemy in his universe, no Tarrant, not even Senzei or Ciani: only this one strange figure, whose need for his help overwhelmed all his defensive instincts, drawing him forward. . . .

And then the paralysis that gripped him shattered like breaking glass. He could hear Tarrant's sharply drawn breath beside him, but he had no time to contemplate its cause—because *they* had turned toward her, all of them, and he could taste the hunger rising in them like some palpable thing, a tide of malevolence that made the bile rise in his throat. They were responding to the same image that he was, drawn by the woman's utter vulnerability. But their instinct was not to defend, but to devour. Not to protect, but to rend. He saw them moving toward her and gripped his sword tightly, then lunged—and felt his sword tip thrust through the back of one of the creatures, just beside the spine. He forced the steel to shove through—blade horizontal, thrusting through ribs and flesh and out again through the chest, steel grating against bone as it passed. Then he jerked it out, hard, and prepared himself for a return assault. But there was none. The creatures were wholly fixated upon their prey, oblivious to all but their hunger and her helplessness. She had stepped back from the road now, into the limited shelter of the trees, and as the creatures moved forward to take her, as Damien moved forward to take *them*, he could almost see the power radiating forth from her, lancing forth to the moons and the stars and back again, a rainbow web of fae that shimmered about her like some translucent silk. *Tidal fae*, he thought in wonder, as he swung again. Targeting the head of one of the creatures. *She's Worked us all.*

The full force of his moulinet smashed into the creature's skull, shattering it in a cloud of blood and hair bits. The body of his victim went flying across the road, brains and bone shards spilling out across the feet of its fellows. It got their attention at last. The nearer one turned and looked at Damien—and blinked, like a man awakening from deep sleep. The priest thrust, but it was too late; the creature managed to dodge him, stumbling, and quickly backed away. He heard a muffled scream behind him, and the blood ran cold in his veins at the sound of it. Ciani? Where the hell was Senzei, and what was Tarrant doing? He didn't dare take a moment to look. The woman's spell was rapidly fading, and the creatures were but an instant away from attacking anew. He braced himself for a second onslaught— how many of them were there, now? Four? Five?—but to his surprise, they made no move toward him. He tried to advance and found himself suddenly dizzy; his left arm was warm and wet and becoming weak. How much blood had he lost? No matter. Against even odds he could stand his ground and parry, but against so many opponents he must press for any advantage, never let them regain the initiative. . . .

They moved. Suddenly. Not toward him, as he had expected. Nor toward the strange woman, or even Ciani. Away. Their legs splattered with the blood of their fallen comrades, their feet treading on bits of bone . . . they ran. Bolted like animals into the brush. Damien moved to follow . . . and then stopped and drew in a deep breath. He fought the urge to look down at his arm and looked instead at the woman. She was still there, but the power surrounding her had faded; whatever she was, she was no longer Working.

Ciani!

He turned back toward the clearing, heart pounding. Toward a tableau that was as chilling as the one which he had just witnessed. Senzei lay on the ground, half-stunned, his stomach and side drenched in blood; barely two feet away lay the body of the creature who must have gotten to him, now decapitated. There was another such creature on the far side of the tableau, similarly dispatched. Whatever else Tarrant's sword might be, it was efficient enough in battle. But as for the man himself. . . .

He stood in the center of the clearing, eyes blazing in hatred and defiance. In his right hand he still held the sword, and its chill glow made his pale flesh look like something long dead. And in his other arm . . . Ciani lay there, limp and unmoving, her one visible hand as white and as bloodless as ivory. Where he pressed her against him there was blood, and it trickled down from under her hair to his shirt sleeve as though binding them together. For an instant it was as if Damien could See the very power that linked them, and he stiffened as he recognized its nature. Hating, as he had never hated before.

"You bastard!" he hissed. "You were one of them all the time!"

The rage in Tarrant's eyes was like a black fire, that sucked the very heat from Damien's soul. "Don't be a fool!" he whispered fiercely. The words came hard, as though he were struggling for speech. "You don't understand. You *can't* understand."

"You did what they did," he said. Seeing the flow of power between them, sensing the new emptiness inside her. "You took her memories. Deny it!"

Tarrant shut his eyes for an instant, as if struggling with something inside himself. Damien gauged the distance between them, Ciani's position, his own fading strength—and then the moment was gone, and the black gaze was fixed on him again. Shadowed, as if in pain.

"I became what she feared the most," the man whispered. "Because that's what I am." He spoke the words as if he didn't quite believe them himself, and as he looked down at Ciani he seemed to shudder. Senzei, behind him, began to stir weakly—and the look that Tarrant shot at him told Damien that not all of the man's wounds had been imposed by the enemy.

"Tried to stop him," Senzei gasped. "Tried. . . ."

Slowly, Damien sheathed his sword. Pain pierced through his arm like fire, but he gritted his teeth and managed to ignore it. Ever aware of the hot blood that was dripping from his wounded arm, he snapped open the pouch affixed to his belt. Inside it, in a carefully padded interior, two special flasks lay side by side. One was silver, and now held most of the Church's precious Fire—the Patriarch's gift. The other, its original vial, was glass; if he threw it hard enough it would shatter on contact, and the moisture still clinging to its inner surface should be enough to burn the life from any nightborn demon.

"Don't be a fool!" Tarrant hissed. He seemed to draw back—but whether in fear or in preparation for a Working, Damien couldn't say.

"You claiming power over this as well?" He drew it out—and even as little moisture as remained in the fragile vial was enough to send beams of golden light lancing through the clearing. Tarrant breathed in sharply in pain as they struck him, but made no effort to escape them.

"You idiot . . . do you really think you can hurt me with that? I can blast the ground beneath your feet faster than you can move— or the air between us, before you can take a breath."

"Give me Ciani," Damien said coldly.

Tarrant winced. Seemed to be struggling within himself. At last he whispered, hoarsely, "You can't help her now."

"Give her to me!"

If he didn't throw the flask then, it was because of the expression that came over the man's face: so human, so strangely tormented, that for a moment he was too shaken to attack.

Tarrant's voice was hoarse. "I vowed once that I would never hurt this woman. But when that woman's Working hit, with the full force of the tidal fae behind it . . . it awakened a hunger too intense. I *feed* on vulnerability, priest—and she was too close. Too helpless. *I lost control.*"

"So much for your precious vow," Damien growled.

Something flickered in those lightless eyes that was not rage or hatred. Pain? "The true cost of that is beyond your comprehension," he whispered.

Damien took a step forward. The clearing spun dizzily about him. "*Give her to me,*" he demanded.

Tarrant shook his head, slowly. "You can't help her," he said. "Not without killing me."

His fingers tightened on the flask. "Then we'll just have to try that, won't we?"

The Hunter tensed. He raised his sword overhead, a gesture more of display than of active aggression—and if Damien hesitated for an instant, it was in the hope that the man would let go of Ciani before he attacked. So that she would be out of danger. But then the blazing sword was suddenly thrust point downward into the earth, deep into the dirt between them—

And earth-fae met earth-fae in an explosion that rocked the entire ridge. The ground erupted toward Damien, a wall of dirt and shattered stone that hit him like a tidal wave. He was knocked to the ground with stunning force, half buried by the clumps of earth and gravel and rotting wood that the explosion had thrown at him. With a moan he tried to move, but the effort was too much; he tried to close his hand, to see if he still held the precious vial, but his fingers were numb and packed in earth, helpless to move. He made one last effort to get himself up, or at least to dislodge some portion of the debris that covered him . . . but it was too much, or else the blood loss was too much, or all of it was too much combined. He slid down slowly into darkness—and even the curse that might have accompanied his passing was muffled by the earth, and went unheard.

Twenty-two

Dirt. Clogging his nostrils. *Dirt filling his mouth and throat, mud-wet with blood. Pounds upon pounds of it, covering him over like grave-filling, burying him alive. He struggles, coughs, tries to take in air. Fights to free himself from the monstrous weight that pins him down—tries to turn over, or sit up, or even just raise up an arm, any sign of life—but the earth clings to him like an incubus, mud-fingers gripping his clothing, pulling him down. . . .*

"Damien."

He pits all his strength against the weight of the earth above him and feels himself move at last, so that he can strike out at the fingers that clutch at him—

"Damien!"

Hundreds of them gripping his skin, holding him down. He strikes out with all his strength at the creature that must be out there, somewhere, whose hands dig so deeply into his flesh that it seems they must draw blood—

"Damien, you hit me once more, I'll give it to you good. You understand me? Damien!"

He drew in a deep breath, slowly. No dirt. The hundreds of fingers became dozens, became ten. He opened one eye—the other seemed to be swollen shut—and studied a hazy outline that might or might not be Senzei.

"Thank the gods," the sorceror muttered. "You all right?"

It seemed that the words had miles to travel before they got to his mouth. "I . . ." He coughed heavily, and the dirt-filled mucus that clogged his throat loosened; the words came easier. "I think so. Where's Ciani?"

"Gone." Senzei's face was coming into focus now—pale, bruised, hollowed by misery. "He took her."

"Where?" He tried to sit up. Pain lanced through all his limbs and his head—especially his head—with such searing force that he fell back, gasping. "Where, Zen?"

"Take it easy." There was another hand, now, smaller and gentler, and it laid a cool cloth against his brow. Damien snatched it away.

"Where, Zen?"

He hesitated. "The Forest is my guess. As good as any. She said he went north—"

He managed to get his other eye open; a second Senzei swam hazily in his vision. "Who said that?"

"The woman."

"The one who . . ." He floundered for words.

"Yeah. That one."

"Merciful God." He raised up a hand to rub his temple, but the touch of flesh against flesh burned him like acid. "What happened, Zen? Tell me."

The sorceror reached out and took his hand, and gently put it down by his side. "Take a deep breath first." Damien started to protest, then obeyed. He coughed raggedly. "Again." The next one went down a bit easier. He took a few more voluntarily, until the flow of air seemed a bit more reliable.

Then he forced both eyes open and took a look around. It was a small room, windowless; Senzei was standing by the bed on one side, a plain, middle-aged woman was seated on the other. An older man in more formal clothing stood at the foot of the bed, scowling in disapproval. After seeing that Damien was both conscious and coherent, the latter figure stalked out.

"Tell me," the priest whispered.

"After Tarrant—" Senzei drew in a shaky breath. "There was an explosion. Most of it went your way, I think. It must have knocked you out. It hit me, too, but not nearly as hard. I thought I saw a figure picking its way over the mounds of earth . . . it must have been him. I couldn't see Ciani. No details. I passed out. No idea how long. When I came to again . . ." He bit his lower lip, remembering. "There was something on top of you. Feeding. The woman was pulling it back, twisting its neck so it would let go . . . it had scaled wings, and a tongue like a snake, and its mouth was dripping with blood . . . she snapped its head off. Just like that. And threw it over the edge, harbor-side. Then she . . . she dug the dirt out of your mouth, so you could breathe. And she took something out of her clothing and rubbed it on your arm, where the wound was. She did some other things—I couldn't see clearly, I was barely conscious myself—and then she stood, and this . . . some kind of animal came to her, walking like a horse but it looked like something else, and it had two long horns, like rainbow glass. . . ." He closed his eyes, remembering; his voice sank to a whisper. "I asked, where did he go? For a moment, she didn't acknowledge me. Then she looked out toward the northlands, and pointed there. "Forest," she said. "Where men devour men." He coughed heavily. "Then she mounted and rode off. I tried to get to you, so I could help—but I couldn't. I couldn't move. The pain was so bad . . . I thought I was dying. Then the sun rose, and they came to help."

"They?"

"From the inn. They'd heard the explosion." He glanced at the woman, then away. His voice was bitter. "They waited till dawn before they went outside. Afraid for their precious skins. So we lay there without help till then. The sun rose, and they came outside and got us. They did what they could for our wounds. They gave us blood. You were delirious. It's been hours. . . ."

Damien tried to sit up. The room swirled around him, and blood pounded hotly in his temples . . . and he tried it again. And again. On the third try, he succeeded.

"We need to go," he muttered.

Senzei nodded. No questions about why, or where. He understood. "You're in bad shape," he warned.

"How bad?"

"The doctor said you'd be out for days."

"So much for that diagnosis. What else?"

"Blood loss, concussion, possible internal damage—he wasn't sure on that last one, might have thrown it in just to cover all the bases. The wound in your arm seems to be closing up all right—whatever she put on it seems to have kept it from getting infected—but all the stitches in the world won't keep it from opening up if you use it too much. And you're bruised like all hell."

"That's par for the course," he said. "What about you?"

Senzei hesitated. "Took a thrust in one side. Pretty ugly, very bloody, but nothing vital was hit. Or so it seems. Hurts like hell— but that goes without saying. The doctor said not to exert myself until it heals."

Damien noted the stiffness with which he moved, the thickness about his middle where bandages were no doubt layered. "She didn't do anything for you? The woman, I mean."

Senzei looked away. "No," he said softly. "I've been thinking about it a lot since it happened. At this point I'm not even sure she meant to save our lives. I mean, the timing was certainly fortunate, but it seems like a chancy way to enter a fight. I think she meant it as a kind of . . . test, maybe. To see what we would do. I think . . . she helped you because you tried to save her. Because that was your first instinct, when her Working hit."

"So what was yours?" Damien asked quietly.

Senzei bit his lip. Shook his head. "Let's not discuss it, all right? Few of us are as perfect as we'd like to be."

Damien forced himself to look away. "All right. You're hurt, I'm hurt . . . simple flesh wounds, maybe an infection or two. Nothing I can't Heal."

"Oh, yeah? Using what fae?"

Damien stared at him. And realized what he meant. "Shit."

"I've been a Worker all my life, you know. Moved the toys near my crib without touching them, and all that. Now . . ." He wrapped his arms about himself and shivered. "It almost killed me in Kale. It'd be a thousand times worse here, this close to the Forest. I think I'd rather bleed."

"We can't wait for nature to heal us before we leave."

"I know that," he whispered.

Damien swung his legs over the side of the bed. The pounding in his head—and the pain—had subsided to a mere throbbing drumbeat. "He can only travel at night, right? It was well past midnight when he left here. Dawn came soon after that, and the sun's still up. That means he got, what, three hours of travel time on us? We push hard, we've got him." He looked at Senzei. "*If* we leave now."

"All our things are packed," Senzei said quietly.

"Can you make it?"

The sorceror looked at him sharply. "Can you?"

"No question," he said. "He's got Ciani."

Senzei nodded. "Same here."

Damien drew in a deep breath, tried to gather his thoughts. "If we're moving fast, we won't want all the horses. We'll keep three— two for us, one for backup. And for Ciani. Drop off some of the duplicate supplies in Mordreth, hopefully where we can get at them later . . . but if not, not. We strip down and travel fast. Get that son of a bitch before he knows what hit him."

"You really think we can take him?"

"Oh, I've killed nastier things. None of them were quite so elo- quent . . . but remember, we're not playing by his rules this time. And I do have a weapon that'll hurt him." He reached for the padded pouch at his belt—and suddenly panicked, when he realized it wasn't there. "Zen, they—"

"It's here." He reached to the side of the bed, where the pouch and its supporting belt lay coiled atop a small table. "They took it off you when they cleaned you up. I didn't let it out of my sight."

"Good man." He opened the flap of the pouch, and saw both the silver flask and the crystal vial cushioned within. The latter had dirt encrusted in its delicately etched surface; he picked at it with a fingernail and muttered, "I'm surprised this survived."

"You had it gripped so tightly it didn't have a chance to get broken. Even in your delirium you wouldn't let go; we had to pry it out of your fingers."

Damien tried to fasten the belt around himself, but his wounded arm—swollen, stiff, and throbbing with pain—lacked the dexterity. Senzei helped him.

"You sure you can make it?"

Damien glared. "I have to. We both have to." He patted the pouch into place over his hip, felt the outline of the flat silver flask within. "I guess if we're going to leave the extra horses behind, we should try to sell them. We've been going through capital like water—"

"I sold three of them this morning," Senzei told him. "Not a great price, but it covered the medical bills. And I gathered our things—what was left of them—and settled with the people here, for their time and supplies. And I found this." He dropped a small golden object onto the bed beside Damien. It took the priest a moment to realize what it was.

"My God," he whispered. He picked it up, and held it by the broken chain so that the earth-disk dangled before his eyes. Its reverse side, engraved with a delicate sigil, caught the light as it turned.

"I found it near where he'd been standing. She must have pulled it off him when he attacked her. Damned lucky accident, don't you think?"

"Knowing Ciani, I would say . . . not an accident at all." He imagined her in that last moment of terror, some precious particle of her mind clinging to sanity long enough to reason out what they might need, striking out in seeming chaos until his tunic front was torn open, until her fingers closed over the precious gold and pulled. . . .

"What a woman," he breathed. "Give me ten like that, and I could take an empire."

Senzei forced a smile. "It's getting hard enough just keeping track of one."

Slowly, Damien eased himself forward. He braced both his hands against the edge of the bed—and paused for a minute, breathing heavily. Then he pushed upward, forcing his legs to bear the weight. Pain shot like fire up his left arm—but it was going to do that for quite some time, he might as well get used to it. After a moment, he managed to stand. A few seconds more, and the room stopped spinning. He managed a step. Two. The room was steady. The pain in his arm subsided to a stabbing throb.

"All right," he said. He looked at Senzei. "Let's do it."

"And no more going unarmed," he said harshly, as the ferry carried them across to Mordreth. "I want you with a weapon on you at all times. That means if you go behind the bushes to take a piss, you have a sword in your hand when you do it. You go off to bed a woman, I want a sword on the pillow next to you. Got me?"

Senzei looked out over the water. "I guess I deserve that."

"Damn right you do. It's a miracle you didn't get yourself killed out there. And miracles rarely repeat themselves."

There were a number of small tables at the center of the ferry, a few of them occupied by travelers: eager merchants conversing over lists of merchandise, a group of laborers quickly bolting down sandwiches, a nursing mother. Damien found them a vacant table and pulled over two chairs for them.

"Let's get to work."

He spilled out a box of ammunition on the table between them, picked one bolt up and turned it about, thoughtfully. The short wooden shaft had a metal tip on one end, a curved band on the other. He took out his pocket knife and, with the tip, tried to pry off the two metal pieces. The tip came off easily. The band at the base was tight, and took some work.

"Wax," he muttered. "Adhesive."

Senzei rummaged through the pack that held their smaller supply items. After a few minutes he managed to find a small chunk of amber wax. The stick of glue took longer.

"Would there be any point in asking what you're doing?"

"Preparing for war," Damien muttered. "Watch and learn."

He laid the naked shaft before him on the table, and rolled it over until he was satisfied with the placement of the grain. Then, carefully, he used his knife blade to split it open. It took little encouragement to get it to crack open along the grain, down the length of the shaft.

He looked about to see if anyone was watching. But the other passengers were perusing their own work at their own tables, or sitting on the long benches that flanked the staircase to the second

level, casually chatting, or else standing at the rail that guarded the
edge of the deck, watching the muddy green water course by.

He took the silver flask out of its pouch and carefully—reverently—
opened it. And he dribbled a few precious drops down the exposed
center of the wooden shaft, until the Fire was absorbed into the wood.
The shaft glowed dully, like cooling charcoal.

"Now." He capped the flask and put it beside him—carefully, oh
so carefully—and took the glue from Senzei. The halves went
together easily, with only a narrow scar where his knife had been
applied. Next he briskly rubbed the wax onto the surface of the shaft,
until the whole of it was coated. The metal tip and anchoring band
he glued carefully back in place.

"There." He set the finished product before him. It looked little
different than the other bolts, and Senzei had to fight to keep himself
from Working his sight to see if there was indeed a difference. The
change would be visible enough when molecules of the Fire, seeping
through the dry wood, reached the surface of the shaft. Maybe.

"You think it'll work?"

"I think it can't hurt to try. A few dozen drops of Fire at risk . . .
and if it works, it gives us one hell of an arsenal." He looked up at
Senzei—and for an instant, just an instant, the sorceror thought he
saw a flicker of fear in the priest's eyes. He felt his own throat
tighten, knowing what it must take to cause such a thing.

*You're the brave one, Damien. If you give in . . . I don't know if I
can handle it.*

"You okay?" the priest said quietly.

He met his eyes. And managed to shrug. "I'll be all right."

"There's nearly two hours of daylight left. We should reach the
Forest's border by then. He can't be too far ahead of us. If we can
find a physical trail—"

"And what if we can't?"

Damien forced his knife into the center of another shaft. The wood
snapped apart with a sharp crack, into two nearly equal halves.

"Then I'll have to Work to find one," he said quietly. "Won't I?"

Mordreth. It was a mining town, a gold rush town, a trapper's
camp . . . and all the worst elements of those things combined, with
none of their redeeming features. It was a transitory camp somehow
made permanent by sheer persistence on the shoreline, by the need

for its dismal bars and rat-trap inns and cheap entertainment halls, as well as the manpower that was its most precious commodity. But if the inhabitants of Mordreth had any hunger for beauty, they clearly indulged it elsewhere. The place was gray: muddy gray along the water, dirty gray in the streets, weathered gray about the houses. The only color that existed in the town was in a few garish signs, a tattered line of pennants, and occasionally the undergarments that the whores wore as they gathered in the brothel windows, beckoning to passing strangers.

Damien and Senzei rode through the muddy streets at a rapid pace; the horses seemed as anxious as they were to get through the town quickly. The place had an aura of entrapment about it—as if by staying too long within its borders, one might lose the will to leave. By the time they reached the far side of the dingy settlement Senzei was shivering—and not from the cold.

"You really want to leave our supplies here?" he asked.

Damien shook his head grimly but said nothing.

They rode through a long stretch of flatlands, the only vegetation sparse patches of dead grass that reminded them how very close at hand winter was. The ground was hard, nearly frozen. Which was something to be grateful for, Damien pointed out; in another season, it might have been mud.

Senzei was beginning to understand why he had never traveled.

A few miles later they came upon the first signs of human life. A scrap of cloth, lying in a clump of dead grass. The shards of a packing crate, long since dismembered. A circle of stones, blackened by fire, and beside it the marks of a recent encampment. Damien glanced at the latter once but gave it no more notice; their quarry would not be camping.

They rode on. The sun dropped lower and lower in the west, the colors of dusk adding their own special tenor to that sullen, swollen star. Greenish-yellow light spilled across the landscape: skies before a storm. It was becoming easier to spot the artifacts on the ground around them now, outlined as they were by vivid black shadows. They came to a low rise, then another. And another. Shallow rises became rolling hills: the vanguard of a mountain range. How far north had they come?

Senzei watched it all pass by, clutching himself against the chill of nightfall. The pain in his side was growing worse and worse, each jolt of the horse on the uneven ground driving spears of fire deep into his flesh. He tried to ignore it, tried to overcome the faintness that threatened to overwhelm him, the grayness that had fogged all but the very center of his field of vision. Because they couldn't afford to slow down, not for him. Slowing down meant losing Ciani. *Taking time to heal now is as good as committing her to death,* he told himself. And so he clung unsteadily to the saddle beneath him, and somehow managed to keep riding.

And then they came to it. Damien first, topping a particularly high rise. He pulled up suddenly, to the confusion of his mount. Senzei followed suit. The extra horse snorted in alarm and tried to break away, but their own two mounts were calm enough and a sharp jerk on the reins of the third served to discipline him for the moment.

They regarded their destination.

In the distance were trees. They began suddenly, a solid wall of brown and black and beige trunks jutting up from the half-frozen ground, overlaid by jagged branches and brown, dying leaves. The Forest. From their vantage point Senzei and Damien could see far into the distance, over the treetops to the mountains beyond. The Forest's canopy stretched out for miles upon miles, a thick tangle of treetops and dead leaves and parasitic vines that smothered the entire region like some vast, rotting blanket. Here and there an evergreen peeked out, a hint of somber green struggling for sunlight. Yellow-green light washed over it all, sculpting the canopy with light and shadow so that it seemed like a second landscape, with hills and valleys and even meandering river beds all its own.

That was what caught their attention first, and held it for several long minutes. Then, when they had taken it in, their eyes traveled downward. Into the valley before them.

Where men were gathering.

They were camped just before the tree line, where the shallow earth had guaranteed that nothing but grass and simple brush would take root. Their encampments were crude and severe, *functional* rather than *comfortable,* and a sharp, ammoniac smell arose from the land they had claimed, as though some territorial beast had sprayed every tent in the place. There were several cabins—crudely built— and a structure that might have been meant to serve as outhouse, but otherwise the make-do shelters that dotted the landscape were transient structures of pole and canvas, unenduring. There were a few wooden frames with animal skins stretched across them, a few cooking fires, a single laundry line. And men. They were gathering at the foot of the hill, as though preparing to welcome the travelers— or challenge them. Damien glanced at Senzei, about to issue instructions—and then looked again, more closely, his eyes narrowing in concern. "You all right?"

Senzei managed a shrug. "I'll live," he muttered. And though that was all he said, they both understood what he meant; not *I'm sure*

I'll survive this, but rather, *I understand our priorities. We have to keep moving. Don't stop for me.*

With a brief nod of approval, Damien started down the hill. He made no move for his weapon, but Senzei knew from experience just how quickly he could get to it if need be. He wished he had half the priest's skill at combat; if a fight broke out here, he'd probably wind up skewered before he could get his own blade halfway out of its scabbard.

Say it right, he told himself. *It wouldn't be a fight. Not with two against this many. That's called a slaughter.*

The two slowed their horses as the locals gathered around them, until they were brought to a full stop at the base of the hill. The locals were all men, for the most part hardy types in their prime, functionally dressed. All were possessed of that particular hard expression that said, *we don't need strangers, or their questions. Justify your presence or get out of here, fast.*

Damien rose up in his saddle; Senzei could feel the crowd tense. "We're looking for someone," the priest said. His voice was carried crisp and clear by the dry autumn air; a preacher's voice, strong and unhesitating. "He would have come through just before dawn—a tall man, with a woman in tow." He looked out over the sea of faces—neither hostile nor sympathetic, but coolly *unresponsive*—and added, "We'll pay well for any information."

There was a murmur at that, and several glares, passed between the men. One voice spoke up, openly hostile. "Yeah, we've seen one. A Lord of the Forest, that one. Came through like fire—untouchable, y'know? We don't look, we don't ask. Them's the rules."

Damien looked toward the source of the voice. "Did he have a woman with him?"

The men looked at each other; it was clear they were debating whether or not to answer Damien. "Think so," one said at last. "Across his saddle?" "Yeah," another confirmed. "I saw it."

A man who was close to the horses stepped forward and tried to put his hand on Damien's mount, in warning. The horse, well-trained, backed tensely away.

"You understand," he said to Damien. "We're not supposed to notice that kind. It's death to interfere with 'em."

"Interference is my business," Damien assured him. "You know where he went?"

"Listen to me," another said. He, too, stepped forward, divorcing himself from the crowd. A middle-aged man, silver-haired, with dark weathered skin and a workman's hands. "Three or four times a year, His people come through here like that. And right behind them, often as not, a herd of men comes galloping along in hot pursuit. Brothers and fathers, husbands, lovers—sometimes hired swords that were paid to fight alongside them—all of them determined that *this* time, *this one* time, the Hunter won't get what He wants." His eyes narrowed as he regarded Damien. "You hear what I'm saying? Men just like you two, with questions just like yours. Armed to the teeth and ready for anything. They think. So they ride into the Forest with a curse against the Hunter on their lips . . . and never come out again. *Never.* I've watched a dozen, two dozen go in . . . and not a single one ever showed his face on the outside again, in all the years that I've been here."

Damien looked at Senzei; there was something cold in the priest's expression that hadn't been there a moment before, as if some terrible thought had just occurred to him. It took Senzei a minute to realize what it was—and when he did, he felt his hands tighten involuntarily on his reins, his heart skip a beat inside his chest. Was Ciani to be hunted? It was a possibility that hadn't occurred to either of them. But if she was alive, and vulnerable, and the Hunter got hold of her—

"Where's he headed?" Damien demanded. He turned to the silver-haired man. "You seem to know what goes on here. Where's he gone? How do we follow him?"

The man just stared at him like he'd lost his mind. And maybe he had. At last he said quietly, "There's a fortress in the heart of the Forest; they say it's black as obsidian, impossible to make out in the shadows—unless He *wants* you to see it. That's where He stays, the Hunter, and never leaves, except to feed. They'll have taken her there."

Damien looked the men over. "Have any of you ever seen this place?"

"No one's seen it," a man answered quickly. "No one that ever lived to talk about it. You hear me? If you go in there searching for Him—for any reason—you'll never come out again. Not with the woman, or without her. Ever."

"The Hunter's merciless," someone muttered. And another urged, "Give it up, man."

"The Hunter can take his Forest and shove it," Damien said sharply. "How do we get to this black fortress of his?"

They were silent for a moment, stunned by the force of the blasphemy. At last the silver-haired man said, "All roads lead to the Hunter's keep. Go in deep enough—so the shadows can herd you along—and you'll get there, all right. Whether you *see* it or not is another thing. But there's no way back, after that," he warned them. "Not by any path a living man can follow."

Damien looked toward the Forest. Where the trees parted some-what there was a well-worn trail. As he watched, a pair of men on horseback broke free of the Forest's confines and cantered over toward where their fellows were gathered.

"You go in there," Damien challenged. "And you come out again."

"Sometimes not," someone muttered. Damien heard whispered curses. A rugged man in a black wool jacket said harshly, "That's because there's stuff in there that's worth that kind of risk. Plants that don't grow anywhere else, that sorcerors want—animals that mutate so fast, each generation has a different coat. There's a pack of white wolves in that Forest, belongs to the Hunter himself—you kill enough of them to make a man's coat from the skins, I can point you to a buyer who'll pay a small fortune for it. Yeah, we'll risk going in. Because we know the rules. Do as you like in the daytime . . . but if you're in the Forest after nightfall you're His. Period. So we do it fast and clean. Mark ourselves a good trail. Get out before sunset." He glanced nervously toward the leading edge of the Forest; a shudder seemed to pass through his frame. "Not as easy as it sounds," he muttered. "Not when you can't see the sun. Not when the place plays games with your mind."

"All right," Damien said; clearly he'd heard enough. He reached into his tunic front and drew out a small purse. He looked around, then threw it to the silver-haired man—who let it fall before him and made no move to pick it up.

"Save your money," he said. "It's one thing in the Hunter's eyes to trade a little gossip—and quite another to sell His secrets for profit." He glanced toward the fringe of the Forest and added soberly, "He reminds us of that distinction, every now and then."

"Your choice," Damien responded. He left the pouch lying where it was and began to ease his mount forward. Senzei moved to follow—but for a moment his legs wouldn't move, and his hands were strangely numb. "Damien. . . ." In his side the sharp pain had become an amorphous fire that throbbed in time with his heartbeat. "I can't. . . ."

The priest twisted in his saddle, studied his companion's face. Senzei could imagine the things that were going through his mind: *He's weak. City-born. Never suffered a serious wound in his life, and now this. But no one can do a Healing here without losing his soul to the Forest. And if we stop to rest, even for an hour, that might cost Ciani her life.*

"I'm fine," Senzei managed. And when Damien kept staring at him, he added, "Really."

After a moment, Damien nodded. He turned back toward the Forest, and kneed his horse into motion once more. Gritting his teeth from the strain of it, Senzei managed to get his body to obey him. Slowly, his horse moved to follow Damien's. And the third in line, behind him, took its accustomed place behind his. *You'll be all right,* he told himself. *You will. It's a question of mind over matter. You can't afford to be sick, therefore you will get well. Right!*

But mind over matter—or any other conscious control of the flesh—required the fae. And for the first time in his life, Senzei was beginning to understand what it meant to do without that.

Twenty-three

There were seven of them now, and they lay along the northern crest of Morgot, staring hatefully at the distant shore. One was wounded. Three had died. Of the original band that had traveled to Jaggonath, only one remained—and if he acted as the leader of the backup team that had met them in Morgot, it was because he alone had been there since the start of it.

They had a sorceror! one whispered angrily.

The leader answered quietly: *They are all sorcerors.*

You know what I mean. That one—

It was that bitch from the plains, another interrupted. *If she hadn't interfered—*

You should have killed that sorceror-woman in Jaggonath, one of the newcomers accused. *Then this wouldn't have happened. None of it would have happened.*

Yes, the leader said quietly. *I agree.*

So why didn't you!

I had other orders, he answered simply.

But it was the same woman! a newcomer demanded. *You're sure of that!*

Yes. Very sure. The disguise was good, but her mind still tastes the same. He licked his lips, remembering. *So good, these human souls.*

They stared out across the water. At Mordreth. Toward the Forest.

Are we going in after them? one asked nervously.

No need, another whispered. *They will come out. They must come out. And we'll kill them then, when they do.*

And if the plains bitch interferes again?

One hissed angrily. Another clenched his hands into fists, as if readying himself for battle.

The plains bitch is gone. She refused to enter the Forest. I saw her arrange passage to the rakhlands; by now, she must be within the Canopy. I say . . . we deal with the humans when they leave the Forest. And kill the plainswoman later, when we pass through her own camp.

He added, in a hungry whisper: *She can serve as food, for the long journey home.*

Twenty-four

Just before they reached the tree line, Damien signaled for Senzei to stop. He had seen to it that they each were carrying a springbolt, disassembled. Now he removed his from its worn leather saddlepack and motioned for Senzei to do the same.

With quick, efficient motions he assembled both their weapons. Senzei's was brand new, a gleaming, polished weapon that had been purchased for the journey. Damien's was an older model, heavier about the grip, whose well-worn finish and blood-stained shaft spoke of much use, not all of it at projectile distance.

"Ever use one of these?" he asked Senzei.

"Arcade sports." He said it apologetically—as if somewhere in his citybound upbringing he should have seen fit to practice on live targets.

"Same theory. Heavier weapon." He eased his horse over, close enough that he could point to details. "It'll hold two bolts; keep it loaded at all times. There's the safety; make sure it's on if the weapon's cocked—which it will be, at all times." He watched while Senzei hefted it up to eye level, left hand forward to hold the barrel ready.

"Try it," he directed. "That tree."

He sighted carefully, and pulled the trigger. There was a snap as the upper spring was released, and the metal-tipped bolt shot out from the barrel. Straight toward the tree and almost into its bark; but it missed by an inch and whistled past the target, into the Forest's darkness.

"Close enough," Damien muttered. "We'll put in some practice time when we get out of here." Not *if*, Senzei noted; *when*. The man's confidence was unbelievable. "You've got a blade on the barrel tip and some heavy brass on the shoulder piece; if anything comes in close, use it. If something's coming at you, don't even try to reload; it's a fifty pound draw, you'd have to wind it back, and that takes too long." He took the weapon from Senzei and forced it back to a cocked position with a single draw; the pulley mechanism meant to ease such a procedure spun silently below, as if in protest of his strength. "And here's the special ammo." He pulled a bolt out of his forward pocket—and whistled softly. "Look at that, will you?"

The bolt's shaft was glowing. A soft light, that would have been all but invisible in the daytime—but with the darkness of the Forest looming up before them, and God knows what waiting there in the shadows . . . the effect of the Fire was clearly visible. A glow from within the heart of the shaft, resonating against the impermeable wax surface as if it chafed at its imprisonment.

"Gods of Erna," Senzei whispered.

"This power was bound by the Church, for Church purposes." Damien slipped two bolts into the loading chamber, saw that they were settled properly. "Please have the decency not to invoke other gods while using it."

Senzei started to force a smile—then realized that Damien was deadly serious. He nodded and managed to take the weapon back. It was a heavy piece, almost more than he could lift. He didn't remember that being the case when they had bought it. He must be losing strength rapidly. . . .

"All right, then." Damien's voice was grim. "Now listen: if you see Tarrant, if you have an opening, you shoot to kill. No questions, no conversation. Got it?"

"What kills that kind?"

"Go for the heart. There's leeway for error that way; leave the fancy targets to me." He glanced at Senzei. "You ready?"

He wasn't, he never would be—but he nodded, all the same. No other answer was possible.

With a last grim glance at the dying sun—now half-lost behind the horizon's edge, powerless to aid them—Damien turned his horse toward the narrow path and led them into the Forest.

And night closed over them. Close-set trees, their upper branches intertwined, formed a thick canopy overhead that was reinforced by vines and dead foliage and gods alone knew what else, until no more than a mere hint of sunlight was capable of seeping through. By the time they had gone a few hundred yards into the Forest the road ahead of them was already lost in shadows, indistinguishable from the woods beyond. Senzei glanced back the way they had come and saw no more than a faint carmine glow at the place where the road left the Forest: the last vestige of sunlight, rapidly dying. But even that vision seemed to waver as though viewed through running water, or flawed glass. And though he could make out the road's starting point—barely—it was impossible for him to focus on it. He wondered if even now they had lost the option of turning back. Would that part of the road still be there if they wanted to use it?

"Dark fae," Damien muttered. "Makes sense."

"What's that?"

He indicated the trees that loomed over them, the thick canopy of vegetation overhead. "No direct sunlight ever reaches the ground here," he whispered. "Think of what that means! Have you ever watched during the true night, how quickly the dark fae moves out into the open, how powerful it gets even in that limited time? A very hungry, very volatile power, that tends to manifest man's darker urges. But here—imagine this place in the summer, when those branches are thick with leaves . . . my God! Morning, even high noon . . . no light would ever touch the ground then. The dark fae would live on, oblivious to sunrise, and it would grow, and it would manifest—"

"Damien."

The priest twisted around to look at him; his horse nickered softly.

"If there's no sunlight here," Senzei said slowly, "or very little, anyway. . . ."

He could see Damien's hand tighten on the springbolt's grip. He thought he heard him curse.

"So Tarrant didn't have to stop," he whispered. "Damn him! We should have guessed that." He reached into the pouch at his side and drew out the Patriarch's crystal vial; in the gloom of the artificial night it glowed twice as brightly as before: a star in the measureless gloom. "We have a light, at least." His voice was grim as he affixed the vial to his saddle. "And one the Hunter won't like. That's something, anyway." But his voice was far from optimistic. Was he thinking what Senzei was—that with a whole day's head start on them, Tarrant might have delivered Ciani to her destination already?

They rode. Not slowly, as they might have done if Ciani were with them. Not cautiously, by any measure. Ahead of them the light of the Fire etched out details of their road in sharp relief—and their horses' hooves pounded quickly past, as the mounts choose the most solid ground with certain instinct. No doubt there were dangers out there for which they should be watching—but the need to reach Ciani as quickly as possible, to make up for the time lost in Morgot, overwhelmed any need for caution.

Senzei hungered for his Sight. He wanted to see the road ahead as it really was: dark earth seething with the violet hues of the night-fae, delicate tendrils of that hungry power reaching out like fingers to grasp at the horse's hooves . . . and then curling back, burning up, turning to mist as the Fire's light struck it. Or perhaps withdrawing into some secret place, to venture forth again when the threat had passed. Maybe somewhere in the distance, unseen, Senzei's fears were already sculpting the dark fae, manifesting his uncertainty. How ancient the power must be here—and how sensitive, how deadly! He longed to see it on its own terms, to do battle with it directly. And for a moment—just a moment—the key to a Knowing was on his lips. He tasted the words . . . and then bit them back, forcing himself to swallow them. The currents had nearly dragged him under in Kale; here, in the Forest itself, he would be swept away to his death before he knew what hit him. And while even that might have tempted him once—to taste such power, even for an instant!—he had Ciani to think of. He hungered to cast himself into the black sun, drink in its power—but for now, it would have to rise without him.

The path they followed became less and less defined, a mere hint of direction as opposed to the well-worn road they had started out on. The light of the Fire fanned out before him, illuminating the road ahead. Despite the fact that no threats were visible, Senzei began to feel a prickling along the back of his neck. As if someone—or something—were watching. He glanced behind them as best he could, saw only darkness. The feeling persisted. Not *watching*, exactly. *Anticipating. Waiting.*

Instinctively he began to key a Knowing—and though he stopped himself after a single phrase, those few sounds were enough to unlock a fearsome Working. Currents of earth-fae roared past his ears like a flood; the force of it nearly knocked him from his saddle. He had to hold on for dear life as the currents battered him, enveloped him, attempted to drag him under . . . it was so deep, so very deep! How could there be so much power in one place? He tried to cry out—in panic, in warning, in an attempt to banish his Knowing—but the current was too strong, and too swift for him. In the instant it took him to focus on a portion of the fae, that portion swept past and was gone. And what replaced it was new and hungry, untamable, a force as inexorable as the tides or the winds, as powerful as a newborn tornado. . . .

He managed to cry out. Somehow. Damien twisted back to look at him, his right hand raising the springbolt to firing position, thumbing off the safety catch—and then something black and sinuous launched itself from a shadowed tree trunk, directly at him. He must have heard it coming—or seen its flight reflected in Senzei's eyes— for he turned back even as its claws reached out for him and discharged the loaded weapon point-blank into its gut. Senzei felt the bolt strike home as if the flesh it tore through was his own, and he cried out in agony as the Fire began to consume him. Striking out at Damien in primal fury—and then being struck across the base of the skull with the brass butt of the springbolt, claws tearing loose from horse and saddle and spinning, spinning, down into the raging current. . . .

"There are more!" he gasped. The bulk of his voice was lost in the flood; he prayed that Damien could hear him. The wounded beast was writhing in pain on the ground before them, and Senzei had to fight not to share its convulsions. Had to fight not to share its descent into death, as the Fire at last consumed it. "Others!" he managed. He fought against the pounding of the current and managed to bring up one arm. To point. He whispered the key to an Unseeing, desperately, as he fought to bring his own weapon up. To find enough strength to hold it, and pull the safety free.

He did so.

Just in time.

They came from the woods, silent and smooth as shadow. Their souls sang loudly of hunger and of hate, chords of death that reverberated along the current, making Senzei's blood run cold. He braced the springbolt against his shoulder, praying for the strength to fire it. They had come up from the rear, which meant that Senzei had to turn to face them; Damien was behind him. All that was before him was the unmanned horse, rearing up in terror—or trying to, the reins didn't quite allow it—and four dark, sleek shapes with eyes that burned purple and breath that stank of hate. He muttered the Unseeing once, twice, again, as he waited for them to come close enough that he could be certain of hitting his target. The roar of the flood subsided somewhat—enough that he could hear Damien shouting instructions, not enough that he could make them out. The hand that was holding the barrel shook slightly—from fear or weakness?—as he centered his sights on the leader of the pack, directly between its eyes. And fired. He heard the sharp snap of the springshot's release, saw a spark of light shoot out from the barrel, heard the crack of bone as it struck home, a sudden burst of brilliance as the Fire took root in its victim . . . he forced himself not to watch, not to think, just to turn and aim again and listen for the click that meant the second bolt was safely engaged . . . and fire. Not as clean a shot as his first, but it struck one creature solidly in its hindquarter and sent it off screaming into the woods. That was two. He reached to his pocket for another pair of bolts, suddenly remembered Damien saying something about not reloading—and then one of the beasts was on him, claws digging into his horse's flank, purple eyes burning with hunger. Without even thinking he rammed the point of the weapon into its face and felt the blade bite into flesh, the cold wash of its nightborn blood as it gushed out blackly over his hand. He fought not to vomit. His horse bucked, panicked by its pain, and for a moment it took everything he had not to fall off. When he at last got it to stand still again, he saw that the reins of the third horse had been snapped off from his saddle; dizzily he looked around, trying to see where it had gone.

"Back off!" Damien barked. The voice gave him a sense of direction, and purpose; he forced his mount a step backward, then two. In that two of the beasts were struggling with the riderless horse not far from where they stood, Senzei's mount was happy to move as ordered. It surprised him for a moment that it didn't just turn and run, overwhelmed by the experience. But Erna had bred its equines for transportation in some of the most dangerous parts of the human lands; any beast that gave way to blind fear would have been weeded out of the breeding stock long ago.

Damien pulled up beside him; his springbolt was cocked and raised and splattered with black blood. He aimed quickly and fired at the nearest of the creatures. The screaming horse reared up, nearly getting itself in the way of the shot—but then the bolt drove home in a sleek black throat, and one of the attackers was down.

Before he could turn to fire at the next one, the terrified horse kicked out; its tripart hoof took the last beast in the head, and sent it flying backward into a nearby tree. There was a sharp crack as it hit, and when its body struck the ground it was twisted oddly, and all its limbs were still.

Senzei reached out to catch the bridle of the free horse—too far, too hard, pain lanced through his side, forced him back in a sudden spasm of agony. The animal reared up, blood running from its legs and a wound in its neck, and then took off into the depths of the Forest, screaming in rage and pain. Senzei gasped, and held tightly to his saddle. The pain was like fire in his veins, the whole world was spinning about him . . . but at least the currents were invisible again. Powerless to claim him. Thank the gods for that.

"You okay?" Damien whispered. Senzei tried to find his voice, tried to make his mouth form words—and then a sudden screaming split the night to the west of them, a sound of equine terror and agony that came from just beyond the reach of their Firelight.

Wordlessly, Damien reloaded for both of them. There were long scratch marks across his knuckles, and crimson blood had welled up there in thick, parallel lines. He didn't even glance at it. With a nod toward the source of the screaming he eased his mount westward between the trees, springbolt braced against his shoulder. Senzei followed suit. Wondering if the path would be there when they tried to get back to it. Wondering if they would last long enough to try.

Barely a hundred yards forward, their Firelight driving back the shadows, they saw where the horse had fallen. A heavy steel trap had snapped shut on its ankle, breaking through the flesh to crack the bone beneath. Blood gushed out on the ground as it struggled to right itself. Senzei heard Damien curse the trappers under his breath as he moved forward toward it—and this time it was the sorceror who stopped him, with a touch of his springbolt barrel to the priest's nearer shoulder.

There were things coming out of the ground. Wormlike things, dark and sinuous. They came in response to the horse's heat, or its blood, or its screaming. They came, and they fed. Slick black worms as wide as a man's wrist, with a circle of viciously pointed teeth at the forward end. They lunged for the warm flesh and hooked themselves onto it, then began to burrow in. Half a dozen at least, that fixed themselves onto the horse's belly and began to work their way toward the soft inner organs.

Senzei felt the bile rise up at last, and this time he couldn't fight it. He leaned over to the far side of his mount and vomited helplessly onto the ground—aware, even as he did so, that the warm fluid might attract the very things that revolted him. When he looked up again Damien was taking aim at the writhing horse. There was a look on his face more grim, more terrible, than anything Senzei had ever seen there. He waited until the horse lay still for a moment, exhausted by its struggles, and then he fired. The bolt lodged in the horse's neck, seemingly in well-padded flesh. Then the animal moved again—the shaft of the bolt broke off—and a river of blood gushed out of its neck, spurting in time to its heartbeat.

"Carotid artery," he muttered. "Once that's opened up, they're quick to die." He wiped one hand across his brow, smearing blood on his face. "He was carrying the extra supplies, right? Nothing vital. Nothing we have to risk . . . *that* for."

"No." Senzei's voice was a hoarse, shaken whisper. "Nothing."

"All right, then." The horse's screams were dying down; the gurgle of blood was audible. Damien wheeled his mount around, hands dripping blood on the reins. "Let's get the hell out of here."

They bandaged their wounds while on horseback, and did what they could for their mounts from the same position. Damien thought it might have been body heat that had attracted the worm-things, and the horses' thick hooves would insulate against that better than their own thin-soled boots. Nevertheless they kept moving as well as they could, even as they wound the lengths of gauze around their damaged hands. Senzei felt a warm trickle run down his side also but said nothing; this was neither the time nor the place to stop and examine his wound.

Twenty-four hours ago. It felt like days—years—another lifetime. He thought of Damien, traveling from city to city through regions of such desolation that even traders feared to go there, braving realms that had been given over to the products of man's worst nightmares . . . and for the first time he understood just what that meant. To choose to do that kind of thing over and over again, without even a fellow traveler to back one up, to stand guard while one slept . . . he couldn't imagine it. Couldn't imagine why one would choose such a life. Couldn't imagine what it would be like to be filled with such a faith, that when your god wanted you to go on such a trip you did so, with no thought for the dangers of the terrain you were facing.

And their god gives them nothing in return. No special favors. No easy miracles. Nothing but a single dream, which may never be fulfilled.

They rode. Damien observed the foliage—or some other equally subtle sign—and announced there was probably a river running just east of them. Which was good, he explained. Fewer faeborn things would come from that direction. And once the sun rose the river would mean safe refuge, should they need it.

If it ever rises again, Senzei thought. *If we live long enough to see it happen.*

They rode as fast as they dared, taking into account the stamina of the horses. Damien was very clear on that: to wear out their mounts in pursuit of Ciani so that they were left on foot in this haunted wilderness was as good as committing all three of them to death. The Fire cast a light just far enough ahead that if the road suddenly ended, or was blocked by some faeborn antagonist, they would have just enough time to pull up before riding smack into it. Barely.

Thus it was that Damien's nerves were trigger-taut, and he pulled back on his reins the minute he saw a flicker of movement reflecting back at him from the endless tunnel that was their road. Senzei, some yards back, managed to follow suit without running into him— mostly because his mount had picked up on the fact that it was supposed to be doing whatever Damien's horse did. Side by side they paused in the center of the barren path, trying to make out moving forms in the lightless shadows. Between their legs the horses stirred anxiously, no doubt remembering the clawed creatures that had come running out of the woods mere minutes—or hours?—ago.

And then the shape moved close enough to become visible. Human in its general form, but strangely hunched over; Damien raised his springbolt to eye level as he watched it stagger toward them. The shadowed form resolved into a true human shape, and as it entered the outer boundary of the Fire's light it was possible to see that it staggered in exhaustion, and perhaps in pain. It came closer and lifted its head, its eyes half shut against the pain of so much light after the darkness of the road.

Ciani.

Senzei felt his heart skip a beat, and adrenaline poured into his bloodstream like a tidal wave: from fear, from joy, from concern for her life. She was a mere shadow of her former self, dressed in tattered remnants of her traveling attire. Blood pooled beneath her bare feet as she came to a stop, swaying weakly, and she shielded her eyes with her hand so that she might see them against the Fire's glare. A whisper barely escaped her lips, too fragile a sound to cross the distance between them. A name, perhaps. A plea. There were bruises about her face and arms, and long scratch marks on one side of her face. She seemed to have lost half her weight overnight, and most of her color with it.

"Thank god," she whispered. "I heard the horses. . . ." Tears choked her voice and she took a step forward—then fell, her legs too weak to support her. Tears poured down her face. "Damien—Senzei—my god, I can't believe I've found you. . . ."

The sense of shock which had frozen Senzei's limbs released him at last. With a cry of joy he slid off his horse—and his wound stabbed into him like fire, like a blade of molten steel, but what did that matter? They had found her!—and he ran toward her as best he could, his legs weak and shaking and stiff from hours in the saddle—

And something whizzed past his ear. A bolt of light—a spear of fire—a searing bullet, that left the air hot where it passed. He barely had time to recognize what it was, what it must be, before it struck her. The glowing bolt hit her square in the chest, slightly right of center: through the heart. With a scream, she ceased reaching for him and clutched at the projectile—so close, she had been so close, he had almost touched her!—but it was buried deep within her flesh, and she couldn't pull it out. And then, without warning, she ignited. The whole of her body went up in an instant, like dry leaves sparked

by heat lightning. Senzei cried out as he shielded his eyes against the
glare of her burning, fell to his knees as the pyre roared up before
him. Tongues of Fire licked at the canopy far overhead, and small
black shapes fell—screaming, smoking—onto the road. Only slowly
did it sink into him what had happened. Only slowly did it sink in
what Damien had done. And why.

As the Fire died down at last—leaving no bones to mark the place
where Ciani had stood, nor even any ash, only a faint smell of sulfur—he looked up to where Damien sat, one hand on the reins of
Senzei's horse and the other still bracing the springbolt against his
shoulder.

"How?" he gasped. His whole body was shaking. "How did you
know?"

The priest's expression was grim, his face deeply lined. It seemed
he had aged a decade in the past few hours. "She wouldn't come into
the light," he said. "Ciani would have known that the Fire meant
safety for her, and come to it at any cost. She invoked my god, not
hers. She called you by your formal name—which she's never done
before, at least not in my presence. Do you want more?"

"But you weren't sure!" he exclaimed. "You couldn't possibly be
sure! And what if you were wrong?"

"But I wasn't, was I?" His face was like stone, his tone implacable.
"You'd better learn this now, Zen. Some of the things that the darkness spawns can take on any form they like. They read your fears
from the fae that surrounds you and design whatever image they need
to break through your defenses. And you only get *one* chance to
recognize them, *one* chance to react. If you're wrong—or if you hesitate, even for an instant—they'll do worse then kill you." He looked
off into the darkness; Senzei thought he saw him shiver. "Compared
to some of what I've seen, death would be a mercy."

The Fire had died down. Senzei stared at where it had been, heartbeat pounding loudly in his ears. Why did it suddenly seem so hot?
Had the Fire somehow affected his perception, so that even after it
was gone something inside him continued to burn? He felt overwhelmed. He wanted to cry out, *I can't make it! I'm out of strength!
How can I do anything to save her, like this!*

Damien said nothing, allowing Senzei the time to pull himself
together. Then, suddenly, he stiffened. In a voice that was quiet but
firm, he ordered, "Mount up. Now."

Senzei looked at him, saw him reloading the springbolt. The
priest's eyes were turned to the west, his gaze fixed on something in
the distance. "Mount up!" he hissed.

Shaking, Senzei obeyed. Pain speared through his side as he slid into the saddle and he thought, *I can't do this again. If I get down again, I won't be able to get up.*

And there was peace in that thought. A dark kind of peace, in knowing that soon all fighting might be over.

He took the reins of his horse from Damien and followed the priest's gaze, slightly ahead and to the left of the road. There were two points of light that winked at them out of the darkness, set a yard or so above the ground. Bright crimson, like blood.

"Let's move," Damien muttered.

They rode. At first slowly, watching the lights as they went. Then more quickly, when they saw that the crimson sparks were keeping pace with them. Soon after, another pair of lights joined the first. Then a third.

Eyes, Senzei thought, *reflecting the Firelight. Gods help us.*

They broke into a fevered gallop.

The eyes stayed with them.

There were more and more of them now, too many to count. They would flash bright as stars as their owners turned to assess their prey, then become invisible a moment later as the beasts turned their attention to the ground underfoot, or the Forest ahead. Whatever manner of creature they were, they were swift and seemingly tireless. Try as they might, the travelers couldn't lose them. Senzei heard Damien curse under his breath, knew that he hated to drive the horses this hard for any length of time—but no matter how fast they rode, the gleaming eyes managed to keep pace with them.

Finally Damien slowed, and Senzei did the same. His horse was covered with sweat, and it shivered as the chill night air gusted over it. He was suddenly acutely aware of how desperately they needed these animals, of how little good it would do them to get where they were going—even to rescue Ciani—if they had to walk back through this place. *We wouldn't last an hour.*

Damien lifted his springshot to eye level and cursed, "Damn them!"

"What?"

"They're just beyond firing range. Exactly the right distance. Damn! It means they're either hellishly lucky . . ."

He lowered his weapon. "Or experienced," he said quietly.

Senzei whispered, "Or intelligent."

There was a moment of silence. "Let's hope not," he said at last.

Something stepped out into the road.

It looked like a wolf, at first—an unusually large wolf, with bleached white fur and blazing red eyes. But there were differences. In its paws, which were splayed out like human hands. In its jaws, which were broader and more powerful than even a wolf's should be. And in its bearing, which hinted at more than mere hunger: a subtle malevolence, not at all bestial.

It moved to the center of the road and stood there, as if challenging them to ride over it.

Damien moved. His mount, responsive to his needs, broke into a sudden gallop. Despite his misgivings Senzei followed suit. The priest charged directly at the wolflike beast, as if daring it to stand its ground. But its only response was a low snarl and a twitch of its lips: a mockery of human laughter.

Then, when he was almost upon the beast, Damien veered off toward the right. Off the path. The move sent them toward the river, and their horses were forced to make their way through thicker and thicker brush. Damien's mount stumbled once but managed to stay on its feet. After they had ridden parallel to the river for some distance the priest turned west again; Senzei realized that he was hoping to circle around the pack, and regain the road. But as they went farther west, they saw that the eyes were already there, waiting for them. Arrayed at an angle that seemed just a shade too calculated, as though they meant for the pair of them to reach the road at one particular point.

Herding us, Senzei despaired. Evidently the same thought had occurred to Damien; with sudden determination he pulled his sword free of its sheath and made ready to hack his way through their line. Senzei clutched his springshot to his chest and tried to pray. He wondered if Damien was praying as well—and whether the priest thought his prayers would be answered, or used them only to discipline his mind.

They broke from the trees, back onto the road. At least a dozen animals were arrayed before them, red eyes gleaming hotly; each of them was clearly capable of taking a man and a horse to the ground, and enjoying the fight.

And then Damien pulled up short, and motioned for Senzei to do the same. Confused, he did so.

In the middle of the road, poised tensely before them, was a man.

He was thin and lanky, with hair the same bleached color as the animals' fur and skin that was nearly as white. He had red eyes that reflected the Firelight like crimson jewels. His skin was thin, translucent—so much so that it was possible to see the veins throb in his neck, deep blue veins running down into a white silk collar. He wore a white shirt and sleeveless jacket, white leggings, white leather boots. As if he, being albino, would only wear such animal produce as came from beasts that shared his affliction.

He smiled, displaying needle-sharp teeth. One of the beasts moved to his side; its claws flexed as it waited.

Too many, he despaired. *How can we fight that many?*

Apparently, Damien thought the same thing. He didn't sheathe his sword, but he lowered it. With his other hand he reached into his pocket, and drew out the golden earth-disk.

The man grinned, a bestial expression. In a voice that was half hiss, half laughter, he challenged Damien: "You claim to be a servant of the Hunter?"

"I'm looking for one of his people."

"Then you're brave, sun-man. Or stupid. Or both." He squinted toward the Fire. "Put that thing away."

Damien hesitated. "Light a torch," he ordered. It took Senzei a moment to realize that he was talking to him. He fumbled in one of his packs for a brush torch and matches. Finally he found them. And managed to get the thing lit. His hands, and therefore the light, shook badly.

Damien slid the crystal flask out of his belt and into the neck of his shirt. The Firelight faded, replaced by Senzei's flickering orange flame.

"Much better." More of the beasts had come onto the road; Senzei could feel his horse trembling, anxious to flee the smell of danger. "It hurts the eyes."

"I'm looking for Gerald Tarrant," Damien told him.

"Yes. He knows that."

"You know where he is?"

The thin man shrugged. "In the keep. The Hunter's warren. Where he belongs."

"And the woman he had with him?"

The red eyes sparkled. "I don't keep track of the Hunter's women."

Damien tensed; for a minute Senzei thought that his rage would get the better of him and he would attack the man. He looked at the two dozen animals waiting to take them, and despair filled him. *Prepare to die,* he thought, and he gripped his weapon even more tightly.

But Damien didn't attack. Instead he said coldly, "You'll take us to him."

Something flashed in the albino's eyes. Irritation? Anger? One of the white wolves growled. But then he answered, in a voice as smooth as silk, "It is what I came to do."

He looked to the south, where the road behind them was swallowed up by darkness. For a moment it seemed that his eyes gave off a light of their own, a crimson far more brilliant than mere reflection could account for. He whispered something into the air—a Working?—and then waited. After a moment, a pounding could be heard in the distance. Rhythmic. Familiar. Horses' hooves? Senzei wished that Damien was facing him, so that he might read his expression. But the priest refused to be distracted, and kept his eyes fixed on the albino sorcerer. When a horse broke into their circle of light and galloped past them, he didn't turn. Not even Senzei's horrified gasp was enough to bring him about, although his body went rigid in anticipation when he heard it.

It was their horse. The one they had left behind, the one that Damien had killed. Now it was drained of all its color as surely as it had been drained of life. Thin rivers of blue coursed down its hide where red blood once had spilled. Its eyes were empty, unfocused, its expression unresponsive. And from its belly—

Senzei fought the urge to gag, succeeded only because there was nothing left in him to bring up. Or no strength left in him to vomit. Out of the horse's belly hung the tail ends of the worm-creatures, which writhed from side to side as their forward halves, buried within the beast, sought out choice morsels of horse flesh.

The white man swung himself up onto the ghastly animal. One of the worm-ends, responding to his proximity, wrapped itself around his ankle—and then snapped back suddenly, as if burned. After a moment, it shuddered and went limp. The rider grinned.

"Since you will not be driven," he hissed, "then you must be led. Yes?" He kneed the gruesome mount into motion, one hand tangled in its death-bleached mane. "Follow me."

And he laughed softly—a silken, malevolent sound. "I believe the Hunter is expecting you."

Twenty-five

I'm going to kill him, Damien thought.

It wasn't anyone in particular that he meant, so much as a general desire to strike out at the source of his frustration. The Hunter would serve. So would the courteously arrogant Gerald Tarrant. Even this albino henchman of the Hunter would do nicely—although if it came down to trying to unhorse him in combat, Damien didn't know if he could bring himself to kill the same animal twice.

But he was checked in his rage by a single thought, which echoed in his soul with unaccustomed power. *Ciani.* She was still alive. He sensed it. If he gave in to his fury, and by doing so caused her to suffer more . . . no. It was unthinkable. Alone, he could have risked such action. God knows, his sword had gotten him out of worse situations than this. But now he was traveling with others and was responsible for their well-being. It was an unaccustomed burden, and sometimes it chafed as sorely as manacles. It would have been far, far easier to deal with this situation if he were alone.

But let's be honest, shall we? If it wasn't for the others you wouldn't be here in the first place.

He twisted back in his saddle to take a look at Senzei, who was following somewhat behind him. The man was flushed with fever, and the bruise on his forehead shone livid purple in the flickering torchlight. His hand on the reins trembled slightly—not from fear, Damien suspected, so much as from weakness. He looked bad, in the ways that Damien had come to recognize as life-threatening. He should never have let him come this far. But what other choices had they had, realistically speaking? Should Senzei have remained behind in Morgot so that the rakh-creatures could make a second attempt to kill him? Or stopped for a rest in mid-Forest, in the hope that a doctor would just happen by? Damien wished he dared to Heal his companion, or even do a Numbing. That was the most frustrating part of all of this: riding through a land of such incredible raw power, and being unable to Work it to save the ones he cared about. But he remembered Senzei on the roof of the hotel in Kale, trying to throw himself over the edge in order to embrace something he later described as a "black sun." If the current had been that bad there, then Working it this close to the center of the whirlpool would be tantamount to suicide.

I'd do it, Damien thought grimly. *If I thought I could Heal him before it got me, I'd do it in a second.*

They reached the base of yet another steep incline; Damien felt his horse shudder in exhaustion. And for the first time all night he felt a touch of true despair. All of his assorted skills couldn't save them if his mount gave out; they might free Ciani and even manage to heal Senzei, but without horses they would never make it out of the Forest alive.

The trail switchbacked several times, growing steeper and steeper as they went. They were near the mountains, then. Perhaps even among them; it was impossible to gain any sense of their true position with the canopy overhead, and the endless exhausting miles behind them. He patted his horse firmly on the neck and heard it nicker in response. They had been through worse together. They would get through this. Senzei's mount, on the other hand, was city-trained; Damien wondered how much longer it would last.

And then they came around a turn and it was there before them: a soaring edifice of black volcanic glass that broke through the canopy high above and laid bare the night sky beyond it. Prima's silver-blue crescent crowned the central tower like a halo, and cold moonlight shivered down the glassy stone walls like gleaming mercury, caught in the streaks and whorls of the obsidian brickwork. It was surreal. Breathtakingly beautiful. And, to Damien, disturbingly familiar.

Where had he seen it before? He tried to pin down the memory, but nothing would come. Maybe it wasn't the castle itself that he remembered. Maybe just something like it.

Something like the Hunter's keep!

They rode into the courtyard and for a moment simply sat still on their horses, stunned by what was before them. The volcanic glass of the castle's facade reflected their torchlight back in pools and arcs that shimmered across the brickwork like living things. Finials rose like tiny black flames from the tips of sweeping arches, and a tracery of fine black stone guarded narrow windows that reached up toward the moonlight. Revivalist, Damien observed. The pinnacle of that style. And for the first time in his life, he understood what the allure of the period must have been.

Dear God. What must this place be like in the sunlight? He stared at the perpendicular windows, wondering if the dawn would reveal patterns of tinted glass. And again, a sense of familiarity flickered in the back of his mind.

Where do I know this building from?

The albino had dismounted, and he came to where Damien and Senzei's horses stood. He waited. After a moment Damien dismounted, careful to favor his wounded arm. And Senzei did so also— or tried to. Fortunately, Damien was close by, and he was at Senzei's side the instant he began to fall. He caught him about the chest and helped lower him to the ground, until his feet were steady beneath him and it seemed that he could stand unaided. His flesh was distressingly hot, and it burned like fire even through the fabric of his shirt. *He needs rest,* Damien thought grimly. *He needs a Healer. But how likely are we to get either one of those, in this place?*

Shadows came at them from one of the archways—human-shaped figures swathed in black, that reached out to take their mounts. A muttered warning from Damien was enough to cause them to draw back, long enough for him to remove their more valuable possessions from his and Senzei's horses. God alone knew if they would see the animals again. He patted his horse one last time to calm it, then gave its rein over to the black-cloaked men. Senzei's they simply took, assuming—rightly so—that the wounded sorceror had neither the strength nor the will to oppose them.

Side by side, the travelers entered the Hunter's keep. Black volcanic glass gave way to black numarble, streaked with random bits of crimson. In the light of Senzei's torch, it made the floor look bloodstained. The furniture was black as well, heavy novebony pieces that were as intricately worked as the building's facade, cushioned in jet black velvet. Red silk tassels and fine red fringe edged black velveteen draperies, fixed permanently shut over the high arched windows. There were bits of gold visible here and there—drawer handles, locks, opulent doorknobs—but the dramatic darkness of the castle's interior was only intensified further by the contrast.

At last they came to a door at which the albino paused. "You can wait here if you like," he said. "I think you'll find this room . . ." He grinned. "Comforting?"

He pushed the door open. For a moment, Damien could see nothing. Then the torch that Senzei was holding began to pick out details of the furnishings within—

And he stepped inside, motioning for Senzei to follow him. Not quite believing what he saw. Not knowing how to react to it.

It was a chapel. A room dedicated to the God of his faith, outfitted in the Revivalist style. No black stone here, nor any hint of visual blasphemy; the place might have been lifted out of Jaggonath a thousand years ago, and set down here without a single alteration. Which was, simply . . .

Impossible. Damien walked to the altar, let his fingers brush against the fine silk damask that covered it. He hungered to be able to Work, to Know for himself that this was indeed what it appeared to be, that no subtle malevolence was at work here, defiling the very patterns of his faith. But even in such a place as this he dared not use the fae. *Especially* in such a place as this, he told himself.

There were oil lamps flanking the door, and the albino lit them. "No need for open fire," he said, and he pried the torch carefully out of Senzei's fingers. Holding it at a distance as if in distaste, he turned to Damien. And smiled, clearly amused by the priest's reaction.

"His Excellency is a religious man," he said. As if that would answer all their questions. "I'll tell him you're here. Please feel free to make yourselves at home here . . . if you think you can."

He turned to leave, but Damien stepped forward quickly and caught him by the arm. His body was as chill as ice, and the scent of his flesh was like carrion—but that might be just a perceptual Working meant to discourage physical contact, and Damien held on.

"His Excellency?" the priest asked tensely. "You mean the Hunter?"

"He prefers his Revivalist title," the albino said. He closed a hand over Damien's own—cold, so cold—and then pulled it off his arm. "Your people knew him as the Neocount of Merentha. He prefers Revivalist custom in general, I might add. You would do well to indulge him." Lamplight glinted off the points of his teeth as he grinned: a ferocious expression. "I'm sure he'll be delighted to find out that you made it here."

He left them. Shutting the door firmly behind him, as if by leaving it open he might contaminate the rest of the keep. Senzei looked at Damien—and found him leaning against the altar for support, his face as pale as a ghost's.

"Merentha Castle," he whispered. "It's a copy. That's why—oh, my God. . . ."

His hand on the altar clenched, catching up a fold of damask and crushing it. "Zen . . . do you understand? Do you know who the Neocount of Merentha *was?*"

"I know he was one of the figureheads of the Revival. A strategist of Gannon's, yes? A supporter of your Church—"

"A *supporter?* My God, he wrote half our bible. More than half! His signature is on nearly every holy book we have. The dream that we serve is *his*, Zen. *His!*"

Senzei looked confused. "What about your Prophet?"

"He *is* the Prophet. Don't you understand? That was the name that they gave to him, when . . ." He shut his eyes; a shiver ran through his frame. "A name for the first part of his life. The time when he served God and man, and designed a faith that he believed could tame the fae, if only humanity would accept it. How could we follow in his footsteps without recognizing the source of our inspiration? But the Church didn't dare use his name, because that might have invoked something of his spirit. They struck it from the books. And after . . . after. . . ."

He turned away. He didn't want Senzei to see the tears that were coming. He might misread their source, assuming weakness—when in fact they were tears of rage. "He was an adept," he whispered hoarsely. "One of the first. And the premier knight of my Order. One day he . . . snapped. We don't know what caused it. We're not even sure exactly what happened. But those who searched through Merentha Castle after his disappearance found the remains of his family, gruesomely slaughtered. Apparently he . . . vivisected his wife. His children." He turned back to Senzei. "You have to understand," he whispered urgently. "In our tradition, there is no greater evil. Because he was, before he fell, all that we venerate. All that we strive to become. And then he threw it all away! In an act of such brutal inhumanity that there could be no question that he had damned his soul forever. . . ."

"And no one knew where he went, after that?"

"They thought he died! They thought that hell had claimed him. And of course, yes—there were rumors. There always will be, after something like that. His brothers died in violent accidents, and he was blamed. His fiercest rival was found with his throat torn out, and of course it wasn't mere animals that had done it. The ghost of the Neocount was given credit for at least a hundred crimes—but there never was any proof, not for any of it. And when several lifetimes had passed since his disappearance, it was reasonable to assume him dead. Mortality is the one constant of human existence." He shook his head in amazement, and struck his fist against the altar top; a candelabra trembled. "It's been almost ten centuries, Zen. Ten centuries! How can a human being live that long?"

"Maybe," the sorceror said nervously, "by becoming something that's no longer human."

Damien stared at him.

And the door swung open.

It was the albino. His red eyes took in the picture, and he smiled. It was a faint, fleeting expression that barely touched the edges of his lips; the eloquent minimalism of it reminded Damien of the Hunter's other servant, Gerald Tarrant.

"He's ready for you," the albino told them. And he gave them a moment of silence in which to realize that he wasn't going to ask them if they, too, were ready. Because they couldn't possibly be. The Hunter knew that.

"Follow me," he said—and though his heart was cold as ice, Damien obeyed.

They walked through halls of gleaming black numarble, past tapestries of black and crimson silk, over rugs so dark that only their texture made them visible: velvet black against the glistening mottled stonework of the floor. Though candles set in golden sconces along the wall had been lit some time ago, the cold stone sucked in their light as soon as it was cast. The albino sorceror, with his white hair and clothing, seemed to glow like a torch by contrast.

And then they came to a pair of novebony doors, and the albino stopped. With a grin he pushed against the heavily carved surfaces—panels of hunting scenes, battle scenes, the Dance of Death—and announced, "The Neocount of Merentha."

Beyond the door was an audience chamber, whose vaulted ceiling and decorative arches all drew the eye to the center of the room and the man who waited there to receive them. Haughty, arrogant, he wore the robes of an earlier age: delicate silks in graduated layers, the longest of them sweeping the ground about his feet. And on his shoulders, a broad collar of beaten gold, worked in a pattern of overlapping flames: the mark of Damien's Order.

For a moment, rage nearly got the better of Damien. He thought of the weapons at his disposal—the Fire, the springbolt, the clean steel edge of his sword—and only with effort did he keep his hands from going for one of those tools. Only with a supreme act of will did he keep himself from succumbing to a fury so dark and terrible that it seemed he must give vent to it or burst. But he was not so blinded by anger that he lost sight of the power of the man who faced him, or the vulnerability of his own position. Not to mention—as always—Senzei and Ciani.

Hands shaking, thoughts reeling, he somehow managed to find his voice. "You vulking bastard. . . . "

Gerald Tarrant chuckled. "The soul of courtesy, as always. You surprise me, priest. I would think that the premier of your Order deserved more respect."

"You're no servant of the Church!"

"Oh, I am that. More than you could possibly understand."

"Where's Ciani?" Senzei demanded.

The Hunter's expression darkened. "Safe. For now. You needn't worry about her. There's no place on Erna safer for her to be right now than here."

"I doubt that," Damien said coldly.

Tarrant's eyes narrowed. "You'll get the lady back. Healthy and fit and full of all the memories that I inadvertently drained from her. It was to restore those to her that I brought her here. And the three of you will go to the rakhlands, just as you planned. In addition, your chance of success has increased considerably—because I will be going with you."

"Like hell you are!"

The pale eyes glittered. "Exactly." And before either of the men could respond he added, "I see that I've failed to communicate a vital point. *You have no choice.*" He paused; an expression flitted across his face that was strangely vulnerable—and then, just as quickly, it was gone. "I, too, have no choice," he said softly.

"You expect us to trust you? After what you did to Ciani?'

"*Because* of what I did to Ciani." His expression was strained, his manner tense. Damien cursed his inability to read the man. "You would be fools not to have me. You realized that in Kale, when you thought I was merely an adept. Is it any less true now?"

"We don't need your kind of help," the priest spat.

"On the contrary—it's *exactly* what you need. A mind not so blinded by dreams of vengeance that it will fail to ask the right questions. As you have failed, priest—you, and your friend."

"Such as?"

The silver eyes fixed on him. "Why has the lady lost her adeptitude?"

For a moment the silence in the chamber was absolute; so much so that Damien could hear the slow sizzle of wax from one of the room's few candles. Then Tarrant continued. "Adeptitude isn't a learned skill. It's inborn. Inseparable from the flesh. A woman like Ciani could no more forget how to interact with the fae than she could forget to breathe, or think. Yet that's precisely what happened. I question how. You believe that her assailants were constructs of the fae that sustain themselves by feeding on human memory. But the worst part of what was done to her had nothing to do with memory, and everything to do with power." He paused, giving that thought a moment to sink in. "Which means one of two things. Either these creatures aren't what they appear to be ... or they're allied to something else. Something far more dangerous and complex. Something powerful enough to—"

He stopped as Senzei moaned softly; he turned toward the sorceror, and his expression darkened. Damien turned to his friend, just in time to see him crumple to the floor. Quickly he moved to his side, careful to place his bulk between the two men, protecting Senzei. With one hand he pulled open his collar, with the other he tested his forehead for fever. The flushed skin burned like fire, an ominous heat. Senzei's eyes were open, but glazed and expressionless; his mouthed opened and closed soundlessly, shaping a whisper.

"The scent of death is on him," the Hunter said quietly.

"I'm surprised you can make it out in this place." Damien felt his hands shaking as he felt for his friend's pulse—weak and rapid, like the heartbeat of a frightened bird—and knew that he was going to have to Heal him. Here. Now. It was that or let him die.

I should never have let you go on this long, he thought grimly. *Forgive me.* And then the hardest admission of all, one he rarely made: *I was afraid....*

Senzei gasped. A broken voice forced its way through his swollen throat. "Sorry. . . ."

"It's all right," the priest said quietly. "It's going to be all right." *If it has to be done, so be it.* His heart was cold, as if the chill of the Forest had already invaded his flesh. He began to draw inside himself, to gather his consciousness in preparation for Working— when Tarrant's presence stabbed into him like a knife, breaking his concentration.

"You can't Heal him," the Hunter warned. "Not here."

Damien stood and faced him. The fear inside him gave way to rage; his hands balled into fists at his side as he demanded, "What the hell do you suggest? That I just let him die? Is that what you want?"

"I'll deal with him," the Hunter said calmly.

For a moment Damien just stared at him, speechless. "You're telling me you can Heal?"

"Not at all. But that isn't the skill your friend requires right now."

He began to move toward the fallen sorceror, clearly intending to Work him—but Damien grabbed him by the tunic front and forced him back, all his anger transmuted into sudden strength.

"You stay away from him!" he spat. "I've had enough of your Workings—and so has he. You think I'll let you do to him what you did to that boy?" He shook his head angrily. "I only make a mistake once, Hunter."

Something flashed in Tarrant's eyes, an emotion so human that Damien had no trouble at all interpreting it. Hatred—unbridled, undisguised. The honesty of it was strangely refreshing.

"You *will* trust me, priest." His voice was a mere whisper, but the power behind it was deafening. Ripples of earth-fae carried the words deep into Damien's brain, adhered their meaning to his flesh. "Not because you want to. Or because it comes easily to you. *Because you have no choice.*"

He reached up and pulled Damien's hand from his tunic front. His flesh was like ice; Damien's hand spasmed once in his grip, then went numb. Tarrant pushed him away. Then he glanced down at his clothing and scowled, as though the sharp creases Damien had left in the fine silk were distortions in his own flesh. "As I must serve the lady's cause, in this." His tone was bitter. "I, too, have no choice."

He looked toward the door. Damien felt the power rise in him, tides of fae responding to his will like a dog coming to heel for its master. The priest clutched his injured hand to his chest and wondered just how fast—and how effectively—his other hand could draw and strike. Could he get to the Fire before Tarrant realized what he was doing?

Then the doors were flung open and a pair of men entered. Tarrant nodded toward Senzei's body.

"You did a brave and foolish thing in coming here," he told Damien. His polished mask was back in place, his tone once more aloof and controlled. "I'll admit that I didn't expect it of you. But now that you're here and I'm forced to deal with you, it's time you faced the facts." The men were gathering up Senzei's body. "We are allies, you and I. You don't have to like it. I curse the day it became necessary. But you *will* accept it—for the lady's sake. As I must." He glanced toward Senzei and back again, meaningfully. "I suggest you accept my service while it's still available, priest. Your friend has very little time left."

It's that or Work the fae myself, Damien thought. And he knew, with sudden dread clarity, that he would never survive such an immersion. The evil in this place was too deeply entrenched; it would draw the life from his wounded flesh before he had the chance to whisper his first key.

We have no alternative, he thought bitterly. *We have run out of options.*

"For now," he responded. Not in years had he spoken such distasteful words—but the Hunter was right. There was no other choice. "This once."

God help you if you betray us!

They carried the body to an upstairs room, a vaulted chamber that had clearly been outfitted for guests. There they laid Senzei atop a velvet-draped bed, beneath a heavy brocade canopy supported by four carved posts. The wood of the bed was dark, as was all the room's furniture; even the heavy curtains were a carmine so deep that it might almost have been black. But the fire that had been kindled in the room's large fireplace cast a crisp, golden light across the room, and picked out features of the decor in reassuring amber. Compared to the jet black rooms below, it was almost a human place.

Tarrant wasted no time in superficial examination. With a slender knife that he had produced from somewhere on his person, he cut through the layers of Senzei's clothing with the innate skill of a surgeon and laid his dressing bare. The thick white bandages were stained with a motley of dark, unpleasant colors, and a fetid smell arose from their surface. Damien was dimly aware of the two servants leaving them as Tarrant's knife slid beneath the blood-soaked cloth, dividing it. Slowly, he peeled the crusted layers back from the sorceror's skin. A putrid scent filled the room: the stink of advanced infection. It was a smell Damien knew all too well—the smell of flesh failing, of a body too far gone into death for any mere Healing to save it. With a sinking heart he watched as Tarrant took out a handkerchief—fine white linen, edged in gold embroidery—and carefully wiped Senzei's side clean of the rotted gore that clung to him, so that the wound itself might be seen.

His entire side was black and swollen; the sides of his wound gaped open like the mouth of a fish, despite the stitches that had been meant to close it. Within, it was possible to see the damp sheen of muscle and the sharp edge of a lower rib, both darkly discolored, both smelling of decay. Damien studied it for a long, despairing moment, then looked up at Tarrant—and found the man watching him, pale eyes made gold by the firelight.

"You may See, if you wish." The Hunter's voice was quiet, barely discernable above the crackle of the flames. "The currents are safe enough for you here. But don't interrupt me, or try to interfere. To do so would cost your friend's life. You understand?"

Stiffly, he nodded.

The Hunter turned back to Senzei and fixed his eyes on the wound. Slowly, soundlessly, his lips formed words; a key? Damien considered Working his own vision, felt a chill of fear flood through him—and carefully ignored it, as he envisioned the patterns that would give him Sight.

Delicately. Only a word, a thought; he had no desire to touch any more of the Forest's fae than he had to, Worked or no. Malevolence rose about him like a black, ice-cold lake; he dipped his thoughts into it just briefly, then quickly withdrew. The lake subsided, though its cold had invaded his veins. And his Sight—

Was as it had never been before. Or was it simply that the fae was so different here, which made its form so alien? Dark purple power pooled about the bedposts, slithered up the carved wood like deep violet serpents—and then slid across the coverlet, seeking Senzei's flesh. Damien had to stop himself from reaching out to Banish them. Though he sensed in every fiber of his being that the purpose of these things was to devour, to destroy, the Hunter's last words echoed in his brain: *Interfere, and it will cost your friend's life.*

And his other words, even more ominous. *You will trust me . . . because you have to.*

Damn you, Merentha!

He watched as the tendrils of violet dissolved, becoming a thick purple fog that surrounded Senzei, clinging to his skin. There seemed to be movement within its substance; Damien Worked his senses to let him take a closer look—and stiffened in horror as he Saw. For the cloud was not a cloud at all, but a swarm of creatures too tiny for the unWorked eye to see. Wormlike, hungry, they searched the surface of Senzei's skin until they found a pore or other opening large enough to admit them. Then they slithered in, their microscopic tails lashing from side to side as they worked their way deeper and deeper into his flesh. Damien caught the flash of teeth at one forward end, and remembered the creatures that had devoured their horse; these were clearly their kin, though made of much less solid stuff. He had to fight to swallow back the rising tide of disgust inside him. If this was supposed to be some kind of Healing . . . but no, it wasn't that. Tarrant had made that very clear.

They were under Senzei's skin, now, working their way into his bloodstream. Where his veins were close enough to the surface it was possible to see them moving, the skin rippling as they passed. Thousands upon thousands of them had entered Senzei's body already, enough to tint his blood deep purple, and more were digging their way in each second. It seemed that his entire body had become filled with purple fluid, filled near to bursting. Damien looked at the wound itself and saw larger creatures nestled in the rotting flesh, feasting on its putrescence. Sickness rose in the back of his throat, and he struggled not to give in to it. He had seen more terrible things in his life, but never under conditions like this: watching them devour a traveling companion while he stood impotently on the sidelines. Suddenly he hated Tarrant with a passion that surpassed even his religious abhorrence of the man; this was personal, intensified by his suspicion of just how much the man enjoyed having him in such a position. As if frustrating a member of his former Church was itself a triumph, to be savored.

And then, the cloud withdrew from Senzei. The fog, now black, seeped from his veins like blood, and hovered over him silently, a storm cloud waiting to break. Where the firelight played on its substance it sizzled, and thin filaments could be seen writhing on its surface. Then Tarrant muttered the key words of a Banishing, and it vanished. Not slowly, like a fog being scattered by the wind, but immediately—as though his will, which commanded the action, knew no middle ground.

Damien looked at the wound, saw the clear red of untainted blood slowly pooling in that opening. The carrion-eaters were gone, or at least invisible; he had no real desire to find out which. He looked up at the Hunter—and saw that the man's face was white with pain, as if the healing of Senzei were somehow wounding him.

"Now the fever," the Hunter whispered. He held out a hand, palm up, over the body. Slowly it began to give off a strange glow, a cold silver light that illuminated little of what surrounded it, but burned the eyes to look upon as if it were an actual flame. "Coldfire," he whispered. He molded it in his hand like some nacreous clay, forming it into the shape of what it was not: true fire. And it burst up suddenly in his hand, like a flame devouring fresh fuel, and flickered like its namesake—but there was no heat that came from it, and little of its light reached beyond its brilliant surface. Staring at it, Damien felt the warmth drawn out of him, gone to feed something at the heart of the non-fire; with effort he drew back, and erected a barrier that he hoped would suffice to protect him.

"As volatile as true fire," the Hunter whispered. "And as dangerous." He brought his hand down to the wound and tipped it over; the coldfire slid into the wound like a viscous liquid. As it made contact with his flesh, Senzei cried out—a scream of pain, of terror, of utter isolation. Damien leaned forward and took him by the shoulders, not to hold him down so much as to reassure him, by that touch, that he was not alone. Beneath his fingers he could feel the chill of the Hunter's coldfire as it worked its way through Senzei's veins, consuming the heat of the fever with mindless hunger. As it passed through the thick veins in his neck, toward his brain, Senzei stiffened; then, with a sudden sharp cry, he went limp. Damien turned back sharply to the Hunter—who was leaning back, clearly well satisfied with his work.

"He'll sleep now," Tarrant said. "I've cauterized the wound as well as my skills will allow. True Healing is denied me—it would cost me my life to attempt it—but the coldfire is an adequate substitute, in some things. His fever is down and shouldn't rise again. It will take some regeneration of living flesh to close the wound properly . . . but the Workings of life are no longer in my repertoire. I must leave that to you."

Damien was about to answer when a gong suddenly sounded in the distance. In answer to his unspoken question the Hunter said, "Dawn. And I have work to do before the keep can be shuttered for the day." He pulled something out of a pocket in his outer tunic and threw it to Damien; a small key. "For the window." He paused. "I'm sure you'll understand that I cannot allow you free run of the castle during the daylight hours. Not yet, anyway."

The exhaustion of the last few endless days was taking hold of Damien; he found that he lacked the strength to argue. "What about Ciani?"

"Tomorrow night. I promise you. In the meantime . . . I will see that you're brought suitable food." His eyes narrowed as he studied Damien's person. "And a bath. There's a chamber adjoining this one, with amenities between; you may make free use of both. The doors beyond this suite will be locked until dusk, except when my servants attend you. I'm sure you could easily overwhelm my people if you wished—if you dared to leave your friend here alone. . . ." The threat in his voice was unmistakable. "But I still have the lady, don't I? So it would behoove you to cooperate." He nodded toward Senzei. "See that he's exposed to the sun when it rises. That will destroy any remnants of my power which still adhere to his veins. I recommend you don't attempt a Healing until that's done." The distant gong sounded again: a deeper, more resonant note. "If you will excuse me."

Without further word or gesture he left the room. There must have been a bolt on the outside, for it was that rather than the turning of a lock that Damien heard. The priest turned toward the window— and felt his physical defenses giving way at last, to a tide of hunger, exhaustion, and hopelessness so powerful that it had taken all his reserves to hold it back this long. He tried to estimate the hours since they had awakened on Morgot, but couldn't; it seemed like days—years—a lifetime. As if they hadn't just arrived in the Forest, but had always been there—subject to its hungers, its fears, its eternal darkness, the fierce currents of its power. . . .

With effort, he managed to reach the window. He reached up and pulled the heavy curtain aside, only to find two heavy planks of wood that served as internal shutters, holding back the light. He fumbled for the key that Tarrant had given him and fitted it into the small golden lock between the two panels. The key turned easily, but the heavy wood shutters required all his remaining strength. When he had them pushed back halfway into their storage slots, he paused and leaned against the wall to one side, breathing heavily. And he contemplated that there was only so long a body could function in overdrive, without sleep or food to sustain it.

In the distance, a dark gray light was seeping across the horizon. He estimated how long it would take the sun to rise to the height of this window, then checked to see that Senzei was lying in the path of its light. It was all he had strength to do. The pain in his side, denied for so many hours, lanced through his torso with fresh reminder of his own weakness, and the strain of forty hours with no more rest than a brief fit of delirium in Morgot added its weight to his exhaustion. He stared at the horizon for a few more moments, watching for a change that he knew would occur too slowly for him to see—but by the time the white sun of Erna had cleared the horizon and the first few stars of the galaxy had grudgingly succumbed to its light, he was lost in a sleep so deep, so insulating, that not even the thought of sunlight over the Forest was enough to awaken him.

They came for him at sunset, as soon as it began to grow dark. They gave him time to see that Senzei was well, to affirm that the Healing he had done at midday hadn't been banished by the coming of night—and then they directed him to follow them, through the castle's upper corridors. For once, he was not afraid to leave his companion behind. It seemed unlikely that the Hunter would have invested so much effort in saving Senzei's life if he was only waiting for Damien's absence in order to kill him.

Food and rest had done much to renew his confidence—not to mention a much-needed bath and a timely shave. His face was raw but no longer stubble-covered, and his skin had been rubbed clean of both Forest grime and caked blood. He had even toweled down Senzei, scraping off the residue of gore that encrusted him to find clean, pink flesh beneath, rapidly healing. The latter was a monument to the Forest's earth-fae, which, once tamed, intensified each Working a thousandfold. He wondered if it was just his room that had been guarded from the ferocity of the currents, or the entire castle; if the latter, it meant that he and the Hunter were on much more equal ground.

Then they took him into the guestroom where the Hunter was waiting—and where Ciani lay, as still and white as Senzei had been.

He ignored the adept and hurried to her side. Her flesh was cool to the touch, but the pulse that throbbed beneath his fingertips was regular. No sooner had he acertained that than her eyes fluttered open—and she was in his arms, shivering in a mixture of fear and relief, her tears soaking the wool of his shirt as he held her.

"You see," the Hunter said quietly. "As I promised."

"Her memory is back?"

"All that I took." The adept seemed to hesitate. "Perhaps . . . more."

Damien looked up at him, sharply. In his arms, Ciani trembled.

"This reunion will be managed better without my presence," the Hunter said shortly. "You should know that these are her first waking moments since Morgot—she knows nothing of what you've done, or what has passed between us. You'll need to bring her up to date. When you're done here, have my servants bring you to the observatory. We have plans to discuss."

And he left, without further word. Not until the heavy door had closed behind him did Ciani draw back from Damien. Her eyes were red, her breathing unsteady. "Tarrant. . . ."

"Is the Hunter," he said quietly. And he told her—what they knew, what they suspected, what they feared. She drank it all in hungrily, as though somewhere in that sea of knowledge the key to life was hidden. And it was, for her. Even in such a state, that much remained true.

In time, she grew calm. In time, he was convinced that what the Hunter had said was true: her memories were intact, back to the day of the attack in Jaggonath. He had returned them.

"It hurt him," she whispered. "I think . . . I think it almost killed him, to absorb so much of my psyche. As if the sheer *humanity* of my memories was somehow a threat to him. I sensed that. Without knowing where I was, or what was happening." She shivered. "I sensed it . . . as though his thoughts were my own."

"Anything else?"

"He was furious with you. For entering the Forest. Furious because he would now have to deal with you, instead of just settling things with me. Any entanglement with the living is a threat to him . . . as if it somehow could cost him his life, I don't understand it exactly. He blames you for that."

Damien's eyes narrowed. "That's fair enough. I blame him for a lot."

A hint of a smile crossed her face; the old Ciani, showing through. "What did he mean, we have plans to discuss?"

"He says he's going with us."

There was fear in her eyes—but only for an instant, and then it was subsumed by something far stronger: her curiosity. "It's what we wanted, isn't it?"

"It's what *you* wanted," he reminded her. "But now there's no way to avoid it. I don't believe we can get out of here without his help, and he's raised questions. . . ." He hesitated. He didn't want to bring that up, not now; Ciani had enough to deal with without facing the fact that her assailants were perhaps merely tools for some much darker, much more powerful force. "If this honor really binds him, as he insists, we may be safe enough."

"It does." Her eyes stared out into empty space, as if looking out upon a remembered landscape. "It's the glue that holds it all together for him. The last living fragment of his human identity. If he lets that go . . . he'll be no more than a mindless demon. Dead, to all intents and purposes. A tool of your hell, without any will of his own."

"Not a pretty concept."

"He's very proud, and very determined. His will to live is so strong that every other force in his life, every other concern, is subordinated to it. That's what's kept him alive all these years." She shuddered. "If he didn't feel that the question of honor was so linked to his personal survival—"

"Then we would all be dead," he finished for her. "That explains a lot. What I don't understand is that he's returned the memories to you—along with a few of his own, I gather—and now we're all here together, restored as a group. He's undone the damage he caused. So why is it so necessary for him to come along? How does Revivalist honor play a part in that?"

Her eyes were wide, her voice solemn. "He promised someone," she whispered. "Just that. He promised someone he would never hurt me . . . and then he did. He betrayed himself. The force of his self-hatred. . . ." She looked away. "You can't imagine it," she breathed. "But I remember it, as though it were my own. And . . . there aren't words. . . ." She clutched herself, as though by doing so she could keep his memories from coming to her. "He perceives himself as balanced on a very fine line, with death on both sides of him. And if at any moment he fails to choose the course that will maintain his balance—"

"He dies," Damien muttered.

"Or worse," she told him. "There are far, far worse things than mere death that lie in wait for him now."

Yes, Damien thought, *there would be. A thousand years or more of hell in the making, with new devils spawned by each sinner. And all of them gunning for him, the one arrogant adept who escaped their clutches. . . .*

He kissed her on the forehead. "You've earned your keep," he told her. And despite all his fears, and the long hours of despair behind him, he smiled. "Lucky for us that when he returned your memories he did so this imperfectly; the information you picked up from him may give us enough control over the situation to make traveling with him viable—"

"As he probably intended," she whispered.

Startled, Damien fell silent. Long enough to consider what he knew of the man—and just how hard it would have been for the Hunter to discuss such things openly. To bare his soul as it must be bared, lest the group refuse to travel with him. In which case it would mean that his honor couldn't be vindicated. In which case—

"Yes," he said quietly. "In control, as always." He glanced at the door, felt his arm about Ciani tighten protectively. "Even when he's not here."

He got up from the bed, and helped her to do the same.

"Come on," he said. "I think it's time we had a little talk with our host."

The observatory had been established on the roof of the castle's highest tower, surrounded by a low crenellated wall and a panoramic view of the Forest far below. A number of farseers had been set about the edge, alongside more arcane machinery whose form gave no hint as to its purpose. Far below, white mist veiled the Forest's canopy, and the distant mountains jutted through it like islands rising from a foamy sea.

In the center of the roof was an unusually large farseer with an intricate viewpiece. Surrounding it, carved into the black stone surface of the tower, was a circle of arcane symbols, precisely aligned. It struck Damien as odd that an adept should require such things. Generally it was only the unschooled who relied so heavily on symbology.

Gerald Tarrant was busy adjusting the largest farseer when they arrived, but he quickly looked up from the faceted eyepiece to acknowledge them. He bowed formally to Ciani—the gesture of another time, another world. He might have been born of a different race entirely, so much had Erna changed since he had last lived in it.

"You have decided," he said. A question.

Before Ciani could answer, Damien snapped, "I don't see that we have much choice."

"Just so," he agreed. He turned from them to gaze out into the night, as if reading meaning into its darkness. "It might interest you to know that your enemies have staked out the road to Sheva as your most likely point of departure from the Forest."

"They won't enter the woods, then?" Ciani asked.

"If they did, it might save you all some trouble; nothing within my borders can withstand me."

"How many are there?"

"Six. A formidable company. They've established a false trail leading to the Serpent, meant to convince you that they departed for home . . . but their presence is like a cancer at the edge of my realm. It would be impossible for me to miss it." His gaze came to rest on Ciani, lingered there. "I regret, my lady, that your own assailant no longer seems to be among them; apparently he left soon after the incident in Morgot. Perhaps they sensed that if he were with them, we need only destroy that small company to see that your faculties were returned to you."

Damien's tone was bitter. "As it is . . ."

"We must do what you originally planned, and enter the rakhlands to hunt him down. Only now you must travel at night."

Damien refused to rise to the bait. "I take it we avoid Sheva?"

"And have them on our tail all the way? No." The Hunter smiled. "I have other plans."

When he said nothing more, Damien prompted, "Share them with us?"

"Not yet. When the preparation is complete. Have patience, priest."

Overhead, the clouds shifted. From Prima's disk, now visible, silver light spilled across the landscape. Tarrant's eyes flickered toward the moon, and his hand tightened on the body of the farseer.

"Stargazing?" Damien asked.

"Call it an ancient science." He studied the pair of them as though considering how much to tell them. Then he stepped back and gestured toward the heavy black machine. "Take a look."

Damien glanced at Ciani; she nodded. Somewhat warily, he stepped into the warded circle. If the ancient symbols focused any Working on him, he didn't feel it. He lowered his right eye to the viewpiece, saw Prima leap forward from the darkness to confront him. The leading edge of Magra Crater was a fine line on the silver horizon, and just below were five long channels, stretching like fingers across the face of the globe.

When he had seen his fill of the familiar lunar features he stood up again. "Seems like a lot of excess bulk for that kind of magnification."

"Is it?" the Hunter asked softly. "Work your Sight, and you may think otherwise."

"In this place? The current would—"

"I insulated your rooms, so that you could Heal there. What I did here was . . . similar. You're quite safe where you stand. Go ahead," he urged. "The view will educate you."

Damien hesitated; the degree to which the man knew exactly how to bait him was beginning to get on his nerves. But at last curiosity won out over caution. "All right." He envisioned the first key of a Seeing in his mind, let it mold the earth-fae to his will—

And nothing happened.

Nothing at all.

He tried to Work his other senses. The result was the same. The totality of his failure was staggering. It was as if the fae had somehow become . . . unWorkable. As if all the rules he had come to take for granted had suddenly been unwritten.

"Inside that circle," Tarrant said quietly, "there is no fae."

He heard Ciani gasp, almost did so himself. "How is that possible?"

"Never mind that," the Hunter put his hand on the barrel of the farseer. "Look now."

Damien lowered his eye to the viewpiece—and saw the surface of Prima, just as before. Magnified exactly as it had been, with the farseer still fixed on the features he had chosen.

He stood, but said nothing. Words had failed him.

"Damien?" It was Ciani.

"The same," he managed. "It's still . . . the same." The truth was almost too fantastic. "It's not a farseer."

Tarrant shook his head. "The old Earth word was *telescope*. He stroked the black tube proudly, possessively. "Crystal lenses, ground to precise specifications. Distanced apart at intervals determined by Earth-science. And it works. Every time. No matter who uses it, no matter what they expect, or what they might hope for, or fear . . . it works." There was something in his voice that Damien had never heard there before. Awe? "Imagine a whole world like that. A world of unalterable physical laws, where the will of the living has no power over inanimate objects. A world in which the same experiment, performed at a thousand different sites by a thousand different men, would have exactly the same result each time. That is our heritage, Reverend Vryce. Which this world denied us."

He looked at the telescope and tried to envision a world such as the Hunter described. And at last could only mutter, "I can't imagine it."

"Nor I. After years of trying. The magnitude of it staggers the imagination. That a whole planet could be so utterly unresponsive to life . . . and yet life as we know it evolved on its surface."

"Advanced life."

The Hunter smiled faintly. "We do like to think so." He looked toward Ciani and indicated the telescope; an invitation. As she came forward and lowered her eye to the viewpiece, he said quietly, "Are you prepared for another question?"

Damien felt himself stiffen. Ciani looked up.

"Let's hear it," he said.

"What was it the lady's assailants wanted, in Jaggonath?"

"You mean when they attacked me?" Ciani asked.

"Exactly."

"Revenge," Damien told him. "Ciani had escaped from them—"

"Hell of a long trip, for vengeance."

The night was very quiet.

"What are you suggesting?"

"I suggest nothing. I merely . . . ask questions. Like what would have happened if the lady's assailant had returned to the rakhlands after crippling her—as he supposedly intended." He gave them a moment to digest that, then continued, "According to what we know about the Canopy, when he crossed to the other side of that barrier, the bond that joined them would have been severed. Banished. From the lady's standpoint, I imagine . . . it would be much the same as if he had died."

"She would have been freed!"

"Not exactly an efficient vendetta, eh? A week or two of misery for her, and then it would all be over." His pale gray eyes were fixed on Ciani, drinking in her response; there was a hunger in him that made Damien uneasy.

"You think they had something else in mind."

With obvious reluctance, he forced his eyes away from her. "I think they intended one of two things. To kill her . . . or take her with them. Either way they would have benefited from having her disabled, by loss of memory and adeptitude. Except that in the former case, it wouldn't really be necessary. A knife thrust through the heart is as fatal to an adept as it is to your common man on the street; if they had her under their control long enough to disable her, it seems unlikely they would have failed to kill her. *If that was what they intended.*"

Damien moved closer to where Ciani stood, to put a reassuring arm around her. She was trembling. "You think they meant to take me back?" she whispered.

"I'm afraid I do, lady. It's the only explanation that makes sense. They must have come to Jaggonath for that purpose, then panicked when your shop's defenses hit them. Had your assistant not faked your death they would surely have come back for you. As it was, they thought you were beyond their reach."

"So they started home."

"And met with reinforcements. Perhaps more of their kind who had been left behind, to cover the trail; perhaps some who came later, after the initial attack was launched. No matter. They guessed your friends' intention to be a mission of vengeance on your behalf and joined forces to deal with you. And prepared to ambush you all in Morgot, because they knew you would have to pass through that port to reach their homeland.

"They know who she is now, I'll bet."

"So much for disguise. What next?"

"That depends on why they want her. They may try to capture her again. Or they may simply settle for killing the whole party, just to have the matter ended. Three of their kind have already died at our hands, I'll remind you. They must be questioning whether the game is worth the cost."

"Either way . . ."

"We'll be ambushed in Sheva," Ciani said quietly. "Because of me."

"We'll be ambushed in Sheva because we're hunting them down like the dogs they are," Damien corrected her.

"We will *not* be ambushed in Sheva." Tarrant said irritably. "I've already launched a Working that will take care of that. By the time your friend is fit to travel, that small army will be long gone. Which leaves us with several larger problems to confront." Overhead the clouds had covered Prima's disk, darkening the night a thousandfold. It was impossible to see Tarrant's face as he told them, "The lady would be safest if she remained here."

"No," Damien said firmly. And Ciani stiffened proudly, as if somehow the suggestion had poured fresh strength into her veins. "I can't just sit back and wait," she said. "I can't! It's my fight, more than anyone's."

"As I expected." Tarrant said quietly. "But it had to be said. It has to be your decision. So: the lady comes with us. We cross under the Canopy. And discover what force is allied to these creatures, that hungers so desperately to possess her. There is no alternative to that course of action if the lady's to be freed.

"But consider this," he said—and his voice took on something of the autumn night, its darkness and its chill. "If we take the lady into the rakhlands, whatever our intentions may be . . . might we not be doing exactly what our enemy wants?"

Twenty-six

They waited alongside the road to Sheva, as they had done for many nights. But despite the doubts that several had expressed, the one who guided them insisted that they were right, that this was the correct place to be; and so they waited, hungry and uneasy, anxious to obtain their vengeance and then hurry home. As one of them had done already, in order to report to the Keeper.

And then the humans came.

They emerged from the Forest's edge barely an hour after dusk. Two men and one woman, the same trio that had left from Jaggonath so many days ago. Only now it was possible to see past the woman's makeup, as though her nights in the Forest had somehow compromised her skill in applying it. Even the newcomers could recognize her, from the description given them in the rakhlands.

So she's not dead! one hissed.

Not yet, another responded hungrily.

They could hear the humans speaking now, and as the trio drew closer they could make out words. The woman was angry at the Hunter for what he had done to her and wanted to get away from him as quickly as possible. The large man—who had been so much trouble in Morgot—insisted that it was all for the best, that if she hadn't demanded they leave without the Hunter, he would have insisted on it. Only the tall, pale one was silent, but it was easy to see as he adjusted his Worked spectacles that he had been through much, and not recovered well.

Excellent.

The attackers were still six strong, twice the number that had first set forth on this ill-fated mission. Compared to the puny human force that faced them, they were little less than an army.

The sorceror isn't with them! one exulted.

They refused to travel with him.

Our luck.

Yes. . . .

He had taken them by surprise, that one. He, and that damnable bitch from the plains. *She* had gone right home after the battle, driven off by the raw malevolence of the sorceror's domain. So now she was out of the picture. As for the sorceror himself . . . who cared where he was, as long as he was absent? The humans were alone. That was all that mattered.

We kill them, one of the newcomers instructed. *Quickly. And make sure of it this time.*

There were murmurs of protest—of hunger, of fear—but they soon settled down. The newcomer was right. They had tried a more complicated plan, and the humans had come hunting them. Now it was time to end it.

The Keeper would simply have to accept that.

The humans were closer now; it was possible to hear them arguing. The six tensed, waiting for the right moment.

"This is a mistake—" the thin man was saying.

"You're outvoted, Zen" The large man's voice was brusque, unyielding. "Tarrant's just too vulking dangerous. I'd rather face a horde of these demons, unarmed, than have that kind of power behind my back."

"But—"

"He's right," the woman said quietly. Her voice was tense, her manner strained. She looked as though she hadn't slept for days. "We don't know anything about his motives. Except that he thrives on human terror—and if he traveled with us, we'd be the only humans in range for quite some time." She shivered. "He fed on me once. Once is enough."

They charged.

They ran silently, slipping from shadow to shadow as fluidly as though they themselves were composed of nothing more solid than darkness. The humans were so wrapped up in their argument that it was seconds before they noticed that anything was amiss. And seconds were enough. The first of the attacking army was within arm's reach of the nearest horse when the priest cried out, "Heads up!" and the battle was joined.

Too late, for the humans. Even as the priest whipped out his sword, the nearest attacker had his horse by the bridle; with a sharp jerk he twisted the creature's head at an angle it was loath to adopt. The horse staggered wildly, and the priest's swing went wide of its target.

Another twist and the horse went down violently, slamming onto its side. The priest rolled free, barely. A second attacker leapt onto him while he was still completing his roll, while his sword was still trapped beneath his body; claws raked the suntanned face, drawing rivers of blood. The priest shivered, feeling the first touch of their cold hunger invade his flesh. He kicked out with all his might—and his strength was considerable, for a human—but though his assailant's leg cracked sharply and swung free at an odd angle from the knee down, the attacker managed to hold onto his prey.

The priest fought desperately—as did his companions, each locked in their own small knot of combat—but the attackers knew their tricks now, and would not be defeated the same way again. Besides, the tall and deadly sorceror had not yet come to help the humans—which meant that he would not come at all, that he had abandoned them as thoroughly as they had abandoned him.

Hunger surged in the priest's opponent as the fresh exhilaration of victory charged his limbs with newfound energy. He was beginning to drink in the man's substance now, and flickers of memory formed in its brain—images so rich in content that he hissed in delight even as his claws dug into the priest's protective collar and began to close on his windpipe. He absorbed the priest's aspirations, his conquests, his fears. His loves. He experienced the passion of a woman's embrace as this man had known it—wild and intoxicating, obsessive, uninhibited—and the thrill of battle, which felt much the same. He drank in all these things and more: childhood memories, adult desires, dreams and hopes and the terrors that came at midnight, all of them—and as he did so he gained in substance, his pale, translucent flesh taking on the color and texture of life, his empty eyes filled with the warm light of earthly purpose. In that moment, for an instant, the priest's attacker was *human*—and that was a thing that none of his kind had ever been before. Not perfectly. Not until tonight.

Then the rivers of blood that had pulsed out over his hands, from the wounds his claws had made in the man's neck, ceased. Likewise, the memories ceased to flow, and with it the warming pleasure that came from a kill. *Make sure*, the attacker told himself, and he cut deeply into the man's flesh, severing a vital artery that was lodged in his throat. No more than a thin stream came forth; no more than that little bit was left in him. He lapped at the trickle, felt the man's memories pulse in him like a second heartbeat. And then even that was gone, subsumed into his hunger. The priest was dead.

Sated, the attacker climbed to his feet. The battle was over. At the far end of the field the pale human lay, and he saw that his eyes had been torn out in the heat of that battle. His companions sat between the bodies, licking warm blood from their hands and faces, shivering with the pleasure of stolen memories. He looked for the woman— surely she hadn't escaped—and found her where she had been felled, not far from her thinner comrade.

Dead. Her horse had reared up, terrified, and she had been thrown from the saddle. She had struck an outcropping of granite headfirst, and her cranium had split open like an overripe melon. A thick, wet mass oozed out between the cracks and dribbled wetly onto the ground.

Dead, he whispered.

They gathered around him.

Dead, another agreed. And a third added, *Without question.*

Who will tell the Keeper that we lost her?

They looked at the bodies, the fallen horses, the roads . . . anywhere but at their fellows.

The Keeper will know, one said at last. *When we enter the home-land. As soon as we do.*

They considered that. Several of them shivered.

We could . . . choose not to go home.

For a moment there was silence, as they all considered that option. But it really was no option, and they knew it. The rage when the Keeper learned of their failure would be nothing compared to what they would suffer if they tried to flee. The Master of Lema was wise, they told themselves, and experienced, and would know that these things happened. Surely their punishment would not be too harsh.

They looked at the bodies—and licked the blood from their lips— savoring the last echoes of the humans' screams. And then they turned south, toward the outskirts of Sheva, and began the long journey home.

Twenty-seven

Gazing out into the night, Gerald Tarrant thought, *It's done.*
The black stonework of his observatory was barely visible even to
him, cloaked as it was by the absolute darkness of the true night.
Soon, however, Casca would rise in the west, shedding its maverick
light upon the landscape. And then the most delicate wisps of the
dark fae—which were also the most powerful—would dissolve into
nothingness, and take their Workings with them.

Good enough. The job was done. The demons from the rakhlands,
secure in their triumph, had already turned toward home. In a few
days' time they would cross beneath the edge of the Canopy, which
barrier would then keep them from realizing the truth—that they had
been tricked, and tricked thoroughly.

He watched with his special vision as his Working faded in the
distance, as the three humans he had altered regained their original
identities. It didn't matter now. The demons had already moved on
and wouldn't see the change. Only with the dark fae was such an
illusion possible—one that was maintained not only on the gross
physical planes but in the arena of thought as well—but the dark fae
was a fickle, impermanent force, and could hardly be bound now to
sustain an illusion that no longer had purpose. He would have to lead
the lady's people along a slightly different path, to avoid the questions
which the presence of bodies might raise. . . .

Listen to yourself, he thought angrily. *You're catering to them!*
Better that they should cater to you.

Three nights, at most. Maybe less. Then he would leave the Forest
which had been his home—his shield—his refuge. The land which
was him, as much as the flesh he wore.

And what if some idiot lights a match while I'm gone? He looked out over the thickly webbed canopy and considered calling rain. With enough effort he could establish a weather pattern that would guarantee regular precipitation for months . . . but with winter coming that could as easily mean snow, and too much snow meant its own special perils. No. Let nature take its course. Amoril could handle the Forest. The albino couldn't Work the weather yet—possibly he'd never be able to—but his skills were strong enough in other areas. And if at times he seemed to lack . . . say, a sense of aesthetics . . . he more than made up for that with his enthusiasm.

And besides, no one would know that the Hunter had left. He must remember that. No one would know that the Hunter had passed beyond a boundary through which no human thought could travel, and was cut off from that source of power which he had cultivated for centuries. . . .

He felt a tremor deep within himself, as if some part of the human self he had buried had trickled through to the surface. Fear? Anticipation? Dread? He had lived for so long within the Forest's hospitable confines that he could no longer remember what it was like to be afraid. Somewhere along the line he had lost that, too, as if fear and love and compassion and paternal devotion had all been a package deal, discarded together in that first red sacrifice which took him from one life to another.

And if he feared, was there something that would feed on that? As he fed on the fear of others—that last delicious moment when the human mind abandoned all hope and the defenses of the soul came crashing down? Man had arrived on this planet little more than a millenium ago, and already there were myriad creatures that relied on him for sustenance; why should the food chain stop there?

In the quiet of the night, the Neocount of Merentha mused: *How long does evolution take, among the damned?*

CITADEL
OF
STORMS

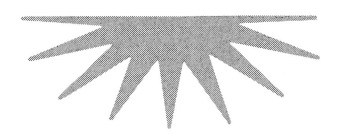

Twenty-eight

They left the gloomy replica of Merentha Castle promptly at dusk. Or so they were told. High up on the ramparts it might have been possible to see the sun, possible to verify that day had indeed ended and the reign of night begun. But in the closed corridors of the castle's interior and beneath the Forest's thickly woven canopy, one had to take such things on faith. The Hunter's faith.

They had no other choice.

Tarrant provided horses for Ciani and himself, jet-black creatures with muscular limbs and rich, glossy coats. They left behind them a trail of crescent indentations, as unlike the three-toed marks left by Damien's mounts as those of another species would be. Their proportion, likewise, seemed strange to the eye, almost but not quite identical to that of their southern brethren. Damien was hard pressed to put his finger on the difference—but he knew, whatever it was, that it was both controlled and intentional. With a thousand years of leisure time on his hands and the nearly unlimited potential of the Forest's fae, the Neocount of Merentha had completed his most ambitious task. Erna now had true horses.

Without a word, as if they feared that the noise of speech might somehow put them in danger, the party rode east. The foliage of the Forest parted before them like a living thing—and on those occasions when it failed to do so, the Hunter's coldfire would flare in the path ahead of them, clearing the way. When they passed, then, they would find the plant life frozen and brittle; the tree branches that had previously hindered them shattered into frigid dust at the mere sound of their passage.

They rode for hours. At last it was Damien who called a halt, judging that the horses would need a breather if they were to continue at pace until dawn. He looked at Tarrant and gestured toward the ground, as if questioning its safety. After a moment the Hunter smiled—faintly, ever so faintly, as if traveling with mere humans had sapped him of humor—and then drew his sword. Silver-blue light filled the air, and a gust of frigid wind went sweeping past Damien, sucked toward the Worked steel. Then the Hunter thrust downward, casting his weapon into the earth. The ground seemed to shudder and cracks appeared, jagged lines that radiated out from the invading swordpoint. The front end of a wormlike creature broke ground and then stiffened—and shivered into a thousand bits of crystal that sparkled like fresh snow on the frozen ground. After that, there was no further movement.

"You can dismount," the Hunter assured them.

Damien and Senzei fed their mounts from the stores they had brought with them; the Hunter's black horses, weaned on the Forest's vegetation, seemed content to crop the leafless stalks that flanked the cleared area. Damien wondered what adjustments he had made to their digestive systems that allowed them to thrive in this dismal place. Did their massive hooves keep them safe from Forest predators who might otherwise track them through the heat of their trail? What adaptive purpose had such thick armor plates served on Earth, where a beast might tread the ground without fear of heatseekers?

"When we reach Sheva," Tarrant told them, "and from then on, I would prefer you not use my title. Or refer to my true identity."

"They seemed to recognize you outside Mordreth," Senzei challenged.

"As a servant of the Hunter. Not as the Hunter himself."

"It makes so much difference?"

"Enough. When a man thinks of killing the Hunter's servant—or even disobeying him—he must take into account what the master's reaction will be. Which is very different from how he will act if he imagines that he might, through the luck of a single kill, dispose with the master altogether." And he added dryly, "It spares me the inconvenience of killing every time I travel. Surely you find that appealing."

Through gritted teeth, Damien muttered. "Surely."

Night. *True* night reigned below, blind to what was happening in the heavens; even Domina's light couldn't pierce the thick canopy, which had been designed to keep the sunlight out. Thick, white-skinned vines glittered in the lamplight as they passed, their leafless lengths twining upward about the tree trunks until they reached a height where sunlight was available. Research in the castle's library had revealed that the Forest was once a fairly normal place, unique only in that it was located near a natural focus of the Earth-fae. The Hunter had changed that. It was he who had evolved the Forest's special trees, which trapped their own dead leaves in a webwork of hair-fine branches, so that even in the dead of winter no light would reach the ground below. But what other adjustments must have been made to this ecosystem to keep it functioning? The perpetual darkness would have killed any light-dependent species within the Forest's confines, throwing the whole ecosystem out of balance. He must have Worked it all—plant by plant, animal, insect, and bush alike— until he had stabilized thousands of species in a new, light-starved balance. And created a few new ones, to facilitate its functioning. Damien thought of the wormlike creatures, and realized that even they must play their part. A biosphere with so little energy input had no room for waste.

What kind of a mind did it take to think on that scale? To take on such a project and then succeed with it, rather than making the Forest into a lifeless wasteland, whose survival was compromised by the lack of one special insect, or one minute step in the food chain ladder? The sheer scope of the project was staggering. —But with a thousand years of spare time on his hands, a very special man could succeed. A man like the Neocount of Merentha, who had spent his last living years redefining man and God, evolving human society with the same precise attention to detail that he gave to horses and Forest flora. . . .

And then there was light on the path ahead of them, ever so little— but it silhouetted the Hunter as he passed between the final trees and flooded the land beyond with the clean, subtle promise of dawn.

"Almost daylight," Tarrant said distastefully. He gestured toward the east. "Sheva's five miles further, at most. You can find shelter there."

"Not as dismal as Mordreth, I hope," Senzei muttered.

It seemed that the Hunter might have smiled, but a quick glance at the lightening sky sobered whatever humor he might otherwise have exhibited. "Mordreth is a special case," he assured them. "But the autumn nights end too quickly for prolonged conversation. Save your questions for the darker hours, and they may get answered."

"This much light doesn't seem to be hurting you," Damien challenged.

Tarrant shot him a quick, searing glare—and it was hard to tell exactly what was behind it. Exasperation, irritation, disdain . . . or all three. "Any man who can stand under the stars can survive the touch of sunlight, priest. It's simply a matter of degree." He dismounted gracefully, making no sound as his boots struck the earth. "I have no desire to test my limits."

He held his reins out to Damien. After a moment, the priest took them. "Feed the animal with your own," the Hunter instructed. "Give it whatever you imagine horses eat. It'll survive."

"You mean you're not joining us for breakfast?"

"I doubt that witnessing my appetite would do much for yours." He glanced again at the eastern sky; Damien thought he saw him tense. "Do as you will with the daylight hours," he said softly. "I'll be back soon enough."

"How will you—" Senzei began. But the man had stepped into the shadows of the Forest once more, and its darkness closed about him like the folds of a cloak.

"Not much of a morning person," Damien observed.

It was good to be in a city again, surrounded by live human beings. Good to be in whitewashed rooms inside brick buildings, with bright quilt coverlets on modern beds and thin curtains that failed to block out all of the glorious, wonderful sunlight. Good to be surrounded by the bustle of human activity once more—even if it meant that getting to sleep was a little bit harder for all the noise. Not to mention the sunlight.

It was good for a few hours. Only that. By the time the sun set they were anxious to move again, and when Gerald Tarrant finally rejoined them there was almost an air of relief about the party.

We want to be there, Damien thought. *We want to get it done.*

They rode east. Soon Sheva gave way to open ground, the floor of the Raksha Valley. They found the river Lethe and followed it southeast, through some dozen small settlements that had been established along its banks. When they needed a break, they ate real food in real restaurants. While Tarrant watched silently, delicately sipping a glass of fresh blood, or—if that was lacking—a northern wine. What he did for his main sustenance, in the short time after each sunset that he assigned to his own needs, Damien had no desire to know. But during the day he dreamed of a thousand possibilities and often awoke in a cold sweat, his hand groping for his sword, aware that he had just witnessed some terrible dreambound atrocity, and that Tarrant was the cause. And he wondered how much longer he could be the cause of that man coming to his region, without feeling responsible for the human suffering that must be littering their trail in the Hunter's wake.

And then they came to it. A small city encircling a tiny harbor, whose business was not in trade so much as tourism. Sattin: close enough to the rakhland border that on a clear day it was possible to gaze out across the Serpent and see the jagged cliffs guarding that secret land and—just possibly—the curtain of power that protected it. The city overflowed with tourists, even in this harsh season, who had paid good money and traveled many days in the hopes of seeing what one pamphlet described as *the last bastion of native power*. Which it wasn't, by any strict definition of *native*, or even *bastion*. But the phrase made good press.

There were sorcerors here, enough to populate a minor colony on their own, and as a record of their presence they left headlines splashed in bold print across the gray of cheap northern paper: *Southern Sorc Feeds the Serpent: Suicide or Sacrifice? Sorceress finds Hunter's Mark Carved on Bedpost.* And, inevitably, *The Ghost of Casca is Back—Local Sorceror Reveals the Terrifying Truth.* Their advertisements lined the streets, and filled the windows of shops and taverns. Offers to *Share a Seeing*, boat rides to *Take you close enough to touch the Canopy*, and *Seer Reads the Future—Reasonable Rates.*

If Sattin's tasteless commercialization of the rakhland's defense system amused Damien, it seemed to irritate Gerald Tarrant no end. Either that, or something else was eating at the nightbound adept. More than once he snapped at Damien in a manner unbefitting his normally smooth demeanor; once the priest thought he even saw an emotion flash in those quicksilver eyes that might have been fear, or something akin to it—but the expression was gone so quickly, and was so out of character for the Hunter they had come to know, that in the end he decided he'd been mistaken. What was there in a place like this for the Hunter to fear?

It was while they were sampling what passed for dinner in one of the city's many restaurants—overpriced fare with no pretensions of quality, hardly preferable to their own dried traveling rations—that Tarrant went seeking a vessel to take them to the rakhland's rocky shoreline. It took him a surprisingly long time, given his past record with such things, and several dismal courses had come and gone before he returned to join them.

"They're cowards, all," he informed them. "Ready to risk the Canopy's edge for a handful of tourist gold, but ask them to sail through it. . . ." His fingers tapped the tabletop as he spoke, a gesture of tension that was uncharacteristic of him; Damien wondered what prompted it. "I found a man who'd risk the trip. His price is high. If

I were of a mind to criticize such business practices, I would call it robbery—but never mind that." He saw Damien about to speak, waved short his interruption. "I have the funds. And my Jahanna coinage may cause him to think twice before dumping us into the Serpent."

Startled, Ciani asked, "You think that's possible?"

"My lady, the human soul's a dark place—who knows that better than I?—and greed is a powerful master. Add to that man's passion for self-preservation . . . and yes, I think it very possible that a man we hire to take us to the Achron's mouth might find it expedient to . . . shall we say, *lighten his load* before reaching shore? I would even call it likely. There's a real danger in that landing, and not all men like the smell of risk. I suggest we be careful."

"I could Work—" Damien began.

"So could I. More efficiently than you. And then, when we passed under the Canopy, all that would be gone. Do you want our pilot's murderous instincts suddenly unleashed at the very moment we're least able to defend ourselves? When even an unconscious Working might backfire on us all?" He shrugged; there was a weariness in the gesture that seemed oddly human. "I chose the best man I could. I paid well and threatened carefully. Coercion is one of my skills. Let's hope it works." He turned to Ciani. "Lady, I've scanned the city three times over—and its environs, and the Serpent, and each and every current of power that passes through or near this place. You have no enemies here. Our pilot says we must wait two nights for a suitable syzygy—a high tide will make the rakhland shore considerably more accessible—and that means waiting here. Which I regret. The place is . . ." he scowled. "Distasteful, to say the least. But it is safe. I want you to know that. Your enemies passed through here days ago, and they left neither ward nor watcher behind. I made certain of that."

"Thank you," she said softly. "That's worth . . . a lot. Thank you."

"And now." He pushed his chair back from the table and stood; his pale eyes fixed on Damien, their depths brimming with hostility. "You're not my ideal of a traveling companion, priest, and I know I'm not yours. Since the lady is safe and our transport assured, may I assume that you would have no objection to my passing my time in other company until we depart?"

"None whatsoever," Damien assured him.

And he wondered: *What the hell's eating him!*

The hill was some distance from town, and not easy to climb. Which was why it was empty of tourists, despite its position overlooking the water. It took her some time to reach the top, and when at last she did she rested for a moment, trying to catch her breath.

He stood at the crest, utterly still. Dark cloak rippling slowly in the night breeze, pale eyes fixed on a point somewhere across the water. Or perhaps on nothing. Coming closer, she saw no other motion about him, nothing that hinted at life. Not even breathing. Did he need to breathe, she wondered, when he wasn't speaking? Exactly where was he balanced, in that dark gulf between life and unlife?

And then he turned and saw her. Surprise glittered briefly in his eyes—then there was only control once more, and his expression was unreadable. "Lady." He bowed. "Alone?"

"You said it was safe here."

"I said your enemies were gone. There are still the assorted muggers, rapists . . . etcetera. It is a city," he reminded her.

"I'm city born and bred," she told him. "And well armed, as you may recall. Even without the fae, I think I could give a mugger a run for his money."

He studied her for a moment; something that was almost a smile softened the corners of his mouth. "Yes. I believe you could."

Then he looked out over the water again, and the softness fled from his expression. His nostrils flared, as if testing the air.

"You came to find me," he challenged her.

She nodded.

"They let you come here?"

"They don't know."

He looked surprised. "They think I'm in my room," she said defiantly. As though daring him to criticize her. "You said I was safe."

For a moment he said nothing. Then, very quietly, he told her, "You understand that it's somewhat jarring for me to hear a woman refer to my presence as safe."

"Isn't it?"

"For you? Absolutely. But your men don't seem too certain of that."

"They haven't seen inside you. I have."

He stiffened, turned away from her. Gazed out across the water. "How did you find me?"

"It wasn't hard. There aren't many places in this region where one can be alone . . . and an adept would want a view of the Canopy. I asked the same questions I thought you would have, to find such a place. They brought me here." She followed his gaze across the water, to the blackness of the nightbound horizon. "What do you See?"

He hesitated—then answered, "Nothing."

"Maybe when we get closer—"

He shook his head. "You misunderstand me. I can see the Canopy quite clearly from here. There's no mistaking it. It's as if the world ends suddenly at that point, as if there's a line beyond which nothing exists. Oh, I can see the water beyond, and mountains in the distance . . . but those forces which are visible only to the adept's eye come to a halt in midair, and beyond it is—nothing. Absolute nothingness. A wall of nonexistence, beneath which the water flows."

"And you think it'll kill you."

He stiffened. She saw him about to respond in his usual manner— eloquent and misleading, dryly evasive—but then, his voice strained, he answered simply. "It may. I don't know. I can't read into it at all. If no fae can be Worked in that zone . . . then the power which keeps me alive may well be inaccessible there." He shrugged; it was a stiff gesture, clearly forced. "Your priest knows this? Your sorceror friend?"

"They might have guessed. I didn't tell them."

"Please don't."

She nodded.

"Is that what you came to find out?"

Instead of answering him, she asked, "Is there anything I can do to help?"

He looked at her, and she could sense him trying to read her. Trying to keep himself from using the fae to do it. "Just keep them away from me," he said at last. "The boat has a secure cabin, and I have the key. It was one of the requirements. But who can say what damage they might do if they tried to interfere? Even if they meant to help." He laughed; it was a mirthless sound. "Unlikely as that is."

"I'll try," she promised. And she nodded, gently, "*That's* what I came to find out."

She turned from him, then, and began to make her way down the rocky slope, heading back toward the city.

"Lady."

She stopped where she was, and turned to him.

"You could have the fae back."

For a moment she just stared at him. Then, in a voice that trembled slightly, she asked, "How?"

"Not as an adept—even I can't give you that. But you could still learn to Work, as sorcerors do. It wouldn't be the same as before. It wouldn't restore your Vision. It would require keys and symbols, volumes of catch-phrases and mental exercises—"

"Are you offering to teach me?" she breathed.

His pale eyes burned like coldfire in the moonlight; it hurt to look directly at them. "And what if I were?"

She met his eyes—and drank in the pain, the power, all of it. "What would you say," she asked him, "if, when you were dying, someone offered you life? Would you question the terms—or simply grasp at the bargain with all your strength, and live each moment as it came?"

"That's a loaded simile," he warned her. "And I don't think I have to tell you what my own answer would be. What it *was*, when I had to make that choice."

"Then you know my response."

He held out his hand. Without hesitation, she took it. The chill of his touch shocked her flesh, but the cold of it was pleasure—promise—and she smiled as it filled her.

"When can we start?" she whispered.

They left for the rakhlands as soon as the sun set. Their captain grumbled about the time of their departure, and about the horses, and the weather, and a thousand other things that weren't exactly as they should be . . . and then Gerald Tarrant came to where he stood and simply looked at him, as eloquent in his silence as a snake about to strike. The complaints quickly ceased.

But there were some very real problems, with no easy solutions. The matter of the horses, for example. This boat was smaller than the one that had taken them across to Morgot, and its shallow draft and simpler deck meant that there was really no place to stand where one was not acutely aware of the water just underfoot, and no place to safely shelter the animals. Damien found himself wishing for a deeper vessel with more enclosed cargo space, even though he knew damned well that such a boat couldn't navigate the treacherous shallows of the rakhland shore. Tarrant couldn't even Work to calm the animals, as he had done before, without risking that his efforts would be negated—or even worse, reversed—as their ship passed under the Canopy. There were drugs made that could render the animals more tractable, and the party had discussed the possibility of using them, but that entailed its own special risk; their landing might prove dangerous, and any drug-induced lethargy on the part of the animals might cost them dearly. So they had settled for blindfolding them according to the captain's instructions, in preparation for crossing the Canopy, and binding them as securely as they could, in a place where they would hurt no one if they tried to break free.

We have to be prepared to lose them, Damien told himself. In anticipation of which they had already taken their most precious possessions from the horses' packs and affixed them to their own bodies, feeling more in control that way. But how much good would that do if they had to swim? Given the choice between approaching their enemy unarmed and trying to avoid drowning with two heavy weapons strapped to his back, Damien would be hard put to choose the better course.

The situation's bad. There's no way around that. We'll do the best we can. —And pray for luck, he added.

For now, things seemed to be going well enough. Despite the captain's muttered complaints the Serpent was reassuringly calm, and it gleamed like quicksilver in Domina's light. In the east Prima had already risen, and her quick pace rapidly consumed the degrees of the sky that stood between her and her more massive sister. Syzygy would occur at midnight, or thereabouts: Erna's two larger moons would pull at the tides in conjunction, deepening the Serpent until the worst hazards of the rakhland coast were buried under several feet of water. Or so they hoped. It was all a matter of degree, and inches might well mean the difference between safety and disaster. Damien hoped that their captain knew the deadly coastline as well as he claimed. And that it hadn't changed too much; in this geologically active zone, no feature was permanent.

And then, looking out over the water, he thought he saw something. A wisp of fae-light, rising from the surface. He tried to focus on it, to make out what it was, but its form eluded him. Each time he tried to fix his gaze on it his eyes would start to wander, or—when he managed to hold them still—his mind.

"The Canopy's edge," Tarrant said from behind him. For once, he didn't start to find the man so close; it made sense that the adept would be here, eyes as still and as glisteningly cold as the water they gazed out upon. After a moment Ciani touched Damien's arm lightly, letting him know she had also come up beside him. To her left was Senzei, face flushed pink from his recent Healing, hands resting lightly on the thick brass railing that guarded the vessel's bow.

"Don't try to See," the Hunter warned. Softly, as if cautioning a child. For some reason Damien had the impression that his words weren't meant for him and Senzei, but for Ciani. He looked up sharply at the adept, meaning to question him—but before he could speak the Hunter stiffened, like a wolf catching the scent of prey. His eyes narrowed, and his hands clenched at his sides. In fear? Was that possible? Or was Damien reading his own unease into the adept's manner, injecting a dose of human emotion into a man who had left his humanity behind long ago?

He looked out toward the south, following the Hunter's gaze. And the Canopy was there, or at least its leading edge; clearly visible, even to their unWorked sight. Not as a physical object would be visible, nor even something so substantial as a cloud. It wasn't so much a *thing* as an *impression*, that touched the brain quickly and then fled, leaving a bright afterimage etched into one's mind. Wisps of it danced about the surface of the water, and Damien was reminded of the mirrored surface of lake water, when seen from underneath: crystal clear, gently rippling, a fluid, fickle reflector. Like the stars at the border of the galaxy, they sparkled in and out of sight, teasing the edges of his vision. If one looked closely enough, it was possible to make out more solid images in the distance, viewed through that glittering filer: the rakhland's shoreline, jagged rocks and looming cliffs edged in double moonlight, and the whitewater surf of its shallows. For a moment it was reassuring, to see anything so solid. But then, as Damien watched, even the outlines of the cliffs seemed to alter—as though the shoreline itself were transforming, as if the rocks were no more solid than the veil of rakh-fae that hung before his eyes. *Illusion*, he told himself, The thought was cold, fear-filled. If the Canopy could affect their vision across miles of open water, how were they to navigate? How were they to land? It would be impossible, he realized. They would have to reach the other side of this barrier before trying to wend their way through the shallows, or else there was no way on Erna they could manage it. He tried to remember what the Canopy's parameters were in this region: its width, its rhythm of fluctuation, its average distance from shore. But the knowledge wouldn't come. He turned to Tarrant, certain that the adept would know—he seemed to collect all manner of arcane knowledge, why not that?—but when he looked back to where the Hunter had been, he found only undisturbed air. Neither shadow nor chill to witness that the man (if man he could be called) had ever stood there, or to explain why he had left.

The captain joined them where they stood. He was grinning. "It's said that when fish swim from one side to the other, they come out different from what they started," He wiped his hands one against the other, smearing streaks of dark oil on both. He seemed about to say something else—equally reassuring, no doubt—but Damien interrupted him.

"Where's Mer Tarrant?"

"You mean his Lordship?" He nodded sharply toward the center of the vessel, where a locked door guarded his own private cabin. "He's just taking a rest, of sorts. You don't go bothering him now, see? That's the deal."

Damien glared, and began to move toward the cabin. Ciani grabbed his arm and held it.

"Let him be," she said quietly.

"What's he pulling now—"

"*Please*, Damien. Just stay here. He'll be all right."

He stared at her for a moment, not comprehending. And then it all came together for him. The Canopy. The Hunter. The constant Working that must be required, to maintain that unnatural life. What the Canopy would do to such a Working, and to the man who required it—

He must have started to move again; Ciani's grip tightened on his arm, and kept him from leaving her.

"Let him be," she insisted. Quietly, but firmly. "Please. There's nothing we can do except make it worse."

"How bad?" he said hoarsely. God in Heaven, he had just come to terms with that man's presence. How like Tarrant it would be, to leave them just when he was becoming useful. . . .

He saw the concern in her eyes, the unvoiced fear. Not just for a faceless adept, an ancient evil, but a man. Jealousy flared in him— and he bit back on it, hard. No place for that now. No time for it, not for days to come. Better get used to that right now.

And then the Canopy touched them. Gently at first, disarmingly, like a breeze that whispered at the leading edge of a hurricane. He saw Ciani's face waver in his vision, no longer the solid, dependable picture he had grown accustomed to, but a foggy duplicate that wavered as the night air passed through it and grew thin upon the breeze until it was possible to see through the back of her eyes, to the shoreline in the distance. He drew in a breath—and the air was fluid, molten, stinging his lungs as it passed into his body, igniting his blood as he absorbed it. There was a music in the air, it seemed, but even that was inconstant: subtle one moment, complex and cacophonous the next, passing from delicate chimes in perfect harmony to a brassy, earsplitting screech, like that of an orchestra attempting a crescendo with all its instruments warped out of tune. Damien found himself shaking, more from confusion than discomfort. Behind him one of the horses whinnied, its voice pitched high in panic, and hooves struck noisily against the varnished wood of the deck. And that, too, became a sort of music, and the glittering fae struck up a harmony, as if zoofuls of animals had begun screaming in sympathy. The gravity beneath Damien's feet began to shift, so that it pulled at him from beyond the bow, from out in the depth's of the Canopy's power; it took effort for him to stay where he was, to resist its strange siren song of weight and stability. It was no longer possible to see anything clearly, least of all Ciani. He was no longer certain if her hand—or both her hands, or perhaps more than two of them—still rested on his arm. He reached out for the ship's railing, found it shifting lithely beneath his hand, like the body of a snake in motion. Behind him a horse screamed in terror, another in pain as the first struck out blindly about him. He thought he felt Ciani fall into his arms—or was that a wisp of fog, taking her shape?—and suddenly he was no longer even certain that she was with him, or that the deck of the boat was underfoot. Something coursed about his feet, chill as the Serpent's waters, and began pull at him. Sweet-smelling, sweet-sounding, seductive as a woman's embrace. He had to fight to maintain his grip on reality—limited as that had become—and remain firmly rooted on the boat's deck where he belonged. As the Canopy thickened, it became harder and harder. His survival instinct said he should Work to save himself—but he knew that would be dangerous and might well cost him his life. At best, the Canopy would simply negate his efforts; at worst, it would turn them against him. He closed his eyes, trying to close out the chaos that surrounded him—how lucky the horses were, to enter this region blindfolded!—but he saw through the lids of his eyes as though they were glass, as a storm of discordant colors descended on the small ship. *No!* He forced himself to close his eyes, inside and out. Forced himself to *believe* that he had closed them. He worked to remember darkness, how it felt and tasted and what the smell of it was, the feel of it against his skin; he recreated it within his brain until it began to seep outward from him, conquering the intrusive vision. And at last darkness came, responding to his summons: cool as night, it soothed his fevered brain. Never had he thought it would be so welcome.

After what seemed like an eternity—and it might have been, who could say how time progressed in such a place?—the deck began to grow solid again beneath his feet. With tortuous slowness, gravity resumed its natural balance and its accustomed force. The fog by Damien's side became more solid, and took on a familiar form and scent: Ciani. The strange lights faded. Music withered. The fear which had gripped him loosened its hold, enough that he could breathe again. He closed an arm about Ciani, protectively, and felt no more than the flesh of a woman, her heat and her trembling.

She whimpered softly, and he whispered, "Shhh"—gently, meaning to comfort her. But the sound came out a hiss, distorted by the power of the Canopy's fringe; she tensed in his embrace. By the cabin he could make out a form that might be Senzei, but the visual distortion engendered by the Canopy made it impossible to be sure. It might as easily be the captain—or something wholly fantastic, which the wild fae had conjured.

Just wait it out, he thought. *There's nothing you can do to hurry it along. The worst is over. Just wait.*

And for a moment he was so glad to be seeing normally again that he forgot the danger they were in, and how quickly they needed to get in control of things again. As Tarrant had suggested, this was the most effective moment for treachery on the captain's part; if he meant to unencumber himself by casting them into the Serpent, he would do so while they were still partially incapacitated. He forced himself to open his eyes and look around—but it was like coming to a stop after spinning in circles. The world spun about him with dizzying speed, he found himself losing his balance ... then his foot banged into a brass railing post, and he was falling. He hit the edge of the waist-high rail and was about to go over into the dark, churning water, when a warm weight fell on him, brought him back down inside the rail, bore him down to the wooden deck with force enough that the world about him settled, illusion driven from his mind by the presence of real and immediate pain, of his head striking the hard wooden planking.

He dared to look up, saw a sky without stars. His head throbbed sharply. Ciani's face came into focus, her expression taut with worry.

"You almost went over," she whispered.

He twisted onto his side, searching for the captain. This time he found him. The man was in the back with one of his crewmen, checking on the turbine. Discussing in low tones whether the crossing had affected its mechanism. When he saw Damien looking at him, he grinned mischievously and winked, as if he were aware of exactly what was going through the priest's mind. As if the whole thing had been staged to amuse him.

"Rough passage," he called over to him. "Just about over. Sit tight."

Senzei staggered over to where they lay, and helped the two of them to their feet. That meant everyone was accounted for—except for one man.

"Where's the vulk's Tarrant?" Damien muttered.

Ciani hesitated. "He'll be out," she promised. But she sounded less than certain. She glanced at the cabin door and then away again, as

if somehow her fear might adversely affect the adept. "Soon," she whispered.

"Land ho!" the captain called over to them. And he added: "Looks like your horses made it through."

Damien looked toward where the animals were bound. His practiced eyes found the man's optimism a bit premature. One of the horses was covered in sweat, panting heavily, and another was clearly favoring a hind leg. But still, they were alive. They were here. It could have been worse, he told himself. Much worse.

He looked to Ciani and saw her eye still fixed on the cabin door. She seemed to be shivering. He touched her cheek gently, felt her start at the contact.

She's afraid. Of him, or for him?

He forced his voice to be gentle, his tone to be nonconfrontational. "Is he hurt?"

She hesitated. "He could be," she said at last. Lowering her eyes, as if somehow saying that was a betrayal. "He said the Canopy might kill him. He was willing to chance it, to help me. . . ."

He was willing to chance it to save himself, he thought irritably. But he managed to keep his voice neutral. If Tarrant was dead, so be it. If he was alive—or whatever passed for alive, in his state—there was nothing to be gained by adding further tension to their already strained relationship. "Maybe you'd better check," he suggested.

It was then that the door opened. And Tarrant stepped forth, blinking as if the moonlight hurt his eyes. For a moment he just stood in the doorway, hands gripping the edges of its frame as though he required such support in order to stand. He looked terrible—which is to say, as he should have under normal circumstances: haggard, drawn, unnaturally pale. It occurred to Damien that for the first time since he had met the man, he genuinely looked undead. The thought was strangely unnerving.

"You're all right?" Ciani asked.

It took him a moment to find his voice. "I'm alive," he said hoarsely. "As much as that word can apply." He started to say something else, then shook his head. His head dropped slightly, as if he barely had the strength to hold it up; his hands tightened on the doorframe. "That's all that matters—eh, priest?"

"You need help?" Damien asked quietly.

"What would you do—Heal me? That kind of power would be more deadly than the Canopy, to my kind."

The adept looked to where the horses were milling nervously about their bonds. He seemed to flinch at the thought of having to Work them, but nontheless forced himself away from the doorframe.

Slowly, somewhat unsteadily, he walked to where he might touch the animals. His movements were agile enough that they might have seemed natural in another man, but Damien had traveled with him long enough to see the awkwardness that haunted his gestures, to guess at the pain that shortened his steps, that made his footfall uncharacteristically heavy on the damp wooden planking.

As he had done in Kale, Tarrant tried to Work the horses. But this wasn't Kale, and he clearly wasn't at full strength. Each Working seemed to cost him, in strength and energy; each effort was preceded by a moment of silence and a long, deeply drawn breath, and accompanied by an almost indiscernible shiver that might have been born of exhaustion, or pain.

Damien walked to his side, watched as the horses lowered their heads one by one to graze on imaginary lush fields of grass. At last he said, conversationally, "Water's deep, here. The fae must be hard to access."

For a moment the Hunter said nothing, merely stared out at the water. Finally he whispered, "That, too."

"You all right?"

"I'm surprised you care."

"Ciani was concerned."

The Hunter's eyes fixed on him, hollowed and bloodshot. "I've been through worse." Then a faint smile touched his lips, a pale, sardonic shadow of humor that did little to soften his expression. "Not recently," he amended.

At the bow of the ship Senzei had begun to Work, his attention fixed on the water that flowed before them. The captain had brought them in to the east of the Achron's mouth, which was the smoothest stretch of shoreline in this region—but even that was peppered with hundreds of unseen obstacles, pinnacles of rock that rose from the Serpent's bottom, carved by the conflicting tides of Erna's three-moon system and split into jagged shards by the tremors that repeatedly shook this region. Some were avoidable, most were not. But all were visible to a Worker's Sight, by virtue of the earth-fae that clung to them. Shallow waters would glow with power, deeper recesses shadowed in insulating darkness. One by one Senzei noted the obstacles and pointed them out to the vessel's pilot, who made subtle adjustments to his course to compensate. Under normal circumstances no ship of this size would brave such waters; that job would be left to the smaller canoes and rowboats—at most to tugs—whose safety lay in their maneuverability. But the party's desire to bring their mounts to the rakhlands had made that option unviable; a horse could hardly be expected to balance itself in a canoe.

Inch by inch, yard by yard, they approached the shore. The splashing of the twin paddlewheels had slackened to near-silence, and the boat drifted forward with agonizing slowness. The captain stood by Senzei's side, nodding approval as each new instruction was passed on to his crew. And Ciani stood by his other side, her eyes fixed steadily upon the waves. To see her there like that nearly brought tears of pain to Damien's eyes. How like a sorceror she stood at that moment!—how like a Worker she concentrated all her energy on studying the shallow waters, as if she might somehow See the faelight that coursed beneath it. Like a blind man might stare at the sun, he thought—as if doing that might burn the darkness from out of his eyes.

I can't even imagine her pain, he thought. *Can't even pretend to understand what it means to her, to have lost what she had. But so help me God, we'll get it back for her. I swear it.*

At last the captain seemed to see something promising in the distance; he pointed toward the east, and nodded for Senzei to take a look. The sorceror squinted, trying to focus—and then nodded, hesitantly at first but then with greater confidence as they drew nearer to the point in question.

"You ought to hire out," the captain told him. "There's good money for that kind of skill, around these parts."

"You found a place we can land?" Damien asked.

"I found a place we can come in damned close without tearing the hull to bits . . . and that's as good as we're going to get in this region. Let's hope it's good enough." He nodded toward the lifeboat. "I can give you that to take you in, with one of my men to bring her back. The horses will be a problem—"

"They can swim," Tarrant said coldly.

"You sure of that?"

The pale eyes fixed on him with clear, if tired, disdain. "You mean, am I sure they were born with that instinct? I made certain of it."

He left the captain standing there openmouthed—not unlike a beached fish—as he went to the bow to watch their progress. And Damien thought—somewhat guiltily—that it was nice to see Tarrant's arrogance directed at someone else for a change.

The shoreline passed by in jagged bits. Repeated tremors had split the cliff walls in at least a dozen places, and the cascades of sharp-edged boulders that had fallen to the earth blurred the borderline between water and shore until distinguishing between the two was all but impossible. Not a hospitable place, Damien thought. And it was probably worse when the tide was out. How many dangers were passing submerged beneath their feet, that another few hours might uncover?

The Captain knew what he was doing, when he scheduled us to come in during syzygy. In that it reflected on the man's general competence, it was a reassuring thought.

What the captain had spotted, and Senzei had confirmed, was a ledge of rock that stretched out into the water, a diagonal shelf flat enough to be safe and just deep enough to suit their purposes. The water over it was relatively still, without the whitewater eddies that dominated so much of the shoreline. As they came in closer the captain nodded his approval, and exchanged a few words with Senzei that seemed to satisfy him further. Seeing the relative calm on the man's face—knowing just how worried he had been about this part of the journey, Damien thought, *We're going to make it.* And then added, somewhat more soberly, *This far, anyway.*

It was about time something went right.

Suddenly something brilliant flashed from a clifftop, a brief glint of light that was gone almost before he noticed it. He turned toward where he thought it had been and scanned the cliff with wary eyes— but he could see nothing other than jagged rock walls and the trees that clung to them, their roots trailing down to the water like thirsty serpents. He Worked his sight, carefully. It was hard to contact the earth-fae through the water, but with effort he managed it. And Knew—

Metal ornaments—light glinting off glass beads—human eyes that mirrored nonhuman thoughts, and the acrid smell of hatred—

He shivered, and broke off the contact before the creature he saw could Work it against him. Clearly, their efforts were being observed. By what he couldn't say—the contact had been too brief, his touch too wary—but it wasn't human, and he didn't think that it was friendly. After a moment he steeled himself, and dared to Know again. But the watcher was already gone, and any fae-mark he might have left behind was too far away, or else too weak for Damien to identify.

He was suddenly very glad that they'd gotten a good night's sleep in Sattin. He suspected they weren't going to get one again for some time to come.

"Something wrong?" It was Tarrant.

He nodded toward the cliff wall, looming tall in the double moonlight. "Some sort of lookout, I think. Not human."

"Rakh," the Hunter whispered.

Damien looked at him sharply. "You Know that? Or are you guessing?"

"Who else would guard these cliffs so carefully? Who else would know the very spot where a safe landing might be made, and set a sentry to watch over it?" He paused, considering the site in question. "This land is the rakh's last refuge, priest—I would be very surprised if under those circumstances they didn't at least set a watch over it. And defend it with vigor, against man's intrusion."

"You think they'll attack us?"

"I don't think there's any doubt about that. Our only question is when."

"You can't Divine that?"

"If you mean read the future, no one can do that. And as for reading the present clearly enough to make a reliable prediction . . . not now. That takes strength, clarity of mind. . . ." His voice trailed off into the darkness, his silence proclaiming his weakness more eloquently than any words could. Damien looked at him, wished he had some scale against which to judge his condition. How long did it take the undead to heal themselves? For as long as Tarrant was incapacitated, the danger to all of them was increased.

"Coming in!" the captain called; the tone of relief in his voice reassured Damien. The man watched while his crew prepared to disengage the turbine and drop anchor, and then, when he was satisfied that all was going well, came to where the priest and the Hunter stood. And looked out at the shoreline flanking them, whose deepening shadows might hide any number of dangers.

"This is safe as it gets," he assured them. "You could practically walk in from here. Wish I could take you in closer—but if I run aground in this tide, I won't get off till doomsday."

"You did well," Tarrant said quietly. He took a small leather purse from his pocket and held it out to him; if the coins inside were of gold, there was an impressive amount of them. He offered it to the man. It was a gratuity, Damien knew. Tarrant had paid for the trip in advance.

The captain made no move to take the purse—but he bowed ever so slightly, acknowledging the offer. "Tell the Hunter I served him."

"When I return, I'll do that. Until then. . . ." He took the man's hand in his own and turned it palm up, then placed the small purse in his palm and closed his fingers over it. "Say that he is pleased with your service."

The man bowed deeply—a formal gesture that his sincerity made graceful—and then took his leave, to oversee the last moments of their journey.

When he was safely out of hearing, Damien said to Tarrant, "I know heads of state who would give their lives to have half your influence."

The Hunter smiled—and for the first time since the Canopy there was life in his eyes, and a hint of genuine humor.

"If they truly gave their lives," he said, "they might have it all."

The disembarkation went no worse than they had anticipated—which was to say that it was tense and strenuous and very, very difficult, but they finally made it ashore. So did the horses. Tarrant had Worked them again, and though his strength was clearly waning—or perhaps the fae was harder to access here, it was hard to be certain— he did manage to get them off the ship and into the water. By the time they had been driven ashore the horses had managed to get everyone thoroughly soaked, but that was a small inconvenience when weighed against their need for having mounts for the long journey ahead.

They stood on the shore and watched as the small ship withdrew, watched until the night swallowed it once more and the moons shone on nothing but the Serpent's froth. And Damien thought, *We're here. Praise God—we made it.* They were wet and they were tired and they were freezing cold, but they were inside the Canopy at last, and that was all that mattered.

He turned back to study the cliffs again—to see if their watcher had returned, or if some other danger had taken its place—but before he could complete the motion a terrified screech from one of the horses forced his attention back to the shoreline once more. It was Ciani's horse, a magnificent black animal that had so far come through the journey unscathed. Something had shifted underfoot as it waded through the shallows and it was down, thrashing at the water as it tried in vain to stand up again. From the sharp angle of its forward leg Damien judged that the bone had broken, and badly. In pain and fear it lashed out at Senzei, who fell back just in time to keep his face from being crushed by its flailing hooves.

Tarrant and Ciani were there in an instant. She helped Senzei out of the water, safely away from the terrified animal. Between the horse's dark coat and the water it was impossible to see the extent of the wound, but Damien thought he smelled blood. He started into the water himself, to try to reach the beast, but Tarrant's hand held him back.

"Wait."

The adept's brow was furrowed in tension as he tried to Work the earth-fae at their feet so that it would serve his will above the surface of the water. Not an easy task under any circumstances, and the Hunter was clearly not in the best of shape. Damien heard the sharp intake of breath, almost a gasp of pain, but the adept's attention never wavered. The horse's body jerked spasmodically, as if from seizure, and then stiffened. Froze, as though its skeleton had locked in place. Damien could see its forelimbs trembling, the gleam of terror in its eyes.

"Go," the Hunter whispered.

He waded to the animal's side, cold water chilling his flesh anew. The leg in question was underwater. He looked back at Tarrant, who nodded slowly, his eyes narrow with the force of his effort. Damien grasped the damaged leg. The horse shuddered and snorted once, but otherwise seemed incapable of motion. He moved the leg gently, to bring the break above the water's surface. It was bad: a compound fracture that had broken through the skin in two places. Probably worsened by the horse's own fear, Damien thought; the fae could do that.

Carefully, he began to Work. It was difficult reaching down through the water to tap the earth-fae, unlike anything he had never experienced before. And even allowing for the interference of the water— which clung to the fae like glue, making it almost impossible to manipulate the stuff—the current itself seemed weak. Insubstantial. As though somehow the earth-fae had been drained from this place, leaving little more than a shadow of what had once been.

As for Tarrant's holding the horse steady for him . . . he tried not to think about that. Tried not to think how much was riding on that man's power right now—his power, and his "honor." Tried not to think about how easy it would be for him to ease up just a little— just for an instant—and let fate take care of the only member of his party who seemed willing to challenge him.

He's left us alive this long because he perceives that Ciani needs us. What happens if he changes his mind?

With effort, he concentrated on Working. He could feel the horse's flesh trembling as it fought Tarrant's control, and knew it would take only a momentary slip on the part of the adept for the creature to strike out at him. As he manipulated the bone fragments, first by hand and then by Touch, he could feel the pain coursing up the animal's leg. But with the current as weak as it was and the water interfering, there was simply no way to anesthetize the beast. Relying upon his Seeing to show him what must be done, he wound strands of healing fae about the bone ends and slowly drew them together. The horse screamed once, in agony—and then Tarrant's power silenced it. Damien prompted the equine flesh to deposit calcium where he needed it, and accelerated the production of new bone a thousandfold. *Hold onto him, please. Just a short while longer.* Spongy tissue filled the gap and then hardened; bone chips were absorbed by the body, to fuel the new construction. Damien felt a cold sweat break out on his face, and channels of that and the Serpent's spray coursed down his neck as he Worked. *Just a little bit longer.* He felt the horse shudder beneath his hands as the adept's control slipped, just a little. *One more minute!* And then the leg was whole again and he jumped back—just in time. The muscular animal staggered to its feet, nostrils distended in outrage. But its leg was whole and the pain was gone, and the whole experience was fading rapidly from its memory. That was part of the Healing, too, and Damien was relieved to see it take.

Shivering in the chill of the night, he finally led the animal ashore. Ciani had opened his oilcloth-wrapped pack and laid out dry clothes for him; with no thought for modesty, he changed into them, glancing at the cliff only once as he used an extra dry shirt to wring the water from his hair.

Then he looked for Gerald Tarrant.

The adept was nowhere in sight. Ciani saw Damien searching and nodded toward the west, where an outcropping of rock hid part of the shoreline from view. But when he passed by her on the way there, she grasped his arm and held it.

"He's in bad shape." She said quietly. "Has been since the Canopy. The horse took a lot out of him. Just give him time, Damien."

He disengaged himself from her gently. With a last glance toward the clifftop to check for enemies—there were none—he walked cautiously in the direction she had indicated, to where a boulder, grotesquely carved by wind and water, hid some of the shoreline from view.

He was there, behind it. Eyes shut, leaning against the rock as if, without its support, he would surely go down. He didn't hear Damien approach—or perhaps he simply lacked the strength to respond. A delicate shudder ran through his body as he watched, a glissando of weakness. Or pain.

"You all right?" Damien asked softly.

The adept stiffened—but if there was a curt response on his lips, he failed to voice it. After a moment the tension bled out of his frame; his shoulders slumped against the rock.

"No," he said. "No, I'm not." His voice was little more than a whisper. "Does it matter to you, priest?"

"If it didn't, I wouldn't be here."

Gerald Tarrant said nothing.

"You're hurt."

"How observant."

Damien felt himself stiffening in anger—and forced himself to relax, his voice and body to be calm. "You're making it pretty damned hard for me to help you."

The Hunter looked at him, hollowed eyes gleaming in the moonlight. "Is that what you came to do? Help me?"

"Part of it."

He looked out into the night. Shut his eyes once more. "The Canopy drained me," he whispered. "Is that what you want to hear? The Working that sustains my life had to be renewed minute by minute, against a turbulent and unpredictable current. Is it any surprise I'm exhausted? I almost didn't make it."

"So what you need is rest?"

He sighed. "When *you* do strenuous work, priest, you eat to sustain yourself. My chosen fare may have changed, but the need remains the same. Is that what concerns you? Be reassured—I have no intentions of feeding on your party. God alone knows if the rakh are sophisticated enough to offer me what I need, but the currents speak of other human life inside the Canopy. I have no intention of starving to death," he assured him.

"What is it that you need?" Damien asked quietly.

He looked at the priest. A flicker of evil stirred in the depths of his eyes, and a cold breeze stirred in the air between them.

"Does it really matter?" he whispered.

"It does if I want to help."

"I doubt you would be willing to do that."

"Try me. What is it?" When the adept said nothing, he pressed, "Blood?"

"That? Merely an aperitif. The power that sustains me is demonic in nature—and I feed as the true demons do, upon the vital energy of man. Upon his negative emotions: Anguish. Despair. Fear. Especially fear, priest; that is, by far, the most delectable."

"Thus the Hunt."

His voice was a whisper. "Exactly."

"And that's what you need now?"

He nodded weakly. "Blood will suffice for a while—but in the end, I require human suffering to stay alive." The cold eyes fixed on him. "Are you offering that?"

"I might," Damien said evenly.

"Then you're a brave man," he breathed. "And a foolish one."

"It's been said."

"You trust me?"

"No," he said bluntly. "But I don't think you want me dead just now. Or incapacitated. And I don't see that you're much good to us, the way you're going." *And I want you on your feet before the others think of trying to help you. Senzei couldn't handle it. Ciani isn't strong enough.* "Is there a way it could be done, just this once, without . . ." He floundered for the proper phrase.

"Without you dying?" He nodded. There was a new note in his voice, a sharper undercurrent. Hunger? "There are dreams. Nightmares. I could fashion them in your mind, to inspire the emotions I require . . . but it would take a special link between us to allow me to feed off them. And that wouldn't fade when the sun came up. Are you willing to have such a channel established—for life?"

He hesitated. "Tell me what it would entail."

"What any channel does. A path of least resistance for the fae, that any Working might draw upon. Such a thing could never be banished, priest. Not by either of us."

"But if it wasn't used?"

"It has no power of its own, if that's the question. Nor would it fade with time. Only death can sever that kind of link—and sometimes not even that."

He thought about that. Thought about the alternatives. And asked, grimly, "Is there any other way?"

"Not for me," the Hunter whispered. "Not now. And without sustenance my strength would continue to fade . . . but I'm surprised you don't find that preferable."

"You're part of our company now," Damien said sharply. "And from the moment we passed under the Canopy until we get out from under it, we're all in this together. That's how I see it. If you have any trouble with that attitude, now's the time to let me know."

Tarrant stared at him. "No. None at all."

"You obviously can't feed off the horses or you would have done that already—and I won't let you touch Ciani or Senzei. Period. That leaves me. Or else you stay as you are, and we all suffer from the loss of your power. Right? As far as I'm concerned, your company isn't so pleasant that I would keep you around just for conversation. —So are you going to tell me what you need to establish this link between us, or do I have to guess at it?"

For a moment the Hunter was still. Then he said, in a voice as cool as the Serpent's water. "You never do cease to surprise me. I accept your offer. As for the channel we'll be establishing . . . that's potentially as deadly for me as it is for you. If it's any consolation."

He pushed himself away from the boulder, and managed to stand unsupported. It clearly took effort. "Before we deal with that, I suggest we move on. Find somewhere where there's shelter, from prying eyes and sunlight both. A place where we can camp in safety. Then. . . ."

He looked at Damien curiously. The hunger in his eyes was undisguised.

"It's been a long time since I've tasted a cleric's blood," he mused.

Twenty-nine

Deep within the House of Storms, in a room reserved for Working, the Master of Lema halted in mid-invocation, startled by a sudden change in the current. A quick movement of a gloved hand and a well-trained mind served to Dispel the entity that was slowly taking form in the warded circle, and a muttered key established a Knowing in its place.

After a moment—a long moment—there was a nod. A hungry nod.

"Calesta." The name was a whisper—an incantation—a command. "Take form, Calesta. Now."

Out of the darkness a figure formed, a shadow made solid by the power of sorcerous will. The shape it wore resembled that of a man, but no single detail was wholly human. Its skin bore the hard black gloss of obsidian, and its clothing flowed like smoke over its limbs. Its features were somewhat human in shape—if carved volcanic glass might be said to resemble humanity—but where human eyes should have been were faceted orbs, mirror-surfaced, which reflected back the object of the figure's attention in a thousand fractured bits.

The demon called Calesta bowed but made no sound. In its silence all things might be read, all manners of obesance to the one it served—to the one who was called Master of Lema, Keeper of Souls, The One Who Binds.

"Taste it, Calesta." A hungry whisper, tense with anticipation. "She's entered the Canopy. Can you feel it? And another, with her. An adept. *Two* adepts. . . ."

"Shall I send the Dark Ones after them?" The demon's voice was something more felt than heard: a whisper of fingernails against a dry slateboard, the feel of teeth scaping on chalk.

"Worthless fools!" the sorceror spat. "What good are they? I gave them the richness of an adept's soul to feed on and they acted like children at a banquet—dropping their food as soon as there was some new game afoot! No. This time *you'll* do it, Calesta. First find out who they are. Where they're going. Tell me that. Then we can make our plans."

The One Who Binds tasted the current again. And shivered as the anticipation of conquest, like a newly-injected drug, prompted a torrent of adrenaline within.

"The adepts are *mine*," the Master whispered.

Thirty

Dusk. A *swollen, sallow sunset. Dust strewn across a barren landscape, naked hills swelling lifeless in the distance. Sharp cracks that split the air: rhythmic, like a drumbeat. Death.*

He staggers onto the field of battle, exhaustion a sharp pain in his side. To his left thunder roars, and the ground explodes in mayhem. Explosives. They're using explosives. In the distance another patch of ground erupts, and a cloud of dust rises to fill the murky air. Warded explosives, he decides. Designed to ignite when some living thing comes too close. A very dangerous Working, rarely dared; that the enemy has applied it says much for their skill, and for their confidence.

Another hundred yards, and he comes upon the bodies. They litter the ground like volcanic debris spewed from a festering cone. Bits of arms and legs and fragments of shattered skull pepper the ground as far as the eye can see—some bodies still twitching, whole enough to feel pain as they bleed out their last life into the dusty ground. He staggers to one of those and prays for strength: the strength to persevere, the power to Heal. Explosives fire like a sharp drumroll in the distance, the crack of a hundred pistols perfectly synchronized. He feels a sharp bite of fear at the sound, at the unnaturalness of it. What kind of Working must it take, to make it possible for so many guns to fire successfully, with such planned precision? More than he has ever witnessed, or imagined possible.

The swollen sun, storm-yellow, watches in silence as he kneels by the side of the fallen, as he gathers himself to Work. The woman lying before him moans softly, her face half-covered in blood. It's a painful wound, but not a deadly one; if he can master enough fae to stop the bleeding, the odds are good she will survive.

He Works.

Or tries to.

Nothing responds.

Shaken, he looks over the battlefield. To the south of him black earth spouts upward suddenly, accompanied by the thunderclap of explosives. He tries to Work his sight, to See what the currents are like here—the place is strange, unfamiliar to him, maybe the patterns of the fae need to be interpreted before they can be Worked— but he sees no fae, he Works no vision, there are only the dead and the dying about him. Nothing that speaks to him of power—or hope.

He shivers, though the air is warm.

With effort, he forces himself to his feet again, and staggers over to the next body. A man, with his left hand blown off. Thousands of small wounds pepper his body, sharp metal shards still lodged in some of them. He touches the tender flesh and wills all the power to come and serve him, using all the skill that the years have given him. He focuses on his own hunger to Work and the need to Heal— the desperate need to Heal—and the faith that has sustained him past pain, past death, into realms where only the holy may enter—

And nothing responds. Absolutely nothing. The planet is dead, unresponsive to his will. He feels the first cold bite of despair, then, a kind of fear he's never experienced before. Danger he can deal with, death he's confronted on least a dozen occasions, but there's never been anything like this before—never such absolute help-lessness in the face of human suffering, such sudden awareness that his will doesn't matter, he doesn't matter, he has no more power to affect the patterns of fate than the dismembered limbs on this field, or the cooling blood that turns the dry earth to mud under his feet.

For the first time in his life, he knows the rank taste of terror. Not the quantifiable fear of assessed risk, but the unbounded horror of total immersion in the unknown. Guns fire once more in the distance, and for the first time since coming here he realizes why they can function with such regularity. Man's will has no power here— not to kill and not to heal, not to alter the world and not to adapt to it. The whole of this world is dead to man, dead to his dreams, impassive to his needs and his pleas and even his fears. The concept is awesome, terrifying. He feels himself falling to his knees, muttering a key as he tries once more to Work the fae, to find some point of stability in this alien universe. Anything. But there is no response. No fae that he might use, to bind his will to the rest of the universe. The world is closing in around him, like a dead hand closing about his flesh. The claustrophobia of total despair chokes him. He cannot breathe. He—

Woke. Gasping for breath, shivering. Cold sweat beaded his forehead, and his heart pounded like that distantly remembered gunfire. It took him a moment to remember where he was. Another long, painful moment to realize what had happened.

"Zen?" His voice was hoarse. "Cee?"

There was no response. He looked about, saw their bedrolls neatly bundled by the cavern's entrance. There was little light, which meant the sun was setting—had set?—which meant, in turn, that he had slept for hours. Too many hours. Despite the fact that he had retired from his last watch well before noon, he felt as though he had never closed his eyes. As though he had spent his daylight hours in constant battle, his muscles and his soul still aching from the effort.

He forced himself to his feet and stood with one hand against the cavern wall until the worst of the shaking subsided and he felt he could walk again. As the Hunter had instructed, he had told Ciani and Zen that he should be allowed to sleep until he awakened naturally. He had never thought that it would take so long.

They must be worried as hell. How much should he tell them of what had passed between the Hunter and himself? On the one hand, it would upset them to no purpose—and on the other, if some kind of permanent channel had been established, didn't they have the right to know? His head swam with trying to decide.

Steady, Vryce. One step at a time. Time to move again.

His will gripping his unsteady legs like a vice, he sought the cavern's entrance. There, sheltered beneath a lip of granite, Gerald Tarrant sat—eyes shut, utterly relaxed, breathing steadily in contentment. From further down on the beach (if *beach* it could be called) a tiny cookfire flickered, a dark figure huddled over it. Ciani, he guessed. Senzei would be on watch.

He looked down at the Hunter, found that the man's obvious contentment grated on his nerves more than all his nightmares combined. "I hope you're satisfied," he whispered hoarsely.

"It was adequate." Tarrant turned to him, pale eyes brimming with languid malevolence. Damien was reminded of a sated predator, lazily contemplating his prey. "You seem surprised, priest. That I could inspire such fear in you? If so, you fail to give yourself credit. That was my seventh attempt, and by far the most complex. My victims are usually more . . . vulnerable." Then his voice dropped to a whisper and he added, with soft intensity, "That was Earth, you know."

"Your vision of it."

"It's the dream you serve. A future the Church hopes to make possible. A land in which the fae has no power, to alter fate or man . . . how do you like the taste of it, priest? The special savor of Terran impotence."

"They got to the stars," he retorted. "In less than twelve centuries, our Terran ancestors went from barbarism to galactic colonization. And what have we done in that much time? Settled two continents on a single planet—and barely that. And you dare to ask me if it's worth a price to regain our lost heritage? Any price, Hunter. *Anything.*"

"Your faith is strong," he mused.

"Damned right. *Your* legacy, Neocount. *Your* dream. Some of us were foolish enough to stick with it. Now, are you feeling better, or was all that effort wasted?"

"It wasn't wasted," the Hunter said softly. "Given three more nights and total control over your environment I could have managed better . . . but for what it was, it served well enough."

"You can Work now?"

"If the currents allow. The fae was fairly weak as I recall—or at least it seemed so when we landed. I wasn't in the best of shape then."

"But you're all right now."

"Yes." For a moment he seemed to hesitate. Searching for the right words? How many centuries had it been, since he had last been indebted to a mere human being?

"Thank you," he whispered at last. The words clearly came hard to him. "I am . . . very grateful."

Somehow, Damien managed to shrug.

"All in a day's work," he assured him.

The watcher hadn't come back. That was the first piece of news that greeted them when they made their way down from their protective niche in the cliff wall. Whatever manner of creature had watched them as they made their way to shore, it had not returned. Damien wished he could read something optimistic into that, but it was still too early to judge. And optimism could be dangerous, when it was founded on mere guesswork.

While they ate—a haphazard stew of dried rations and the meat of some reptilian creature Senzei had managed to shoot during his first watch—Gerald Tarrant withdrew, ostensibly to test the currents. When he returned to them, his expression was grim. Yes, he said, the earth-fae was sparse here, and the currents that governed its motion weak and insubstantial. Which made no sense, he told them. No sense at all. He seemed almost angry, as though the fae were

somehow consciously plotting to frustrate him. When Senzei started
to question him further, he went wordlessly to where their packs
were stored and withdrew a thick tube of maps from among his own
possessions. The heavy vellum sheets had come through undamaged,
rolled tightly inside waterproof, wax-sealed containers.

"Here," he said, and he unrolled one of the precious maps before
them. Firelight flickered on its surface as he weighted its corners
down with stones. "See for yourselves."

The map—undeniably ancient, certainly from the time before the
Canopy had been raised—depicted local currents in the region they
were now traversing. They could see rich currents of earth-fae flowing
along the fault lines, eddies of power that swirled about the foothills
of the Worldsend Mountains and the eastern range, just as it should
be. Tarrant stared at the maps, as though trying to reconcile them
with the reality he himself had observed, and at last shook his head
in frustration.

"The fae here is weaker than it should be," he said finally. "There's
no natural law I know of that would account for its being so—but it
is. Unquestionably. Which means that all our Workings—including
my own—will be that much less effective."

"What about our enemy?" Senzei asked.

"Probably the same for him. But I wouldn't bet my survival on
that," he warned.

"You don't think this could have occurred naturally?"

"The earth-fae is, and always has been, a predictable, ordered force.
Faithful to its own laws of motion and power which, when understood, can be manipulated. Or have you forgotten your Prophet's
teachings?" he asked dryly.

"Excuse me for challenging your canon."

His pale eyes glittered with amusement.

"What about its reactive power?" Ciani asked him. "That's not
predictable, is it?"

He hesitated—as if a dry, mocking answer was ready upon his lips,
about to be launched into their company. Then he swallowed that,
with effort, and said simply, "It is. Utterly predictable. The complica-
tion with man's Working it is that there are too many levels to
human consciousness, and the earth-fae doesn't distinguish between
them. If man's fears resound louder than his prayers, the former is
what will manifest results. The fault lies within ourselves, lady—not
with the fae." He looked down at the ground beside him and touched
a slender finger to it: observing the current, Damien decided. Using
his adept's sight to determine its strength. "With every new seismic
event, earth-fae rises to the surface of the planet. Eventually it con-

gregates, in pools and eddies and currents that we can map. Except that here those aren't what they should be. Not at all." He paused, and looked at each of them in turn—studying them for reaction? "To my mind, that hints at outside interference."

But the scale of it! Damien thought. *What kind of creature—or force—could be responsible?* He envisioned that vast atomic furnace which was the planet's core, tons of magma thrusting upward against the crust of the planet until the continents themselves shifted in response, earth buckling and cracking from the pressure of the assault—seismic shockwaves releasing that power which they had come to call the *earth-fae*, in quantities so vast that no human being dared touch it, so powerful in its pure form that the merest attempt to Work it was enough to fry a man to cinders. And here it was weakened. How? By what process? What had happened here, in the centuries since the rakh had claimed these lands, that had altered the very nature of Ernra?

Or is it simply our understanding that's lacking? Damien wondered. *What clue is here we're not seeing? That we perhaps don't even know how to look for?*

Carefully, Gerald Tarrant withdrew another sheet from its protective tube. Its value was evident in the way he handled it, in the reverence of his motions as he carefully unrolled it and weighted its corners down with smooth, water-polished stones.

At first, Damien couldn't make out what it was. He moved one of the lamps in closer, saw the tenuous outline of a continent subdivided by several sharp red lines. The shoreline was unfamiliar to him, but after a while, by looking only at the larger forms, he began to make out familiar shapes. The eastlands. The rakhlands. The Serpent. With a start he realized that the Stekkis River coursed westward rather than to the north, and met the sea at Merentha. The Lethe had also shifted, and the coastline by Seth was markedly different.

"It's old," he murmured.

The Hunter nodded. "Over twelve hundred years. And not designed for permanence, even then. If not for my Working, it would have crumbled to dust long ago."

"Over twelve centuries?" Senzei asked sharply. "That would mean—"

"It's a survey map," the Hunter informed him. "A tectonic extrapolation. Done on board the Earth-ship, before the Landing. According to one document in my possession, that was standard procedure aboard such vessels. They would scan each possible landing site for seismic activity—and other variables—to assess the dangers that the colonists might face. It normally took five to ten Earth-years to determine whether or not a planet was suitable for colonization. In the case of Erna, nearly ninety were invested." He tapped the map with a slender forefinger. "This was the reason."

"Seismic activity." Damien's tone was bitter.

The Hunter nodded. "Enough to make colonization difficult, if not downright impossible. Maybe if there'd been an alternative, the ship would have moved on. Maybe somehow it knew that there was nothing beyond this—that it had come so far, rejecting so many planets along the way, that if it rejected this one there was nowhere left to go. It was balanced on the brink of the galaxy, with nothing but darkness ahead of it, and it knew only two options: wake up the colonists and settle them here, or move on. No turning back. No going home. Those were the rules."

"They were crazy," Senzei whispered

"Maybe so. As were those men and women who braved the eastern sea to find out what lay beyond it, and those who traveled to Novatlantis despite the constant eruptions in that place . . . and the lady here, who passed through the Canopy unattended, to explore forbidden lands. It's a human craziness, the need to explore. The hunger for a new frontier. But since we are its children, I would say we have little right to criticize."

He tapped the map with a slender forefinger, indicating a point some three hundred miles to the east of them. "Assuming we do indeed have an enemy," he said quietly, "this is where he will be located."

"How can you be so sure?" Damien demanded.

"Simply put: because there is no better place." His finger traced a red line that coursed upward through the eastern mountain range to where another, sharply angled, intersected it. "Look at the fault lines. Three continental plates meet here, each forced against the other by earthly powers too vast to contemplate. The plates collide, continents crumple into mountain ranges, rivers are rerouted . . . and a vast amount of raw power is released each time it happens." He sketched a circle around the intersection of the fault lines, approximately forty miles in diameter. "This is what we call a *point of power*—a wellspring of the earth-fae—and if there's anything in this land that feeds on the fae, or Works it . . . it will be here. Somewhere within this periphery."

"Why not on the point itself?" Ciani asked.

He looked up at her, and there was something in his eyes that made Damien tense. Not his usual amusement at an ignorant question, or his customary derision toward the rest of the party. Something far more subtle. More *intimate*. Damien was reminded of the seductive undulations of a snake, as it mesmerized its prey.

"Only a fool builds his fortress on a fault line," Tarrant assured her. "It's one thing to ward against the tremors of an earthquake— and quite another to try to maintain a structure when half the ground beneath it suddenly rises, or sinks, or moves to the west of that which remains. Even an adept will die if the roof falls in and crushes his head, lady. Especially if it happens at the one time he dares not Work to save himself."

"I see," she whispered.

"What it means," he said, rerolling the map, "is that we have a difficult journey ahead of us."

"And an enemy who knows we've arrived," Senzei added soberly.

Tarrant looked up at the cliffs; his eyes narrowed as if somehow he might see the watcher again if he looked carefully enough.

"Impossible to read that trace," he muttered. "Damn the weakness of the currents here! In the Forest I could have told you who it was that saw us, and what his or her intentions were. . . ."

"Or *its*," Damien reminded him.

A cold breeze gusted in across the Serpent. For a moment there was silence, broken only by the sound of the horses feeding. The shifting of sand as Ciani began to douse the fire.

"Yes," Tarrant said at last. Clearly not liking the taste of the word, or its implications. "His, her, or *its*."

"Come on," the priest said. "Let's get moving."

It had never occurred to Senzei that he might wind up the most powerful of them all. No, not powerful exactly . . . more like *useful. Adaptable.*

Maybe it came from all those years of watching the currents at home, of focusing on their intensity with a desperate need to perceive minute changes, as an affirmation of his skill. Maybe it was from all those years of watching Ciani Work, of honing his Sight while she refined more concrete skills, knowing that whatever else he might choose to do she could do better and more easily. Whatever. The end result was that here and now, in this special place, Senzei Reese had exactly the skills required to get his companions from one point to another in safety.

Trudging through the chill autumn waters, mostly on horseback, sometimes on foot, his eyes fixed on the swirling liquid before them, he used his Sight to feel out the currents that lay beneath that saline froth. Used his Sight to ferret out the rock formations that might cause them to stumble, the hairline faults and pebble-filled hollows that would cause the ground to shift if too much weight was put on it. Each was reflected in the earth-fae as it shimmered up through the water, each had its own special flavor, its own peculiar light. As he had guided their boat through the rakhland's shallows, he now guided his party along the shoreline, across terrain that shifted from pebbled beach to half-submerged boulders to waist-high waters in a matter of minutes. And no one else could do it as well as he could. That was simple fact. The priest specialized in Healing skills, the arts of Life; the adept Gerald Tarrant, for all his awesome power, seemed ill at ease Working through the water, and preferred to leave that duty to another. And Ciani ... it hurt him to think he was benefiting from her disability, but the truth was that he had never experienced this kind of pleasure before—this absolute certainty of being needed, of having the skills which the moment required and needing to use them. Of being the only one who *could* use them. His years with her had been rich ones, in both experience and friendship, but he realized now just what it had cost him to function in her shadow all these years. How much of him had never *lived*, before this moment.

Step by step, obstacle by obstacle, the four of them worked their way westward, toward the Achron's outlet. At times the shoreline was almost hospitable, a narrow beach of worn pebbles and broken shells overlaid with thick strands of seaweed that allowed them to ride as quickly as their horses could find footing. But then it would drop away suddenly and the sheer palisades would meet the water without junction, leaving them to work their way through pools of deep, ice-cold water, their horses struggling to find firm footing amidst the potholes and the undertow that were invisible beneath the black waters. It was a dangerous route, rife with tension—but he, Senzei Reese, led them through. Skirting deadly pits which the tides had carved at the base of the cliff walls, finding the one solid path across a mud-covered landscape, sensing the hollows in which venemous creatures hid, obscured beneath mounds of rotting seaweed ... with a constant Working on his lips to support his special senses he read the oh-so-subtle variations in the earth-fae, and then used that vision to find the one safe path amidst a thousand deadly ones. It was exhausting work, and by the end of the night his head rang with pain from the exertion. But it was a wonderful pain. An exhilarating pain. A pain that was as exquisitely sexual as the first time he had entered a woman, all the heat and the giddy fear and the sense of *rightness* combined, in one blinding agony of exhaustion.

This is what I was born to do, he thought, as he lifted a hand to rub one throbbing temple. *Persevere, where the adepts falter.*

They paused once along the way, for food and a brief respite. The horses nibbled uneasily at the rations they were offered, grainy cakes that combined nutrition with a high-calorie supplement; it was better than nothing, but the animals clearly weren't happy about it. Damien muttered something about hoping they found proper grazing ground before their limited supply of the stuff ran out. They discussed stopping for a while while they were still on hospitable ground, but it was no real option; Tarrant's presence among them meant they couldn't travel during the daylight hours, which in turn meant they needed to cover as much ground as possible during the night. So they wrung out their clothing and waited while the priest tamed enough earth-fae to ward off sickness and stabilize the temperature of their flesh—not a sure thing in these currents, he warned them, but better than no effort at all—and they continued.

Their first indication that they were nearing their objective was a faint roaring sound in the distance, not unlike the noise one might hear cupping a shell to one's ear to catch the sound of blood surging within the body. It had no rhythm, unlike the waters at their side, no heartbeat of surf breaking over an inconstant shore, but was more like the rush of water surging through a confined space: river rapids, Senzei thought. He saw Damien's head snap up as he first became aware of the sound, and the priest's expression darkened slightly. *Not good?* he thought despairingly. He didn't dare ask. Even his own skills would be of little use in river whitewater, and the footing . . . he shivered as he envisioned it. Gods willing, the land there would be solid enough to serve them.

It took nearly another hour to reach the mouth of the river, across such difficult terrain that for a while Senzei thought they might not make it. But then, when the roar of whitewater had grown so loud that they could hardly speak to one another without shouting, they came around a bend and it was there before them, in all its violent glory. A break in the cliff wall to their left, through which the river poured like a herd of wild beasts in desperate stampede, casting themselves upon the mounds and mudbars that time and the tides had erected. Roaring white surf capped the Serpent's waters, and moonlight shattered into a million sparks on its wild, frothing surface. A fog of spray rose for yards above the water, and eddies of mist curled like phantoms within it, ghostly forms that were barely born before the water and the wind swallowed them up again.

Senzei moved closer to the cliff wall, blinking the spray from his eyes. It was hard to see, hard to get any sense of where they were, or where they needed to be. He tried to Work, but he had always depended upon vision for his focus—and here, clear vision was impossible.

"There!" He heard Tarrant's shout with unexpected clarity—but of course, the adept would have augmented his voice. He tried to respond, but his horse had begun to back away from the spectacle before them, and he had to fight to bring it under control before he could look where the Hunter was pointing. Damien's hand was on Ciani's reins and he could see that her mount was ready to bolt, might have done so moments ago if not for that restraint.

"There," the Hunter told them, and he pointed to the cliff wall.

For a moment, it was impossible to see. Then—perhaps by chance, perhaps in response to Tarrant's will—the worst of the fog parted before them. It was now possible to see the gap where the river poured out, to a short but violent waterfall that met the Serpent in thunder. It was also possible to see that the river had once been higher—or might be again, in a wetter season—and that a narrow ridge, erosion-carved, paralleled the course of the waters. Ten yards above them, perhaps half a mile away. It might as well have been on another planet.

"How are you at parting the waters?" Damien yelled to Tarrant—and it must have been some kind of religious joke, because the Hunter smiled dryly.

There's no going back, Senzei thought grimly. *And this is the only way forward.*

As if in answer to his thoughts, Damien slid from his mount's back, to stand on the pebbled ground. He fumbled for a moment among the horse's several packs, withdrew one, and strapped it to his own shoulder. And looked toward his companions. His expression was dark but determined, and in it Senzei read his absolute certainty that somehow, with or without a horse beside him, he was going to get himself up to that ridge. Were they with him? Senzei looked at Ciani, felt his heart lurch as he saw the determination in her eyes— and recognized its source. Not courage, or even resolution; she simply had nothing left to lose.

They dismounted. Tarrant had packed few special possessions for the journey, but his horse had been carrying a share of the camping equipment for the party; Damien removed those bags which were the most important and, without a word, shouldered them as well. Ciani's horse reared back as it felt her weight leave its back—but a sharp word from Tarrant, that carried above the roar of the water, made it shudder into submission.

Leading the horses, they walked with care, blinking constantly against the force of the spray. They felt their way across the narrow

bit of solid ground by touch even more than by sight. The roar of the water was like thunder, an utter cacophony that made speech impossible, thinking nearly so. Somehow, Senzei managed to keep his feet. Ciani stumbled once, but he managed to reach out and grab her by the arm, holding her steady until she managed to get her feet back under her. It amazed him that the horses were still with them, though the animals were clearly unhappy about their destination. Maybe Tarrant had helped with that, somehow; gods knew, they needed all the help they could get.

At last they were at the base of the cliff wall, as near as they could get to the break itself without swimming. Senzei saw Damien point upward, but he couldn't make out what the priest was pointing at. Blindly, he followed. Stumbling up an incline made slippery by water and algae, trying to guide his mount to safe footing when he could scarcely find it himself. He could feel panic building in the animal, powerful enough to affect the fae and manifest before him: a cloud of equine fear that engulfed him as he tried to move forward, driving spears of animal terror into his own flesh. He stumbled, felt his ankle twist and nearly slide out from under him. Desperately, he tried to Work—there was solid ground under him, therefore there must be earth-fae accessible—and he managed the ghost of a Banishing, barely enough to dissipate the fear directly before him, not enough to keep its fringes from affecting the rest of his party. *Not good enough.* Gritting his teeth against the tides of fear that were rising within him—his own and the animal's, and gods alone knew who else's— he threw all his will into his Working, every last bit of power that he could possibly manifest. And the dank cloud of terror wavered, thinned, and dispersed at last into the mist.

Exhausted, he climbed. And somehow managed to get both himself and the frightened horse up to the top of the incline, to a narrow ledge of rock that looked over the Achron. Damien grasped him by the arm and helped him along—was the man ever bothered by anything?—and then the spray was behind him, the thunder dimming to a mere roar, and smooth, solid ground was underfoot once more. He tightened his hand about his horse's reins—and then doubled over and retched, helplessly, as though that might somehow cast the fear and the exhaustion out of him.

When he finally straightened up again he found his companions with him, as soaked and exhausted as he was but yes, every one of them had made it. Even the horses. He saw Damien strap his pack back onto his mount's back, and managed weakly to grin in acknowledgment. They had made it. The worst part was over. *This* worst part, anyway.

Tarrant took some minutes to soothe the last of their mounts' fears—perhaps blinding the animals to the dangers of their path, perhaps merely numbing their emotional response—and Ciani seemed as grateful for the break as Senzei was. She wrung the water from her hair and tried not to look down at the river beneath them. There, mere yards below their feet, the glassy current had already begun to froth, as if anticipating the drop soon to come.

Senzei looked out over the seething waterfall, toward the Serpent. He could see nothing but clouds—white clouds, silver clouds—rising like steam from the water's surface. And perhaps, ever so elusive, sparks of liquid illusion that shimmered in the air like sea-spray. The Canopy. This close?

He turned back and found Damien watching him. When the priest saw that he was all right, the concern in his eyes gave way to wry humor; the grimace of tension softened to a smile.

"Welcome to the rakhlands," he told him.

The Achron had carved its meandering path through the rakhlands over the course of eons, and now was seated in a twisting, steep-walled canyon, whose eroded strata made for narrow ledges that flanked the water like roads. They followed one, single file, until at last it widened to a more hospitable proportion. Then, when they could move about without the constant fear of falling into the swift current beneath them, they finally stopped to catch their breath. Ciani was pale, and her body shook as she lowered herself to sit on the ground, legs unsteady beneath her. Senzei felt little better. Even the tireless Damien Vryce looked exhausted, wrung out by hours of fighting the cold waves and the treacherous rocks, and the fears that had crowded about them like specters ever since nightfall.

"That," he gasped, "was one hell of a climb."

"We should build a fire," Ciani said.

"Dry out," Senzei agreed.

"Find shelter," Tarrant said quietly—and something in his tone drew their attention to him, so that their eyes followed his up the rock wall beside them, to a point some twenty yards above their heads.

"We're being watched?" Damien whispered tensely.

The Hunter shook his head. "Not now. But the trace is there." He narrowed his eyes in concentration, then murmured, "The same trace. But old."

"How old?" Damien demanded.

"One day. Maybe two. I would guess it was part of the same watch system that spotted us when we landed; perhaps even the same individual, riding from one post to another. The impression is very similar."

"But not identifiable?" Damien pressed.

The Hunter looked at him. His expression was unreadable.

"Not human," he said quietly. "Isn't that enough?"

Damien stared up at the sheer wall and cursed softly. "They set the watch right here," he muttered darkly. "It's the first place any traveler could rest in safety, after getting to the canyon."

"Our enemy chose his vantage points well," the Hunter agreed. "I only wish. . . ."

His voice trailed off into darkness.

"What?" the priest demanded.

Tarrant seemed to hesitate. "In another place, I might . . . but not here. Not with the fae this weak."

"See, you mean?"

"That, too. I meant reconnaissance. But the point is moot," he said quickly, waving short Damien's response. "I can't do it. And certainly none of you can."

"I can't make it much further," Ciani whispered.

"And neither can the horses," Tarrant agreed. "I've been supplementing their strength up until now . . . but my own has its limits, as you know." And he looked at Damien—very strangely, Senzei thought—as if reminding him of some secret knowledge that the two of them alone shared.

"We'll camp as soon as we can," the priest told them.

Somehow, they managed to get to their feet. Managed to move again, though all their flesh screamed in protest of further exertion. As they progressed, the walls of the canyon grew closer overhead, the river deeper. Mica glistened erratically in the stratified rock, like spirits trying to manifest upon its surface. Already the moons had dropped low enough that no light shone directly into the canyon; the lanterns they had lit might banish mere darkness, but it was hardly enough to dispel the dark fae that was slowly gathering about them. Once Senzei thought he saw a face begin to form on a glistening outcropping of rock—but he quickly muttered the key to a Banishing, and the face disappeared. Once or twice he heard Damien whisper a word that might been meant to key a Working, and his stomach lurched in fear as he envisioned what manner of things might manifest in such a place as this. He even thought he heard a whisper of Working from Ciani—but that just said how frightened he was, how potentially irrational. How could Ciani be Working? Only Tarrant was silent, clearly at peace with the night and its darkness. And why not? Half the things that might hunger for their life, that might take on familiar form to gain access to their blood and their vitality, were kin to him. What did he have to fear?

As if in answer, Tarrant reigned up his horse. Peering, and then pointing, into the darkness ahead.

"There's shelter, of sorts." He looked up at the cliff wall that towered over them, as if searching for something. A hint of daylight? "The sun will be up soon."

Damien peered ahead into the darkness ahead of them, saw nothing. "Your eyes are better than mine, Hunter."

"That goes without saying." He pointed slightly ahead and to the left. "That crevice, there."

Squinting into the darkness, Senzei could barely make out the form of a cleft in the rock. It was narrow, but passable, and might open into a larger space within.

"You think it's safe?" he asked.

"I think nothing here is safe," he said shortly. "But to continue onward in your current condition avails us nothing—except greater risk. Our enemy is waiting for us. The sun is about to rise. And I, for one, have no intention of confronting either at this time. You may do as you will."

He dismounted and walked toward the opening. His horse was either too well-trained or too numb from exhaustion to do anything other than stand there and wait for him; he made no attempt to secure it. Senzei watched with growing despair as Tarrant approached the dark crevice, studied it, and then slipped within. It was as if he could feel the jaws of a trap closing about them, the eyes of an unseen watcher fixed on their backs as they went about securing shelter, hordes of unseen warrior-creatures awaiting only a word to strike . . . he shivered, from cold and misgivings both, and wrapped his arms tightly around himself. As if that could somehow still the tide of fear inside him.

Think rationally, Zen. Like the enemy does. They knew where we would stop to rest—but they weren't there when we arrived, were they? They don't know that we have to travel only at night, therefore they can't second-guess our schedule. And they also don't know that we need an absolute shelter from the sun, that a cavern would draw us in like honey in an insect trap. . . . The words sounded good, but they did little to quell the fear inside him.

Suddenly a snarl sounded from beyond the cavern's mouth, followed by a wild, bestial howling that made his skin crawl in horror.

He saw Damien start forward, then stop himself, forcibly. The priest's expression was grim. The howling rose in pitch, a war cry of pain and terror and territorial urges—all cut short, suddenly. Sucked up into the utter silence of the night.

Tarrant reappeared. Brushing lightly at one shoulder, he dislodged a bit of cave-dirt that had stuck to his clothing. "Shelter enough for one day," he announced—and it might have been Senzei's imagination, but it seemed there was a glint of red about his teeth as he spoke.

"Unoccupied?" Damien asked.

Tarrant's eyes glistened coldly. "It is now. You may help yourself to . . . dinner, if you like. There's meat for it." And he added, with an ominous smile, "I've already dined."

They stared at him for a moment, all three of them. No one more anxious than any other to see what manner of place he had found for them, or what manner of carrion it now harborerd.

Then: "What the hells," Ciani muttered. She slid from her horse's back, and somehow managed to stand steadily despite the obvious weakness in her legs. Gods, they were all near collapse.

"As long as it's dry," she said.

There was something going on between them, Damien decided—something happening between Ciani and Gerald Tarrant that he didn't like at all. He couldn't quite identify what it was—but it was there, without doubt. Like a channel had been established between them. He could almost See it.

As they made their preparations for the day's encampment, he kept half an eye on each of them. Tarrant explored the back recesses of the narrow cavern, making certain there were no hidden dangers there—and Ciani accompanied him. Tarrant took it upon himself in the last hour of relative darkness to see that the horses were rubbed dry and calmed, and tethered within reach of edible brush—and Ciani, who had little experience with such duties, went to help him. Damien was aware of whispers passing between them, things more felt than heard: a subvocal purring of conspiracy, of coalition. But what purpose could it possibly serve? Without knowing, he told himself, he had no right to interfere. Ciani had every reason to be curious about the adept, and if Tarrant was answering her questions, the more power to her. And if that was all it was, Damien had no right to interfere. But what if it wasn't? Did Ciani really understand how dangerous the Hunter was—how utterly corrupt a soul must be, to sink from the Prophet's heights to such a murdering, parasitic existence? The thought of prolonged contact between the two of them made Damien's stomach turn, and he watched them carefully. Trying to stay within hearing distance. Hoping for any excuse he might reasonably use to keep her away from their deadly companion.

The cavern which Tarrant had found them—little more than a cleft in the cliff wall, six feet wide at its broadest point and considerably less than that as it angled back into the stratified rock—had clearly been occupied, and for some time. It reeked of generations of animal occupancy: the oils of mating, the exudations of birth, the pungent spray of territorial markings. Not to mention the carrion that Tarrant had provided, a tangle of bloody fur and moist meat that still stank of animal terror. But it was dry and safe, and the floor was layered in insulting dirt, and at this point that was all any of them wanted. They unpacked their bedrolls along its length, rendered Tarrant's kill down for its edible portions and threw the rest into the Achron, and laid their wet clothing—which was most of what they owned—out on the ledge by the cavern's mouth, to be dried by the rising sun. Watches were scheduled. A minimal fire was kindled. The cave's former occupant became a satisfying, if somewhat gamy, repast. And they waited for the sun to rise, knowing that only for a few hours would it shine directly down into the gorge which the Achron's current had scoured into the land—waiting to see what manner of place they had come to, what patterns of promise and danger the light of day might reveal.

Once, when his watch had ended, Damien made his way to the rear of the cavern, where Tarrant had isolated himself, to see how the adept was doing. A slab of rock that had fallen from the ceiling in some past earthquake concealed the back recesses of their shelter from immediate view; when he made his way past it, he found that a wall of coldfire had been erected in the lightless recess. Utterly frigid. Utterly impassable.

"Well, fine," he muttered. "Just fine."

And then—hoping the Hunter could hear him—he added, "I trust you, too."

The land through which the Achron coursed was a rich, three-dimensional tapestry of geological history, whose cross-section had been revealed by the cutting action of the river's progress. From a layer of granite through which the water coursed, up through layers of black basalt and alluvial sediment and compressed volcanic ash, it was possible to read the history of this region in the patterns that decorated the cliff walls—volcanic eruption and glacial invasion and always, as elsewhere, the violent geo-signatures of earthquakes. Where the narrow strata had once comprised an ordered map of geo-history, it had now been split by successive upheavals into a jagged mosaic that lined the walls of the gorge like some immense, grotesquely abstract artwork. Winds had grooved the junctures of strata, widened fissures, and eroded away the underpinning of various outcroppings, so that ragged columns and angular arches loomed overhead, a giant surreal sculpture that had been abandoned to the elements. Vegetation had taken root wherever it could, but for the most part the upper reaches of the walls were utterly lifeless: a bit of lichen, a patch of coarse grass, perhaps a few dried roots to mark the place where a desperate tree had once tried to grasp hold. No more than that. Unclimbable, at any rate. Which meant that they were doomed to traverse the river's bed until some variation in the canyon's structure allowed them to ascend to the rich lands surrounding it.

At sunset they moved again, Senzei concluding the last watch of the day as they urged their horses back onto the narrow path. There was still no sight of the watcher, or any other attempt at surveillance. Damien was beginning to think that maybe something positive might be read into that. Maybe whoever had seen them land was merely an independent observer who had chanced upon the spot, with no lasting interest in what became of them, no dangerous allies to mobilize—

Right. Damned likely. Dream on, priest.

They rode. The horses were clearly less than thrilled about their chosen road, but a good day's rest in a relatively dry place—not to mention fresh food and water—had given them back something of their accustomed spirit. Damien had little trouble convincing his mount to lead the way along the narrow ledge, and the struggles of the previous night receded into hazy memory as the rhythm of travel engulfed them all.

When Casca's three-quarter face cleared the western wall, they stopped for a short while. In the shadow of the grotesque natural sculptures they nibbled at bits of meat and cake and discussed, in guarded murmurs, the possibility of finding a way out of the canyon in the nights to come. Tarrant took out his maps again and located several points of possible egress: tributary junctions in the Achron's course, which might or might not involve some variation in the canyon's structure. He seemed to feel that the odds were good—and since it was the first real optimism the man had expressed about this journey, Damien found it doubly comforting. For once, things seemed to be going their way.

But then he thought: *When we get up to the plateau, that's when the real work begins. The real danger.* It was a sobering thought, and one that he didn't share with his companions. Let them enjoy this last bit of security while it lasted; such things would become rare soon enough.

In time Casca set behind the eastern wall, and a nearly-full Prima took her place in the skies. The presence of any moon above them weakened the dark fae which might otherwise harass them, and Damien was grateful for the current lunar schedule. Not long from now there would be a period of true night, when no natural light was available; by that time, he hoped, they would be out of the canyon, not trapped on some twisting path beneath walls that were prone to fracture, with the angry black water waiting just beneath them, and all their fears manifested by the power of the ultimate Night.

Tarrant will gain strength, then, he thought. *He'll come into his true power for the first time since our landing.* It was a chilling thought, but somehow it lacked the power of his previous fears. Was it possible that Tarrant's usefulness was beginning to outweigh the abhorrence of his nature, in Damien's mind? That was dangerous, the priest reflected. That was truly frightening. That worried him more than the true night itself—more than all the rest of it combined. Could one become inured to the presence of such an evil? So much so that one lost sight of what it truly was, and saw no further than the elegant facade which housed it? He shivered at the thought, and swore he would keep it from happening. Prayed to his God that he *could* keep it from happening.

Gradually, the canyon narrowed. The water could be heard to course northward with a far more violent current than before, and although he hesitated to look down—the view was dizzying—Damien knew from the sound of it that there was now white water below their feet, that the walls here had fragmented and fallen often enough to place a thousand obstacles in the river's path—obstacles over which the water now coursed angrily, obstacles against which any fallen creature would certainly be crushed. All the more reason not to fall from the ledge. He eased his horse farther from the edge and hoped his companions would follow suit. As long as they were careful—and the ledge grew no narrower—they should be in little danger.

Then they came around a bend, and his heart went cold within him. He signaled for a stop, forced his own horse to stand steady as he studied the road ahead as well as he could by moonlight. The apprehension of his fellow travelers was like a tangible thing, a cloud of pessimism so thick that he could hardly breathe through it.

Finally he gestured to Tarrant, signaled for him to come to the front. "Your night vision is best of anyone's," he said. "What do you make out?"

The Hunter dismounted, and made his way on foot to the front of the procession. There he gazed into the darkness for some time before responding.

"The path continues to narrow," he said. "And I don't like the look of it. The water has eaten its way underneath that shelf, and there are visible damages . . . it's not as solid as what we've been traveling on, by any means."

"Can it support us?" Senzei asked tensely.

Tarrant's expression tightened, and the concentration that Damien had come to associate with his Working flashed briefly in his eyes. "As it is now, it will," he responded. "If nothing interferes."

"Are there alternatives?" Ciani asked him.

He looked up to her, cold eyes fluid, like quicksilver. "None that I see here, lady. Except going back, of course. That's always an option."

She stiffened. "No," she whispered. "Not while I have the strength left to move."

"Then there are none."

"We go on," she said firmly.

The Hunter nodded and remounted. Without a word, they began to move forward onto a section of ledge that was scored by faults. They moved slowly, carefully, ever aware that a single overemphatic hoofbeat might crack something loose underfoot and send them plummeting to the white water below. As they rode, the ledge narrowed. After a time Damien could no longer keep his horse to the path without his left leg scraping against the wall of the gorge periodically; small bits of rock showered to the ground beneath him after each such contact, and bounced off the ledge down into the shadows beneath to disappear into the hungry river.

Even if we wanted to turn back now, we couldn't. Not without backing the horses up for miles—and they'd rather jump into the water than put up with that.

God help us if the ledge peters out, he thought—and then, because there was no constructive way to think about such a possibility, he put it forcibly out of his mind. The ledge *would* continue, it *would* be sound enough to support them, and if it wasn't they would manage to do . . . *something.*

They traveled in tense silence, each cocooned in his fears. Beneath them the river coursed, noisily now, and white froth glittered in Pri-

ma's light. The edge of that moon had already dropped behind the
eastern wall of the gorge, with the rest soon to follow. What would
they do when its light was gone? Could they traverse a path this
dangerous, with nothing but lamplight to guide them? Damien felt
like he had been traveling forever, leading the way along a path so
narrow, with a surface so irregular, that it seemed only a matter of
time before one of them stumbled and fell. His own horse was
unlikely to lose its footing; that animal was experienced in handling
such situations and knew what it meant to test each footstep in
advance. But would Senzei's animal, city-bred, slip from the path? Or
the Forest beasts, which had known only packed, level earth before
this? If anyone went down into that angry water . . . it was better not
to think about such things. Better just to keep the mind blank and
hope the horses got them through.

Finally—after what seemed like an eternity—the ledge began to
widen. Slowly, almost imperceptibly—but at last the point came
when the travelers' legs no longer brushed against the wall, when his
horse's easier gait informed him that the animal now felt more secure
about the ground underfoot. "On our way," he whispered. He began
to think they would really make it through. Damien allowed himself
the luxury of a few deep breaths, and stretched his cramped feet in
their stirrups to bring life back into them—

"Heads up!" The Hunter called. "And don't Work, whatever you
do!"

The urgency in his voice made Damien twist back quickly. The
adept had one hand raised as if to shield his eyes from light. But
there was nothing in the canyon that Damien could see, and Senzei
and Ciani seemed similarly confused. What force had the adept's
vision disclosed, which would suddenly become so bright—

"Hells!" he heard Ciani whisper as she realized what was happening. A rumbling filled the air around them—which meant an earthquake, very close and very bad. Damn it! Not now! The rock
overhead began to tremble visibly, and he could feel his horse shift
its weight nervously, responding to signals half-sensed, half-felt, from
the ground beneath its feet. He tightened his hands on the reins,
spasmodically—but there was nothing he could do, absolutely nothing. They were utterly at the mercy of Nature, and she was known
for her ruthlessness. He tried to urge his horse a step closer to the
cliff face, but either the animal didn't like that strategy or it was so
far gone in its own mounting terror that it simply didn't acknowledge
the command. He decided he would be safer on his own two feet and
began to dismount. Suddenly the cliff wall overhead split, with a
sound like thunder, and segments of rock the size of a man's head

crashed to the path right before them. The horse reared back, squealing in terror, and nearly crushed Damien against the jagged wall behind them. He didn't dare let go lest the animal trample him, but nor did he have a secure hold on its saddle; as falling rocks pelted them like hailstones he struggled to stay in control, tried to calm the beast. But all his practiced words and signs could do nothing to lessen its terror. Maybe it could sense from him just how dangerous their position was. Maybe the fae had taken his own fear and injected that into the animal, so that it must deal with human terror along with its own. Or maybe the tremendous surge of earth-fae that had blinded Gerald Tarrant was capable of amplifying all their reactions so that logical decisions were drowned out in a deluge of primal fright.

Something struck Damien. Hard. Sharp rock cut deeply into his skull, as though he had struck the wall—or the wall had struck him. He felt something massive come down onto him, crushing him against his saddle, driving both him and the horse to the ground. Only the ground wasn't there anymore. His horse's feet struck wildly at where the ledge should have been and found only emptiness. The flawed rock had crumbled—and they were tumbling downward, the two of them, blood pouring down into Damien's eyes as the river rushed up hungrily to meet them. He felt darkness closing in on him and fought it, fought it back with everything in him that hungered for life—because to lose consciousness now was to die, plain and simple. Head pounding in pain, hands shaking, he somehow managed to yank his foot out of its stirrup and twist himself so that when the animal landed he wouldn't be beneath it. They struck with a force that sent water flying high up onto the cavern walls. The horse screamed in pain as it landed, began flailing out wildly. Rock rained down like hail about them as Damien struggled to get out of range of the animal's hooves. Then the current grabbed him and he went under; ice-cold water filled his mouth as the river's angry force slammed him against rock—once, twice, again. He reached out for anything to serve as anchor, to fight against the current, but his fingers met only slick rock and slid off, leaving him to the mercy of the water. Dimly he was aware that the current had dragged him down deep, very deep, and was taking him out into the middle of the river. His lungs already throbbed with pain, and he had to struggle not to try to breathe as he tried to determine which way was up. But all was chaos about him, a churning hell of icy water and rock that had neither direction nor order. He felt one shoulder strike bottom with a force that nearly drove the last air out of his lungs, and for one desperate moment he thought that he might Work to save himself—but the ground was still trembling, and the rumble of the earthquake still sounded even below the water, which meant that a Working meant death. Absolutely. Only a fool would even try it.

Or a dead man.

He gathered himself, knowing with one portion of his mind that he was about to be fried to a crisp—and knowing with another that if he did nothing he would certainly die. The river was too strong to fight. He needed air. Blood-red stars exploded before his eyes as his lungs began to convulse spasmodically, but he kept his throat closed as he gathered himself for a Working. The cold of the water had numbed him with a chill that was strangely warm. Was this what dying was? Time, now. Grasp the power—

And then something jerked him, hard. The stale air burst from his lungs and before he could stop himself he breathed in; water poured into him, drowning out his life. But something had taken hold of his harness, was dragging him back. Stars were swimming in his vision as he reached out toward the source of the movement. A strong arm grasped him, hand to wrist, and held. He was yanked upward—and he broke the surface gasping, water pouring out of his nose and mouth as he retched helplessly, dragged above the level of the river's surf by a grip even colder than the water, colder than the river and the freezing wind and all his fear combined. He stumbled as he was pulled through the icy current. The grip on his wrist was so steady it could have been made of solid rock; the hand that drew him upward was the center of his universe, the only thing he saw as the red stars slowly receded into blackness, as his lungs finally acknowledged the presence of air and drew it in, aching from the effort.

He looked up, saw Tarrant's visage highlighted by moonlight. The man's expression was strained, his hair plastered down about his face like wet seaweed. But despite the whitewater current that threatened to drag them both under again, his grip was like steel as he drew Damien up, inch by inch, until he was safely above the level of the water. The priest gasped for breath, tried to mouth something useful. Like, *Thank you.* Or, *Thank God.* Or perhaps, *What took you so damned long?* But it took too much effort just to breathe; he had to settle for gasping like a beached fish as the tall man held him, while the current swept hungrily about their knees.

"It's over," the Hunter told him. "That one, anyway." By which he meant, of course, the first shock wave. With a quake of that intensity, there could be several. Many. It could go on for days. "We need to move."

He managed to nod, felt his head explode with raw pain. Something red ran down into his left eye. "Zen—Ciani—" He managed to twist so that he could see back the way he had come, toward the figures

that still clung to that precarious ledge. He caught the glint of moon-light on Ciani's hair, recognized Senzei's lanky frame. Both safe, then. Thank God. The figures were hazy, masked by a distance that was greater than he had expected; the river must have swept him far downstream before Tarrant had managed to save him. He counted the horses—or tried to, the dark figures bled into each other at this distance—and it seemed to him that one was missing. But whose? And with what equipment? Their lives might well depend on the answer to that.

And then he sensed Tarrant's stillness, and looked down. At the river about them. At the three figures who stood in it, knee-high in the swirling water. All were human, in general form—and anything but human, in the details of their features. Golden eyes stared out of faces that were insulated in matching fur, and tufted ears swung forward to test the breeze, as a cat's might. He was aware of thick manes that covered both the shoulders and chests of the creatures, and trinkets of metal and shell that had been knotted into them. Aware most of all of the weapons they were holding, sharp-tipped spears that were aimed at the humans' midsections with obviously hostile intent. Hatred glimmered in the golden eyes, far more intense than anything the moment should warrant. It was the hatred of an entire people, that had been festering for decades. The hatred of an entire species, for Damien's own.

As for Tarrant . . . he was staring at the spearpoint directed at him with an expression that was half bemusement—was someone daring to threaten him?—and half something darker. Anger? Fear? Would the Hunter die if his heart were pierced? *A knife through the heart is as fatal to an adept as it is to anyone else,* he had said. And with the earth-fae still surging in the quake's deadly aftermath, he didn't dare Work to save himself. For one dizzying instant Damien thought that this was indeed what Gerald Tarrant would look like when fac-ing his own mortality. When facing the fact that in one moment all the work of centuries might be thrown away, and a single spear-stroke commit his soul to the hell he had been determined to avoid.

Then the Hunter looked at him—and something that was almost a smile passed across the man's lips. Something that was almost humor glittered in his eyes.

"I do believe," he said quietly, "that we have found the rakh."

Thirty-one

The demon Calesta took form slowly, like blood congealing in open air. The scent of the river still clung to him, and it clashed with the musty closeness of the Citadel's confines until at last the former was abolished, freshwater breezes choked out of existence by the cloying sweetness of the Master of Lema's favorite incense.

"You found them," came the whisper.

The demon bowed.

"Tell me."

"There are four: the woman, an adept, and two others. The adept is the most dangerous."

"Of course." Hunger was an echo behind the words. "Also the most satisfying. Their purpose?"

"To kill you. And, en route, your servants. As well as any other hungry thing foolish enough to cross their path."

"An ambitious plan."

"It is the priest's. He dominates."

"And the adept?"

"He endures."

A chuckle sounded. "You'll take care of them, yes? It's so easy, with that kind. You'll read what's in their hearts, and know what to do. As always."

The demon bowed.

"Spare the adept, of course. And the woman. Weaken them if you can, by all means, bring them as near to death as you like—but bring them to me intact. I . . . hunger for them."

The demon's voice was a hiss, a low screech, the sound of metal on metal. "I understand."

"As for the others . . . it's no concern of mine whether they live or

die. Do what pleases you, Calesta—provided their power is neutralized. You have such marvelous instincts regarding these things. And
they're coming here, yes? Marching here right into our hands. How
very convenient."

"The adept, my lord, is sun-sensitive."

The One Who Binds stiffened. And nodded, slowly. Anticipation,
like a drug, coursed through veins that had been jaded by time; the
thought of conquest surged through ancient flesh like orgasm.

"That's sweet news indeed," came the whisper. "And power
enough, for any who know how to use it. He was a fool to come
here! And the woman—more than a fool, that one. I had her once. I
will have her again. And when I am done . . . you, Calesta, may have
what remains. Serve me well, and I promise it."

The demon bowed. The hint of a smile played across its obsidian
visage; the mirrored eyes flashed hunger.

"As you command," it hissed.

Thirty-two

For a moment, no one made a sound. The tension was eloquent enough, with its accompanying kinesthetic signals: a rakhene hand tightening on a spear haft. A rakhene body testing the river bottom for stability, preparing to thrust. Rakhene eyes filled with a terrible hatred, that looked simultaneously upon the present moment and a horrifying past: the attempted obliteration of an entire intelligent species. In the shadow of such a holocaust there was nothing to say, no way to say it. Attempts to bargain would have been an insult. Pleas for mercy would have seemed a joke. Man's own actions had provided him with a far more ruthless enemy than anything the fae might invent.

Breath ragged, water surging about his knees, Damien itched to reach for his sword. Not so much to bring it into play as to make sure it was still there; the harness was loose about his shoulders, clearly damaged from the fall, which meant that the river might well have disarmed him. He flexed his shoulders ever so slightly, trying to judge the weight—and a spear point bit into his flesh, deeply enough to draw blood. He checked his motion, glanced up at Tarrant. The man understood—and nodded carefully, an almost imperceptible gesture. *Yes*, it said, *you're armed*. But the grim expression on his face told an additional story, and when Damien looked down he saw that the man's Worked sword—and its scabbard, and the heavy belt that supported it—were gone. He must have taken it off before entrusting himself to the river. *Shit!* How good was the Hunter at hand-to-spear combat? With his sorcerous skills made off-limits by the earthquake—

A call sounded from the cliffs high above: half speech, half animal yowling. Damien's captors tensed. The one holding a spear to Tarrant's torso glanced up at the cliff just long enough to bark out an answer—and Damien could see the Hunter gathering himself, muscles tensing secretly in that precious, unguarded instant. But then he checked himself, and his mouth tightened in anger and frustration as the furred warrior turned back to him. Not moving. Not saying a word.

Because of us, Damien thought. *He could have saved himself— but not Ciani. Not when the fae is still too hot to handle.*

He could see dark figures gathering about the ex-adept, could see Senzei tense as if he were about to fight them. *Not now,* he begged silently. *There are too many of them. Our position is too desperate.* Even while he prayed, he saw the figure fall back. Saw the dark figures closing in on it. And he wondered at the man's inner courage—or was it blind devotion to Ciani?—that would allow him to even consider resistance under such overwhelming circumstances.

There's a strength in him that's never really been tested, he thought grimly. And: *God willing, that'll never be necessary.*

Something flew down the cliff wall toward them, and then snapped to a stop mere feet from the bottom. A rope, of sorts—more like a tapestry, or an intricate knotwork sampler. Mere seconds later a figure slipped over the edge and climbed rapidly down toward them, fingers—or claws?—slipping in between the knots and out again with fluid efficiency. It dropped the last few feet in silence, landing on the ledge above them. Smaller than its fellows, it was dressed in layers of patterned cloth that swathed its limbs tightly to the wrist and ankle. No place for a shoulder-mane beneath those garments, nor any need for it. What this rakh lacked in raw mass it made up for in feline agility. And as it shifted its weight in the moonlight, so that the shadows no longer obscured its form—female, undeniably female— Damien realized why this one seemed so familiar.

"Morgot," he whispered. And the Hunter answered softly, "Just so."

She called out toward them—and though the words were unintelligible to Damien, the sharpness of the sound made it clear that its message was either a warning or a command. Or both. The language the creature used was one of hissed consonants and sharp vowels, utterly foreign to Damien's ears—and yet, without question, the cadence of it was familiar. Somewhere, sometime in the distant past, his own language had influenced this one.

They had no language when they left the human lands. That must have evolved here, in isolation. What else did they develop, that humankind knows nothing about?

One of their captors barked out a response, in tones so harsh that it was clear what manner of action he would prefer. Damien was aware of a cold wind blowing across his body, freezing his soaking clothes and hair until they felt like ice against his skin. A shivering had begun deep inside him, a last desperate attempt on the part of his body to generate warmth. The current that pushed at his legs was frigid, insistent. He was afraid—and also angry. At having to feel his life bleed away into the cold, when he could be spending his last moments in battle. Taking some of them with him.

If these bastards argue long enough, I'll die of hypothermia. But he could do no more than fight to keep his teeth from chattering—they'd probably use the sound as an excuse to kill him—as they continued in their conversation. Because there was, as always, Ciani to consider. And if her presence had tied the Hunter's hands in this situation, it did the same to Damien ten times over. He dared take no action that would bring rakhene wrath down on her head.

At last some manner of conclusion seemed to have been reached. One of their captors barked out an order toward them and prodded Damien sharply in the chest. Blood began to spread from the point of contact, staining his jacket carmine. But if the wound was meant to anger him, to make him lose control, it accomplished just the opposite. He held himself utterly still—as much as was possible in the swift river current—as one of the rakh jerked his arms behind his back and bound them together, coarse rope biting into his wrists. A jerk to his harness strap from behind told him that he had also been disarmed. He saw Gerald Tarrant being bound in the same manner. The look in the adept's eyes was one of pure murder—but he endured it, just as Damien did. There was no other choice.

In a nightmare journey they were forced upriver, back to where their companions waited. And then beyond that point, with Senzei and Ciani prodded forward on a course parallel to theirs, picking their way carefully along the broken ledge. Stumbling, often slipping, without their hands to steady themselves, the priest and the Hunter were forced to rely on their captors' occasional supportive grasp to keep them on their feet. Often it came too late, and several times Damien fell to his knees, hard, water swirling cold about his chest. Once he lost his balance entirely, and it was a clawed, alien hand that pulled him out of the water, jerking him up by the neck of his jacket as though it were the scruff of a cub's neck, meant for that purpose.

The look in Tarrant's eyes was murderous. What must it be like, Damien wondered, to have a soul that could command the ages, trapped in a body that could be made so vulnerable? He imagined the force of the rage and fear that must be building inside the man—and was glad he wasn't going to be at the receiving end of it when it broke. The man who killed sadistically for a hobby must be even more vicious when dealing with his enemies.

At last there was a shore, of sorts, and they were prodded toward it. The ledge which they had once traveled upon had dropped to nearly the level of the water, and widened also. Ciani and Senzei had been bound, he saw, and the two surviving horses were being led by rakhene warriors. Damien recognized Senzei's mount and one of Tarrant's animals. Which one of the true horses had they lost—and with it, which supplies? He thought of his own horse, fallen screaming to the rocks, and his gut tightened in anger. And sorrow. That animal had crossed through the Dividers with him, had seen vampires and smashers and an earthquake that leveled half a city, and come through it all unharmed. And now . . . the loss was an emptiness, an aching pain that stabbed at him even through the numbness of his frozen flesh.

Damn you! he thought, as a frigid wind gusted over him. As if somehow the horse could hear him. *You picked a hell of a time to die, you know that?*

They were forced up against the edge of the ridge, and then strong, clawed hands lifted them up onto it. Talons biting into cloth and flesh alike, like meat hooks digging into a fresh carcass. Damien saw Ciani's face was white with shock, Senzei's driven equally pale from fear. Hell, at least those two were dry. He felt like a fish on ice.

Then the rakh-woman was before them, alien eyes glaring out at them from a harsh, fur-sculpted visage. "You come," she hissed, "or you die. Simple. You understand?"

He nodded stiffly, was aware of his companions doing the same. Then she pointed to the Hunter and snapped a sharp command in her own tongue. The rakh standing behind Tarrant pulled a strip of cloth from out of his belt—heavily decorated, some kind of ornament—and before the adept could respond, bound it across his eyes. Damien heard Tarrant draw in a sharp breath, saw the muscles in his shoulders tense as he tested the ropes binding his arms, felt his rage engulf them all like a dark cloud—but whatever he might have tried to do to free himself, he didn't manage it. The blindfold was fastened tightly about his head, denying him both his earthly vision and his Sight. Damien wondered if an adept could Work the fae without seeing it . . . and then realized what the answer had to be. The woman had seen him in Morgot, and knew his power. She had bound him well.

Grimmer and grimmer, Damien thought.

She turned, then, to guide them south. A rakh dug his claws into

Tarrant's collar and forced him forward; a sharp prod in the center of Damien's back, that bit through cloth to break his flesh, forced the priest to do the same. *Give me half a chance and you'll eat that vulking spear,* he promised silently. He could feel Ciani and Senzei behind him—the heat of their bodies, the sharp tang of their fear. They should never have come this way, should never have been so unguarded . . . but what choice had they had? They'd taken every possible precaution. In the end, the land itself had turned against them. How could a man defend against that?

Limbs nearly frozen, he staggered onward. To the left of them the river gradually widened, until it formed a small lake between the steep canyon walls. From ahead came the sound of water falling, and Damien pictured the first tributary marked on Gerald Tarrant's map. A sheer drop from the surface of the plateau to the Achron, he guessed. No way up, then, for horses or men. How long would they have had to continue on, without ever gaining the plateau?

But as they came around one final bend, a new landscape revealed itself. A portion of the canyon wall had split off and fallen into the river, and on the resulting slope of rubble a crude road had been built. No, hardly a road; a slender path, that wound its way through hairpin turns on the side of the towering cliff wall, just barely wide enough for a horse to travel. Damien glanced behind him once as they ascended, to where an impatient rakh forced the blinded Hunter forward. A good thing the adept didn't know just how narrow the path was. Damien thought. It was a bad enough climb with one's eyes open—the thought of having to thrust one's enemies to guide one along it was enough to make his stomach turn. He managed to make fleeting eye contact with Senzei, who nodded stiffly in grim encouragement, but Ciani's eyes were fixed on the hazardous road ahead of them. He thought he could see her trembling.

At last they reached the top, and the humans were allowed a few brief seconds to catch their breath. Damien was shivering violently, knew he wouldn't last much longer if he didn't get his body temperature up. Did he dare Work, this soon after a quake? How long did the earth-fae take to subside in this place? Damn it, he needed Tarrant's Sight. . . . With a muttered curse, he decided to wait. At least a short while longer. Every second that passed made it safer.

There were beasts waiting for them at the top of their climb, horselike in general form, but as unlike true horses in the finer details of their anatomy as the rakh warriors were unlike men. They tossed their heads impatiently as the party approached: silk-fine fur rippled in the cold autumn breeze, pearlescent horns gleaming with reflected moonlight. *Xandu,* he thought, awed by their wild beauty. They shied away from Tarrant distastefully, as if somehow they could sense what role he had played in their history. And sniffed at the humans' horses with gentler mien, as if pitying them for the grandeur they had lost. Roughly, Damien was jostled toward one of the horses. He wasn't sure whether they meant for him to mount it as he was—a dubious endeavor—or whether they intended to unbind him temporarily. He never found out. Because in that moment, Tarrant moved. Blue flame flickered first at the edges of his blindfold, then consumed the fabric utterly. An unearthly chill swept through Damien, as if somehow all remaining warmth had been leached from the air around him; when he breathed, his breath turned to white fog that misted toward Tarrant. Then the adept stepped away from the rest of the company, and as he did so the blue fire died—and the blindfold shattered like glass and fell to the cold earth around him in a thousand tiny slivers.

Cold silver eyes regarded the rakh, and Damien knew from experience just how much power was behind them. Half of him was jubilant to see a member of his party freed—and the other half of him shuddered at the thought of the slaughter that might take place if Tarrant's fury was fully unleashed. Was there any way to stop that from happening? Did he have any *right* to stop it from happening? Coldfire flashed again, and coarse rope snapped into a thousand brittle fragments: Tarrant's hands were freed. One of the rakh began to move toward him, spear raised into an aggressive position; Tarrant's eyes narrowed and he dropped the spear with a sudden cry of fear and pain. There was flesh adhering to it, frozen to its surface; from his hand, dark blood dripped slowly.

Tarrant turned to the rakh-woman; his expression was dark. "If you meant to kill us, you waited too long. If you have any other intention, now's the time to make it known. I find myself short of patience."

One of the other warriors started to move forward, but she warned him back with a quick gesture. "*You* live because you saved his life." She nodded sharply toward Damien. "Because somewhere in that wretched thing you call a soul, that much of value still exists." She looked at them all, with varying degrees of disapproval. "My people are torn between wanting to know why you came here, and wanting your heads for souvenirs. I've convinced them to swallow their death-hunger long enough for you to answer questions. That's why the rest of you have been spared. Whether you remain alive after they have their answers . . . is up to you."

"Untie my companions," Tarrant said quietly.

She made no response, other than to step back a bit. Giving him room.

After a moment the Hunter stepped forward and applied himself to Damien's bonds. The priest's flesh was so numb from the cold that he couldn't even feel it when his hands were at last freed, but observed them as they swung down by his sides as though they were strange to him, the limbs of some other creature. He forced himself to acknowledge them, to use one to try to rub warmth into the other, as Tarrant untied the two other humans.

Then the adept turned, and faced the rakh-woman again. Even soaking wet—his hair plastered messily to the side of his face, his clothing torn in a dozen places by the application of claws and spear-point—he was possessed of a regality that commanded a power all its own. A dark charisma, which even the rakh must respond to.

"You touch my companions again," he warned—and his eyes scanned the warriors as he spoke—"and you die. Instantly." His eyes fixed on the rakh-woman. "Tell them," he commanded.

For a moment the woman just stared at him. Then, without answering, she walked to where her xandu stood. With a motion as fluid and unpredictable as a cat pouncing suddenly on its prey, she gained its back. And twisted one hand into its mane, sharp claws entangled in gleaming silk.

"They understand you," she told the Hunter.

And she smiled coldly, displaying pointed teeth. "They understand more than you think."

The xandu rode like the wind. The horses rode like overtired, overwrought horses, who'd had enough of earthquakes and waterfalls and long rides without rest, and who hadn't collapsed before now only because no one had let them stand still long enough to do so. It didn't help that Senzei and Ciani were sharing a mount, or that Damien— a heavy man to start with—was carrying twice his weight in water-logged clothing. But at least they'd been spared a fourth rider.

Damien looked up at the sky, at the great white predatory bird that soared high above their company, and felt a cold, unaccustomed awe fill him. Shapechanging wasn't supposed to be possible, at least not for the flesh-born—but he had seen it done, and the memory chilled his blood more than weather and river-water combined. Against his will, he recalled it: a budden burst of coldfire brilliance, so frigid that it blinded, human flesh dissolving as if in an acid bath, features running together like water in a whirlpool—and then, in that last instant, white wings rising up out of the conflagration, bearing the Hunter's new body into a moonlit sky. But it wasn't the transformation itself that made Damien's blood turn to ice in his veins, or even the memory of human flesh dissolving before his eyes. It was the look on Tarrant's face, in that last moment before he entrusted his life to the earth-fae. Utter discipline, total submission—and an echo of pain and fear so intense that Damien, remembering the man's expression, still shivered before the force of it.

I couldn't have managed it, he thought. *Not for all the power in the world. No sane man could.*

Unsane, unconquerable, the Hunter soared high above them. Periodically a rakhene warrior would glance up at him, and the fur-bordered eyes would narrow. In defiance? In fear? It wasn't unreasonable to hope for the latter. Damien's small party needed every advantage it could get in dealing with these creatures—and if the rakh decided that Tarrant was a man to be feared, so much the better.

He'd feed on that, too. Draw strength from it.

He nodded grimly, and thought, *Good for him.*

Miles passed beneath the pounding hooves, flat land layered in thick black soil and the dying remnants of summer's bounty. In places the browning grass was so deep that the horses' legs sank into it a foot or more, before withdrawing; In other places it was so sparse that a shoulder of granite might be seen, forcing its way through the moist black cover of the earth. Damien wrapped himself as tightly as he could in the thick woolen blanket he had taken from their stores, which did little to raise his body temperature but at least kept the wind off his soaked hair and clothing. *Just a little bit farther,* he promised himself. *Body heat is an easy thing to conjure, once you're standing still. No damage has been done that you can't undo, if they'll just leave you alone to Work.* But the likelihood of them doing that was very small indeed, and the dry clothing he would have liked to change into must be halfway down the Achron by now, still strapped to his horse's corpse.

It was Tarrant who first spotted the rakhene encampment—and he let out a shrill shriek to warn his companions as he circled down lower, overseeing their arrival. Seconds later the leader of the rakh drew a finely engraved horn from out of his belt and blew on it, presumably to alert the camp to their presence. The rakhene formation pulled in tighter about the humans, spear-points nearly touching the horses' flanks, forcing them to a halt. After a few minutes Damien could see a second company riding toward them, maned warriors who gripped their weapons tightly as they approached, as if impatient to use them. They glared at the humans as they approached the raiding party, and angry words passed between the leaders of the two groups. The cadence of the newcomer's speech resonated with fury as he indicated Damien's unbound hands, and those of the other humans. Their captors responded defiantly, and Damien could only guess at his argument: the humans were disarmed, they were wounded and exhausted, they were sharing two mounts among three of them—how much damage could they possibly do? At last, with an angry nod, the leader of the second group agreed to lead them in. His companions went galloping on ahead, presumably to warn the camp that they were coming.

The great white bird swooped low overhead: a warning to the rak-hene warriors, a gesture of support to the three humans. Despite his anxiety, Damien smiled.

Never thought I'd be this glad to have you around, you son of a bitch.

They rode to the top of a gentle swell, where thick autumn growths crowded about their horses' ankles. From here it was possible to see the rakhene encampment, a village of tents and lightweight structures that stretched as far as the eye could see. Xandu grazed between the primitive dwellings, with no hobble or leash to bind them in place. Despite the lateness of the hour there were numerous people about, going about the day's business as if the sun were still high in the sky. Children darted out into the moonlight and then were gone again, small golden forms as naked as the xandu who indulgently made way for them. Full-grown rakh tended cookfires, carved new weapons, sat around low-banked fires with bowls of steaming drink in their hands and made noises that might have been laughter. There were warrior-rakh like the ones who had captured Ciani's party, broad-shouldered, heavily maned males with glittering ornaments woven into their fur; slender females, clothed from neck to ankle in finely gathered cloth, layered necklaces cascading down the front of their tabards; other females, aggressively naked, whose few, carefully chosen ornaments served only to highlight full rounded breasts, a sensitive strip of hairless skin that ran the length of their abdomen, hips and thighs that swayed as they walked in a motion at once exotic and familiar: the timeless dance of sexual desire. There were others, too, whose dress or manner blurred the dividing line between those groups, but they were gone too quickly for Damien to identify. Castes? Genders? What manner of society did these creatures develop, when human-style intelligence first began to stir within them?

With a brusque, barking sound, one of the rakh ordered him to dismount. Damien tried to obey. But his legs, weakened by the exer-

tions of the night and numbed by the searing cold, were barely able to support him. He held onto the horse for support and breathed deeply, trying to will the feeling back into his flesh, praying for the strength not to look as weak as he felt in front of his enemies. Ciani and Senzei dismounted quickly, without being ordered to, and came running toward him. There were spears placed in their path, but Zen shoved them aside; for once he seemed more angry than afraid. Then, suddenly, a shadow swept cross Damien's face. The rakh nearest to him drew back—fearfully, it seemed to him. Then, in the space that they had cleared, the great predator-bird landed. Feathers gave way to burning coldfire, which melted in turn into flesh; Tarrant caught Damien before he could fall, and for once his skin was no colder than the priest's own.

"Good flight, I hope," the priest whispered.

"I've had better." He held Damien steady while Senzei rewrapped the blanket around his shoulders. "You need to get warm, fast."

"Tell me something I don't know."

A group of rakh were approaching from the camp. Damien managed to stand up straight, though he could feel the strain of it pounding in his heart. Beneath the blanket he grasped at Tarrant's arm, hoping such weakness went unseen. Whoever thought that man's presence would be so reassuring?

They waited, side by side, as the strangers approached. Seven in all: three males, two females, and two that might have been either—slender figures, fully clothed, whose form and manner offered no hint of gender or social status. Eunuchs? Adolescents? Not knowing their society, Damien couldn't begin to theorize.

The newcomers seemed to command some special respect, and warriors hurried out of their way as they joined the raiding party. They came to within several paces of where the humans stood and studied them. So focused was he upon staying on his feet, denying his own weakness, that Damien almost missed it when the rakh-woman joined them. Clearly, she was one of their number.

It was Tarrant who spoke first; his tone was harsh. "If you mean to kill us, now's the time to try it. If you intend anything else, I think it's time you told us about it." It was hardly a speech calculated to make friends—but there was very little time left for diplomacy, Damien realized. In less than an hour's time the sun would begin to rise, and Tarrant would have to leave them. He was trying to force some kind of confrontation before that happened.

It was the rakh-woman who responded. "It's your intentions that need to be judged—not ours."

"We came to heal one of our own kind. Not to do battle with the rakh."

"Our peoples are at war," a male challenged him. "Do you deny that?"

Damien stiffened. "That war ended centuries ago."

The woman hissed softly. "Not for us, human. Not for us."

Damien was about to respond when Ciani broke in. "Please . . ." she said softly. "We're exhausted. Can't you see that? We don't have the strength left to hurt you, even if we wanted to." Damien felt Tarrant stiffen at his side, as aghast as he was at her admission of weakness. What in hell's name did she think she was doing? "Please. We need . . . a fire. Something to drink. A minute to breathe. Just that," she begged. "We'll do what you want. Whatever you want, after that. *Please.*"

For a moment, utter silence reigned. Damien trembled—in disbelief, and apprehension. He'd never imagined that such words would ever come from her lips, such an abject admission of weakness . . . and not here! Not now! Not when they needed so desperately to establish themselves on strong ground. But because she was Ciani— because she must have *something* in mind, some reason to act this way—he bit back on the defiant words that were half-formed on his lips, and forced himself to be silent. To wait. To let her speak for the four of them.

The rakh conferred among themselves, sharp phonemes passing like animal hisses between them. At last the woman looked back at them. For a few seconds she just waited, perhaps to see if one of the men would protest Ciani's message. But Senzei and Tarrant had clearly come to the same decision that Damien had—in fact, Tarrant was nodding slightly in approval.

"Come with us," the rakh-woman said. "You'll be fed, and given warmth—and then you can explain yourselves."

The woman's small group surrounded them in guard formation, herding them to the north. As for the real guards, the rakhene warriors, they hissed disapprovingly as their prisoners were taken from them—but they did let them go, which said much for the status of the woman's group.

Damien glanced up at Tarrant, who put a slender finger to the side of his face. Through the contact of flesh-on-flesh a Working formed, that widened the channel between them until words could pass along it.

Very clever of her, don't you think? Assuming that animal instincts would still be active among them. Enough so that a display of abject submission might be enough to short-circuit their aggres-

sive instincts. She seems to have earned us a place—however low—
within their hierarchy. Which means the hierarchy may now afford
us some protection.

Quite a woman, he thought, and his words resonated with admiration. *She's put us all to shame, for not having thought of it before.*

It surprises me that the Hunter can still experience shame, Damien
thought back.

Very rarely, he admitted. *It's not my favorite emotion.*

The hand fell away from his cheek, fine skin grating on several
days' stubble. Time to shave, Damien thought—or maybe time to
give up on it and just let the beard grow. Sometimes that was the
best thing to do, while traveling. It occurred to him that Gerald Tarrant seemed to have no such problem—and it was faintly amusing
that a man of such power should have devoted a portion of his skills
to something as inconsequential as facial hair. But then he glanced
at Tarrant—at the clean, delicate profile, the perfect skin, the eyes
brimming with vanity—and thought. *No big surprise. The man's got*
his priorities straight. Appearance tops the list. And he smiled to
note that the adept's hair, though still wet, had been Worked back
into a smooth, gleaming mass; the holes that the rakh had poked in
his finely woven garments had been cleaned of blood and repaired,
with similar finesse. He looked like a refugee from a garden party.

The tent that the woman led them to was a large one, situated at
the western face of the encampment. As they ducked beneath the
flap she raised to enter it, Damien was aware of faces peering at them
from behind the protection of its bulk: young faces, mostly, anxious
and curious and clearly fascinated by the presence of these strangers
among them. In some there was no hostility, merely a desire to learn
what these strange creatures were—which meant that the former trait
was learned, not faeborn.

What was learned can be unlearned, Damien thought. It was a
promising sign.

The tent was a large one, that easily accommodated both the
humans and their self-appointed guards. In its center was a low fire,
mere glowing embers beneath a blanket of ash. But that was more
heat than Damien had seen in hours, and when the woman gestured
toward it he settled himself gratefully on a coarse rug laid before it,
and shivered in relief and pain as the unaccustomed warmth of it
began to drive the deadly cold from his body.

The tent itself was made of the skins of various animals, stitched
together with painstaking care. But that surface was nearly invisible
from the inside; tapestries and arras, richly worked, hung from the
tent-poles in carefully orchestrated layers, trapping warmed air

between them. Rugs were scattered across the floor, so numerous and
so carefully overlapped that not a hint of grass was visible. Small
sculptures hung from the juncture of tentpoles—wards, perhaps, or
some rakhene equivalent—and they rattled like wind chimes whenever some harsh wind shook the structure. There was furniture—
short tables engraved with intricate designs, screens and mirrors,
chests and shelves—and bits of jewelry, shell and colored glass, that
lay strewn about the interior like fallen leaves. These people might
have had nomadic roots, Damien reflected, but he doubted that they
traveled much now; there was enough stuff here to keep a moving
company busy for days.

They settled themselves in a circle about the fire, humans on one
side and rakh on the other. A constant tinkling accompanied the
movement of their hosts, delicate necklaces and hair ornaments and
mane-beads striking against each other as the rakh took their positions about the fire. Such noise would alert prey or enemies from
quite a distance; the warriors must shed enough decoration to move
silently in the field, before they left the camp.

Drink was passed, a hot, bitter brew reminiscent of tee. Damien
gulped it down with relish, felt its heat spread quickly through his
veins. The aching relief of it nearly brought tears to his eyes. There
was food, mostly meat, and Damien registered the fact that the early
rakh had been carnivores; any taste for plant life that they might
have developed would have come after man's Impression had begun
to alter them.

Their hosts waited until they had eaten their fill, as silent and still
as a beast stalking game. No words had passed among them since
the time they entered the tent, yet it was clear that a hierarchy had
somehow been established. When the last cup of steaming drink had
been emptied, when nothing remained of the strips of roasted meat
but a thin puddle of juice on carved wooden plates, one of the maned
rakh stirred, and with an air of obvious authority addressed the
humans.

"You should know what we are, before you begin. Our rank among
this people—that of *khrast*—has no translation in your tongue. It's a
rakh-thing, born of the persecution time—"

The woman hissed sharply. A few words of the rakhene language
passed between the two of them, sharp, biting phonemes with obvious anger behind them. Damien sensed a wealth of emotion that
reached back into the rakh's early years, when a species torn between
human potential and bestial inheritance was forced to flee from the
very race that had brought it into being. The male's tone, when he
spoke again, was filled with anger and resentment. And something

else, perhaps, that lurked about the edges of his words, nearly hidden behind his facade of racial aggression. Fear? Awe?

"What I mean to say," he amended gruffly, "is that although our people are familiar with your tongue, we seven alone are fluent. Our ancestors foresaw a time when we might need such fluency, perhaps to bargain for our lives—and so they captured women of your tribes, and sometimes men, and forced them to interact with our young. Until your *English* took root here, and our few *khrast* families were established." With a short, sharp gesture he indicated his companions. "Each one of us has spent time in the human lands, among your kind, absorbing the vernacular. Some have passed as demons, some as visions, some—occasionally—as humans. We've traveled in your world; we know your ways. We seven can interpret your words so that our people will understand what you have to say. That's all. We have no other rank but that; nothing in common as individuals, beyond the *khrast* tradition. No authority as a group, beyond that which we may wield as individuals."

"We understand," Ciani said.

The rakh-woman leaned forward; her eyes flashed viridescent, like a cat's. "Tell us why you came here," she commanded.

It was Senzei who answered. In a voice that trembled only slightly, he told them what manner of creatures had come to Jaggonath, and with what intention. He described the attack upon Ciani—and its devastating result—in terms so passionate that Damien felt as though he had witnessed the incident himself. Then, for a moment, Senzei's overpowering grief at Ciani's loss stopped the words from coming. For a moment he shook silently, the pent-up anger and frustration of the preceding days finally getting the better of him. That, too, seemed to communicate something to the rakh. When he spoke again, they seemed . . . different. More receptive, somehow. As if he had finally reached them on a level they could relate to.

"They came from your lands," he concluded. "Demons that feed on the memories of others, and keep intelligent beings like farm animals to feed on. We came here hunting them. One demon in particular. All we ask is the right to pass through your territory in order to reach it. In order to free our companion from that curse."

Damien glanced at Ciani, saw that she was trembling. Merciful God . . . if it was hard for Senzei to describe these things, how much harder for her, who had suffered in ways he could barely comprehend? He longed to take her hand, to offer her that minimal comfort, but dared not. Who could say what manner of interaction might anger these creatures?

After a silence that seemed painfully drawn out, one of the slender rakh spoke. "I've seen such things," he muttered. "In the east, near the House of Storms. Seen, but not believed."

"Human demons," a maned male spat. "Born of human fears."

"Inside the Canopy?" a female challenged him.

"Humanity is like a disease. It spreads without limit."

With sharp rakhene syllables, the male who had spoken first silenced their bickering. "It's not our place to make decisions for our people," he said firmly, "merely to interpret for them." He looked the small group over; his expression was cold. "We'll pass on what you've told us and let the others decide. But you should know this: We're not a forgiving people, and our hatred of your kind runs very deep. The punishment for humans who trespass in our lands has always been death. In all my years, I've only known of one exception to that rule. One human who managed to bridge the gap between our species, and earn the respect of a southern tribe, so that they permitted her to live. *One.*"

He stood. His amber eyes were fixed on Ciani. "I remember that woman. I remember her scent." His voice dropped to a soft hiss. "And the fact that you don't remember me, Lady Faraday, says more for your suffering than a volume of human arguments ever could."

He drew back a tent flap, allowing the warrior-rakh who were waiting outside to enter. The other *khrast* gathered themselves to leave. Clearly, the interview was over.

"I'll do what I can," he promised.

The camp of the rakh did not lend itself to the maintenance of prisoners. As negotiations between their captors were hissed in low tones, Damien reflected upon what the maned rakh had said, and the implications of it. *The punishment for humans who trespass in our lands is death.* It meant that the rakh had no experience in dealing with human prisoners—and if they handled their political affairs with the same animal instincts that they used to establish their local hierarchy, they might not even have experience in holding rakhene captives.

He glanced at Ciani as they were led from the tent, herded like milk-beasts. He expected to see fresh pain evident in her face, the anguish of lost memory suddenly brought to light. And there was certainly that, in considerable measure. But something more, also. Something that gleamed in her eyes with aggressive fervor, as she watched the rakh respond to unspoken, almost unseeable signals.

Something that was coming to life in her, here . . . as it must have come to life the first time, so many years ago. They had sensed it in her, and it had saved her.

Hunger. A thirst for knowledge, as powerful as Senzei's yearning for power—or Tarrant's hunger for life. Or my—my what?

What did he hunger for? If his life were to be rendered down to one ultimate statement of purpose, if the energy that kept him fighting were to be attributed to one driving force, what would it be?

To know, when I died, that my descendants would inherit Earth's dream. To know that my children's children would possess the stars. To believe that I've changed the world that much.

Then: *Nice thought,* he reflected dryly. *You need to stay in one place long enough to have children, if you want all that.*

They were driven through a good part of the rakhene camp, to a modest tent some distance from the center of things. In response to a barked command the tent's owner came forth from its confines, ducking in order to pass through the minimal opening. He was a slender rakh, maneless, and not dressed for company; he hurriedly wrapped a patterned robe about him as he emerged, allowing one brief flash of a minimal loinskirt adorning a thin, lanky body.

The warrior-rakh's mane-beads rattled as he issued a command, the hair about his shoulders rising so that considerable bulk was added to his already sizable frame. Looking at the two of them, it was hard to imagine them being from the same species. As the thin rakh protested—weakly—Damien thought he caught sight of a small ruff of fur about the neck that might be the remnants of a mane. Or the undeveloped promise of one? Male, then, most likely, and either young or poorly formed. Such a creature would rank low in any animal hierarchy.

And—let's be honest—among humans, too. Would I have gotten half as far as I did without the physical capacity to back up my intentions?

Clearly resentful, the rakh finally relented. As he ducked back into the tent to collect a few treasured belongings his back was rigid with resentment, and his teeth were bared in a whispered hiss—but all that was gone when he faced the maned one, defiance giving way to the power of a pecking order he lacked the strength—and courage—to challenge.

Prodded by spear-point, the party was forced into the small tent. All but Tarrant, who paused by the door flap and turned east, to look at the sky. Dark gray, Damien noted; still somber in tone, but no longer lightless. There was perhaps half an hour left.

"You stay here," he said sharply. "I'm going hunting."

The maned one stiffened as he tried to withdraw, and blocked his way with the shaft of a spear. "You all stay here until we release you," he said sharply. The rakhene accent made his words hard to decipher, but his intentions were clear. His fur bristled stiffly, mane ornaments jingling like wind chimes. "You understand? You go in, with others."

A spear was leveled, poised to strike through Tarrant's heart at a moment's notice. Damien tensed—and wished he had his sword, his springbolt, even a heavy rock—but with a tight knot building in his gut he realized he was more weaponless than he had ever been in his life. Tarrant had damned well better know what he was doing— because three unarmed humans against eight of these sturdy rakh wouldn't even buy him a moment's time. Not when every weapon was already leveled against them.

In answer to the rakh, Tarrant simply stared. Something in his expression warned Damien to look away . . . but fascination overrode that instinct, and he watched as the pale gray eyes seemed to take on a light of their own. An unnatural light, that seared one's vision but offered no real illumination: coldfire. For a moment even the rakh were fascinated, and though no weapon was lowered it was clear that, for the moment, no one would strike. *Like animals led to the slaughter,* Damien thought grimly, *mesmerized by a flash of sunlight on the butcher's knife blade.* Then, suddenly, the lead rakh cried out. His body convulsed in wavelike spasms, which rippled through his flesh with almost audible force. A cry escaped his lips—pain and terror and fury all combined, a wordless screech of agony that made Damien's flesh crawl—a sound so like the death cry of Tarrant's last kill that for a moment it was almost as though they were down in the canyon, listening to that cry again. And then, as quickly as it had begun, it was over. The rakh's body fell to the ground, spasmed once, and then was still. Thick blood, blue-black, stained the fur about its mouth, oozed from the eyes and ears. And its groin. Damien felt his own testicles draw up in cold dread as he forced himself to look away, tried not to consider what manner of internal damage might give birth to such a seepage.

For several seconds the remaining rakh were too stunned to move. Damien wondered if they had even seen human-style sorcery before, or if this kind of killing had been made doubly horrible by their ignorance of the power that caused it. Either way, it was now clear to them that Tarrant was a force to be reckoned with. Damien could see their fear and their anger warring with hierarchical instinct, hatred and awe comprising a volatile mixture in their half-bestial, half-human brains.

"Any other objections?" Tarrant asked quietly.

If there were, no one dared to voice them.

Coldfire flared about the adept's form, close enough to Damien that he could feel its flame—a thousand times colder than mere ice, or winter's chill—lick his flesh. Then the man's body was suddenly gone, and in its place a glorious hunting bird rose from the ground. Black this time, with feathers that gleamed like shards of obsidian and claws that glittered like garnets. It was a powerful form, and one clearly designed to impress the rakh; they backed away as the glistening wings beat hard above them, and a thick smell that might have been fear rose from the place where they stood.

Damien saw Ciani slip her hand into Senzei's, saw the man squeeze it tightly in reassurance. And he felt something inside himself tighten as if in loss, to see her turning to another man. Jealousy? *That isn't rational,* he told himself. *Certainly not with Zen.* But he wondered in that moment if he had ever known so close a friendship as the two of them shared—or if he could ever establish one, for as long as he kept moving. That simple contact—so slight, yet so eloquent— was years in the making.

He forced his thoughts back onto their circumstances, and forced his gaze to follow theirs, to the fallen rakh's body. Already it had begun to decompose, as if the flesh itself was anxious to decay. As they watched, deep purple carrion larvae crawled in the body's shadowed contours. He looked up at Tarrant and shivered, despite himself. Guessed at the death-hunger which must burn inside the man, to foster a power of that nature. So carefully controlled. So masked, by that elegant facade.

Thank God he's on our side, he thought.

And then added, with grim honesty: *For now.*

It was light outside when the delegation came to them, and the three humans winced as they exchanged the close darkness of their prison-tent for the searing light of day. All about them the camp was still; the few figures that moved about did so with obvious reluctance, doing their chores quickly and then disappearing once more into the shadowy confines of a patchwork tent. Occasionally, several children would scamper out into the open. Then the sharp cry of an adult would ring out, and the youngsters would disappear again, into their parents' dark haven. Clearly, the rakh were nocturnal creatures.

"You come," an aged female announced. Her fur was yellow-white, stripped of its color by her many years, or perhaps by stress. The *khrast* female was with her, as was a male of that group. There were several others as well, but their attitude made it clear that they were subservient; Damien focused his attention on the dominant threesome.

They were led through the camp to a large and ornate tent near its center. The older rakh hissed a few short words into the doorway and received an equally short response. She stood aside and beckoned for the humans to enter. From the doorway wafted a familiar odor, animal musk tinged with a vinegar scent. Fear? Damien ducked within—

—and saw a tableau of mourning, a sorrow so passionate that despite its alien form the full force of it was communicated, and set his priest's soul vibrating in sympathy. He glanced around the tent as Ciani and Senzei entered behind him, noted ornaments draped in soot-blackened cloth, tapestries turned to the wall, rugs rolled up to reveal dry, dead earth. A woman knelt in the center of the room, and she looked up as Damien studied her; her fur was caked with thick black mud in what was obviously mourning-custom, and her eyes were red-rimmed from sleeplessness. By her side, on a plain woven mat, the figure of a maned male lay still. But for his shallow breathing, one might have assumed him to be dead. But for his open eyes, that gazed out into nothingness, one might have thought him asleep.

Damien's first instinct was that they had brought him here to Heal—and then he realized that these people knew nothing of his vocation, and must therefore have some other purpose. He looked at the *khrast* female for explanation—and saw a measureless anger fill her eyes. It was not directed at him.

The older rakh muttered something to him, hissed phonemes and whispered gutturals; the *khrast* woman translated. "She says, do you see, this one has been emptied. Totally. In humans there are many parts of thinking, so that when they eat your thoughts maybe only one part of the soul is consumed; the rest remains, and can function. But when they eat from the rakh, all is one: one brain, one soul, one heart. One meal, for the eaters. Everything is gone, but life."

"When did it happen?" Damien asked.

The *khrast* questioned the older woman briefly, then answered, "Five nights ago. He was on watch, by the river. The next watch found him . . . like this."

He felt Ciani close behind him, felt her fear like a palpable thing between them. And her fascination. So: the demons that had consumed her memory had struck here, too. Fresh from the human lands, they had stopped off for a snack on their way to . . . wherever.

He looked into the male's eyes—empty, so empty!—and wondered how many others there were. Empty bodies strewn along the path of these demons, marking the way to their homeland. God in heaven, how long had this thing been going on? How much more suffering would they discover, as they came ever closer to its demonic source?

"We came to kill them," he told her. "We have reason to believe that when they die, their victims may recover. Whether that will hold true for your people, as well as for ours. . . ." He didn't finish. He didn't need to. The rakh might seem alien to him, but they were certainly intelligent enough to realize what was at stake here: not only Ciani's health, Ciani's recovery, but that of their own people. And ultimately, the safety of their species.

"This is your purpose?" the older woman asked.

"It is."

"This is reason you come here?"

"Our only reason," Ciani assured her.

"And Mer Tarrant's, as well," Senzei added.

She considered that. She considered each of them, in turn—and her face shadowed briefly as she considered their absent companion. At last she indicated the soulless body that lay before them, and demanded, "You help this."

Damien hesistated. "If we kill these demons, he may heal. But we can only do that if you let us go free."

"And your . . . *friend*," she said coldly. "The one who kills rakh. Speak of him."

"Tarrant's a weapon," Damien answered sharply. "He can turn the fae against these creatures, better than any of us. If you want these demons killed, this man freed . . ." he indicated the body on the mat. "Then we need him. We four must work together."

She hissed softly, but made no other response. Clearly, Damien's answer was not to her liking.

"We think," she said at last. Harshly. "We talk, to rakh *hris*. Own kind." She looked to the younger woman, who explained, "Your fate is no longer in the hands of our fighting males. No longer subject to their temper. That is, for as long as you behave as you should . . . there'll be no harm done to you. You understand? Not to you, or your possessions. *If* you behave."

"We understand," Ciani said quietly.

"When does the killer return?"

It took him a moment to realize whom she meant. "Tarrant?" He hesitated. "Maybe this afternoon—maybe not until tonight." He wondered just how much the woman knew about them. Whether she knew that Tarrant could be killed by sunlight, a fact he was trying to obscure. "Certainly no later than that."

"You come then," the older rakh commanded. "We talk, all rakh and human four. Together."

She looked at the body on the mat—at the mud-covered figure mourning by its side—and whispered, "There is maybe something here we hate, even more than you."

Thirty-three

"Our purpose in coming here," Gerald Tarrant said, "is to kill one demon, and free our companion. Nothing more."

Damien had known him long enough to sense the fury that lay behind those words, but the Hunter masked it well. There was no way for his rakhene audience to know how close he was to killing them all, how much it infuriated him to negotiate with them like this, bargaining for freedom rather than simply claiming it. Damien didn't doubt for a minute that the man's tainted soul would much rather rend their flesh and spirit and leave their camp a shattered ruin, for the audacity of having interfered with him. And he blessed whatever remnants of honor still existed in the man, for forcing him to follow a gentler course.

At least they were according him—and his party—some small measure of respect. His display of murderous sorcery seemed to have earned not only their fear but a grudging deference; now, when the humans were herded about they were no longer treated like animals, more like . . . *loaded weapons*, he decided. And yes—that's exactly what Tarrant was. Loaded, cocked, and itching to fire.

With one half of his mind he listened to the adept describe their travels to date, a version that he diplomatically edited to suit their current purpose. With the other half he studied their audience. A good portion of the village must be gathered here tonight, ranged around them in concentric ranks so numerous that the outermost rakh were beyond the reach of the firelight; only the occasional flash of green eyes betrayed their presence at the edge of the gathering. In the center, grouped about the bonfire, were the humans and their rakhene judges: elders, a handful of heavily maned males, and of course the seven bilugal *khrast*. A gathering so disparate that it was hard to imagine them coming to any manner of agreement, least of all on a matter as complex as this one.

Then: *Not complex at all*, he thought grimly. *They want us dead. Period. We're fighting to earn the right to live. The fact that we're using words rather than weapons doesn't make it any less of a battle.*

Quietly, he tried to shift his weight into a more comfortable position. The ground was rocky, and the rakhene clothing they had given him did little to cushion him from its assault. He stopped himself from cursing the shortcomings of his hosts, decided to be grateful that they had accorded him even this much hospitality. His personal possessions were God alone knew where, swept downriver along with his horse. His only clothes had been those on his person when he arrived, soaked through and nearly frozen solid. Once the rakhene elders had decided they were going to wait for Tarrant's return, they had outfitted him as best they could ... and it was hardly their fault that none of the rakh were of his stature. The largest garment that could be procured—a kimonolike robe decorated with colorful pictoglyphs—fell several inches short of covering his chest, and ultimately it had to be combined with with an underrobe and female tabard to do its job. He must have looked extremely odd, judged by their custom ... but that was still an improvement over displaying his bare chest to the winds. Not to mention exhibiting his relative hairlessness in a tribe where such a quality was associated with females and runt males.

Holding all those layers in place was his thick leather belt, which he refused to relinquish even for a moment. He hadn't dared to check on its contents for some time after their capture—he was afraid that if the rakh observed how much he valued it they might take it away from him, as they had his sword—but as soon as the humans had been left to their own devices he had unlaced its closure, and drawn out the two precious containers. Both were still intact—thank God!—though neither was wholly undamaged. The silver flask had a dent in one side, which spoke of some severe impact; the crystal flask, still glowing with the pure golden light of the Fire, had developed a jagged flaw that followed the line of its engraved surface pattern, but was still apparently airtight enough to safeguard the few drops of moisture remaining within it. Relief was so strong in him when he saw that the Fire was safe, he could taste it in his mouth. God help them all if that most precious weapon were ever lost.

Tarrant had finished with his narration now, and there was no way to tell whether it had fallen on sympathetic ears or not. The rakhene faces were unreadable.

"You came to kill one demon," an elder female challenged them.

It was Damien who spoke. "We came to see to it that one demon dies, in order for our friend to be freed. As for the rest of them . . ." he hesitated. What was it they wanted to hear? What words would buy his party safe passage? "I think we would all rather see them dead than feeding on the living. Wouldn't you? But whether that's something we four can accomplish remains to be seen."

The high-ranking rakh whispered among themselves in their native tongue, an occasional English word thrown in—usually mispronounced—to clarify a given point. Damien noted that one of the *khrast* women was nearly naked now, her few minimal garments adorning rather than concealing full, heavy breasts, dark nipples, rounded hips and thighs. She fidgeted restlessly as she listened to the proceedings, unable to concentrate on any one focus for more than a minute or two. Periodically her eyes would wander over to one of the inner circle's males, and fix on him with candid hunger. *In heat?* Damien wondered. The thought was oddly disquieting.

"There is more than demons in our east," an elder female announced at last. "There is a human also."

Across the circle, he saw Senzei stiffen. His own heart doubled its pace excitedly as this new information hit home.

"What manner of human?" he asked her. "Where?"

It was clear that she lacked the words she needed to answer his question efficiently. "In Lema," she offered. "Which is place most east, before water. In the place of storms. *Assst!*"

Clearly frustrated, she turned to the *khrast*. The female they knew from Morgot took over. "Our people call it the House of Storms, because when the human first came and built his citadel there were great storms that gathered there—lightning that filled the sky for months on end, thunder so loud it made speaking impossible. There are still more storms than there should be, in that region. No one knows why."

"Who is this human?" Damien asked. "What's he doing here?"

The *khrast* woman exchanged quick words with her elder, then explained, "They call him the *One Who Binds*. And other names, equally descriptive. He came here over a century ago and established himself in the region we call Lema. No rakh has ever seen him—but we can taste his human taint on the currents, and smell his stink along the eastern Canopy."

"Over a century," Ciani whispered.

"More than a single lifetime," Tarrant agreed. And he explained to the rakh, "Avoiding death takes more than mere sorcery, among our kind. What we're dealing with here is either an adept . . . or he's made one hell of a Sacrifice."

"Or both," Damien said grimly.

The rakh spoke among themselves in quick, sharp syllables; no doubt considering how much they would tell the humans, and in what manner.

At last: "Bring her," an elder ordered, and a lesser male sped from the circle to obey.

A few minutes later he returned, a small female in tow. Unlike all the others she was dressed in unpatterned cloth, and her fur was thin and matted. Her fearful, darting gaze made her seem more animal than any of the others—indeed, when judged against her standard, they seemed doubly human by contrast.

"This one came from the east many greatmonths ago," the *khrast* woman explained. "She's been sheltering with one of our southern tribes, here in the plains. Our *hris* sent for her last morning."

The woman came nervously into their circle; Damien had the impression she was ready to bolt for cover at the first sign of danger. He felt driven to comfort her, to ease her terror—but he knew that he lacked the custom, the language, and the knowledge needed to do so. If she would even let a human that close to her, which was doubtful. He forced himself to stay where he was as she approached, and to say nothing to her—but he fumed at his own enforced impotence.

She knelt near the center of the circle, facing the tribal elders. A female addressed her gently. "You are from Lema,"

The girl hesitated, then nodded. Damien guessed that her English was poor.

"Tell us," an elder male prompted. "Tell us, in human speech, what you saw there."

She looked around the circle, seemed to notice the humans for the first time. She almost cried out—but the sound seemed to die on her lips, and though she started as though to flee the motion was cut short, aborted before it began. Damien glanced at Tarrant, saw his pale eyes focused in a Working. A Tranquilizing? No. Probably something more malevolent, that accomplished the same end. Anything that close to a Healing would be too out of character for him.

"I see ... in Lema ..." She drew in a deep, shaky breath; there was moisture under her eyes. "I see ... my people are in fear. Many go to feed the hungry ones, disappear from family. Large years, it so. Many of those, eaters of souls. All hungry. Always hungry." She shivered, and a gust of fear wafted over Damien; rakh emotion, tainting the earth-fae. "All rakh fear. All work in day, unnatural, live in sun to be free from fear. Is pain in day, *sisst?*—but safe. Yes? More safe than dark. *They* hunt in dark."

"Tell us about the hungry ones." Tarrant's voice was low and even, filled with quiet power. Damien could almost see the link he had established with the terrified woman—perhaps because of his own link to the Hunter, quiescent though it was. He felt the adept's mesmerism as though it were directed at him. As though the man's knowledge of English was flowing into him, not the woman—and with it, the Hunter's enforced calm.

"They came from the east," she whispered. "In big ships, like the humans use. From across the Sea of Fire. Many, many years ago. There were few of them then. For a long time, there were few. They hunt like animals, in night. Some rakh die, but not many. Some rakh . . ." She hesitated, shivering as some particularly painful memory passed through her. "They eat rakh thoughts. They leave the body, eat the mind. Sometimes rakh hunt them like animals, kill them. But the hungry ones hide. Hide good. Come again, later. But always, before, there were few of them. In the past."

She looked about the circle, studying her audience. Her eyes fixed on Tarrant for a long, silent moment, and suddenly Damien knew what manner of Working had quieted her. No: what manner of mesmerism made her *seem* so calm, while the Hunter drank in the sweet savor of her terror. Damien started forward instinctively, stopped himself only with great effort. *There's nothing you can do,* he told himself bitterly. And: *He needs it. He's got to feed. If he doesn't live off the fear he finds here, he'll have to go out and inspire some of his own. And that's even worse—isn't it?* But his soul ached to free her from that malignant bond, and only by reminding himself, *Tarrant's power is the only thing keeping her lucid,* did he manage to keep himself from interfering.

Damn you, Hunter. For making us need you. Damn you for everything.

"Tell us about the human," an elder prompted.

"I . . ." She hesitated, struggling with her fear. Damien didn't dare look at Tarrant, for fear of seeing the pleasure that must light his eyes. He might kill him if he did. "I think . . . it was when the human came. That there were more of the eaters. Suddenly many more, and they begin to hunt in groups. Whole families of rakh disappear. I see . . . I see . . ." she shook her head in frustration, unable to find the proper word. "Rakh with no mind, rakh with half-mind, dead and damaged and wounded, so many. . . ." Her voice shook; her shoulders were trembling. "Lema is half dead, many try leaving, but the hungry ones hunt the borders. . . ."

"You escaped," a female elder said gently.

She shook her head stiffly: yes. "Very few get out," she whispered. "Very hard. No riding animals in Lema, like you have, must walk . . . more than one day to walk that way, and in night *they* come. . . .''

She lowered her face to her hands and shook; short gasping sounds that might have been rakhene weeping came from beneath the muffling fur.

After a brief consultation with the elders, the *khrast*-woman told the humans, "She can't tell you any more than that, not even in our own tongue. All she has left are fragments of memory—and fear."

"We understand." Damien said quietly. He watched as Tarrant dissolved the bond between them—regretfully, it seemed—and waited until the male who had brought her to the circle escorted her out of it once more. Waited till she was safely out of hearing, so that their conference might cause her no further pain.

Then he challenged, "They've taken over a whole district."

The *khrast*-woman's amber eyes fixed on him. Her expression was alien, unreadable. "It would appear so," she hissed softly.

"With the aid of a human. As protector? Servant? Probably the former, if he's an adept." He exhaled noisily. "No wonder you hate our kind so much."

"This incident is the least of it," she assured him.

Senzei spoke up, unaccustomed strength in his voice. "Look. You all want the same things we do. The death of these creatures. The fouling of their plans. If you would just let us go, let us do what we came to do—wouldn't that help your people?" He hesitated. "Isn't that what you want?"

"Is not easy, now," the elder's spokeswoman informed him. "Before, yes. Four humans, four horses, weapons, supplies, plans. You go east, and maybe die. Or maybe not. Maybe you kill the ones who eat rakh soul. But now. . . ." She paused meaningfully. "Is not enough, just humans go. Just be free. Four humans with *two* horses, half of supplies, few weapons. If you go now, like that, you die sure. You *fail*." It was clear from her voice that the latter was what disturbed her. "You understand? My words enough good? Need translate?"

"No," he said quietly. "We understand."

"To make you free now, no more than this, is same as to kill you. Why not just kill? More easy, yes? And we keep supplies. But if humans go free—if humans go to kill Dark Ones—then rakh must help. And to help humans. . . ." She shivered dramatically.

It was Ciani who spoke. "You've already decided."

She hesitated, then nodded. "We have decided."

"And?" Damien pressed.

She looked at the *khrast* woman. Who told them, coolly, "You'll need fresh mounts. We have xandu. You'll need weapons. Ours are primitive by your standards, but they'll spill blood readily enough. We have food and cloth to spare, and oil for your lamps." She looked at Damien. And added, somewhat stiffly, "You'll need a guide."

He nodded his understanding. "A rakh."

"A *khrast*. One who knows your people as well as ours—and the land itself, which few of our people travel. Someone to get you safely to the east, so you can do what you came to do . . . and liberate our people from this horror, as well as your own. That's the deal," she concluded. "Serve us as you serve yourselves—or die, and fail us both."

"Not much of a choice," he pointed out.

She grinned, displaying sharp teeth. "It wasn't meant to be, human. So what do you say?"

He looked at his companions, saw in their eyes exactly what he expected. He nodded, and turned back to face the *khrast* woman.

"We accept," he said. "Thank you."

"This is debt," an elder male warned him. "You come back here, tell what you see. Understand?"

"We do," he assured him. "And we'll do whatever we can, against these demons. I promise it."

He looked around at the various *khrast*, saw the half-clad woman rubbing against a thickly maned male. Saw amber rakh-eyes, narrow and resentful, luminous with species hatred.

"So who's the guide?" he asked.

"Who should it be?" the *khrast*-woman countered. "One who knows you better than any. One who's seen you in the human lands, among your own kind. One who's recently tolerated the combined stink of your species, so that her senses are numb to the reek of a few individuals."

"In other words, you."

Her thin nostrils flared. "Unless you have someone else in mind."

From somewhere he dredged up a hint of a smile. "I wouldn't presume."

She turned to face the others of his party. "Is this acceptable?" One by one, they assented—Senzei with vigor, Ciani with relief, Gerald Tarrant with . . . hell, did he ever look agreeable? At least he nodded. But there was hatred burning just behind the surface of that carefully controlled facade, and Damien suspected he knew just how little it would take to fan it to a full-blown conflagration.

Not now, Hunter. Just hold out a little bit longer. Please. We'll be out of here soon enough.

"I believe," the rakh-woman said, "we have a bargain."

The springbolt was a mess of battered wood and bent fixtures, and under normal circumstances he would simply have replaced it. But the nearest supply outlet was a good two hundred miles away, and so he took the damned thing apart, piece by piece, and filed and clipped and sanded—and prayed—and then put it carefully back together, in the hopes that it would work again.

The rakh-woman watched silently while he worked, still as a statue. *Or a hunting animal,* he thought. He flexed the loading pin once, twice, and was at last satisfied with its performance. The stock clipped into place with a reassuring snap. To his left he saw Senzei wiping down his sword blade, Ciani oiling their other remaining springbolt. That their weapons had finally been returned to them should have been cause for rejoicing—but instead it had driven home just how much they'd lost at the river, and how very unprepared they were going to be when they reached their enemy's stronghold at last. As for Tarrant . . . he was off wherever adepts went to, when they wanted to Work in privacy. Or maybe he just didn't like the company.

I still have the Fire. That's something our enemy can't possibly anticipate—and a power no single sorceror can negate. As long as we're armed with that, there's still a chance we might succeed in this.

—Albeit a slim one, he forced himself to add.

The special bolts were gone, along with the rest of his personal arsenal. For the tenth time that night, he tried not to resent that fact that it was *his* horse which was lost—along with his notes, his clothing, and all his special traveling gear. He had made a few replacement bolts, but hesitated to commit too much of the Fire to that one purpose; with only two springbolts between them, it was unlikely they were going to rely too heavily upon such ammunition.

With practiced care he braced the reassembled springbolt against his shoulder and pulled back on the trigger; the sharp crack of its mechanism assured him that it was, for the moment, in perfect working order. With a sigh of relief he lowered it. At least they had two of the powerful weapons left; things could have been much worse. He tried not to think about the loss of his horse as he wound back the tightened spring, forcing its lever up the length of the stock. And then he cursed, loudly and creatively, as the pulley system broke and the lever went flying forward.

"Problem?" the rakh-woman questioned.

"Damned draw system. The thing'll fire—and I can cock it—but as for Cee and Zen . . ." He shook his head, his expression grim. There were no finely milled parts here to replace those which were damaged, nor even the kind of steel he would need to jerry-rig a replacement. Damn it to hell! What good would it do them to have the vulking thing in working order, if half their party couldn't load it?

The rakh-woman reached out for the weapon; he let her take it. Her tufted ears pricked forward as she studied the half-open mechanism, her eyes as bright and curious as a cat's. "What's the problem?"

He indicated the cocking lever with a disgusted gesture and muttered, "Damn thing will only draw straight, now. Fine lot of good that does us! I suppose I could ease up on the pull . . . but it wouldn't have much power then. Hell! I—"

She had curled one claw around the lever, and now she pulled it. Backward, in a motion as fluid and graceful as a dancer's extension. Her layered sleeves and loose tabard hid whatever play of muscle and bone supported her as she drew the lever back, far back, all the way to its primed position. And locked it there. Effortlessly. And looked at him.

"Damn," he whispered.

"Is that good enough?" Her expression was fierce. "Good enough for killing?" There was an edge of hunger in her tone so primal, so intense, that it seemed to fill the small tent; he felt something primitive deep within him spark to life in response, and quelled it forcibly.

"Oh, yes," he assured her. His muscles ached in sympathy as he considered her strength. Considered her ferocity. "More than enough."

And God help the creature that gets in your way, he added silently.

The Hunter stood alone on a gentle rise, black against black in the night. Staring into the distance as if somehow mere concentration could bridge the hundreds of miles between him and his object. And perhaps it could; Damien wouldn't put anything past him, at this point.

He came to his side and waited there, silently, certain that Tarrant was aware of his presence. And after a moment the adept stirred, and drew in a deep breath. The first breath he had taken since Damien's arrival.

"Things are going well?" The Hunter asked.

"Well enough. We lost a lot at the river . . . but how much that will cripple us remains to be seen. I meant to ask you—your maps—"

"Are probably in the Serpent by now."

He drew in a slow breath. "I'm sorry.'

"So am I. Very. They were priceless relics.

"I know collectors who would have killed for them."

"I did," the Hunter said coolly.

Damien looked at him, bit back his first response. At last he offered, "You were hard to find."

"I apologize for that. It was necessary for me to get away. Not from you," he amended quickly. "From the rakh. They overwhelm the currents, making it impossible to Work cleanly. I needed to get clear of their influence."

Damien looked toward the east, saw nothing but darkness. "You're trying to Know the enemy?"

He affirmed it with a nod. "And trying to keep the enemy from Knowing us. The current flows east here, which means that our every intention is carried toward him. Like a scent of confrontation on the wind: easy to read, simple to interpret. I tried to Obscure it. Whether I've succeeded. . . ." He shrugged, somewhat stiffly. "Time will tell. I did what I could."

Then he turned to face Damien, and the pale gray eyes fixed on him. Silver pools of limitless depth that sucked in all knowledge: for a moment Damien nearly staggered, made dizzy by the contact. Then the eyes were merely eyes again, and the channel between the two men subsided into quiescence once more.

"Why did you come here?" the adept asked.

He had considered many different approaches, a host of varied words and phrases that differed in degrees of diplomacy. But when the moment came, he chose the simplest of his repertoire—and the most straightforward. "I need to know what you are," he said quietly.

"Ah," he whispered. "That."

"This trip is getting more dangerous each night. It's difficult enough planning for four instead of one; I won't pretend it comes easily to me, or that I like it. But it has to be done. And I can't do it efficiently when I don't even know what I'm traveling with. Already we've been in one situation when I didn't know what the hell to do, to try to help you or just leave you alone . . . I don't like feeling helpless. And I did, back at the river. I don't like traveling with ciphers, either—but you're forcing me to do just that. And it makes everything that much harder for all of us." He waited for a moment, hoping for a response; when he received none, he continued. "I think they could have killed you, back at the river. I don't think you could have stopped them. Am I wrong? Centuries of life, more power than other men dare to dream of—and I think they could have ended it all with a single spearthrust. You tell me, Hunter—do I misjudge you?"

The adept's eyes narrowed somewhat; the memory of that night clearly disturbed him. "If I'd had only myself to consider, they could never have taken me. But being indebted to the lady, and therefore you . . ." he hesitated. "Complicates things."

"We've got a job to do, together. You and I may not like that fact, but we've both chosen to accept it. I've done my share to make that partnership work—you know that, Hunter. Now it's your turn."

Tarrant's voice was low but tense. "You're asking to know my weaknesses."

"I'm asking *what you are*. Is that so unreasonable? What manner of man—or creature—we're traveling with. Damn it, man, I'm tired of guessing! Tired of hoping that we won't get caught up in some situation where my ignorance might really cost us. I might have been able to help you, back at the river—but how was I to know what you needed? What really might bind your power, as opposed to what they *thought* might bind it? The closer we get to our enemy, the more powerful he looks. Some day very soon we're going to face the bastard head-on, and you may have to count on one of us for support. God help us then, if all we have to go on then is my guesswork. You want to bank your life on that?"

The Hunter looked at him. Cold eyes, and an even colder expression; his words slid forth like ice. "A man doesn't explain his vulnerabilities to one who intends to destroy him."

Damien drew in a sharp breath, held it for a minute. Exhaled it, slowly. "I never said that."

A faint smile—or almost-smile—softened the Hunter's expression. "Do you really think you can hide that from me? After what's passed between us? I know what your intentions are."

"Not here," Damien said firmly. "Not now. Not while we're traveling together. I can't answer for what happens later, after we leave the rakhlands—but for now, the four of us have to function as a unit. I accept it. Can't you read the truth in that?"

"And afterward?" the adept asked softly.

"What do you want me to say?" Damien snapped. "That I approve of what you are? That it's in my nature to sit back and watch while women are slaughtered for your amusement? I swore I'd be your undoing long before I met you. But that vow belongs to another time and place—another world entirely. The rules are different here. And if we both want to get home, we'd damn well better cooperate. After that . . . I imagine you know how to take care of yourself once you're back in the Forest. Do you really think mere words can change that?"

For a moment, Tarrant just stared at him. It was impossible to read what was in those eyes or to otherwise taste of the tenor of his intentions; he had put up a thorough block on all levels, and the mask was firmly in place.

"Bluntness is one of your few redeeming traits," he observed at last. "Sometimes irritating . . . but never unenlightening." The wind gusted suddenly, flattening the grass about their feet. Somewhere in the distance, a predator-bird screeched its hunger. "You ask what I am—as though there's a simple answer. As though I haven't spent centuries exploring that very issue." He turned away so that Damien might not see his expression; his words addressed the night. "Ten centuries ago, I sacrificed my humanity to seal a bargain. There are forces in this world so evil that they have no name, so all-encompassing that no single image can contain them. And I spoke to them across a channel etched in my family's blood. *Keep me alive,* I said to them, *and I will serve your purpose. I'll take whatever form that requires, adapt my flesh to suit your will—you may have it all, except for my soul. That alone remains my own.* And they responded— not with words, but with transformation. I became something other than the man I was, a creature whose hungers and instincts served that darker will. And that compact has sustained me ever since.

"What are the rules of my existence? I learned them one by one. Like an actor who finds himself on an unfamiliar stage, mouthing lines he doesn't know in a play he's never read, I felt my way through the centuries. Did you think it was different? Did you imagine that when I made my sacrifice, someone handed me a guidebook and said, 'Here, these are the new rules. Make sure you follow them.' Sorry to disappoint you, priest." He chuckled coldly. "I live. I hunger. I find things that will feed the hunger and learn to procure them. In the beginning my knowledge was crude, and I found crude answers: blood. Violence. The convulsions of dying flesh. As my understanding grew more sophisticated, so did my appetite. —But the old things will still sustain me," he warned. "Human blood alone will do that if nothing else is available. Does that answer your question?"

"You were a vampire."

"For a time. When I first changed. Before I discovered that there were other options. A pitiful half-life, that . . . and gross physical assault has never appealed to me. I find the delicate pleasures of psychological manipulation much more . . . satisfying. As for the power that keeps me alive . . . call it an amalgamation of those forces which on Earth were mere negatives—but which have real substance here, and a potential for power than Earth never dreamed of. *Cold,* which is the absence of heat. *Darkness,* which is the absence of light.

Death, which is the absence of life. Those forces comprise my being—they keep me alive—they determine my strengths and my weaknesses, my hungers, even my manner of thinking. As for how that power manifests itself . . ." He paused. "I take on whatever form inspires fear in those around me."

"As you did in Morgot."

"As I do even now."

Damien stiffened.

"The lady knows that I can mimic the creatures that attacked her, make her relive that pain any time it pleases me. That's fear enough, don't you think? With Mer Reese the matter is much more subtle. Say that I embody the power he hungers for, the temptation to cast aside everything he values and plunge into darkness—and the fear that he will do so only to come up with empty hands, and a soul seared raw by evil."

"And myself?" Damien asked tightly.

"You?" He laughed softly. "For you I've become the most subtle creature of all: a civilized evil, genteel and seductive. An evil you endure because you need its service—even though that very endurance plucks loose the underpinnings of your morality. An evil that causes you to question the very definitions of your identity, that blurs the line between dark and light until you're no longer certain which is which, or how the two are divided. —That's what you fear most of all, priest. Waking up one morning and no longer knowing who or what you are." Pale gray eyes glittered hungrily in the moonlight. "Does that satisfy you? Is that what you wanted to hear?"

For a moment, Damien said nothing; emotion was too hot in his brain for him to voice it effectively. Then at last, carefully, he chose his words. "When all this is over—when our enemy has been dealt with and we're safely out of the rakhlands—I will kill you, Hunter. And rid the world of your taint forever. I swear it."

It was hard to say just what wry expression flickered across the Hunter's face. Sadness? Amusement?

"I never doubted that you'd try," he whispered.

They left at sunset. A tremor struck the camp as they were mounting up, which made tent ornaments jingle like windchimes and rakh children run howling about like banshees—but despite the noise of the small quake, it did little real damage. And since it meant that for a short while there would be fresh earth-fae—strong currents—Damien considered it an excellent omen.

On the surface, they seemed a well-supplied company: five travelers, five mounts, and supplies enough to get them all to the east coast and back again. None of them had discussed how likely it was that not all would survive the round trip journey; packing a full store for each of them had been a ritual of hope, a gesture of denial—a necessary armoring against the presence of Death, as they began a journey into his domain. Nevertheless, Damien could not help but notice how the various elements of their small company seemed a composite of opposites: Ciani and Senzei seated on xandus, the rakh-woman clutching a springbolt, himself dressed in clothes made from quickly-woven cloth, fashioned in the rakhene style. He ought to have been grateful for the thick woolen shirt, for it kept out the autumn chill far better than his human wardrobe, but the vivid pictures that had been hurriedly painted onto it seemed somehow . . . conspicuous. Mere color had never bothered him, of course, and he had worn the stuffed and padded styles of Ganji-on-the-Cliffs without reserve, but to have his exploits—as the rakh understood them—splashed in vivid hues across his person . . . he wondered if there wasn't just a hint of sarcasm hidden in those cryptic pictoglyphs, some little bit of rakhene humor at his expense. Or was the sight of his personal history splayed across his belly humor enough for their kind?

As for Tarrant, he was . . . well, Tarrant. Tall and elegant and fastidiously arrogant, he rode the last remaining Forest steed as though it always had been and always would be his mount. There had been no question of his taking a xandu, of course; the animals wouldn't have him, and he clearly considered them to be inferior stock. Much to Damien's surprise, the party had no sooner left the rakhene camp than the adept urged his black horse forward into a point position. It was as if he was wordlessly daring their enemy to strike at the party through him.

Which means he knows damn well that no one's going to attack us now, Damien thought. *The man's not a fool.*

Then: *Not fair, priest. Not fair at all.* He reminded himself what the adept had done for him. Not only saved his life at the river, but later cleansed him of the illness that had taken hold in those terrible, frozen hours. He shivered to remember the touch of coldfire in his veins, the pain and terror that racked his body (no doubt feeding the Hunter as it did so) while the killing cure took hold—but the end result was more than he could have managed himself, in his weakened state.

Call it what you like, he thought to the Hunter. *It looked like a Healing to me.*

Technicalities. He knew now what a true Healing would do to the adept's compact. Any act of life—or fire, or true light—would negate the power that kept him alive. A hell of a price to pay, for a single act of compassion.

What a thin line you must have to walk in order to travel with us.

Then he looked at the adept's back—and beyond it, into the darkness that obscured their enemy's domain. And he shuddered.

What a thin line we're all walking, now.

Thirty-four

It scared Senzei, that their enemy might See them coming. It scared the hells out of him. Sometimes he found it hard to control his fear, to go about the motions of traveling and camping and foraging and guarding without the fear taking hold of him utterly, making it impossible for him to do anything other than crawl into his bedroll and shiver in terror. How did his companions deal with it? Did they not experience such feelings at all, or were they simply better at hiding it?

For a while he'd been all right. On the way to Kale, through the Forest itself, right up to the border of the Canopy. Because their enemy had been not a man, then, but a measureless abstraction. A faint whiff of evil, a shadow of threat—not a creature with a name and a homeland, a being with armies and citadels and weapons that one could only guess at. An enemy who knew how to read the currents, who might well be watching their every move as they progressed slowly across his realm. Tarrant's Obscurings might give them some cover, but was it enough? Their presence in the rakhlands, so alien to the local currents, sent out waves of identification so clear and intense that only a blind man could fail to read them. Or so Tarrant told them.

Damn him, for sharing that truth.

There was no other way; that was what Damien told them. No other path to take to get them where they were going, and no better way to travel it. The risk was real but unavoidable. Tarrant Worked each morning and night to reinforce the patterns that would keep their enemy from reading their true identities, the extent of their arsenal, their intentions . . . but whether such a subterfuge was possible, or just a wasted effort, only the gods could say. They did what they could. And hoped it was enough.

And prayed.

For days there was nothing but grassy plains to cross, a seemingly endless expanse of flat land that was host to a thousand varieties of life. Wild xandu grazed on autumn's browning stalks, and eyed their domesticated brethren warily as the party moved past them. Small tufted scavengers leapt through the grass, then fell to the lightning strike of a sharp-toothed predator. When the company was silent, they could hear that the air was filled with chirpings and cluckings and a thousand varieties of rustling; nature's kingdom, winding down for winter. Periodically Senzei would Work his vision and See the patterns that dominated this land: even, steady currents, delicate in design, whose gentle whorls and eddies linked predator to prey to carrion hunter, and all those beasts in turn to the fauna around them, the sunlight that warmed them, the weather that supplied them with moisture. Against such a landscape, the humans' own presence stood out like a fresh wound—livid, swollen, seething with intended violence. It was impossible to imagine that Tarrant could Obscure such a mark—or even mask it in any way. If their enemy had Sight, he could certainly See them—and there was no doubt, in any of their minds, that this was indeed the case.

Gods help us, Senzei thought feverishly. *Gods help us all.*

At night the demons would come out, bloodsuckers and their kin— but they were mild creatures compared to the denizens of the Forest, or even Jaggonath's demonagerie: constructs of the party's fears that had manifested enough flesh to make a fleeting appeal for sustenance, but little more than that. They lacked the substance it would take to withstand even a mild Dispelling, the kind of solidity that comes only from years of feeding on one's host/creators, of drawing life from the pit of darkness that resides in every man's soul. Even Senzei could banish them, with hardly a whispered word to focus his Working. Clearly, whatever convolutions of human character created such demons, the rakhene mind had no equivalent. The land Erna's natives had settled was more peaceful than any the travelers had seen, nearly free of the nightmares that had devoured the first colonists.

So where did the memory-eaters come from? Senzei wondered. *Surely one mind couldn't be strong enough to manifest horrors on that scale.*

Mile after mile of featureless terrain passed beneath their mounts' hooves, each one indistiguishable from the last. Slowly, gradually, the distance behind them blanketed the Worldsend peaks in a haze of soft blue fog. One morning Senzei looked about and discovered he could no longer see any landmarks: not the mountains behind them, nor the eastern range ahead of them, nor any feature to mar the perfect flatness of the earth. In that moment it seemed they might travel forever without seeing any variety in earth or sky, only a few wispy clouds that floated languidly, casting fleeting shadows upon the ground beneath.

Then, without warning, a call came. A whistle, followed by an animal cry—or perhaps a voice crying words, that were almost but not quite English. The thick grass parted to make way for a rakhene warrior, who established himself before them with a bristling mane and obviously hostile intentions. Others followed—a hunting party— fierce nomadic warriors clearly ready to deal with any humans who happened to cross their path. Their tempers were so animal, so volatile, that the one time Senzei dared to See them they left their afterimage seared into his retina, as if he had stared too long into the sun.

It was their rakhene guide who saved them, who bargained for their lives. Hissing commands and arguments in the native dialect, posturing herself to convey a plethora of kinesthetic signals: territorial combat fought with words and hisses, hierarchical issues resolved with the ruffling of fur, the stiffening of neck muscles. Eventually, resentfully, the hostile tribes parted to let them pass. Deep growls sounded low in rakhene throats as the hated odor of humankind drifted past their sensitive nostrils, but they made no move to harm their chosen enemies—and soon enough they, too, were gone, swallowed up by the endless sea of grass that stretched from horizon to horizon, without surcease.

They encountered other tribes, with much the same result. And Senzei came to realize just how lucky there were that the *khrast*-woman was with them. They had survived the Forest's worst, they had maneuvered through deadly surf and earthquakes and an ambush by their enemies, but they would never have made it through the plains without her. The rakh were simply too many, too hot-tempered, too eager to kill humankind. They would have been spitted like shish kebob before the first words of parley came out of their mouths.

Tedium began to eat at their nerves, an all too human response to the endless, identical miles. Tempers flared hotly in the featureless days, petty annoyances transformed into grievous trespasses by the joint powers of fear and boredom. How many hours could one ride thus, sandwiched between terrible dangers but unable to address oneself to them—riding endless miles in the constant company of others, without even a moment of true privacy in which change one's clothes, or bathe, or defecate, or even just *get away!* At least Tarrant left each morning. That helped. Senzei could almost see the cloud lift from about Damien when the Hunter finally transformed, adopting the broad feathered wings that would bear him to a daytime shelter. Tarrant refused to take shelter with the rest of the company, and clearly that was the wisest course; who could say when the temptation of an easy kill might overwhelm all prior agreements in the priest's mind, when all that was required to rid the world of the Hunter forever was the lifting of a single tent flap? The land was riddled with shelters, Tarrant told them, and his adept's vision easily picked out the subtle variation in earth-fae currents that betrayed the presence of a suitable cavern. So he rested in the earth, like the dead, while they camped and slept and stood uneasy watches. And when he returned each night there was as much regret as relief in Damien's eyes, that he had managed to get through the day safely.

Nightmares began to plague them—violent images, full of dire, unnatural symbols. More often than not the humans would awaken with pounding hearts, pulses throbbing hot with terror, all hope of sleep banished for that day. Even the rakh-woman wasn't immune, but shivered in the grip of some half-bestial nightmare that brought snarls and hisses to her lips as she thrashed about angrily, cocooned in her blankets. True rest became nearly impossible, something garnered in fevered snatches between the dreambound assaults.

And assaults they well might be, in a very literal sense. That was the most frightening thought of all. That their enemy might be watching them so closely that he was able to Send these images to torment them, to rob them of sleep until they arrived in his realm mere shadows of their former selves. Because that was a real possibility—and a frightening one—they fought it. All of it. The nightmares, the fear, the growing claustrophobia that came from being too close to other people too long, the burning need to be *alone.* It was Tarrant who unWorked the nightmares themselves, burning some precious document he had tucked about his person; the value of his sacrifice flared hot, like sunlight, and seared the vicinity clean of whatever taint might have formed about them. Perhaps it would last for a day, or two; Senzei had his doubts.

They traveled southeast, as the rakh-woman advised. It would bring them to a break in the eastern range where the mountains folded upon themselves to create a lowland pass. They debated long and hard the efficacy of such a route—wasn't it exactly what the enemy would expect of them?—but in the end they decided that they had no choice; in this harsh season, there was no other viable crossing. Besides, did they really think secrecy was possible in this place? Did they really imagine they weren't being Known anyway, every step they took, regardless of where they went?

At last it was Tarrant who convinced them to take the lowland course. *The current will be strongest in the mountains,* he said, *and it flows toward our enemy. Thus far, that's been to our detriment; it takes all my strength just to block the flow, to keep our intentions from reaching him. But when we get to the mountains, and the earth-fae is stronger, I can turn that same current against him. Create a simulacrum of our party, to take our place and draw his attention. So that we can move unobserved.*

A Distracting, Damien mused.

Far more complex than that, Tarrant assured him. *But the results are much the same.*

Are you sure it will work? Senzei had demanded.

The pale eyes turned on him—utterly lifeless, utterly cold. *It has once already,* he said dryly. And he left them to wonder just what manner of imposture had taken place at the Forest's edge, that had saved their fragile flesh.

Senzei wanted power like that. He wanted to taste it, just once in his life. Feel what it would be like, to have the fae pour through his soul like light through glass: focused, pure, powerful. Once would be enough, he told himself—but he knew even as he thought that it wouldn't be, it couldn't be, he could never give up such a glorious vision. Never! Never suffer as Ciani had, to have it taken from him. . . .

I would die first, he thought. And he shivered, to imagine it.

Then, at long last, the eastern mountains appeared before them. Misty purple peaks contrasted against a glistening dawn, velvet blue and gray slopes to frame the rising sun. The company stood there for a short time in silence, each mouthing his own prayers of thankfulness. The mountains were not of naked granite, like so much of the Worldsend range, nor covered with the spotty brush and narrow pines that typified so many northern ranges; these were lush, fertile hills, whose slopes were still stained orange and red and sunlight gold by the palette of late autumn, whose thickly forested heights gave way to snowy peaks with obvious reluctance, high in the distance.

"Beautiful," Senzei whispered. He heard the priest mutter something; a thanks to his god, perhaps, that they had succeeded in getting this far. The rakh-woman—who had given her full name as *Hesseth sa-Restrath*—hissed something in her native tongue, and for once the coarse rakhene words seemed gentle in tone. Almost loving.

We made it, Senzei thought, as he urged his mount forward.

And then he added, in unhappy honesty, *This far, anyway.*

They camped in the shadow of trees, by the side of a small stream. It was the rakhene woman who chose their campsite, using senses Senzei could only guess at to find them a source of water. Smell, perhaps? Or perhaps some rakhene Working. He remembered her manipulation of the tidal fae in Morgot and shuddered, despite himself. *She has more skills than she's admitted to*, he thought. *What does that mean, for the rest of us? Will she help us if we need it— or leave us to sink or swim, as our human limitations dictate?* He strongly suspected the latter. To date she had spoken little to the party, and when she did her conversation was limited to practical concerns: estimations of travel time, course advisement, foraging instructions. *No*, he thought. *Correct that.* The rakh-woman had spoken little to the *men*. To Ciani she vouchsafed a few parcels of genuine conversation, even went so far as to ride beside the woman several times in order to converse while traveling. Now and then Senzei caught snippets of their conversation, tidbits carried back to him on the evening breeze: Rakhene history. Rakhene custom. Rakhene legends.

Alien knowledge, he thought, with awe. Even without her knowledge, her confidence, the skills of an adept, Ciani was very much the same person she had been—hungry for knowledge the way most men are hungry for food.

Or power.

He wondered what it was like, to want something that could be obtained so easily. His own hunger had become a hole in him, an emptiness, a vast wound incapable of healing. The adepts spoke of the music of life, which filled every living thing with song and echoed from each molecule of inanimate matter, an endless symphony of being; he ached to hear it for himself. The rakh-woman could see tidal fae flicker into being across an evening sky, a vast aurora of power shimmering like the light of a thousand jewels; he yearned to possess that vision. Ciani had Shared her special senses with him once, but that wasn't the same thing. That had been as much pain as ecstacy, as much *wanting* as *having*. He had withdrawn from it confused and hurt, too shaken to manage his own Workings for some days afterward. They had never tried it again.

What I want, no one human being can give me. It was the truth of his existence—but it hurt no less for being familiar to him.

At sunset, promptly, Gerald Tarrant rejoined them. That he did so when the sun had barely dropped below the horizon warned his companions that something was amiss; generally he hunted for his own sustenance before returning to them.

He wasted no time on preliminaries, but addressed the group as soon as his form was human enough to allow for speech. "Do you know the date?" he demanded, as the last of his feathers melted back into flesh, hair, the intricate weave of clothing. "Do you realize what happens in a few hours?"

For a moment, no one responded. Then Damien stiffened—and Senzei likewise, as he realized what Tarrant was driving at. Like the rest of them, he had lost track of human calendrical reckoning in their trek across the rakhlands; now he looked up at the sky, his blood running cold in his veins as he realized what the Hunter was driving at.

In the east, half-veiled by trees, Casca was already setting. In the west, following the sun in its course, Domina and Prima would soon do the same. And the last stars of the Core would be gone within the hour. Then: darkness. Utter darkness.

"True night," someone whispered.

"Just so," the Hunter agreed.

They had forgotten. They had all forgotten. Even in the autumn such times were rare, and the last few true nights had been so short ... Senzei thought of how long this one might last, with all three moons just now setting, and he shivered in dread. It was madness to be outdoors at such a time. Absolute madness. But what other choice was there?

"How long will it last?" Damien asked.

"Hours," Tarrant told him. "No way to know the precise time without a good lunar chart—and mine was lost back at the river. But Casca will have to rise again before the dark fae is driven back—and a good part of the night will pass before that happens."

Senzei tried to keep the fear from his voice as he asked, "Do you think they'll attack us?"

"Our enemy, you mean?" Tarrant considered it, then shook his head. "Not now, I think. Not here. There'll be enough nights like this later on, when we're in a position more favorable to assault. But we can certainly expect to be hit with a Knowing, or similar probing. Something of unusual strength. But I can block those easily enough, once the sunlight is gone." An expression that was almost a smile flitted across his face. "The true night is my time, also."

"So is there anything you do feel we need to watch out for?" Damien asked tightly.

"Not so much *watch out for*, as *do*." The Hunter turned to Ciani; his pale eyes gleamed silver in the moonlight. "Lady?"

She drew in a deep breath, slowly. There was a strange intensity about her—fear and desire combined, an almost sexual excitement. Something about it made Senzei's skin crawl. "Is it time?" she whispered.

"If you're ready for it."

She shut her eyes tightly. And nodded, a barely perceptible notion. Senzei thought he saw her trembling.

"Time for what?" Damien demanded. "Now's not a good time to play at mysteries, Hunter."

"No such thing was intended. The lady and I have discussed some . . . arrangements. I think tonight would be a good time to test them. It'll take some courage on her part—but I've never found the lady to be lacking in that."

"You wouldn't care to be more specific, would you?" The priest's voice was carefully controlled, but not so much so that Senzei didn't hear the edge of violence in it. As if the mere threat of the true night had begun to dissolve his inhibitions, those precious checks and balances that must exist in order for him to tolerate Tarrant's presence among them. Or pretend to tolerate it.

The Hunter explained, "You know that there's a bond between Ciani and her attacker, which was established in the initial attack. You yourselves intended to manipulate that link once you reached the enemy's domain. Wasn't that the very reason you brought her along? With a simple Knowing, carefully planned, you would be able to locate her attacker, pick him out from among the dozens of his kind . . . an admirable scheme, given your knowledge and your power. But tonight, in the true darkness, I can do much more than that. Give us an advantage that the enemy can't foresee." He bowed toward Ciani. "*If* the lady is willing."

Senzei saw Ciani's hands clench and unclench, her flesh made colorless by fear. Damien saw it too, and said harshly, "You won't do anything that increases the risk to her. Understand? She's in danger enough."

Tarrant's eyes flashed angrily. "Don't be a fool, priest. The risk is already tremendous. She's the one that our enemy wants, not us—and he's going to try to claim her as soon as we cross these mountains. By bringing her this near to his domain you've placed her in greater danger than any other course could have done. And yes—you had your reasons. I agree with them. But now it's time to use the tools our enemy has provided, Because to *fail* to use them, to fail to turn them against him by whatever means possible . . . is to fail *her*, Reverend Vryce. And I remind you that I have a very strong personal interest in the success of this mission. One which I will not allow you to jeopardize." He paused. "Am I making myself clear?"

For a moment there was silence between the two men: chill, acidic, sharp with hatred. Then Damien found his voice, and managed to make it civil. "Go on."

The Hunter looked at Ciani. "Through her," he told them, "I can reach the mind of her tormentor. It's a dangerous process. Using earth-fae alone I would never chance it—our enemy is clearly as fluent in that domain as I am, and could easily turn such a Working against us. But using the dark fae, in those few precious hours when it dominates this land . . . that force is my substance, priest. My *life*. No mere man can best me in that arena, without first making a Sacrifice to equal mine."

"Damned unlikely, that," Damien muttered. His reaction to what the Hunter had done was strong enough to taint the earth-fae surrounding him; the valley was filled with the scent of blood, the heat of his revulsion. "So what will this accomplish? *If* you succeed?"

"If I succeed—and the odds of that are excellent—we will have far more information regarding our enemy than any other technique might procure. We'll learn his whereabouts, his intentions, perhaps even his weaknesses. We'll know what this link with Ciani means to him, and how he might use it against us."

"And if you fail?" Damien challenged.

"If I fail?" He looked at Ciani—and she met his eyes boldly, a faint nod saying that yes, she knew the risk, and yes, she was willing to try it. But her hands were trembling violently, and Senzei thought he saw a tear glitter wetly in the corner of one eye.

"If I fail," the Hunter said softly, "then there will be no point in continuing this expedition. Because he will have her. I will have given her to him."

For a moment, there was nothing in the camp but stillness. The fire, dying, crackled in its embers and spewed forth a few meager sparks. The rakh-woman tensed as if in anticipation of combat, but there was no way to read her intentions. Damien looked toward Ciani—and read something in her eyes that made his expression darken, deep furrows across his brow giving silent voice to his misgivings.

"All right, then," he said at last. "If Ciani's willing. If there's no better way."

"I am," she whispered.

And Tarrant assured them, "There isn't."

Dark fae. Strands of it, fine as spider's silk, drifting out from the secret places in the earth. Deep violet power that twined like slender serpents out from the shadows, snaking along the ground in rhythmic patterns as primal—and as complex—as human brainwaves. Power so responsive that the mere act of watching it was enough to make it shiver in its course. Power so volatile that it could manifest human fears long after their original cause had faded from memory. Power so hungry that it fed on darkness, devouring the very essence of the night in order to reproduce itself over and over again, filling the night with its violent substance.

"Ready?" the Hunter whispered. His voice was little louder than the breeze, and as chill as the night which was swiftly descending on them. Senzei shivered as he watched him prepare to Work, and not merely because the air was cold.

"As ready as I'll ever be," Ciani murmured.

With care he bound her, wrists and ankles tightly affixed to stakes driven deep into the ground. Another rope, tightened across her chest, would keep her from rising up. Such preparation was necessary, Tarrant had explained, in case her attacker should gain control of her body—but it made Senzei queasy to see her like that. Damien had told him how the Neocount's wife was bound, when they found her body. Too similar, he thought. It made his gut knot just to think of it.

"All right," the Hunter said. He looked at each of them in turn— and though Damien managed to meet his gaze without flinching, Senzei couldn't. It was as if something in those pale gray eyes had come to life, something dark and terrible. And hungry. "I need silence. Absolute. And you mustn't interfere—no matter what happens. No matter what the cost may be of completing this Working. Because to interrupt it midway is to give her soul to the enemy. You all understand that?" His words might have been meant for all of them, but his eyes were fixed on Damien. After a moment the priest nodded stiffly and muttered, "Go on."

No matter what happens. Already Senzei could see forms taking shape about the circle of their campsite, the company's fears given life and substance by the malignant fae of the sunless hours. Tarrant had assured them that nothing would approach—his own nature fed on the dark fae, and would devour any manifestation that made it past his wards—but even so Senzei shivered, as the legions of creatures that their fears had spawned flitted about the warded circle, seeking entrance. He was tempted to unWork his vision, to let that terrible vision fade . . . but the alternative was far, far worse. This way at least there was light; the deep violet essence of true night's power might not be wholesome illumination, but at least it was something. Without it, the autumn night would be utterly lightless: cave-black, cellar-dark, in which a man might raise his hand before his face without seeing it—in which the darkness seemed to close in until one could hardly breathe, until one wanted to run desperately for light, any light . . . only this time, in this place, there was nowhere to run. And the darkness would last for hours. Even the minimal illumination of night's special fae was preferable to that.

Slowly, like wisps of smoke, the fae began to gather about Ciani's body. Senzei saw her shiver, though whether it was in pain or simply in dread he had no way to see. She certainly had cause enough for the latter. As she breathed in, thin violet strands caught hold of the breath and followed it into her lungs, her flesh; the air she breathed out was merely dark, liquid swirls of onyx blackness that had been leached of all power. She slowly closed her eyes, but even as she did so Senzei could see the violet light that shimmered in their depths, radiant as the green that would sometimes flash in a cat's eyes at night. She had absorbed the dark fae.

"Submit to me," the Hunter whispered. His voice was a chill caress, that made Senzei's flesh crawl. "With every thought, in every cell of your being." And then he added, in a tone that was almost tender, "You know I'd do nothing to hurt you."

She nodded. Then a shudder seemed to pass through her body, and Senzei thought he heard a faint sound—a moan?—escape from her lips. Tarrant's Worked fae was thickening about her, and he could see it connect to the wild fae beyond—creating what might be a lifeline, an umbilical cord. A connection that pulsed with its own special life, in time to some unheard heartbeat.

"You hunger," Tarrant commanded. Chanting the words: a mantra of possession. "For memory. For life. For fragments of the past, which you draw from the souls of others. The hunger is constant, all-consuming. It torments you. It strengthens you. It drives you to feed—and gives you the power to do so." In his voice was promise, commiseration, a dark seduction that went beyond mere recitation of demonic qualities. How much of his own nature was he drawing on in order to establish this rapport? As he reached down to touch Ciani, to lay one slender hand over her heart, it struck Senzei for the first time just how like their enemy he was. The Hunter and Ciani's tormentor might feed on different emotions, but they both served the same dark Pattern.

When Tarrant touched her, Ciani cried out—and then was suddenly still, so much so that Senzei feared for her. For a moment she lay like one dead, so utterly unmoving that Senzei found himself searching in vain for any sign of breathing, any tremor of a heartbeat. There was none. Then she trembled, and her eyes shot open. Black, utterly black, with no sign of iris or white. Pits of emptiness, which anything might fill.

"Who are you?" the Hunter demanded.

In a voice that was Ciani's but not Ciani's, she answered, "Essistat sa-Lema. Tehirra sa-Steyat. Ciani sa-Faraday. Others." A ghastly sound escaped her lips, that might have been intended as laughter. "I don't remember all the names."

Tarrant looked up at Hesseth, who nodded shortly. *Rakh names,* the gesture indicated. For once, the *khrast*-woman seemed as tense as the human company.

The Hunter turned his attention back to Ciani. "*Where* are you?" he asked.

Again the ghostly laugh—then, in a cryptic tone, "Night's turf. Hunter's den. The basement of storms."

"Where?" Tarrant pressed.

The thing that was Ciani shut her eyes. "In darkness," she whispered at last. "Beneath the House of Storms."

"In the earth?"

"No. Yes."

"In caverns? Tunnels? Man-made structures?"

Her eyes shot open, fixed on him. "*Rakh*-made," she corrected fiercely. "Where the Lost Ones dwelled until we drove them out. We fed on their memories, too—but those were narrow things, all tunnels and hunger and brainless mating. Not like the memories of the other rakh." She closed her eyes, and a shudder passed through her frame; strangely sexual, like the first shiver of orgasm. "Not like with the humans," she whispered. "Nothing like that."

Again Tarrant glanced at Hesseth, and this time he mouthed the words. *Lost Ones?* Her brief nod sufficed to indicate that she knew the reference, would be willing to explain it later. Or so Senzei hoped.

Tarrant returned his attention to Ciani. The black depths of her eyes gleamed like obsidian as she watched him.

"Do you fear?" he asked her.

"Fear?"

"As the rakh do. As humans do."

"Fear? As in 'for my life'? No. Why should I?"

"You feel safe."

"I *am* safe."

"Protected," the Hunter probed.

"Yes."

"Efficiently."

The empty eyes opened; a hint of violet light stirred in their depths. "Without question."

"How?"

She seemed to hesitate. "Lema protects. The Keeper shields."

"Against what?" When there was no answer, he pressed, "Against the rakh?"

"The humans," she whispered. "They're coming for us. That's what Lema said. They're coming, with a Fire that can burn away the night. Can burn *us*."

"But you're not afraid."

"No." The voice was a hiss. "Lema protects. The Keeper is thorough. Even now—"

She hesitated. Gasped suddenly, as if in pain. Tarrant said quickly, "It took a lot of planning."

"Not much," she answered. Her body seem to sag into the ground, as if in relief, and her voice was strong once more. Senzei sensed that some barrier had been not overcome, nor destroyed, but somehow sidestepped. "Only a misKnowing. The rest is up to us."

Senzei saw something flicker in Tarrant's eyes, too subtle and too quick for him to identify. Fear? Surprise?

"A misKnowing?" he whispered.

"Yes. The demon said that would be best. To turn their own Workings against them. To let them feel confident in their knowledge, while all the while they were walking into a trap. That's the only way to take an adept, Calesta says. Trick them, using their own vision."

For a moment, there was silence. Shadows of forms began to shiver into existence about the Hunter's body, bits of misgivings seeping out from his soul, given shape by the night. A death-mask. A spear. A drop of fire. In another time and place such images might have gained real substance, but his hungry nature swallowed them up again as quickly as they were formed. Only a brief afterimage remained, black against black in the night.

"Tell me," he whispered tightly. "The misKnowing. What is it?"

Ciani seemed about to speak, then hesitated.

"*Tell me.*"

She gasped soundlessly, like a fish out of water. Seemed incapable of making the words come.

He reached forward and grasped her by the upper arms; his power flowed into her like a torrent, purple fae marked with his hunger, his purpose. "Tell me!" he demanded. She tried to resist, tried to pull away—and then cried out, as the cold power wrapped itself around her soul. Senzei saw Damien start forward, then force himself back.

Because she might die if he interfered. Only because of that. But there was murder in his eyes.

"Tell me," the Hunter commanded—and Senzei could feel him using the dark fae to squeeze the information out of her, like juice from a pulped fruit.

"Sansha Crater!" she gasped. There were tears running down her face, and she was shaking violently in his grip. Information began to pour out as if it had a life of its own, words and concepts struggling to get free. "The humans' Knowings will lead them there in search of us. They'll believe that our stronghold is there, beneath the House of Storms. Most important, *he* will believe it—their adept—because Calesta took the image from his mind. When he looked at his maps and said *this is where the enemy will be,* the Hungry One noted it. And the Keeper will let them think that he was right, warp his Knowings to serve that end . . . and the adept's own Workings will lead them into ambush."

For a moment Tarrant was still, and utterly silent. The look in his eyes was terrible—shame and fury and blind, raw hatred, intermingled with even less pleasant emotions that Senzei didn't dare identify—but Ciani, or whatever manner of creature now inhabited her body, seemed oblivious to it. Had his own word not bound him to protect her, Senzei was pretty sure the Hunter would have struck out at the body before him, Working the dark fae so that it would transmit the damage to Ciani's possessor; but he *was* bound, and by his own will, and so his rage went unexpressed.

"Where is the House of Storms?" he hissed. Dark purple tendrils swirled about his rage, dissolved into the night. "Where is your people's stronghold?" When she didn't answer him his eyes narrowed coldly, and she gasped; Senzei could see the last of her resistance crumble.

"On the point of power," she whispered. "Where the earth-fae flows in torrents, hungry for taming. Where the plates sing in pain as they crush the power out. Where the Keeper—"

Ciani's body went rigid. She mouthed a few words, soundlessly—and then a spasm of pain racked her body, traveling from head to foot like a wave. "No!" she cried out—Ciani's voice, Ciani's pain. She pulled against her bonds with a force that almost dragged the tent pegs from the earth. "Gerald!" But the adept did nothing to help her.

"Stop it!" Damien hissed. He started forward—and then forced himself to halt, though his fists were clenched in fury. *To interrupt this Working is to give her soul to the enemy.* "Stop it, damn you! She can't take any more!" As if in answer to him, blood trickled from

Ciani's mouth. And Tarrant did move, at last. He put his hands to the sides of her face—and she tried to bite him, wild as a wounded animal—but he grasped her firmly and held her head back against the earth, while her body struggled against its bonds. Fixing his eyes on hers, pinioning her to the ground by the power of his gaze. A power that Senzei could see, a vivid purple that vibrated with the force of his hatred.

"Let go," he whispered fiercely. "This is not your flesh, not your place. Obey me!" She struggled in his grasp—helplessly, like an infant. Blood poured down her cheek and smeared on his hand, deep purple in the fae-light. It dripped to the ground. He took no notice of it. *"Obey me,"* he whispered. And the power that flowed from him was so bright, so blinding, that Senzei had to turn away.

For a brief moment, the whole of Ciani's body went rigid; her bonds creaked as she strained against them. Then, suddenly, all the strength went out of her. She lay on the bloodied earth like a shattered doll, her intermittent gasping for breath the only sign of her survival. After a moment, Tarrant released her. Her eyes—now human, heavily bloodshot—shut. She shivered, as if from cold.

"Take out the Fire," the Hunter said quietly to Damien.

"You're sure—"

"Take it out!"

He stood as the priest complied with his command, and put a few hurried steps between himself and the rest of the party. Nevertheless, he was clearly loath to go too far from Ciani; he remained close enough that when the Fire was uncovered its light burned a swath across his face that blistered an angry red as he watched her.

For a moment, Senzei could see nothing: the Fire's light was brilliant, blinding. He felt his Seeing fade, knew that it would be long minutes before he could conjure such vision again. But there was no need for it. The dark fae was gone, consumed in an instant by the force of that Church-spawned blaze. And with it, whatever remnants of the night's power that had clung to Ciani. She whimpered softly as Damien went to her, clung to him as he severed her bonds and gathered her up in his arms, the light of the Fire pressed into her back.

"She'll be all right," the Hunter promised. "Keep the Fire out until Casca rises. No. Until the sun comes up. She'll be safe, once she's exposed to true sunlight; neither his power nor mine can cling to her then."

"But if you—" Damien began.

"You'll have to function without me," he said sharply. "There are several things that want looking into, and I can handle them best alone."

"Not to mention the Fire," Damien said queitly.

Tarrant turned toward him, slowly, and let him watch as the sanctified light spread across his features. The skin of his face and hands reddened, tightened, began to peel—but his cold eyes gazed steadily at Damien, and there was no hint in his manner of any pain or hesitancy.

"Don't underestimate me," he warned. Blood pooled in the corner of one eye, and he blinked it free; it traveled down the side of his face like a tear. Still he did not turn away, nor shield himself from the Fire's light. "Don't ever underestimate me."

"I'm sorry," Damien said at last.

"You should be," he agreed. And he bowed to Ciani—a minimal gesture, hurried but graceful. "It's vital that you don't discuss what happened here tonight—any of it—until the sun rises. Otherwise your attacker might learn . . . too much. Lady?"

She whispered it. "I understand."

He stepped—and was gone, more quickly than the eye could follow. Reddened flesh fading into blackness, burnt skin swallowed up by darkness. Salved, by the true night's special power.

"The Fire didn't hurt him," Senzei whispered, "Not like it should have."

"Of *course* it hurt him," Damien said sharply. "And it would have killed him if he'd stayed here long enough."

"But he didn't seem—"

"No, he didn't, did he? And what gets to me is that he would have stayed there, endured the pain—till the Fire fried him to a crisp, if that's what it took. Just to prove a point."

He drew in a ragged breath, and closed his arms tightly about Ciani.

"That's what makes him so vulking dangerous," he muttered.

Rain fell. Not the gentle rain of days before, a chill but tolerable mist that wet the land without truly soaking it, but a downpour that swept in from the East, borne on winds that had coursed over thousands of miles of open sea, scooping up foam and spray and converting them into thick, black storm clouds. If Casca rose, they never saw it. Water fell in sheets, interspersed with bits of hail and clumps of crystal, as if it couldn't decide what form it wanted to take—but it was all cold, and dark, and drenching.

They huddled inside the rakhene tent, thick hides stretched across hollow poles to form a cone-shaped shelter. The women, that was. Senzei and Damien stayed outside long enough to fashion a primitive shelter for their animals. Already the real horses were straining at their tethers, and the xandu, unbound, milled nervously about the campsite as if they were beginning to regret their faebound allegiance to the rakh-woman and her companions. But the two men managed to find a granite overhang near the camp, and jam enough branches into a crevice above it that when soaking leaves were stuffed in between them they stayed in place. The downpour became a trickle within the shelter, a turbulent sheet at its edge. Good enough, Damien indicated. They led the drenched animals inside, the light of the Fire casting harsh shadows across jagged granite walls, and saw that they were safely settled there before returning to the camp.

Tarrant, perhaps predictably, did not return. Damien muttered something about him not wanting to get his hair wet, which Senzei assumed was facetious. The men wrung out their clothing as well as they could, exchanging their soaked cloth for cold but dryer garments. In the tent's narrow interior comfort was difficult, privacy impossible—but four warm living bodies in that narrow space slowly warmed it until the air was tolerable, and by the time dawn came at last Senzei discovered that he had fallen asleep sometime in that interminable darkness.

Dawn. They assumed it came, because the sky grew slowly lighter. But the sun was hidden by deep gray storm clouds, and its light was filtered through sheets of rain. Several times Senzei saw Damien hunch over toward the tent's small opening, studying the sky with narrowed eyes. Waiting for sunlight to break through the cloudcover. Because until Ciani was exposed to the sun's cleansing power, none of them dared talk about what they had seen, or heard, or feared in the night. Nor could they make plans.

It was the longest day they had ever spent together.

Toward sunset, a break came at last. A glimmer of light in the distance, that broke up the downpour into a thousand glittering jewels. A break in the clouds that showed first the sun, then the Core. White light commingled with gold warmed the frozen land slowly, and broke up the rain into a fine silver mist. Soon a patch of clear sky passed overhead, and then another; nevertheless, it was many long hours before Ciani could stand in the full light of day, shivering in pain as the solar fae burned the last vestiges of true night's Working from her flesh.

Gerald Tarrant returned at sunset. By then they had reclaimed their mounts—the animals were skittish and hungry, but otherwise unharmed by the downpour—and found enough dry twigs beneath the tent, and in other places, to kindle a feeble fire. The four of them sat about it, silent, while Tarrant reestablished his wards. Guarding against eavesdroppers, Senzei guessed. At last he seemed satisfied, and lowered himself to a place by the fire. His hair, Senzei noted, was not only dry but perfectly groomed.

"I had hoped for several more nights of travel before certain decisions were necessary," he told the group. "We need more information than we have, and I'd hoped to find it in Lema. But I think it's clear we've run out of time. Our enemy has anticipated us, and the result is that we nearly walked right into his hands. So we have to decide a few things here and now—what we're doing, and how we mean to do it—so that we can set everything in motion now, before our enemy realizes that we're on to him."

"Without knowing the land we're traveling to?" Senzei asked.

"One doesn't win a war by letting one's enemy write the rules. And he's trying to do just that. We need to plan—quickly, and thoroughly. Otherwise we may as well march into Sansha Crater and deliver the lady to him ourselves."

"What are the chances he's aware of what you did last night?" Damien asked.

Tarrant hesitated. "In a general sense, that's unavoidable. No sorceror could miss it. In a specific sense . . . I was very, very careful. And the dark fae is my element, remember; its manipulation is as natural to me as breathing is to you. If he investigates the matter, he'll discover that we tried to use the link between Ciani and himself to facilitate a direct assault. And failed. Not that information flowed in the opposite direction, toward us." He turned to the rakh-woman. "There are some facts we need, before we make any decisions. He mentioned some names that were unfamiliar to me. They may be crucial. And you seemed to recognize them."

"The Lost Ones."

"And Calesta."

She shook her head. "That name is unfamiliar to me. But the Lost Ones . . . that's a rakhene term for a tribe of our people that disappeared back in the years of the Changing. You understand, we had no language then, and our form was still unstable; each generation differed from the last, making social continuity nearly impossible. We have only oral records from those times, and even those are uncertain. Bear that in mind as I speak.

"The rakh who came here—the ones who survived the Worldsend

crossing—spread out across the land, each group establishing its own territory. They weren't even tribes then, more like . . . extended families. Many settled in the plains because that land was so hospitable. Others went south, into the swamplands. Or east. Our ancestors were territorial creatures, who needed their own space as much as your people need food and water; it was humanity's intrusion into our lands in the first place that caused—" She drew herself up sharply, inhaled through gritted teeth. "That's dead and gone, now. Our people spread out. They changed. We gained language. Sophistication. *Civilization.* Eventually the plains rakh began to travel, to see what our world had become, and learn more of yours—thus the *khrast* tradition—and slowly, warily, the scattered tribes made contact once again. We discovered two things: that even though man's Impression still dictated our general evolution, we had adapted to our chosen lands. The rakh who hunt for sustenance in the southern swamplands bear little resemblance to my people, or any other tribe; in some cases the differences are so great as to preclude intermating, implying— according to your science—that we have become several species.

"Second, we discovered that during the time of our dispersal a large number of rakh were lost. They had chosen to settle in the mountains—these mountains—and had lived there during the early stages of their development. We found artifacts of their civilization—tools, trash heaps, broken ornaments—but never any hint of where they had gone. Legend says,"—and here she breathed in deeply—"that they went underground. That there was a time of terrible cold, when debris from an upland volcano cut us off from the sun's warmth, and the mountains were covered in ice. Certainly, most rakh would rather seek shelter under their territory than abandon it utterly. If so, they never came out again. Only legends remain."

"And now this testimony," Damien said. *"Where the Lost Ones dwelled, until we drove them out.* If we knew how long ago these demons moved into Lema—"

"Three centuries," Tarrant said coolly. "give or take a decade or two."

Damien stared at him in astonishment. "How do you know that?"

"The rakh-girl from Lema. Remember? I . . . interrogated her."

For a moment, Damien was speechless. Then he hissed, "You *bastard.*"

Tarrant shrugged. "We needed information. She had it." His eyes glittered darkly. "I assure you, any interest in her emotional state was strictly . . . secondary."

Damien made as if to rise, but Ciani put a hand on his shoulder.

Firmly. "It's over," she said. "You can't help her now. *We have to work together.*"

He forced himself to sit back; it clearly took effort.

"Go on," he growled.

"Three centuries ago," Tarrant repeated. "The Lost Ones were alive and thriving then, and they built their tunnels. Or adapted them from existing caves—our informant seemed to indicate both. Then came this foreign sorceror. Lema's human Master, who built his citadel above their warren. And the demons who served him took refuge in the caves beneath, driving out their former inhabitants. So that they might be protected from sunlight."

"Three centuries," Ciani mused. "The lost rakh might still be alive."

"Adapted to the darkness—and thus very photosensitive. I doubt that they care much for sunlight themselves—in fact, it stands to reason that their underground domiciles would be interlinked. So that they might go from one to the other without ever coming aboveground."

"Including—" Senzei began.

Tarrant nodded. "That one."

"Underground access," Damien whispered.

"If their tunnels were rakh-made, no. The new tenants would have sealed those off, for defensive purposes. Or they'd have them guarded. But if we're talking about natural caverns, with all their infinite variety ... there's a real possibility of finding some way in that our enemies don't know about. Or creating one, through adjoining chambers."

"Coming in through the back door," Senzei mused.

"Just so."

Damien turned to the *khrast*-woman. "What's the chance of finding these underground rakh? Of communicating with them, if we do?"

"Who can say where they are—or even if they still exist? No one's seen them for centuries. As for communication ... they wouldn't speak English, I'm sure; that was a later development. They might still speak fragments of the rakhene tongue ... or they might not. Too much time has passed to be certain."

"But the tunnels will be there, regardless," Tarrant said.

Damien turned to him. "You think you can find them?"

He chuckled. "Just what do you think I do every morning, when it comes time to find shelter? Locating caves is child's play for anyone who can See the currents. It's much the same skill that Senzei

used, bringing us to shore. But locating the *right* caverns. . . ." He
nodded thoughtfully. "That will take some effort."

"All right, then," Damien said. "Let's say that we may have a way
to sneak up on them. And we have an effective weapon, if they're
sun-sensitive." He patted the pouch at his hip. "There's time enough
ahead to decide how best to use it. As for our enemy's ambush . . .
now that we know what game he's playing, we should be able to
counter it. Which leaves us with only one question left—"

"Where the hell we're going," Senzei supplied.

Tarrant withdrew a sheet of vellum from his pocket; it had been
folded so many times that it was barely as wide as two fingers, yet
it opened up to display a sizable map of the area. "I sketched this
from memory, soon after losing the original. I can't guarantee its
accuracy, but I believe that the general form is right." He spread it
out before them. It was a map of the rakhlands and its surrounding
regions, superimposed over a webwork of jagged ink lines.

"Fault lines," Damien whispered.

Tarrant nodded. "Missing a few minor ones, no doubt, but I believe
the major plate boundaries are all in place." This map, unlike the
first, was labeled. *Greater Novatlantic plate. Eastern Serpentine.
Lesser Continental.* He pointed to where those three plates met.
"Here's the single point of power for this region," he mused. "I
assumed he would have settled somewhat near it. According to our
informant, however, he's sitting right on top of it."

"I thought you said—" Damien began.

"That only a fool would do that? I did. And I'll stand by it. Don't
ask me how he's kept his citadel standing, in a region this seismically
active. Wards alone won't do it. He must be counting on something
else. Maybe luck. The girl said there hadn't been a quake in this area
for a long time. Years."

"That's impossible," Damien muttered.

He nodded. "Certainly odd, to say the least. The small ones sometimes go unnoticed, of course . . . but even so, we're talking about a
considerable seismic gap in this region. I just hope it holds long
enough for us to get where we're going."

"Speaking of which," Damien said, "is there any way to keep the
Master of Lema from tracking us? He seemed to read through your
Obscuring—"

"You can't blind a man to the obvious," Tarrant said sharply. "But
you can divert his focus. Last night I prepared a Working that should
do that. It will take effect . . . here." He indicated a point on the map
some two days' journey east of them. "We have to stay with the pass
this far to get to Lema; he knows that. But once the five of us reach

this point, I've arranged for simulacra to take our place. They will continue along this path,"—his finger traced a line through the mountains, into Lema, toward the place where the three plates met—"to here." He indicated a point some twenty miles to the east of that place of power, and looked at the rakhene woman for confirmation.

She reached out and moved his hand a few inches southward. And nodded. "The crater is there." She looked up at him. "And the ambush."

"While they travel toward it, his Workings will be drawn to them. We will be all but invisible."

Damien stared at him. Something in his expression made Senzei's skin crawl.

"You used people," he said quietly. "Rakh."

"A good simulacrum can't be created out of thin air. Such an illusion wouldn't fool an adept for an instant. There has to be enough substance that when one probes beneath the surface—"

"*Innocent* rakh."

The Hunter's expression darkened. "This is a war, priest—and in a war, there are casualties. The innocent are sometimes among them."

"You have no right!"

"*But I have the power.* And that's all there is to it. I won't argue this point. Not when my own survival is at stake. I have far too much already invested in that, and one hell of a reception awaiting me if I die. The Working exists. I've already warded it. When you reach this point," and he tapped the map aggressively, "five simulacra will leave for Sansha Crater. And because my Working was bound to living flesh they will be convincing, and our enemy will watch them, *not* us, until they die." He shook his head slowly. "I don't intend to perish here, priest. Certainly not for your morals. You'd better come to terms with that."

Speechless, Damien turned to Ciani. "Cee—"

"Please. Damien. He's right." She put a hand on his arm; he seemed to flinch at the contact. "We have no choice, don't you see? We need this Working, or something like it. Otherwise, we might as well just give up now. And I can't do that, Damien. Can't give up. Can you?"

Wordlessly, he pulled away from her. His expression was unreadable—but there was a coldness in it that made Senzei shiver.

"You have me," he muttered at last. "I won't interfere. I can't. But you'll pay for those lives—in blood. I swear it."

The Hunter laughed softly; it was an ominous sound.

"Those and a thousand others," he agreed.

Morning. Next day. She came to Senzei while he was gathering wood. And startled him so badly that he nearly dropped his bundle.

"Ciani?"

Sunlight poured down through the half-stripped branches above them, illuminating her pallor. Her weakness. The possession of two nights before had taken more out of her than any of them wanted to admit.

"I thought you might like company," she offered.

The words were out of him before he could stop them. "You shouldn't have left camp."

She shrugged; the gesture, like all her gestures, was a mere shadow of her former state. Even her gaze seemed weakened. "You worry as much as he does." She looked about for something to sit down on, settled on a broken stump. "Which is a little too much, sometimes." She lowered herself onto it with a sigh. "Sometimes you have to get away . . . from fears, from people." She met his eyes, held them. "You know what I mean?"

He could feel the color come to his face; he fought the impulse to turn away from her. "It's too dangerous, Cee. You shouldn't be alone, not even for a few minutes."

"I know," she told him. "And yet . . . it's as if too much risk numbs the mind to danger. Is that possible? Sometimes I have to consciously remind myself how close we are to our enemy, how much power he has . . . but even then it's distant, somehow. Unreal. As if I have to work to be afraid."

She looked down at her hands, as if studying them for answers. And at last said, quietly, "I never had a chance to tell you. About the memories. Just bits and pieces . . . but I had them again, for a time. During Gerald's Working. As if, while that creature used my body, I could sense something of his. My memories, stored in his flesh." She looked up at him; her brown eyes glistened in the sunlight. "I relived . . . when you came to me. Do you remember, Zen?"

It had been so long ago—and was so much a part of a different world, to which he no longer belonged—that it took him a minute to recall it. To recall himself, at that age.

"Yes," he said softly. And he winced, remembering.

"You were young. So young. Do you remember? That was the image I got when we made contact. Your face—what I saw in it— what I Knew of you. But what I remembered most of all was your youth. Gods, you were so young. . . ."

"I'm only thirty-four now," he said defensively.

"Yes. Still young. Body not aging yet—not irrevocably, anyway. Still at an age where the fae can regenerate flesh. . . ." She let the thought trail off into silence. Let him finish it for himself. "Do you remember why you came to me? What you wanted?"

The color was hot in his face now, and he did turn away. "Cee, please. . . ."

"It's nothing to be ashamed of."

He shook his head slowly, and bit his lower lip; it alarmed him that the memory could still awaken such pain. "It's not shame, Cee. It's . . . I didn't understand. That's all. I wanted the world to be something that it wasn't."

"You came to me seeking vision," she said softly. "Not power, not wealth, not even immortality . . . not any of the things that other men seek. Just the Sight."

He kept his voice even, but it took all his self-control; beneath that surface he could feel himself trembling, his whole soul shivering with humiliation. "And you explained the truth. That I couldn't ever have it."

"Yes. I had to. Dedication like yours deserved honesty, no matter how much the truth might hurt. And maybe, if the knowledge hurt that much, it was in part because so many people had lied to you— had led you to believe that there was some kind of hope, when there wasn't—"

"They weren't adepts," he said quickly. "They couldn't know."

"It's just—I'm sorry," she whispered.

He shut his eyes; his soul ached with regret, with the pain of shattered dreams. "You did what you had to."

"It was what I believed. What we all believed. That adeptitude was an inborn trait; one either had it or one didn't. That no act of man, no manner of Working, might cause the Sight to exist in one who hadn't been born with it."

He heard her draw in a deep breath. Gathering her courage? "I was wrong, Zen."

He turned to her. Not quite absorbing her words, or what they might mean. The shock was too great.

"I *believed* what I told you," she assured him. "And any adept would have said the same—any honest one. But that's only because none of us had lived long enough to understand—"

She stopped herself suddenly, as if her own confession distressed her. He could feel his hands shaking, with need and fear combined, and he felt as if he stood on the edge of a precipice. Balanced at the edge of a great yawning Pit, about to topple into it.

"Long enough for what?" He could barely manage the words. "What are you saying, Cee?"

She whispered it—furtively, as if afraid that some other might hear. "No *act of man* could do it, I told you. No act of man could wield enough power to break down the soul's own barriers . . . no act of a *single* man," she stressed. "But what if hundreds of sorcerors were to combine their skills—what if *thousands* were to pour all their vital energy, all their hopes and dreams, into one all-powerful Working— wouldn't that be enough? Couldn't the laws of Erna be altered with such a force as that?"

He stared at her in disbelief, could find no words to say.

"Gerald made me aware of the pattern. Showed me what to look for. He was around when that kind of power was first conjured, saw with his own eyes what it could do . . . but I don't think even he thought of this. Or would have told you, if he did." She leaned forward, hands on her knees. Her voice was couched low, but there was fever in her tone. "The *Fire*, Zen. That's what it is. The power of thousands, concentrated in that one tiny flask. Tamed, to serve man's will." She paused, giving the words time to sink in. Their meaning burned like flame. "I believe it could free you. I believe it could give you what you want."

She rose from where she sat and came to him; not close enough to touch, but nearly. "I don't have all my old knowledge," she told him. "I can't know for sure that it'll work. But the more Gerald tells me about the kind of power that was wielded in the days of the Holy Wars, the more I think . . ." She drew in a deep breath. "It could *change* you, Senzei. Give you what you dreamed of, in those days. You still want it, don't you?"

"Gods, yes. . . ." Was it really possible? He had worked so hard to bury that hope, so that he might not destroy his life with it. Now, to consider it again, after all those years. . . . For a moment he could hardly speak in answer. He was afraid that in the place of words might come something less dignified, like tears, or gasping, or simply speechless trembling. The emotion was almost too much to bear.

"Does he know?" he managed. "Damien. Did you tell him?"

"How could I?" she said gently. "He'd never let you have it. Such a use would be . . . blasphemy, to him."

"Then isn't this—your being here—isn't that a kind of betrayal?"

"I don't share his faith," she reminded him.

"But doesn't that mean—I mean, Damien—"

"Don't mistake me. I care for him, deeply. But philosophically . . ." She seemed to hesitate. "We're from different worlds, it seems sometimes. The faith he serves . . ." She shook her head. "It's not that I don't respect it, or him. But gods! They're living in a dreamworld, filled with misty hopes and misguided passions . . . and I'm simply a pragmatist. A realist. This is my world. I accept it. I *live* in it. And if you give me a source of power, I'll use it—as the gods intended."

She touched a hand to his cheek, gently; the storm of emotion inside him made the contact seem an almost alien thing, oddly distant from him. "Romance between man and woman is such a fleeting thing," she said softly. "You of all people should know that. But the devotion of a true friend . . . *that* endures forever. My loyalties are just what they should be, Zen. And I'll stand by them to my grave."

He should have had so many misgivings, so many fears—but the pounding of his heart drowned them all out, until it was hard to focus on any one thought. Feebly—mechanically—he protested, "It's his weapon. *Our* weapon."

"And do you think this will lessen it? Would the whole pint of Fire be so diminished by a few drops? He spared that much to Work his weapons, back in Mordreth. And again in the rakhene camp." Her voice was a whisper, barely audible above the sound of the breeze stirring the leaves—but he heard every word as though it were a shout, felt her meaning etched in fire upon his soul. "One drop, maybe two," she whispered. "That's all it would take. I *know* it. And think, Zen, if it worked . . . then *you'd* be our weapon. You'd be able to use everything that's inside you, instead of keeping it all pent up in your brain. Take the hunger of all those years and turn it into power . . . and he'd still have nearly a pint left. He'd never even know it was gone! And Zen . . . you'd be able to help us, like you never could before. Wouldn't that be a fair trade? If you could only manage that, then we wouldn't have to rely so much on—"

She stopped suddenly, and wrapped her arms around herself as if her own words had chilled her.

"The Hunter?"

She whispered it. "Yes."

He chose his words carefully, tried to keep his voice steady. "Damien wouldn't give it to me."

"No. Not willingly."

"Is there any other way?"

She hesitated. He felt mixed emotions—elation, terror, need—flood his soul. "Please, Cee."

"I can Distract him," she said softly. "Gerald taught me how. He didn't mean it for this purpose . . . but he wouldn't have to know, will he? I can give Damien dreams while he's sleeping. Keep his attention fixed on them, so that he doesn't wake up. You'd only need minutes. Later . . ." She breathed in deeply. "Later you could Work him yourself. Like an adept, Zen. *You'd be an adept.*"

He shut his eyes, felt a violent trembling course through his body. The dream, the need . . . it was almost too much to bear. The hope itself was too powerful, too overwhelming; like an ocean tide, it threatened to drag him under.

"Dangerous. . . ." he whispered.

"The sun-power? The church's fae? How could it be? That's a force born of pure benevolence, bound together for cleansing purposes. What could be possibly be safer? You saw him use it last night—saw him hold it against me, to protect me from the dark fae. Did it burn me? *Could* it burn me?" When he said nothing, she pressed, "What's the only Working that his church will tolerate, even now? Healing. Because that's what his faith is all about, Zen—that's where their power lies. *That's what the Fire is.*"

He had lost his voice, and with it his resistance. The dream had hold of him again, and the hunger that had burned in him for so long had become something else—a lover, a seduction—no longer fever-hot but cool, blissfully cool, like the touch of a woman whose skin had been chilled by the night, all fluid ice and liquid passion and burning need at once. . . .

Then she touched a finger to his lips and whispered—so low that he could hardly hear her—"We can't discuss this again, you understand that? There's a link between Damien and me, strong enough that he might read your intentions through it. And as for Gerald . . ." She turned away from him; a shiver seemed to pass through her flesh. "There's nothing I can keep from him now. Nothing. Not after I submitted my soul to him." She shook her head. "It would be too dangerous, you understand that? He depends on his adept's skills to control the party. And me. If he thought for a moment that there was a way you could challenge his dominance—"

He shivered in fear—but the fear was enticing. Challenge Gerald Tarrant? "I understand," he whispered.

"I think I can keep him from knowing, for a time. Despite . . . what's between us. But I can only manage that if I can pretend that nothing's happening. Pretend I don't know myself what you're planning. So we can't discuss it again, ever."

"But if you do that—I mean, how can you—"

"Help you?" She turned back to face him. Her eyes were bright. "I can Work Damien's dreaming ahead of time. Gerald taught me how. If I do that, and then you go to his side when he's sleeping, nothing short of a quake would wake him up. I promise it. You don't even have to tell me your decision. It would be safer if you didn't—for both of us. Only . . ." she hesitated. "If you do it, it has to be soon. We don't have many more days before . . . before . . . gods." She lowered her head, and he thought he saw her tremble. "We'll be in their territory," she breathed. Her voice so soft that he could hardly hear it. "Soon."

"Cee. You'll be all right. I promise you." He put his arm around her—her flesh was cold, her skin so pale—and she cupped his nearer hand in hers and squeezed it. So much love in that simple gesture. So much support. He ached to know how to return such emotion. If he only had the skills of an adept, with which to Work a suitable response . . . he ached with longing, just thinking of it. The old dreams were taking hold of him again. The old recklessness. *Soon,* he promised himself. *Soon.* If the Fire freed him, then all the rules could change. For the better.

"Be careful, Senzei," she whispered.

In a party of four, only so many duty combinations were possible. With two of the company sleeping and two sharing watch at any given time—and at least three days' travel left before they reached Lema's western border—the odds were good that chance would favor Senzei, and give him the opportunity he required.

Or so he told himself. Because *waiting and hoping* was easier—and safer—than *doing.*

I don't want the power just for myself, he told himself, as the cold sweat of guilt kept him from sleeping. *I want to be able to help Ciani. I want to be able to do my share, like she said. And I could, if the Fire would free me.*

He wanted it so desperately. And feared it, with equal fervor. Most of all he wanted the decision to be out of his hands; wanted the dreadful balance of *need* versus *betrayal* to swing one way or the other without him, so that he might be spared such an awesome responsibility.

It's not betrayal. Not if I take what the Fire gives me and use it to help others. Is it?

Ciani, I need your counsel! But her warning had been a sound one: to speak of anything, in this company, was to risk being heard by all. And he couldn't afford that. Not if he meant to do it. Any of them would stop him. Any one of them. . . .

*Damien, I wish I could confide in you. I wish your faith would
allow it.*

On the second day, during the late afternoon shift, his chance came
at last. Hesseth and Ciani took the watch together, removing themselves to a nearby promontory from which they might view the surrounding area. Damien and Senzei were left to get what rest they
could ... but there was no question of Senzei sleeping. Long after
Damien had wrapped himself in blankets against the chill of the
afternoon, long after his husky snoring indicated that he, at least,
had found some respite, Senzei's pounding heart kept him awake,
and the rush of adrenaline through his body made him tremble with
need.

Now. Do it now.

Carefully, he pushed back his own blankets. Quietly, he dressed
himself. Thick shirt and jacket, worn leather boots. The weeks of
traveling had taken their toll on his wardrobe; nearly every layer was
patched or repaired in some place.

When he was done, he crept to where Damien lay and settled there,
watching him. The priest slept clothed, as always, and his sword was
laid out by his side. Ready for battle, even in slumber. Ready to
respond to the slightest disturbance with a lunge for that sharpened
steel, and—

Stop it!

A cold sweat filmed his forehead as he studied the sleeping form.
Would Ciani's Working take? Would it hold? How would he know
when—or if—it was happening? But even as he watched, a change in
the priest's demeanor became apparent. His eyes flickered rapidly
beneath closed lids, as if scanning some dreambound horizon. A soft
hiss escaped his lips, and his brow furrowed tightly. His hands began
to flex, like a sleeping animal's, and the muscles across his shoulders
tightened as if in preparation for combat. Whatever dream had him
in its thrall, he was wholly its creature.

Now. Do it.

Gently he folded the priest's blanket down to his waist, then
crouched back nervously to see if there was any response. None. With
trembling hands, then, he reached out to where the small leather
pouch was bound to the man's belt and somehow managed to slide
open its clasp. Damien groaned once, noisily, but the sound was clearly
in response to some dreamworld menace, not Senzei. Carefully, gently,
he slid the silver flask from its housing. Golden light warmed his hand,
made his skin tingle with anticipation. Even the few drops of moisture
still trapped in the crystal vial had that much power; how much more
was in his hands, in that precious pint of fluid?

Shaking, he managed to get the pouch closed again. It was important to leave things just as they should be, so that if Damien awoke too soon he wouldn't suspect what had happened. Would Ciani's Distracting work again so that Senzei could return the Fire to its housing? He didn't know; he should have asked. But that was the least of his concerns. By that time—gods willing—he would be an adept himself, capable of protecting his own secrets.

For a moment he simply sat there and cradled the silver flask in his hands; its warmth soothed his nerves, drove out the chill that had been part of him for longer than he cared to remember. If he had feared that the Fire might harm him, the touch of its light was utter reassurance. Like the sunlight that it mimicked, it had no power to harm an ordinary man; the force of its venom was directed at the nightborn, the demonic, creatures that shied away from the source of life even as they fed upon its bounty.

With care he crept from the camp. Gods alone knew what would happen to him when he took in the Fire, what form such a transformation of the soul might take; he didn't want to risk waking Damien and facing both his rage and the Fire at once. Hand closed tightly about the precious flask, he found his way through an insulating thicket of trees, and did not stop until he was safely out of sight of his companions' camp. Only then, safe in a tiny clearing, did he dare to unfold his fingers and regard the smooth polished metal, and the light that seemed to radiate even through its substance.

"Gods of Erna protect me," he whispered. And with shaking hands, he unstoppered the small container.

Light spilled out from it, a cloud of purest gold. Even in the brilliant sunlight it was visible, driving back the afternoon shadows that filled the tiny clearing and suffusing the air with clear, molten luminescence. For a moment he just stared at it, at its effect, drinking in the promise of its power. And fearing it. The hunger was so strong in him that he could barely hold his hand steady, and it was several minutes before he dared to pour out a few drops of the precious elixir. With utmost care, he gentled them into his palm. And raised his hand to his lips, that his body might drink and absorb that cleansing power.

I willingly accept change, in whatever form it comes. I willingly accept the destruction of everything I have been, in order to create what I must become.

He touched his tongue to the precious drops and shivered in fear and need as his flesh drew the moisture in. Heat surged through him, not the essence of the Fire yet, but something from a far more human source: a heat in his loins that made him stiffen with need, the hunger of his soul made manifest in his flesh. His heart pounded wildly as he swallowed the church-Worked water, its beat so loud in his ears that he couldn't have heard his companions if they'd called to him. For a moment, sheer anticipation surged through his veins— and with it a giddy ecstacy a thousand times more intense than sexual excitement, more intoxicating than a gram of pure cerebus. He nearly cried out from the force of it. Pure hunger, pure need, coursing through his veins like blood; he shook from the onslaught, embraced the pain of it, felt tears come to his eyes as the desperate need of an entire lifetime was coalesced in one burning instant.

Do whatever you want to me, he thought—to his gods, to the Fire, to whatever would listen. He felt tears coursing down his cheeks— and they were hot, like flame. *Whatever it takes. Whatever will change me.*

Please. . . .

The Fire was inside him now, and its sorcerous heat took root in his flesh. His muscles contracted in sudden pain as the burning lanced outward, heat stabbing into his flesh like white-hot knives. The pain pulsed hotter and hotter with each new heartbeat: the agony of sorcerous assault, of transformation. With effort he gritted his teeth and endured it, though his whole body shook with the effort. Tears burned his face like acid as they coursed from his eyes to his cheeks, and then dropped to the ground; he thought he heard them sizzling as they struck the grass, and the thick smell of dry leaves smoking filled his nostrils, crowding out all oxygen. Inside him, he could feel his heart laboring desperately to keep pace with the transformation, and its beat was a fevered drumroll inside his ears.

He had shut his eyes in the first onslaught of pain; now, somehow, he managed to open them. The trees about him had been stripped bare as if by fire, and he could see between their blackened trunks to the sun beyond, a thousand times more bright and more terrible than any mere sun should be. With one part of his mind he acknowledged how deadly it was to gaze upon that blazing sphere for more than an instant—but then he knew with utter certainty that it had changed, that *he* had changed, and that no mere light could harm him. And so he stared at it defiantly even as new pain racked his flesh; kept his vision fixed on it as his muscles spasmed erratically, pain overwhelming him in spurts of fire. The very woods about him seemed to be burning now, with a flame as pure and as white as that of the sun itself; he heard its roaring eclipse the sound of his racing pulse, felt the song of its burning invade the very marrow of his bones. The clearing he was in was surrounded by fire, and white flames licked at him, smoking his clothing, scalding his flesh. He fought the urge to flee, to scream, to try to unmake the bond that was transforming him. *Whatever it takes!* he repeated, as fresh pain speared through his flesh. Blood sizzled in his ears, his fingers, its red substance boiling within his flesh. *Whatever is required!* The whole sky was ablaze with light, the whole forest filled with fire— and he was a part of it, his flesh peeling back in blackened strips as he embraced the flames, his blood steaming thickly in the super-heated air. A sudden pain burst in his eyes and his vision was suddenly gone; thick fluid, hot as acid, poured down his cheeks.

It was then that he began to fear. Not as he had before, but with a new and terrible clarity. What if he didn't consume the Fire, but rather, *it* consumed *him?* What if its power was simply too vast, too untempered, for mere human flesh to contain it? He tried to move his body, but the roasted meat that his flesh had become would not respond. *Daylight can't hurt you,* Ciani had said—but it could, he realized suddenly, in enough quantity. It could burn, and dehydrate, and inspire killing cancers . . . he struggled to move again, to gain any sense of control over his flesh, but the precious nerves that connected thought to purpose had sizzled into impotence, and his body would not respond. Uncontrolled, his body spasmed helplessly on the dry, cracked earth. Flame roared skyward with a sound like an earth-quake—and then was suddenly silenced, as the mechanism that allowed him to hear split open and curled back in blackened tatters, releasing one last bit of moisture into the conflagration.

And somewhere, amidst his last fevered thoughts—somewhere in that storm of pain, that endless burning—the knowledge came to him. Not a knowing of his own devising, but one placed there: a last sharp bit of suffering to make the dying that much more painful, so that the creature who fed on it might be wholly sated. Knowledge: sharp, hot, and terrifying. Despair burned like acid inside him as he saw her approach—as he submitted to the vision that was placed in his brain, in the absence of true eyes to see it with.

Ciani. Cold, and dark against the fire. She came to his side and knelt there. Not concerned, not upset . . . only hungry. And he could feel the hot tongue of her hunger lapping at his suffering, as he slid down into the fevered blackness of utter despair.

The last thing he saw was her eyes. Backlit by fire.

Gleaming, faceted eyes. Insect eyes.

Ciani!

Damien scanned the sky anxiously. In the east the sun had already set, and the bloodstained bellies of the farthest clouds were the last vestige of a short but dramatic sunset. Soon the last of the stars would follow, leaving Domina's crescent alone in the heavens. Dark, it was nearly dark. So where the hell was he?

"There." Ciani pointed. "See?"

In the distance: white wings, gleaming like silver against the evening sky. Not for the first time, Damien wondered at the Hunter's choice of color; black seemed much more his style, both for its ominous overtones and its very real value as camouflage. Of course, it was always possible that he did it just to irritate the priest. That would be very much his style.

While the three of them waited anxiously, Tarrant circled twice above the camp, checking out the surrounding terrain before he landed. Damien wondered what he would find. Would his bird's-eye view give him some insight into what had happened, and make explanations unnecessary? Or would he come to ground as ignorant as they were, and thus dispel the last of their fevered hopes? Something in Damien's chest tightened as he watched. *He doesn't know what happened,* he told himself. *So if he doesn't see anything special in the currents, it might be because he doesn't know what to look for.*

The Hunter came to ground before them, wings curling so fluidly to brake his flight that the action seemed a ballet, a dance of triumph of one man's will over mere avian flesh. Then coldfire blossomed, consumed him; white features melted into flesh with practiced efficiency, a display that never ceased to awe. But this time Damien had other more important things on his mind, and the few minutes that it took for the Hunter's flesh to readopt its human form seemed a small eternity. At last, when the coldfire finally faded, he searched the Hunter's face anxiously, looking for some hint of what the man might have discovered. But the adept's expression was the same as always: cool, collected, a smooth stone mask meant to frustrate prying eyes. If he had seen anything useful, it couldn't be told from his face.

So he said the words, and made it official—the act, and the fact of their ignorance. "Senzei's gone."

The Hunter drew in a breath, sharply; he didn't like it any more than they did, though probably for other reasons. "Dead?"

Damien felt that bitter sense of helplessness rising in him again, which he had been fighting all afternoon. The frustration of total ignorance. The shame of forced inaction. "Missing. Sometime in the afternoon. He was in the camp with me, sleeping ... and when I awoke he was gone." He shook his head tightly. "No sign of why or where."

"Did you track him with the fae?"

Damien's face darkened in irritation. "Of course. And we found a trail leading to the edge of the forest. That ended there. Abruptly. As if—" He hesitated.

"Something had erased it," the Hunter supplied.

Damien felt something cold stir inside him, that was half fear and half anger. "Possibly."

"Did you search for him? Bodily?"

It was Ciani who spoke. "As much as we dared." Hearing the tremor in her voice, Damien took her hand and squeezed it. Her flesh was nearly as cold as his own. He explained, "It meant dividing the party so that one of us would be alone. Or leaving the camp unguarded. We didn't dare—"

"No," the Hunter said shortly. "Because if something had waylaid Mer Reese for the express purpose of rendering you vulnerable, you would be playing right into its hands." He glanced at the party's mounts—packed and dressed and ready to go—and at the campsite, already scrubbed clean of any sign of human habitation. "Did you find—"

"Nothing," Ciani whispered. She lowered her head. "No sign of him beyond that which led to the edge of the camp. No trail."

"We could hardly scour the woods at random," Damien said.

"You did exactly what you should have done, and—more important—you avoided doing those things which might have gotten you killed." The silver eyes fixed on Damien and seemed to bore into him. "To feel any guilt over the matter—"

"That's my business," the priest said harshly. "And if I want to feel lousy because a friend of mine might have been in danger—dying, possibly—while I had to sit here and twiddle my thumbs until night fell . . . you just stay out of it, all right? That's part of being human."

The breeze had shifted direction, bringing a gust of cold toward them from the east. Tarrant blinked a few times, as if something in the chill air had caught in his eyes. "As you wish," he said quietly. "As for the trail, or lack thereof . . ." He turned to the rakh-woman. "Did you search with them?"

Her lips parted slightly, displaying sharpened teeth. "I packed the camp," she told him.

"She hasn't tracked in the woods before," Damien said. "I asked. She wouldn't know the kind of sign—"

"Maybe not. But there are senses which atrophied in humankind that may still function among the rakh. And if our enemy doesn't yet know that a nonhuman travels with us, he might not have allowed for them."

"You mean, that a trail might still exist for her."

"Precisely. His attempts to obscure—"

He coughed suddenly, and brought his hand up to his mouth in unconscious reflex, to mask the rasping sound. Such behavior was so uncharacteristic for him that no one said anything, merely watched as he breathed once, heavily, as though testing the air. And then coughed again. When at last it seemed that the spasm had ended, he lowered his hand from his mouth and seemed about to speak. And then he looked down at his hand, and all speech left him. What little color he had faded into white—the hue of fragile vellum, of corpses. It made Damien's blood run cold.

"Gerald?" It was Ciani. "What is it?"

Silently he opened his hand, and turned it so they could see. Moonlight illuminated a smear of deep carmine. Blood. His.

"Something's very wrong," he whispered. He looked up, and out into the night. His manner reminded Damien of a hunting dog, testing the air for a scent of its prey. Or perhaps of a deer, seeking the smell of predators.

At last he turned to the priest. His eyes were bloodshot, their pupils shrunk to mere pinpoints. His face was flushed, as if from fever. Or sunburn?

In a voice that was tense, he asked, *"Where's the Fire?"*

It took Damien a moment to realize what he was asking, and why. When he did so, he reached to the pouch at his side and hefted it slightly in answer. But the weight that should have been in it wasn't. He fumbled with the catch, finally got the small pouch open. The crystal vial was still intact, and it glowed with reassuring light—but the silver flask, its companion, was gone.

Gone.

He looked up at the Hunter. The man had one hand raised, while the other was shielding his eyes. It was clear that he was Working— or trying to. His breathing was labored, and obviously painful. After a moment, the wind shifted direction. After several moments, it held.

The Hunter lowered his hand from before his eyes—they were red, a terrible red, like balls of congealed blood—and asked, in a hoarse whisper, "Is it possible that Mer Reese would betray you?"

"Never!" Ciani cried, and Damien muttered, "No. Not that."

"Are you sure?" He looked at each of them in turn, fixing them with his bloodshot gaze. "So very sure? What if our enemy offered him what he wanted most of all—an adept's vision, in return for one simple betrayal of trust? Wouldn't that tempt him?"

Damien shook his head—but something in him tightened, something cold and uncertain. "Tempt him, maybe. Seduce him, no. Not Senzei." His voice was firm, as if he was trying to convince not only Tarrant but himself. Was he? "Not like that."

Ciani offered, "He might have gone off alone if he thought there was something he could do that way, to help—"

"He didn't have that kind of courage," the Hunter said harshly.

"He had courage enough to put his life on the line for a friend," Damien said sharply. "That counts in my book."

"Can you find him?" Ciani asked. "Can you use the Fire?"

He turned his eyes on her; already the redness was receding, but he was still a terrible sight. "I can't, in any form, shape, or manner, *use the Fire*. But we do have a direction in which to search, now." He looked eastward, toward the source of the Fire-laden breeze. "With that, and Hesseth's senses, we may succeed in picking up his trail." He looked at the rakh-woman; she nodded. "Only one thing worries me—"

"That the wind was no accident," Damien supplied.

He looked at him sharply. "You felt that?"

Damien shook his head. "Call it good guesswork."

"There's the touch of a foreign hand on the weather patterns. Fleeting, evasive . . . and the Fire burns too brightly. I can't read its origin. But it's a good bet that someone—or something—wants us to go after him."

The priest walked to where his horse was tethered and patted it once on the neck. He removed the springbolt from its pack, and pulled back on it hard, to load. "Then we go armed," he said. "And we go damned carefully. Right?"

For once, they all agreed.

They found him in a small clearing perhaps a mile from the camp. Hesseth had picked out the smell of death and led them toward it, so they already knew what they might find. Nevertheless it was a shock to see him lying there—lifeless, so utterly, obviously lifeless— that for a moment no one could say anything, only stare at the corpse of their companion in terrible, mute silence, as the magnitude of the loss only slowly hit home.

Senzei was dead. And he had not died easily; that much was clear from the condition of his corpse. His mouth was open, as if in a scream. The eyes were wide, and rolled up into his head so that the pupils—mere pinpoints, hardly visible—lay at their upper edge, against the lid. Every muscle of his body was rigid, as if death had merely frozen him in his suffering; his muscles stood out like gnarled ropes along his neck, wrists, and face, giving his skin the striated texture of a mummy. His body was arched back in the manner of corpses left in the sun to dry, and his fingers were splayed apart in a grotesque mockery of a Working-sign.

"He died in terror," the Hunter told them. "Or perhaps, *of* terror."

Damien approached. Behind him, he heard the soft scrunch of grass as Ciani did the same. She went to the body. He went to the place some feet distant from it, where a single glint of silver in the moonlight hinted at an even more terrible loss.

It was there, lying on a bed of browning leaves. The silver flask, unstoppered. Open. Empty. There was still a faint shimmer about the ground where it had fallen, but the light was so dim compared to the Fire itself that it was clear the thirsty earth had drawn the water down, deep down, where no simple act of man might retrieve it. What little had remained for the air to claim had been carried to them on the wind, and was now dissipated. The Fire was gone.

He picked up the emptied container, and its metal was cold to the touch. Almost as cold as his flesh. Inside him was a bleak and terrible emptiness, as if all the accustomed warmth of his soul had deserted him. Sorrow took its place. And in its wake, shame.

He turned back to the body. Ciani was kneeling by its side, clasping Senzei's hand in hers as though somehow the contact could bring him back to life. But the emptiness in her eyes told a different story.

"He's gone," she whispered. Her voice, shaking, was barely audible. Her hands tightened about Senzei's. "I did . . . I can't . . ." She looked up at him; her eyes were wet with tears. "For me," she whispered. "He died because of *me.*"

"He did what he felt he had to." The words of comfort came automatically, dredged up from some distant storehouse of priestly wisdom. "That's all any of us can do, Cee. You can't blame yourself."

"The Fire's gone?" It was the Hunter.

He shut his eyes, felt the shame rising again. *Damn you, Tarrant. Damn you.* "Yes," he said quietly. "The Fire's gone." He looked at Ciani, felt a wetness on his cheeks to match her own. "We'll bury him," he said softly.

It was the Hunter who responded. "There's no soul here to do honor to—surely we all know that. To waste time administering to empty flesh—"

"Burial isn't for the dead." He looked up at Tarrant, found the man's eyes and skin already healing. He wondered if the wounds in his own soul would heal as fast. "It's for the living," he whispered. "Part of the healing."

"Even so, we can't—"

"*Hunter!*" He could feel the coldness come into his own gaze, like ice, could hear it in his voice. "You don't understand. You *can't* understand. That part of you's been dead for so long you couldn't remember it if you tried. And you don't want it back," he whispered hoarsely. "You willed it to die. All right. You succeeded. The living have their needs. You have yours. So just go, and leave us alone. Stand guard if you want—or go kill something if it makes you happy. Anything. Just *leave*. You have no place here."

Tarrant's expression was unreadable—and for once, Damien had no desire for insight. Then he turned, and with a swirl of his cloak disappeared into the deepening shadows. The depths of the forest hid him from sight.

A soft noise from Hesseth caused him to look in her direction. The rakh-woman had taken out a small shovel from among their camping supplies, and was offering it to him. Wordlessly, he took it. And began to dig.

And he prayed: *Forgive me, God. Forgive me, for my human weaknesses. Forgive me, for my failure to rise above the distractions of day-to-day life, and keep my spirit fixed on Your higher ideals. Forgive me, that in that moment of shock I forgot Your most important lesson: that a lost object might be replaced, a lost work recreated, a lost battle rejoined . . . but a human life, once lost, can never be restored. Forgive me, that I forgot that primal truth. Forgive me that when I came here my first thought was for the Fire—a mere object!— and not for the loss of a human life, or the sorrow of the living.*

He dug his blade deep into the chill earth, pressed onto it with a booted foot to drive it even deeper.

And help me to forgive myself, he pleaded.

Thirty-five

Gerald Tarrant thought: *It has to be here. Somewhere.*

Beneath his wings the vast expanse of the eastern divide rippled with the currents of fae pouring over rocks: brilliant blue earth-power, the rainbow flicker of tidal forces, strands of vibrant purple that licked forth from the deepest shadows as if testing the air for sunlight. To the east of him the sky was already lightening, midnight black and navy blue giving way to a sullen gray, first harbinger of the dawn. He should be in hiding by now. He should have found some place deep beneath the earth and already be settling himself into it. So that the powers that hid from sunlight might wrap him in their soothing chill, and renew his failing strength.

But not yet. Another few minutes, another few miles. It must be here, somewhere. . . .

In the east, slowly, deep gray gave way to a sickly green; he winced as the light burned his feathers but kept on flying. He had chosen a white form, and that should protect him for a while; nothing short of direct sunlight would make it past that reflective coat. Nevertheless, his eyes felt hot and tender, and his talons throbbed painfully in time with each wingbeat. Time to land, soon. Time to take shelter. How many minutes left till sunrise? He was cutting it damned close, that was certain.

Taking chances, Hunter! Not like you.

Hell. This whole damned trip isn't like you.

With careful eyes he scanned the ground beneath him, searching for . . . what? What shape would the Lost Ones' caverns take, that would be reflected in the currents above? What kind of sign would there be, and would he know how to read it? Most important of all—would he find such a sign before the sun's hateful light drove him underground once more, so that he might return to his companions with some measure of hope?

Damn them all, he thought darkly. And: *Damn the fate that brought me to this place.*

He would be hard put to say exactly what drove him to continue, as dawn's increasing light made each wingstroke harder to manage, each rational thought that much harder to muster. He had already found two caverns that would have been more than adequate shelter for the coming day, but had entered neither of them. Instead he had turned toward the north and begun to search for some sign of the Lost Ones, some gesture of hope that he might bring back to his grieving party. And even while he searched, it irritated him that he cared enough to bother. Cared enough to risk the pain of sunlight in service to their cause. That was dangerous. That was *human.* But the feeling was there, too strong to ignore. Not born of sympathy, however, but of anger.

My failure, he thought grimly, recalling Senzei's body. It wasn't the man's death that bothered him so much; that life was as valueless as any other, and in another place and time he might have snuffed it out himself, with no more passing thought than one gave to the squashing of an insect. No—what bothered him was simply the fact that he, Gerald Tarrant, had been *bested.* Tricked. His own Working had been turned against him, without him even sensing it. *That* burned him, more than Domina's light and the coming dawn combined.

You're going to die, my enemy, and not pleasantly. I promise you that.

He searched the land with an adept's eye, reading the currents that coursed beneath him. It was no hard task to locate mere caverns; the eddies that formed above them made them as visible as rocks in running water, and he easily assigned to each a location, size, and probable shape. But he was looking for something different this time. A smoother flow, perhaps, or staccato burst of turbulence; something that would indicate a cave-but-not-cave, an underground structure that rakh, not nature, had created.

And then, just as the sky turned a forbidding gold at its lower edge—just as he knew that he must take shelter immediately, with or without reaching his goal—he saw it. His attention fixed wholly on the ground ahead of him, he banked to a lower altitude. And studied the area closely. Yes. There.

A unique pattern of earth-fae marked the western slope of the mountain beneath him, a succession of whorls and eddies too uniform to be wholly natural. The ground above tunnels might look like that, if the tunnels were uniform enough. He looked about, saw other slopes with the same pattern; the whole area must be riddled with tunnels. He fought the urge to explore further and dropped down to the earth, seeking shelter. His muscles burned from the light of dawn; overhead, the stars of the Rim were already fading from sight. He searched the ground about him quickly, looking for some sign of the enemy's presence; there was none. At last, satisfied that he was safe—for the moment—he let the current take him. Let his flesh dissolve, so that no more than his faith remained to maintain the spark of his life. It was terrifying, never ceased to be terrifying, not in all the years he had practiced it. And it was made no easier by the rakhland's currents, which were barely strong enough to support a simple Working, much less one of such vital complexity. But one did what one had to, in the name of survival. There was no other option.

The changing drained him of the last of his strength, and because the humans weren't present he allowed himself to *be* drained, to take a precious second and indulge in the sheer exhaustion of it. He had been growing weaker nightly, forced to rely upon primitive rakh and sometimes even more primitive animals for his sustenance. If the fae had to come from within him instead of being garnered from without, he would have been forced to stop Working long ago. The humans had no idea how much this trip was draining him—and they damned well weren't going to find out, either. It wasn't that he was afraid, exactly. Certainly not of that brash, swaggering fool of a priest. It was more a question of . . . pride. Stubbornness. And of course, self-defense.

Fat lot of good that'll do you if you stay outside past dawn.

He searched for the patterns of earth-fae that would indicate some sort of entrance. This was where the tunnels began, so didn't it stand to reason that there was some kind of opening here? He searched for long minutes, using all his skill and all his strength, and at last he found it. Barely in time. Already the rising sun had cast its first blazing spears across the sky, to light up the western peaks in warning. Even that much reflected light was enough to burn him, and he felt his exposed skin redden and peel as he tore away the tangled brush that hid the entrance to the rakhene tunnels. Barely in time, he crept inside. And worked his way to where a large protruding rock cast shadows of true darkness beyond. There he rested, while dawn slowly claimed the valley he had just left, and the mouth of the tunnel behind him.

Playing it close, Hunter. He put a hand up to his face, felt a blister split beneath his fingertip. *Too damned close.* Ahead of him, cool darkness beckoned. Utter blackness, soothing and sweet; the healing power of total lightlessness. For the first time since he had overseen Ciani's possession, he felt something akin to optimism. And when some of his strength had returned to him—not all of it, by any means, but enough—he pushed himself away from the rock at his back and began to make his way into the lightless labyrinth.

Soon dark fae began to gather around his feet, humming with the power of the underearth. The song of it was a subtle symphony compared to the blazing cacophony of day, and he drank in the delicate harmonies with relish. Behind him the last notes of dawn crashed their way through fissures and passages, but the light—and the sound—could not penetrate this far. He breathed a sigh of relief, knowing himself safe at last. And penetrated further, into the Lost Ones' ancient lair.

The underground rakh had settled themselves in a system of interlinked caverns, altering the natural pattern only when necessary. The larger rooms were thus exactly as nature had carved them, vaulted cathedrals filled with the limestone residue of a million years of erosion. The tunnels connecting them, on the other hand, had clearly been enlarged, and chisel marks scoured the rock where ceiling and walls had been altered to allow for easy passage. There was no sign, anywhere, of recent occupancy. On the contrary, the one relic Tarrant found—a slender knife blade chipped from obsidian—was affixed to the floor by a thin film of limestone, that told of centuries passing since its deposition.

A good enough place to rest, at least. And I do need that. Sleeping in this secure a place would give him a chance to renew himself, and he needed that desperately. Time enough later to explore, when the darkness had healed his wounds.

Suddenly, there was a sound behind him. A faint whisper only, like the breath of silk against flesh. But it was enough. He had Seen that there was nothing alive in these caverns, would never have taken shelter here otherwise. So whatever might greet him here was not alive, neither human nor rakh—and therefore, it was likely to be dangerous. He braced himself to Work, took a precious second to bind the wild power to his will, then turned—

And froze. Only for an instant—but that was enough. His concentration shattered. The fae he had bound broke free of his will, and dispersed into the pool of its making. In that instant, that terrible instant, he knew just how much danger he was in, and he drew his sword in a last attempt to save himself; coldfire blazed forth from the Worked steel, filling the cavern with icy light.

And *she* stepped forward. Flawless in beauty, as she had been the day he'd killed her. Red-gold hair gathered about her shoulders like an aurora of light, warm skin and delicate blush defying the harsh illumination of the fae. Almea. . . . It couldn't be. It wasn't. The dead never returned once Death had claimed them; at best this was a Sending, mindless and soulless, that had taken on her face in order to gain access to him. Or a demon, with some even darker intent. He forced himself to move, to strike—but it was too late already, he saw that in her eyes. Even as he unfroze, she moved. Delicate hands turning, canting forward an object whose surface flashed purple and blue as it moved. A mirror. Even as he raised his sword it fell into position, caught hold of a slender beam that had filtered down somehow through a crack in the earth—

Sunlight. It struck him full in the face, hard enough to send him reeling back against the rock. He shut his eyes against the terrible pain of it, felt his hands spasm helplessly as they burned, his sword dropping noisily to the rock beneath his feet. The dark fae sizzled and smoked about him, the reek of its dying thick in his nostrils. He tried to move, to find some kind of shelter—anything!—but the beam of light followed him. He tried to Work, gritting his teeth against the pain of it—but the earth-fae was too weak here, or else he was simply incapable, the pain of it was making concentration impossible. . . .

He reached back with numbed hands to the rock beneath him, and closed his shaking fingers about the thick folds of his cloak. And raised it, so that the cloth might cover his eyes. At least he might have that much darkness. But even as he did so, the light was diverted upward. A prism hidden deep in a fissure caught the beam, and divided it. Mirrors set in the rock reflected it once—again—a thousand times—until the whole of the cavern was filled with it: a vast cacaphony of light, a symphony of burning. It wrapped about him like a web and speared through his skin at every unguarded point— pierced through the cloth itself and seared his flesh within, so that his muscles refused to obey him and he fell helplessly to the wet stone floor, unable to protect himself.

The lines of light connected, bent, became a terrible prison of pain that surrounded him on all sides. Gleaming mirrors reflecting the killing light of the sun down onto him, prisms dividing it into a thousand beams, a thousand colors, each one a separate note of agony, a separate flame in his flesh. Slowly, his struggles subsided. His body, incapacitated by the light, refused to respond to him; only his will remained, trapped within it like a caged animal. But even that was being drained of strength. The light was like a massive jewel, and he was in its center; there was no escape. Slowly darkness came to him—hot darkness, desolate of comfort—and the brimstone scent that lurked behind it was almost enough to start him struggling again. Almost. But the sun had burned him dry of life, and nothing remained but fear. Pain. And the absolute certainty of what awaited him, on the other side of death.

The last thing he heard was his dead wife's laughter.

Thirty-six

"He's not coming back."

For a moment, silence. Only the words, hanging in the air between them like a knife. Sharp and chill. Even in his absence the Hunter had that kind of power.

Ciani wrapped her arms around herself and shivered. "Or he'd be here by now," she whispered. She stared out into the night as if daring it to contradict her. Her voice was shaking. "He's not coming back, Damien."

The priest bit back at least a dozen reponses—sharp answers, empty optimisms, they were unworthy of her. Something cold was uncoiling inside him. Dread? Fear? He fought it back with effort, tried to keep the sound of it out of his voice. "Something must have happened," he agreed. He forced his tone to remain even, unimpassioned. Now, most of all, they needed his strength. Now, most of all, *she* needed him.

Dusk. Twilight. Nightfall. They had waited through it all, the various stages of evening, and had received no word or sign from the Hunter that might explain his absence. How long did one wait, before finally giving up hope? Before admitting that the enemy's *divide and conquer* policy seemed perfectly capable of taking on a single man and destroying him? Even such a man as Tarrant was. Preternaturally fae-fluent. Utterly cautious. If the enemy could take on someone like that, what hope did that leave for the rest of them?

He was trying not to think about that. And failing, miserably.

"What now?" Ciani whispered. "What do we do now, Damien?"

He forced his voice to be calm, though the rest of him was anything but. "We go on," he said quietly. He reached out to touch her, gently—and then took her into his arms. He felt her soften, as if her flesh was a hard clay warmed by the heat of human contact. Slowly the stiffness of her fear gave way to the weakness of utter desolation, and finally exhaustion. Her face buried in the thick wool of his jacket, she wept. Gave way to the pressure of the last few weeks at last and let it all pour out, all the terror and the hope and the striving and the loss. *Too much,* he thought, as he tightened his arms around her. *Too much for anyone.* He could feel the tears building inside himself, tears of frustration and rage, but fought them back; she needed him now, too much for him to let go. First Senzei's death. Then the loss of the Fire. Now ... this. His thoughts were a jumble, fear and mourning and hatred and dread all tangled up so thoroughly that it was impossible for him to isolate any one emotion, to analyze its source. Which was just as well. Some things didn't stand close inspection.

"We go on," he repeated.

"Can we?" She drew her head back and looked at him. Her eyes were bloodshot, red-rimmed from lack of sleep. It struck him suddenly how very fragile she looked—not like Ciani at all. When had her strength given way to this? Or was that only a trick of his mind, that insisted on seeing her vulnerability plastered across her face? "If they could get to Gerald—" she began.

"That means nothing," he said firmly. Keeping the doubt carefully out of his voice. He had to sound confident for her sake. "Tarrant was vulnerable," he told her. "Powerful, yes, and manipulative, ruthless ... but fatally flawed, in the Working that sustained his flesh. Remember what the Fire did to him, even from a distance? All our enemy would have had to do was keep him from finding shelter before daylight and he would be finished. That simple. It wouldn't even require a direct confrontation." He drew in a breath, sharply. "*If* he knew how to do that." How did one entrap the Hunter? It frightened him more than anything that their enemy had figured out how.

"He should have stayed with us. We could have protected him."

"Yes. Well." He drew in a slow breath, tried to calm his own shaking nerves. "There wasn't much likelihood of that, was there? He trusted me only slightly less than I trusted him. And now we're both paying the price for it."

Him more than me. A thousand times more. What kind of hell awaits a man like that? He tried to imagine it, and shivered. *I wouldn't wish that on any man. Not even him.*

"What now?" the rakh-woman asked. "What plans, without the killer?"

He turned to face her. In the light of Prima's crescent she looked particularly fierce, blue-white light glinting off her teeth like sparks of coldfire. His stomach tightened, to think of that power lost. That deadly potential.

"We wait out the night," he told her. "Let him have that much time before we give up on him for good. If by morning he hasn't come ... then we make other plans." *Plans that don't include him or the Fire. Or Senzei.* He tried not to let his face betray his misgivings. *Too much. Too quickly. How does one compensate for something like this?*

He pulled his sword from its sheath, felt its leather grip warm to the touch of his hand. Already there were shadows gathering about the edges of their camp that were more than mere darkness: bits of the night given independent will—and hunger—by the party's misgivings. How solid would such things become in the rakhlands' inferior currents? How many such creatures would come to hover about the camp, thirsting for a taste of the human minds that had helped birth them? Ever since Tarrant had joined the company in Kale his presence had driven off such threats, in a manner they had come to take for granted. Now, how many of their own fears would Damien have to kill—or at least frustrate—before the light of dawn scoured the landscape clean of such monstrosities?

Damn you, Tarrant, he thought grimly, as he hefted his sword. *You picked a lousy time to die.*

Maps. Spread out in the sunlight, dappled leaf-shadows mottling their surface like lichen. The breeze stirred and their edges lifted, struggling against stone paperweights.

"These are all we have left," Damien said grimly.

"Not the survey map."

"No. He must have had that on him when ... whatever." It was safest not to speak of what had happened. Speaking led to questioning, which led to wanting to Know. And Knowing was dangerous. Whatever force had bested Tarrant might be waiting for them to establish just such a channel, in order to take them all. They dared not risk it. Not even to lessen the sting of ignorance.

"I've copied the important information, so we can each have a copy. In case we get separated." He saw the fear coalescing in Ciani's eyes, reached out to squeeze her hand in reassurance. Her flesh was cold, her eyes red. Her face was dry with exhaustion; had she slept at all since Senzei's death? It bothered him that he didn't know.

"We have to plan for it," he told her, gently. "We have to plan for everything. I don't like that any more than you do, but it's suicide to do otherwise. The enemy's strategy is clear: pick us off one by one, before we can get to his stronghold." *Leaving only the one he wants,* he thought. *You.* But he didn't say that. "God alone knows how he got to Tarrant, but with Senzei we can venture a guess. And when you've got an enemy that can play on your weaknesses like that ... we've got to be prepared, Cee. For anything."

"Do you still think there's hope?" Her voice was a whisper, utterly desolate. "Even after all this?"

He met her eyes, and held them. Tried to will strength into his gaze, that she might draw on it for courage. "Very little," he admitted. He wished he had the heart to lie to her. "But that's as much as there ever was, on this trip. As for our chances now ... remember, we planned this journey before we even met Tarrant. We'll manage without him."

"And Zen?" she asked softly. "And the Fire?"

He looked away. Forced his voice to be steady. "Yes. Well. We'll have to, won't we?"

He pulled the nearest map toward him and studied it, hoping she would do the same. Hesseth was silent, but her alien eyes followed his every movement. Carefully, he circled a few vital landmarks. Sansha Crater. Northern Lema's focus of power. The trigger-point that Tarrant had Worked, so that when they reached it their duplicates—their simulacra—would begin the hazardous journey into ambush. The taste of that plan was bitter, but there was no stopping it now. And part of him was grateful. God knows, they needed a good Obscuring now. More than ever. He hated himself for feeling such gratitude.

Damn you, Hunter. Even in your death you haunt me.

"According to this, we've reached the point Tarrant meant us to." He looked eastward—as though somehow mere vision could pierce through rock and span the miles, so that he might see that doomed quintet of doppelgangers. Quartet? Trio? How many? "Which means that even now the simulacra are setting out, to take our place."

"So the enemy will focus his attention on them."

"We can only hope so."

He said it would be automatic. Said that when we reached this point, five rakh would depart for the Crater, wearing our forms. But we're no longer five ourselves. Did he allow for that possibility? He

*was a thorough man, who anticipated so much ... but would he
ever make allowance for his own death?*

He couldn't imagine Tarrant doing that. And if not, then the whole
scheme was wasted: five innocent rakh were marching toward death
for no purpose. Because the minute their enemy saw that the numbers didn't match, he would know that something was wrong. The
thought of it made Damien sick inside—and he tried not to think
about whether it was the death of five innocents that bothered him
most of all, or the failure of Tarrant's deception.

Carefully, he folded the maps. "We go north," he said. "Toward
the House of Storms. And we try to make contact with the Lost
Ones. If we're lucky—and Tarrant's Working is a good one—we won't
be watched on the way."

"And if not?" the rakh-woman asked.

He looked at her. And cursed the alien nature of her face, which
made it impossible to read. "You tell me."

"Can you back it up?" Ciani asked. "Do an Obscuring independent
of Tarrant's, in case the simulacra ..." She hesitated.

"Don't work?" he said gently.

She nodded.

"That would be very dangerous," he said. Not meeting her eyes.
"There was a ... a channel, between the Hunter and myself." *Don't
ask me about it,* he begged silently. *Don't ask me to explain.* "If I
were to attempt such a Working, while the fragments of his own still
clung to the party ... I could very well open up a clear channel
between ourselves and the force that killed him." *And anything that
could take on the Hunter could probably destroy us without pausing
for breath.*

"So all we have is what he did," she said quietly. Eyes downcast;
voice trembling slightly.

"Maybe."

She looked up at him.

"*I* can't do it. And neither can you. But that leaves one other person." He looked at Hesseth meaningfully. "And I think she might
have exactly the skill we need."

The *khrast*-woman's lips parted slightly; a soft hiss escaped
between the sharp teeth. "I don't do human sorcery."

"But it wouldn't be human sorcery, would it? And it wouldn't
involve the kind of fae that humans could manipulate. Would it?"

"The rakh don't Work," she said coldly.

"Don't they?" He turned back to Ciani. "Let me tell you something
I discovered about the rakh. I was going through Zen's notes last
night, you see, and I found a bit of early text he'd dredged up some-

where and copied. About the rakh's ancestors. They were true carnivores, it seems. Unlike our own omnivorous ancestors, they were utterly dependent upon hunting for their foodstuffs. No agriculture for them, or the complex social interaction that farming inspires." He glanced at the rakh-woman. "They were pack animals. As we were. But with a markedly different social structure. The males spent their lives in competition with each other, expending most of their energy in sexual display and combat. When they hunted they did so in large groups, and only went after dangerous game. The risk seemed to be much more important than the food, and their social hierarchy was reshuffled—or reinforced—with each hunt. What they killed they ate on the spot, or left to rot."

"Sounds like some men I know," Ciani said, and Damien thought he saw something that might be a smile flit across Hesseth's face. Briefly. Then it was gone again, replaced by guarded hostility.

"The females hunted for the rest of the pack," he explained. "And fed them, in accordance with the local hierarchy. Dominant males first, then children, then themselves. With scraps for the lesser males, if any remained. Mammalian social order at its finest."

He leaned forward tensely. "Do you see it? *The females did the hunting.* Not for show, but for sustenance. Not to display their animal machismo, but to feed their young. And the fae would have responded to their need, as it does with all native species. And what two skills does that kind of hunter need the most? Location and obscuring. The ability to find one's prey, and the capacity to sneak up on it unobserved." He looked to the rakh-woman, met her eyes. There was challenge in his tone. "If a rakh female were to Work the fae, wouldn't those be the two areas in which her skills would be strongest? The two very skills we need so desperately right now."

The *khrast*-woman's voice was quiet but tense. "The rakh don't Work."

"Not like we do. Not with keys, pictures and phrases and all the other hardware of the imagination. They don't need that, any more than a human adept does." He paused, watching her. "But it isn't wholly unconscious anymore. Is it? Somewhere along the line your people ceased to take the fae for granted and began to manipulate it. Improved intellect demands improved control. Maybe on a day-to-day basis the old ways were enough . . . but I know what I saw in Morgot," he told her. "And that was deliberate, precise, and damned powerful. A true Working, in every sense of the word." When she said nothing he pressed, "Do you deny it?"

"No," she said quietly. "As you define your terms . . . no."

"Hesseth." It was Ciani. "If you could work an Obscuring—"

Her eyes narrowed. "That's a sorceror's concept, I can't—"

"Call it whatever you like," Damien interrupted. "We'll find a rakhene word for it, if that makes you happy. Or make one up. Damn it, can't you see how much is riding on this?" *Careful, Damien. Calm down. Don't alienate her.* He forced himself to draw in a deep breath, slowly. "Tarrant's gone," he said quietly. "So's Senzei. Even if I could Work this myself, my skills in this area are limited; sneaking up on enemies isn't a regular part of Church service. Whatever cover the Hunter Worked for us is going to fade away now that he's dead—if our enemy doesn't Banish it outright."

"*Could* you help us?" Ciani asked her. "If you wanted to? Could you keep the enemy from finding us?"

She looked them over, one after the other. Reviewing her natural hostility to their kind, perhaps, and seeing how far it would give.

She picked her words carefully. "If you were my kin," she told them. "My blood-kin. Then I could protect you."

"Not otherwise?"

She shook her head. "No."

"Would you, if you could?" Damien challenged her.

She looked at him. *Into* him: past the surface, past his social conscience, into the heart of his soul. The animal part of him, primitive and pure. Something unfamiliar licked at his consciousness, warm and curious. Tidal fae?

"Yes," she said at last. "If that comforts you. But you're not my blood-kin. You're not even rakh. The fae that answers to me wouldn't even acknowledge your existence."

"Then force it to," Damien told her.

She shook her head. "Not possible."

"Why?"

"The tidal fae never has—"

"—and never will? I don't buy that kind of reasoning." He leaned forward, hands tense on his knees. "Listen to me. I know what the rakh were, when humans first came here. I understand that those animal roots are still a part of you. *Have* to be a part of you. But you're also an intelligent, self-aware being. You can override those instincts."

"Like the humans do?"

"Yes. Like the humans do. How else do you think we got here, ten thousand light-years from our native planet? Of all the species of Earth, we alone learned to override our animal instinct. Oh, it wasn't easy, and it isn't always reliable. I don't have to tell you what a jerry-rigged mess the human brain is, as a result. But if there's any one definition of humanity, that's it: the triumph of intelligence over an animal heritage. And you inherited our intellect! Your people could be everything to this planet that we were to ours. All you have to do is learn to cast off the limitations of a more primitive time—

"And look where that got you!" she said scornfully. "Is this supposed to be our goal? To have our souls divided, with each part pulling in a different direction? Like yours? Vampires don't haunt *us* in the night; ghosts don't disturb *our* sleep. Those things are humanity's creation—the echoes of that part of you which you've buried. Denied. The 'animal instinct' which screams for freedom, locked in the lightless depths of your unconscious mind." She shook her head; there was pity in her eyes. "We live at peace with this world and with ourselves. You don't. That's *our* definition of humanity."

She stood. The motion was smooth and unhuman, silken as a cat's. "I'll do what I can—on my own terms. *Rakh* terms. And if the fae will respond to me . . . then I guarantee you, no human sorceror will read through it."

"And if it doesn't?" he asked quietly.

She looked northward, towards the point of power still far in the distance. Observing the currents? Or imagining the House of Storms, and its human master?

"Then your own Workings had better be good," she said. "Damned good. Or we'll be walking right into his hands."

Thirty-seven

Power. Hot power, rising up from the foundations of the earth. Sweet power, filtered through the terror of an adept's soul. Raw power, that reverberated with pain and fear and priceless agony of utter helplessness. The taste of it was ecstacy. Almost beyond bearing.

The demon asked: "It pleases?"

"Oh, yes." A whisper of delight, borne on the winds of pain. That delicious pain. "Will it last, Calesta? Can you make it last?"

The faceted eyes blinked slowly; in the dim lamplight they looked like blood. "A thousand times longer than any other." His voice was the screech of metal on glass, the slow scraping of a rust-edged knife against a window. "His fear and the pain are perfectly balanced. The earth itself supplies the fuel. It could last . . . indefinitely."

"And he'll cling to life."

"He's terrified of death."

"Ah." A deep breath, drawn in slowly and savored. "How marvelous. You do know how to please, Calesta."

"The pleasure is mine," the demon hissed.

"Yes. I'm sure it is." A low chuckle, half humor and half lust, sounded from the Master's lips. As raw power lapped against the smooth stone walls, staining them with blood-colored fae. The color of pain. The color of delight.

"See that you have something equally suitable arranged for when *she* gets here."

Thirty-eight

Snow. It wasn't unexpected—Hesseth had smelled it coming, and even Damien had made note of the ominous color of the sky that morning—but that was little consolation. The last thing they needed now was for winter to begin in earnest. Damien cursed himself for failing to anticipate such weather, even as he beat the powdery white stuff from his jacket. He should have checked for it regularly. Weather was hard to predict, but not impossible—general trends betrayed themselves some days in advance—and he could have turned this choice bit of misery into something else, if only he had Seen it coming. A little push to the wind pattern there, perhaps a little shove to the jet stream . . . there were a dozen and one ways in which the weather might be Worked, but all of them involved advance planning. And Damien had been too wrapped up in other things to remember that a good winter storm might lay ruin to all their plans.

The snow deepened to ankle height, gusted in billowy dunes to the level of their mounts' knees, caught in their collars and their boot-cuffs and trickled down inside their clothing as ice-cold water. Still they pressed onward, making what progress they could. They couldn't afford to slow down, not now. Once or twice the snow turned to hail, or hail mixed with freezing rain, and they were forced to stop. Battered, disheartened, they took what shelter they could find and waited for the downpour to lessen. And began moving again as soon as they could, anxious to make up for lost time.

He wondered, in those cold times of waiting, if their enemy might not have sent the storm. Certainly it seemed the perfect tool for his purposes, in that it struck at both their strength and their spirit. And there was damned little Damien could do about it, either way. Oh, he tried. But weather-Working had never been his forte, and trying to alter a storm once it had actually begun was a task that would have given an adept nightmares. The best he could do was to Know it carefully, which allowed him to reassure his party that the worst of it had in fact passed them by; the flatlands east of the mountains had received a tempest ten times worse. But as cold, dark days gave way to icy nights, that was little consolation.

Tarrant could have shifted it away from us, he thought. *Tarrant would have seen it coming, and known what to do.* Bitterly he tried to drive such thoughts from his head, but they kept returning. It bothered him that he had any positive feelings about the Hunter, even so vague a one as that. Whatever worth the man had once possessed had become buried beneath so many centuries of corruption and cruelty that the resulting creature was more demon than man, and hardly a suitable subject for admiration. Especially for one of Damien's calling.

But he was of my calling, too. A founder of my faith. How do you reconcile those two identities?

They traveled in somber silence, their passage soundless but for the crunching of fresh snow and ice beneath their animals' hooves. The xandu were growing restless, in a way that made Damien uneasy. Apparently it bothered Hesseth, too, for when they finally made camp she tethered the animals as though they were horses, so that they might not wander off. Over dinner she explained that the mountain snows of the Worldsend often triggered a migration instinct in the beasts, driving them to lower ground. Perhaps they were responding to that ingrained mandate. All night Damien could hear the xandu struggling against the pull of the leather leashes, snorting in indignation at their bondage. When it came his turn to sleep, he tried to shut out both the noise and the cold with a thick cocoon of blankets, but he was unsuccessful. The best he could manage was a restless half-slumber that refreshed his body but did little for his nerves.

Through calf-deep snow they resumed their travels in the morning. The clouds parted just long enough to confirm that the sun had risen, then closed overhead and plunged them into a timeless dusk of cold, white flurries alternating with sleet. Once Damien's horse slipped and nearly fell, while precariously close to the edge of a sheer drop— but it managed to stay on its feet somehow and edged past the dangerous spot.

I feel like a jinxer, the priest thought. *Like some poor fool who Works the earth-fae without even knowing it—only it does the exact opposite of what he wants. Isn't this how it works with that kind?*

You just manage to figure how bad things really are, and just then another disaster crops up.

Would it be possible to use that as a Cursing? To take a mind that affected the currents naturally, and warp it so that its effect was negative? After several hours' contemplation—and a cold lunch, eaten hurriedly beneath the half-shelter of a rocky overhang—he decided that it would be impossible. There were too many variables to account for; too much was still unknown about the relationship of brain and fae. If you tried to Work a system like that, the whole thing would come crashing down around your ears. Only nature could alter biology on that scale and get it right.

But then he remembered the trees of the Forest—a whole ecosystem, redesigned to suit its human master—and he shivered, thinking of the kind of man it took to Work that. And what manner of sacrifice he had made, to conjure that kind of power.

A man who could Work the Forest could do it. A man like that could do anything, Then: *Anything except save himself,* he added grimly. And he tightened his knees about his horse's cold flanks, and tried not to think about how much this weather—cold and lightless— would have pleased the Hunter.

He's dead. And you wanted him dead. So forget him. But the memory of the man hung about him like a ghost. Was that because of the channel that had been established between them? Or simply the force of the man's personality? It was impossible to say. But sometimes when he looked at Ciani he saw the ghost there, too—a fleeting image, in the back of her eyes. What had gone on between the two of them, in the Hunter's last days? Damien hungered to know—and didn't dare ask. It was dangerous to pose questions, when you weren't sure you could handle the answers.

All day, the snow continued to fall. They rode. And somewhere in the distance, an unknown number of unknown rakh hiked northward, snow blinding them to the sight of their destination. Five of them, or perhaps three. Wearing alien faces, marching to an alien purpose. Struggling their way through this very storm. To their deaths.

Or—Damien thought suddenly—had that Working dispersed when its maker died? That was a frightening thought. What if the simulacra had never started out in the first place? What if, now that Tarrant was dead, the party had no cover at all?

Then we must depend on Hesseth's skill, he thought. And he looked at the rakh-woman, and wondered just how strong her power was. And how willing she would be to harness it to their need if all other defenses failed them.

Fire. Brilliant, like sunlight: white-hot, molten, filling the air with a blazing heat. Senzei's face, like wax: melting, sizzling, running down into the grass like Fire, sucked down into the soil. Flesh running free like water, blood and bones dissolving into liquid fire, essence burning, dissolving . . . transforming. Until the hair is Core-golden, soft strands tangling in the thermal gusts. Until the eyes are silver-white, hot as metal freshly poured into a wound. Until the mouth is solid enough to voice a scream—and it screams, and the screams resound along with the roar of the flames, across the burning heavens, and as far beneath as the gates of hell and beyond.

The Hunter's face.

The Hunter's eyes.

The Hunter's screams. . . .

He awoke. Suddenly. Not because of the dream. He was too exhausted for a mere nightmare to awaken him, too in need of the sleep that had been shattered. Besides, he'd seen those images before. Never in that form, never with such terrible clarity . . . but ever since Tarrant's disappearance he had been envisioning fire, both waking and sleeping. Had dreamed of Tarrant, in fire. Ciani had also. He'd had to reassure her that such dreams were only natural, given their recent experiences. Her dreaming brain was combining the elements of Senzei's and Tarrant's deaths, fusing the two disasters into a single, gut-wrenching nightmare. It was frightening, but only that. Not meaningful, he assured her. It couldn't possibly be meaningful.

Could it?

Carefully, he freed himself from his blankets. More than anything else he hated this weather because of the vulnerability it fostered. The tight cocoon of blankets which he needed to combat the cold was the last thing he wanted to be trapped inside if danger came calling. Even fully clothed it was bad enough—and he knew damned well that if he *really* wanted to be warm he should be naked inside that cocoon, his body heat warming the blankets and the air inside it rather than lost to his clothing. But that was where he drew the line. He'd once had to fight off a pack of ghouls in below-zero weather with nothing on but a pair of socks, and it wasn't an experience he was anxious to repeat.

He looked about the campsite, quickly took in details: Ciani, curled tight in uneasy slumber; Hesseth crouching by the campfire, springbolt in claw; the mounts half-asleep, restless. Nothing else amiss—or at least, nothing that was immediately obvious. Thank God, the snow had stopped at last.

He came to where Hesseth was and crouched down beside her. But the position which came so naturally to her rakhene form was painful for his cold-stiffened limbs, and after a moment he simply sat.

"How goes it?" he asked quietly.

She nodded toward where their mounts were tethered. "The horses are starting to get edgy now."

"And the xandu?"

She shook her head. "Increasingly restless. There's obviously something here they're responding to . . . but damned if I know what it is."

"Scent of a predator, perhaps? If something were following us—"

"I'd smell that," she reminded him.

He drew in a sharp breath. "Of course. That was . . . human of me." He managed a halfhearted grin. "Sorry."

She shrugged.

He looked out into the night, wondered what unseen dangers the darkness was obscuring. As he had done each night since Tarrant's death—and each day, and morning and evening besides—he Worked his sight and studied the currents. They were harder than ever to see now, faint blue veins of shadowy light barely bright enough to shine through the blanket of snow that covered them. But after a few minutes he was able to focus on them and discern their current state. Which was just what it had been yesterday, and the day before, and probably countless days before that as well. Weaker than earth-fae should be here. Weaker than earth-fae should be in any mountain range.

It's as if there was no seismic activity here, he thought. *None at all.* But that simply wasn't possible. Even on Earth the mountains weren't *that* quiescent. Or so logic dictated. Certainly the colonists had been familiar enough with the nature of seismic disruptions to scan for such activity when they arrived—which said that they understood the nature of that particular danger, because they had experience in dealing with it.

Weak currents. Inexplicably stable terrain. A nest of demons. And a human adept who had settled himself right at the juncture of three crustal plates, heedless of the risk which that entailed. How did those elements fit together? It seemed to Damien that if he could only determine how they were interlinked, he could find the answers they so desperately needed. But the more he studied the puzzle, the more it seemed as if there was a vital piece missing. One single fact, which might make the whole pattern fall into place.

If we knew how they trapped Tarrant we might understand them better. We might understand them enough.

With effort he forced himself away from that train of thought and turned his attention back to his companion. Animal-alert, she was scanning the brush around their camp for any sign of movement.

"How's your Working?" he asked her.

She shrugged. "As humans would say, I *Called*. Last night, when the moons passed overhead and the tidal power was strong. If the Lost Ones are anywhere within hearing, they'll come to us—or we'll go to them. Either way, we'll meet." She shook her head slowly, as her eyes scanned the white-shrouded land encircling their camp. "There's no saying how, of course. Or when."

"Or if?"

Again she shrugged.

"Is that how Zen called you to us?"

"Very similar. In my case I read his message directly, and decided to respond to it. But the result is much the same. If this attempt succeeds, my call will fix on a Lost One whose path might cross our own—if such is available—and the currents will shift in response, to maximize the odds of our meeting. If the Lost One is conscious of the currents she may be aware of that process. I was. If not . . ." She raised her hands, palms open, suggestively.

"You say *she*."

The corner of her mouth twisted upward in a slight smile. "They are rakh," she pointed out. "If they have anything similar to a Worker, it will be a female. Our men generally lack the . . . time for such pursuits."

"And the interest?"

"Their interests are quite limited," she agreed. She looked him over, top to bottom; it was an appraising glance, clearly meant to assess the features of his manhood. "But they do have their uses," she told him finally.

"It's nice to be good for something," he said dryly.

"I meant *rakh* men," she corrected. "Who knows what humans are good for?"

She stood, in one fluid movement that belied the discomfort of her previous posture. And threw the springbolt to him so that he caught it in his lap.

"Your turn to stand guard," she told him. "I'm going to try to get some sleep."

Then she looked over to where their mounts were tethered, and her whole body suddenly tensed. Eyes narrowed, her attention focused on ... what? What special signs were visible to her rakhene senses, that went unnoticed by his human sight?

"Watch the xandu," she said quietly. "If anything happens ... it seems to be focusing on them. Watch them carefully."

"What is it?"

"I don't know," she whispered. "But I don't like the feel of it." She shook her head slowly. "I don't like the feel of it at all."

Nightmares. Of Tarrant and conflagration, and the two combined. Of pain, bright and molten, that shot through the brain like burning spears. And fear—so primal, so intense, that they shook from the force of it long after their bodies had awakened, their minds still vibrating with otherworld terror.

Nightmares. Identical. Every time he and Ciani shut their eyes, every time they tried to rest. The same dreams for both of them. But *only* for both of them. Neither their rakhene guide nor the animals were bothered. It seemed that only humans could dream such dreams ... or perhaps, only those who had established a blood-link with the Hunter.

And it was Ciani who first voiced the fear. Or was it a hope?

"I don't think he's dead," she whispered.

Riding. Endless miles of snow-shrouded earth. And questions that needed to be asked, no matter how painful the answers might be.

"What happened between you two?" he asked Ciani. He spoke softly, but even he could hear the strain in his voice. How could he keep his tone light when his spirit was anything but?

The ice underfoot crunched beneath the horses' hooves, broke beneath the xandu's toenails. It made for a complex rhythm, not unpleasing.

"You really want to know?" she asked him.

"I think I should."

White ground, snow-shrouded trees. The creaking, tinkling sound of limbs overburdened with ice. Periodically a bough would crack loose and fall to the path before them, scattering snow in its wake.

The worst of the storm had passed to the east of the mountains, but it would be long before the destruction truly ended.

"He apprenticed me," she said quietly.

He felt something tight and cold coiling inside him, forced it to loosen its death-grip on his heart. *She was desperate for sorcery, in any form. It would have been worth the price. . . .*

"Anything else?" he asked stiffly.

And she answered gently: "Isn't that enough?"

There was no more intimate link in the world than that. A true apprenticeship would color one's development for the rest of one's life—long after the training period itself ended. Even if her memory was returned to her now, all her Workings would bear the Hunter's mark. His taint.

The woman I loved will never come back now. Even if her memories are restored to her, she'll be . . . different. Darker. That taint will always be there.

And the part that hurt most was not that it had happened. It was knowing that she didn't care—knowing that the very aspects of the Hunter which made him so abhorrent to Damien were little more than items of curiosity to her. Never before had the gap between them seemed so wide, so utterly impassable. Never before had he so clearly understood its nature.

"And you?" she asked him. "What was there between the two of you?"

He shut his eyes and told her, "I bled for him."

Even now, I bleed.

It was Hesseth's warning cry that woke him up. He came to with the reflexes born of a decade of living with danger—fully awake, fully armed, and half free of the blankets that bound him before he even paused to take in his surroundings. Domina's light filled the camp, which meant it was near midnight; the full orb of Erna's largest moon made it easy to locate the source of the disturbance, to see—

The xandu. They seemed to have gone mad, were striking out at everything in their vicinity. Pale manes flying, sharp horn tips stained with blood. He could see where one of the horses had gone down, and the other was straining at its tethers, trying to get as far away from the maddened animals as possible. The fallen horse was lying still, and blood pooled thickly about its chest; nevertheless the nearer

xandu impaled it once—twice—again with its horns, as if maddened
by its refusal to fight back.

Hesseth was drawing near the creatures, as if intending to calm
them. "Stay back!" he ordered. The maddened squealing of the animals made it hard for him to make himself heard. "Back!" She glared
at him but at last gave ground, springbolt braced against her shoulder.
As he approached the horses, she scanned the surrounding woods
quickly for danger. A good move. The screams of the animals were
deafening; anything that hadn't known they were in this part of the
mountains sure as hell knew it now.

His practiced eye picked out details of the fight, and he struggled
to make some sense of it. The horses seemed terrified, but no more
than was reasonable under the circumstances; any attempt on their
part to break free seemed to be survival-motivated. And it seemed that
one of the xandu—the louder one—was fighting to defend its flesh,
rather than struggling for freedom. That left only one out of four to be
causing the trouble, and with only three riders to be carried—

He swung his sword in a powerful moulinet, stepping in quickly
on the downstroke. Gleaming horns passed within inches of his chest
even as the steel blade struck leather and parted it, and he jumped
back quickly. The xandu reared back in rage, as if intending to crush
him—but when it realized that it was free it turned about and bolted
from the camp, almost toppling itself in its mad rush for freedom.

Hesseth looked at the other animals, then at him. "Follow?" she
asked.

He glanced at the remaining animals—somewhat calmer, but still
agitated—and nodded curtly. "But we don't separate, under any
circumstances. And we don't leave without our gear. For all we know
this is some new gambit to split us up . . . or to separate us from our
possessions. We've got good light; there'll be a visible trail. Let's pack
it fast and move."

"It could be a trap," Ciani said. Her voice trembling, ever so
slightly.

"It could be," he agreed. "And we're going to be damned careful
because of that." He nodded in the direction the xandu had fled mere
seconds before. "But if we don't find out what the hell happened
here—and why—it may happen again, later. And that would leave us
with too few mounts. Not to mention no answers."

They broke camp quickly. Within minutes their possessions were
bundled onto the three remaining animals, pack straps carefully tightened. It took longer to affix the saddles, as the animals were still
highly nervous; Damien had to spare a precious moment to do a
Calming, in order that they might be mounted.

Then he knelt by the side of the fallen animal and took its measure. A large, ragged hole had gouged it through one side; the froth that formed on its lips as it struggled to breathe was stained deep red. He put down his sword long enough to draw a knife from his belt, and with one quick motion sliced across the animal's neck. Quickly, and deeply. There was no struggle, no cry, only a gush of blood that stained his blade and the surrounding snow crimson as the animal died.

He caught Ciani's eyes on him as grabbed the reins of Tarrant's horse—the only true horse remaining—and mounted. "Carotid artery," he muttered. "Kills almost instantly."

He gestured to his two companions, assigning them positions behind him. "You in the middle," he told Ciani, "and stay there. Because if you get picked off . . ." *Then there's no point in any of this*, he finished silently. Her grim nod said she understood, and she pulled in behind him. Followed by Hesseth, and then—

Into the woods. Ice-laden branches creaking as they passed, miniature avalanches spilling to the ground before and after them. Damien had his springbolt out, braced against his shoulder in a one-handed grip. He could fire it that way if he had to, with his other hand tight on the reins. Not for the first time he wished for his own mount, that had drowned in the river. That animal could have been guided by his knees alone, leaving both his hands free for battle . . . but it was dead and gone now, and wishing for it was no use to anyone. This was what he had to work with, and at least it was a proper horse. —And probably a damned good one, given that Gerald Tarrant had raised it.

The trail was easy to see but hard to follow, a furrow gouged into the snow that wheeled erratically between the rocks and trees as if the xandu itself had no idea where it was going. And maybe it didn't. Maybe some Working had stung it on the ass—so to speak—and it was fleeing blindly, with no particular destination in mind. Which was marginally reassuring. If the xandu was supposed to lead them into ambush it would probably be following a more direct course, one designed to bring them in at the right angle, at the right time, and in the right frame of mind.

He shouldered his springbolt and aimed at the treetops ahead, watching for motion. But unlike the trees of the Forbidden Forest these had been stripped of their mass by the coming of winter; moonlight clearly illuminated a canopy bereft of life, that offered neither threat nor cover.

And then they came upon it. In a clearing, spacious and well-lit by moonlight. Damien heard his horse's hooves break through ice as he approached, felt the cold spray of water about his ankles. A stream, frozen over by winter's chill. He warned the others with a wave of his hand, heard them fording it carefully. The xandu was before him, and it snorted as if in rage—but its eyes were fixed on nothingness, its hot gaze utterly empty. It seemed to be struggling—but with what, Damien couldn't say. It was almost as if some unseen rope was pulling it backward, while all its brute instinct urged it to flee; animal flesh versus some unseen power, with the latter slowly winning. There was foam on its lip, speckled with red, and when it struck the ground with its front feet Damien could see that it had sprained an ankle, or worse. He glanced back worriedly at the other xandu ... but whatever madness had claimed this one, it did not extend to the others. It was almost as if whatever power had focussed in on it was content to claim one animal and leave them the rest. A truly chilling concept.

Then the xandu staggered backward, and the ground gave way beneath its feet. First the area directly beneath it, then the ground surrounding—as if the earth itself had lost all support and was falling in on itself. It screamed and struck out blindly—but there was no solid footing, not within reach, and as the ground opened up it fell, limbs flailing, into the lightless hole beneath.

And then a scream pierced the night. One scream, utterly horrible. It was pain and fear and confusion combined, the dying scream of a soul drowning in terror. Damien's skin crawled to hear it, and he had to pull back on his reins to hold his mount steady. Beside him he could hear the others doing likewise, and he glanced at them briefly to see how they were doing. Hesseth's eyes were scanning the clearing with fevered urgency, her hand tight on the springbolt's stock. Ciani's face was white, but her sword was drawn; fear hadn't immobilized her. Good.

And then: silence. Utter silence, unbroken by anything save the ragged breathing of their three mounts.

After a moment Damien slid from his saddle; his boots sank deeply into the snow as his horse snorted anxiously, concerned. Ciani's eyes met his, and she seemed about to say something—and then simply nodded and took his reins from his hand.

He walked forward slowly, utterly cautious. Long sword probing the ground ahead, testing for weakness. The snow was deep here, which made for uncertain footing, but he made certain of each step before he committed himself to the next one; he couldn't afford to be off-balance, not for a moment.

He could hear sound now, from the place where the xandu had fallen. A soft scraping sound, like that of cloth against snow. Or flesh? Something about it made his skin crawl. Inch by inch, he worked his way to the place where the earth had given way.

—And stared down into a massive pit, splattered with blood. There were wooden stakes set in the bottom, a good six feet long, perhaps two feet apart from each other. Easily as thick as a man's arm, but narrowing to a slender point. The sharpened tips pointed upward, as neatly arrayed as soldiers in formation; waiting for some animal to fall through the earth and impale itself, with such utter finality that struggle was meaningless.

And in the center of the pit, their xandu. Or rather, the collection of meat and hide that had once been a xandu. Now, blood-splattered, it was barely the shell of its former self, a mere parody of life; its rainbow horns, coated with blood, were stripped not only of beauty but purpose, and its flesh was so ruptured by its brutal impalement that it was hard to imagine its owner running free on the ground above only moments before.

A hunting call, Damien thought. *That's what got it. Something needed food, and its hunger Worked the fae.* He stared down at the trap and corrected himself. *Not something—someone.*

"Damien?" It was Ciani.

"Come look," he murmured. "Carefully."

Something was moving in the depths of the pit, between those sharpened stakes. Something that dipped in and out of shadow, its form utterly elusive. And then another one. They were clearly mammalian, though something about their skin reminded Damien of a slug. Then one of them looked up at him. He was dimly aware of details: a long tail, hairless, like a rat's. Immense pale eyes, filmed with a thick mucus. Hands shaped like the human extremity, but with fingers that seemed stretched to twice their accustomed length, that twined like nervous serpents as their owner looked up at him.

Not skin, no. Fur, short and close-lying. Ears flattened down against the skull, but a small tuft was still visible at their tips. And in those eyes . . . a hint of amber?

He looked up as Ciani and Hesseth came up beside him, their horses tethered to trees far behind them. "What is it?" Ciani asked, as she came to the edge of the pit. But his eyes were on the *khrast*-woman. She came to where the earth had caved in, and gazed at the tableau below—and then drew back, hissing, her claws unsheathing as she braced herself for conflict. Her ears had flattened, in self-defense, and there was no mistaking the shape. Or the resemblance.

"It's the rakh," he told her. "The Lost Ones."

There were five of the creatures in all. The sight of their dead-white eyes and altered limbs made Damien's skin crawl, but he managed to bury his revulsion deep inside him. Jelly eyes, tentacle fingers . . . he looked at Hesseth, saw her body go taut with hostility. A reaction to the scent of the strangers, no doubt—an instinctive response to the right-but-not-right odor of their presence.

"Hesseth." He hissed the name softly, and as a result it sounded truly rakhene. He waited until she looked at him before he spoke again. "You can't follow your instinct here. You *can't*. It's fine for territorial conflict, but it won't get us where we're going." The eyes were gleaming with feral hostility. "Hesseth. You understand me?"

After a moment, she nodded. Stiffly. A shudder seemed to pass through her flesh, as though pain had suddenly racked it. Her lips drew back from her teeth and she hissed: a warning. But then her ears seem to relax somewhat, and they lifted slightly. The fire in her eyes became a mere smolder. Her claws sheathed—halfway.

"Human tricks," she hissed.

He nodded grimly. "It's the name of the game right now."

Beneath them, four of the five misshapen rakh crouched tensely, waiting for them to make a move. The fifth had gone forward to the xandu carcass, and was beginning to carve it up into manageable chunks with a crude obsidian blade; but even she was wary, and she cast frequent glances at the travelers standing above her to make sure that they were keeping their distance.

She. Four of them were female. The fifth was male, but nearly as slight of build as his companions. A lesser male, Damien guessed, who had adopted a female role in order to get access to food. He hoped for all their sakes that the male was firmly ensconced in his new role; that way, they might get through this meeting with no need for macho heroics.

"Talk to them," he urged Hesseth. "See if they understand you."

For a moment, she seemed incapable of speaking. Then, quickly, she barked out a few sharp phonemes. It was obviously taking great effort for her to speak at all, much less in a civil manner. The lone male looked up at her, his alien face utterly unreadable. After a moment he stepped back to where his companions stood, his tentacular fingers wrapped tightly about the base of his blade.

"Try *hello*," Damien prompted.

She shot him a searing glance, then turned back to the Lost Ones. And rasped out some other sounds, that sounded like a cross between a command and an invective.

This time they reacted. The male glanced at his companions, then handed his knife to one of them. And dropped back into the shadows that veiled the back of the pit, and from there into darkness.

"Not good," Damien muttered. "Gone back for reinforcements?"

"How bad can it be?" Ciani asked. "We're armed, and it would take them time to climb from the pit—"

"No need to. You saw what they did to the xandu." His expression was grim. "Their enemies come to them."

Ciani turned to Hesseth. "What did you say to them?"

"What had to be said," she answered sharply. "With words, since they lack all the other signs."

Damien looked down at the agitated foursome and realized, suddenly, just how much of a barrier there was to communication. Their alien physique would certainly alter their body language, and it was clear that they lacked the right scents . . . that left only words, and words were a poor second in rakhene communication. No wonder Hesseth was edgy.

That, and her instinct. God give her strength to override it . . . and the desire.

They waited. In silence, the nervous pawing and snorting of their mounts the only sound within hearing. Damien shifted his weight cautiously, as the wet snow began to invade one boot; otherwise, there was no movement.

And then the shadows in the back of the pit stirred to life, and several figures emerged from it. The lesser male. Two others, like him. And a figure nearly twice their height, a male who was clearly decades past his prime. His fur hung in patches on wrinkled skin, folds of loose flesh hanging from his bones like an oversized tunic. His skin was pierced: not merely in one place, or a dozen, but all over the surface of his body. Thorns, sharpened twigs, thin blades whittled from bone, pins carved from precious stone, all those had been thrust through the soft folds of skin to serve as a gruesome adornment. A thin shaft of shell, clearly precious, had been thrust through one cheek, and tiny beads dangled from its larger end; delicate needles of carved jet had been passed through the skin of his penis. It made Damien's skin itch just to look at him.

The pierced male addressed them—and there was no mistaking his authority, even without a common tongue between them. It surrounded him like an aura; it seeped forth from him, like blood from his manifold wounds.

Without consulting the humans, Hesseth answered. She had no time to translate before the next question came, or the one after that; the ghastly figure voiced his challenges too quickly, and she dared not hesitate in answering. But though he understood none of the words and even less of the kinesthetics, Damien grasped what was happening. *Who are you?* the pierced rakh was asking. *What are you?*

Why are you here? He wondered what Hesseth considered suitable answers to be—and wished that it were possible for her to confer with him before she answered.

Watch it, he told himself. *She's smarter than you give her credit for, and she knows her people better than you ever will.* He studied the pierced rakh as he spoke, and he shivered in sympathy. What was his position in the social hierarchy, and why was he ... like that? Damien had seen no equivalent among the plains rakh that he might compare it to. He envied his ancestors, whose knowledge-base had encompassed an entire planet with thousands of diverse cultures; how much easier this would have been for them, with so many different examples of primitive behavior to draw on!

At last the pierced one gestured shortly. There was a scurrying sound behind him, in the shadows. Then footsteps. Then the slow scraping of metal on rock as something was dragged out of the shadows. And into the open, where they might see it.

Tarrant's sword.

It was every bit as brilliant as he remembered it, and every bit as malevolent. Its vivid unlight filled the pit's interior with disarming color, turning human skin a pasty white and the Lost One's skin an even less wholesome color—and yet it did nothing to dispel the shadows that ranged close behind it, or to otherwise illuminate the scene. The darkness that had gathered beneath the lip of the pit seemed to draw fresh life from the sword's presence and became even blacker. The shadows became sharper-edged, unyielding. A cold wind swept upward from where the Lost Ones stood, and Damien shivered as it touched him—not wholly because of the temperature.

The pierced one spoke to them. It was a short question, harshly voiced. Hesseth turned to them to translate.

"He asks, is this yours?"

Damien drew in a deep breath, glanced toward Ciani. But her eyes—and her attention—were fixed on the sword. On what it meant, that the sword was here.

"Tell him ... that it belongs to one of my people. One of my blood-kin," he chanced.

He thought he saw her nod slightly in approval as she translated. It was clear that the Lost Ones' dialect differed greatly from her own—which was only to be expected, given their isolation—but there seemed to be enough common ground that the pierced one understood her.

"Ask him where he found it," Damien said quietly.

She did.

"He says, far south of here. Many one-walks. His people ... *sensed* that it was there and went to investigate." She hesitated. "The language is very different, I'm not sure of that one. Perhaps, *heard* it?"

"Ask if there was a body nearby when they found it."

It all centered on that. He wished he knew what answer it was that he wanted to hear.

"He says, no."

Beside him, he felt Ciani stiffen. He forced himself to speak again, to keep his voice even.

"Or anywhere near it?"

She asked, and the pierced one answered. "No."

"Did you find any part of a body? Or . . . personal equipment?"

She conversed at length with the pierced rakh; it seemed they were defining terms. At last she turned back to Damien, and told him, "Nothing. Only the sword. No a sign of how it had gotten there."

"That means he's alive," Ciani whispered.

"Or was, when they took him," Damien corrected.

Hesseth looked at them sharply. "Can you be sure?"

He shook his head. "No. But it's only logical. If their only concern was to kill him, they would have left the body where it fell. Or whatever remained of it. If they wanted the kind of power you can conjure from a corpse—or needed his flesh for some symbolic purpose—can you think of anything more powerful, or more personal to him, that *that?*" He indicated the sword. "Even if they killed him and then got rid of the body, they would have included the sword in their plans. Would have had to, to keep his spirit from wielding further influence. But if all they wanted was him, alive . . . what would it matter that his weapon of choice was left behind? It only meant that much less danger for them."

Hesseth's tongue tip touched the edges of her teeth as she considered that. Ran over them, lightly. It was a ferocious expression.

The pierced one spoke again; clearly some sort of command. Hesseth stiffened, and barked back a sharp response.

The pierced one snarled. The rakh in the pit tensed, as though readying themselves for battle.

"What was that?" Damien demanded.

"He says that if this is a thing of your blood-kin, then it's now yours. You must come and take it."

He looked at the glowing blade, felt something inside his gut go ice-cold at the thought of touching it. "Okay," he said quietly. "That's fair enough."

"He means . . ." She floundered for the proper English words to describe it. "That is . . . he *challenges* you to come get it."

And suddenly he understood. Understood all the levels of status that were involved, all the crucial posturing. And the risk.

Their females hunt for food. Their males hunt for status. —And the more dangerous the prey, the better.

"All right," he said at last. He began to move toward the edge of the pit, looking for a way down. And hoped he was guessing right about their customs.

"Unarmed," Hesseth added.

He looked up at her and said sharply, "What?"

"Unarmed," she repeated. "He said that. Actually, *naked of threat* is what he said."

He looked at the pierced one. And something in him darkened— some part that had had its fill of tact and diplomacy and was very near the breaking point.

"Tell I'll be happy to disarm," he said coldly. "Provided he removes his teeth and claws."

"They have no claws."

"Then translate the rest."

She looked at him somewhat oddly, then did so. The pierced one snarled but otherwise said nothing.

"I'll take that as a yes," the priest told her.

"Damien—" Ciani began. She hesitated, then whispered, "Be careful."

From somewhere he dredged up a hint of a smile; it cracked ice crystals from his beard, that had set in a harder line. "I think we're past that point."

He found a place where the nearest stake was several feet distant from the wall of the pit, and lowered himself down. But the seemingly firm earth crumbled to bits beneath his fingertips and he was forced to drop the last few feet, landing unceremoniously on his side as the icy ground refused him purchase.

The Lost Ones watched.

He gained his feet quickly, noting for future reference that the ground down here offered little traction. Undoubtedly the snow drained into this area when it melted, only to freeze again come nightfall. He made his way carefully between the sharpened stakes, noting that their bases were set deep into the ice; a permanent hunting site, then, or at least semipermanent. Coarse wood caught at the wool of his coat as he passed; sometimes he had to press the stakes aside in order to squeeze his bulk between them.

Couldn't draw a sword in here even if I wanted to. He passed by the carcass of the xandu, felt a momentary pang of loss at seeing such an elegant creature reduced to formless carrion. And then he was clear of the deep-rooted spears and opposite the Lost Ones. They seemed larger from up close than they had from the ground above, and their smell was rank and musty, the reek of enclosed spaces. He could see now that their fur was edged with green, as if some species of mold had adopted them as its habitat; rosettes of pale gray marked the shoulder of one and muddy brown the haunches of another. Those growths added their own smell to that of their hosts, the odor of mildew and decay. In addition it seemed that some of the pierced one's ornaments were olfactory in nature; the sharp smell of pine needles and the pungence of musk drifted about his person like fog, a miasma of adornment.

He came as close as he could to his challenger and postured himself opposite the creature. Though the Lost One was taller he was also considerably thinner, and he lacked Damien's layers of insulating wool and fur. Though he tried to provide an imposing presence, he was no match for the priest's hefty bulk—and his ritual hostility was nothing compared to the potential for violence that lurked beneath the priest's carefully controlled facade, waiting for its first excuse to surface.

"You make one wrong move," Damien growled, "and I'll cut your vulking head off. —Don't translate that," he warned.

"No chance of it," Hesseth assured him.

The pierced one hissed angrily, but made no move to harm the priest. Instead he stepped aside, so that the sword behind him was visible. The malevolent power of it blasted Damien in the face like an arctic wind; it took everything he had not to react visibly, so that the Lost Ones wouldn't know his weakness. With a cold, tight clenching in the pit of his stomach he went to where the sword lay. And regarded it. He glanced over his shoulder to make sure the Lost Ones were keeping their distance from him—they were—and then reached down to where it lay, and closed his hand about the grip

—and pain exploded in his hand, like spears of ice thrust suddenly into his flesh. He could feel all the warmth in his arm coursing down toward his hand, through it, drawn out to feed that hungry steel. He gritted his teeth and raised the weapon up, his fingers numb from the searing cold of it—but he held on, despite the pain, despite the panic that was rising up inside him. *The Hunter feeds on fear*, he told himself. *His weapons would be Worked to inspire it.* He fought the panic down, forced his fingers to stay wrapped about the leather-bound grip even as the killing power flowed into his flesh—his lungs—his heart. He had submitted to Tarrant's coldfire once, and this felt much the same—a hundred times more powerful, a thousand times more terrifying, but its nature was clearly similar. He closed his eyes and remembered that ordeal, used it to fortify himself as the power filled him, remade him—*tested* him, against some dark and terrible template—and then withdrew, until the pain became bearable. Somewhat. Until the cold, though still piercing, was no longer a direct threat to his survival.

He turned to the Lost Ones, fingers still wrapped tightly about the sword's grip. His hand was still numb from the cold of it, but the blade seemed to have a life of its own; he had no doubt that if he had to wield it, he could.

And it will drink in life, like its owner does. It will drink in the terror of the wounded. . . .

The pierced one spoke. His tone was challenging.

"He says, that thing has killed many."

Yes, Damien thought. He noted the rope still wrapped about its quillons, which they had used to drag it here. *And the only reason it didn't kill me just now is my link to Tarrant. The sword knows its own.*

"It belongs to my blood-kin," he repeated. The weight of it was like ice in his hand, but he refused the temptation to put it down.

The pierced one spoke again.

"He says, it eats souls."

Damien drew in a deep breath, forced himself to think before answering. "Tell him . . . that we came to kill an eater of souls. An eater of *rakhene* souls. Tell him . . . sometimes it takes power of the same sort to kill one like that."

He could see them react as Hesseth translated. He waited. Dark power flowed up his arm, wrapped itself around the circuitry of his brain. *Kill*, it whispered. *Kill, and be done with them.*

He shifted his grip on it and tried to block out its message. Tendrils of malevolence continued to seep into his brain, but he refused to acknowledge them.

"There is only one eater of souls here," Hesseth translated for them. "In the . . ." she hesitated. "I think he means, the House of Storms."

"What did he say, exactly?"

"I'm not sure. Their speech is so different. . . ."

"Then don't try to translate the concept—just give me the words."

Her brow furrowed tightly as she considered. "The place of . . . blue lightning?"

"Blue lightning?"

"I'm not sure. I—"

"*Blue* lightning?"

"I *think* that's the word. Why?" she demanded. "Is it so significant?"

He was remembering the sky over Jaggonath, when the earthquake struck. The blinding spears that had shot up from the earth, filling the heavens with light. So much like nature's lightning, only a hundred times more intense. And, of course, silver-blue—earth-fae blue—as opposed to nature's white.

He tried to recall what it was that Hesseth had described, back at her people's encampment. *Lightning, she'd said, that filled the sky for months on end. Thunder so loud it made speaking impossible.*

That's what it was. That's what the storms were. Not real lightning at all. Power; *bound* power.

My God, the implications. . . .

"Tell him what we need," he ordered. He could hear his voice shaking as he spoke, tried to steady it. So much seemed to depend upon a display of strength, with these people. "Ask him if he'll help us."

An overload, firing heavenward. But an overload of what? There are no earthquakes in this region. And the currents here are so weak. . . . It was hard to think clearly with the power of the Hunter's sword chilling his brain. Even so, he sensed that he had glimpsed the last piece of the puzzle. Finally. He had only to see where it fit into the whole picture, and then they would know where to strike. . . .

Tarrant would have understood it. Then he corrected himself, grimly: *Tarrant still may.*

"He'll lead us," Hesseth told them. "As far as the . . . *region of no,* is the phrase."

"Forbidden zone?" Ciani offered.

"I don't know. What he says . . . it's not a concept I'm familiar with."

"Can we get from there to the House of Storms?" Damien asked. "To the tunnels underneath them? That's all that matters."

"He says . . . that region is a place of dying. The tunnels beneath the House of Storms are filled with dying. Those are the . . . the *places of no.*" She shook her head. "I'm sorry."

"Taboo," Damien guessed. "As any dwelling place would be, once demons moved in." He looked at the pierced one. "Tell him yes. Tell him that's what we want. What we *need.*"

He looked to the dirt wall behind the Lost Ones, to the tunnel mouth that waited there. Somewhere at the far end was their human enemy. Ciani's assailant. And—just possibly—Gerald Tarrant.

"That's our entrance," he whispered.

Thirty-nine

The winter wind howled across the eastern flatlands, flinging snow across everyone and everything in its path. It was a bitter wind, fresh from the arctic regions, and the moisture it had picked up while crossing the Tri-Lakes area and the Serpent made it doubly vicious. There was nothing to do but find shelter from the storm and stay there, and the various inhabitants of eastern Lema had done just that. The local rakh huddled in their tents, gathered tightly about their fires, and waited for the storm to pass. Flatland browsers were packed tightly in their caves and their tunnels, yawning as the first waves of hibernation dulled their minds with drowsiness. Even winter's predators had taken shelter, and they paced restlessly in their cramped hiding places as they waited for the worst of the storm to pass, so that they could follow the trails made by their prey in the smooth, white snow.

It was no time for animals or rakh to be abroad, and all the inhabitants of Lema seemed to know this.

All but three.

They walked like humans, though their anatomy was clearly rakhene. It was a mismatch of body and purpose, as though somehow a human persona had been welded to native flesh. They were furred, like most rakh, and heavily clothed, but the wind that whipped across the open plains was more than a single coat could ward against. Beneath the thin fur, warm flesh was already turning white with death. Extremities first: the fingers and toes, then nose, lips, cheeks ... in the frigid cold of winter's first storm they labored for breath, and the moisture of their lungs gathered like frost on their lips as they exhaled, gasping, into the wind.

Mindlessly they staggered forward, their legs knee-deep in snow.

Driven to stagger forward, by a force they could neither comprehend nor fight. It had taken their memories, this alien force, and replaced them with others. Foreign pictures; alien recall. Names and places and hungers and needs, feelings so intense that their own memories were mere shadows beside them. Shadows that faded as day turned into night turned into day again, as the hours of travel became endless and the goal ahead—if there was one—seemed forever beyond their reach.

The wind gusted suddenly. And one of them fell. It was the youngest of the three, a female barely old enough to mate. Exhaustion had robbed her limbs of strength and she lay in the snow, her face cracked and bleeding from the cold. Panting lightly, as if she lacked even the strength to breathe.

The other two looked at her. They were her father and sister, bloodkin to her flesh . . . and they looked at her now, and were unaware of any kinship. Were unaware of anything save the force that drove them northward, and its demands.

For a moment was silence. Within them, and without; a precious moment of non-being in which the alien memories ceased their clamor, and the flesh was emptied of all thought. A single instant of peace, in the midst of their nightmare journey.

And then it came, as a whisper. Invading their flesh, their souls. *Two is enough*, it said. *Move on. Leave the dying one here.*

The female hesitated, then turned away. The male looked down at his daughter. Some memory stirred in the back of his mind that might have involved warmth and paternal devotion . . . but then it was gone, crowded out by alien images. *Human* images. He fought them for a moment, but the force that had implanted them was stronger than he was—and at last he gave way, and the old memories died within him.

Slowly, he, too, turned away. Slowly they began to move again, breaking a trail through the knee-deep snow. Two of them, now. But two was enough. The force that had bound their wills made that clear.

In the snow behind them, in a shallow grave of crystal and ice, the simulacrum who had once been their blood-kin breathed her last.

Forty

They let the horse and the xandu go free. They could hardly take them underground, and had no way to lodge them safely until they returned. *If* they returned. So they let them go. Th⌐ xandu were born to the wild, and could easily return to it. As for the Forest steed . . . Damien debated killing it, to spare it a slower death by freezing or starvation. But the horse had ridden beside the xandu for so long that when they were freed to go it tried to go off with them, like one of their number. Well enough, Damien decided. It was the Hunter's stock, after all; doubtless it could manage to fend for itself.

The sword was another matter. That had to come with them, there was no question about it. But even wrapped in multiple blankets it radiated power, and its aura of malevolence was so intense that Damien wondered how long he would be able to carry it. The mere thought of contact with the Worked steel made his blood run cold with dread, and revived echoes of a voice—and a person—he would rather forget.

Just like him, too. Even in death his evil affects us.

Or in imprisonment, he corrected grimly.

Carrying their most vital possessions on them—the rest had been buried, or given to the Lost Ones—they entered the narrow tunnel that led from the back of the hunting pit. Dark earth closed in about them, walls too close and ceiling too low and the whole of it damp, rank with the smell of that mildewed species. Damien could see Hesseth shiver in revulsion as they descended, deep into the reeking earth, and he prayed that she could hold out. Her sense of smell was stronger than all the humans' put together, and the odor seemed to awaken some primal fight-or-flight instinct within her. He hoped she had the strength—and the desire—to overcome that response. For all their sakes.

As the moonlight faded far behind them, no light took its place that unaltered humans might see by. The pierced one seemed to wend his way by the light of the earth-fae, his pale eyes split wide to reveal a glistening pupil, as broad as Damien's palm. If the tunnels descended deep enough, Damien thought, only the dark fae would be available for illumination. He debated using the Fire to facilitate his own sight, or even kindling a small lamp. But in the end he simply Worked his own vision and saw as the natives did. He turned to check on Ciani, to offer her a similar service—and found to his surprise that it wasn't necessary. She had Worked her own vision, using the techniques that Tarrant had taught her.

Good for her, he thought. But his soul was sick as he contemplated the cost of that Working, the darkness that would slowly be taking root inside her.

She'll never be what she was, he thought grimly. And what bothered him most of all was not that it was happening, or that he didn't know how to stop it. It was that she didn't care. Didn't even recognize the problem.

It's all the same power to her. He's just another adept. More interesting than most, perhaps—but that only makes him more desirable. The cost of it means . . . nothing.

By the light of the dark fae alone they descended, so deep into the earth that only a few wisps of earth-fae coursed about them; Damien felt strangely naked, in a world without that omnipresent power. He cast about with a cautious Working, anxious to catch wind of any threat to his party before it manifested. But he found himself incapable of Working on that level, and the truth of what Tarrant had said to them earlier finally hit home: *The power does not come from within us, but from without.* Which meant that in a place where the earth-fae was scarce, there was no Working. Period. It was all he could do to maintain his altered vision, and who knew how long he could keep that up? If their Workings should fail them they would be trapped here in true darkness, hundreds of feet beneath the earth. Totally helpless. He reached back instinctively to feel the haft of his sword, to comfort himself that even facing such adversity he could hold his own. But his fingers closed about the grip of Tarrant's sword instead—he had strapped it to the same harness, as a means of carrying it without having to look at it—and its chill power shot up his arm with stunning force. He tried to release it immediately, but his hand was slow to respond. Ice-cold power slammed into him, and the tunnel errupted in violet iridescence. Twisting threads of light filled the air about him, too bright to look at directly. They tangled about his feet, clung to his clothes as though seeking the flesh beneath. And burned, with a purple brilliance that was blinding. He forced himself to release the sword, and after a moment—a very long moment—the power subsided. And with it, the vision. He forced himself to breathe steadily, slowly.

The dark fae, he thought. Awed by the vision, so unlike anything he had ever seen. *Is that how it looks to him?* It was an incredible concept, that the man who seemingly thrived on darkness lived in a world of such brilliant light. Never lacking illumination, because his vision was always Worked.

Ciani was like that. That's what she lost. And his hands clenched at his sides, remembering what the loss had done to her. *That's what we're getting back for her.*

The pierced rakh led them onward without a word, through an underground labyrinth of dizzying complexity. Natural tunnels met and merged in combination with rakh-carved corridors, that twisted back on themselves and merged again and opened out into natural chambers, with a thousand nooks and crannies in which the dark fae lurked ... Damien tried to memorize the pattern of their progress, but it was impossible. Which meant they had no hope of finding their way back, or of locating any other exit, without the pierced one's help. It was a kind of helplessness he despised—and it was all the more frustrating because there was nothing he could do about it.

After a time the rakh-made caverns altered in nature. The ceiling became more even, the cave floor more regular. And the walls ... they had been reinforced with the bones of the Lost Ones' prey—long, sweeping femurs and radia cemented into place beneath fragile stone formations, like the armature of some ghastly sculpture. These increased in number as they progressed, their sheer profusion giving the tunnels the aspect of a behemoth's rib cage seen from within. Those gave way in turn to larger spaces, in which Nature had seen to the decorating: huge vaulted chambers whose ceilings dripped limestone formations like icicles, waterfalls of crystalline calcite that gleamed like fresh snow in the dark fae's light, underground lakes that were no more than an inch or two deep, but that seemed fathoms in depth—and always there were the veils of memory that the dark fae conjured, that parted like silk curtains at their approach and fluttered slowly into misty darkness behind them. Evidently their fears had no power to manifest in the pierced one's presence, which was fortunate for all of them.

Damien was exhausted—from walking, from Working. When they at last stopped to rest, he kindled a small tin lamp and let his eyes take a break. Ciani dropped down by his side, equally exhausted, and he saw her rub her eyes as if they hurt her. He put his arm around her, tenderly, but there was little comfort he could offer. Except to whisper that he would keep the lamp out from now on, that its light was inferior but they would have to make do with it. They couldn't keep Working forever.

"But we tried, yes?" she whispered. And despite their redness her eyes gleamed with pride, because she had Worked as long and as well as he had.

It was hard for them to get moving again. Even Hesseth seemed to bend beneath the weight of her pack, as though it had doubled in weight since she had last borne it. The pierced one watched them in silence, and seemed to need no rest; his own body was clearly more accustomed than theirs to the rigors of underground hiking. And in the end it was his searching gaze that got them moving again, the sight of his mucus-filmed eyes searching for weakness in them. Any weakness.

And then—hours later, miles later, who could say how far they'd come, or how long they'd been traveling?—there was life. At last. First the smell of it: musty and close, like the Lost Ones themselves. Then a faint whiff of smoke, that drifted tantalizingly past them and then, just when they had noticed it, disappeared. Followed by the pungent aroma of the rakh's fur-mold, which they could now see clinging to the damp cave walls, as well as to the pelt of their host. And the scent of warmth—of fire—of blessed heat, that drove the last of winter's chill from their weary limbs and promised at least a brief respite from their exertions.

The corridor turned, and widened. And opened into a vast chamber filled with the wide-eyed Lost Ones. They were gathered in small groupings—families?—whose members huddled close together as they stoked their small fires, scraped and polished bones, carved ornaments, picked at each other for parasites. The nearer heads shot up as the party entered the vast common chamber, and Damien caught the glint of firelight on ornaments, thin needles of stone and shell thrust through cheeks, nostrils, even eyelids. Mostly on the men, he noted. And the stronger ones wore more of them and courted more painful placement. What manner of rakh did that make their guide? Damien glanced at the pierced one, saw him studying the inhabitants of the chamber with clear authority. Some sort of leader, then. Or priest. Did the cave-rakh have priests?

The walls were ornate, albeit primitive in design, and had been painted with charcoal and bits of lichen in crude but intricate patterns. Once more, the Lost Ones had used the bones of their food-animals to reinforce the walls, but here the effect seemed more decorative than structural. Polished to a gleaming white, the bones glittered like candleflames in the relative brilliance of the rakhene cookfires. Toe bones and hand bones and slender fingers, worked like mosaic tiles into some sort of native cement—

And then he looked closely at those gleaming bits and hissed softly, rakhlike, as he recognized some of them. He felt his arm muscles tensing as if for battle, had to forcibly keep himself from reaching for his sword.

Not here. Not yet. Find your way out of this warren first.

He took care to position himself so that the women had no chance to see the wall behind him; he could only hope there were no similar displays elsewhere. He felt despair growing inside him, the impotence that came of feeling totally powerless. And he was, indeed, made powerless: by the darkness, by the labyrinth, by the lack of Workable fae in this place—but most of all by their enemy's all-Seeing power, which was probably even now scouring the rakhlands in search of them. There was some small comfort in that, at least—as long as they were this far underground, not even he would be able to find them.

The cave-rakh began to gather around them, half-crawling, half-walking, coming as close as they dared and then sniffing noisily, white nostrils distended as they tried to catch the strangers' scents. Tails whipped urgently behind them, twining about each other like serpents in the darkness. How they could smell anything over the moldy reek of their own bodies was beyond Damien; this close, their odor was nigh on overwhelming. He gathered Ciani close to him, a protective arm about her shoulder; Hesseth he kept behind him, lest the like-but-unlike quality of her scent should trigger some violence among these creatures.

The pierced male spoke to them. After a moment of waiting, he snapped another few phrases in the rakhene tongue, hurling them at Hesseth like knives. With effort she composed herself, barely enough to translate, "He says these are the fringe-folk, who live on the borders of the . . . the no-place. He says . . ." She drew in a deep breath, shaking; it was hard for her to translate calmly when all her animal senses were screaming at her to flee. "He is the dream-one, the seeing-one, and they'll respect his wishes. Because he asks it, they'll keep us here, so that we may sleep in—in—I'm sorry," she said, flustered. "I just don't know that one."

The pierced one continued. "From here they can show us the House of—the place of blue light," she corrected herself. Damien could hear the strain in her voice, echo of a self-control that was alien to her and her kind. *That's it*, he thought approvingly. *Keep it up.* "He says that the tunnels we want are under this place, but they are not easy tunnels. The small ways are too narrow, and the walls are . . . *falling-threat*, he says. Which is why the tunnels were abandoned." He saw her nostrils flare in terror, innate response to some half-sensed threat. Once more she drew in a deep, slow breath, as if struggling for air. "Very dangerous," she gasped. Was she translating the dream-one's words, now, or referring to their general situation? "In past times there was much death, in the no-place. No rakh ever goes there, now. No rakh *will* ever go there." The pierced one grinned, displaying crooked teeth. "But I will go there," she translated, as he slapped his breast proudly. A thin drop of blood welled forth from the base of a pectoral ornament he had struck. "I, the seeing-one, the dream-one, who dares the places of no, I will take you there." The filmy eyes fixed on Damien with clear hostility. "I think this is some kind of male statement—"

"I understand it," he told her. Oh, yes: the social pattern was very familiar. Primitive, even bestial . . . and not without its congruent among human males. He remembered one young boy braving the true night alone, in order to achieve the status that only foolhardy courage could earn. Because of a dare, he remembered. It was always because of a dare.

"Tell him yes," he said brusquely. "Tell him I want to see if he can lead us there, to the place where no rakh go. I want to see if his . . . if his *seeing* is stronger than his fear. —Say it that way," he urged her.

He watched the pierced one's face as his challenge was voiced. And therefore did not see the faces surrounding them, as several rakh gasped in response to his audicity.

But the pierced one merely nodded, once, tightly, as he accepted the challenge. "After sleep, then," he told them through the *khrast*-woman. "After you have seen the lightning-place. We go then." We waved to one of the local females, who scurried off ratlike into the darkness. "The fringe-folk give you shelter, for resting in. You will not be sleeping together, so—"

"*We stay together*," Damien said sharply. And he sensed, rather than saw, relief in Hesseth's eyes. "At all times."

The pierced one fixed wide black eyes on him, as if trying to stare him down. *Fat chance*, Damien thought. He stared back with equal vigor. At last the rakh nodded, somewhat stiffly. "All three together," he pronounced. The myriad impalements of his face made his expression particularly grotesque. "You come, then, and the fringe-folk will bring food—"

"No food," Damien said sharply. He said it again, when the pierced one hesitated. *"No food."*

It seemed to him that several of the smaller rakh giggled—or some gurgly equivalent—and for a brief moment nausea washed over him, as he recognized the source of their mirth. But he kept his expression stern, puffing himself up in his best rakhene-male manner. And after a moment of silent confrontation, the pierced one nodded stiffly.

"There will be no food," he agreed. "Come," He waved back the mildewed crowd, giving them room to move. Just in time, Damien reflected; the air had become nearly unbreathable. He kept a protective arm about Ciani as they fell in behind him, and a close eye on Hesseth.

"I gather you got the upper hand," Ciani murmured to him, as they were led from the common chamber. "I don't suppose you'd care to explain what that last little bit was about?"

He glanced back toward the vast cavern, towards its ornamented wells, and shivered. "Don't ask," he muttered. "Not till we're out of here, at least." *Don't ever ask,* he pleaded silently.

And he remembered the polished bones that he had seen on the cavern wall, remnants of the Lost Ones' meat-animals applied to decoration. Much as a man might make a rug from the hide of his kill, he thought, or hang its head on the wall. There had been hundreds of bones in that place, all of them smooth and gleaming, some of them carved in intricate patterns . . . and among them at least one hand, nearly human-sized, that was not from a beast. He remembered the fingers of that one—remembered them very clearly—slender bones with rakhene claws at the tip. The retractable talons of the plains-rakh, without doubt. Glued to the wall like some grizzly trophy, a momento of past feasts relished.

He hoped with all his heart that Hesseth hadn't seen it. He wished with all his heart that he hadn't, either.

"I didn't think their food would agree with us," he muttered.

Darkness. Closeness. The chill of stone, close about them. Packed earth, at their backs. In a sleeping-crevice so narrow that the three of them were forced to huddle together, like a family of Lost Ones might have done. It was not uncomforting, under the circumstances. But it was a bad position to be in, should they be attacked.

Damien cradled the clear vial of Fire against his chest, and let its light drive back the dark fae that even now was trying to reach them. As soon as the cave-rakh had left them, that dark force had begun to manifest their fears, with the result that several amorphous shapes were now lying in sliced-up bits around the party. But that was before. The golden light of the Fire was enough to keep it at bay, and Damien meant to keep it out until the Lost Ones returned to them. After one-sleep, they had said. Whatever the hell that meant.

Beside him, cradled against his chest, Ciani moaned softly, trapped in the grip of some nightmare. He nudged her gently, hoping to urge her out of the dream state without quite awakening her. On his other side Hesseth slept fitfully, deep growls and animal hisses punctuating the soft, whistling snore that counterpointed her slumber. And he . . . he needed sleep desperately, but didn't dare succumb to it. There was too much here that was unknown—too much that was dangerous. If the Lost Ones considered their cousins to be food-animals, what would they make of the humans, who were even more unlike them? He was acutely aware of the stone shelf close overhead, of his inability to swing a sword without first climbing down from the sleeping-crevice. But to take up guard elsewhere meant that either he or his companions must be without the Firelight, and that was simply unacceptable; the dark fae was too responsive, their fearful imaginations too fertile. They would be overwhelmed in moments. So the best he could do for them was to remain where he was and doze as he had in the Dividers: mere moments of sleep, quickly claimed and quickly abandoned. Mere moments of darkness, punctuating long hours of alertness

Too many hours. Too long a vigil. But who could say how long the night took to pass, in a place where the whole world was darkness?

"There it is."

They stood upon a ridge of naked granite which the wind had scrubbed clean of snow, and tried to adjust to the harsh morning light. In the distance, barely visible to the naked eye, the House of Storms rose from the ground like some sharp, malignant growth. All about it the land had been flattened, a no-man's waste of barren ground that made their enemy's tower all the more visible by contrast. Whatever defenses their enemy might value, invisibility was clearly not one of them.

"Don't Work," Damien warned Ciani. "Whatever you do, don't

Work to see it. Or for any other reason." Not knowing how much she remembered—or, more accurately, how little—he explained, "Any channel we establish can be used against us, no matter what its purpose. We're too close now to chance that."

"And it would let him know we've arrived?"

"If he doesn't already know," he said grimly.

"What's the chance of that?" Hesseth asked.

"Hard to say. We've had nothing happen since Tarrant's death, to further thin the ranks of our party ... but that could just mean that he considers us sufficiently weakened already."

"Or that his attention's fixed on the simulacra instead."

He hesitated. All his gut instinct warned him not to bank his hopes on that one deception—*never count on anything you can't See yourself*, his master had cautioned him—but to deny Ciani such a small hope now was little less than cruelty. "Let's hope so," he muttered. And he raised the small farseer to his eye.

The fortress seemed to leap toward him: slowly he coaxed it into focus. And drew in his breath sharply as its bizarre design gradually became clear.

"Damien?"

"No windows," he muttered. "No windows at all." But even those words couldn't capture the oddity of it. The utterly alien quality of its design. "He's a paranoid bastard, that's for sure."

What rose up from the distant ground was a polished obelisk of native stone, whose slick surface betrayed no hint of doorway, viewport, or any structural joining. It was as if it had not been raised up from the earth, but rather carved from the mountainside itself. A massive sculpture of cold, unliving stone that required no petty adornments—such as entrances or windows—to proclaim its purpose. He studied its surface for many long minutes, and had to bite back on his urge to Work his sight further. That would be too dangerous. He sought mortar lines, the thin shadows of juncture, any hint that mere mortals might have erected that eerie sculpture, but there were none. Not a single crack in the polished surface, that might serve as handhold to an invader. Not even a tiny viewport, through which weapons or gas might enter. *Or an agile invader*, he thought. Fear of attack was written across every inch of the structure.

"Utterly defensive," he muttered. "To say the least." He handed the farseer to Ciani, heard her gasp as she brought the strange edifice into focus. For a moment he looked at her, concerned; was it possible that old memories were surfacing, this close to her tormentor's fortress? Her hands shook slightly as she held the farseer, and she drew in a long, ragged breath as she stared through it. But no, that was impossible. Her memories weren't buried, but wholly absent. Taken from her. And if he made the same mistake Senzei had—of confusing *absence* with *suppression*—he might well be courting a similar fate.

"Cee?"

"I'm all right. It's just that it's so . . ." She fumbled for an adjective, shivering. "That's it, isn't it? Where we're going."

"That, or somewhere beneath it." He took the farseer back from her and handed it to Hesseth. Who looked it over with catlike curiosity before finally raising it to her eye to look through it.

Naked stone, polished to an ice-slick surface. A six-sided tower that rose up from the earth like a basalt column, as though Erna herself had vomited it up from the volcanic depths of her core. A structure that widened as it rose so that the walls were forced outward, doubly discouraging anyone who might try to scale it.

It was structurally impossible, plain and simple. Earthquakes might not strike here, but the sun still shone and the seasons still progressed, as in any normal place. And any mass that huge, that solid, was bound to develop flaws as Nature went through her paces. Uneven expansion and contractions, the erosion of wind and ice, the deforming pressure of its own top-heavy mass . . . such a monument could not exist and therefore it did not, simple as that. Not even a Warding would hold it together, against such complex forces. Which meant that something else was involved.

"Illusion?" he mused aloud.

The women looked at him. "You think?" Ciani asked.

" 'When one is in the presence of the seemingly impossible, that which is merely unlikely becomes more plausible by contrast.' That's a quote, you know, from—" He stopped suddenly, even as the words came to his lips. And forced himself to voice them. "The Prophet," he told them. "His writings."

"Gerald," Ciani whispered.

He said nothing.

"He's in there, isn't he?" Her voice was low and even, but in it was such yearning, such hurting, that it made his soul ache to hear it. "Trapped in there."

"That's likely," he agreed. Knowing, even as he spoke, that it was more than likely. It was certain. He could feel that in his bones, as if his link to the Hunter had allowed knowledge to take root there, without his even knowing it. "Whatever's left of him," he said quietly. "Remember the dreams of fire."

She nodded, remembering. More than mere dreams, but less than true Knowings. How much could they trust such visions?

She stared at the distant citadel, and whispered, "He's in pain."

"Yeah." He forced himself to look away, toward the citadel in the distance. "So are a lot of other people, whose lives he destroyed. Not to mention the hundreds he's killed."

"Damien—"

"Ciani. Please." He knew what was coming, and dreaded it. "He took his chances. If he's—"

"We have to help him," she whispered.

He could feel his chest tighten—in anguish, in fury. But before he could speak she added quickly, "It's not just because he needs help. That wouldn't be enough for you, I understand that. It's because we *need* him." With slender hands she turned him to face her, so that his eyes were forced to meet hers. "In that citadel—or beneath it— are three things. A human sorceror, who's already proven himself capable of killing our best. A high-order demon who may be defended by dozens—if not hundreds—of his kind. And a single man who can wield more power than you and I could ever dream of—and *will* wield it, in our defense, if he's free to do so. Don't you see?" She shook her head tensely, her bright eyes fixed on him. There was wetness gathering in the outer corner of one of them. "It's not a matter of sentiment, Damien, or even ethical judgment. It's the odds against us, plain and simple. Gods, I want to come out of this alive. I want to come out of this *whole*. And now, with your Fire gone, Senzei murdered . . . don't we stand a better chance of success, with Tarrant's power on our side?"

"I would sooner walk through the gates of hell," he told her, "than loose that man on the world again. Do you realize what he is? Do you realize what he *does*? The hundreds of people who will suffer because of him—the thousands!—because we set him free?"

"You had an agreement with him. You said that for as long as we were traveling together—"

"And I damned well stood by that agreement, though every minute I encouraged him rather than cutting him down will count against me at my day of judgment. No, I wouldn't have made a move against him while we were traveling together—but God in heaven, Cee, am I supposed to go in after him now that someone else has? Risk my life to save him?"

"He's trapped in there because of *me*—"

"He's in there because he values his own vulking life more than fifty of yours—and mine—combined! Because some little footnote in his survival contract dictated that he come here in order to safeguard his own existence. Nothing more than that—nothing, Cee! The man's a monster—even worse than that, a monster who once was human. That's far more dangerous than your average demonkind. Do you think he really cares for you? Do you think he cares for anything, other than his own continued existence? He'd sacrifice you in a minute if you stood in his way." The words were pouring from him like a flood tide, and with it poured all his anger. All his hatred for the man and what he represented. Everything he had been suppressing for weeks. "Do you know what he did to his wife, his family? Do you imagine you'd rate any better, if he thought that it would profit him to kill you? Do you think he values you more than he valued those of his own blood? He would kill you without a second thought—and worse, if he stood to gain from it."

"Don't get me wrong," she said quietly. "I have no illusions about his nature. I think maybe I even understand him a little better than you can"—and her eyes narrowed—"seeing as I'm not half-blinded by theological prejudice. Let me tell *you* what he is. Strip away the sword and the collar, and all the accoutrements of his evil . . . and what you come up with is an adept, plain and simple. *What I was.*" She just stared at him for a moment, giving the words time to sink in. "We're the same," she whispered, "he and I."

"Cee, you're not—"

"*Listen to me.* Try to understand. It's not what you want to hear, I know that. Why do you think I never said it before? For all our closeness, there's a part of me you never really knew. A part you didn't *want* to know. A part no nonadept could ever understand . . . except maybe Zen. I think, sometimes, that he did."

She put a hand on his arm—but the contact felt cold, and strangely distant. Uncomforting. "We were born the same way, Gerald Tarrant and I. Not like your kind, in the midst of a comprehensible world, born to parents who could foresee your troubles and prepare for them. Most born adepts don't make it past infancy. Or if they grow up, they grow up insane. The infant brain just can't handle that kind of input—it's too much, too chaotic, they can't sort it out. We spend our lives trying to adapt, fighting to impose some kind of order on the universe. He did it. So did I. Different paths, but the end goal was the same: stability. Of ourselves, and of our world."

"And now, suddenly, you remember all this?" he asked sharply. He hated himself the minute the words left his mouth, for how they might hurt her. But it was as if the hatred had opened a floodgate; he could do nothing to stop the words from coming.

"I Shared his memories. He offered," she said quickly. "And why not? It's a means of learning, isn't it? They weren't memories from the . . . not from the time after he changed. Not that, oh no. But from his human years. And gods, the richness of them, the depth. . . ."

He closed his eyes, understanding at last. The darkness within her.

The taint he had sensed, without knowing how to define it. Tarrant had poured his soul into her, to fill the empty places in hers. And in the short term it had probably assuaged her pain, somewhat. It had certainly given her a knowledge base to replace what she had lost, something to draw on. But in the long run . . . he had to turn away from her, lest she see the rage in his eyes. The hate. And the mourning. . . .

She would be unable to leave him behind. Physically unable, due to his influence. Period. No matter what he said or did, it could be no other way.

"As for what he is, that's just his adaptation," she said. "Don't you see? To you it means something else, it's all tied up with questions of faith and honor—but to me it's just that. A terrible adaptation, it's true—I don't deny that—but does that make it any less of an accomplishment? He's *alive*. He's *sane*. Not many of our kind can lay claim to that much."

"I wonder about the sanity," he muttered, bitterly.

"Damien." She said it softly, her tone so gentle that it awakened memories of other places, better times. She touched the side of his face with a soft hand, chilled by the morning breezes. "Don't you want him on our side? Don't you want that kind of *power* on our side?"

And live with that, all the rest of my life! He shuddered at the thought. *The knowledge that I was the one who made it possible for the Hunter to feed again. All the hundreds he would torment, feast upon, kill . . . their deaths would be on my head, all of them. A multitude of innocents who would have been alive, but for me.*

"I can't," he whispered. "I can't do it."

For a moment there was silence. Then a hand touched his arm. Strong, and with sharp nails that pierced through his sleeve. Not Ciani.

He opened his eyes, and saw Hesseth standing before him.

"Listen to me," she said softly. Her voice a half-whisper, half-hissing. "It's not just your species at risk here, remember? I was sent with you because rakh are dying, in every part of this region. People every bit as real and as 'innocent' as the humans you ache so to protect. Suffering, no less than the victims of your Hunter. Are all those lives worth nothing to you?" She glanced back at Ciani. "I despise your killer companion. I sympathize with your hatred of him. But I also tell you this: Our chances of success in this are next to nothing without him." She bared her teeth, an expression of warning. "You tell me to bury my primitive instincts, act with my head. Now it's time for you to do that. Because if we fail here, we doom my people to more and more attacks like the ones that take place in Lema now. Maybe even outside the Canopy, later, among your own people. Is that what you want? To waste all our effort? She growled softly. "I say we go to this place and see what our options are. If we have a clear shot at our enemy, we use it. But if not, and we think we can liberate this Hunter of yours . . . then we'd be fools not to, priest, and that's the simple truth. And I have no tolerance for foolishness when it threatens my life."

For a moment he couldn't answer. For a moment the words were all bottled up inside him, like a wine under pressure. Waiting to explode. And then he exhaled slowly, slowly; an exercise in self-control. Two breaths. Another. At last he spoke, in the low monotone of one who has choked back so hard on his feelings that nothing, not even normal emotions, can surface in his speech.

"All right," he said. "As you say. We'll see what the situation is, first, and then decide. The three of us." He felt somehow polluted, shamed by his betrayal of . . . what? His people? The rakh? The matter was too complex for simple answers, and he knew it. But he felt as though he had betrayed his faith—himself—and the shame of that burned like fire. He turned away from them both, lest they see the hot reddening of his cheeks. Lest they guess at his shame. Lest they realize that beneath his bitter hatred of Tarrant there ran an undercurrent of something else. A sharp sense of relief, that when they finally went into battle they might have Tarrant's power backing them. And that shamed him more than anything.

Damn you, Tarrant. Damn you to hell.

"All right," he whispered. Hoarsely, as though the words hurt his throat. "Let's do it."

You'd better be worth it, you bastard.

Forty-one

Caverns. Not like the tunnels of the Lost Ones, which had
been carved and plastered and buttressed and adorned for rakhene
convenience; these were empty spaces, utterly lifeless, whose silence
was broken only by the slow drip of water as it wended its way down
from the surface, chamber by chamber. Tunnels that were comfortably six feet in height would shrink to a mere crawlspace yards later.
Room-sized chambers that accommodated four people would be
reduced to mere crevices at their farther end, requiring a painstaking
divestment of all supply packs before the party could pass through.
Steep inclines dead-ended against blank walls and pits dropped down
into seeming nothingness, while shallow lakes, mirror-surfaced, made
it all but impossible to guess at the hazards that lay underneath.

Under the best of circumstances, progress would have been slow.
With what they had to deal with—inadequate lighting, lack of proper
tools, and an enemy who might turn their own Workings against
them—it was maddeningly frustrating. Though they knew that they
were only a short distance from their objective, it was impossible to
travel a straight line in the torturous underground system. Sometimes
the most promising route would double back on itself, returning
them to a point they had passed by hours ago. The pierced one was
doing what he could to guide them, but even his rakhene sense of
direction could do them little good in such a place. They could only
fight their way forward step by step, chamber by chamber, and hope
that *ground gained* exceeded *ground lost* in the long run.

What kept them going was the knowledge that there was, for them,
no other way. Unless they were ready to break into the citadel itself,
this was the only known entrance to the labyrinth beneath it. And
so they fought on, and kept their weapons tightly in hand as they

wended their way through the underearth—ever aware that if the demons attacked them, it would be without light, without warning, and without mercy.

At last, wary of the weakness that exhaustion would conjure, they found themselves a chamber more defensible than most and slept. Briefly. Having no knowledge of how many hours had passed since they had first entered the random tunnels, or whether sunlight or darkness reigned in the world above. They stood guard in teams, as they had above ground, but silently Damien questioned the efficacy of such an arrangement. If the demons they sought could shed their human form, then there was no truly defensible place; the earth was too full of mysterious cracks and crevices, and dark pits that extended to other levels of the labyrinth. So he made sure that his sword was close at hand and napped in a sitting position, springbolt braced against his knees.

How much time did they have to search? He wished he knew. Even if Tarrant's Working had succeeded in buying them cover it would only work for as long as the party's doppelgangers were alive. The minute those poor doomed souls reached Sansha Crater and the ambush took them, the deception was ended forever. And in that moment their enemy, who very likely knew the party's purpose—or at least guessed at it—would begin to search his domain with a fine-toothed comb, searching for them.

He hoped that the simulacra would take longer than expected to reach their goal. And hated himself for doing so. He hated himself for wanting the deception to work at all; for being grateful that five innocents had been doomed to a grisly death, instead of his own party. But worst of all were those rare instants when he was honest enough to admit that he was grateful to Tarrant for making that move without asking him. Without giving him the chance to stop it. That gratitude was like a cancer on his soul, a growing uncleanliness which he lacked the knowledge—or perhaps the will—to eradicate.

It's what he said he would do to me, he thought darkly. *Exactly what he described.* The thought of going in to rescue the man was doubly abhorrent because of it. But the longer they traveled, the closer their destination loomed in his mind, the more Damien was forced to admit that they needed him. Plain and simple. As for the ramifactions of that . . . he would deal with them later.

When he slept he dreamed of fire, and it burned in his brain with such an intensity that his skin was actually flushed with fever when he awakened, as though the fire burned within him. From the place where Ciani lay curled up, asleep, he heard soft moans of anguish, and he knew without needing to ask that the same dream had her in thrall. Neither Hesseth nor the pierced one seemed troubled by such visions, but who could say whether the mechanism of their sleep bore any similarity to a human standard? There was no way to judge whether something was in the currents that only humans might respond to, or—a far more alarming possibility—whether Tarrant himself was the source of those visions, using his links with Damien and Ciani to communicate in symbols what he lacked the ability to send in words. But fire? From the Hunter? He considered many possible causes for that, in the hours they traveled, and all of them were chilling.

It wasn't until long after their sleep break—when they were taking a brief rest in a large, dry chamber—that he thought to mention it to his rakhene companions. To his surprise the pierced one responded immediately.

"It is the *fire of the earth*," Hesseth translated. Suggesting by her hesitation a far more complex phrase, with connotations that had no parallel in her own dialect. "It lives in this place."

Damien heard Ciani's sudden indrawn breath, felt excitement stir within him. "Fire of the earth? What is that? Ask him?"

She did so. And listened to the answer at length, and questioned him about it, before turning again to her human listeners. "I'm not sure of this," she warned them. "His language is very unclear. Highly symbolic. But what I make of it is that here, somewhere in these caverns, is a fire which the earth itself supplies with fuel. He says it burned when his people first came here, and kept burning in all the time they occupied this region. Before the falling-threat finally drove them away. It has some kind of . . . spiritual significance, I think."

"The word is *religious*," Damien said quietly. "Go on."

"That's all he knows. They don't have the kind of oral tradition we do; all he remembers are snatches of stories, that were retold because of their dramatic value." She smiled slightly. "I gather the young of his kind are threatened with being thrown into this fire if they misbehave too often."

"A fire of the earth," Ciani whispered.

And he nodded. Not in response to what she said, but to what she was thinking. Because there was no question about it: the fire of the earth was Tarrant's fire, the same yellow flame that haunted their dreams and their thoughts, which seemed to guard the secret of their dark companion's disappearance. As soon as he even considered that connection he knew it for the truth. It was as though some some vital circuit in his brain had finally closed—or as though the channel between Tarrant and himself allowed that much knowledge to flow, before distance and distaste could occlude it. And he knew, without asking Ciani, that her experience was the same.

"Tarrant's fire," he muttered. "Fed by the earth? I'd guess fossil fuel, in some form. Probably solid, or a shifting of the earth would have cut the supply channel at some point."

"Except that the earth hasn't moved here," Ciani reminded him.

"It's moved some. Maybe not enough to shake the ground hard—maybe so little that no one's ever aware of it—but it moves. It *has* to." He turned to Hesseth. "Ask him if he knows where it is. Ask him if he can tell us anything of how to find it."

She talked to the pierced one again, and this time it was clear he was the one having difficulty. After a time he answered her, haltingly, and she told the humans, "Deep down. Very deep down. I'm not sure whether he means the lowest caverns in this system, or the lowest caverns not underwater. Or even the lowest caverns not rakh-made; there might be tunnels that were dug below that level, later."

"Good enough," Damien muttered.

"Damien?" Ciani put a hand on his arm; he noted that she was trembling slightly. "What are you thinking?"

"That it may be a safe way in," he told her. He put his own hand over hers, and squeezed it tightly in reassurance. "We can't Know the caverns, because then our enemy would See exactly where we are. We can't Locate Tarrant, because the minute we tried we'd be opening up a channel that our enemy could use to strike at us. But a fire? A simple fire? A straightforward Working, fixed on that . . . it would be doubly safe, because he'd never anticipate it. How could he know that we'd even heard of the *fire of the earth?* How could he anticipate that we would understand its significance? It just might work, Cee. *Safely.* We just might get away with it."

In a voice very still, very fragile, she asked, "You'll go after him?"

For a moment there was only the darkness around them, and the chill silence of the underworld. Then, choosing his words very carefully, he told her, "I said I'd take the best way in, didn't I? I said if it turned out the best thing to do, I'd go with it." *You have no idea what it's going to cost me to save that man,* he thought grimly. *Or of what it will cost our world, to have him free in it. But Hesseth was right. If his strength and his knowledge can help end this plague, then I have no real choice, do I? We use the tools we must.* "If nothing else, it gives us a clear road in. And God knows, we need that."

Then he took her hand in both of his, warmed it between his palm. "The relationship you had with him means that you know him better than I can," he said softly. Trying to keep his voice utterly neutral, trying not to let his tone and manner betray how appalling he found that fact. "He knows how abhorrent I found him. He knows how much I despised him, for everything he represented. Tell me this, if you can ... if he were in trouble—captured, let's say, and in pain, incapable of helping himself—does he think that I would come after him?" When she hesitated, he added, "Or that I would let our party come to help him? Or does he think I would leave him to die—perhaps even be grateful to our enemy for arranging it?"

For a long time she stared at him, as if by doing so she could read what was in his mind. But he was careful to keep his expression neutral, and at last she answered, "There's not any real question about that, is there?

"He believes it."

She hesitated, then nodded.

"He believes it *utterly*."

This time the nod came faster.

"What is it?" Hesseth asked. "What does that mean?"

"If our enemy were rakhene, nothing. But it has to do with the way human sorcery works—with the way that our enemy would naturally use Gerald Tarrant as a focus for any Working that concerned us."

"He would take the knowledge of our plans from his mind?"

"Either that, or use it as a ... say, a filter of sorts, for a more general Knowing. But either way...." His hands tightened about Ciani's. A familiar excitement was beginning to course through his veins, driving out all memory of fatigue and frustration. This was the approach they needed, at last; it felt *right*, in a way that years of experience had taught him to trust. "He wouldn't see us coming," he whispered fiercely. "If Tarrant thinks what you say he does, if he's that certain of it ... why would the enemy assume him wrong? It means that way would would be only lightly guarded, if at all. And probably not Worked against us. But most important ... it means we have a way to find our way through this damned labyrinth without being caught at it. Praise God," he breathed. "Now, let's just hope that when we get that bastard back...."

He released Ciani and lifted his springbolt. And tested the draw, to make sure it was tightly cocked.

"Let's just say he'd better earn his keep," he warned her.

Caverns. So deep within the earth that the earth-fae itself faded to a whisper: a mere hint of power with no sense of motion about it. A shallow pool of unWorked potential, utterly unlike the swift-flowing currents that coursed on the planet's surface. But for what Damien intended, it was enough. He cast his will out upon the mirror stillness of its surface and shaped it slowly, carefully, to serve his intentions. After a moment, there was a ripple—more felt than seen, like a shadow of thought that flitted through the mind without taking form—and then the fae began to flow. Slowly. Not as it would have done on the surface of the planet, where the power born of seismic disruption was constantly pouring into it, stirring it to life. But moving nonetheless, with clear direction. It was enough.

"Toward the fire," Damien whispered. And they Worked their sight—with effort—and followed it. Wading downcurrent, following the whispery power as it clung to the edges of water-carved stone, marking a path that they might tread. The pierced one was silent now, his jangling ornaments bound up with bits of cloth so that they might not betray the party. Nor did he speak, but climbed through the caverns lost in the web of his own thoughts. Communing with his gods, perhaps, or contemplating his masculine bravado. Whatever it was, it served their purpose well enough; Damien encouraged it.

And then they came to a place where the last chamber narrowed, until all that led from it was a low-ceilinged crawlspace, barely wide enough to accommodate a man. Small formations edged its upper surface like teeth, and two stalagmites the thickness of a man's wrist rose from its mud-covered floor. Damien looked at it dubiously, was about to speak—and then heard a gasp behind him that caused him to whip about with his weapon at the ready.

It was Ciani. Pale as a ghost, shivering as though she had just seen—or heard—something utterly terrifying. She had her hands up before her face as if trying to ward off some terrible danger—but when Damien turned back in response to that gesture, to seek out the cause of her terror, he saw nothing more than he had previously. Only empty stone corridors, weakly coursing fae, and glistening of moisture on slender calcite branches.

"The smell," she whispered. "Gods, I remember. . . ."

He came to her then, handed his weapon to Hesseth—who understood, and was ready to take it—and took the ex-adept into his arms. And held her tightly, making his body into a shield that might protect her from all dangers.

"I smell it," she whispered. "Can't you? I remember running. . . . Gods, I must have come this way. There were places . . . I thought . . . but I had so little light, then, and so little strength . . .

and these caves all look the same, don't they? But I thought . . . oh gods, don't you see, I've *been* here. . . ."

Then she lowered her head to his chest and sobbed softly there; he stroked her hair gently and wished he could will some of his own strength into her. It had been bound to happen, this outburst, and he'd been expecting it . . . but he knew that there was even worse to come, and so he just held her, gently, and let her have her tears. God knows, she'd been holding them in long enough.

Soon she'll remember all of it. All of it! Her capture, her captivity, whatever torture she endured at the hands of these creatures . . . it'll all return to her in an instant. A single blow. What will that be like! So much terror pouring back into her, all those years of suffering relived in an instant . . . this is nothing, compared to it. Her hardest moment will be the one in which we restore her to what she was.

When he thought she was capable of listening to him, he said to her gently, "You couldn't have come this way, Cee. Think about it. You'd have had to come through that tunnel, and you'd have had to break the formations to do it. Right? They're still there."

"It's the smell," she whispered. Her whole body was shaking. She clung to him desperately "It's like that all through their tunnels. Can't you smell it? I couldn't escape it. I ran and ran, and I couldn't get away from it. . . ."

He tested the air, caught a faint whiff of sourness coming from the tunnel. Too faint, or else too unfamiliar, for him to identify; he looked to Hesseth and saw her nod grimly.

"Carrion," she hissed softly. And the pierced one concurred. "Rotting carrion," she translated for him.

The region of no, he thought. *The place of dying.*

"All right," he muttered. "We're going through. The fae'll guide us to the fire all right, so if we see anything move we shoot—or swing, or whatever—and worry about what it was later. Agreed?"

Ciani nodded, as did Hesseth. When the *khrast* woman translated for their pierced companion, he bared his teeth and hissed aggressively, his naked tail curling at the tip. *I'll take that for a yes,* Damien thought.

He approached the narrow passageway and studied it. Had it been clear of mud and monuments it might have been wide enough for him—barely—but as it was, there was no clear way through.

"How strong are those things?" he asked the pierced one, pointing to one of the slender stalagmites.

It took the Lost One a moment to realize what he was driving at. Then he answered, "When small, very brittle. When that large,"—

and he pointed to the two stalagmites rising from the mud-covered floor—"they will still crack, if much force is applied."

"Good enough," he muttered. He opened the buckles on his sword's harness and lowered the sheathed weapon from his back. "Hand this through as soon as I'm out," he said, giving it to Ciani. Tarrant's sword had been affixed to the same harness, but he unfastened it so that it would come through separately. All he needed in a moment of trouble was to grab the wrong one. Even through its multiple layers of wrapping the cold sword throbbed with malevolence, and Damien thought he perceived a certain . . . call it *hunger*. Was that because it sensed it was close to its master/creator? Or because it knew that soon it might be going into battle, with all the mayhem that implied?

He divested himself of all the layers he could: outer jacket, fleece vest, thick overshirt. He left on the thick leather undervest which had saved his life on so many occasions, and hoped that its bulk wasn't too excessive. "Leave the general supplies here," he ordered. "Take weapons, tools, some food and water. We'll come back here when we're done." *If we can.* "Take light," he added. And he removed the precious pouch of Fire from his belt and hung it about his neck instead, so that it might not impede him in the narrow passageway.

Then: head first, shoulders brushing the uneven walls as he crawled slowly through. He had a long knife clasped in his teeth so that whatever danger might lurk on the other side would not find him unarmed, or unready. Thin calcite spines caught on his shirt as he passed, snapped off like burrs as he pressed onward. Good enough. He elbowed his way forward, through a tunnel that grew narrower and narrower, until he could feel the stone walls pressing close on both sides of him. Then he came to the first of the slender formations, and he leaned all his weight against it; it snapped off cleanly near the base, and he set it to one side. The same with the second. The tunnel widened somewhat, enough that he could crawl through. And then opened suddenly, without warning, into a much larger chamber.

He thrust himself into it and rolled to his feet, and then reached back the way he had come. Ciani had followed after him, close enough that when she extended his long sword toward him he was able to grasp its hilt and draw it. Thus armed, he surveyed his surroundings. A large room, empty of adversaries but filled with the reek of their presence. He saw where a tunnel opposite had been widened to allow for more comfortable passage, and he thought with grim satisfaction, *This is it. This is where they'll be.*

"Come through," he whispered. "Carefully."

They did, with considerably less difficulty than he'd had. He noted that if they fled this way he would need to make sure he went through last, in order that they might not be delayed while he squeezed his bulk through the passage. Not a cheery thought.

"Can you See?" he asked Ciani. And even more than listening for her answer, he watched for her response. But she seemed to be somewhat under control, and she nodded as she gazed down at the fae.

"Barely," she whispered. "It's very weak."

"But it'll have to do. We can't use real light in here; they'd see it coming miles away." Again she nodded, and he extinguished their illumination. It had only been minimal to start with, a bare spark of fire in a mostly hooded lantern, but now it was gone. He handed the lantern to Ciani, who hooked it to her belt. And looked down at the earth-fae, to see which way his guiding current was flowing.

"This way," he whispered, and he led them into the heart of the demons' lair.

It was dark, and cold, and rank with the smell of death. The chill of it seemed to exceed the natural cold of the underneath, as though some force had leached the heat from the very stone about them; Damien thought of the Hunter's sword—now strapped again to his harness—and wondered at the similarity. An eater of souls, the pierced rakh had called it. Like the ones they were hunting. How similar were they, really?

And then Hesseth whispered Hssssst! in warning, and Damien fell back. The cold stone behind him pressed Tarrant's sword even closer, so that its unnatural chill lanced into his back muscles; he had to fight not to alter his position, to remain utterly still and utterly silent while his companions also hid, waiting for any sight or sound that might tell him what the danger was. And after a moment, it came. The padding of flesh on stone, the whisper of clothing. The hoarse breathing of one who has no need to be silent, the muttered conversation of one who knows no reason to fear.

Then they came around the corner, and Damien paused just long enough to acertain that there were only two of them before he swung. He put all his strength into it, knowing that the unWorked steel was all but invisible to their fae-sight. And the full force of it hit the first creature at neck level and sliced through muscle and bone with a crack, coming out the other side with some speed still left in it. The creature's head struck the wall, bloodily, and caromed off it to the floor; its body sank slowly, as if not yet fully cognizant of the fact of its death. Damien turned to the other one, quickly, ready to face whatever manner of defense the surprised creature could muster—

but the face that stared at him had a black hole in the place of one eye, from which acrid smoke and golden sparks issued as he watched. He caught sight of the rear metal band of a bolt as the creature twitched, the Fire spreading in its veins like poison. And he turned back to see Ciani standing with springbolt in hand, an expression that was half fear and half pride suffusing her countenance.

"It seemed like the thing to do," she whispered.

Damien leaned down to inspect the headless body. Vaguely human in shape, it was dressed in an assortment of mismatched garments, haphazardly arranged. Barefoot. After a moment he placed his hand on its flesh and muttered "Warm. The body's alive. Not just a demon, then. Truly embodied."

"What does that mean?" Hesseth asked.

"It means they bleed. It means they die." He looked up at her; he could feel the fierceness in his own expression. "It means that whatever these things are, the odds in our favor just got a little better."

They hid the bodies as well as they could. They couldn't wash the blood from the ground or drive the reek of burning flesh from the area, but at least if someone passed through quickly they wouldn't see what had happened. The earth-fae was faint enough here that whoever relied upon it for sight might miss seeing details. The dark fae, though far more intense, clearly had no love of carrion; it withdrew from the corpses as it would withdraw from cold, unliving stone, and therefore offered no illumination.

"Good enough," Damien muttered at last.

They went on. Damien in the lead, with Hesseth right beside him. Her senses of hearing and smell were clearly more accurate than his, so he trusted her to be on guard for approaching danger. He studied the current, and the walls, and tried to get some feel for the lay of the land. At least this cavern system had been modified so that a man might walk through it upright. He had given one springbolt to the rakh-woman, and Ciani carried the other. Damien preferred his sword, not because it was more efficient—it wasn't—or even because it was marginally quieter—it was—but because it was . . . well, *familiar*. A weapon he had wielded through so many battles, relied upon in so many tight situations, that using it was like using part of his body. Second nature. *And besides*, he told himself, *it doesn't need reloading*. The pierced one carried a slender wooden spear, brought with him from his home caverns. If the look on his face was any guide, he knew how to use it.

Well armed and more than ready, he thought grimly.

They passed through a number of chambers and passageways, including some where several routes intersected. At each of these he paused, and worked to commit the place to memory. He didn't dare mark the walls here as he had during their descent; the marks he made would be as likely to lead their enemies to them as serve any purpose of theirs.

And then they came to it. It was the pierced one who felt it first, and hissed sharp sounds to Hesseth in warning. "Heat," she translated. "From up ahead." They looked at each other. "I don't feel it," the rakh-woman whispered.

"You wouldn't, necessarily," Damien whispered back. "Specialized senses. The temperature belowground is so constant, any change would have significance." He nodded his approval—and his admiration—to the pierced one. And checked the current carefully before he moved again.

Now, if possible, they were doubly alert. If there were guards at all, they would be here. Damien felt a breeze brush by his face, something far more suited to open spaces than this underground warren. And then he understood: the fire. Drawing oxygen, and with it air. Creating suction as it burned, so that fresh air would be drawn to it. How else could it keep burning so long, regardless of its fuel?

"Very close," he whispered. He signaled for them to stop, and strained his senses to the utmost. The fetid stink of the demons' lair was stronger here, perhaps concentrated by the fire's pull. Not certain that Hesseth would pick up any smell besides that foul odor, he listened for a hint of movement. None. Not a sound or a smell to hint at the presence of any other being in this chamber, or in any adjoining passage. It was almost too good to be true.

He doesn't expect us here, he reminded himself. There was a chance—just a chance—that the fire wasn't guarded. At all. If so, they might even make contact with Tarrant before anyone realized they were there. . . .

And then all hell breaks loose. Because no matter what their enemy was doing with Tarrant, he'd damn well be monitering the results. Which meant that the moment they interfered with his plans, he'd be aware of both their presence and their purpose. They'd be lucky if he didn't blast them right on the spot; if he lacked that kind of power he'd certainly send his people after them, and it was a good bet the resident soul-eaters knew this labyrinth better than Damien and his company.

We'll deal with that when we get to it.

There was light, now, flickering and faint—but real light, golden light, like the kind that came from a natural fire. It seemed to Damien that now he, too, could feel heat on his face, as if each few steps brought him into a place where the air was noticeably warmer.

He felt a cold buzz course up his back, as though Tarrant's sword was somehow upset by the concept of warmth. *Tough shit,* he thought to it. He turned a sharp corner and squeezed around an obstruction—the light was much brighter now, and it seemed that in the distance he could hear the roar of flames—and then

Fire. Burning so brightly that he had to turn away from it. Burning so hot that the skin of his face reddened, just from standing before it. For a moment he saw nothing but the fire itself, a narrow-based bonfire that blazed upward a good fifty feet before licking even farther into a wide crack in the cavern's upper surface. The chamber it was in was a good forty feet wide, if not more, and a jagged crack ran down the center of the floor; it was the middle of that which had broken open, giving access to the limitless fuel beneath. Sometime in the distant past someone or something must have ignited it—but that moment was little more than legend now, if that. As far as the Lost Ones were concerned, the fire had burned forever.

He forced himself away from the entrance so that the others might follow. And scanned the chamber as well as he could, for any sign of enemy activity. But for as much as his darkness-adapted eyes could see past the blazing fire, it seemed they were alone. Except for a pile of fabric against the far wall, and a long, slender object that lay atop it. . . .

He walked toward it, half-aware that the others were following. He had a terrible feeling about what it was and fervently hoped he was wrong. But when he got to the pile at last, he saw that it was indeed what he had feared. Midnight blue silk and fine gray worsted, in layers that were all too familiar. And atop it all an empty sheath, its surface inscribed with at least a dozen ancient symbols . . . Tarrant's sheath. Tarrant's clothing. He felt sick, realizing why they were here.

He looked at the bonfire—squinted against its glare, and tried to make out details—and at last muttered, "He's there. In that."

Ciani shivered, and looked at the fire. And then said, "But it isn't Worked. How could it hold him—"

"He can't Work fire," Damien said tightly. "Or anything connected to it." It seemed to him that for a moment he understood what that meant, what it felt like for a being that powerful to be rendered impotent—utterly neutralized—by so simple a means. And the pain of it, the utter *humiliation* of it, was so intense that he nearly staggered back, as though struck. For a man of the Hunter's arrogance to be trapped thus . . . he wondered if that fierce pride could survive such an experience. If the identity he knew as Gerald Tarrant could emerge from it unscathed—or even recognizable.

"I think," he said slowly, "if there's any one facet of our enemy that terrifies me . . . it's how well he knows us. How well he knows how to get to each of us."

He walked toward the fire slowly, his eyes filling with tears as the heat of it seared his face. He came as close as he dared and then stopped and stared into it. Into the brutal heart of it, the blazing core of its heat.

And he could barely make out, amidst the dancing flames, the black figure of a man. Stretched out across the opening, arms spread out in a cruciform arrangement. The fingers—if there still were fingers—would be just inches short of the fire's edge. Damien looked for some kind of support, saw the blunt ends of coarse steel bars resting on both sides of the crevice. The metal glowed with heat where it lay against the stone floor. If he lay on that framework, perhaps bound to it . . . merciful God. No doubt it was the powerful air currents, fire-stirred, that kept the smell of roasting flesh from reaching them. Damien had no doubt that it was there, in quantity.

"We have to turn it off," he muttered. His mind racing as it considered—and discarded—at least a dozen options. "I can't get to him while it burns."

"Smother it?" Ciani asked. She was by his side, a hand shielding her eyes as if from bright sunlight.

"Can't. There's air coming in, all along there." He indicated the narrower portions of the crevice. "If not from underneath, too."

"Block it?" Hesseth asked.

He bit his lower lip as he considered that. "Going to have to try," he said at last. "The earth-fae's weak, but I can't think of another good option." He turned back toward the chamber's one entrance, saw that the pierced one had taken up guard there. "They'll be on us the minute I Work. It may take them time to get down here, but they'll come. In force. As soon as I alter the fire."

"Then we'll just have to be ready for them," the rakh-woman said fiercely, and she braced the springbolt against her shoulder.

He went back where Tarrant's possessions lay, and considered them. Then he removed the coldfire blade and unwrapped it, carefully. The Worked steel blazed with a chill blue light, as blinding as snow—and then was extinguished, as he thrust it deep into its warded container. He tested the handle, and sensed no active malevolence. *Thank heaven for that, anyway.*

He positioned the other members of their small company as best he could, to prepare for the arrival of the enemy's servants. But: *Our best won't be good enough,* he thought darkly. Without Tarrant's power behind them they were no match for a horde of demons, flesh-dependent or no; they would have to work fast and get out quickly, and hope that Tarrant could be restored before battle commenced.

He looked at the body within the flames, and felt despair uncoiling within him. *If he can be restored,* he thought grimly. *What if we're doing all this for nothing?*

He gathered himself for Working, and stared into the fire. Stared beneath it, to where the sharp lips of rock gaped wide above the earth's store of fuel. He Worked his sight—no easy task, with the earth-fae so thin—and tried to look deep down into that opening, to assess its structure. But there was no place immediately below where the walls of the crevice drew any closer together. With a sigh he resigned himself to Working its upper edges, and braced himself for the effort.

And air roared past him, sucked up by the conflagration. Earth-fae swept past him, too thin to grasp. He tried to enclose it in his will, to force a form and purpose upon its tenuous substance—but it ran through his fingers like smoke and was sucked up into the inferno. *Not enough of it,* he despaired. *Not enough!* He was used to the currents of Erna's surface, so deep and rich that the simplest thought was enough to shape it, the simplest Working enough to master it . . . but here, Working the fae was like trying to breathe in a vacuum. There simply wasn't enough power for what he needed to do.

But there has to be, he thought darkly. *Because we have no other choice.* Already he could feel the malignant thoughts of their enemy closing in around him, like a fist being clenched. How long did they have before he struck? Mere minutes, he guessed. He poured everything he had into his Working: all the force of his hatred for Tarrant, his love for Ciani, his despair at losing her twice—first to the assault in Jaggonath, then to Tarrant's corruption. If raw emotion could master the earth-fae, then he would use that as his fuel. His will blazed forth in need, in pain, and he grasped at the elusive power. And fought to weave it into a barrier, that might bridge the mouth of the crevice. But there simply wasn't enough fae there to do what he needed. Again and again he tried, until his soul was scraped raw by remembered anguish, until his whole body shook from the force of his exertion. But his Bindings dissolved even as he made them, and the force of the fire broke through his every Working.

"I can't" he gasped at last. "Can't do it." His brain was on fire, his whole body shaking, his plans in chaos. *What now?* he thought desperately. *What now?* Behind him he could sense Ciani's despair, and it cut into him like a knife. *I failed her. I failed them all.*

How much time had passed, while he wrestled with the earth-fae?

He didn't dare ask. But every second they spent here increased their danger. Already their only escape route might be cut off—

Think, man. Think! The earth-fae isn't strong enough here. The dark fae can't be used to bind fire. There's nothing we can do by physical means alone. What else is there? What? Think!

He knew, suddenly. And turned to Hesseth.

"Tidal power," he gasped. "Can you—"

"Not stable," she warned. "Not for solid work. There would be danger—"

"To hell with the danger! It's that or nothing." He was drenched with sweat but refused to move back from the fire. *"Can you do it?"*

For a moment her eyes unfocused, and she stared not at him, but past him. *Through* him. He remembered the tidal fae fluxing over Morgot, the brief rainbow power that had suddenly filled the sky with brilliance, then vanished with equal rapidity. It was a fickle power, utterly impermanent. Dangerously unstable. And right now, it was the only hope they had left.

"I can try," she said at last. "But you understand—"

"Just do it!" He was counting down the seconds in his mind, wondering how long it would take their enemy's soldiers to reach them. "Do it fast," he whispered. Was it possible that the enemy's attention had been elsewhere when they struck, delaying his response? He prayed that it was so. Every minute counted now.

Hesseth turned her attention to the fire, and he followed her gaze. He tried to See the forces she was summoning, but the delicate power eluded him. How much fae would be available to her, and how long would it last? The tidal patterns altered minute by minute, as time and tides progressed about the planet. Even if she could conjure a barrier for them, would it remain solid long enough for them to do what they had to?

"There it is," Ciani whispered. Pointing to the crevice. It could be seen at one edge of the opening, now: a fog, a darkness, that grew solid even as they watched, and eclipsed the fire behind it. He felt his heart pounding as he watched it extend—several inches into the crevice, a foot, two feet, now halfway across it—and he wiped the sweat from his face with a salt-soaked sleeve. *Go for it, Hesseth. You can do it.* The remaining fire was ragged now, as if struggling against some unseen bond. Smoke was beginning to seep from other places along the crevice, desperately seeking egress from the pit of its birth. For a moment he feared that the fire would break out elsewhere, that Hesseth's Working might force it to break through the very rock beneath their feet. Then the last of the Fire spurted upward, licking the ceiling with its orange tongue—and was suddenly gone, vanished beneath the shadowy blockage.

It wasn't hard to see what the enemy had done to Gerald Tarrant; the grating that supported him still glowed red-hot, supplying them with more than enough light. Atop the thick steel bars lay a body that had been burned and healed and burned again, so many times that its surface was little more than a blackened mass of scar tissue. Where cracks appeared red blood oozed forth, and it sizzled as it made contact with the superheated skin. Damien didn't look at the face—or what was left of it—but he felt hot bile rise in his throat as he studied the man's bonds. Wide metal bands bound the Hunter to his rack at the wrist, upper arm, ankle and neck; they, too, glowed with heat, and had burned their way deep into his flesh until the edges of bones were visible.

"How long—" he began.

"Eight days," Ciani whispered. "If they brought him right here." She looked up at him; her face was drenched with sweat, or tears. Or both. "What do we do?" she begged him. "How do we get him off it?"

He fought back his growing sickness and tried to Work. It wouldn't take much fae to break those bonds; that was a simple exercise, a straightforward molecular repulsion. But either Hesseth's Working had affected the earth-fae or he was simply too exhausted to Work it. He fought with the fae until his vision began to darken about the edges, the whole of the room swimming about him. And then knew, at last, that he was defeated. The best of his efforts couldn't conjure more power than there was in this place, and there simply wasn't enough. Tarrant might have been able to do it. He couldn't.

He looked up, and saw Ciani's eyes fixed on him. Not despairing, now, but filled with a feverish excitement. And with a terrible fear. The combination was chilling.

"The coldfire," she whispered. "The sword."

It took him a moment to realize what she meant. "Too dangerous—"

"*Not for me.*"

He remembered the malevolence housed within that blade, and shuddered. "Can you?" he whispered. "Can you control it?"

She hesitated. "*He* controls it," she said hoarsely. "But I think I can use it. For him."

She went to get the blade. He tried to fight back his growing sickness, his sense of horror at what she was attempting. If she tried to master that power and failed, what would the cost be? He remem-

bered the hunger he had sensed while handling it, that had so horrified him. What had the Lost Ones called it—the Eater of Souls?

And then she was back, and the sword was in her hands. She hesitated just an instant—and he knew in that moment that she feared
it every bit as much as he did—and then drew it from its sheath. The
containment wards let loose their hold, and the chill power of Tarrant's coldfire blazed forth freely.

Hot versus cold. Expansion and contraction. If she could gain control of that frigid force, if she could focus it finely enough . . . it might
be enough to break through those bonds and free the Hunter. But if
not. . . .

He saw the barrier flicker for an instant; a burst of flame shot
through it, enveloping Tarrant's torso, and then was gone. He looked
at Hesseth, saw her whole body tense with the effort of Working.
Hang in there, he begged her. *Hold onto it. . . .*

Ciani touched a hand to the blade—and cried out as the blue-white
power shot up that extremity, up to her shoulder. Her skin took on
the ghostly pallor of long-dead flesh, and frost rimmed her fingernails.
Then she grasped the haft of it with that hand, at it seemed that her
fingers froze closed about the grip. Slowly she extended the Worked
weapon toward the nearest of Tarrant's bonds; he could see her struggling to bind its power, fighting to impose her own focus on its chaotic essence. Then the tip of the sword touched the red-hot metal,
and sparks flew. Coldfire arced upward with electrical brilliance, and
snapped like lightening in the charged atmosphere. Then it was gone,
and the sword was withdrawn . . . and the steel band that had bound
his wrist was shattered, its frosted pieces falling like shrapnel to the
fae-worked barrier beneath.

Smoke spurted and curled upward through Hesseth's Working as
she struggled to move the sword again. *Hold onto it!* Ciani's face had
taken on the same ghastly pallor as her hand, and he could almost
hear her heart laboring to maintain its beat as the Hunter's killing
cold invaded her flesh. Damn the man! Would they free him from
death, only to lose her? He watched her face as a second metal strap
shattered into frozen crystals, saw the pain—and the fear—that was
etched across her brow. Still she continued. Tarrant's neck was freed
now, and Damien's hand closed tightly about the grip of his own
sword. They could cut through the man's other wrist if they had to,
and even his ankles; let him regenerate the flesh at his leisure, once
they were out of here. He thought he could hear footsteps now, a
distant pounding as if from running feet. The fourth bond shattered.
The sweat on Ciani's face had frozen, and ice crystals rimmed the
bottoms of her eyes. Five. He started to move forward, saw a wall of

flame erupt before him. *Ciani!* But it was gone as quickly as it had appeared, and though her hair was singed and the skin of her face burned, Ciani seemed unharmed.

Hang in there, Hesseth. Just a few minutes longer!

He moved as the sixth bond shattered, so that by the time Ciani reached to free Tarrant's second ankle he had hold of the man's flesh, was grasping him tightly about the wrist. Hot blood scalded his hand, but he knew there was no time to experiment with less direct measures. As soon as Ciani had broken the last steel band, he pulled with all his strength. The body moved like a broken doll, burned flesh pulling loose from it as it was jerked from the red-hot framework, scar tissue sizzling as it was dragged across the grating—and then they were both out of the danger zone, and just in time. Thin flames licked upward through Hesseth's barrier and then suddenly, with a roar, shot upward toward the ceiling, burning with newfound energy. He felt his own hair curling from the force of the heat, could only pray that Ciani had made it back in time.

He dragged the body back from the flames, tried to wipe some of the sweat from his eyes so that he could see. There was blood on his sleeve; his, or Tarrant's? It no longer seemed to matter. He was dimly aware of blisters all along his palm, from where he had grasped the body. His sword-hand, too—damn, that was careless!

"They're coming!" Hesseth hissed.

He took up his sword in his right hand, wincing as his burned palm closed about the rough grip. And saw Ciani throw a length of cloth about the body—Tarrant's cloak?—so that when they wanted to move it they might do so safely.

And then they came. In numbers, as he had feared. Not a trained guard, but six of the soul-eating creatures who inhabited this underground lair. They were only the first wave, no doubt, the ones who had been closest to the fire when the enemy spotted their activity; there would be others to follow, dozens more, better armed and far more dangerous. But for now, these were enough.

The heat of the fire blazed across his back as he turned to face his attackers. A bolt shot past his head, from Ciani, but she had fired from too far back; it missed its intended target and struck the wall, wooden shaft splintering from the impact. Hesseth had picked up the other springbolt and she fired it point-blank into the gut of one of the creatures; even as it pierced his abdomen and came out through his back he grabbed at the weapon, long claws scoring her arm as he fought to claim it. A second bolt whistled past Damien's ear, and this one struck; a shot to the arm that began to smolder in the pale flesh. Only two of the creatures were armed, but though they bore sizable swords they used them clumsily, like men unaccustomed to armed combat. As Damien engaged the first, trying to keep his back close enough to the fire that none would circle behind him, he wondered what manner of contact was required for their most deadly mode of attack. Mere touch? Bodily penetration? He parried his opponent's sword down to the stone floor and slammed his foot down on it, hard; the cheap steel snapped with a crack, and the momentum of it made the creature stagger off-balance, into his own waiting blade. He wrenched the steel from between the creature's ribs and swung about just in time to duck a blow that was coming at him from the side; it cut his arm, but not deeply, and he moved to take control of their interplay. Where the hell was the pierced one? He saw Hesseth struggling hand-to-hand with an attacker, was dimly aware that one was burning, one had gone off after Ciani, and he could account for two . . . that left a creature missing, as well as one of his own party. He prayed fervently that the pierced one knew how to take care of himself; the thought of trying to find a way out of these caverns without him was terrifying indeed.

He heard a sudden scream from somewhere behind him—it didn't sound like one of his companions—and the smashing of a heavy object into a metal grate. The screaming became a shrieking as flesh began to sizzle, as the creature Ciani had forced into the fire roasted in its core.

Good for her. He parried a cut that was meant to decapitate him and managed to get his back against a wall. One, two, three accounted for . . . there was still one missing, by his reckoning. Gone for help? That was bad. He saw Hesseth go down, her assailant on top of her, and knew with a sinking feeling in the pit of his stomach what manner of attack was taking place. But there was no way he could help her, not with sharp steel thrusting at his gut from one side and sharp claws threatening his face from the other. He brought his own blade around two-handed, forcing the thrust aside—and kicked out at his other attacker, taking him right in the kneecap. Whatever manner of flesh they wore, it was as fragile in that joint as its human counterpart; the creature went down, howling, and it was no hard work to follow through with a second sharp kick, into the face. Bone snapped and blood gushed and he was down for good—and then Damien's other opponent left himself open along one side of his rib cage and he was down, too, blood spurting from a gaping wound in his side.

He looked about, saw nothing but blood and dead flesh about him. He stepped over one of the bodies and ran to where Hesseth lay, her assailant only now coming to his feet by her side. Her eyes were dilated, glazed, like the empty stare of a fish stranded on dry land. Her attacker's glee made it quite clear what manner of exchange had taken place between them, and the eyes that gazed out from that death-white pallor were so like Hesseth's in shape and expression that Damien felt fresh horror take hold of him as he raised his sword to strike—

—and light blazed past him as a Fire-laden bolt hit home, piercing the creature's eye and driving deep into his brain. He screamed and fell back; dark blood gushed from the socket, and other less wholesome fluids as well. With a twitching motion he fell, and as the Fire began to consume his brain the whole of his body shuddered, ripples of pain coursing through his flesh as he soundlessly mouthed screams of agony.

Ciani came to where Hesseth lay and helped her up; dazed, the rakh-woman seemed uncertain as to where she was, or exactly what had happened. Then she saw the body of her assailant, and memory returned to her. All of it. As Ciani helped her to her feet, she whimpered softly in terror.

"The Lost One—" Damien began. But before he could finish Ciani directed his attention upward, to the wall of the cavern just over its entranceway. There, clinging to the jagged stone surface, the pierced one displayed the body of the last attacker to them proudly. It hung by one ankle, which was wrapped in the cave-rakh's prehensile tail. Its throat had been torn out. When he saw that they had witnessed his kill, the Lost One released the body; it fell to the floor like a bag of wet cement, bones snapping as it struck. The cave-rakh then climbed down, serpentine fingers taking purchase in the tiniest of crevices, tail grasping at convenient stone protrusions for support.

Damien looked about, and counted the bodies. Six. All accounted for—but there'd be more, soon enough. "Let's get out of here," he muttered. He went back to where Tarrant's body lay, now covered in the folds of his cloak, and hefted the weight of it up to his shoulder. It was impossible to tell if any life was left in that limp form, but at least the heat of it had cooled somewhat. Time enough later to analyze its condition.

They ran. As well as they could, considering Hesseth's wounds and Damien's burden. The rakh-woman turned back once or twice briefly as if to Work, but whether she had the strength to do so effectively was something Damien couldn't begin to guess at. He held his own wounded arm tightly against him as he wended his way through the demons' labyrinth, hoping that no blood was dripping to the floor— because if they left a trail that distinct, all the Workings in the world couldn't hide it.

At last they came to the narrow tunnel that had been their entrance into this area. Ciani, who had caught up Tarrant's possessions in her flight, now threw down a long silk tunic to cover the rough stone bottom and crawled through. Tarrant's sword went with her, now safely sheathed. Hesseth followed, her bright blood staining the folded silk as she crawled over it. Then the pierced one. By now Damien though he could hear the faint sounds of pursuit from the area they had just left. He lowered Tarrant's body down from his shoulder—still warm, still bleeding, still utterly lifeless—and, with great effort, managed to get it far enough into the tunnel that the pierced one could pull it through. The cloak Ciani had wrapped around it kept the broken flesh from tearing on the sharp formations, but he could see at the end of the tunnel where dark blood, seeping through the wool, had stained the stone beneath. Quickly Damien divested himself of his weapons and passed them through the narrow space, then balled up Tarrant's bloodstained tunic and threw that after it. Then, somewhat awkwardly, he began to back himself into the passageway. Voices sounded from a nearby corridor as he forced himself through the narrow space. As his feet reached the other side he felt hands close about his ankles, meaning to pull him through— but he kicked them off and halted midway, fumbling in the darkness for the two stalagmites he had broken earlier.

The earth-fae was weak here, but this Working was a minor one; it took only seconds for him to use that force to bind the two slender spires back in place, so that the passage was once more impassable. Then he thrust out his feet behind him and let his companions grab hold and pull; stone edges scraped his sides as the neck of the tunnel finally let him pass, and he was through—not a second too soon. Even as he dropped below the lip of the tunnel he saw a flash of light coming from its opposite end, and clearly heard voices from the adjoining room.

They crouched there, hearts pounding, and waited. Hesseth had Obscured their path, but how well? Had they made it through without leaving a telltale path of blood behind them, or a more subtle trail of sweat and scent that the demon-creatures might follow? It was because Damien had considered that possible that he had risked a few precious seconds to Work the two stone pinnacles back in place. Now, as best they could make out, it appeared to be that move which turned the trick. The creatures stared down the tunnel for some time, evidently considering it a viable exit from the area. But it was clear that no man-sized being could have made it through that space and left the formations intact, and so at last they moved on.

"They'll be back," Ciani whispered. "They don't understand how we got away, but their master will."

"That'll take time," he whispered back, hoarsely. "First, we bind up these wounds so we don't leave a trail of blood behind us." He nodded toward Hesseth—whose golden fur was scored with at least a dozen deep, bloody gashes—and indicated his own injured arm. "Then we get as far from this place as we can, preferably high up enough to work a good Obscuring. If that's possible. Then . . ." He felt fresh pain wash over him, and the weakness of exhaustion. How deep was his wound? How much blood had he lost? "We see what we rescued," he whispered. "We see if Gerald Tarrant still exists. We see if he can help us."

"And then?" Ciani asked.

From somewhere, he dredged up a grin. Or at least, the hint of one. It hurt his face.

"Then the real work starts," he told her.

Forty-two

"Calesta!" The voice rang out imperiously, echoing in rage. "Calesta! Attend me, now!"

Slowly the demon's form congealed, drawing its substance from the nearby shadows; when the figure was solid enough to bow, it did so. "My Master commands."

"They took him, Calesta. Out of the fire! You said he would burn there forever. You said they would never come—never!—that they would let him burn. And I believed you. *I believed you!*"

"You commanded me to look into his heart," the demon responded. "I did that. You told me to read his weaknesses. I did that. You bade me devise a way of binding him to your purpose, so that he would be helpless to free himself. I did that also. As for the others, you said, *Leave them to me. . . .*"

"They came for him, Calesta! How? They were miles from here when last I Knew them—miles! I—"

"They were never there," the demon said coolly.

Blood drained from the enraged face, turning it a ghastly white. "What? What does that mean?"

"It means that you were wrong. It means that your Knowing was misdirected. It means that these humans anticipated you, and made false replicas of themselves to draw your attention."

The word came, a whisper: "Simulacra."

The demon bowed its head.

"Why didn't you see it happening? Why didn't you warn me?"

"I serve," the demon answered. "I obey. Those were the parameters you set when you first Conjured me. Had you ordered me to inspect the strangers, I would have done so. You didn't."

"So you stayed in the caverns, to feed on the adept's pain—"

"I never fed on the adept. I've never fed on any of your victims." The faceted eyes glittered maliciously. "I think perhaps you mistake my nature."

Pacing: quickly, angrily, to the window and back again. "I must have him back. You understand that? Him, and the woman. And I want no room for error this time—none at all. You hear me, Calesta? We work out the best way to go after them, and—"

"That won't be necessary," the demon interrupted.

"Meaning what?"

The demon chuckled. "You need only wait. They'll come here by themselves."

The pacing stopped. The tone was one of suspicion. "You're sure of that?"

"Their nature demands it."

"After *me?* Not after the woman's assailant?"

"They understand now that the two are linked. They recognize you as the stronger force. The priest will insist that they deal with you first. And the adept will demand your death—or worse—for what you did to him." The demon paused. "Do you require more than that?"

"No," came the answer. "That's enough." The voice grew harsh. "They're coming here? Good. Then we'll be ready. That's an order, Calesta. You understand? Watch them. Neutralize them. Take them prisoner. No taking chances, this time. Nothing fancy. Just bind them and bring them to me. *To me.* I'll deal with them."

Calesta bowed. And it seemed that a hint of a smile creased the obsidian face, gashing its mirrored surface.

"As you command," the demon responded.

Forty-three

Not until they were near the surface did the four travelers stop, and lower their various burdens to the muddy floor beneath them. As soon as it was clear that they would be staying in one place for more than a few minutes Hesseth sank to the ground, and sat with her head lowered between her knees, her breathing hoarse and labored. Ciani came to where Damien stood and helped him lower Tarrant's body to the ground. It was a dead weight, cold now, and though neither would voice such a thought they both feared that the Hunter's spirit might truly have deserted them.

And what then? Damien thought. *What if all this was for nothing?*

Carefully, the two of them unwrapped the battered form. Bits of burned flesh and crusted blood adhered to the wool, tearing loose from the Hunter as the cloak was removed from him; fresh blood dripped from the resulting wounds, making his flesh slick and hard to handle. By the time Damien had freed him from his wrappings the priest's hands were coated in blood, and the black ash of burnt flesh stuck to his skin as though glued there.

"Look," Ciani urged. She pointed to where the Hunter's arm lay exposed, to the deep gash seared into it by the band of red-hot steel. Blackened skin curled back from the wound, displaying muscles and nerves that had been seared to a bloody ash. But the bone itself was no longer visible. Damien drew in a sharp breath as he realized that, and he turned the man's arm over, to make sure of it. "My God. . . ."

"He's healing," she whispered.

He looked at the body—which displayed no other sign of life, and numerous signs of death—and felt awe creep over him. And horror. "He must have had to repair his flesh constantly in order to survive. Drawing on what little fae there was, to replace what the fire destroyed . . . my God." He looked at the man's face—or what was left of it—and felt his sticky hands clenching into fists at his side. "It could have gone on forever. He could never have Worked the fire itself, never have freed himself . . . only this." He worked himself a Knowing, with care; the mere act of Working was painful. "He's trapped in it," he whispered. "Lost in a desperate race against the fire. He doesn't even know he's out of there."

"Can you Work through to him?"

He shook his head. "He would suck me in, as fuel. Never even know who or what I was."

"So what do we do?" she demanded. There was an edge of hysteria in her voice that he had to force himself not to respond to. It was all too easy to abandon reason, and let blind emotion reign.

He reached up to where his sleeve had been sliced open, over his wound. The makeshift bandage was already soaked with blood, and as he wound it off it dripped carmine spots on the floor. He felt dizzy and his arm throbbed hot with pain, but that had been the case for so long now that he had grown accustomed to it. He gritted his teeth as he pulled the bloodsoaked length free at last and flexed his arm to keep fresh blood from flowing. With his other hand he bunched up the cloth and brought it to Tarrant's lips. What remained of his lips. And squeezed.

Red blood, warm and thick. It dribbled onto the corner of his mouth, coated his lips with glistening wetness. He squeezed again, and forced a trickle between the parted teeth.

"Drink it," he urged. His voice was a hoarse whisper, half hate and half anxiety. "Drink, damn you!"

"Damien, he's not a—"

"He *is*. Or at least, he was. And he said he could feed this way again, if he had to. I'd say he has to." He pressed the bunched-up cloth against his arm again; it soaked up the fresh blood like a sponge. "Drink," he whispered, squeezing the precious fluid out into Tarrant's mouth. "Or so help me God, I'll take you back down there and stick you in the fire myself. . . ."

He thought he saw movement, then. A flicker of wetness, within the mouth: a tongue tip? He squeezed harder, and saw the lips move slightly. The skin of Tarrant's throat contracted slightly, and crusted flesh cracked off from its surface. Beneath, the tissue was pale and moist.

Damien began to collect more blood—and then cast the bandage aside, and lowered his gashed arm to the Hunter's mouth. Sharp teeth bit into his flesh, a blind and desperate response to the presence of food; he bore the pain of it with gritted teeth as the cavern swayed about him, telling himself, *He doesn't know where he is. He doesn't know who you are.*

And then, at last, with a shudder, the teeth withdrew. He pulled back and pressed the wound closed, watching the man's face closely. The blackened crust was flaking off, and beneath it new tissue gleamed moistly in the lamplight. The process reminded Damien of a snake shedding its skin.

"Come on," he muttered. "Come back to us." He Worked his vision and saw the dark fae gathering about the Hunter's body, saw it weaving a web about the man's flesh that acted as a buffer between him and the light. Between him and the world. Cutting him off from the source of his pain—and with it, the rest of the living universe. "Tarrant!" He grasped him by the shoulder, but his blood-slicked hand slid off—and took with it a layer of burned flesh, revealing the newmade skin beneath. Cell by cell, layer by layer, the Hunter was restoring his body.

Hesseth hissed softly to get his attention and held out a flask of waxed leather toward him. He took it, somewhat perplexed, and smelled the stopper. And then nodded gratefully. The smell was familiar to him, the same odor that had clung to his flesh after their fight on Morgot. He poured a bit of the rakhene ointment into his right palm and rubbed it into and around his wound. And thanked her.

Then Tarrant stirred. A shiver passed through his frame, as though somewhere inside that battered flesh a spark of life was fighting to manifest itself. Damien reached out to him—and then, remembering what the Forest's monarch had said about Healing, used the hand that was free of ointment to grasp him by the shoulder. No telling what the rakhene liniment might do to a man who thrived on death.

"It's over," he told him. "Over."

"The fire. . . ." It was hoarsely voiced, barely a whisper—but it was speech, and it was audible, and he used it as a lifeline to reach the man.

"Gone. Left behind." He dared a comforting lie: "Extinguished."

The eyes opened, slowly. Fresh new lids of smooth, pale flesh, smeared with blood and black ash. For a moment he gazed emptily at the ceiling; then he shivered, and moaned softly. His eyes fell closed again.

"Tarrant. Listen to me. You're out of there. *Safe.* It's over. You're with us now." He paused. "Do you understand?"

The lids blinked open, tears of blood in their outer corners. For a minute or two the Hunter stared without seeing, silver eyes fixed on nothing. Then he turned, slowly—painfully—and met Damien's eyes. There was an emptiness in his gaze that made the priest's flesh crawl.

"Where?" the Hunter gasped. "Where is this?"

"We're in a cave, near the surface. Judging from the earth-fae, that is." He hesitated. "Tell me what you need. Tell us how to help you."

The pale eyes shut again, as if keeping them opened required more strength than the Hunter had. "More blood," he whispered. "But you can't give me that. I've already taken as much as your body can spare."

"Gerald." It was Ciani. She crawled over to where the Hunter lay and seemed to be about to reach out to him, but Damien warned her back. "I can supply—"

"Don't," the priest warned her.

"But I wasn't wounded. I haven't lost—"

"*Don't.*"

"Damien—"

"Ciani, think! He takes on the form of whatever his victims fear the most. That means that if he feeds on you, he'll become more like *them*. The ones who hurt you; the ones we're hunting. I don't think he's strong enough to fight it now. I don't think we can afford to risk it."

"But if we don't—"

"He's right," the Hunter whispered. "Too much risk. . . ." He shivered, as if from some secret pain. "I would hurt you. I might even kill you. And . . . I would rather die, than do that."

Damien watched for a moment as he lay there—his breathing labored, his movements weak—and then asked, "You going to make it?"

The Hunter raised a hand to his face, rubbed his eyes. The fingers were whole, but stained with blood. Flakes of charred skin fell from his face as he rubbed, revealing smooth white skin beneath. "I think . . . yes. They didn't do anything that time won't heal. Not to my flesh, anyway." He tried to force himself to a sitting position but fell back, weakly. "How long?" he gasped.

"In the fire?" Eight days, Ciani figured."

"It seemed like so much longer. . . ." He looked about weakly—at Ciani—at Hesseth—at the pierced one. His gaze lingered on the latter, and for a moment curiosity flared in those silver eyes. Then exhaustion took its place, and he turned away. "You saved my life," he whispered. The pale eyes fixed on Damien—and in the back of them, deep in the shadows, was a flicker of something familiar. A faint spark of sardonic humor, reassuringly familiar in tenor. "I didn't expect it of you."

"Yeah. Well. That makes two of us." He got to his feet, and brushed at some of the caked mud which clung to his clothing. "You get some rest, all right? Finish putting yourself back together, if you can." He looked at Hesseth. "Will the Lost One stand guard? I think he's the only one of us left with the strength to do it."

She murmured rakhene sounds to the pierced one, who grunted. And then assented, in phonemes that were becoming familiar to Damien.

"All right." He turned down the lantern wick as far as it would go, trying to save oil; of the store of fuel they had brought, only half a flask remained. When that was gone . . . he shuddered to think of it. One could only Work one's sight for so long.

"Let's all get some sleep while we can," he urged his party. "It may be our last chance." His body felt weak and drained, almost incapable of moving; the combined fatigue of loss of blood and too many nights without slumber. He lay back on a tangle of clothing and blankets, and listened to his heart pounding in his chest: a metronome of exhaustion. Then, slowly, he slid down into darkness. Warm and sweet and utterly welcome.

For the first time in eight days, he didn't dream of fire.

When he awakened, things weren't where they should be. It took him a moment to place the wrongness, to fight off the dizziness of his recent blood loss and think clearly. The light wasn't coming from where it should, he decided. Which meant that the lantern wasn't where he'd left it. He looked around the cavern, saw a spark of light at the far side of the chamber. And a tall figure who held it, whose body eclipsed its minimal light as he moved, casting Damien into utter darkness.

Tarrant.

The man had apparently found his clothes—what few items Ciani had salvaged—and had managed to pull on a silk shirt and woolen leggings, which hid most of his ravaged skin from sight. Where his hands and feet were visible his flesh was a chalky white, utterly bereft of living color; it bothered Damien that he couldn't remember whether that was his normal hue or not.

The Hunter had unhooded the lamp and turned up its wick, and was casting its bright light upon the length of an oddly twisted column. As Damien approached, he reached out and touched the glistening stone, running his hand down its finely grooved surface. And then did so again, more carefully.

"Not right," he whispered, as the priest came to his side. "Not possible."

Damien studied the formation. It seemed to be oddly shaped for its kind, and there were tiny ridges up and down its length, but otherwise it looked like all the others. And he had seen enough cave formations in the last few days to last him a lifetime.

"It isn't just this one," the Hunter whispered. "They're all wrong. Every column in this chamber, every formation that bridges between two surfaces. So wrong. . . ." He shook his head in amazement—and even in that simple gesture, so sparingly performed, Damien could read his weakness.

"What is it?" the priest asked quietly.

He turned down the lantern's wick again, to save the last of the oil. Then he put one hand against the gnarled formation: his fingers, like the rest of him, were lean and wasted. "See these ridges," he whispered. "Each of these is where the column cracked when the earth shifted beneath it. Slowly new minerals would seep in and fill the cracks . . . but they left scars. Thousands of scars." He gestured with the lantern, toward formations Damien had never noticed before. Fallen stalactites. Severed columns. Jagged shapes, all of them, that defied the normal pattern. "Do you see?" the Hunter whispered. He turned the lantern until its light shone on a slender column nearby; looking closely, Damien could see that it had been split cleanly through the middle, and its upper and lower halves no longer lined up with each other. "This isn't the result of secondary vibration. We must be right in the fault zone. The earth is deforming right here, all about us, and the cave formations reflect it. Lateral movement along a major fault line. To be reflected in the stone. . . ." His hand closed about the narrow column as if he needed it for support. Damien had to fight the urge to reach out and hold him upright.

"There's nothing recent," the adept whispered. "Nothing at all. Not here, not in any place I could look . . . and that's just not possible. Not possible! But all the fractures have been filled in, and that takes centuries. . . ." He shook his head in amazement. "Am I to believe there's been no movement here? For that long? That defies all science."

"The rakh said there have been no earthquakes here. Not for a century, at least."

"That's not what I mean. Not at all. What's an earthquake? A series of vibrations that informs us the crust of the planet has shifted beneath our feet. We measure it by how much it inconveniences us—

how much we're aware of it. The earth could move so slowly that all our instruments would never detect it—and it would still add up to the same motion, in the end. The crust of the planet acts in response to the currents of Erna's core. How could that simply cease? And cease only in one place, while all surrounding areas continued on as normal? Because they do, I know that; I monitor these things. The land all about here is normal, utterly normal. Except in this one place. How?"

"Our enemy built his citadel right on the fault line," Damien pointed out. "You said only a fool would do that. But if he wanted the power of this place at his disposal, and could keep the earth from shaking . . ."

For a moment the adept looked at him strangely. "No one man could ever bind the earth like that," he said. "No one man could ever hope to conjure enough power to offset the pressures of the planet's core. And besides . . ."

He turned away. And shut his eyes. And whispered, "The Master of Lema is a woman."

"What?"

"The Keeper of Souls is a woman," he breathed. "Our enemy. My torturer. The architect of the House of Storms. A *woman*."

For a moment Damien couldn't respond. Then, with effort, he managed to get out, "That doesn't make a difference."

The Hunter turned on him angrily; his eyes were red-rimmed, bloodshot. "Don't be a fool," he snapped. "Of *course* it makes a difference. Not because of gender, but because of *power*. Raw physicality. What can you know of it—you, who were born with the size and the strength to defend yourself from any physical threat? What can you know of the mind-set of the weak, whose lives are centered around vulnerability? When you hear footsteps behind you in a darkened street, do you fear being kidnapped? Raped? Overcome by the sheer physical strength of your attackers? Or do you feel confident that with firm ground and a reliable weapon in your hands you could hold your own against any reasonable threat? How can you possibly understand what it means to lack that confidence—or what it can drive a human to do, to try to gain it?"

"And you do, I suppose?"

The Hunter glared. "I was the youngest of nine sons, priest. My brothers took after their father, in form and spirit: a hulking, crude beast of a man, who believed that there wasn't an enemy on Erna he couldn't bring to his knees if only he swung his fist hard enough. I grew up among them, sole inheritor of our mother's mien—and I didn't come into my height until late, or my power. Now, you think

about the cruelty of that kind—and of sibling youths, in general—
and the brutality of my age, which was at the end of the Dark Ages—
and then tell me how much I don't understand." He turned away. "I
think I understand it very well."

"They died," Damien said. "Within five years of your disappearance. All of them."

"It was the first thing I did, once I had gained the power—and the
moral freedom—to work my will upon the world. And those eight
murders are among my most pleasurable memories." The cold eyes
fixed on Damien, piercing him to the core. "What they were to me,
you and I are to her. The whole world is that, to her: a thing to be
mastered, defeated. *Broken*. Do you understand? Power has become
an end unto itself; she feeds on it, demanding more and more . . . it's
like a drug that has slowly taken over her body. Until she lives only
to assuage its demands, to do whatever will blunt the edge of that
terrible hunger." His brow was furrowed as if in pain. As if even the
memories burned him. "And I'll tell you something else, priest. I've
seen that hunger before. Not in such a blind, unbalanced form . . .
but it might have become that, in time. In fact, I believe that it
would have become that, if not for Ciani's influence."

It took him a moment to realize what Tarrant meant. He felt something tighten inside, when he did. "You mean Senzei?"

Tarrant nodded. "I think so. I think this is what a man can become,
when that kind of hunger goes unchecked—when it continues to
grow, like some malignant cancer, until it devours the very soul that
houses it. Until all that's left is an addiction so terrible that the flesh
lives only to serve it."

"But that would imply that he . . . that *she* isn't an adept."

"I don't believe she is," Tarrant said quietly. "and I wonder if—"
He swayed, and shut his eyes for a moment. "Not now," he whispered. "Not here." He looked up, as if seeking some opening in the
water-etched ceiling. "Up on the surface, I could be sure. If there's
any Working in this region, it would be where the currents were
strongest. I could read it there."

"What are you thinking?"

He hesitated. "Something so insane that I wouldn't even suggest
it," he whispered. "Except that I've seen with my own eyes just how
insane she is. God in heaven, if she were that blind—but no. I
shouldn't talk about it until I can test my suspicions." His silver
eyes were ablaze with hatred—and he seemed to draw strength from
the emotion. Slowly he released the slender column at his side, so
that he stood unaided. And it seemed to Damien that he trembled
only slightly as he did so.

"She was able to take us because she knew what we were," Tarrant said. "She knew what the flaw was in each of us. And if I'm correct in what I'm thinking . . . then I may know hers, as well." The pale eyes fixed on Damien, and in their depths was a flicker of power. Faint, weak, barely discernible—but it was there, and that was more than Damien had seen in him since the rescue.

"And I will be no less ruthless in exploiting it," the Hunter promised.

The surface of the planet was bitterly cold, and windswept snowdrifts coursed down from the peaks like waves of sea froth, frozen in midmotion. In the distance it was possible to see the enemy's tower, a gleaming black chancre on the white landscape. Tarrant looked about, then pointed away from it. His eyes were narrowed, as if trying to focus on something in the distance. What? Domina's light was strong enough that the dark fae would have withdrawn from the surface of the planet, and Damien's Worked sight revealed no other special power. What had the adept's vision uncovered, that merely human sight was incapable of making out?

They followed him, struggling across the snowbound landscape. Tarrant seemed somewhat stronger than before, but that could simply be the force of his hunger for revenge making itself felt. Damien wondered how long it would support him.

He led them through knee-high dunes and ice-clad gullies, hesitating after each obstacle was passed to study the lay of the land again, and perhaps shift their direction slightly. He gave no hint of what he was seeking or how long it might take them to reach it. Though Damien knew that the Hunter's cold flesh thrived on the chill of the icy peaks, he nevertheless shivered as the wind whipped Tarrant's thin shirt about his haggard frame. How much longer could the man go on, with no more than a single draft of blood to sustain him?

And then the Hunter stopped, and stiffened. His sudden alertness reminded Damien of an animal, ears pricked forward to catch the sound of danger. The adept began to walk forward, more quickly now, stumbling through the ankle-deep snow that cloaked this part of the mountain. And then he knelt and touched one hand to its whiteness. Again there was the sense of utter alertness. As if his whole body was tensed to respond to the slightest sound. Then he began to brush the snow away. After a moment, Damien knelt beside him and helped. He Worked his vision in the hope of catching some glimpse of what the adept had seen, but though the currents coursed clearly beneath the insulating snow—more and more visibly now, as they cleared away that obstacle—Damien was forced to admit that he could make out no sign of what was drawing his companion.

And then his fingers touched something which was neither earth nor stone nor frozen brush. "Here," he muttered, and the Hunter's efforts joined his own in clearing the snow from it. Slowly a disk came into view: black onyx, carved with an intricate motif. The snow which caught in its etchings made its pattern doubly visible, and Damien struggled to place the design in his memory.

When he did, at last, he looked up at Tarrant. And said—not quite believing his own words—"A quake-ward?"

Ciani knelt down by his side; her fingers, cold-whitened, touched the etched surface delicately. "But what would it protect?" she whispered. "The citadel's too far away."

For a moment the Hunter just stared at it, as if not believing his own find. Then, slowly, he reached for his sword. And drew it. Cold-fire blazed along its length, doubly bright against the whiteness of the snow. Damien remembered the last time he had seen that power used, and flinched. But Ciani was gazing at it—and the Hunter—with hunger.

"You had better all stand back," Tarrant said quietly. "You might need to move rather quickly."

"What are you going to do?" Ciani asked.

"See what this is linked to. See where it leads." He touched a hand to the ward's icy surface; snow clung to his fingertip, unmelting. "See what it's warding," he whispered.

They stood back. Too fascinated to feel the cold, or the bite of the wind on their faces. Damien heard Hesseth whispering explanations to the pierced one—but how much did she really understand herself? He watched as the Hunter took his sword in both hands, watched as he bound its power to his purpose, to trace the lines of Warding—

—and light shot out from it, brilliant and blinding. Pale blue fire, that blazed about the etched tile and then arced out from it, coursing over the surface of the earth like streamers of azure lightening. A branch of light struck the earth some distance from them, and snow shot up in a thick white plume, baring the ground beneath. When the air had cleared they could see the glint of moonlight on another ward-stone, its etched patterns filled with the gleaming coldfire. And south of that, yet another. Soon the land was alive with ward-fires, and the gleaming network of power that bound them together in purpose.

Damien looked at Tarrant, could see his haggard face rigid with strain as he fought to control the coldfire. *The power may come from outside us,* the priest thought, *but the order we impose on it must come from within.* And then, apparently, the strain was too much. The Hunter shut his eyes and fell to his knees. The sword in his hand blazed bright as an unsun as it struck the earth, and all the power that had gone out from it slammed back into the Worked steel with a force that made the man reel visibly, trying to control it. Damien had to stop himself from moving forward to help, knowing the cold power would drain him of life before he could get close enough to touch the man. What had the Lost Ones called the blade— the Eater of Souls? He looked at Ciani, worried that she might move forward to help the Hunter without realizing how dangerous it was. But though her eyes were on him, she did not approach. Instead she reached into her jacket pocket as though seeking something. After a moment she pulled out two small items: a folded knife, and a piece of not paper. Damien recognized Senzei's handwriting on the latter as she twisted it tightly with trembling fingers into a funnel formation. He started to object as he realized what she was doing—and stopped himself. And forced himself to take the paper cone from her hand, that she might be free to open the knife. To use it.

She sliced quickly across the ball of her thumb, a cut that slid just beneath the skin. Maximum blood, with minimum damage. He held the makeshift cup for her as she squeezed out a thin stream of red into it, and wondered that his own hand wasn't shaking. Could one become so inured to the Hunter's needs that they no longer seemed unreasonable?

When the cup was full, she took it from him and knelt by Tarrant's side. His nostrils flared as he caught the scent of her offering, and hunger flashed in those silver eyes. Then he turned away, and whispered hoarsely, "Please don't. I can't."

"The cut's already been made," she said quietly. "The blood's already been shed. You wouldn't be hurting me by taking it." When he didn't respond, she whispered, "Gerald. Please. There'd be no risk this way." Blood dripped from her hand to the snow, staining it purple in the coldfire's glare. "*I need you.*"

"Don't you understand?" he gasped. "I gave my word. And keeping it is the only thing that keeps me from becoming like *she* is." He nodded back toward the citadel, shivering. "Don't you realize what an addiction power is? *Any* power? If you don't impose some order on it, it consumes you—"

"Honor is one thing," Damien told him. "Stupidity is another.

Take the blood, man—or do I have to pour it down your goddamned throat?"

The pale eyes fixed on him. And the Hunter nodded slowly. "I believe you would," he whispered.

"Take it."

Slowly he raised one hand from the grip of the sword and closed it about Ciani's. And raised the makeshift cup to his lips, and drank. Damien could see a tremor pass through him as he absorbed the precious fluid. Pleasure? Pain? Tarrant made no protest while she filled the cup again, and made no effort to resist the second offering. While he drank, Damien took out one of the cloth strips he had prepared for bandages, so many nights ago, and offered it to Ciani. She wound it tightly about her hand, forcing the wound closed.

Slowly, when he was done, the Hunter moved. With effort he managed at last to sheathe his sword, sliding it into the heavily Worked enclosure that would confine its power. And he sighed—in relief, it seemed—as the coldfire faded from sight.

"Now tell us: what was that all about?" Damien indicated the carved ward before them. "What are those things?"

The Hunter drew in a deep breath, then said, in a voice that shook slightly, "Our enemy has warded the crust of the planet."

"To do what?" Ciani asked.

"To Bind the fault, I assume." His voice was a whisper. "To freeze the earth in its motion."

"I thought you said that wasn't possible."

"It isn't, in the long run. But if one's vision were limited enough—or blinded, by dreams of power. . . ." He looked out across the snow-clad mountains, where a vast webwork of coldfire had so recently burned. Where a vast network of wards had been revealed, that stretched across miles of earth in perfect alignment. A thousand or more quiescent Workings that waited to tap the energy of the earth itself, when the tides of the planet's core released it. "I said she was insane," he whispered. "I meant it. But insanity on such a scale . . . my God. When it fails—and it must fail, some day—what does she think will happen? To her, and to everything she's built here?"

"You mean the wards won't hold."

"How can they? The power of the fae is constant. The pressure along the fault is building. There must have been enough fae in the beginning to make such a Binding possible in the first place . . . but now? After pressure has been building up here for a century, unrelieved? It would require more and more fae just to maintain the status quo—and you see how weak the currents are in this region. Where is the power to come from if the earth isn't moving?"

Damien looked at Hesseth. "What was it your people said? That the storms here were constant, when the Master of Lema first came. And then, after a time, there were fewer." He turned to the Hunter. "The reference was to lightning, apparently. Ward-lightning. Overload."

"There would have been more than enough fae at first for her purposes," he murmured. "When the earth began to shift, the wild power would have surged ... and then her wards would Bind it, and the excess fae would bleed off into the sky. What remained would be safely tamed. *Consumable.*"

"But why?" Ciani asked. "What purpose did it serve?"

The silver eyes fixed on her. "Why did Senzei steal the Fire? Why does any non-adept take in a power wild enough to kill him, if not to satisfy that most primal of all hungers? Every time a quake strikes Jaggonath there's someone fool enough to try to Work it. Here's a woman who tamed the earth itself so that she could drink in its power in safety. But only for as long as her wards hold; that's the catch. Remember what the rakh said? The storms are fewer, now. Not because there's less power, but because more and more of it is required to maintain the Binding. And as pressure continues to build within the earth, that imbalance will increase geometrically, until one day soon mere wards will no longer be sufficient. ..."

Slowly, he got to his feet. "We are standing on a time bomb," he whispered. "Of such immense proportion that it defies description. And if what the rakh say is true ... then it's very near to going off."

"You're thinking you can trigger it," Damien said quietly.

He looked out over the snow-shrouded earth, at the places where the quake-wards lay.

"It's a simple series," he said at last. "Break one, and the rest would go. But would the earth respond immediately? There are so many variables. ..."

"But the odds are high."

"Oh, yes. The odds are very high. Higher than they could ever get without man's interference." He shook his head in amazement. "Only someone with a complete disregard for seismic law would dare something so intrinsically stupid as this. ..."

"Or someone so addicted to the rush of power that she can't think clearly any more. Isn't that what we're dealing with?"

"She fed on me," he whispered. Wrapping his arms about himself, as if that could protect him from the memory. "She used my pain as a filter, to tame the raw earth-fae. That's what she wants Ciani for. As a living refinery for the kind of power she lusts after. As if by using us in this manner she can somehow break through the barriers inside herself, give herself an adept's capacity. . . ."

"I thought that wasn't possible," Damien challenged.

"It isn't. But it's a powerful fantasy, nonetheless. Man has always been loath to accept his limitations. How much easier it is to deny the truth altogether—to imagine that Nature has given us all the same potential, and that a single act of will can suddenly cause all limitations to vanish." He laughed bitterly. "As if Nature were just. As if evolution hadn't designed us to compete with each other, so that only the strong would survive."

"What about the Dark Ones?" Ciani asked. "Where do they fit in?"

"Servants. Symbiotes. She has to remain at the heart of her web in order to maintain its power. They serve as her eyes and ears and hands, to scour the land in search of what she needs . . . and in return they have her protection. Which is no small thing, in a land with no other human sorcery." His eyes narrowed, and a new edge of coldness entered his voice. "If we mean to destroy one of her creatures, then we must deal with her first. That, or have her strike us from behind at a crucial moment."

"If we could release the earth from her Binding, would that do it?"

He hesitated. "There were wards in her citadel. I remember seeing them when I was brought in. But I have no way of knowing what they were, exactly. Quake-wards? If so, the building might endure for a time. Only a few minutes, at most—but that would be enough. Because she'd have warning, remember. The surge of earth-fae that precedes an earthquake would have reached her minutes before, with all its power intact. She would have known then that her precious system had failed her, and if she could get away from the citadel in time—"

Then he stopped. And said, very quietly, "Unless she was Working when it happened. In that case, there would be no escape."

"Can we force that?" Damien asked. "Set her up, so that she doesn't see it coming?"

"How?" the Hunter whispered.

"Some sort of attack. Something she would have to defend against—"

Tarrant shook his head, sharply. "That would require an active assault, which would mean that when the surge hit . . . it would be fatal for both parties. No, she would have to be the only one Working, and I don't see how. . . ."

He stopped suddenly. And drew in a long, slow breath.

"Gerald?" Ciani asked. "What is it?"

His arms tightened about his body. But he said nothing.

"You know a way," Damien said quietly.

"Maybe," he whispered. "The risk would be tremendous. If she were sane, if we could predict her response ... but she isn't, and we can't." He shook his head. "Too dangerous, priest. Even for this expedition."

"Tell me."

The pale eyes fixed on him. Silver in white, with hardly a trace of red; the man was healing.

"You would have come here alone," he said softly. A challenge. "If we had not been available—or necessary—you would have traveled to this place by yourself, and dealt with her unaided. Gone into the heart of her citadel, if that's what it took, with nothing but your own wits and a small handful of weapons. Am I correct?"

"If I judged it to be worth the risk," Damien said warily.

"The rakhlands won't support her forever. Already the currents are too weak to truly satisfy her, drained as they are by her Wardings. Soon she would begin to draw on the Canopy itself, and after that ... I imagine she would move into the human lands. Utterly mad, forever hungry, and backed by a horde of demons capable of reducing her enemies to brainless husks. Would that be worth the risk, Reverend Vryce? Would you brave her citadel alone, for that—risk her rage, and that of the earth itself, to gain the upper hand in this war? Because I think I know a way that she might be rendered vulnerable, but it would have to be done by a single man. Human, and not an adept. There's only one of us who fits that description. How great is your courage now?"

"If I'd come alone, as you say, I would expect to do no less," he said tightly. "What are you thinking?"

"It wouldn't be pleasant, I warn you."

"As opposed to the rest of this trip?"

Despite himself, the Hunter smiled; the expression was edged with pain. "You're a brave man, Reverend Vryce, and true courage is rare. I respect you for it. But there's more than simple risk at issue here." The silver eyes burned like fire. Coldfire, unwarm and uncomforting. "Could you trust me, priest? Without reservation? Could you give yourself to me, for the lady's sake? Entrust your soul to me, for safekeeping?"

Damien remembered the touch of the man's soul against his own, which he had endured once in order to feed him. The mere memory of it made his skin crawl—and that had been but a fleeting contact, with no real depth to it. Even the Hunter's coldfire in his veins, for all the pain and horror it had inspired, had been nothing compared to that. The utter revulsion. The soul-searing chill. The touch of a mind so infinitely unclean that everything it fixed upon was polluted by the contact. He shivered to recall it ... but said nothing in response. The man hadn't asked if he would enjoy such contact, but if he could endure it. If he would *trust* him.

He looked at the man's face, at the taut tissue so recently ravaged by fire. At the weakness that lurked just beneath his facade of arrogance, which had so nearly consumed his life just now. All this, in a man who feared death more than any other single thing. All these things he had risked, and suffered, for the sake of one promise. One word. One single vow, which his present companions had not even witnessed.

"I assume it would be temporary," he said quietly.

"Of course." The Hunter nodded. "Assuming we both survive to undo it."

"I have your word on that?"

"You do." The pale gray eyes glittered with malevolence; toward him, or toward their enemy? "And I think you know what that's worth, Reverend Vryce."

He felt himself on the brink of a vast cliff, balancing precariously on its crumbling edge. But the darkness of the citadel which loomed overhead was even more threatening than the imagined depths beneath, and at last he heard himself say, in a voice that seemed strangely distant, "All right, Hunter. Tell me what you have in mind."

Tarrant nodded. And turned to the pierced one. In all the time he had been awake, he had made no move to acknowledge the Lost One's presence. Now he gazed upon the crouching form, whose cave-pale fur protected it from the night's chill, and seemed to consider what the others had told him about it.

"Go back to your people," he told the cave-rakh. Gesturing for Hesseth to translate his words. "Tell them they must leave this region quickly. The earth will move soon, and the caves here are too fragile to protect them. Tell them they must go down to the plains, or else head west. Away from the fault zone, as quickly as possible. Their lives depend on it." He glanced up at the night sky as if trying to judge the time by it. "They'll have till tomorrow night," he said. "Tell them that. We won't begin until nightfall, and even then it may take some time." He looked at the rakh-woman. "But not much," he warned. "Make that clear."

She stared at him for a minute—suspiciously, it seemed—and then finished translating his words. It took some time for their meaning to sink in; when at last it did, the Lost One rasped a few hurried questions at Hesseth. Her answers were short hisses, and the hostility in them was clear even to those who didn't speak her language. Finally the Lost One stood, stiffly, and looked at the party—looked long and intently at Tarrant with an expression that was unreadable—and then turned away sharply, and moved off into the night. Motion silent in the soft snow, long tail curled tightly in foreboding.

Damien waited until the Lost One was out of sight—and, presumably, out of hearing—and then said to Tarrant, "That wasn't like you."

"No," the Hunter said softly. "I find myself doing a lot of things that aren't like me, these days."

"I wouldn't have thought their lives mattered to you," Hesseth challenged.

The silver eyes fixed on her, filled with a languid malevolence. "They don't. But I do recognize my obligations." He turned back to Damien. "You saved my life. All of you did. But in the Reverend's case ... I know what that meant for you," he told Damien. "We share the same background, you and I—and I remember enough of it to understand what that cost you." *The pain of it*, his expression seemed to say. *The guilt.* He nodded toward where the lost One had gone, now rendered invisible by the shadows of night. "Consider this my small gesture of gratitude. A few hundred less deaths to darken your conscience, Reverend Vryce. It won't outweigh the evil of my existence, in the long run ... but it's all I can offer you without hazarding my own survival. I regret that."

"Just get us through this, and you'll have done enough," Damien said tightly. "That's what I brought you back for."

Gerald Tarrant bowed. And if there was weakness in him now, it was overlaid by such hatred for the enemy that it was hard to make out. The hunger for revenge, combined with Ciani's blood, had replenished not only body but spirit.

"As you command," the Hunter whispered.

Forty-four

The tunnel was long and dark, and filled with the smell of mold. Which told Damien two things: that life passed this way often enough to deposit the fragile spores, and that the tunnel was deep enough to be protected from the worst of winter's chill.

He was dressed in a woolen shirt and breeches, his only other protection a tough leather vest that was concealed by the loose folds of his garments, and matching bracers strapped about his wrists. His heavy jacket had been left at the tunnel's entrance, along with the knitted scarves and overshirts of winter's travel. Such garments might have kept him warmer, but they also added to his bulk—and for once that wasn't desirable. His sheath was no longer strapped to his back but harnessed to the side of his belt: he fervently hoped he would remember it was there when the time came to draw it. Other than that he carried only a single long knife, a length of rope, two folding hooks, a number of small locksmithing tools, and several amulets. Those last were compliments of Gerald Tarrant, who had Worked them with just enough power to justify their presence on his person. He had no springbolt. That had been the hardest thing to leave behind, but it was a bulky weapon, not quickly drawn, and a man bent on assassination couldn't afford to slow himself down. Or so he told himself, as he mourned the loss of its reassuring weight on his arm.

At his hip lay the flask of Fire, safely cushioned in its leather pouch. He should have left that behind, as well ... but if the first stage of their plan went askew—or any other part, for that matter— he might well need some weapon that could drive back the enemy's demonic guard. And he had stripped himself of anything else that might serve.

He felt naked, thus weaponless. But also exhilarated. Because for the first time since leaving Jaggonath, he was on his own. Oh, he still had Ciani's safety to worry about, and Tarrant's Workings were wrapped tightly about him, a cocoon of malevolence that shadowed his every step . . . but that still wasn't the same thing as having them *here*, as knowing that he must watch out for them every time he planned, every time he took a step . . . no, this was much better. This was the way it was meant to be. Every sound that he heard was important because it concerned him—or unimportant because it didn't. There was no middle ground. His progress was a study in black and white, threat and nonthreat, and no other concern existed in his mind but that he must get from *here* to *there* in safety. And then manage what he came to do, with minimal damage to his person.

If that last is possible, he thought grimly. And he remembered what Tarrant had told him about their enemy, running the details through his mind as he crept slowly forward, eyes and ears alert for any sign of danger. He prayed that Tarrant's guesses were right, prayed that he had arrayed himself properly for this foray . . . and then prayed in general, just for good measure. Not because his God would interfere in such a thing—or even care about the short-term consequences—but such prayer was a reminder of his identity. And with Tarrant's taint wrapped about him like a shroud, darkening his every thought, he needed all the reminders he could get.

I only hope he's right. I only hope he understands her as well as he thinks he does. And then he added, somewhat dryly, *The ruthless, analyzing the mad. . . .*

Periodically another tunnel would merge with the one he was following, and he would pause to check it out. *Egresses from the lower caverns*, Tarrant had told him, *that merge with the citadel's escape route.* They were fortunate that the underground system was close enough to Erna's surface to affect the currents above it: otherwise the Hunter might never have managed to locate it at all. As it was he knew only the location of its entrance, and its general route beneath the eastern mountains. It wasn't enough, he told himself. Except that it had to be. Because it was all they had.

At each intersection the priest paused, hooding his lantern with his hand so that no light would precede him. And he listened—ears alert, eyes narrowed, his whole soul focused on *perceiving*. But not with Worked senses. That was impossible, because of what Tarrant had done to him. That was why he'd had to submit to the man, choking on the blackness of that warped morality as the Hunter's mind wrapped about his own, picking at his brain like an old woman picking out the stitches of some tightly sewn embroidery—

Don't think about that, he warned himself. His heart was pounding: he breathed deeply, trying to still the trembling of his hands. All the trust in the world couldn't have staved off the terror of that experience, and Damien's stomach turned as he recalled how the Hunter drank in his fear, sucking the terror out of him as surely as he had once drawn out the blood that ran in his veins. The difference was that this time something had been left behind. A coiling malignance, serpentlike, that slithered in the dark recesses of Damien's mind and licked at his thoughts as they flickered from neuron to neuron—

Stop it!

He moved swiftly between intersections, knowing that the smooth, rakh-made tunnels offered no concealment between those junctures. Time after time he felt himself reaching for his sword, and he had to force his hand to drop back to his side, empty. It was important that he remain unarmed. Every detail of this was important, he knew, which was why every move had been planned out in advance . . . but that was little comfort as he advanced toward certain danger, his palm itching to close about a sword-grip, his arm tensing as if to balance the weight of that defending steel.

And then: he heard it. A noise that whispered behind him in the endless passage. Footsteps? He forced himself to keep moving forward, tensing his ears to catch the sound. Soft, rhythmic . . . yes, footsteps. Unshod, he guessed. Since there were no signs of any large animal in this place, that left only one possibility—

He turned. Too late. He knew it even as he reached for his sword, even as he cursed himself for going to his shoulder instead of his hip to draw it. Cold, clawed hands tore at him from the darkness, and one grabbed his sword arm and twisted it brutally behind him. His sheath swung into the dirt wall as he struggled, dislodging clumps of earth. He fought to break free, desperately, but pain clouded his vision as his arm was twisted even more tightly behind him, and he knew it was within inches of breaking. Another assailant grabbed him by the throat and squeezed, sharp claws drawing blood through the collar of his shirt. There were too many of them, and they were too fast, too strong. The fetid stink of them filled his nostrils, choking him, as he felt the long dagger drawn from his belt even as the reassuring weight of his sword was snapped from his side. Cold hands felt along the length of his body, and one by one his tools and weapons were located and removed from him. The hooks. The rope. The amulets. The latter were broken free with a hiss of amusement, thin gold chains snapping with a sound like a pennant in the wind. Then sharp fingers pried at the pouch at his belt, opening it—and a cry of pain burst forth from one of the creatures as it backed away from the church-Worked light. There was an instant of chaos that Damien tried to take advantage of, but the Dark One who held him prisoner was on the other side of him, and thus sheltered from the light. He twisted the priest's arm brutally as he struggled, forcing the man to fall to his knees in order to keep it from breaking; a foot forced the leather pouch closed again and pressed down on him as his assailant forced him lower, into the earthen floor. "Let her deal with it!" he heard one hiss. He tried to struggle free, choking on dirt, felt the bite of cold claws digging into his face. Drawing his face upward, forcing his eyes to meet—

Dizzying. Blinding. A whirlpool of raw malevolence, its walls glittering with hunger. He felt himself being sucked down into it, felt the thoughts and memories being torn loose from him as he fell, the rush of them past his ears as the power of the Dark One dismembered, devoured—

And then it ended. Suddenly. As though an impenetrable wall had been slammed down between himself and the Dark One. Damien gasped for breath, heard the demon curse in frustration. Then the cold hand that gripped him squeezed his face even tighter, and he felt that boundless hunger reaching out to him again, the maelstrom forming . . . and it slid from him like claws on ice, unable to take hold.

"Can't do it," he heard a voice rasp. And another, hungry, hissed, "Let me try!" He felt his head turned forcibly to one side, as blood from a claw-wound dripped into one eye. For a moment there was the sensation of falling, of a power so vast that it must surely overwhelm the barrier Tarrant had established in him . . . and then that, too, dispersed, and he was left shivering in pain as they debated, hotly, the cause of their failure.

"Let her deal with him," one hissed at last, and the others agreed. Damien felt himself jerked to his feet, his other arm pulled up sharply behind him. Then the pressure on the first mercifully let up, and through his fog of pain and confusion he could tell that they were binding him, using the very rope he had been carrying on his person. They tied tight knots about his leather wristlets, binding wrists that he made taut with tension as he tried to fight them. But the creatures knew by his weakness that though they had failed to drain him of memory, they had served his flesh from his spirit; bereft of passion, securely bound, he appeared all but helpless in their hands. He snarled fevered curses as they dragged him forward, but his words were impotent weapons; the creatures chittered sharply as they gathered up his steel and the rest of his equipment, in some dark equivalent of laughter. And one stopped to lick the blood from his face— as if to remind him that they fed on his kind, that once they managed to break through the barrier which Tarrant had Worked in him, he would be no better than an evening's snack to them.

They dragged him down the length of the corridor, his neck leashed like an angry dog's. And as he stumbled along behind them—weaponless, bleeding, his face and arms stinging from the prick of their foul claws—it was all he could do to reflect upon his purpose, and keep from pitting his full strength against the bonds that had rendered him helpless. Because helplessness was what he needed right now. It went against his every instinct to accept that, to play along with it, but Tarrant was right; if the Dark Ones could not have rendered him helpless, they would have been forced to kill him. Their primitive minds knew no middle ground.

As he stumbled towards the enemy's stronghold, he thought grimly, *So far, so good.*

The citadel was a jewel, a prism, a multifaceted crystalline structure that divided up the night into a thousand glittering bits, turning the sky and the landscape beneath into a cubist's nightmare of disjointed angles and broken curves. Domina's cold blue radiance reflected from the mirror-bright surfaces in seemingly random splinters, making it impossible for Damien to isolate any one structure as cohesive as a wall, or a doorway. When they walked he was forced to rely upon his feet to feel out the structure of the floor; stairs and inclines were all but invisible, masked by that visual chaos.

A reflection of her madness, he thought. He was appalled, but also impressed. What would the place be like in the sunlight? Or in Corelight? Brilliant, he decided. Disturbingly beautiful. It was clear to him that the Master of Lema was no creature of the night, as her servants were.

She came, then, down a staircase that glittered like diamonds in the fractured moonlight. He couldn't make out the edges of the stairs beneath her feet, but judged their size and shape by the action of her long robe upon their surface. Silk sliding over glass, a waterfall of color. Mesmerized, he watched until the delicate fabric was level with his own feet, until that signal informed him that the Keeper of Souls had entered the very chamber he was in.

A taloned hand forced him to his knees; he didn't fight, but dropped down as though beaten. And watched her intently, as she approached.

She was not a young woman any more, though her skill with the fae had kept her from aging too badly. She might have been beautiful once, but decades of obsession and the relentless power of her addiction had robbed her face of whatever natural elegance it might once have possessed. Her eyes were deeply hollowed, underscored with carmine lines where the bone edges pressed against the sallow tissue. Her skin was dry and taut with the inelasticity of enforced youth. Her lips, once full, were textured with a webwork of fine lines, that left only a hint of what must have once been vital sensuality. Only her eyes blazed forth with life, and they were so filled with hunger— with raw, uncaring *need*—that despite all he had known of her nature, Damien shuddered as he met her gaze.

"So you're the one," she said shortly. Her eyes flickered up to meet those of her captors; it seemed to him that the Dark Ones flinched before her. "What were my orders?"

"To claim his memories, Keeper."

She hooked a hand beneath Damien's chin and forced his head upward, to face hers. Studied his eyes, and all that was behind them.

"You disobeyed me," she said softly. "Is there a reason?"

"We couldn't do it," one of Damien's captors rasped, and another offered, "There was a barrier. . . ."

"Ah." The eyes pierced into him, burning his brain—then withdrew, and were merely eyes once more. "A Shielding. Very good. They have both intelligence and power." She let go of his head. "But not enough."

She stood back. "Get him up."

Sharp claws bit into his upper arms as two of the creatures jerked him to his feet. He was careful to appear unsteady, as if from pain or weakness, but feared it would do little good. Carmine cloth swept from her shoulders to the floor, draped over an armature of padding that was clearly meant to lend aggressive mass to her frame. Even so, she was considerably smaller than he was, and he knew to his despair that no feigned emotions could counteract the sheer power of his bulk—or the threat she would read into it.

She nodded to one side, and the Dark Ones scurried to lay out Damien's weapons before her. She waited until they were done and then said in a disdainful tone, "Is that all?" She reached down and took up a handful of amulets; thin gold chains slithered down between her fingers, like serpents. "Did you really think these would affect me?" She opened her hands and let the precious medallions slip through her fingers like so much refuse. "I think you underestimate me." And a smile, faint and unpleasant, wrinkled her lips. "I know that *he* did."

She came back to him and cupped a cold hand beneath his face. Sharpened nails bit into his skin, not unlike the talons of her servants. "I want him," she said. "And I want the woman. Tell me where they are, and I'll let you go."

Elation filled him, at the realization that Hesseth's efforts had paid off; the human sorceress couldn't read through her tidal Workings. But he kept it carefully from his face as he said, in a tone edged with fear, "I won't betray my friends."

She smiled coldly. "Oh, you will do that. No question about it. All that's at issue is how long it will take . . . and how much pain has to be applied in the process." An odd hunger flickered in the depths of her eyes; her tongue tip touched her lips briefly, as if in anticipation. "Well? Will you answer me now? Or do I have to break you to get what I want?"

Damien's heart was pounding so loudly he wondered that she couldn't hear it. What was the safest way to answer? He had to goad her into specific action, without bringing down the full weight of her wrath upon his head. He tried to remember what Tarrant had told him, tried to weigh all his alternatives—and at last he gasped, in a tone that he hoped was more fearful than defiant, "I can't. Please. Don't ask that."

Her expression hardened. She reached out to him again, and took his face in her hands. Gripped him tightly, so that his blood pounded beneath her fingers. So that he was incapable of looking away. "You'll serve me," she told him. "Like it or not, you will." She willed him to look up at her, into her eyes; fae wrapped about him like a vice, forcing obedience. "I need to know where they are and what they're doing. You're going to tell me that." Hot thoughts slithered into his mind, wrapping about his brainstem like serpents. Stroking the centers of pleasure and pain within him as she practiced her control. "Submit to me," she whispered. He shut his eyes, tried to fight her off—but she was inside him, her hunger filling his flesh, her thoughts stabbing into his brain. Where the hell was Tarrant's barrier now? He tried with all his will to force her out of his mind—to sever her control—but without a Working to focus his efforts he didn't have a prayer. And he didn't dare Work, not now.

Amused by his struggles, she stroked his brain anew; waves of sensation, shamefully erotic, reverberated through his body, followed by a pain so intense that it would have doubled him over if not for the fae that bound him upright. She was playing his flesh like an instrument, there was no place he could hide, no way he could stop it . . . but knew that if he gave in, even for a moment, if he let his human intellect be swept away by the tide of her madness, that he was lost forever. Her hunger knew no middle ground.

And then, suddenly, the sea turned cold. The lust became darkness, and ice shot through his veins. His body shook as the essence of the Hunter filled him—unclean, inhuman, but oh, so welcome!—forcing out the foreign influence, chilling his burning flesh. His stomach spasmed as the force of Tarrant's unlife filled it and he vomited suddenly, as if by casting out the bitter liquids within him he might also cast out that influence. Never before was the Hunter's essence so alien, so physically intolerable. And never before was it so welcome.

When he came to himself he saw her standing back from him, rage burning like wildfire in her eyes. Somewhere in the back of his numbed brain he remembered something about a signal, his link to Gerald Tarrant . . . what was it? He grasped at the fact, used it as a lifeline to restore his reason. Something about a sign, and the wards . . . that was it. This was what they'd set up, as the trigger: their enemy, trying to break through Tarrant's barrier. The Hunter would have sensed that and taken it for his starting sign. Even now, the quakewards were being broken.

Which left very little time. Minutes, perhaps. Or so he hoped. He tried to focus on what he needed to do and how fast he needed to do it, tried not to think about what might happen if the earth failed to respond to its newfound freedom. Because that possibility was enough to chill him to the bone. The longer it took, the less was the likelihood that this woman would be Working when the wave hit— and for him to be here, bound and helpless, with her still alive and whole, and knowing what they had intended . . . it was unthinkable. She would destroy him. She would destroy them all.

"You're a fool," she said angrily. "Do you really think your precious adept can protect you? After I broke him? He couldn't even save himself—how on Erna is he going to help you?" The voice became seductive, cloying. "Tell me what I want to know, and you can go free. Isn't that the easiest way? Or else . . . I might have to dissect your mind, thought by thought, until I find what I need. Until there's nothing left in you, but that one bit of information and enough strength to voice it. Not a pleasant prospect." Her eyes narrowed to slits, her expression drawn. "The choice is yours, priest."

And he took his chance. Daring her rage. Daring her hatred. Because it was her obsession he wanted, and that must be directed at him. Quickly, before the quake-wards failed.

"Go to hell," he spat.

He was struck from behind on the head, hard enough to draw blood. He allowed the blow to drive him to his knees, gasping audibly as a thin, warm trickle began to seep down the back of his collar. Defiance, laced with weakness: that was the winning formula. Play it right, and he would goad her into Working him without doing him permanent harm. Play it wrong . . . he shuddered. She was perfectly capable of maiming him—or worse. He had put himself in her power. If she had been sane he would have been confident, but she wasn't— and the victims of addiction, any addiction, were notoriously unstable.

The taloned fingers caught in his hair and jerked his head up, so that he was forced to meet her eyes. Hatred was hot in her gaze, and a disdain so absolute that he knew for a fact she would never see the blow coming. Not if he could get her Working. Not if he could keep her involved.

"You made a fatal error," she informed him. "Not just in coming here, but in guarding yourself against my pets. That interrogation would have been far more merciful than this one will be."

—And her power hit him, full in the face, a wall of searing force that drove the breath from his body and left him stunned, half-blinded. The fire of her addiction focused in on him, became a red-hot spearpoint that probed deep inside his flesh, testing for weaknesses. If she had used a real blade, she couldn't have made the pain any greater; his nerves rang out as though scraped by sharpened steel, his body shaking uncontrollably as pain consumed his universe.

He struggled not to fight back. That was harder than all the rest combined: forcing himself *not* to respond, as she played his body like some terrible instrument. It went against every instinct in him, against all his years of learning and experience. But any Working now might mean death, if luck and Erna turned against him. And so he swallowed back on all the ingrained keys that might unlock his defenses, and banished the images that floated in front of his eyes, before they could Work the fae to save him. And he drank in the bitter draught of utter defenselessness as her will probed sharp within him.

And then—an eternity later—she released him. He would have fallen, but clawed hands had taken hold of his shoulders and they held him upright. The woman's face was a mask of rage and indignation—*How dare you defy me!*—with a desperate edge that might well blossom into something more dangerous.

"Please," he whispered. Daring a subterfuge. "I can't. Don't you understand? I can't!"

The burning eyes narrowed suspiciously. She turned to regard a figure who stood just behind her left shoulder—he had not been there before, Damien was certain of that—and demanded, "Well?"

Faceted eyes in an ink-black face. Glassy surface that refracted the light, like chipped obsidian. Damien had seen figures in his nightmares that looked more forbidding—but not many. And not often.

"The adept has Worked a barrier," the surreal figure rasped. The quality of his voice—like sandpaper on an open wound—made Damien's skin crawl. "And he's Warded it into this man's flesh, so that it requires no sustaining power. In fact, you empower it every time you try to break through it." The glistening eyes fixed on Damien, and seemed to pierce through him. What was that creature? What if it could read the truth in him? "Well Worked," the dark figure rasped.

"Spare me your admiration," she snapped, "just tell me how to break it."

"You can't. Not directly. Its power feeds off yours. The more force you use, the stronger it gets."

"You're telling me I can't get inside him?"

"I'm telling you that mere force won't succeed here. You'll have to dismantle it, step by step. Reversing the process he used to erect it in the first place. Assuming you can," he added.

"I can do anything," she said acidly.

She took hold of Damien again, sharpened nails tangling in his sweat-soaked hair. "You'll regret the day you decided to serve him," she promised the priest.

"—Or of course," the black figure interjected, "there's always physical torture."

She looked back sharply at him. And Damien could barely hear her words, so loud was the pounding of his heart. "Would that work?" she demanded. Hunger echoed in her voice.

"Who can say? It would certainly be . . . interesting."

"I can't," Damien whispered. Trying to will as much fear into his voice as he could muster. In the face of possible torture, it wasn't hard. "He said the barrier wouldn't permit it. Said that his blockage was absolute, from both directions. . . ."

"So that you can't betray him," she concluded. "Not even to save yourself from pain." Disappointment flashed briefly in those hollow eyes. "A shame." Then her expression hardened once more; the grip on his hair tightened, pulling his head back. "Not that it will help you," she whispered.

He shut his eyes this time, so that he didn't have to see the inhuman depths in hers. There was something in her so blindly ravenous that the mere thought of contact with her made his stomach tighten in dread. This wasn't just a hunger for vision, like Senzei had known, or even an obsession with power. It had gone beyond that—far beyond that—into realms so utterly corrupted that barely a fragment of her human soul remained, clinging to the flesh that housed it as if somehow the two could be reunited. Could mere hunger do that to a woman? Or would it take something more—some outside influence, that fed on the soul's dissolution? He thought of the obsidian figure standing beside her and wondered at its source. At their relationship.

Then: Her hunger enveloped him. Dark, unwholesome, utterly revolting—and focused, this time, in a way it hadn't been before. He felt her mental fingers prying at the edges of Tarrant's barrier, trying to Work it loose from his flesh. Though he didn't doubt the Hunter's skill, he knew that her tenacity went far beyond anything a sane mind might conjure—and he shivered to think of what would become of him if she managed to dismantle Tarrant's Warding before the faesurge struck her.

Where's your earthquake, Hunter? He imagined all the things that might have gone wrong—Gerald Tarrant too weak to Work, the quake-wards too strong to be broken, some secondary defense system, hitherto unnoticed, coming into play—but nothing frightened him more than the simple fact that the earth might not move. Period. Even if all their planning had been perfect, even if Tarrant had succeeded in all he set out to do . . . the nature of seismic activity was random, and all the Workings in the world wouldn't make it otherwise. The odds had been in their favor, true—but what if odds weren't enough? What if the earth betrayed them, and took its sweet time in responding?

Then I'm dead, he thought darkly. Behind his back, his fingers played with the edges of his bracers. Thick leather, but soft; he unsnapped them. The Keeper's thoughts burrowed inside his mind—like so many worms—but her attention was fixed on Tarrant's Warding.

Keep Working, he begged her silently. *Just keep Working.* It seemed that time had slowed down for him, that something in the enemy's assault had altered his temporal functioning; he was aware of long minutes passing as he pushed at the forward edge of his bracers, forcing the leather back through the ropes that bound his wrists. Buying himself additional slack, through that action. He told himself that he had to be ready, in case their plan failed. Had to be ready to free himself and move quickly. He tucked one thumb against his palm and tested his hand against his rope, seeing if he had gained enough slack to force his hand through. Coarse rope bit into his skin, but the fit was promising. One good jerk—and the loss of some skin— and he might be free. He gauged the distance between himself and the woman, reached out with his senses to Know the whereabouts of her servants—and then stopped himself, sickened by his carelessness, and forced himself not to Work. Not to Work at all. It seemed to him that hours had passed, that while he had been lost in the mechanics of bodily defense she had launched whole offensives against the structure of Tarrant's Warding. And still the earth hadn't moved. Had Tarrant managed to dispel the quake-wards, or was he still struggling with them? Was there still some hope that the adept might succeed, and trigger the surge they required?

And then she drew back from him, and the world spiraled out into her eyes. And he saw the anger there, and knew with dread certainty that she had sensed some hidden purpose in the barrier. Enough to stop her from Working.

Which meant that it was over. It was all over . . . and they had lost.

"I think," she said coldly, "we may try torture after all."

He looked about himself, desperately, as his hands prepared to pull loose from their bonds. As he steeled himself to move, and move quickly, in a sudden bid for freedom. But then his eyes fell on the eastern wall, at the soft glow rising up from its base—and he flinched, as the meaning of that became clear. As the full measure of his vulnerability hit home.

Light. Gray light, rising in the east.

Dawn.

He was suddenly aware that the Dark Ones had left them, no doubt withdrawing to some protective recess deep within the earth. Tarrant was powerless now. If he hadn't broken the quake-wards yet, he wasn't going to. Not in time to help Damien. The priest's last hope had died with the night.

"What is it?" she demanded. Sensing that something was amiss with him, not knowing what. She turned toward the eastern wall, back to Damien. "What new trick . . ." Her eyes grew hard, and he heard her mutter something; a key? He felt a Knowing taking shape around him, felt it working to squeeze the information out of him, examining his link to the dawn, to Tarrant—

And then it struck. He saw it, for an instant, through her eyes— for one terrible instant, in which the whole world was ablaze. Power surged through the crystalline walls, dashed against the mirrored steps, cycloned fiercely about them. Earth-fae fresh from the depths

of Erna, hot as the magma that spawned it. She screamed as it struck her, screamed in terror as it blasted its way into her, its power filling and then bursting each cell in her brain.

He threw himself back. The distance somehow seemed to sever the contact between them, and the terrible vision was gone—but her screaming went on, rising in pitch to a fevered shriek as the earth-power poured through her. He tried not to listen as he jerked hard at his bonds, fighting to free himself. The coarse rope cut into him as he tried to force his hand through it, drawing blood—but with that lubrication, and a near-dislocation of his thumb, he managed to pull one hand free. Burning suns swam in his vision, an afterimage from the fae; he blinked as though that could cool their glare and tried to see past them to locate an exit. The shrieking numbed his brain, made it all but impossible to think clearly. How had he come in? He had no hope of finding a true exit from the citadel, not in time; his only chance lay in getting himself underground, and in hoping that the coming quake was merciful to whatever space housed him. With luck he could find his way back to the entrance tunnel—which would lead him down to the plains, and relative safety. . . .

He grabbed his sword as he ran, sweeping it up from the crystalline floor—now spattered with blood and vomit, therefore visible. He didn't dare be unarmed, not now. Thank God mere steel was enough to dispatch the Dark Ones. He ran, trusting to blind instinct to guide him. Stumbling, as unseen steps trapped his feet, hitting one mirrored wall hard enough to shatter it. Where was the exit? Where was the passage down? He tried to remember all the turnings they had taken on the way in, tried to reason his way through the glassy labyrinth— and then he took his sword and slammed its pommel into an obstructing wall, hard. Crystal shivered into bits, revealing the dark mouth of a tunnel beyond. *Praise God*, he thought feverishly. *Please, let it be in time.* Bits of mirror crunched underfoot as he fought his way toward the entrance, slipping and sliding on the glassy frag-ments. And then the earthen wall was beside him, and his hand was upon it, and he was stumbling down into the depths—

And the earth convulsed, with force enough that he was thrown from his feet, headfirst into a hard dirt wall. Overhead the citadel tinkled, like a thousand wind chimes in a stormy sky—and then began to shatter, wall by wall, staircase by staircase, as the ground swelled up and broke beneath it. Huge chunks of crystal crashed to the earth behind him, sending fragments like spears down into the tunnel at his feet. Half-stunned, he forced himself to move again, to work his way down into the heart of the trembling earth. To his side, a wooden support snapped and came loose; chunks of rock and dirt hailed down on him as bits of crystal caromed into the depths. *Too close to the surface,* he thought, despairing. *Too close!* A shockwave threw him off his feet, and dirt rained down on him as he struggled to recover his balance. *Must get deeper. . . .* He struggled on blindly, not pausing to consider whether greater depth would really mean safety—not stopping to question whether any place could be truly safe, in such an utter upheaval.

It should only last seconds. Shouldn't it? What were the parameters of a quake like this, that had been decades in the making?

The tunnel grew dark about him, dawn's dim light filtered through a rain of dirt and gravel that fell from its ceiling. He staggered down the length of it by feel, praying for enough time to save himself. But even as he did so he knew that if the quake had already begun, his time was just about up.

And then a support overhead broke loose, and swung down into him. It knocked him against the far wall, hard, leaving him stunned where he fell. The motion loosed a fresh avalanche of dirt and rock that rained on him as he struggled to right himself. All around him he could hear the tunnel collapsing, the roar of the earthquake as it raged through the planet's crust. His hand clenched tightly about his sword grip as he struggled to his feet—as if that weapon could somehow protect him from the fury of the earth itself—but then the ground beneath him spasmed furiously, and the whole of the ceiling gave way at last. Pounds upon pounds of dirt and rock poured down upon him, battering him into the ground. He tried to fight free, but the torrent of earth overwhelmed him. Gasping for breath, he choked on dirt—and as he struggled to clear his lungs, something large and sharp struck him hard on the head. Driving him down, deep down, into the suffocating depths of Nature's vengeance.

Forty-five

Light. Blinding. He shrank back from it—or tried to—but a strong hand had hold of him, long fingers entangled in his shirt. It jerked him up, forcing his mouth above the level of the earth. He gasped for breath, winced from the pain of the effort. Then his lungs spasmed suddenly, and he began to cough up the dirt that had filled them. Retching helplessly, as the strong hands continued to pull him out of his earthbound tomb.

The light faded slowly to a mere star, to a tiny lamp flame. By its glow he could see that the tunnel was mostly gone, and what little that remained was filled with dust. Even while he watched, a fresh trickle of gravel began to course down from what remained of the ceiling.

"Can you move?" Tarrant asked.

His limbs felt numb, but they responded. He nodded.

"Then let's go. This place is death."

The Hunter wrapped an arm about his shoulder—so cold, so very cold, who could ever have thought that the man's chill could be so comforting?—and with his help, Damien somehow managed to make his way to open space. He paused there for a minute, shivering.

"Close?" Tarrant asked softly.

"Too close," he whispered. A wave of sudden weakness washed over him; he let the Hunter support him. "Ciani," he breathed. "Where—"

"Right ahead of us. With Hesseth. No one's being left alone anymore till this is over."

"Did she—" He was afraid to voice the words. Afraid of what a negative answer would mean. "Is she—"

"Whole? Recovered?" He shook his head, grimly. "Not yet. But this is just the beginning. If her assailant isn't killed in a cavern collapse, I'll hunt him down later. Now that his protector is dead, it should be easy enough."

He looked up at him, sharply. "You know that?"

"She fed on me," he answered quietly. "A channel like that works both ways, you know. Did you think I wouldn't drink in her terror when she died? She owed me that much."

He struggled to get his feet firmly beneath him. "Good meal, I hope."

"Damned good meal," the Hunter assured him. "Let's move."

Together they crept through the remains of the access tunnel, through passages made dangerously narrow by earthfall. At times they had to dig their way through, heaving aside rocks and mounds of earth to make enough room for a body to squeeze through.

"You came in this way?" Damien asked.

"It's still collapsing, if that's your question." He grasped a fallen support beam and pulled; a narrow passage opened up to receive them. "Somewhat less violently, farther along. That's where the women are. —But I wouldn't like to be here when the next shock wave hits," he added.

"I'm surprised it hasn't yet."

The Hunter looked at him; there was a faint smile on his lips. "That may be because I left some of the quake-wards intact. I Worked them to kick in again after the first tremors ended. They won't hold long, of course, not without the rest of the series . . . but every minute counts."

"You're very thorough."

"I try to be." He wiped dirt from his eyes with the back of a sleeve. Damien tried to do the same, and his hand came away from his face sticky with blood. The quantity of it unnerved him. "Much further?"

The Hunter glanced at him. "You'll make it."

He thought of the dawn light he had seen from the citadel. How much time had passed since then? What kind of safety was there for his dark companion, if the sun had risen? "What about you?"

He jerked loose a piece of splintered wood that blocked their path; dirt showered down in the narrow passageway. "I'm strong enough, if that's the question."

"I meant the sun."

For a moment the Hunter was still. Damien thought he saw a muscle tense along his jaw, and the pale eyes narrowed. "Let's deal with that problem when we get to it," he said at last—and he heaved the broken timber from him, hard enough that it gouged the far wall.

"If you think—"

"Talk won't make the sun set," he said sharply. "And we're still far from getting out of here. Look." He pointed to the far side of the passageway, to a hole that yawned in the far wall. "Can you see it? In the currents. They're stirring, underground. The ones that survived the first shockwave will be coming to the surface, where they imagine things are safer. Idiots! If they knew their science, they'd stay where they are, where the surface waves can't reach—"

"You're afraid," Damien said quietly.

The Hunter began to protest, then stopped himself. "Of course I'm afraid," he muttered. "I'd be a fool if I weren't. Does that satisfy you?" He kicked loose a thick clod of earth, clearing the passage ahead of them. "I suggest we get to the lady and Hesseth before our subterranean friends do—and worry about fear later. There'll be time for it, I assure you."

He gave the lamp to Damien—his own sight didn't require it—and led the way eastward, through the ruins of their enemy's escape passage. As the tunnel cut deeper into the earth the damage seemed to be lessened, but it was still a struggle to make good time through the ravaged warren.

Periodically Tarrant would turn and look back, his eyes narrowed as he focused on the weak underground currents. But if he saw anything specific that disturbed him, he kept it to himself. Once, at the mouth of a narrow tunnel that led down to the Dark Ones' realm, he paused to listen—senses alert as a hunting animal's, nerves trigger-taut in tension—but he said nothing. His expression grim, he nodded eastward, urging the priest away from the citadel.

And then they came across the body. It was half-buried in dirt, as though in its fall it had loosed some new, private avalanche. Tarrant turned it over, brushed the dirt from its face—and breathed in sharply as the charred hole of a Fire-laden bolt became visible, right where one eye should be.

He looked up, lips drawn tight, and muttered, "Come on." And ran. In time they passed another body—this one's chest had a gaping hole, with fresh smoke rising from its Fire-seared edges—but they didn't stop to examine it. The smell of burning flesh was thick and sharp, doubly acrid in the tunnel's claustrophobic confines. They passed a turn where the earth had fallen, kicked a hurried path through loose clods of dirt that barred their way—

And found them. Springbolts in their hands, determination in their eyes. There were bodies here, too, and the scent of their blood was fresh. Tarrant had been right: the Dark Ones were surfacing.

Damien went to where Ciani stood—her back braced firmly against the wall, her hands gripped tightly about the weapon—and put one bruised arm around her. She softened, slightly, just enough to lean against him, barely enough to accept the reassuring gesture. Then she put her free arm around him, too, and squeezed.

"Thank the gods you're still alive," she whispered.

He glanced back at the adept. "Thank Tarrant, in this case."

"We'd better move," the Hunter warned them. He grabbed up a supply pack that had been left by Hesseth's feet, swung it to his back. "And fast."

"How much ammunition is left?" Damien asked the women.

"Plenty," Hesseth responded. "But only three with the Fire." Her teeth were half-bared, as if in a dominance display. "You think there'll be more of them?"

"I think there's no doubt of it," Tarrant assured her. "The only question is how fast they'll come."

"He hasn't died yet," Ciani whispered. "I would know that . . . wouldn't I?"

My God, will you know it. The memories will smash into you like a tidal wave—like the surge of fae that killed your enemy. The experience of an entire lifetime, reabsorbed in an instant. He hated himself for dreading that moment. Hated himself for wondering, with steel-edged calculation, whether that moment might not be the most dangerous of all.

They ran. And they were not alone. Close behind them, back the way they had come, something else was moving through the tunnels. Something that chittered in half-human speech, as it followed the path they had cleared. One demon—or many? With a sudden start Damien realized that his sword was still buried near the citadel, the rest of his weapons inside it. All he had left was the flask of Fire—if that was still intact—and he couldn't draw that out without burning Tarrant. Still, if Tarrant could survive it, and if it could drive back their enemies . . . he fingered the flap of the pouch as he ran, made sure that it was free to open. Tarrant would understand. Strategy demanded it. *Survival* might demand it.

And then they came around a turn, and there were the Dark Ones. A good four of them at least, and perhaps more in the shadows beyond. They were bruised and bleeding, and more than a little disoriented—but their eyes blazed with hatred, and hunger, and their nostrils flared as they caught the scent of human fear. Of food.

"Don't let them touch you," Hesseth whispered. A tremor of fear was in her voice; was she remembering when she'd been drained, back at the earthfire? Damien stepped to Ciani's side and took the springbolt from her. "Get back," he whispered. Out of the corner of his eye he saw Tarrant reach out to her—for a moment he was lost in Morgot again, as the tidal power Hesseth had conjured dissolved all their barriers, and set loose the Hunter's evil—and then he nodded, and gestured for her to go to him, knowing that there was no place where she would be safer than by the adept's side.

And then the creatures fell upon them. Mindless as animals gone rabid, and ten times as deadly. He brought one down with a shot to the gut, fired point-blank into the demonic flesh. And then cursed himself as he brought the second bolt into line, for failing to ask which one of the weapons had only one Worked bolt in it.

And then one was upon him, and his weapon was still uncocked— so he brought the brass butt up into its face, hard, cursing it as he did so. There was blood, and the sharp crack of bone splitting, but the blow did nothing to slow the creature down. One clawed hand grasped the barrel of the springbolt, another grabbed at Damien's arm. He tried to throw the creature off, but a strange numbness had invaded his arm; he found it hard to move. Shadows began to fill his mind, and his thoughts were slow in coming. He needed to fight it. Didn't he? He needed to drive it back from him, before it . . . what? What would it do? He found himself shaking as the numbness claimed more of his flesh, found himself filled with a dread and a fear that was all the more terrible because he couldn't remember its cause.

—And then the Dark One howled, and fell back. In its chest was a smoking hole, where the point of a Fire-laden bolt had pierced through the flesh. Hesseth was ready behind it, her blade poised as if to decapitate the creature, but the Fire made that unnecessary. With a last desperate cry, the Dark One fell—and memories flooded Damien's brain like some wild dream, a thousand and one disjointed bits pouring into him with nightmare intensity. He staggered, trying to absorb the onslaught. Trying to brace himself for further battle, even as he reclaimed his humanity. But beside him the cold blue light of Tarrant's sword filled the tunnel, and he could see by its glow that an icy path had been etched through the flesh of two of their assailants. Carmine crystals glittered where the great veins had been severed, and a frosty steam arose from the newly chilled flesh.

"Let's go—" Damien began, but Tarrant ordered, "Wait."

He walked several yards down the tunnel, back the way they had come. And studied the ceiling overhead as if searching for something. After a minute had passed he seemed to find it, and he raised up his sword so that the glowing tip brushed the packed earth overhead. And then thrust up, suddenly. Chunks of dirt burst outward from the point of contact in an explosion that echoed down the length of the tunnel. And when the dust cleared, they could see that passageway behind them was filled. There might be Dark Ones still ahead of them, but none would be coming from behind. Not without a digging crew.

The Hunter resheathed his sword. "Now we go," he whispered. His posture was tense, in a way that Damien had never seen before. Had the enemy touched him, as well? Or was it just that the odds against them were growing, too swiftly for the adept's liking?

If he's afraid of them, Damien thought grimly, *what does that mean for the rest of us?*

They passed other openings that offered access to the lower regions. Half of them were already filled with rubble, rendering them useless to the Dark Ones. The other ones they left alone. There were simply too many, and each one that Tarrant chose to seal meant another delay, another chance that their enemies would get ahead of them . . . Damien caught sight of the adept's expression as they passed by a particularly large opening, and it was utterly colorless and grim. And he remembered the sunlight that awaited them all, if they ever did reach the end of this passage, and wondered what the man could do to save himself. Was it safe for him to stay down here until sunset? With so many Dark Ones coming to the surface, half-mad with rage and hunger?

I won't let him do it alone, Damien thought darkly. Remembering the hands that had pulled him from the earth, which might just as easily have left him there. Feeling a loyalty which might have shamed him, in another time and place, but which now felt as natural as breathing.

"They're coming," Tarrant whispered, and he turned to look behind them. There was nobody visible there, not yet, but Damien knew enough to trust the man's senses. He was about to speak when Ciani cried out, sharply—and the look on her face was one of such abject terror, such utter despair, that Damien's blood chilled as he recognized what the cause must be.

"He's there," the Hunter said. Giving voice to her fear. "He's coming."

"Is he aware of us?" Damien asked him.

The pale eyes narrowed as Tarrant studied the fae. "Not yet," he whispered. "But he will be soon. He listened for a moment longer, then added, "There are many of them together. Too many to fight."

"Then we move," Damien told him. "The entrance can't be much farther. If we can make it out before they get to us—"

He stopped. Met the pale eyes squarely. "Then Ciani can be safe in the sunlight," he concluded, "while you and I deal with her assailant."

They had just started to move again when it seemed, for an instant, that the earth trembled beneath them. Damien felt his heart skip a beat, and he prayed wildly, *Not now. Please! Just a few minutes more.* As if his God might really interfere. As if the guiding force of the universe was concerned with a handful of human Wardings, or the lives that might depend on them.

They ran. The walls and ceiling of the earthbound passage began to rain down fresh dirt on their heads, but they shielded their eyes with their hands and continued onward. Knowing how close they must be to the tunnel's eastern exit, knowing how close that exit was to the relative safety of the plains, they pressed on—through dirtfall, over rock-strewn drifts, across huge heaps of splintered wood and boulders—they scrambled over obstacles as quickly as they could, not daring to take the time to study their surroundings. Again the earth trembled, and this time a dull roar could be heard. "They're going," Tarrant muttered, and Damien whispered, "God help us all." The tunnel seemed at least twice as long in this direction as it had been when Damien first entered it; where the hell was that exit?

And then the worst of it struck. Not nearly as violent as its predecessor—but such violence was no longer necessary. The supporting structure of the tunnel had already been weakened, and its walls were riddled with gaping holes. It didn't take much to shake loose what was left, so that the remaining ceiling fell in huge chunks behind them, on top of them, directly in their path. Damien threw himself at Ciani just as a massive shard of stone hurtled down from the ceiling above her; he managed to roll them both out of its path, barely in time. Gravel pelted them, and earth that had been packed to a bricklike consistency. He sheltered Ciani with his body and prayed that the other two were all right. And that their enemies weren't. Wouldn't that be convenient, if the earth itself swallowed up Ciani's assailant?

But when he finally raised himself up from where he lay, and looked at her, he knew that they'd had no such luck. Her face betrayed none of the joy—or the disorientation—that returning memories would have brought.

He felt sharp nails bite into his shoulder, heard Hesseth hiss softly. "I think you'd better look at this," the rakh-woman told him. She nodded toward the east, down to where the tunnel turned. He paused for a second to make sure the tremors had ceased—they had—and then got to his feet and followed her. The space remaining was barely large enough to admit him, and his shoulder pressed against damp earth as he forced his way through. To where the passageway turned, just prior to its ascension. . . .

It was filled. Completely. The weight of the earth had collapsed a whole segment of the tunnel, rendering it impassable. Damien felt despair bite into him, hard, as he regarded the solid mound before him. They might dig through it, given enough time and the right tools . . . but they had neither, and there was no telling how far the blockage went. If the whole tunnel between here and the surface had caved in ahead of them, then there was simply no way to get through it. No way at all.

He made his way back to the others and prepared to tell them the bad news—and then saw that it wasn't necessary. Tarrant had read the truth in the currents, and Ciani's eyes were bright with despair. The single lantern which remained to them shed just enough light to show him that her hands were trembling.

"We're stuck," he muttered.

"Can we dig out?" Ciani's voice was a whisper, hoarse and fragile. "Dig up, I mean."

Damien glanced at the ceiling. And then at Tarrant.

"We're near the surface," he said quietly. "I can hear the solar fae as it strikes the earth. Can almost feel it. . . ." He paused, and then Damien thought he saw him shiver. "If the earth above is soft enough to dig, but solid enough not to bury us when we begin to disturb it . . . it would still take time," he said. "A lot of time." He looked back the way they had come. "I'm not sure we have that," he said tensely.

Damien listened—and it seemed to him that he could hear a scrabbling in the distance, like rodents. "They survived."

"Enough of them," the Hunter said grimly. "More than we can handle, without using the earth-fae."

Damien glanced at Hesseth, but she shook her head. Whatever combination of tides she required in order to Work simply wasn't available now. It might be, in the future . . . if they lasted that long. If there was any future for them.

Louder, now; the sounds were approaching. Damien heard voices among them, hissing human phonemes. He looked about desperately, trying to think of some way out, or some new way in which they could defend themselves—but there was nothing. They were trapped. Even if they could fight off the Dark Ones for a time, they were still too close to the surface; the next quake would bury them.

And then the Hunter turned away from them. And put one hand up against the dirt at his side, as though he required its support.

"There is a way," he whispered hoarsely. "One way only, that I can think of. It would save the lady."

The voices were getting louder. Damien came close to where the adept stood so that they might talk quietly. "Tell me."

Tarrant looked up at the ceiling, as if searching for some sort of sign. It occurred to Damien with a start that this was how he had searched before, in the moments before he brought down a whole section of the tunnel.

"I could blast a way out," the Hunter muttered. "There's enough tamed fae in the sword that I could do it, without having to use the currents. Only . . ."

"The sunlight," Damien said softly.

Tarrant turned away again.

"You can't," Ciani whispered. "Gerald. . . ."

"I appreciate your concern," the adept breathed, "but there's no real alternative. Other than dying here beneath the earth, our souls gone to feed those . . . *creatures*." He shook his head, stiffly. "Even I can't Work an adequate defense, without the earth-fae to draw on. There are so many of them, and we have so few weapons left . . . it would only be a matter of time."

"Until nightfall?" Damien asked.

The Hunter shook his head, grimly. "Not that long, I regret." He turned to Ciani. "This would free you," he whispered. "I could open this part of the passage to the sunlight, and if your assailant was here at the time . . . it would free you."

"And you?" Damien asked. "Could you survive it?"

He hesitated. "Probably not. Sunlight is relative, of course; I've stood in the light of three moons, and beneath a galaxy of stars . . . but this is different." A tremor seemed to pass through his flesh. Damien recalled the fire underground, and what it had done to him. If a mere earthly blaze could wreak that kind of damage, what chance would the Hunter have when facing the sun itself?

Then: "I see no other way," he said grimly. And he drew the cold-fire sword from its sheath.

The voices were coming closer now. Ciani moved to his side, reached out as if to touch him—and then drew back, trembling. "Gerald."

"Lady Ciani." He caught up her hand in his free one and touched it quickly to his lips. If she had any sort of negative response to the chill of his flesh, Damien didn't see it. "I owe you a debt of honor. I've risked much to fulfill it. If this succeeds, and your memory is restored—"

"Then I would say your honor is satisfied," she whispered. "And I free you from any further obligation."

He let go of her hand. And bowed. "Thank you, lady."

"If you can find shelter—" Damien began.

"There'll be no shelter when I'm done." He gestured for them to move back, clearing the space nearest to him. And studied the ceiling again, looking for a workable fault. "You'll have to move quickly. Gain the surface as fast as you can, and then get away from here. Fast. You don't know how long those *things* will take to die, or what damage they might do to you in their death-throes. The best defense is distance. Don't even pause to look back," he warned them—and Damien wondered if his concern was for their lives, or that they might see the Hunter burning.

"Now," he hissed. "Get ready."

The voices were approaching. Damien stood back, and gathered Ciani to him. Hesseth pressed close by his other side, springbolt at the ready. He began to shield his eyes—and saw Tarrant's pale gaze fixed on him.

"Good luck, Hunter," he said quietly.

And they came. Climbing over the mounds of earth like oversized rodents, inhuman eyes blazing with hunger. The first one saw them there and pulled up, hissing a sharp warning to its fellows. Then they came into the lamplight as well, swarming about him like hungry insects, filling the far end of the tunnel. Wary, because Tarrant's sword was drawn and they clearly sensed its power.

And then one of them fixed its eyes on Ciani and hissed softly, in pleasure. A sharp tongue tip stroked the points of its teeth, and Damien knew by the tremor that ran through her that this was the one, the demon who attacked her in Jaggonath. The one who contained her memories.

"*Now,*" the Hunter whispered.

The demons began to move.

He thrust. Up into the earth, deep into the fault he had located. The force of the coldfire-bound steel took root and expanded, exploding outward with all the force of a bomb. Dirt bits slammed into Damien and his companions, and the force of the compression struck them like a fist. For a moment there was nothing but a hailing of dirt and rocks, like shrapnel. And then: light. Blinding. The brilliance of the morning sun, to eyes that had spent days in darkness. He threw up his arm across his eyes, as the pain of it seared his vision. The whole world was white, formless, utterly blinding . . . he forced his arm down, remembered Tarrant's last warning. *Get away from here. Fast.* Against the glare of sunlight he could barely make out shapes, now, hot white against the hotter white of the morning sky. He clambered toward one of them, felt a newly-formed wall of earth take shape beneath his fingertips. He pulled Ciani over to it and guided Hesseth to follow. "Climb!" he whispered fiercely. He could barely see the ground beneath him, but trusted his hands to guide him. The earth here sloped back in smoothly curved walls, like that of a meteoric crater; he tried not to think of Tarrant as he struggled up that slope, as he tried to gain solid purchase in the shifting, inconstant earth, helping the others to climb along with him—

Ciani screamed. It was a sound of pain and terror combined, so utterly chilling in its tenor that for a moment Damien froze, stunned by the sound. Then he saw her slipping as her body convulsed, and he grabbed out for her. Caught her by the sleeve of her shirt, and tried to keep her from sliding back down to the tunnel below.

"Can't," she gasped. "Gods, I can't—"

"Help me!" he cried—and Hesseth reached out from the other side, grabbing Ciani's arm. Together they held their ground as she shivered from the onslaught of her own forgotten memories, all the pain and fear of a lifetime compressed into one burning instant. Her skin was hot to the touch, but that might have been because of the sun. After weeks among the nonhuman and the semihuman, wounded and tired in cold, dark tunnels, Damien would be hard pressed to remember what normal body temperature felt like.

They began to drag her upward. Slowly. Afraid to move on the treacherous slope, but even more afraid to stay where they were. That Ciani's assailant was now dead was all but certain. But how many others remained, who might find a short climb into sunlight an acceptable price for revenge? Inch by inch, carefully, the two of them worked their way up the earthen slope. Beneath them clods of earth broke loose and tumbled down into the crater's depths. They fought not to tumble down with them. The slope grew steeper, and Damien had to drive his hands deep into the soil to get the support he needed. Ciani moaned softly, utterly limp beneath his grasp, and he could only hope that the climb was doing her no damage. He reached into the crumbling earth, and caught hold of something solid at last. A root. He looked up, and against the glare of the sun he could make out the form of trees, not far above them. With a prayer of thanksgiving on his lips he grabbed at the firm root, and used it to pull himself up the slope. Hesseth, on the other side of Ciani, saw what he was doing and followed suit. The soft earth gave way to a tangle of vegetation, gave way to the underearth limbs of mature trees. . . .

And they were over. All three of them. Damien lay gasping on the ground for a moment, his legs still resting on the edge of Tarrant's crater. Then, with effort, he forced himself to his feet. Ciani was utterly still, but the look on her face was one of peace; lowering his head to her chest, he could hear her measured breathing. He lifted her up into his arms, gently, and murmured, "She's all right." Cradling her, as one might a child. "She's going to be all right."

And the winter chill was nothing to them as they staggered away from the site of their recent trials. Because the sunlight was streaming down on them, and that was life itself.

The series of earthquakes which Tarrant had triggered continued for nearly three days, but none were as violent as those first few had been. Trees had been torn down, mountains reshaped, whole cavern systems refigured—but in the end the land survived, and that was all that really mattered.

They camped on the plains, on open ground, until the worst of the aftershocks had ended. Only then did Damien dare to climb back up, to that place where they had so recently escaped from the earth's confines. The landmarks had all changed, and massive rockslides made climbing all but impossible . . . but in the end he found it, a circle of land devoid of trees, where the ground sloped down in a gentle arena of freshly-turned earth.

It had been filled in, almost to the brim. The repeated tremors must have done it, shaking the broken earth until it sought its own level, like water. Whatever Tarrant had done to the demons—and to himself—it was buried forever in the mountainside, along with the remains of his body.

He tried not to think of what that burning must have been like, as he knelt in the soft earth to pray. Tried not to remember the Hunter's charred flesh as it had been in his hands, as he softly intoned the Prayer for the Dead. Pleading mercy for a soul that had never earned mercy, for a man who had so committed himself to hell that a thousand prayers a day, offered up for a thousand years, would not negate one instant of his suffering.

"Rest in peace, Prophet," he whispered.

He hoped that someday it would be possible.

Forty-six

Winter had come early to the plains—but it was nothing compared to the frigid abuse of autumn in the mountains, and Damien was grateful for it. After nearly two hundred miles of travel it was good to be clean again and in fresh clothes, and knowing that he and Ciani were safe was a luxury he had begun to despair of ever experiencing. And if she had changed somewhat, if she was no longer the woman he had known . . . hadn't he seen that coming, in the last few days? Hadn't he seen it building in her, all the way back from the eastern range?

That doesn't help, he told himself, bitterly. *It doesn't help at all.*

He looked toward the center of the rakhene camp, where even now a celebration was taking place. The night was dark, almost moonless, but the jubilant rakh had set it alight with over a hundred torches, and their triumphal bonfire blazed like a sun in miniature from the center of their camp. And *she* danced among them—not like one of them, exactly, but not like a human woman, either. An adept who had chosen to suspend herself between two worlds, so that she might bridge the gap between them. A loremaster. He turned away, remembering the word. Resenting it. And hating himself, for the unfairness of his reaction.

She was never really yours. You never really knew her.

It didn't help. Not a bit. But then, cold reason never did.

He felt restless. Confined, by the nearness of so many tents. So many rakh. The ranks of Hesseth's tribe had been swelled by numerous visitors who had come to hear the tales and see the relics and gaze in fascination upon the hated, fearsome humans. He sensed power games going on all about him, on levels too complex for him to interpret, as tribes who normally avoided each other tried to sort themselves out into a new, all-inclusive order. *Human society*, he thought. *We've planted the seeds.* In time there would be nations, and treaties, and all the ills that came of such things ... he didn't know whether to feel glad or guilty, but he suspected the latter was more appropriate. God willing the Canopy would remain intact so that the rakh could make their own fate, in peace, before having to deal with humankind again. God willing.

Slowly, he turned from the camp. It was cold outside, but the heavy garments which the rakh had made for him were more than sufficient to ward off the wintry chill. He tucked his hands into his pockets and began to walk eastward, away from the starkly lit celebration. The noise of rakhene chanting faded behind him, as well as the occasional burst of human laughter that sparkled in its midst. *Her* laughter. He pulled his jacket tightly about him and increased his pace. The trampled earth of the rakhene encampment gave way to half-frozen slush, which in turn gave way to snow: pristine, unsullied, a glistening white blanket that draped over the plains like the softest wool, cushioning the land in silence.

He walked. Away from the camp, from the noise. Away from all signs of life, and all protestations of joy. He had put in one hard night's celebration, and now he was ready to move again. Restless, as always. To the west of him the Worldsend Mountains loomed, sterile and foreboding. He knew that all its passes were frozen by now, would remain frozen for months to come, and that its slopes were ripe with avalanches in the making, and a thousand other hazards of winter. He would never have risked such a route in this season, not with others by his side—but he might do so alone. Now that Senzei had found his peace, and Ciani had found ... other things.

And then a movement caught his eye, back the way he had come. And he turned, to see who had followed him from the camp, what rakhene business would disturb his solitude.

When he saw, he froze.

The figure stood with the moon to its back, so that all of its front was in shadow. Thick fabric fell from its shoulders, enveloping it like a cloak, rendering its form doubly invisible. Its face was no more than an oval of blackness, its body an amorphous shadow. But there was no mistaking its shape. Or its identity.

"I see that the lady is well," the Hunter whispered.

Relief surged up inside him—and moral revulsion also, as fresh within him as the day on which he'd learned the Hunter's name. The force of the admixture was stunning, and it rendered him utterly speechless. He was grateful that he had no weapon on him—glad that he was thus spared the trauma of having to sort out his feelings, having to decide whether or not this was an appropriate moment to remind the Hunter of their natural enmity.

At last he found his voice. "You survived. The sunlight. . . ."

"It's all a question of degree, Reverend Vryce, as I told you. Fortunately, the Dark Ones lack such sophistication. Since they had no knowledge of any other option, they died." His voice was a mere breath, hardly louder than the breezes of the night. It seemed also to be coarser than usual—but it was so hard to hear him at all that Damien couldn't be certain of that. "I thought you would want to know that I lived. I thought you had that right."

"Thank you. I'm . . . glad."

"That I survived?" he asked dryly.

"That you didn't die . . . like that." He meant it sincerely and knew that could be heard in his voice. "I intended . . . something cleaner."

"So you'll still be coming after me when you leave the rakhlands. I regret that, priest. There's a quality in you that I would hate to destroy. A certain . . . recklessness?"

"But you'll manage it anyway."

"If you try to kill me? With relish."

"Then I'm sorry to ruin your sport," he said, "but I'm afraid you're going to have to wait for that particular pleasure." He watched the dark figure carefully as he spoke, wondering what it was about it that seemed so strained, so very . . . *wrong*. "I'm going east."

The voice was a whisper, no louder than the wind. "East is the ocean. Novatlantis. The deathlands."

"And more than that, I'm afraid." He nodded toward the camp; its fires were invisible in the distance. "The Lost Ones returned, you know. The males, that is. I think the risk appealed to them. They're cleaning out the last of the Keeper's warren, braving rock falls and tunnel collapse in order to hunt down her servants. For food, they told me. The last of the Dark Ones will be their winter sustenance."

"That's impossible," the cloaked figure muttered. "Demonic flesh wouldn't be—"

"It isn't demonic flesh," the priest said quietly. "Because the Dark Ones aren't constructs." He looked east: toward the mountains, toward the fallen citadel. "Hesseth found a body. We examined it. We thought we could determine what sort of construct it was, maybe find out how had come into being . . . only it wasn't a construct at all. Hesseth was the first to suspect it, and Ciani confirmed it. The truth." He drew in a deep breath, remembering that moment. Reliving it, as he spoke. "It was rakh," he told Tarrant. His own voice little more than a whisper. "The Dark Ones are rakh."

For a moment, Tarrant's form was utterly still; Damien imagined he could hear the man's thoughts racing, aligning fact with fact like the pieces of some vast puzzle. "Not possible," he said at last. "That would mean—"

"Someone—or something—has been evolving them. Like you did to the Forest, Hunter. Only this time on a grander scale. This time with high-order intelligence." He felt the tightness growing inside him again, the same restless tension he had felt when the truth first became apparent. His hands in his pockets tightened into fists. "Nature couldn't do it. Nature *wouldn't*. Take a tribe of intelligent, adaptable creatures, and bind them to the night like that? Suppress their own vitality, so that they could only live by torturing others? Those Dark Ones *died* when you exposed them, Hunter—and you didn't. You, who've spent a thousand years avoiding the sun—whose very existence depends upon constant darkness—*you survived*. Why would Erna imbue one of her creatures with such a terrible weakness? What point could it possibly serve?"

"You think someone's done it," he whispered. "Deliberately."

"There's no question in my mind," he said grimly. "And it would have to be on a massive scale, to succeed like that—the corruption of a whole environment. There's nothing like that in the human lands. Remember what the rakh-girl said? *They came from the east.*"

"So you're going after them."

"Five expeditions have tried to cross that ocean. Two in your own age, three in the centuries after. None were ever heard from again. But that doesn't mean that they failed, does it? For all we know, humankind managed to populate those regions . . . and gave birth to something which has warped the very patterns of Nature. I think that what we saw here . . . that's just the tip of the iceberg. I think we need to know what the hell is going on over there before something far worse comes over." He looked at the dark figure before him, and felt something stir in him that was not quite revulsion. Not wholly abhorrence.

"Come with me," he whispered. "Come east with me."

The figure stiffened. "Are you serious? Do you know what you're asking?"

"A chance to strike at your real enemy. The one behind all this; the force responsible. Doesn't that appeal to you?"

"In the past few weeks," Tarrant said darkly, "I have been bound, humiliated, starved, burned, blasted with sunlight, tortured in ways I will not describe, and nearly killed on several occasions. I, who have spent the last five hundred years building myself a safe refuge from such threats! Are you suggesting that I should court such disasters again? Truly, I shouldn't have taken so much of your blood," the dark figure mused. "The shortage clearly affected your brain."

"You have no curiosity? Or even . . . hunger for vengeance?"

"What I have, Reverend Vryce, is a haven of absolute safety. A domain that I have built for myself, stone by stone, tree by tree, until the land itself exists only to indulge my pleasure. Should I give that up? Commit myself to the eastern ocean, with all the risk that entails? I'm amazed you want me with you in the first place."

"Your power's unquestionable. Your insight—"

"And it would keep me out of trouble, eh? For as long as I was with you, there would be no hunting in the Forest. No innocent women suffering for my pleasure. Isn't that part of it? Isn't that how your conscience would deal with the fact of my continued existence, when you've sworn on your honor to kill me?"

Despite himself, Damien smiled. "It has its appeal."

"Let me tell you what that ocean means, to my kind. Thousands upon thousands of miles of open water, too deep for the earth-fae to penetrate. Do you understand? The very force that keeps me alive, that I require for most of my Workings, would be inaccessible. Which means I couldn't help you, or myself, if anything happened. One good eruption out of Novatlantis when we're in that region and no power of mine or yours could do anything to save us. Why do you think no one crosses that water? Why do you think it was only attempted five times, in all the years that man has been here? *And*, I would be all but helpless. At your mercy. Do you think that appeals to me? Such vulnerability is unthinkable, for one of my kind."

"I gave you my word before. You know I was good for it. Try me," he dared him.

The figure stared at him in silence for a moment; unable to see the Hunter's expression, Damien was unable to read its cause.

"I thought you traveled alone," Tarrant said at last.

"Yes. Well." He looked back toward the camp. "Hesseth's going. She insisted. You should have seen her when we learned the truth, when she realized that her own species was being corrupted. . . ."

"And the lady Ciani?"

His expression tightened; it took him a moment to find the proper words. "This is her life's work," he told the Hunter. "The rakhlands. Their culture. I didn't know that before because she didn't have the memory . . . but then, I didn't know so much about her."

For a moment there was silence, then: "I'm sorry," the figure said softly.

He forced a shrug. "It was good while it lasted. That's the most you can ask for, isn't it?" He forced his hands to unclench inside his pockets. Forced his voice to be steady. "We're from two different worlds, she and I. Sometimes you forget that. Sometimes you pretend it doesn't matter. But it's always there." He looked up at the figure, toward where his face would be. Like all of him, it was sheathed in darkness. "There's something growing in the east," he said. "Something very powerful, and very evil. Something that's had both the time and the patience to rework the very patterns of this planet, until Nature was forced to respond to it. Don't you want to know what that is? Don't you want to make it pay for what it did to you?"

"Set evil against evil, is that it? In the hope that they might destroy each other."

"You were the one who recommended that. Or don't you remember?"

"I was very young, then. Inexperienced. Naive."

"You were the voice of my faith."

"Past tense, Reverend Vryce. Things have changed. *I* have changed." The figure stepped back, breathing in sharply as it did so. In pain? "Years ago, I decided that I would sacrifice anything and everything in the name of survival. My blood. My kin. My humanity. Should I render all that meaningless now, by courting death at this late age? I think not."

Damien shrugged. "We'll be leaving from Faraday if you change your mind. In late March or April, probably; it will take at least that long to work out the practical details. I'll save you a private berth," he promised. "With no windows, and a lock on the door."

For a long moment, the dark figure just stared at him. Though the silver eyes were lost in shadow, Damien could feel them fixed on him.

"What makes you think you know me so well?" the Hunter asked hoarsely. "What makes you think you can anticipate me, in ways that go against my nature?"

"I know who you were," Damien answered. "I know what that man stood for. And I'm willing to bet that somewhere in the heart of that malignant thing you call a soul is a spark of what that man was—and the boundless curiosity that drove him. I think your hunger to know is every bit as great as your hunger for life, Neocount. I'm offering you knowledge—as well as vengeance. Are you telling me that combination has no appeal?"

The figure lifted one arm, so that the folds of his cloak fell free of it. "Appeal or no," he whispered. "The price is too high."

Moonlight shimmered on the wetness of bloody flesh, on muscle and veins stripped bare by the force of the sun's assault. Sharp bone edges poked through strands of shrunken flesh, their tips charred black by fire and crusted with dried blood. The fingers were no more than seared bits of meat, strung together along the slender phalanges like some macabre shish kebob. If a scrap of silk or wool adhered to that flesh, or any other bit of clothing, it had been so torn and so bloodied that it was now indistinguishable from the man's own tissue.

"Enough is enough," the Hunter whispered. The arm dropped down, and the cloak fell to cover it. The voice echoed with pain, and with the soft gurgle of blood. "The answer is no, Reverend Vryce. And it will stay no, through all the years that you remain alive." He gestured toward the distant camp, across the field of spotless snow. "You may consider the life of these tribes my parting gift, if you like—I had once sworn to kill them all, for their audacity in binding me."

"A few less souls to darken my conscience?" he asked sharply.

"Exactly."

The Hunter bowed. And the effort that it took was so apparent, his pain throughout the motion so obvious, that Damien winced to see it. How many muscles had been burned to ragged strands, that a man would require for such a gesture? How much blood was being made to flow, for that last show of elegance?

"Good luck, Reverend Vryce," the Hunter whispered. "I suspect you'll need it."

Epilogue

Deep in the bowels of night's keep, in a chamber reserved for the Lord of the Forest, a figure lay still atop a numarble table. There, where the sun would never shine its baleful light, where earthquakes had never yet disturbed the carefully warded walls, the body of the Hunter lay immersed in dark fae, purple power clinging to his death-pale skin. Utterly cold. Utterly lifeless. Silk robes spilled over the sides of the polished table like a waterfall frozen in motion, their contours hinting at the items that lay beneath. For if this castle was a duplicate of Merentha's citadel in every other regard, so was its underground workroom a dark reflection of the Neocount's original—and the straps which had bound Almea Tarrant in her dying adorned the polished worktable like some macabre ornament, now parted to receive the Hunter's body.

Power: not weakened by sunlight—or even moonlight—and not compromised by the presence of some local primitive mind. Pure power, deep and swift-working—a death-hungry power, that had been building in these caverns for longer than man could remember. It gathered around him like a blanket—a shroud—a barrier against life— and any observer would be hard pressed to say whether the flesh thus protected was cradled in the true chill of death, or in some macabre facsimile.

In that place where no sound had been heard for so many days, footsteps now resounded. Soft and measured, slowly approaching. There was a rattle at the door as the great lock was opened, then the slow creak of steel hinges overweighed by the mass of their burden. Fae-light shimmered on an albino's brow, purple light reflecting bright magenta in the pigment-free depths of his eyes. He regarded the figure that lay before him, then bowed, ever so slightly. And reached out a tendril of his own dark will, to touch the currents that guarded that motionless form.

For a moment, nothing happened. Then, with infinite slowness, the pale eyelids opened. The dark fae parted as the Lord of the Forest spread his fingers, flexing his hands into motion once more. Stretching his arms, likewise. After a moment he levered himself to a sitting position—and though he winced as though in pain while doing so, it was clear from his movements that the worst of the sun-spawned damage had been repaired.

"Forgive me," the albino said. "I know you didn't want to be disturbed—"

"How long has it been?"

"Nearly a long month, Excellency."

"So long." He closed his eyes and drew in a deep breath slowly, as if savoring the air. "You wouldn't bother me without a reason, Amoril, I know that. What is it?"

"You have a petitioner, my lord."

The pale eyes shot open. Their depths sparkled violet in he faelight. "Indeed? What manner of petitioner?"

"A demon, Excellency. High-order, if I read him right. He said that you would know him, and respect his business. He gave his name as Calesta."

For a moment there was silence. Then the Hunter said, softly, "I know him. And I think I know his business, as well."

"Is he the one you fought, in the rakhlands?"

He swung his legs over the side of table, and tested their strength against the floor. "He was a symbiote of the one that I fought. And that kind can't last long, without some kind of human partner." He chuckled softly. "I'm surprised I still rate that designation."

"Partner?"

"Human."

"You think he wants to link himself to you."

"Let's say I consider it possible."

"After what he did?"

"Demons aren't whole people, Amoril. Like animals they know only blind hunger and a channel to the hand that feeds them. And the desire to survive, as passionate as anything humans might experience." He eased himself onto his feet, until he was standing free of any support. "Calesta's symbiote is dead. His enemy lives. It's to his advantage to placate that power which might still destroy him—and perhaps even court it. Demons rank themselves according to such alliances."

"And would you ally with him?"

The Hunter's expression grew dark. "I haven't forgotten what he did to me. But we're in my realm now, playing by my rules. Let's see how well he adapts to that, shall we?" He brushed at the silk of his shirt sleeve, binding enough dark fae to smooth out the wrinkles. "Have him come to the audience chamber, and await me there." And he warned, "I may leave him waiting some time."

The albino bowed. "Excellency."

Darkness. Absolute. He let it fill his eyes and his heart for a moment, let it seep deep into his soul to where the sun-born wounds still throbbed. And then he let himself See, and Hear, and breathe in the power of the Forest. A symphony of power rising up out of the earth, all dark and cold and rich with his signature. *So beautiful,* he thought. *So very beautiful.* He felt the presence of the trees that dwelled there, remade to serve his special need; the predators that stirred above and below the earth, responsive to his will; the blood-filled life that hovered at the edges of his domain, all restlessness and greed and human recklessness. Their nearness awakened a hunger in him so intense that for a minute it seemed the whole Forest was filled with their blood, and all its air was ripe with the smell of their fear. And the music of their mortality, almost painful in its intensity.

How long ago had it been since last he'd hunted? He ached for the sweet taste of a woman's terror, for the boundless pleasure of hunting in a land where all life responded to his will—where the land itself could be reshaped, if he so desired it, to force his prey back upon her own path, into his waiting arms . . . he shivered in hunger, just thinking of it. Too many days. Too many nights of rakhene fear and disembodied blood and a need so powerful that it had nearly overwhelmed him. Now there was no need for him to deny himself. Now he could choose his prey and set her loose in these woods, and feed as his nature demanded. Wash his soul clean with killing, until the taint of his contact with humankind was nothing more than an unpleasant memory.

Until you come for me, Vryce, he thought. *Until you do what your nature demands, and try to put an end to me. In my domain. On my terms.* He chuckled darkly. *You haven't a chance in hell, my friend. But I'll enjoy watching you try.*

Dark fae swirling about his feet, silken robes brushing the floor as he walked, the Neocount of Merentha headed toward his audience chamber.

Black floor and dark draperies: they soothed the eye and calmed the heart, nourishing his nightbound soul. His visitor was a different story. Though the demon's chosen body was also black, his form was riddled with flaws and sharp edges that caught what little light there was and magnified it, making it bright enough to sting the Hunter's newly-healed eyes. His voice was likewise irritating, a thing of life and hidden sunlight and the ceaseless cacophony of day.

"Excellency." The demon bowed. "Allow me to—"

"You're a guest in my domain," the Hunter interrupted. "And not a very welcome one. You can design yourself a suitable form for this audience or leave. *Now.*" When the demon failed to respond he added sharply, "I'm prepared to Banish you, if necessary."

Calesta stiffened. "Of course, my lord." The glittering edges of his obsidian flesh began to pulse—and then melted, into a smooth, rippling surface. His voice became a whispering thing, all night air and cool darkness. "Is this better, Prince of Jahanna? Does this please you?"

"It'll do," the Neocount said shortly. "What's your business?"

"Exactly what you expect, my lord. I saw what your vengeance did to my Mistress. I have no wish to suffer a similiar fate." The black form bowed deeply. "I've come to make an offering. A gesture of conciliation."

"With no strings attached?" the Hunter asked dryly.

The demon laughed softly. "You're not the fool that she was, my prince. You know the world, and its workings. Let's say that it would please me if you accepted my offering. It would please me very much."

"I'm listening."

The demon glanced toward the window; faceted eyes glittered in the fae-light. "I've found you a woman. A rare delight. A beautiful, delicate flower of a girl, whom the gods must have designed with you in mind. A fragile spirit and a strong young body married together in perfect unity, so that the one might suffer while the other endures. She could pleasure you for hours, Hunter. Not like the others. This one was born to be devoured."

"And where is this . . . jewel?"

"In your realm, prince. I took the liberty of bringing her here while you slept. I anticipated that when you awakened you might be . . . hungry. See for yourself," he whispered. "It's all there, for the Knowing."

The Hunter gathered the dark fae about him and bound it to his will. Tendrils of power stretched forth, and touched the fleeing woman. He tasted the memory of her looking into a mirror, felt the absolute certainty of her beauty reverberate within him. And that soul! As fragile and as fine as porcelain in its tenor, but utterly resilient in its substance. He stroked her brain tenderly with his power, savoring her capacity for terror; she responded to him on at least a dozen levels, from the personal to the archetypal. A finely tuned instrument, that might produce whole symphonies of fear. It would have been a delight to hunt her under any circumstances; now, with the abstinence of a month or more sharpening the edge of his hunger, she was doubly irresistible.

"You would feed off my pleasure," he challenged the demon.

The dark figure chuckled. "You'd have more than enough pleasure to spare in this hunt."

"I don't support parasites."

"Not true, my prince. Not true at all. What about Karril? You've dedicated more than one hunt to him. While all he does is watch, and cheer you on. I can bring you victims, Hunter. I can read the hunger inside you better than any other, and scour the world for suitable prey. You doubt my skill? Test me, then. This one's a gift. No strings attached—this time. If she pleases you as much as I think she will. . . ." He bowed, deeply. "I live to serve, my lord."

The taste of her was on his lips, in his soul. It was hard to keep his voice steady as he asked, "What have you told her?"

"The Hunter's rules. The Forest's tradition. That you'll track her as a man would, in a man's form, using no Working. That she has three days and nights in which to evade you . . . and if she succeeds, she'll be free of you forever."

"And did she believe that last point?"

"Of course she did. I understand how important that is, Hunter. It's the death of hope, rather than of the flesh itself, which is your true kill." And he added, "I have taken one special liberty, my lord."

The Hunter's eyes narrowed suspiciously.

"This is her third night here. I tracked her myself for two of them, just as you would have. So that her terror would be at its peak by the time you went out to take her. After such a long healing sleep . . . I thought you might be very hungry."

"And you were right," he said softly. "In that . . . and in your choice. I accept your offering, Calesta. If she pleases me as much as I think she may . . . then we can talk about the possibility of future arrangements." He looked toward the window, at the Forest beyond; it seemed he could smell her fear on the wind. "That's all for now," he said quietly. "You may go."

The demon smiled, and bowed again. "Good feeding, Hunter."

The forest air was cold and dry, and her fear was something he could taste on his lips as he breathed it in, testing the wind for her scent. Beneath his feet her imprints were clear, hurried steps that dug deep into the half-frozen earth and then tore it loose—running steps that were skewed as if from exhaustion, a line of imprints that staggered from tree to tree as if she were desperate for some support, but dared not pause long enough to take it. Because resting, even for a moment, meant losing ground before him. And with only hours to go before her last dawn, she dared not waste a precious second.

Run, my fragile one. Run for the sunlight. Only a short time more before your safety is certain . . . and then, in those last desperate moments, I'll take you. And I'll taste your hope as it dies, drowned out in a sea of terror. . . . He could feel her already, a faint flicker of fear against the edge of his mind, and desire filled him. What form should he take, once he had her? Her fears were so many, and so deeply rooted . . . he had never faced such a wealth of options before. The thought of taking her blood excited him, a strange sensation; not since his early days had he taken pleasure in so brutal an attack, or taken on a form so centered in pure physicality. Perhaps it was the result of traveling among humans again, of accepting their blood in cold, measured doses—enough to awaken that hunger again, not enough to satisfy it. Whatever the reason, he found that the thought of such a physical assault made him burn with hunger, and his hands shook as he brushed a drift of dead leaves from her trail, in order to read it more clearly. Perhaps a sexual assault would serve his purpose best. Not that he was capable of sexual congress, or even of mimicking its forms; procreation was an act of life, and it was as forbidden to him as fire was, or the light of the sun. But a woman such as that, who found herself overpowered by a man, who might be rendered naked with so little effort . . . she would come to her own conclusions regarding his intent, and those were nearly as nourishing as the act itself. He imagined the taste of her blood under those circumstances, and shivered from the force of his need. *Calesta knew my hunger well,* he thought. *Better than I knew it myself.*

And then he caught her scent on the wind, and he knew that he was close. Very close. He took care to move quietly, now, avoiding the crisp leaves that littered the ground about him. It seemed that he could hear her labored breathing, underscored by the pounding of her heart. So much blood, rendered so very warm by her terror . . . it seemed he could taste it on his lips already as he followed her trail, seemed that he could feel the rush of her fear as it enveloped him, hot and wild and utterly unfettered. . . .

He ran. Long legs consuming the Forest ground at a pace her own could not possibly equal, sharp eyes picking out the marks of her trail in the near darkness. Calesta was right, he could never have waited. And this way there was no need to. For two nights now the demon had tracked her in his stead, playing all the subtle games that he had perfected in order to bring her terror to a fever pitch. All that remained was for the Hunter to harvest that fear, to drink it in along with her life and the last of her hope—to replenish the strength that two months of traveling with those humans had drained from him. A sweet prospect, indeed.

A clearing. Trees fell back, as though parting for him. At the far side a slight figure paused, then spun about in panic. Black hair whipped across a pale face, obscuring delicate features. Her slender fingers were red with blood, where thorns and rough bark had scraped them raw; her clothing, once fine, had been tattered by three days of flight through the woods. Fear blossomed out from her like a welcoming fire, and he had neither the strength nor the desire to resist its heat. He crossed the ground between them quickly and closed his hand about her wrist. Her pulse fluttered wildly, like that of a terrified bird, and she moaned softly as he pulled her toward him. Too weak to struggle; too overwhelmed to plead. He shut his eyes and let himself sink into the depths of her nightmare imagination, let all the images that were within her surface and take form, so that he might choose from among them. So many, so rich . . . the smell of her blood made him giddy with hunger, and he felt himself pushing the torn shirt back from her shoulders, baring skin as pale as the moonlight itself—

"*You*," she whispered.

The word was like a blow. For a moment the world spun about him, dizzily—and then he managed to regain control, and he opened his eyes. And he released her suddenly, and staggered back. Stared at her, not quite believing.

"I won't run from you," she whispered.

Those eyes, that face . . . he remembered the night he had walked her home, so comfortably arrogant as he played at shielding her from the dangers of the night . . . remembered the promise he had made to her, the vow she didn't know how to value. That the Hunter would never harm her. That *he* would never harm her.

"I promised myself that," she breathed. There were tears in her eyes now—of sadness, not fear, a tender mourning that had no place in his brutal realm. "For what you gave me . . . if you wanted . . .

whatever." She bit her lower lip, fighting for courage. "I won't run," she whispered. "Not from you."

"Son of a bitch," he muttered. He turned away. His hands were shaking—with rage, with hatred. "That bastard. . . ."

He drew in a ragged breath, tried to master his hunger. Tried to dim down the passion that had been driving him, until he could control it. Tried not to think how close he had just come to betraying himself, or at whose prompting it had almost happened. . . .

There was a touch on his arm. Light, like the wingstroke of a bird. "Are you all right?" she whispered. And suddenly he could neither strike out at her, nor laugh at the total incongruousness of the question—but was caught somewhere between the two expressions and thus frozen. Unable to react.

At last he managed, "We were betrayed. Both of us." He turned back to her, tried to still the tide of hunger that rose up within him at the sight of her. So very, very delicate . . . he swallowed back on that impulse, hard, and said, "I promised not to hurt you. I promised the Hunter would never hurt you."

Son of a bitch!

The rage, hot inside him, was finally overwhelming the hunger. It allowed him to think. "Here." He pulled his medallion out of his shirt—on a new chain, made to replace that which Ciani had torn from his neck so many weeks ago—and handed it to her. "Take this. Hold onto it. None of my people will harm you while you have it, and the beasts . . . they obey my will. Nothing will hurt you."

"Thank you," she whispered. Confused, as her fingers closed about the thin disk and its chain. "I don't understand—"

"You don't want to," he assured her. "Ever."

With effort, he managed to step back from her. The smell of her blood was like a magnet to his hunger—but she no longer feared him, and that helped immensely. Even as it amazed him, that it was true.

"I'll send you help," he told her. "Someone to get you safely out of here. You wait, with that . . . someone will come. You show him that. You'll be safe."

Calesta, you bastard . . . you'll pay for this indignity. And so will whoever or whatever spawned you. I swear it!

He turned to go. And he felt her fingers on his arm again; there was fear in her touch.

"Do you have to go?" she breathed. I mean . . . please."

He turned to her in amazement, saw the desperate hope in her eyes. She was afraid—not of him, now, but of the Forest. His creation. He was her island of refuge in a vast sea of terror, the single creature whom she did not fear in all of his domain. The concept was so bizarre he could hardly absorb it.

"I have a score to settle," he told her. And then, because it seemed to suit this bizarre new role that he had made for himself, he added, "You'll be all right."

I promise you.

The harbor at Faraday was bustling with activity, longshoremen swarming across the open docks like insects on honey. By now most of the tugs had put out to sea, and the small skiffs that would transport passengers across the shallow harbor waters were already making their way toward their motherships, whose vast sails and steady turbines stood ready to tame the dangerous eastern waters.

The captain of the *Golden Glory* looked out over the docks and snorted sharply. Then he climbed to where Damien stood, on a shelf overlooking the harbor. And put his hands on the hips, facing the man.

"Tide's going out soon," he informed him. "Another hour."

The priest nodded.

"It's a hard double, this time. Best we'll get. It could take us past the Shelf before anything from outwater could hit us—you listening to me?"

"A hard double tide," Damien repeated. "One hour. Anything else?"

"Only that we've really got to leave, this time. The investors won't stand for another delay—and neither will I. You want a safe crossing, we start now. Otherwise you can find yourself another captain, not to mention another ship."

Damien smiled faintly. "And you think that pack of gold-seekers on board will let you quit, just like that?"

The captain grinned, displaying several broken teeth. "You got me there, Reverend. But look: it's you who got it all together, right? You who found enough bodies willing to cross the sea, to get us some investors to pay the backing costs, to buy yourself a good safe crossing ... so why waste all that? I don't want to be out there in storm season and neither do you. Whatever you're waiting for ... it's had its fair chance, all right? Let's take this one and go."

He waited a moment for an answer—and then, receiving none, shook his head in exasperation and began the long climb down. "One hour!" he called back. "Be there!" Damien watched as he negotiated the dangers of the rubble-covered slope, finally down the last twenty feet or so to the level of the piers. Then he looked up, back toward the road from Faraday proper—and froze, as a tall, lean figure and a single horse stepped out into the moonlight.

He climbed up the remaining slope quickly until he stood face to face with the man. The Hunter's gaze was as cold as ever, and considerably more confident than when he'd last seen it. The pale eyes blazed with anger.

"If you say one smug word about this," Gerald Tarrant warned, "—at any time—anything like 'I told you so,' or, 'What took you so long?'—I will sink that miserable crate to the bottom of the ocean, and swim home if I have to. Am I making myself clear?"

He carefully avoided all the obvious rejoinders, and said only, "Of course, your Excellency. Infinitely clear." And bowed, with only a hint of mockery.

The Hunter glared at him, as if about to speak—and then simply shook his head in exasperation, and began to walk toward the harbor. The night-black horse, laden with several travel bags, followed obediently behind.

Damien watched as the figure faded into darkness, disappearing behind a turn of the switchback road. And then shook his own head, smiling slightly.

"Welcome aboard," he whispered.

ABOUT THE AUTHOR

Having failed at both science and sewing on the high school level, C.S. Friedman decided to devote her life to science fiction and costume design. She presently teaches costume design at a small private college in northern Virginia, and has published patterns for historical costumes, most recently for the English and Italian Renaissance. She has been an active member of numerous historical re-creation societies including The Society for Creative Anachronism, Medieval Studies and Restoration, The Brigade of the American Revolution, L'Epee et la Rose, and the League of Renaissance Swordsmen. She has fenced with both period and modern weapons, and has choreographed combat for the stage. Currently she is doing research for the second volume in the Coldfire trilogy, which begins with BLACK SUN RISING.